BRIGHTNESS FALLS

&

STORY OF MY LIFE

BRIGHTNESS FALLS

&

STORY OF MY LIFE

JAY McINERNEY

BLOOMSBURY

for my father

Brightness Falls first published in Great Britain 1992
Copyright © 1992 by Jay McInerney

Story of My Life first published in Great Britain 1988
Copyright © 1988 by Jay McInerney

This paperback edition published 2004
Copyright © 2004 by Jay McInerney

The author wishes to thank the Corporation of Yaddo, where *Story of My Life* was
written. *Story of My Life* is based on a story that appeared in *Esquire*. An excerpt
from the novel was published in the premiere issue of *Smart* magazine.

Bloomsbury Publishing Plc, 38 Soho Square, London W1D 3HB

A CIP catalogue record for this book
is available from the British Library

ISBN 0 7475 7454 5

10 9 8 7 6 5 4 3 2 1

All papers used by Bloomsbury Publishing are natural, recyclable
products made from wood grown in well-managed forests.
The manufacturing processes conform to the
environmental regulations of the country of origin.

Printed in Great Britain by Clays Ltd, St Ives plc

www.bloomsbury.com/jaymcinerney

BRIGHTNESS FALLS

All the new thinking is about loss.
In this it resembles all the old thinking.

—ROBERT HASS
"Meditation at Lagunitas"

ACKNOWLEDGMENTS

For bucolic shelter from the urban storm I would like to thank Carl Navarre, George Plimpton, James Salter and the Corporation of Yaddo.

For sharing their knowledge in various fields I am greatly indebted to Kate Bonner, Robin Carpenter, William Koshland, Ken Lipper, Mark McInerney, William Norwich, Ellen O'Toole, François de Saint Phalle and Chuck Ward.

For moral, oral and technical support I am very grateful to Gary, Binky, Marie, Morgan, Mona, Michael, Nick, Terry, Bret, Barry, Liz, Carl, Rust, Erroli, Sonny and Garth.

BRIGHTNESS FALLS

The last time I saw Russell and Corrine together was the weekend of the final softball game between the addicts and the depressives. The quality of play was erratic, the recovering addicts being depressed from lack of their chosen medications and the depressives heavily dosed with exotic chemical bullets aimed at their elusive despair. Being myself among the clinically numb, I don't remember the outcome of the game now, though I submit that taken together we were as representative a group as you could hope to field at that juncture in history. It was the fall of 1987. The leaves in Connecticut were bursting, slow motion, into flame; one night, as we smoked on the porch after dinner, a girl in my unit who claimed to suffer from precognition declared that she could see paper airplanes crashing to the pavement of Manhattan, fifty miles away. Of course she would turn out to be right. But this was just before all that, before the big discount of gross expectations.

When they arrived at the hospital that Indian-summer day, I was sitting on the grass above the visitors' parking lot sucking a Marlboro, imagining how I might mince and dice them in their Cuisinart, because they were partly responsible for putting me in that white clapboard Bedlam, and because it was easy to disdain them as types—like a couple in a magazine ad, so patently members of their generation and class. Corrine's yellow hair and Russell's yellow tie flying like pennons of bright promise. Begin with an individual and you'll find you've got nothing but ambiguity and compassion; if you intend violence, stick with the type.

I was sitting with my friend Delia, whose arms were inscribed with a grid of self-inflicted wounds, an intricate text of self-loathing. Totally scrambled by the good life, Delia had once been to a party at Russell and Corrine's, and as they rolled up the tree-lined drive in their open Jeep, her dead raccoon eyes seemed to flicker with recognition. They sprang lankily from their faux combat vehicle, in uniform faded jeans and blue blazers, and the normally mute Delia said, without irony, "Here's the Prince and Princess in their six-horse carriage." Sitting next to Delia on the hospital lawn at that moment, I decided it was almost a viable illusion—such was the contrast of their entitled, courtly bearing as they strode up the hill, with the inverted gazes and the stooped, shuffling posture of the inmates around me. In a sense they had always been that—the royal couple visiting fractured friends in the nuthouse, noblesse oblige. But marriage is a form of asylum, too. When I shacked up myself, I always heard the wild call of the world outside the door. And eventually it seeped under their door, too. But at that moment they weren't aware of being watched as they sauntered glamorously up the golden lawn toward the hospital, still focused on each other, not having made the transition from their separate world to communal space, and at that moment I almost started to believe in them again.

I

Lemoning the sole fillets in the kitchen, Corrine hears her husband's voice louder than the rest, perhaps because it is louder, or because she's especially attuned to it. The voice now approaching from the hall, directed back into the living room but moving toward her: "I like the old version better." Russell didn't talk, he boomed.

"Old version of what," she asks, as he thumps into the kitchen, nearly filling it with his numerous limbs—one of those pre-war New York apartment kitchens not really intended for serious employment, but rather, it seemed, for the three-a.m. scrambling of a few Eggs Benny Goodman, after the Stork Club.

"Did I buy enough fish," he asks, replenishing her wineglass on the counter as he peers over her lightly freckled shoulder at the stove, and then surreptitiously down the front of her dress.

"Nice dress," he says. "Birthday girl."

"Thanks. Now you can complain about my hair."

They often debated her hair before a party: he likes it down, which he thinks is sexy; she prefers to put it up. Tonight it's pulled back in a loose golden French twist secured with black velvet ribbon, and he likes it anyway, approves of the idea of being married to this elegant creature.

"I thought we agreed you were positively going to stay out of the kitchen."

"What do you think of the Condrieu?"

"Please, no speeches about the wine tonight. Promise?"

"Only if you promise not to crawl around under the table orally servicing our male guests. Don't look at me that way. I know you.

Just because you haven't done it yet doesn't mean you're not thinking about it."

"I think Jeff's date will probably beat me to it."

"God, I hope so."

"Where do you suppose he found this one?"

"He lifted up the tablecloth and *voilà!* There she was."

"So where's the colander?"

"Wash wore it home after the last party."

"Do you wish you could date girls like that," Corrine asks, suddenly serious.

"God, Corrine, don't *ask* me that."

"*Russell,*" she groans, turning away from the counter with a crushed lemon half in her hand, looking up at him with doleful eyes.

"I like the old version better," he says again, taking her in his arms.

She reaches back and unhooks his hands. "You shouldn't use that word with a girl who just turned thirty-one. God, thirty is one thing—"

"Which word?"

"The O word."

"You're still my blonde bombshell."

"A mere shell of my former bomb."

He grabs her again. "Have I ever told you you look like the young Katharine Hepburn?" He has, of course. That's why it was important to say it again; like all marriages of any duration, theirs has its ritual incantations. And Russell thought of his wife as embodying certain Kate-like virtues: the flinty beauty suggestive of a sinewy Anglo-Saxon blood-line, the faint smattering of freckles suggestive of a Celt in the woodpile. He is of Hibernian extraction himself, a fourth-generation County Cork Calloway by way of Boston and Detroit.

"I was trying for Grace Kelly," she says.

The formula satisfied, she is self-possessed again.

"Where the hell is Washington? I'm almost ready to serve."

"You know Wash. Probably feeding the dog."

"Five years ago this bad-boy shtick had more charm."

"So says the den mother of the bad boy scouts."

"Is Jeff high?"

"On what?"

"That's what I'd like to know."

"He's fine."

"I think you should talk to him."

"I talk to him every day."

"I mean really talk."

"You mean really *leak*."

"Talking's not leaking. I *hate* it when you say that."

"Drip . . . drip . . . drip. Let's talk about our feelings, girls." Wielding the wine bottle like a microphone, he croons: "Feelings . . . whoa whoa whoa, feelings . . ."

"You're *so* sensitive, Russell."

"It's my curse. I *feel* everything so deeply," he says, grabbing her left buttock by way of illustration.

Corrine and Russell Calloway had been married for five years. They'd known each other eight years before that, having met in college. Their friends viewed them as savvy pioneers of the matrimonial state, as if they had homesteaded one of those formerly marginal areas of the city into which the fashion-conscious were just now beginning to follow. In the years they'd lived in New York, their East Side apartment had become a supper club for their less settled acquaintances, a sort of model unit for those thinking of buying into the neighborhood of matrimony. For the recently conjoined, it was a safe haven in a city that murdered marriages, and the unpaired found relief here from the strenuous formlessness of single life.

Not even their college friends, of whom there were fewer each year, could quite remember them separately. Individually they were both perhaps a little too attractive, but marriage neutered the appeal just enough that men who had been daunted by Corrine Makepeace at Brown, where she was something of an erotic totem figure, could now flirt with her safely while the women confided in Russell, drawing him into the bedroom for urgent conferences. It was a measure of the trust between them that Corrine seldom thought to be jealous on these occasions; a measure of the heat of her passion that, sometimes, frangible objects were hurled in anger. Sophisticated as they could appear, Russell and Corrine shared an almost otherworldly quality, being so long shielded from the bruising free market of romance, having answered that large question early in their lives. Like Scandinavians, they inhabited a hygienic welfare state the laws of which didn't necessarily apply outside the realm, and sometimes, when one of them expressed an opinion, an outsider wanted to say, Sure, that might be true for you two, but the rest of us, we're still trying to find a warm body.

If it seemed exemplary, their estate also looked attainable. Though it commanded a view of the great city spreading south from a small terrace like a buffet of lights, the apartment was only a one-bedroom rental, the antiques juxtaposed with dorm-room salvage. One of the two couches was beginning to divulge its stuffing, and an overflow of books from the built-in shelves in the living room was housed in a low-income unit made of cinder blocks and unpainted pine planks. Photographs of Russell and Corrine and friends, indiscriminately framed in Tiffany silver and cheap plastic, hung between Galerie Maeght posters and signed lithographs. They entertained in a liberal and stylish manner which to some guests suggested an abundance of this world's blessings. In fact, their finances were perennially precarious. They had two incomes, but Russell toiled in the historically underpaid field of publishing and Corrine had been a stockbroker for only two years. Their joint tax return was modest by the boomtown standards of many of their friends and neighbors.

After nearly collapsing in bankruptcy during the seventies, their adoptive city had experienced a gold rush of sorts; prospecting with computers and telephones, financial miners had discovered fat veins of money coursing beneath the cliffs and canyons of the southern tip of Manhattan. As geologic and meteorological forces conspire to deposit diamonds at the tip of one continent and to expose gold at the edge of another, so a variety of manmade conditions intersected more or less at the beginning of the new decade to create a newly rich class based in New York, with a radical new scale of financial well-being. The electronic buzz of fast money hummed beneath the wired streets, affecting all the inhabitants, making some of them crazy with lust and ambition, others angrily impoverished, and making the comfortable majority feel poorer. Late at night, Russell or Corrine would sometimes hear that buzz—in between the sirens and the alarms and the car horns—worrying vaguely, clinging to the very edge of the credit limits on their charge cards.

Socially acute observers could read in Corrine's manner the secret code of American pedigree. But the Makepeace fortune had been dispersed when Corrine's dying grandfather, a quirky liberal, had endowed a science center at a struggling black university, partly out of spite for his only son—and Corrine's only father. Russell's grandfather, an Irish immigrant, had been an autoworker, his father a GM executive of middle rank; Russell possessed the open posture and direct manners of the enthusiastically striving middle class. He and Corrine shared a history of fission in the nuclear family, her parents having divorced after years of violent misalliance and his mother having died at approximately the same time, just as their romance was beginning; a sense of the fragility of familial love lent urgency to their courtship and mortar to their marriage.

Dinner was served. Sommelier Russell managed to refrain from declaiming about the wine as he orbited the dining room table and poured, while Corrine dished up the first course, a pasta. Not really a snob, he was, however, an enthusiast in many areas, tending to throw himself into new pursuits with a convert's ardor, proselytizing his acquaintances. Russell had little capacity for reticence or restraint. As his occasional doubles partner in tennis, for instance, Corrine was sometimes maddened that he always went for the put-away at the net and refused to temper his second serve, whacking it as hard as his first, though this frequently resulted in double faults. A large man, he bumped into things—the kind of guy who walked into rooms without knocking. Crash Calloway. Luckily for the occupants of these rooms, his voice usually preceded him, a sort of air-raid siren. Corrine often worried that he would embarrass her by saying something intimate in front of a store clerk or starting a conversation with the strangers in an elevator. At present, as he dabbed at some wine he'd spilled on the tablecloth, he was confiding loudly about the mushrooms, which had been sent to him by an Italian author whose novel he was publishing. "It's illegal," he informed their six dinner guests, "but he wraps them in plastic and sends them in a cheap leather purse to disguise the smell."

"We used to talk like this about drugs," Corrine said, to clear away the slight whiff of self-satisfied epicureanism.

"We still do," said Jeff, on her right, flashing one of his wistfully roguish smiles. Built like a fillet knife, he sported his usual ripped jeans and washed-out untucked Brooks Brothers button-down shirt, over which he wore his coat of many press clips. Jeff had published a successful book two years before, a collection of stories about an eccentric New England clan that, not so remarkably, closely resembled his own. Everyone listened to him just a little more intently these days, as he listened less attentively to everyone else.

"I used to hate mushrooms so much when I was a kid," squeaked Dawn, Jeff's nineteen-year-old date, who looked like a model with breasts—who in fact *was* a model with breasts. "When we wanted to think of something really bad, like a punishment or something, we'd say, 'You have to eat a whole plateful of mushrooms.' " The Second Law of Social Dynamics, Corrine figured: The single women get younger every year. But what was the first?

"Now we just send you to bed without supper," Jeff said. Then, to Corrine, with the air of someone diverting attention: "How's Mr. Jones?" By which he meant, Corrine knew, the Dow, and the market in general, though it occurred to her that in an earlier era it might have been a reference to the Dylan song.

"The last time you were here," Corrine said, taking a sip of her wine, "somebody asked you what you were working on. And you said, 'Don't ask a writer what he's working on. It's like asking someone with cancer about the progress of his disease.' "

She decided she was unhappy with him for bringing this child to dinner and, having done so, putting the girl down.

"Did I say that? I must have been drunk. I hope you immediately plunged a steak knife into my kidney, or a kidney knife into my steak."

"I should have. But instead I insist that you observe the rules. Rule number one: No boring questions. I don't allow them at my table."

Zac Solomon asked, "Are there any other rules here. I'm not real familiar with eastern etiquette. In California we don't usually even wear clothes."

"It shows," Jeff said. "You definitely haven't got the hang of wearing them yet."

"If you weren't my writer, guy, I'd be forced to take grievous offense at that remark."

"Hollywood producers are not allowed to take offense," Jeff said. "They're expected to give it."

"Just to show you what a self-deprecating character I am," Zac said,

"I'll tell you all the latest joke. There's this producer driving really fast down Santa Monica talking on the phone, and he has this accident, flips his car over, gets thrown out, and somehow his arm is severed in the process, goes flying."

"Is Santa Monica Boulevard a significant detail," Jeff asked, helping himself to more wine.

". . . So anyway, another car stops, the driver gets out and rushes over to the producer, who's lying in the street, and he says, 'Are you all right, guy?' And the producer's looking at the wreck of his car, wailing, 'My Porsche, my Porsche, my Porsche!' So the other guy looks at the stump of his arm, then points at the other half of it lying across the street and says, 'But what about your arm?' And the producer looks across the street and says, 'Oh my God—my Rolex, my Rolex, my Rolex!' "

"We approve of self-deprecation," announced Corrine, who before tonight had never met Solomon. Cute, a little beefy, lingering baby fat or premature business-dinner paunch. Late twenties, according to Russell, and he'd already made millions. He played to the stereotype, tongue in cheek, in a way that made it seem almost okay. Not that you'd necessarily have wanted your daughter to marry one. It was business, sort of, Russell said, and anyway, he was an amusing character. The latter being the only valid point for Corrine, who had an old-fashioned notion that business should be confined to offices.

"Does that mean I can stay," Zac asked.

"Only if you pronounce her name right," Jeff said. "Rhymes with *Mau*reen, a homophone for *chorine*—that's chorus girl to you."

"And only if you're extremely attentive to the single women," said Nancy Tanner, animating her long blond locks with a trademark toss of her head. Russell once suggested the gesture was intended to mimic the effects of a wind machine. She was the ungrounded wire of their extended circle, the single female.

"Last time I heard that joke," Jeff said, "it was about agents. The problem is it could also be about most of our friends."

Colin Becker, who was not a member of one of the agented professions, was talking to Jeff's date now about architecture, while Russell considerately entertained Anne, who was a corporate lawyer and thankfully never talked about it. Corrine suddenly remembered they owed the Beckers a wedding present.

Abruptly, Washington Lee arrived, saying, "Guess who's come to dinner," as he inevitably did. His eyes like crazy marbles, all shiny and bright—Corrine had a feeling this was going be a late one. "Sorry," he announced. "Got caught in a crossfire on Broadway. Bank-robber dudes trying to escape over the rooftops, they had the cops pinned down, traffic stopped cold, spraying the street with automatic fire." Either because they made allowances for Washington's hyperbole or because they were inured to the violence of the city, none of them chose to challenge the statement or ask for elaboration.

Reverting to a primitive male condition, Jeff and Russell hooted at the sight of their buddy, slapping hands and backs.

"It's the Righteous Brothers," said Washington.

"Now that you're here," Jeff said, "we're the Temptations."

"We resist anything *but*," Washington responded.

Corrine sat Washington between Jeff's girlfriend and Casey Reynes, her freshman roommate, whose husband was out of town. Washington immediately put his arms around both of them, to the obvious annoyance of Casey, who flexed her beautiful-rich-girl hauteur.

"So what's the buzz?"

"How come we never talk about politics," asked Nancy, tossing her hair and reaching across the table to put her hand on Washington's arm. "I'll bet *you* have some interesting views," she added, in a tone of voice generally reserved for lewd propositions. Corrine suddenly wondered if they'd ever slept together.

"Shucks, ma'am, I just minds my own business and leaves politics to the white folks."

"Don't get Russell started," Corrine said quickly, knowing how Washington liked to exploit these moments. "We'll be up all night. Russell's greatest regret is that he basically missed the sixties. He's been trying to make up for it ever since."

"I didn't miss the sixties," Russell countered. "I watched them on television."

"Russell's for Gary Hart," Washington sneered.

"Hart *and* sole?" Jeff sighed, pushing his plate away. "Other topics? *Please?*"

"Who else *is* there?"

"Gary Hart and his *new ideas*," said Washington. "What *new* ideas? Tell the dude to read Ecclesiastes."

Soon they were arguing about Nicaragua. As he was publishing a book about the covert war against the Sandinistas, Russell was armed with facts and dates. A Republican, Zac relied on epigrams and lighthearted xenophobia. Parnassian Jeff disdained politics. Washington, who probably knew more than anybody, preferred to play dumb, strategically letting others betray themselves with earnestness. Jeff's girlfriend looked increasingly bewildered—and it wasn't a strategy—almost frightened by this excursion into foreign terrain. It wasn't her fault she was in over her head, Corrine realized. The breasts and the big pouty lips weren't her fault, either. At least she didn't think they were. Corrine was just enough of a prodigy herself to know that this was like inheriting a pile of money at puberty without a trust officer in sight, like climbing behind the wheel of a Ferrari for your first driving lesson. Some generations the little boys got sent to the jungle or the trenches with nothing but a gun, and that was the only way they'd ever begin to have a fucking clue about what it was like to grow up a pretty girl with big tits. If you were lucky you didn't get to New York or Los Angeles until you'd made the tutelary mistakes.

Not that she'd ever had breasts like that. Jesus, Jeff. Were they real? These days, hard to say. Reminded her of a girl at prep school who was voted best couple in the yearbook. Without stopping to think, Corrine said, aloud, "I heard a story that if you have breast implants and you take the Concorde they can explode." Was it her imagination, or did Jeff's date look worried?

"Party tits," said Washington.

Over at the stereo, Russell cued up Roxy Music's *Avalon* and looked over his shoulder to see if Corrine had noticed. She blew him a kiss. "Soundtrack album of our first year of matrimonial bliss," she explained.

Jeff's girlfriend turned to Washington. "Are you married?"

Washington looked at her as if she were insane; Jeff coughed red wine onto the tablecloth.

"They haven't invented the right kind of marriage for me yet," Washington said calmly. "See, I don't understand why there's got to be just one kind of marriage. When you need a place to live it's like you can get a floor of a brownstone, or a loft, or a few rooms in a big shiny tower with a health club, depending on how you want to live, but when it comes to marriage there's just this one basic variety. You're supposed to live together monogamously. You see what I'm saying? One size fits all? No way. Why can't we have different brands of marriage. Color-coded . . . the red kind of marriage, say, where you spend four nights a week together and cruise the other nights, or the green marriage, where you have kids together and lend them out to your impotent relatives and—"

"What color do you want," asked Casey, whose own marriage was, like ancient currencies, based on the gold standard. She was half British and half Du Pont, her husband a venture capitalist from the same registered social circle in Wilmington, Delaware. Russell thought they were snobs, and referred to Mrs. Reynes as "Her Majesty"; Corrine's loyalty had more to do with memories of the leveling storm of adolescence than to current compatibility.

"Please, don't tell us, Wash," Corrine said. "We've just eaten."

"Marriages need a certain amount of slack. A lot of fond-making absence," said Casey, whose husband traveled incessantly on business.

Nancy said, "All men need just four things. Food, shelter, pussy . . . and strange pussy."

"I can't vouch for the first two," Washington confessed. The other men around the table looked embarrassed, it seemed to Corrine—as if they'd just been caught out.

In a sudden panic, she glanced across the table at Russell. Looking flustered, he shrugged sheepishly.

Jeff helped clear the dishes. In the kitchen Corrine said to him, "I don't think she's quite your type."

"Is that understatement?"

"Diplomacy, Jeff."

He put his arms around her. They were old friends from similar worlds, Jeff the late spawn of a dusty Yankee family whose capital, like the soil of his native Massachusetts, was largely depleted. There was an air of unfinished business between them. She'd always thought him attractive, six-three and bone-thin, slightly hunched with the self-consciousness of those sensitive tall people who prefer not to tower.

"What you mean," Jeff suggested, "is that you're sorry to report that she's exactly my type and that I am therefore demonstrably a scumbag."

She looked into his eyes, as though she might read the health of his soul there. The kind of eyes that might belong to a villager in the Middle East, someone encountered on the banks of the Tigris or the Euphrates, the dark eyes of an old soul. Russell had boyish wide blue eyes and was born the day before yesterday.

Dodging her gaze, he said, "The trouble with girls who are my type is that I don't find them attractive."

Corrine laughed. "What?" All at once she realized she was buzzed. Felt good. "I thought you found all women attractive."

"Or else I find them attractive but they're married."

"Sometimes they're attractive *because* they're married."

That, she thought, was a good, sensible response. Deflecting trouble, like a good wife and hostess. Where did she find that? "Are you working? I don't want to know *what* you're working on, just *if* you are."

"Writing a screenplay for Zac, but I'd hardly call that work."

"Then why are you doing it?"

"You're a stockbroker, Corrine. Why do *I* have to be pure?"

Corrine twisted away, feeling dizzy for a moment, almost losing her balance as he let go of her. She moved to the sink and turned on the water. It was true, she sold stocks, bonds, annuities. But in her actual heart she was someone entirely different. A lover and a student of life. God, she couldn't believe she was thirty-one. What had happened to the last ten years?

Filling up the coffeepot with water, she felt Jeff still standing behind her. "Some of us had to become regular people so you could have readers." She turned. "You arrogant shit," she said, doused him with the contents of the pot, and then—she didn't know why—sank to the floor in convulsions of hilarity.

"I was *just about* to ask for some water," he said, his scraggly hair and long, untucked shirttails dripping.

She laughed harder. Until finally she coughed, then paused to say, "Just once I think it would be good for you to be at a loss for words."

"Happens all the time," he said. "Whenever I sit down in front of my word processor." Patting himself down with a wad of paper towels, he added, "by the way, I haven't wished you a happy birthday."

"Damn you, that's a secret."

"Thirty-one, *n'est ce pas?*"

"If you say anything I'll kill you."

"What did Russell give you?"

"Head," she answered, laughing uproariously at her improvisation. I *must*, she thought, be drunk.

"About time," Jeff said.

"Believe it or not," she said, standing up and brushing her dress off with exaggerated strokes of her fingers, "other men are more than capable of making women happy. Some of them are so good they just take our little breaths away."

"That's more or less what Caitlin said before she split," he said.

Dave Whitlock, a colleague of Russell's, turned up with a blonde Brazilian named Elsa who worked as a scout for Mondadori. At least Corrine thought that's what she said; it was curious that a Portuguese-speaker would screen books in English for an Italian publisher. Others arrived, people they'd invited for after dinner. The evening broke up into smaller pieces, a mosaic of shiny and oddly shaped fragments grouted with alcohol. Or so it seemed to Corrine the next day. A party is like a marriage, she decided: making itself up while seeming to follow precedent, running on steel rails into uncharted wilderness while the promises shiver and wobble on the armrests like crystal stemware.

House phone to his ear, Russell asked, "Do you know somebody named Ace? The doorman says *he* says you know him."

"It's okay, send him up," Corrine said, blushing. Ace was a homeless man she knew from the soup kitchen where she was a volunteer; buying mixers for the party at Food Emporium in the afternoon, she'd met him redeeming cans and bottles from a noisy garbage bag, the assistant manager looking weary and pissed off as he helped count them into a cardboard box; Ace explained his appearance in her neighborhood by saying that he liked to spread his business around. "Having a party," Ace asked, seeing her purchases. On a sudden guilty inspiration she asked him if he wanted a job helping with the cleanup. And here he was. She was pleased with herself and with Ace for taking her at her word, but Russell made fun of what he called her Mother Teresa complex. In this case he didn't particularly notice or remark on Ace's arrival, though he was hardly inconspicuous—an unwashed black man in a Mets cap and unlaced Nike high-tops, asking the guests if they were finished with their beer bottles. Corrine saw him drink off the residue of a bottle he had liberated from Jeff.

"Used to be," Russell was declaiming, "you'd read a good short story somewhere, call up the author in his hovel, you'd offer him a couple thou' for a collection and a novel, and he'd dedicate his books to you, offer you his mistress, Eskimo style, promise you his firstborn. Now you've got to transfer a six-figure advance to a numbered Swiss bank account just to get a first look at some creative writing student's senior thesis. And his agent's still all over your back."

"Used to be," said Jeff, "only dweebs, dorks and geeks went into publishing. Second sons and Sarah Lawrence grads. I'm sorry to report that this is still the case."

Each with glass in hand, they clenched in an ambiguous bear hug. Corrine watched as the two friends drifted southward across the carpet, this migrating arc finally intersecting the sideboard, Russell's butt glancing it, unbalancing and toppling a blue-and-white Oriental vase, which fell to the floor, narrowly missing the edge of the rug, and shattered on the parquet floor.

Russell's face betrayed his knowledge of this object's dynastic label and long association with Corrine's family—a wedding present. But Corrine rushed in to say it was nothing, she'd get the dustpan, watch out for the pieces.

"Crash Calloway," Jeff said, using the nickname Russell had borne almost since he could walk, fall or knock things over.

At the time of night when guests become disk jockeys, sifting through the library of records and tapes, the stereo becomes a time machine, stuck in reverse. Neil Young's "After the Gold Rush" blasted abruptly from the speakers. Washington was dancing with Jeff's date, and Ace swayed on his feet like a sailor in a six-foot sea, his hand on Zac Solomon's reluctant shoulder, talking about his plans to cut a rap demo.

Casey Reynes drew Corrine aside on her way out and announced she was pregnant. "It's a secret, Tom doesn't want me telling anyone yet."

Corrine embraced her. "I'm so happy for you," she said, though her happiness was tinged unexpectedly with envy.

Elsa, the Brazilian with the Italian connection, was tugging at Corrine's sleeve. Had she seen David Whitlock, her date?

"How far can he get?" Russell called over. "There's only three rooms."

"I'll call you tomorrow," Corrine said to Casey.

Jeff's date was also missing, according to the insistent Elsa.

"He's probably feeding the dog," Russell said.

"What dog," Elsa asked.

"Check the bathroom," said Jeff. "Until recently, the bathroom was always the center of any good party, as the homely kitchen had been in earlier cultures."

Soon Elsa was pounding on the locked door of the bathroom. When she hurled her glass against it, Russell wobbled over to calm her.

"Broom and dustpan are right inside the closet," Corrine called out to Russell, thinking of Casey, the same age as she.

A few minutes later Jeff was passed out on the couch. Strange, Corrine thought. He usually drank everybody under the table. Then she giggled aloud, remembering what Russell had said about under the table. She was recumbent in an armchair, gathering her strength, when the doorman rang. Wearily she picked up the house phone.

"Black guy down here's trying to carry a VCR out the door. Says he's going to repair it. You want me to call the cops?"

"That must be Ace," Corrine said. "Just ask him to leave it with you, Roger. Tell him we changed our minds about the repair." Then she realized she hadn't paid him and asked the doorman to give him a twenty and not to mention anything to Russell.

What's-her-name, Jeff's date, breasts in tow, emerged from the bathroom, a trifle sheepish, and a moment later so did Washington. Uh-oh. Guilty of *something*. Elsa, who watched as Russell cleared up the broken glass, said, "Where's David?" then began pounding the bedroom door, which had gotten closed and locked somehow. Finally Nancy Tanner popped out of the room. Elsa started screaming at Whitlock. It sounded like a real scuffle in there. "London Calling," high volume, made Corrine think briefly about the financial markets; also, fleetingly, about the neighbors. But no, she didn't care to think about the markets right now, thank you very much, and the neighbors would have to speak for themselves. How can you like the Clash, punk-socialist band, and sell corporate equity at the same time? That was the inexplicable mystery of being Corrine Calloway at the age of thirty-one.

Russell wandered over and put his arm around her. "Another successful party," he said.

＊　＊　＊

"Where's the jelly," Russell asked, groping in the drawer of the nightstand.

"Hell with the jelly," Corrine said, rolling him onto his back. "Don't you think it's kind of a sexy idea, doing it without protection? Wouldn't it be sort of incredibly sexy to make me pregnant?"

He stopped moving. "No."

"No, really."

"Yes, really. Are you nuts?"

"Nuts?" She rose to her knees and looked down on him. "*Nuts?* What's that supposed to mean?"

"It means crazy. As in, not in your right mind. Not in your sane self."

"How dare you," she said, punching the side of his head with a half-clenched fist, hurting her knuckles. She stood up, tore the quilt off the bed and retreated to the living room.

"Corrine, I'm too tired to argue," he called after her.

"Good," he heard faintly.

He meant to go out and get her, but woke a few hours later, at seven, with a bad case of cottonmouth and a vast headache, feeling more or less like a porcupine turned inside out. When he turned to look for Corrine, she wasn't there. It took him several minutes to remember it was a weekend, and to figure out where his wife was. Walking out to the living room, he couldn't remember what they'd fought about, but there she was, on the couch amid the debris of her secret birthday party, pictures askew, dead soldiers standing at attention. Corrine curled into a ball under a corner of the quilt. It was not often Russell saw his wife in repose. Usually still talking when he fell asleep, and awake at some hour, like this one, which he preferred not to hear about.

He picked her up and carried her back to bed. "Where were you?" she murmured, as he bumped down the hall with her. "I was lost in this crowd, a big party, and I kept calling you and you weren't there. It was so real. It started out this wonderful party, all our friends and all these interesting new people, and then we lost our friends and I lost you and the party became ugly and sad."

"I'm here," he said, laying her down in bed, where she immediately returned to sleep.

2

"You don't think it's news that the administration's been running drugs? What do *you* call news over there?"

"We just think there's nothing real new in the story, Russ. These allegations have surfaced before."

"Don't tell me about allegations. I'm talking evidence, documentation, smoking guns out the wazoo. This book's got assassination, dope-dealing, money-laundering, and all of it leading straight to the front door of the White House. Nixon got chased out for less. So what does it take with you guys, a game-show angle?"

"I have a meeting, Russell."

"Can you promise me a review, at least?"

"I'll see what I can find out from the books people."

"Loved the cover story on Michael Jackson, by the way. Hard-hitting stuff."

"Jesus, Russell. I said I'll try."

Russell detached the receiver from his ear and lifted it overhead, then made the sound of an airplane falling out of the sky as the instrument traced a series of descending loops ending with a loud crash on his desktop.

From outside his office a nasal female voice called out: "Any survivors?"

"That's a negative."

After six years of Reagan and almost as many in publishing, Russell thought of himself—though he was alone in this perception—as a fairly jaded character. But when this manuscript came across his desk he knew it was one of the books he'd been waiting to publish. It seemed to him a shameful characteristic of the era that the liberal press lacked all conviction while the yahoos were full of passionate insensitivity. For two years the author had followed the story of the secret war in Nicaragua from El Salvador to Israel to Cuba to Washington to Managua to Little Havana. He'd talked to gunrunners and drug runners, contras and Sandinistas, slept in jungles and had his life threatened, and Russell seemed to be the only one who was terribly interested. For weeks he'd been trying to get the big papers and magazines to pick up some of the more sensational revelations. He'd sent galleys to national-affairs editors, followed up with phone calls, and lunched every contact he had, this last one an alleged friend, an editor at a so-called newsweekly.

Righting his tilted chair, he fired off three darts at the opposite wall, missing Elliott Abrams, three points, assistant secretary of state, but catching Oliver North right on the chin, for five points, with the third dart. Various politicians, book reviewers and indignitaries served time on the dartboard when their behavior earned Russell's disapproval.

On the facing wall were photographs of friends, family and heroes: snapshots of Corrine, his mother and father; a framed, already yellowing page from the Sunday *New York Times*, the review of Jeff's book; a poster of the Karsh portrait of Hemingway circa *The Old Man and the Sea*; a photograph of bearded, bleary John Berryman, chin and cigarette in hand; another of Keith Richards, onstage with tongue out, dripping toxic sweat; a publicity still of Jack Nicholson, signed "To Russ, who gives good book—Jack," souvenir of a movie tie-in edition; as well as the usual author photos and book posters.

The phone trilled—neither a ring nor a buzz but a kind of exotic birdcall.

"Incoming," Donna called out. "Victor Propp."

Russell glanced wistfully at the First World War German infantry helmet on his desk, a trophy his grandfather had picked up in the Argonne Forest in 1918, shortly before losing half of his eyesight to mustard gas.

Punching in the speaker phone, he said, "Victor, how goes life and literature?"

"Life is short and brutish, Russell. Full of S and F, et cetera. Literature—truly endless."

Russell took the latter to mean that the book wasn't finished, hardly a surprise. Victor had been working on it for about twenty years, the deadline for delivery receding gradually into a semi-mythical future. In this unfinished condition it, and its author, had become a local literary legend, the locale in this case being a literary/academic republic encompassing patches of Cambridge, New Haven and Manhattan's Upper West Side.

"Did you see that piece on Roth in the *TransAtlantic*? A very snide reference to me—'unlike those rococo goldsmiths who worry the surfaces of their bibelot sentences . . .' "

Russell decided he just might need the helmet. "Victor, I don't necessarily read that as a reference to you."

"Russell, my dear boy, every literary intellectual in America scans that sentence and says, 'For "rococo goldsmiths," read "Victor Propp." ' "

"Not to worry, Victor. There are only three or four literary intellectuals left in the whole goddamn country." It wasn't that Victor didn't have his detractors; just that he nicely illustrated Delmore Schwartz's maxim that even paranoids have enemies.

"Despite your considerable intelligence, Russell, you are remarkably naive. Do you suppose it has anything to do with coming from the Midwest? Not that it's an unattractive quality. It's very American. The thing about real Americans . . ."

Russell looked at his watch as Victor started sermonizing about the land of the freaks and home of the slaves. Eleven-forty. He wet his finger with saliva and polished the crystal. Scanning a report on his desk, he was pleased to discover that *Scavengers and Birds of Prey*, a selected edition of the Audubon plates, was going into another printing. He had guessed correctly that the fiercer birds would be popular in the current climate. He tuned in on a rising interrogatory note in the great man's voice, though Victor's questions were usually rhetorical.

". . . doesn't he? That is to say, Jeff has this very granitic, Yankee quality in his prose which I quite like, the natural thing that Salinger had to work at so obsessively, being a Jew—believe me, I know. But I wonder how to account for all the press on his book?"

Russell tried to remember if he'd ever told Victor that Corrine once had lunch with Salinger, but decided to leave well enough alone.

"I like Jeff's prose quite a bit, its wonderful loopy vitality, but I'm wondering if we shouldn't be working on getting *me* more press at this point in my career."

"Victor, you don't have a book, number one, and number two, you don't exactly write for the *People* magazine crowd. Don't worry about this shit. Remember what Bob Dylan said, 'He's got everything he needs, he's an artist, he don't look back.' "

Victor probably *was* an artist, one of the few in Russell's wide and arty acquaintance, but he didn't seem to have anything he needed and he was constantly looking back, down, around—as if in a maze or a conspiracy. Not trusting the evidence of his senses, he wasn't about to take reality for granted.

"What I'm saying, Russell, is that I think we ought to work on raising my visibility."

"Let's have lunch and talk about it. . . ." Russell found an opening in his datebook ten days away and was able to hang up just a few minutes later.

Donna slouched in with the mail, her haircut reminiscent of a Punic War–era Roman helmet. Clad in black spandex, wearing an "Eat the Rich" button, Donna was a token punk here in a landscape of tartan and tweed. She had a streetwise sense of humor and a hard-boiled telephone manner, which usefully intimidated importunate authors and agents and infuriated Russell's colleagues. She occasionally irritated even her admiring boss with third-hand anarchist posturing. Punk was already a historical fashion, a reified sensibility—the safety pin through the earlobe only slightly less dated than love beads, and now even love beads seemed on the verge of a comeback. Russell was sometimes tempted to tell her the whole scene was middle-aged by the time he arrived in Manhattan about a hundred years before, in 1980, tell her the meaning and origin of *épater la bourgeoisie*. But nothing very interesting had come along in the way of a counterculture since then, unless you counted a recent infestation of titled Europeans, and having Donna around made him feel in touch with the tonsorial practices and the music around St. Mark's Place.

"What do the rich taste like, do you suppose," he asked her.

"Huh?" Donna stopped in the doorway of the office to consider the question. She shrugged, a chronic gesture. "The ladies taste like tuna fish, I guess. The *gentle*men taste kind of like baked brie."

"Jesus. You're a very nasty person. Forget I asked."

"I'm going to lunch," she said.

"I'll warn Donald Trump."

* * *

Before his own lunch Russell called his broker, a hustler at Corrine's firm named Duane Peters.

"Got some new sophisticated financial instruments you might be interested in," Duane said. "A very hot new commodities futures index."

"Tell me about it," Russell said. He liked the idiom of the financial world, the evocative techno-poetry of the arcane slang. Sophisticated instruments. Mezzanine financing. Takeover vehicles . . . Lately it seemed almost as interesting as the more familiar dialect of lit crit. In college he had scorned the econ majors who lined up for the bank recruiters senior year, and only a few years before now he had been horrified to learn that two-thirds of a graduating Yale class had interviewed for a slot at one of the big investment banks. He had cited this statistic over a dozen dinner tables to illustrate vague theses about the zeitgeist and had commissioned a book called *The New Gilded Age*, an anthology of jeremiads by economists and sociologists decrying the greed and selfishness of the eighties. At that time he began to read the financial publications. And then, rather like a research chemist experimentally injecting himself with the virus he has isolated, he began investing small amounts. With his encouragement, Corrine had started as a broker after quitting her good-girl job at Sotheby's—after a stressful year and a half at Columbia Law School—and his new hobby had gradually become more and more interesting. It seemed so easy. He was winning on paper, though his total capital amounted to only a few thousand.

". . . buy stock on margin and then cover the stock with futures, the ideal being to hedge and bet so you're covered either way, cowboy. If the stock goes up you make money. If the stock goes down you make money. So whatever happens, you win."

Is that possible? Russell wondered. Duane's explanation sounded too good to be true; it sounded, in fact, like a free lunch. But he didn't have the ante to play this particular game. Russell wished he could give Corrine his business, but his hunches and tips made her crazy.

Two doors down from Russell's office, Washington Lee received a call from the receptionist announcing a visitor. There was nothing on his calendar, and unscheduled visitors struck fear into Washington's heart. He feared a certain wronged husband in particular, discarded girlfriends and rejected authors in general. His occasional inability to remember absolutely every detail of an evening's activities tended to sharpen his fear of the unknown caller. Two years before he had received an advance to write a critical biography of Frantz Fanon, which was still in the outline stage, and while he didn't really expect the publisher to send thugs over to collect the manuscript, this small festering patch of guilt only added to his sense of having dodged the bullet when another day ended without a major confrontation. The name that his assistant gave him now had a faint echo, but all these Muslim names sounded sort of familiar. Everybody had a story to tell, and if they were black they eventually sent the story to Washington.

"Say who?"

There was a mumbled conference at the other end of the line. "Rasheed Jamal, the *author*," the receptionist explained.

Washington's hope went south. All in all, he would rather get a surprise visit from the FBI. Three stacks of unread, unsolicited manuscripts towered in the far corner of his office, Rasheed Jamal's possibly among them. Or else he had thoughtfully brought his precious manuscript with him, hand-delivery, the true story of his life . . . a thousand single-spaced pages complete with crabbed corrections that would make them both millions and reveal the true killers of JFK and Martin Luther King, Jr. It was possible, too, that Washington had already read the book and turned it down. Authors who came to argue their merits in person were the worst.

"I'm in conference," Washington proposed. "Probably won't be available for the rest of the day."

"I'll tell him."

Now he would have to cower in his office until the coast was clear. If the siege lasted past lunch, he could slip up the internal staircase to the ninth floor and take the elevator down to the street.

"I'm not in," he shouted out to his assistant. "You see anybody heading this way with a manuscript under his arm, tell him Mr. Lee has moved to Zimbabwe."

He was on the phone talking to an agent when a fat bearded man in a sweatsuit announced from the doorway that no white bitch was going to tell him where he couldn't go.

"I just wanted to see what color you were," the speaker said, a scowl deranging his chipmunk features. He clutched a manuscript box out in front of his huge belly, holding it like a shield as he advanced into the office. Experiencing a rapid liquefaction of his internal organs, Washington attempted to appear cool.

"What's your problem, Jack?"

"My problem is I'm a black artist. I'm, like, twice removed from this American fascist racist so-called culture. And I'm trying to create an Afro-American literature which the white man does not want to know about and the white establishment wants to suppress." Washington's assistant had disappeared. He could only hope she was fetching some serious help.

"What's this got to do with me, bro'?"

The author reached into the half-zipped front of his sweatshirt, pulled out and unfolded a limp, ragged piece of paper and recited, without consulting the text: " 'Dear Mr. Jamal, thank you for letting us see your manuscript. I'm sorry to say that the editorial board has concluded that we cannot publish your work at this time. We wish you luck in finding another publisher. Sincerely, Washington Lee.' What kind of fucking letter is that? *Sincerely?* I show you my life's fucking work, the true story of the Black Experience in Babylon exile, and that's all the answer I get? And what's this 'we' shit? I sent my book to one man, dude called Washington Lee I heard was a brother, not the house nigger on some editorial board."

"Maybe I could take another look at it," Washington said, playing for time. He had no idea if he'd read it to begin with. He looked at hundreds of manuscripts a year, and sometimes looking was all he had time for. Being one of only two black adult trade book editors in New York, he was expected to be an advocate for his ostensible community, which, in his experience, wrote no better as a rule than any other group. Washington was as willing and eager as any man could possibly be to discover the next *Invisible Man*, but being black and writing a book didn't necessarily make you Ralph Ellison.

Not a moment too soon, security arrived: two uniformed, deracinated white men who stood sheepishly in the doorway.

"Get this fucking maniac out of here," Washington suggested.

"Don't you touch me," the author screamed.

The security men hung back, helpless in the face of what they took to be an internecine dispute. Only when the enraged author hurled himself across Washington's desk did they intervene. Rasheed Jamal threw one of the guards to the floor and was wrestling with the other, larger one when Washington said, "Freeze, motherfucker." He pointed a shiny gray Walther automatic at the fat man's belly.

The security guards, recovering themselves, seemed uncertain of their own role in relation to the firearm, till Washington said, "What've I got to do, carry him out my own fucking self?" Each seizing an arm, the security men pulled Rasheed Jamal to the door, then turned sideways to extract him from the office.

"You ain't no black man," he screamed at Washington.

"And you ain't no writer," Washington responded, having finally remembered reading several chapters of the thousand-page-plus novel that lay in two boxes on his desk. It was only through the exercise of enormous willpower that he restrained himself from pulling the trigger until the so-called author was gone. "And haul your garbage out with you," he shouted, knocking the boxes to the floor. Shaken, he aimed the gun at his own mouth and treated himself to several tranquilizing squirts of vodka.

LOST OUR LEASE said the sign in a window down the block from the office. Lot of those signs popping up lately. On the walk back from lunch with an agent, Russell paused for a moment in front of the window to examine the sale carpets, cheery kilims, a jaded Hariz. Russell's office was located in one of those interstitial regions of the city which until recently had been nameless. It was between Gramercy Park and Chelsea, south of midtown but not properly downtown—an area of century-old eight- and ten-story office and warehouse buildings given over largely to light industry, the Oriental carpet trade and downmarket photographers. The Carpet District, he called it, but lately the rug traders had been folding up their tents. Fashion and the kind of money that traveled light—hip retail and restaurants—had found the area and named it the Flatiron District, after its most famous building. Lunch had certainly become easier. Two years before he had had to get into a taxi to find food that wouldn't offend literary agents. Now they were willing to come down to check out the latest Piedmontese trattoria they'd read about in the *Times*.

The Corbin, Dern Building stood in the middle of its block, on real estate that had quadrupled in value since Russell had been hired, a parking lot on one side and a small brownstone on the other. The publishing house occupied the top four of nine floors. The century-old structure had been copied from a nearby McKim, Mead & White building, and had been occupied since the twenties by the trade publishing firm of Corbin, Dern and Company. For writers and readers and reviewers, Corbin, Dern was a resonant dactyl, an invocation of the muses, a top-shelf cultural brand name.

After lunch Russell stopped in on Washington, who was conducting business in his habitual fashion, leaning back in his ergonomic Italian chair, stretched full length, cowboy boots on the edge of his desk, hands clasped behind his head. He put Russell in mind of a big cat, speed and claws concealed beneath a tropical manner. You seldom saw him run or pounce, but in the dry seasons he brought back prey. Just when it seemed there was no choice but to fire him for some radical breach of decorum, he dragged in a best-seller or one of his obscure Eastern European novelists suddenly won the Nobel Prize.

Waving to Washington's assistant, Russell did not wait for permission to clump in and lie down on the couch; unconsciously he mimicked his friend's position, picking up a copy of the *Post* from the coffee table. HOMELESS MAN ATTACKED BY GIANT CAT. He glanced up at Washington, then turned to page three, where he learned that a leopard or possibly a cheetah was terrorizing the Lower East Side, mauling winos and other street people.

"Yeah, man, let me get back to you."

Lee's manner was always furtive, as if engaged in clandestine business or tryst-making. Russell wondered whether Washington really wanted to get rid of this phone call or just didn't want him to hear it.

"Yo, it's my man Russ."

"I gotta get some heat on this Nicaragua book."

"You talk to Harold?"

"I thought he was already behind me." Washington had occupied the office next to Harold Stone's for a year before Russell had come along. They were contemporaries, though Washington had been moving up the ladder while Russell was still in graduate school. Being the only senior editor who fully qualified as a member of a minority group, and fluent in several important languages, Washington was virtually fearless. "I have tenure," he told Russell one night over many drinks. A Harvard scholarship man like Harold, he'd grown up in Harlem, like almost no one else in the publishing industry, and the few people who had the power to fire him felt just terrible about it.

"Two things you got to remember about Harold," Washington said now. "First, he *used* to be a big liberal. Got that? Look at the people he hangs out with now, socialites and neo-con economists, leveraged-buyout dudes. You think they're jamming about Marcuse and Malcolm X at dinner? Social justice and third-world revolutions are definitely not what is happening. Not on Park or Madison, anyway. Nobody wants to change the world anymore. They just want to own it. Harold's no dummy. All that stuff he did in the sixties, it was chic and it paid. Revolution was good business."

"Easy to say now."

"Doesn't make it any less true. Second, don't assume he wants your books to succeed."

This had occurred to Russell. But it was also important not to take Washington absolutely at face value. Though he almost always *intended* to be on Russell's team, he was a man of facets and intrigues so complex they were not always comprehensible even to himself. A good editor, Washington would have been an even better double agent.

"The world is divided into three kinds of people as far as this shit is concerned," Washington said, on a roll. "There's the good people like you, who are surprised and indignant that, whoa, hey, stop the presses, the government's up to no good. There are the people like me, who aren't surprised at all. Who already fucking knew. Then there's the majority, and they don't *want* to know about it, Jack." Washington pointed his Walther at Russell, who opened his mouth for a squirt. "By the way—how do you know the brother who was at your party the other night?"

"What brother?"

"How many *were* there, man?"

"I didn't notice."

"Jesus." Washington had seen other examples of Russell's obliviousness to his environment, though this seemed extreme. But he was not necessarily sorry in this case. He had been to grade school with the dude, and it had disconcerted him to encounter him there, among the white folks, in Russell's apartment. He did not necessarily like the idea of Russell's knowing about his other life in the old neighborhood, so he let it slide. Some shit don't mix.

Distasteful as it was, Russell felt he owed it to his author to grovel. That was the only chance he had to light a fire under this book. He had to go to the great Harold Stone, who was believed by some to have invented publishing, who taught the alphabet to Gutenberg, whose blessing called forth glowing reviews, serious essays, Guggenheim fellowships. Who was *there* when Jesus Christ had his moment of doubt and whatever. Doubt and shame? Doubt and pain? Or doubt and hate? Next rhyme was "fate." If anybody could wire it, Harold could.

Russell padded down the ancient hall carpet to the editor in chief's corner office. For three years he had been right next door to his mentor in a narrow cubicle. But when he had finally been promoted and a bigger office had become available a few months back, Russell had moved a hundred feet away. It was something like leaving home for college. Suddenly he felt awkward when he encountered Harold in the men's room; he would clear his throat, hold his dick and stare at the eye-level tiles. He wasn't sure how this had come about, whether he only imagined a change. But today he realized he hadn't spoken to Harold in almost a week.

"Nice pearls," he said to Carlton, Harold's blonde and toothy assistant, who sat importantly erect, guarding the portal to the chief, like a girl sporting a broomstick internally, flush against her spinal column. A year out of Radcliffe, she wore the regulation turtleneck and strand of pearls and believed totally in Harold Stone's divinity. She held up one hand in a traffic-cop gesture while cradling the phone in the other. "I'll tell him, I'm sure he will." When hell freezes over, Russell thought. Harold was notorious for not returning calls, and he had stopped writing letters some years before.

"Is he expecting you," Carlton asked when she'd hung up the phone.

Russell stuck his head inside the office; Harold looked up from a magazine he was reading. "Now he is." He refrained from adding, *And do try not to be an officious bitch.* Until recently she'd been meek around

Russell, but now she projected an aura of self-importance befitting a senior officer in the company. Still, Harold had always valued Russell's enthusiastic lack of tact, an unusual quality in the timid precincts of book publishing.

Years before, Russell had decided Harold looked like a great horned owl (a member of Strigiformes Strigidae, as depicted by Audubon, plate 236), and the resemblance seemed only to increase over time. Looking up, his yellow-brown eyes blinking irritably through horn-rimmed glasses, he simulated something awakened out of a bad sleep in the crotch of a dead maple; he nodded and made a faintly interrogatory sound. His lack of the recommended minimum social graces seemed a matter of principle, as if charm, manners and the other lubricants of interpersonal contact betokened a lack of high seriousness. He seldom looked anyone in the eye, shunned greetings, ignored questions—behavior that his inferiors tended to read as arrogance, admirers as the gangly awkwardness of genius. His manner of dress had been adopted in Cambridge years and never revised, button-down shirts and chinos, a jacket when he had to, seldom a tie.

"Can we talk about the Rappaport book?"

"The Nicaragua thing?" Harold said.

"Yeah. *The Secret War*," Russell said, irritated that Harold would forget, or affect to forget, the author's name. Harold had encouraged Russell to buy this book.

"I'm still not crazy about the title."

"I'm having trouble getting it out there."

Harold shrugged. Russell sat down on the edge of the long desk. Though Harold had occupied it for ten years, the office didn't look like it belonged to anyone in particular, which said more about its tenant than the clutter of photos, postcards and memorabilia in adjoining offices said about theirs.

"People aren't reading books anymore," Harold observed, looking out the window, which showed a slice of the Flatiron Building to the west and the Empire State to the north. Russell was reminded of a night several months before when he and Harold had stayed late and polished off a bottle of Armagnac. It was the only time Russell had ever seen his mentor drunk or heard him talk about his marriage, his wife's repeated hospitalizations and suicide threats. And later, when Russell had flattered him shamelessly, Harold had waved it off, saying that he'd been living off his intellectual capital for years, that he felt like the man married young to a ravishing beauty, long sated with her charms, who takes his pleasure from the hungry looks of other men. That, he insisted, was how he felt about most of the books he published. It had all been done. At that time, Harold had seemed to Russell like a stoic hero. Now Russell was beginning to think Harold regretted his candor. From that day on, a certain chilliness had seemed to prevail.

Russell stood up and surveyed the neat spines in the bookshelves, which looked like mere display cases for company product. It was impressive in a way, how Harold stood aloof from his immediate physical environment. Only two photographs adorned the lair; one of Harold and Saul Bellow, some twenty years younger, sitting uncomfortably side by side at a dinner table, Harold thinner, almost gaunt, but otherwise the same; and one of Robert Kennedy, smiling at a frowning Harold, friendly politician's hand on the editor's stiff shoulders. Considering the range of Harold's acquaintance among the famous and distinguished, Russell often wondered what process or lack of it had resulted in the selection of these two photographs to represent Harold's life and career.

"I was hoping you could think of somebody outside the book press who might want to do a news story."

Harold nodded thoughtfully, noncommittally, staring just slightly to the left of Russell's ear.

"It's not as if I think we need to hype this. If we can just get it noticed—"

"What's happening with Propp?" Harold interrupted.

After five years Russell still wasn't sure if these non sequiturs of Harold's were part of a conscious strategy for unsettling interlocutors or an innocent eccentricity.

"He mostly wants to know why I can't get him on the *Today* show."

"Is he ever going to finish the goddamn book?"

"Hey, give the guy a break. It's only six years overdue."

"Seven."

"Harold, what do I need to get the Rappaport book out there? Take hostages? Shoot the president?"

"When's Jeff going to deliver a manuscript?"

"Whenever he finishes."

"Is he writing at all? Seems like he's out screwing every model in New York. Maybe he doesn't have another book in him. Some don't."

"Jeff's got plenty of books in him."

Harold had been extremely supportive when Russell—a little embarrassed because the author happened to be one of his best friends—had first showed him the manuscript three years before. He encouraged Russell to buy it, talked it up among his friends in the literary world and, Russell suspected, wired a review or two. Not even Harold could *make* a book happen, but he could help, and he had. The early succès d'estime was followed by an uncommonly large sale for a collection of short stories, pushing it onto the *New York Times* best-seller list for a few weeks. Two of the stories had been optioned for the movies, and the translation had just won a literary prize in France. The rising arc of Jeff's star had lifted Russell's, and now Harold's attitude toward the book seemed complicated, as if he'd let the kids use the garage to build a go-cart and they'd emerged with the prototype for a Formula 1 race car. His attitude appeared to waver between wanting his name on the hood as a sponsor and hoping that it would crash and burn in the early laps.

"What's your wife say about the market?"

"Waiting for a correction. Next couple months."

Harold pursed his lips and seemed to weigh this notion.

"What about Rappaport?"

"I'll think about it."

"If you would," Russell said sarcastically.

"Hey, talk to that assistant of yours, will you?" Harold said as Russell was leaving. "Kleinfeld was down here this morning and almost called the cops when he saw her at the Xerox machine. Wearing some T-shirt that said 'Fuck the Rich.' "

"It was a button that said—"

"Whatever," Harold said. "Tell her to lose it."

"Why?"

"Don't be cute. You're a big boy now, Russell."

Walking back to his office, Russell thought about sending the editor in chief a copy of a widely anthologized essay about the Berkeley free speech movement written by a fiery young polemicist named Harold Stone. Being a big boy presumably meant stifling that kind of impulse.

A junior associate of the old *Partisan Review* gang, Harold Stone had become known as a wunderkind even before he came down from Harvard with an essay titled "Bakunin and the Idea of an Avant-Garde." He took a job at Knopf, shared a girl with Bellow and got his glasses broken by Mailer, thereby sealing his reputation. At increasing intervals, he published essays and book reviews that were much discussed in the closing days of the last literary establishment in New York. Along the way he had married a young Waspy debutante who now led an entirely separate existence in New Canaan, Connecticut, though they remained married.

Fresh from the suburban Midwest, Russell had devoured Harold's editions of Sartre and Camus and Gramsci in college; he had read Harold's essays on Lukacs and Kafka. When he arrived in Manhattan after graduate work at Oxford, Russell had been fortunate to find a job at the venerable publishing house where Harold reigned, and to come to the older man's attention by way of some poems he had had published in a quarterly. Perhaps Harold had felt nostalgic for the idea of literary young men coming to the city, grateful for the idea that young men were still writing poetry at all, in the manner of his friends from the Village days so long past; curious to know what the smart young men were reading nowadays; guilty possibly, because as likely as not he was about to have lunch at The Four Seasons with a millionaire author of espionage thrillers. At any rate, Harold had seen something in the poems. He first took Russell out to lunch and later took him under his prickly, owlish wing.

At seven, as he was leaving for the day, Russell stopped by Dave Whitlock's office. Whitlock was staring gloomily at his computer terminal. He was the numbers man: the numbers always seemed to make him unhappy.

"Don't fret, Whit. I've got an anthology of Serbo-Croatian poetry in the works that should turn us around."

"Not today, please," said Whitlock, waving him off.

Russell's age, he had been at Wharton learning econometric models while Russell was at Oxford reading Blake, and had arrived at the firm almost the same day as Russell. Whitlock's great tragedy as a businessman was that he actually read books. Four years before, he could have started with a consulting firm or an investment bank for twice as much money as he was now making in publishing.

"Sorry about the Rappaport book."

"What about it?"

"You didn't hear? Harold cut the print run down to ten thousand this morning."

"I was just in there today. The son of a bitch didn't say a word."

Harold's door was closed and Carlton wasn't at her station. Russell simultaneously rapped and pushed the door open. Harold was sitting on the couch; Carlton was sitting on Harold. In the moment after they registered Russell's presence, both turned to monitor and cover their immediate exposure, banging heads audibly. In raising a hand extracted from Carlton's blouse, Harold spilled her onto the floor. Their faces betrayed them more than the flash of white cotton and flesh: surprise modulating rapidly through guilt to gross indignation.

In the days that followed Russell Calloway was left to imagine what the prevailing emotion would be. But from the first instant, he was fairly certain that opening Harold's door had not been one of the all-time great career moves.

3

Corrine was getting so tired of parties: dinner parties, birthday parties, publication parties, housewarming parties; holiday and theme parties; opening-night parties, closing-night parties; gallery openings; junior committee benefits for the American Ballet Theater and the Public Library; benefits for the Democratic candidate, the Society for the Facially Disfigured, the Coalition for the Homeless, the American Medical Foundation for AIDS Research; at nightclubs, at the Plaza and the Temple of Dendur in the Metropolitan Museum of Art; in honor of someone named Alonzo, this being his entire name, who is a professional fundraiser and party-giver . . . a party for Pandy Birdsall, who was moving to L.A. because she'd slept with everybody in New York. "Partying is such sweet sorrow," Jeff said that night.

Last night Russell's colleagues had given a party for a departing editor. So after work Corrine schlepped uptown to Russell's office—subway up to 23rd, twirl around till you figure out you came out of the subway some strange new way and had set off in the wrong direction—then stood around smiling foolishly in a stuffy conference room where impoverished editorial assistants surreptitiously devoured the canapés, gratefully calculating what they were saving on dinner, while the senior staff huddled virtuously in aloof constellations, checking their watches until they could slip off for serious cocktails and fashionable dinners on expense account. Harold Stone with his pained scowl showed up just long enough to convey the impression that fraternizing with his colleagues was slightly less pleasant than catheter insertion, poor Crash still worried that Harold would drop the boom on him; Corrine's comment being, if they wanted privacy why the hell didn't they lock the door? Finally a group of them had gone uptown to Elaine's for an endless, boozy dinner with heaping portions of inside publishing dope. . . .

Now, after a few hours of sleep, Corrine had to go to work. Russell was still in bed. Publishing didn't start until ten; she tried to be in her office by seven forty-five so she could do some research before the staff meeting at eight-fifteen, when the senior brokers would pick issues, analyze the performance of the market the day before, discuss what had happened on the Tokyo exchange. Although today she'd be lucky to make the meeting.

After her shower she still felt exhausted. In the dressing area off the bedroom was a vanity; she sat down with a cup of coffee and turned on the little portable television. God, what a wreck of a face, she thought, looking in the mirror. Methuselah, who turned men to stone. Or was it Medusa? She decided to absolutely stop drinking for a while. Robbing her skin of its youth. Mainline collagen instead.

Applying moisturizer, she listened to an interview with Madonna, who seemed to be claiming that she was the reincarnation of Marilyn Monroe. You wish, honey. Marilyn Monroe probably wished *she* was Marilyn Monroe. Being gorgeous hadn't done much for her self-esteem. Still, Corrine thought she'd like to try it on for size . . . 36C or whatever. Russell would be pleased. Hey, there, big boy . . . two inches and one letter bigger. Come up sometime and see me—no, that was Mae West. Inspire him to come to bed a little earlier, with romantic inclinations. Not just pass out. Be nice if, like men, they would get big for sex—so the boys could play with and admire them—and then shrink back down again so they wouldn't get in the way. Why not? Another example of men getting the better deal. Nature was misogynist. She smoothed foundation over the pale skin, lingering on a thin blue vein under her cheek. The night after her birthday party was the last time, almost two weeks before. Could it be that long? Other men seemed to find her attractive enough. On the street, on the subway, at parties. Always at parties.

A tiny mole on her chin that her mother called a beauty mark and her father wanted to have removed. Dab, dab. Cover it up, cover girl. Hopeless. Paper-bag-over-head time. A simple grocery bag for work and around the house, a Saks or Bergdorf bag for evening wear.

Color fix around the eyes. Looking at the raccoon circles underneath. She wondered if all those names starting with M on TV just now had made her think of Medusa. MTV. Was that publicly held? Must check.

Marilyn and Madonna and Medusa. With regard to the market she secretly believed in omens. Not by themselves, but if everything else looked right. You started with the numbers, but in the end sometimes you needed one more piece. But what was the significance of this M motif? Buy Monsanto? Sell Mobil? She needed more input. More M-put. Sometimes she relied on her dreams, but she was so tired she couldn't remember her dreams this morning.

Sibyl. That was what she needed. A dream reader. Did anybody still read entrails? Messy. Like this hair. Was Medusa the one with snakes for hair? Corrine's looked distinctly snakelike this morning. Nest of vipers. Forked-tongue split ends. Sibilant. What she needed was the new, improved shampoo with miracle conditioner that untangles your hair, erases your wrinkles, firms and lifts your breasts and makes your husband want to shave before he comes to bed and fuck you till the cows come home. Lather, rinse, repeat. Daily. Every morning she vowed she would cut all her hair off, it was a pain, and besides, wasn't it girlish to have hair past your shoulders? But Russell would never forgive her. Men have this thing about hair and women. Want lots on your head, hardly any elsewhere.

Still looking like hell, she went out to the kitchen for another cup of coffee. Russell's camel-hair coat tossed over the back of the couch. Once upon a time she would have found this cute. This morning it just pissed her off.

Back in the bedroom she went to work on her eyes. Windows of the soul. Well, windows needed frames and drapes, didn't they? Brushing on eye shadow. Shutters by Chanel. A nice copper shade on the crow's-feet. The bird with the coppery, keen claws. Who was that . . . Wallace Stevens? A thing about birds, that guy. Looked like Hitchcock, too. Parrots, parakeets, flocks of pigeons. Complacencies of the peignoir—she could use a little of that this morning. Her robe was beat—a total rag.

We're here this morning with Johnny Moniker, the latest star on the fashionable downtown scene. . . .

Corrine looked up at the TV set. Guy looked familiar, kind of cute. She hadn't quite caught the name—Johnny Monologue? She was almost sure he'd been at the apartment a few weeks before. Dark, nasty good looks . . . She'd seen him with Jeff, maybe.

Corrine scuttled over to the bed and prodded Russell.

"There's this guy on TV we've seen somewhere," she said.

"Who?"

"That's what I want to know." She bounced childishly on the bed. "Johnny something."

"Johnny got his gun, shot his wife. Because she woke him up."

"No. Come look."

"Somebody we know?" he said, still refusing to budge.

"Not really. We just met him for a minute."

"Johnny we hardly knew ye."

By the time she got him to the TV they were showing spring fashions from Milan.

"Why am I awake," Russell asked.

Sighing, Corrine went to the bathroom for the aspirin. Only Corrine, Russell thought, *would* be surprised to see someone vaguely familiar on TV. That was the whole point of TV, to make everything familiar. It was like her dreams. Almost every morning she would wake him with the words, "I had the strangest dream," as if she expected dreams somehow to be less dreamlike. She was relentlessly logical, like a child. Her superstition, which seemed when he had first met her to be at odds with the general cast of her character, was actually a corollary of this logical bent. She didn't believe in random events, so if the number eleven swam into her ken several times in the course of a morning she felt certain that there must be a good reason, some deep structure of which this was a coordinate, even if she couldn't figure out exactly what it was. As it turned out, the combination of mathematical genius, tenacity and a superstitious nature made her an excellent reader of the stock market.

He climbed back into bed.

"How do I look," Corrine asked after she handed him the aspirin. He shook three out of the bottle and looked up.

"Fabulously gorgeous."

"I do not."

"Yes you do. Got something going at the office? Something on the side?"

"I should. Can't seem to get a rise out of you lately."

"Hey, I'm sorry. Literally working my balls off. Plus all this goddamn socializing. We'll stay home tonight."

"Promise?" She knelt beside the bed and stroked his forehead. "Let's order in and have a fire."

"Shit." He frowned. "I've got dinner with an agent."

"Cancel it." She buried her head in his neck and began to tickle his earlobe with the tip of her tongue.

"I'd do it in a minute, honey, but he's going back to L.A. tomorrow."

"What's all this L.A. stuff?"

"I'm being sucked into the entertainment business, like the rest of the country."

She stood up abruptly and straightened her blouse.

"He's got a client I want to sign for a book. Tomorrow night we'll stay home." Russell sat all the way up in bed to demonstrate good faith. "Promise."

"The check's in the mail," Corrine said. "And I won't come in your mouth." That would put a little blush on his face. She blew him a kiss, turned and walked out with a haughty, rhythmic deployment of her buttocks.

"Great ass," Russell called after her.

"None for you," she responded.

Across the hall, Mrs. Oliver opened her door as far as the chain would stretch and peered out, her pruney face framed between door and jamb, the brass chain pressed above her lip like a mustache, her Yorkie yipping behind her. Since her husband had passed on to that old men's club in the sky, Mrs. Oliver spent her waking hours standing behind the door, waiting for the sound of a footstep on the stairs, as if it were her fondest wish to be a prosecution witness before she departed this crime-ridden world. All day long she opened and closed the door like a bivalve drawing nutrients from the ocean. Corrine waved.

Downstairs, Roger held the door for her and smiled. "Good morning, Mrs. Calloway." Watching her pass, the doorman felt a flutter of desire that was like a shot of helium in his lungs, lifting him up, making him weightless with the exhilaration of her presence, which for one moment he shared with no one else, and when she had passed he felt sad and lumpish with desire.

Out in the air, she started to feel better. Crisp, excoriating January cold. The sky was bright and clear, having, unlike Corrine, gone to sleep at a sensible hour. Joggers passing in bright colors, damn them. Someday she intended to start exercising again. Three Pekingese inspected a fragrant crack in the sidewalk in front of a brownstone while their mistress stood patiently tethered on three leashes, blue-haired, wearing an empty plastic baggie on her free hand.

At Lexington, Corrine smelled pot; two men in suits walking ahead of her were sharing a joint. The phrase "Cola Wars" drifted back to her with the smoke: ad guys, jump-starting inspiration.

After buying the *Journal* outside the subway entrance, she plunged underground into the briefcase-toting army of the employed and stood jam-packed with a thousand other New Yorkers on the platform, thinking that although they looked featureless together, their inner lives seethed beneath the worsted wool—scores of them cheating on their spouses and their taxes, dreaming of murder and flight. If she were to ask she would find herself connected through friends and acquaintances with many of them; if a catastrophe were to strike they would all find themselves linked and bonded, but now they stood silent and remote. The phrase FIND THE CURE stenciled on the post beside her. How many people on the platform had it? What was that old poem Russell had written about at Oxford? "Journal in Time of Plague"? Something about light falling from the air . . .

She lifted her paper and disappeared into the columns of newsprint, to emerge ninety blocks downtown, borne up to the surface by the heavily bundled throngs, pumped out onto Wall Street, which marked the northern frontier of New Amsterdam and was named for the seventeenth-century log wall that had protected the Dutch settlers from the Indians and the British. Shunning the contemporary female custom of wearing running shoes between home and office, Corrine clicked along on calf pumps just outside the limits of the invisible ancient wall, high-stepping over buried ceramic pipe bowls and wine jugs, bent nails, broken glass and brick fragments, partially fossilized pig, chicken and sheep bones, and other detritus that had been regularly tossed over the wall three centuries before, her route so familiar that she was as oblivious to it as she was to what was underneath the pavement, not really seeing the towering temples to Mammon as she walked toward the one in which she toiled, reading her paper in the available light that found its way to the canyon floor.

* * *

"So, people, this could be the day. The big day, the historic day. The market's looking good, it's looking fit and ready. I think we're going to hit two thousand. The big two-oh-oh-oh. And I think we want to use this as our selling point, particularly in our cold-calling situation."

"Go, team," Corrine whispered to Duane.

"We want to say, 'Mr. John Q. Doctor, you've been missing out here, history's being made today, and your neighbors are getting rich. How about you?'"

Sitting beside her in the overheated conference room, Duane Peters involuntarily nodded in agreement, his yellow tie bobbing up and down on his chest like something meant to attract fish. These yellow ties were too much in the morning—Duane and the supervisor both. So was the pep talk.

It was all too much. The Dow Jones would probably hit two grand today, but Corrine thought it was crazy. The economy was in dreary shape, inventories high, GNP slow, but the Dow kept shooting up. It was a kind of mass hypnosis. Castles in the air.

She had to be careful what she said around the office. Wall Street was pumped up. It was like a cocaine jag. Everyone grinning fiendishly, talking too fast, not quite focusing on anything. The clients, too. Especially the clients. Corrine tried to moderate their greed, urging them to look for real value. Though she wasn't above listening to her superstitions, her basic resource was simple math. If an established company was selling at ten times earnings, it was probably a better bet than an upstart going for fifty times earnings. But everybody wanted instant gratification. They wanted to be junior arbitrageurs. They wanted risk without downside. Big beta factors and guaranteed return. They wanted to get in on a takeover prospect right before it went into play and double their money in three days. They wanted whatever was in the headlines that week, preferably on margin. They wanted to be able to tell their dinner guests they sold short on a turkey. They wanted sex and drugs and rock-and-roll.

Russell was the worst. When he and Corrine finally agreed to divide their tiny investment capital in half, he started trading frequently with Duane. Lately Russell had mentioned he wanted to get into options. She told him she didn't want to hear about it. Her portion, less than two thousand—very big deal—stayed in the money market.

The supervisor was messianic on the subject of phone technique. This part Corrine tuned out. After the meeting, Duane walked her back to their adjoining work stations. He was blond, athletically proportioned, a man of his times, and his predominant mood was up. He, too, was a little too much in the morning.

"Any hot ones today, beautiful," he asked.

Corrine shook her head. They walked down a long aisle flanked with work stations, computer terminals with video screens glowing green with numbers. They had been through the training program together and now shared a secretary. Corrine liked their bantering camaraderie, although she was afraid she might have to throw a little cold water on him soon. The problem with Duane, it seemed to her, was that someone had once told him that he was dashingly handsome, and he'd taken it to heart. There was a kind of self-consciousness to his insouciant gestures and his attention to dress that made him seem comic. Maybe it was just youth. He was almost five years younger, having arrived here straight out of Dartmouth—all the kids now rushing headlong into professions they'd chosen in the cradle. Whatever happened to trying things out? Corrine had tried Europe, law school and Sotheby's and felt like the last of a species—almost the oldest broker at her firm. No country for old men, this business.

Duane was talking about a hot tip, biotech.

"Have you checked it out," she asked, just to say something.

"Looking real good, numberwise." As an analyst he was a little flighty, though he was doing well in the current flighty market.

She stopped in front of her own station, demarked by flimsy partitions on three sides, a token of her seniority. "Cold-calling," Duane asked.

"Eventually." She sighed. It was what she hated most about the business, ambushing strangers on the phone, trying to sell them something they didn't know they wanted. At first that was all she did, but now she at least had a roster of regular customers, though not yet enough that she could afford to stop soliciting.

"Look what I have," Duane said, extracting a stapled sheaf of papers from a folder. He held it between his fingers, dangling it like a treat, and made the cooing sound of a pigeon.

"What is it?"

"Only an up-to-the-minute mailing list of every dentist in New York State."

"Where did you get that?" Doctors and dentists, wealthy and financially unsophisticated, were the preferred diet of the small broker.

He brushed the edge of the partition with his fingers and checked them for dust before leaning against it.

"Sorry. Can't divulge my sources. However, if you would join me for lunch today, I could maybe shave off a few of these names with home and office numbers for you. The Q's and the X's, say?"

"Give me the M's."

"Come to lunch."

"Deal."

He handed her several sheets and disappeared, then called from the other side of the partition, "Where, by the way, is the lissome Laura?" His head reappeared. "Isn't she supposed to be our full-time secretary? Or am I mixed up on this?"

"She'll be in by ten," Corrine said.

"Wish *I* could keep banker's hours." He withdrew again.

Corrine didn't want to tell him that Laura was on a go-see. Although she wore a size fourteen and had a troublesome complexion, Laura dreamed of Paris runways and magazine covers and had been attending a modeling academy at night. The brochure claimed to guarantee success in the world's most glamorous career; by the time Laura showed it to Corrine it was too late for her to say anything. Corrine did not expect to lose Laura to the Ford agency, and she covered for her so Laura would have a job to come back to when her dream faded away. Duane, on the other hand, would have been a bit cruel about the whole thing.

Corrine looked at the *Journal*, punched up numbers on some stocks she'd been watching. At about nine-thirty, she began calling.

When Laura returned, she seemed dispirited and said nothing about the go-see. Delivering the mail later, she said to Corrine, "Did you see Johnny Moniker on TV this morning?"

"Yeah, but who *is* he?" Corrine demanded.

"I don't know. I see him in the magazines."

And then a morning of painful dental work.

When the market closed at 2,003, a cheer went up around the trading room. Duane waltzed around the partition and swept Corrine into his arms, taking advantage of the situation to slip her a little tongue.

Corrine was on the phone with a client and twisted her head away. The client was upset because Corrine had him in a stock that had grown only nineteen percent for the first six months of the year, and he had just read in *Forbes* that the market was up twenty-two percent for the same period. She suggested that if he averaged in the dividend he would find himself way ahead of the game. Duane stood off to one side, absently adjusting the gold stickpin that held the two sides of his collar together. She rolled her eyes for him, held up one finger. Corrine didn't think anybody under forty should wear stickpins.

"Get me out of here," she moaned when she finally hung up.

They walked over to Harry's, a basement saloon favored by the boozier traders and brokers and by the news media whenever the market was news, as it was today. A crowd had formed around the entrance; pitchers of beer were being handed around on the sidewalk. Like a flock of fearless panhandlers wielding outstretched paper cups, representatives of the electronic press thrust microphones at every passing face.

"Everybody here seems pretty happy," said a glamorous blonde who aimed her microphone at Corrine.

"Let's hope they're not hung over tomorrow or the next day," Corrine said.

"What do you mean by that? Do you think the market's peaked?" ·

"I hope not," she said judiciously, as Duane yanked her forward.

Eventually Duane managed to get a bottle of champagne, with which he sprayed himself and some of their neighbors.

"You're that excited about the market?"

"This is actually to celebrate our anniversary," he said.

"What anniversary," she asked suspiciously.

"Two years since we entered the training program."

"You're sweet."

"So are you," he said earnestly, his big blond eyebrows nearly meeting in the middle. She could see an attack of sincerity coming on him like a sneeze. "In fact, you're the sweetest girl I've ever met."

She laughed and tapped his glass, and threw back her own. "You must know a lot of citrus queens. So how'd you do today," she asked, and his face lit up as he described a coup, how he'd heard about a company that was about to go into play. "The buzz was takeover and the buzz went out on the wire and the stock went up. Rumor becomes fact. Even if the stock wasn't in play before, it is now. God bless America." He poured another glass.

"Catch that buzz," she shouted, over the din.

As he poured the last of the champagne, which she declined, Duane suddenly became serious. Taking advantage of the privacy afforded by the mob, he said he had to get something off his chest. Corrine wanted to stop him before he got started, but the champagne seemed to have robbed her of her will; she felt like a creature of the savanna stung with a tranquilizing dart, stunned, gazing out from glazey eyes as the biologist scurried in to perform his tasks. . . .

He told her that she was the finest and most beautiful and intelligent woman he'd ever met and that he was in love, even though, sure, he knew he shouldn't be. "I don't know, I'm just saying I'm in love with you and I'd do anything to be with you," he concluded pathetically. She was touched by his sweet adulation. But she had to be firm and she was, pulling away from him and raising the last of the champagne to her lips. She was finally a little more stern than she felt, for part of her was grateful because she suddenly realized she'd needed to feel the way she did when he was saying those wonderful things, and in this celebratory, demi-Dionysian atmosphere it seemed almost appropriate to strip off your clothes and give yourself over to the spirit of the moment.

He was embarrassed, of course, but she summoned her will again and led him gradually out into the clear light of a daytime world in which she was older and married and they were colleagues with an office to return to. But meanwhile she wanted to assuage his hurt pride and show him she wasn't offended, so she ordered another bottle of champagne, though she was going to lay off drinking the next day for sure, and by the time that was gone she felt quite happy with Duane and with everyone around her, part of the great celebration in which she didn't quite believe. Outside, when Channel 4 stuck a microphone in her face, she said, "I don't know, I think basically the emperor's got no clothes. But at the moment he has a pretty good body."

As the champagne wore off in the taxi she realized that it was her night to work at the soup kitchen. She'd completely forgotten. She looked at her watch. There was time to help with the cleanup, but she felt too guilty and disgusted with herself to think about scouring a vat caked with hot-dog stew as a champagne hangover set in.

Russell had left a message on the machine; he was finishing drinks with an author, then dinner with the agent at a restaurant called Cambodia.

Feeling immensely fat and full of high-calorie fermented grapes, Corrine decided not to eat; but eventually she went out and picked up a fruit salad at the Korean market and lay on the couch watching stupid television shows, nurturing the warm sleepy feeling of being wanted, which had stayed with her through the afternoon, but which otherwise had been in rather short supply.

At eleven-ten she was astonished to see her face on TV as she flipped through the channels—*a pretty good body*.

Oh God, some horrible blowsy fat tramp two and half sheets to the wind, and there was Duane with a sort of precoital grin hovering over her shoulder. She was glad Russell hadn't been around to see it.

She was half asleep when he tiptoed in, breathing awkwardly, a little after one. He undressed in the dark and slipped between the sheets. She wanted to let him know she was awake, wanted to hear about his evening, but she wasn't quite sure how she was feeling about Russell: she had a right to be angry, although somehow she was too distant to be really upset.

And then he started to snore.

Nobody ever tells you things, she thought groggily, like about dating, how you are treated as a prize, something rare and special, and that it ends with marriage.

Why don't they tell you things like that?

That night Corrine had a dream. She is in the shower. It is a big communal bathroom like the one at summer camp on Lake Winnipesaukee, except she is all alone and it is many years after her childhood. She is a widow now, although her naked body is still young and fresh. Her husband is dead. He died in the Cola Wars. She is all alone in this white-tiled chamber full of warm steam, washing herself with a white bar of soap. A bar of Ivory soap. Washing all over. She shouldn't be washing herself. For some reason she thinks that is her husband's job. But he's dead in the Cola Wars. She is rubbing herself with the bar of soap, up and down her arms, her hips, up and down, from her toes all the way up her legs, one leg and the other leg and in between. In the naked steam she rubs the soap along the inside of her thighs. It moves up and down because it's so slippery. She feels guilty washing herself, but there's no one else, and then there *is* someone else. It's Johnny Monocle. He is there in the bathroom with her and he says, I'll wash you. He seems to have only one eye, but he is very distinguished-looking with his black patch and sharkskin suit. Corrine is naked. He washes her up and down as she closes her eyes. He has a beautiful touch that makes her think of butterflies brushing her with their wings. Up and down and back and forth all over her body Johnny Monorail makes tracks. The bar of soap is actually his tongue. They are in bed now. Johnny has taken off his suit and he is naked now too as he travels across her body and suddenly she realizes her husband is alive after all but it's too late because Johnny has grown a penis and something needs to be done about it. She can't very well just ask him to take care of it himself. But they can hear the sounds of her husband coming back from the Cola Wars. Not Russell, some other husband, she doesn't know who. Still, they have to escape. It's a very long penis Johnny has, and a smooth one, smooth as ivory. She compliments him on it and he says thank you. But they have to hide it. It is too big to hide under the sheets, and it keeps getting bigger as she talks about it and touches it. It's so big that it disappears over the edge of the bed and out the window. Come on, quick, says Johnny Monolith. He isn't in the bed now, he's calling from far away, from the other end of the penis, which stretches away into the darkness like an ivory banister. She hears footsteps approaching, the footsteps of her husband, returning from the wars. She crawls to the edge of the bed and straddles the smooth banister, then pushes off, sliding down, floating off into the lovely darkness . . . and awoke tingling and guilty, the red numbers of the clock glowing in the dark, her husband asleep beside her, making small holes in the silence with his prickly breath.

In the morning, when she awoke again, she didn't tell Russell about her dream.

4

Glenda Banes hated working with babies. Not that she was entirely wild about encountering them in her leisure hours; she didn't care to think about how many of her friends had recently succumbed to the you're-less-than-a-whole-woman-if-you-don't form of propaganda, under the duress of an alleged biological clock—it's *just* a clock, for Christ's sake, not a *bomb*. Lately Glenda was finding herself at dinner tables from which everyone was jumping up to call home to the baby-sitter instead of the drug dealer, and conversation often degenerated into discussions of private nursery schools and the plague of nanny-napping—*Can you believe our wonderful Jamaican nanny . . . hijacked by some unscrupulous yuppie parent while she was in the park strolling little Brendan, they offered her an obscene wage and a green card and a room with a view and a new* VCR, *it's just incredibly unethical. . . .* Sometimes people actually hauled out *pictures* of their offspring. It was enough to send you racing to the bathroom for a discreet puke and a quick blast of mood freshener, although Glenda had quit that almost a year before.

Glenda knew photography and she didn't think people should have their picture taken until puberty. Immaturity being unflattering in any light. As of this very minute she was definitely telling her agent—No more baby work. Glenda Banes did *not* need this. But right now there was a cranky baby in her studio, and a bratty model, and she had to cope.

Like a huge, vaguely malevolent sea gull, Glenda Banes hovered over the surface of her loft, which in its whiteness extended indeterminately in all directions, flapping her rangy extremities as she seemed nearly to alight on the tripod that rose from the white floor like a piling from a tidal flat, touching her eye briefly to the aperture of the boxy Hasselblad and then lifting off again, squawking, borne away on an angry thermal.

"Give me a reading and unshine her face," she shouted. Two young men dressed in black leaped up from behind a screen, like ballboys at a tennis match, and raced in the direction of the Madonna and Child at whom the camera was aimed.

The model was Nikki Christianson, very hot right now, Glenda had shot her only about a million times and the camera loved her, that big healthy, horsey look which had been coming on the last couple of years. She was fine except for the language barrier, she didn't really understand English, although the gossip columns said she was born and raised in Wyoming, so presumably it was the closest thing she had to a native language. She could be counted on to be sexy no matter what she'd been doing the night before, but here she was supposed to look maternal, which required a little thespian skill on her part. Impersonating a normal, caring mother was work for Nikki, and her union seemed to have a rule against that.

But she was looking good, no question, her waist more pronounced and waspish since she'd had that operation all the models were having now which removed the bottom two ribs of the rib cage. After Adam had gone to all the trouble of lending one of his own. And while she was under the knife anyway, she had had the fat removed from her knees, the other fashionable new operation.

So it was a standoff here in Glenda's loft. No matter how hard Glenda screamed at her four assistants to move the lights, take new readings and reload the film, no matter how sweetly she cooed soothing monosyllables to Nikki and the just about equally sentient year-old baby, it simply wasn't coming together. Nikki had a twitch in her eye, which probably originated in her nose, and in between takes she handed the baby off to the Filipina baby handler as if it were a bundle of rancid fish—which Glenda couldn't really blame her for—while the baby's agent walked over on prissy little Ralph Lauren tiptoes to offer worthless oral memos of anal-retentive advice. The score was three yowling jags and two diaper changes for the baby, one tantrum for Nikki, five milligrams of Valium for Glenda.

Meanwhile, a sneaky, idolatrous kid in red Converse sneakers was pointing an autowind thirty-five at Glenda, photographing one of her photographic sessions for a spread in some German magazine, portrait of the famous photographer at work, kind of like a play within a play or like the cereal box with a picture of a man holding up a cereal box with a picture of a man holding up a cereal box. Click buzz click . . . If she heard that autowind behind her back one more time she was going to stuff his camera somewhere he wouldn't get a light reading.

"Give her some more of those blue eyedrops," Glenda said to the hair-and-makeup kid. "I'm still seeing red."

"Francesco told me they're bad for you," Nikki whined.

"Sacrifice for your art, Nikki. We all do." Besides which, if you were on the goddamn health-and-clean-living program to begin with, we wouldn't need the fucking eyedrops, would we?

"What?" said Nikki.

What what? wondered Glenda. One never knew how far back to go with Nikki's questions. Start with basic definitions of the words, or what? Take it back to the Big Bang and gradually work up to the part where the fish crawled up on dry land, grew long legs and long hair, moved to New York and got discovered by the Ford agency? *Sacrifice* was probably the word she didn't understand, or maybe *Art*. Glenda had not slept in three days, having gone from L.A. to Rio, then directly from the airport to her studio yesterday morning; with two more shoots scheduled for this afternoon, she was sure as shit suffering for something. At the very least for her new summer house on the beach in Sagaponack.

"This chef Carême cooked for Talleyrand and for the emperors of Austria and Russia," Glenda said, not really for Nikki's benefit but for the porky German reporter who had accompanied the squirrelly little photographer. Give him a quotable. "The coal gas they used for cooking was supremely unhealthful. But when Talleyrand or somebody told him not to work so hard, take care of his health and all, he said, 'Shorter life, longer fame.' "

The chubby little reporter hadn't even lifted his pen, she couldn't believe it.

"Does anybody around here speak English?" Glenda screamed.

"All right, let's try again here, shall we?" Glenda said, after her boys had set up the shot and the baby handler had calmed the infant and Nikki had come back from the bathroom.

Nikki would later claim that she thought the baby handler had a good grip on the kid, but the woman had already retreated a few steps out of the frame when the baby hit the floor. One minute Nikki was holding the baby and the next she was fixing her neckline with both hands. . . .

The soft, yielding thud of impact stunned them all into silence until the Filipino woman screamed.

"What happened?" said Nikki, looking down.

The autowind clicked and buzzed. . . .

"It's not moving," said the agent, crouched over the infant client.

"Somebody call nine-one-one," Glenda screamed.

"Oh, God," the agent muttered. "This has never happened to me before."

It was unbelievable—the kinds of things that happened to Glenda. The month before she'd been shooting a fashion spread with an ocelot. First the fucking cat had bitten the model and then it had escaped out the open window. God knows where it was now, but the job was certainly right down the toilet.

Uptown it was lunchtime, but in the East Village, Jeff Pierce break-fasted on a chocolate egg cream and half a blueberry blintz at Kiev.

"Do you know why they call them *egg* creams," he asked the waitress.

"I giff up," she said. Big strong girl with biceps and virgin blond underarm hair, Eastern European accent, trace of Genghis Khan and Company in the Mongol cheekbones. "Why?"

"I don't know. I'm asking you. Where do the eggs come into it?"

"I don't know nothing about that. You want something else?"

"It's not on the menu," he said.

Walking up Second past the B & H Dairy Bar, scene of his first at-tempted breakfast as a fledgling New Yorker, having driven down ten years before from tired old Massachusetts to his new tenement on Bowery with most of his possessions. Not even the discovery that his old 2002 had been stolen sometime in the night had blunted his wonder at waking up in his own apartment in New York. Wandering the steamy malodorous Lower East Side summer streets, moving quickly so as not to seem new, uncool, wanting to eat but somehow afraid to walk into a restaurant or stop long enough to show his uncertainty, afraid of betraying his freshness in the city, afraid he would unwittingly violate some unposted metropolitan code, until he saw this sign, DAIRY BAR, with its rural, mammary intimations. He took a stool at the counter and watched an old man flipping eggs on the grill, talking over his shoulder with customers. Finally Jeff asked for a menu. "You want a menu?" Old misshaven face, hairs sprouting from the nose, eyes veined like bad egg yolks looking him over. Jeff nodding, old guy saying, "Kid wants a menu?" to the room at large. The other diners finding this hilarious. Jeff tried to cling to the belief that requesting a menu was not a provincial custom despite mounting evidence to the contrary. "Tell you what," said the old man. "You tell me what you want, I'll tell you if we got it." Jeff nodded cautiously. "Eggs over easy." His host seemed tolerant. "Side of bacon." Then the rube alarm had gone off again. "Bacon!" The old man raising his wild eyebrows for his appreciative audience. "Kid wants bacon." After milking the other customers for laughs he finally said, "This is a *dairy* restaurant," as if that explained everything. Delivering the eggs he asked, "You ever been in a restaurant before." Three months later—a Jewish girl having in the meantime explained the fundamentals of kosher dining—he returned to the B & H Dairy Bar, and when, finally, the old man asked him if he'd ever been in a restaurant, Jeff answered, "I don't know—you ever worked in one?" After that he was a New Yorker.

Cruising up Second Avenue now a decade later, he admired a sign that said INDUSTRIAL HAIR. Nice notion, nice oxymoronic ring. What did it mean? Did they shave machines? Not quite an oxymoron. And what would *moronoxy* mean—the faith of morons, the beliefs they all shared? Except for those morons who were heterodox. Dropping some change in the cup of the legless Rican. Buy yourself a joint, my man. And the Ukrainian man who ran the SHOE REPAIR taping a "Back in 5 min" sign on his door and locking up, hobbling down the street in beat-up shoes. Cobbler, heel thyself.

Writers, he thought, are people who think of the right retort long after they get home. Retarded riposters. Across St. Mark's Place, secondhand clothing and record stores, secondhand attitudes on the street—tough kids from the suburbs doing the Sid Vicious shamble.

Cabbing up to the Photo District. Ambulance shrieking at the traffic behind him but no one inclined to make way. Sirens and alarms routine now in the city. The photographers had made a little ghetto for themselves in the vicinity of 20th and Sixth. Jeff imagined them going next door to borrow a cup of developing solution, wondered why writers didn't cluster. Only when free drinks were involved. Once he'd been to a writers' colony in New Hampshire, but they asked him to leave after he brought some locals back from a bar for a late-night swim. The other writers, in their beds of inspiration, were not amused. Especially outraged about alleged skinny-dipping among interloping philistines. Jeff censured and excommunicated by his peers. Big solemn meeting—all very humiliating, thanks.

Buzzed into the small, dirty lobby, he pressed the elevator button and listened to the sinister rattle of chains and pulleys as it descended toward him. All in all he would rather go to the dentist than have his picture taken. Give me lollipops, novocaine, gas—whatever you've got, please. But Russell said this was important, some big-deal magazine article.

Two policemen were standing in the hallway when the doors opened. Caught at last. Jeff stood rooted to his spot, fists clenching involuntarily. Looking for him since he was born, charge of original sin. Numerous additional crimes since—repeat offender. But the cops ignored him, waddling into the elevator. He leaped out just before the doors closed.

Glenda Banes's studio looked like the other lofts he'd been photographed in over the past two years, only more so—a lunar landscape dotted with strange equipment on leggy tripods. Earnest young men ran around tending to all this equipment and to the tall, gangly woman in a white jumpsuit and high-top sneakers whom he recognized as Glenda Banes.

"Is that him, finally?" she said, swiveling in Jeff's direction and focusing. "Let's move it, we're late." She walked over and examined Jeff skeptically. "Are you here for the session?"

He nodded, thinking this a reasonable deduction.

"Will somebody please order some sushi before I collapse?" she shouted without removing her eyes from Jeff. "Jesus, this is the best the agency could do?" she said. "So take off your pants."

"Is this a date," Jeff asked.

"Don't be cute. I need to see your legs."

"Okay." Still wearing his sunglasses, Jeff unbuckled his belt and climbed out of his jeans.

"With these legs I'm supposed to sell underwear?"

He had to admit they looked like albino wax beans with hair. Reminding him of why, through his long adolescence—still in progress, actually—he had always refused to wear shorts.

"What the fuck are those?" she said, pointing to the whales on his boxer shorts.

"Whales."

"Why?"

He shrugged. "For purposes of planting a subtle subliminal association in the minds of female viewers who are about to see them removed," he suggested, although the real reason was that some dopey New England relative had given them to him for Christmas.

"Call the agency," Glenda commanded.

"I think there's been a mistake here," Jeff said.

"Your booking agent took some bad drugs?"

"I'm not a model."

"No, so what are you?"

"I'm here to get my picture taken."

"You're here to get your picture taken but you're not a model. Is this a riddle?"

"Well, I'm Jeff Pierce. If that helps."

"Jeff Pierce the writer?"

He nodded.

"Oh my God, Jeff, I'm sorry." Her chagrined expression turned rapidly angry as she looked around the studio for someone to blame. "Why didn't somebody fucking tell me this was Jeff Pierce." And then, turning back: "I didn't recognize you with your shades on. Sorry, I thought you were some stupid model or something. You want a drink? Corona? Perrier? Will somebody get us a goddamn Coke over here, please? Sorry if I was a little . . . abrupt. But we were expecting you yesterday."

"You were?"

"Weren't we supposed to shoot Jeff yesterday?" she hollered.

"Yeah, Tuesday, one p.m.," somebody answered.

"What's today," Jeff asked hopefully.

"Wednesday, actually. Wednesday three-fifteen p.m. Eastern Standard Time. All our instruments agree. Isn't that right, people?"

An enthusiastic chorus of lackey assent echoed through the loft.

"Traffic was pretty bad," he offered.

Jeff wondered which day he'd lost along the way. Usually he was only a few hours off, though longish stretches of his recent life remained unaccounted for.

"Maybe we can do you today," Glenda said. "We've already had a pretty unbelievable day here. Nikki Christianson—you know Nikki, right? inventor of the silicon microchip?—she dropped this baby on its head in the middle of the shoot so now we're waiting to hear from the hospital to see if it's alive and then I've got this underwear shoot that the model is twenty minutes late for but if you don't mind sticking around . . ."

"Do you give lollipops," Jeff asked.

"We give whatever you want."

"Save me," Jeff said, "from what I want."

When the model for the underwear shoot arrived, Glenda demanded that he remove his pants and shirt. "I think we're going to shave your chest," she said to the dismayed model, who was led off whimpering to a dressing room and emerged twenty minutes later in a pair of jockey shorts, smooth of torso and puffy-eyed. It looked to Jeff as if he'd been crying.

"Nice pecs," said Glenda. "Are they real?"

Jeff went to the bathroom, nodded off on a couch in the corner of the loft till Glenda was ready for him.

"I think we're going to light you from the left side to start. You'll want some of these eyedrops, I think the eyedrops are definitely in order here, having a little trouble locating your pupils in there, big fella. . . . Do you want anything to drink, Jeff?"

"Chocolate egg cream . . ."

"Call the deli, somebody. . . ."

"With maybe a little shot of vodka."

"Absolutely."

"Make it a double and hold the egg cream."

One of the assistants seated Jeff in an old wooden school chair, while another wheeled up an antique Remington on a rickety typewriter stand. The retro writer look. From behind, somebody rubbed mousse into his hair. If there was one thing Jeff hated, it was mousse, except when it was for dessert and chocolate. But Jeff gradually disappeared. He had long since learned that his actual presence was not required at these sessions. At one time his face would clench with the self-consciousness of the unwilling photo subject, but gradually he had worked toward a state of Oriental indifference accelerated in this instance by the vodka. Each time his image was reproduced he looked less and less like himself, the flash bulbs progressively bleaching the map of his soul out of his face. With enough exposure he would look like someone else entirely— the perfect disguise for a writer.

Two brand-new models showed up at the studio looking for portfolio shots and Glenda decided to mix them into Jeff's shoot. He was too stunned to protest; they were the kind of mythic feminine creatures rarely encountered in three dimensions. The stylist dressed the blonde in a man's pin-striped suit and gave her a cane. The black girl they stripped and wrapped in plastic ivy. Jeff gathered it was supposed to be laurel. Not being a visual artist, he didn't quite catch the concept. The girls vogued and posed around him like inhabitants of a dream, making him dizzy with fear and yearning.

Somehow he had not envisioned this part of the job, back when he'd decided to be a writer.

A phone rang and presently one of Glenda's functionaries whispered in her ear. "The kid's all right," Glenda announced. "Maybe have a little trouble with algebra down the road, but he's kicking and screaming. So, are we all set here?"

But Jeff was asleep, his elbow propped on the typewriter, his head nestled in the cup of his palm, his breath whistling softly through the cavern of his open mouth.

5

While Russell was in the bathroom Corrine pulled on the new bustier she'd bought at The Pleasure Chest, which lifted her breasts higher than they'd been since she was about seventeen, and nearly spilled them right back over the top of the scalloped translucent black lace cups. She climbed into the unfamiliar garter belt, then stepped into the garters, slid the black fishnet stockings up her calves to her thighs, where she succeeded with some difficulty in attaching them to the garters. The faucet in the bathroom was still singing like a teakettle. Next she pulled her hair back, bobby-pinned it down as quickly as she could, and ran to the closet for the wig box. Adjusting the stiff copper tresses of the Tina Turner wig, she looked around frantically for the lipstick, yanking the tops from several of her old tubes and scattering them, finally finding the new one, a lurid, supernatural shade of red which she hoped never to encounter in real life. A slathering of mascara and she was finished, just as the bathroom door opened.

She ran to the bed, threw herself down across it, and struck an indecent odalisque pose. Emerging naked from the bathroom, Russell was startled to find a strange woman in his bed. But she could see, quite explicitly, that it didn't take him long at all to get the idea.

Once inspired, he didn't require instructions. After all, it was Valentine's Day, or had been until midnight. Russell had risen early and brought her breakfast in bed with bagels and cream cheese and Scottish salmon, and spilled orange juice—very sweet, though she hated to eat in the mornings—along with a card and bottle of Chanel No. 5 on the tray. Inside the card he had written:

Black velvet hairbands and French scented candles
John Stuart Mill and supermarket-tabloid scandals
The song Van Morrison sings
These foolish things
Remind me of you.

As she was dressing after breakfast, she'd noticed the wig box in the closet and remembered the night when they had come home from the Halloween party the year before—how he'd leaped on her while she still had the wig on and how afterward he had confessed that it was like fucking another woman, and she hadn't minded because it was her, after all, and she had been excited by the idea of *being* the other woman.

Not that she had time for this, she thought, as Russell, sated and exhausted from his tumble with Tina, began to snore. But that was the whole point: When it was new you didn't have time for anything else, and after ten years you never had the time. There was always something else, work, sleep, the final chapter of a book. Though it was Sunday, she had to wake up early for a christening, and now she couldn't sleep, thinking about lost ardor and about that terrible story she'd heard from Jeff.

They'd given their annual Valentine's party; at dinner Russell had served a wine called Les Amoureuses, which she had thought was very cute of him until she noted the outrageous price on the tag still attached to one of the bottles. After dinner Jeff had arrived with an entourage of downtowners and demi-celebs, club people, lowlife and highlife types who never went to an office in the morning—a gossip columnist named Juan Baptiste who wanted to talk to Russell about a book; Leticia Corbin, heiress of the publishing family; Glenda Banes, the photographer. After Glenda left, Jeff told a horrible story about a model who'd dropped and killed a baby during a photo shoot. Once the bereaved parents had consulted a lawyer, Jeff said, the modeling agency hired a private investigator, who came up with solid evidence of past marijuana use and probable cocaine use, which the agency threatened to reveal to the father's employer unless the parents settled for a reasonable amount of cash. Fifty thousand, as it turned out, which was tax-deductible for the agency.

Corrine wanted to do something, call up *The New York Times*, organize a boycott. Hours later, she was still so upset that she had to find out if it was really true. She slipped out of bed, padded out to the living room, toxic with smoke and boozy residues, and punched Jeff's number. She wanted to talk, and she was never afraid of waking him up. The machine picked up; she whispered into the receiver for a minute, because he always screened his calls, but he wasn't picking up. "This is your married Valentine calling to check up on you," she said. His night was probably still young. They had all been on that schedule once. Dawn patrol.

But where did Jeff meet these people, she wondered, as she slipped back into bed, and how had his life become so weird, so different from theirs? Apparently once you were sort of famous they sent you a membership card. And the girls, the modules and actress slash waitresses. The piquantly slutty young things who were not without interest for Russell, and whose presence invigorated all of the intoxicated thirtyish men in the smoky apartment.

Socializing was aphrodisiac for Russell. He got excited being charming for strangers. Those few nights when they stayed at home, nights into which Corrine sometimes tried to inject romance, Russell read manuscripts or watched TV, as if unwilling to crank up his engine for her alone. She had decided to take advantage of his exuberance tonight, dust off the lingerie and tease up the wig. She just wondered how long it would be before he got tired of Tina Turner.

6

Sunday is the day of restlessness, dedicated to stale news, guilt and culture. The city lies stunned from its excesses and the inhabitants, when they finally venture out, walk the streets without, for once, appearing to have any immediate destination or purchase in mind.

Dans le musée: Amidst the rocks and trees of Cézanne's Provence, this French girl was shaped like something dreamed by Brancusi, Russell thought, a piece that would be called *Sex Moving Through Space*, this notion provoking a nagging inner voice acquired via the *Times* op-ed and the higher media, progressive girlfriends and old New England schools: *You shouldn't entertain such thoughts, being ostensibly enlightened, liberal, and married besides. Treating women like objects; making low similes out of High Art.* Two violations. Still, it happened. Even here in the Museum of Modern Art, where a not-so-very-*jeune fille* in blue jeans was standing in front of Cézanne's *The Bather* whispering to her friend in the artist's native tongue—even when we should be admiring *Le Château Noir*, usually one of our favorite paintings.

"At least Cézanne doesn't let his ego into the painting," Corrine said.

"Say what?" Russell often had occasion to note his wife's gift for abruptly going public with her interior monologues, plunging him into the middle of a debate the subject of which was still a mystery.

"I was thinking about Hemingway saying he learned how to write from Cézanne," she said. "His descriptions of nature have that same solidity and depth, but it's like all the trees in Hemingway's forest have his initials carved in them, and his brooks burble 'Me! Me! Me!' "

Russell didn't think "Me! Me! Me!" was burbling, and was annoyed at this shopworn revisionism. "Jesus, Corrine, that's so stale."

"It isn't stale to me, Russell, I just noticed it for myself, and if you've heard it before I'm sorry. I'm not a literary critic, okay?"

"And what do you mean, '*at least* Cézanne doesn't blah blah blah'?"

The Frenchwoman looked over, Russell noticed, then slipped into the other room. This made him even madder.

"I just meant," Corrine said, "technically it's great, but Cézanne is so, you know, cold."

"The whole twentieth century couldn't have happened without him," Russell insisted.

"Well, maybe that would've been a good thing."

"Jesus *Christ*, Corrine."

"Russell, will you please not shout. I don't know what your problem is, but you've been snapping my head off over every little thing."

"When was the last time you read 'Big Two-Hearted River'?" Russell boomed, his voice filling the small gallery. Feeling absurd even as he spoke—defender of truth, the mot juste and American literature. "Read it and weep. Then tell me about ego."

"How *old* are you?" Corrine demanded. She turned and fled. Russell watched her go, as did everyone else in the room. Then they looked at him—this philistine in their midst, tormenter of that lovely girl.

Why do we even come here? Russell wondered. Though they'd never had a problem with the Post-Impressionists before. Usually they made it to Synthetic Cubism before they started to argue.

Russell observed the Frenchwoman for a while, conferring with her friend about Rousseau's *Sleeping Gypsy*, but now that Corrine was gone she didn't look quite so hot.

He drifted through the hushed chambers thinking about his wife. He could picture her achingly clearly in her absence, whereas sometimes when she was *right there* he just couldn't see her—the virtues so visible to him now becoming blurred with her actual presence. Smart, funny —the best-looking girl in the room, he thought, though she'd never imagine it, always saying, *I've got to lose a few pounds I felt so dumpy at the party standing next to Gloria she's so thin*, when in fact Corrine is whippet-thin and the lady in question is built along the lines of the pyramid of Cheops.

He remembered the first time he caught sight of her: she was standing at the top of a fraternity house staircase, leaning forward over the banister with a cigarette held exquisitely between her fingers, like a blonde in a thirties movie, gazing down on a party that until that moment had seemed to Russell the climax of his recent escape from home, parents and the Midwest. He'd been drinking everything in sight, huddling with his new roommates, flashing his wit, or so he imagined, at the expense of girls he was still working up the courage to talk to.

Then he saw Corrine at the top of the stairs. He felt he recognized her, took in at a glance everything essential about her character. He stifled his first impulse to point her out to his roommates, not wishing to share the vision, not sure they would see what he saw. Russell believed in his own secret aristocracy, a refinement of soul and taste that he knew he must keep to himself, which much later he would almost forget to believe in. Later, too, he would realize that most of us believe, as he did at that moment, in our ability to read character from physiognomy. While she failed to notice him and his nobility of soul from her aerie atop the staircase, he read intelligence in her gaze, breeding in her slightly upturned nose, sensuality in her lips, and self-confidence in her languid pose. Only in this last would he find he was wrong. As he watched, a boy he recognized as a campus figure appeared on the landing behind her, along with another, radiant couple. She turned, and though Russell could not see her expression, though they did not touch, the air of familiarity and possession between her and the boy was unmistakable; and then the two couples disappeared from view, retreating to the real party, the actual heart of the world, an action that suddenly revealed the event on the lower floor to be a beer brawl—a congress of the second-rate, the meek and halt and lame.

The social accomplishments of his first semester, unknown to Corrine, were committed in her name. He did not have to sleuth hard for news of her; Corrine was a legend in her own right and formed part of the group everyone talked about, which made her seem more desirable and less accessible, as did her liaison with Kurt Sinclair, a basketball star and druggie—a combination that at that time in history made him a formidable competitor. Tall, lanky and slightly bowlegged, he was alleged to be good-looking, although Russell disputed this judgment. Russell bided his time. He had four years, and Sinclair would be gone in three.

Second semester, Corrine Makepeace was in his Romantic poetry class, and without ever actually meeting they became acquainted. He and Jeff, who hated each other at first glance, took turns trying to dominate the class and each other; Corrine couldn't have helped noticing him: he showed off to an extent that he still winced in recalling. In her few forays into class participation, uncovering Coleridge's Teutonic philosophical debts, for instance, she revealed herself to be very bright. A mathematical genius, according to rumor, she was, he felt certain, someone for whom intelligence constituted a desirable secondary sexual characteristic. At registration the next fall he met her coming down the stairs of the administration building and she greeted him as if they were friends. Pleasantly astonished, he affected an air of weariness, as if over the summer break he had rather outgrown this stodgy New England campus, though in fact he'd been home in Michigan. It was a hot September day. Russell admired the contours of her tanned legs, picturing her summer of sailboats and tennis, imagining he could almost feel radiant heat from the waves of her long golden hair. He kept waiting for her to say good-bye. She kept talking.

They jabbered through lunch at Spat's, filling the ashtray and emptying wineglasses. They talked about everything—he had been only half right about her summer, Nantucket and sailing, along with six weeks as a Red Cross volunteer helping build an airstrip for a remote village in southern Oaxaca. The airstrip might have been on one of the moons of the planet Saturn—he couldn't stop looking at her mouth, watching her lips on her cigarette, the dense clouds of smoke that she exhaled seeming to him the visible trace of inner fires. Still smoking and talking, they found themselves by late afternoon in Russell's dorm room, where they suddenly fell on each other—a crisis of lips and tongues and limbs that somehow stopped short of the desired conclusion. She was still going with Kurt, and he was involved with a girl named Maggie Sloan.

Their romance fell dormant for almost two years, till Corrine called up one night and asked in her slightly hoarse voice if she could come over. When she arrived she said she had broken up with Kurt, although she had failed, evidently, to make this clear to him; soon after Corrine holed up he began calling, then coming over to shout drunken threats across Keeney quad. Russell savored the atmosphere of siege, which lent an extra dimension of urgency to their union, an element of danger and illegitimacy which was profoundly stimulating. He ditched Maggie over the phone. Maggie cried and appealed to the weight of tradition—two years of going out. With Corrine at his side—all over him, in fact—Russell was sympathetic but firm, righteous in the heedless cruelty of new love.

Outside the dorm it was a prematurely cold New England fall; red and yellow leaves slipped from the trees and twisted in the wind. For five days they left the room only to get food, staying in bed most of the time, drinking St. Pauli Girls, smoking Marlboros, talking, learning how to make love all over again. In the mornings, Corrine told Russell her dreams in minute detail. Her imagination was curiously literal. She remembered everything—what people were wearing, inconsistencies and illogic which surprised and annoyed her a little, as if she expected dreams to conform to quotidian standards. Her view of the waking world, though, was somewhat fantastic. Certain dates and names were fraught with un-likely significance for her, and more than Russell, the poet, she believed in the shamanistic power of words. She had the kind of faith in hearing herself declared loved, in the physical fact of the words being spoken, the syllables being pronounced out loud, that her heroine Franny Glass had in the repetition of the Jesus Prayer. When, much later, Russell proposed to her long-distance, Oxford, England, to New York, New York, she made him promise never to say the word "divorce."

He mouthed the word now: *divorce.* Nothing happened. He couldn't imagine her not being around; even now, still angry, he could feel himself starting to worry about her. They were both hung over—that was one problem. And he was tense about the situation at work. The Nicaragua book was about to be stillborn and Harold wouldn't even speak to him. Having until a month before been heir apparent, Russell was going to have to think seriously about getting a new job, or something.

After listlessly cruising the circuit of Painting and Sculpture, Russell came upon Giacometti—first *Spoon Woman*, in which a visual analogy is made between the female torso and the bowl of a spoon, suggestive of fertility, maternity, the triumph of the feminine principle. He glanced at it briefly, then stopped short in front of its opposite, a bronze he'd been mesmerized by several times, a sprawl of limblike appendages entitled *Woman with Her Throat Cut*. Whenever he'd come upon this piece in Corrine's company he had always hurried past it, feeling guilty, embarrassed, a participant in all the crimes against her sex throughout history, his guilt stemming from a fascination and attraction he felt for the object, the bronze woman with a wedged declivity in her larynx, arching her back and thrusting her splayed legs upward into space. Although he would not exactly admit it to himself, this piece made him feel he might be capable of evil.

Looking up suddenly, he found himself facing the Frenchwoman, who smiled at him.

Dioramas of late-twentieth-century Manhattan chieftains and their women, the windows at Bergdorf's displayed extravagantly costumed mannequins in the postures of revel and feasting. Having swindled the original inhabitants out of the land and then exterminated them, this tribe flourished until shortly before the millennium. . . . Pausing in her commentary, Corrine, as anthropologist of the future, tried to decide what form of doom had befallen—*would* befall—her own. For lately it seemed to her that the horsemen of the apocalypse were saddling up, that something was coming to rip huge holes in the gaudy stage sets of Ronald McDonald Reaganland. Meanwhile she was selling stocks, a glorified Fuller Brush girl. Hi, I'm Corrine, can I interest you in a sexy growth stock or maybe a cute little annuity?

Must be hung over. Of course. Why else run crying from the museum, not that Russell hadn't been horrible. Pompous ass. She was almost mad enough to go into Bergdorf's and charge up one of these nice Donna Karan ensembles with all the accessories. If it were open.

She kept walking, past the fountain in front of the Plaza—called the Fountain of Abundance, dry now. She always thought of this as the navel of the slender island on which she and Russell had camped for five years, having come together as newlyweds with duffel bags and dreams, after their *Wanderjahre* and grad schools and their halfhearted, experimental attempts to live without each other. Coming here to be grown-ups, she starting Columbia Law, so as to fight injustice in its many guises; he still thinking of himself as a writer then, the publishing job as a temporary expedient, a way of paying the rent till he became a famous poet. And though those two dreams quietly expired, she usually believed she and Russell were happy, that the city had been good to them, that they had been good to each other.

Approaching the apartment building she saw an ancient man attacked by two kids. One kid held him up while the other slapped and punched his face. As they fled, Corrine rushed forward. Having struggled up to a sitting position, the man was holding his hand to his bloodied face. Corrine held out her own hand. "Are you all right?"

"I don't want help," he said, not looking up at her.

"Take my hand. Do you want an ambulance?"

"Go away."

"You're bleeding."

"Can't you see I don't want your help? Leave me alone!" Tears of rage were streaming from his eyes. When Corrine reached down once more he swung his cane around and whacked her hip, flailing at her until she retreated out of range.

"Leave me alone," he screamed.

When Corrine looked back from the next corner he was on his knees, struggling furiously to attain his feet before anyone else offered help.

Her name was Simone. Russell didn't ask what had happened to her friend, and she didn't allude to his wedding band, though she certainly noticed it, just as he noticed the heavy gold tank watch beneath the sleeve of her sweatshirt. On the weekends there were two ways to determine someone's tax bracket: watch and shoes.

Sitting across from her in the museum café, Russell talked about his job—she had heard of Jeff and another of his authors, and had a Gallic as opposed to an American view of the profession of letters, which is to say she wasn't disappointed to find that he was not an investment banker or a soap opera star. She didn't seem to be the kind of person who ever had to settle on any one thing in terms of employment, but most recently she'd worked as a wildlife photographer on an expedition in Tanzania. "I am thinking of joining an expedition up the Amazon," she said, her English flawless though accented, a little more precise than a native speaker's, and it turned out she was one of those people who'd been reared in the middle of the Atlantic—as much a New Yorker as a Parisian. "But

I don't know. I think I'd like to do something completely different this time, you know?"

Russell had been imagining the viscous tropical air of the jungle, the screech of gaudy birds overhead, Simone straddling the bow of a tub reminiscent of the *African Queen*, a profane figurehead with tan thighs scanning the underbrush with a zoom lens . . . tan thighs misted with blond hairs glistening like gold in the bottom of a prospector's pan, tailings from the golden city of El Dorado.

He saw now why his opinion of her charms had varied over the course of an hour; she was not indisputably beautiful in stasis, but the slightest speech or motion exposed a sexual essence.

"Do you like Giacometti," she asked.

He nodded.

"My father has one." She paused and then said, "Maybe you'd like to come over and see it," looking directly into his eyes with just enough intensity to indicate that modern art was only one of her passionate interests.

"That might be nice," he said, trying to clear his throat of a sudden dry constriction. "And what does he do?" he added, to cover his confusion, knowing this was an underbred question but curious about the class of people who owned Giacomettis.

"Oh, he invests the money for my family."

"Good work if you can get it."

"Are you interested in finance?"

"I dabble. I'm afraid I'm vastly undercapitalized."

"Talk to my father. He has too much money."

"It's very sad."

"Yes. I think I'd like you to feel very sorry for me."

Just as Corrine was about to give up on him and cancel for dinner he arrived home buoyant and apologetic. He hugged her, running his tongue along the edge of her ear.

"I'll admit that Cézanne's a little chilly," he said, "if you'll grant that Chagall is a wimp."

"Have I done something recently," she asked. "Have you just lost interest in me?"

"I'm an ungrateful bastard," he said. "But as of this moment I promise to improve my character. Close your eyes—I've got a present for you. Okay, put out your hand."

Her fingers closed around a postcard, a photo of Matisse's *Dance* inscribed on the other side: "I'm sorry. I love you. P.S. This postcard entitles the bearer to romantic dinner tonight at expensive restaurant of choice. Mystery Dance to follow—informal attire." She smiled at the private joke, a reference to a favorite Elvis Costello song.

"You're sweet—in fact, I don't know if I quite recognize this romantic boy who just swept into my apartment. But we've got Colin and Anne tonight, remember?"

"Shit."

"I'm holding on to this, though," she said, slipping the postcard down the front of her shirt and winking.

They returned home after midnight. Corrine was exhausted, but Russell was in the mood so she took advantage. He was very passionate, and attentive, too—sometimes he seemed to forget she was there during sex, as if she were a car he was driving to a private destination.

She fell asleep almost immediately, contented.

Russell lay awake for several minutes thinking idly about a boat chugging up a jungle river, but his conscience was almost clear, in fact it was more than clear. This morning his fidelity had been untested of late, while tonight he was a man who had turned down an invitation to see another woman's etchings—or rather, her father's Giacometti. The narrowness of his escape, the degree to which he had been aroused by the idea had rebounded to Corrine's advantage, the nearness of his infidelity having erotically charged his cells; he'd watched Corrine all through dinner, couldn't wait to get her home, and the happiness he found in this vision of himself as an upright husband had increased his appreciation of the wife for whom he performed this heroic feat of abnegation.

He was barely troubled by the thought that Simone had given him her phone number, since he knew he would never use it.

7

Was it invariably true—a natural law, like the conservation of matter—that there was no free lunch?

Cabbing from the West Village to the Sherry-Netherland in order to partake of the midday meal with his editor, Victor Propp mulled the question from many angles, the chalky cliff of his forehead corrugated in cerebration. Literally speaking, writers never paid for lunch. Agents, editors and journalists did. That was the way of the world, a social convention which approached the status of a universal truth. It was necessary, in Victor's view, that as an artist one remained a child in some sense, spoiled and dependent; a porous, needy, oral creature—a sucking mouth; a monstrous ego for whom all objective reality is composed of mirrors and nipples.

No free lunch. Who said it first? he wondered. It had the pithy quality of a Ben Franklinism. But wasn't that really what it meant to be an American, to believe above all in the free lunch? Dialectically opposed to the Puritan ethic and every bit as firmly fixed in the national psyche was the bedrock belief in something for nothing, the idea that five would get you ten. The free lunch was Marx's Surplus, the bonus of labor that capital claimed for itself. It was the gratuitous vein of gold, the oil gusher, the grabbed land, the stock market killing, the windfall profit, the movie sale. Europeans believed in the zero sum game, that one man's feast was his neighbor's fast. But here the whole continent had been free, almost, for the taking. Or so it seemed to Victor Propp, American novelist.

He did not think of his own mind as being particularly American, however, though he was spawned in Boise, Idaho, the product of a taciturn Swedish mother and a Russian Jewish father who taught high school English and claimed kinship with the great storywriter Isaac Babel. Victor had not remotely felt at home in Boise and had begun to find his place in the world only when he arrived at Yale at the age of sixteen and discovered Europe in the comp lit department. While he did not, like fellow Idahoan Ezra Pound, remove himself across the ocean, he did imagine that he stood outside the culture, critical and aloof, quarantined at an Ellis Island of the spirit with the disease of his art. A hundred years after Henry James had fled the raw continent, Victor mused, the consciousness of his native land remained barely half forged. Americans were still radical materialists. More innocent than Kalahari bushmen, who were adepts at reading signs and symbols, Americans took everything at face value—words, signs, rhetoric, faces—as if reality itself were so much legal tender. For Victor it was a treacherous text composed by a necromancer, diabolically resistant to analysis. Even the phrase "face value" suggested to a mind like Victor Propp's a labyrinth of interpretation, of masks and falsity and deceit, divergences of appearance and reality, rancorous divorces between signifier and signified, the apparent solidity of the words collapsing underfoot, feathering out and deliquescing into Derridean twilight, surfaces giving way suddenly, like the street along which Victor's taxi was bucking at this very moment, ripped up and peeled back after a gas main explosion to reveal networks of pipe and wire and rat-infested tunnel.

In a small notebook, Victor wrote *Free Lunch . . . Manifest Destiny . . . American Mind*. This brought his total output for the morning to some forty words, the past three hours having been devoted to the fashioning of a thirty-three-word sentence fragment and six parenthetical phone calls. Writing was self-inflicted torture, *déjeuner* a blessed relief.

Young Calloway was paying for today's lunch. Propp was intrigued by Calloway's mind precisely because it was so American, so different from his own, standing as if on firm ground where Victor descried quicksand. Calloway reminded Victor of those cartoon characters who were able to walk on the air so long as they didn't know there was an abyss underneath them. Naive, in a word—but an interesting, almost exemplary naiveté, having to do with youth and an admirable brashness. Like an athlete, he had a pure, practical kind of knowledge upon which Victor wished to draw. He had launched the careers of Jeff Pierce and several other not insignificant writers at an age when most publishing slaves were still typing letters. Approaching sixty, Propp often worried that he had waited too long to make his decisive literary move, and he was reassured by the rapt interest of the bright young man. Harold Stone and his peers still ran the show, but Propp knew which generation would pass judgment on his own. And in his darker moments he suspected he had exhausted Harold's faith in his genius, as well as his patience. Russell might just accomplish something noteworthy or even spectacular, particularly if given a push, and Victor had an idea he wished to set into motion. Having renounced the world for his priestly vocation, Victor cultivated a Jesuitical interest in the mechanics of power.

As for the price of lunch, Calloway and his employers expected Propp someday to deliver the book on which he had been working for twenty years; in the meantime the young man considered himself amply rewarded with the company and conversation of the legendary novelist, while Victor tried to probe Russell's innocence, his representative nature as one of the best and brightest of a barbaric native culture. It was a pleasantly disguised system of exchange and credit in which, by Victor Propp's reckoning, he came out way ahead. Propp estimated he had dined five or six hundred times with editors in the course of writing his second novel.

For Russell, the planning and execution of lunch could consume half a day. He didn't doubt that early hunter-gatherers had had it easier— step outside the cave and pick some berries, impale a mammoth on your spear, wait for lightning to strike a nearby tree in order to provide cooking fire, no problem. The late-twentieth-century editor, by contrast, faced daunting logistical problems. If you were the instigator of the meal you had to choose a restaurant—not as easy as it might sound, questions of the status, expectations and physical location of the diners arising at every turn. Also questions of your own ability to command a reservation. Although Victor Propp lived fairly modestly, he was a snob when it came to spending other people's money, and he'd put in a specific request today for the local branch of Harry's Bar in Venice, located in the Sherry-Netherland hotel, which he liked for its Levantine literary associations and its Himalayan prices.

So in pursuit of the daily lunch your assistant called and made a reservation, or, as in this case, pleaded unsuccessfully. Then you panicked. Previously, in another lifetime, you would have called up your boss, Harold Stone, and asked him if he could put a word in, pride-wounding though it was to show him that you, his handpicked successor and an ostensibly happening guy making a name for himself out there in the big world, had not yet made enough of a name to get your own table. But now you doubted that he would get you a reservation at McDonald's. So instead you called Jerry Kleinfeld, the publisher of Corbin, Dern. Subsequently you called your lunchmate to confirm, then usually a cab in midday traffic . . . a wait for the table, the question of whether or not to order a cocktail, a glass of wine with the meal, a bottle of wine . . . not wishing nowadays to appear a hopeless alcoholic or unconscious of the whole health issue while not wishing to look like a tight-ass or tightwad, either. Dining with the old martini-drinking boys of the business, and novelists in general, one had to be prepared to ruin the afternoon in an attempt to keep up. But Victor Propp was a one-glass-of-wine epicurean, so that part was easy. Victor didn't cloud his mind; he kept it clear for self-contemplation, syntax aikido, conspiracy theories and other forms of mind-fuck.

Being entrusted the care and feeding of Victor Propp was presumably a mark of being chosen, although Russell sometimes wondered. Victor was a long-term, highly speculative literary investment, a sophisticated instrument—Corbin, Dern's most exotic holding. In 1961, Propp had published a delicate coming-of-age novel called *New Haven Evenings*. The story of a Propp-like second-generation American who goes to Yale to become a poet and falls in love with a duplicitous Daughter of the American Revolution, it collected respectful, encouraging reviews as well as a Prix de Rome fellowship for the young author. Since then Propp had entered an almost purely theoretical realm in which, as someone once said of E. M. Forster, his reputation grew with each book he failed to publish. The word "genius" was increasingly appended to his name.

Propp's work-in-progress gained stature and renown with each passing year in which it failed to appear, while the fame of his contemporaries waxed and waned according to conventional market principles as they predictably published fifth, sixth and seventh novels. Fragments of the untitled novel infrequently found their way into literary journals, fraught with the Promethean labor of their own creation, somehow conveying the sense of samizdat: scratched on the damp rock walls of the author's prison cell, copied and recopied, memorized, swallowed, and discharged after a tortured routing via Baltic cities and tramp steamers to the sub-basement printing house. The subject of this long-anticipated work seemed to be the author himself, in every phase of his development from the embryo, one of the most famous passages to date being the heroic monologue of the embryonic protagonist recounting the tides, rhythms and developmental struggles of the amniotic world as he delivered himself from the womb by sheer force of will. One feminist critic, wondering about his mother's role in all of this strident creation, complained that, in Propp, "ontogeny recapitulates misogyny." What chiefly dazzled Propp's admirers was the language, reminiscent, as one commentator proposed, of "Henry James with bowel movements"—a Propp sentence being a colonic labyrinth of qualifications, diversions and recapitulations—another enthusiast declaring that Propp was the only American writer of this century who thoroughly understood the semicolon.

Almost alone among allegedly major authors in the late century, Victor Propp was his own agent, and though the man who represents himself in court purportedly has a fool for a lawyer, Propp had outperformed every literary salesman in the business. In 1966, Propp had received a modest advance for this second novel. After five years, Corbin, Dern became impatient for delivery, at which point Propp published a piece of the novel in *Esquire* and let it be known to other publishers that he was available for lunch and dinner; under threat of losing the novelist, whose cult was growing, the young Harold Stone had revised the contract and enlarged the advance. This process had been repeated periodically over the years; to date Propp had collected nearly a quarter of a million dollars on the unfinished masterpiece.

As if to compensate for the aloofness of his publishing stance, the semiblocked author was deeply involved in the intrigues of the literary world and liked to worry about the accomplishments, reputations and crimes of other writers, and particularly of his enemies, whom he imag-ined to be legion. Inevitably Harold and Victor had fallen out. Russell wasn't certain of the exact nature of the dispute, but these men of letters were no longer speaking, though Harold still wanted to publish the book. This crisis was resolved by naming Russell as Propp's official editor.

Russell had admired Propp since college, when Jeff bequeathed to him, like a man imparting hieratic knowledge, a battered copy of the *Paris Review* containing the embryo's monologue.

They talked frequently—Propp spent half his day on the phone and needed many ears into which to pour the torrent of his verbal overflow —and met for lunch once a month. They talked about Victor Propp and those he liked to consider his peers: Richardson, Flaubert, James, Musil and the later James Joyce. (Russell could have sworn he had on one occasion heard Victor refer to him as "Jim Joyce.") Propp wanted to talk with Russell about marketing and pop culture, whereas Russell wished to engage the great man on the subject of Literature. Russell was reminded of George Bernard Shaw's complaint about his meeting with Bennett Cerf—the American publisher wished to discuss art, while the great playwright wanted to talk only money. Now Russell wondered how much he could count on friendship and mutual self-interest. His relationship with Victor and several other authors gave him some kind of minimal job security at Corbin, Dern. If he got fired, he wondered, would Victor come with him?

"How famous is Jeff," Victor asked, not long after he alighted at the table, his raptor eyes and tall white forehead putting his lunch companion in mind of a ravenous bald eagle (Falconiformes Accipitridae, Audubon, plate 107).

"Compared to what?"

"I mean, do people recognize him on the street? Do girls send him scented panties in the mail? I find it fascinating when a writer crosses over into the field of consciousness of tabloid readers and television viewers. How does this dynamic actually work?"

Russell never quite became accustomed to the suction grip of Victor's gaze. When Victor turned interrogatory eyes and italicized eyebrows upon you there was a sense of hanging on to your seat and everything else, the force of his curiosity threatening to suck the inner organs out through your gaping mouth. Semicolons aside, Russell thought he was a master of the question mark. You really wanted to find the right answer for Victor, even when, as now, the question didn't seem particularly interesting. Unlike most writers of Russell's acquaintance, whose corporeal selves seemed mere pasty shadows of their Platonic essence, Victor had a powerful, space-displacing physical presence, which accounted in part for the proportions of his myth.

"Jeff's not famous," Russell responded, almost testily, as if he were tired of this subject. "He's been on a couple of morning shows—but the guy who reads his electric meter doesn't know him from Adam."

Victor seemed disappointed, but undeterred. "I've been thinking about the uses of fame, about the tension between the private imperatives of creation and the imperative of the artist and the finished art object to force itself upon the world at large, to assume a public dimension. For two-thirds of my life now I've cultivated the private at the expense of the public."

"But you've made a legend out of it."

"Do you think so," he asked eagerly. "But I doubt whether people your age know who I am."

"The literate ones do."

"Does anybody outside of New York or, not to put too fine a point on it, outside the subscription list to *The New York Review of Books* know who I am?"

Russell suffered the momentary illusion that he was sitting across from an aging beauty who has called her charms into question in order to hear them defended. It disturbed him that this man he admired for his uncompromising commitment to writing had lately developed such a keen interest in the mechanics of publicity.

"Look at rock and roll," Propp continued, "the visceral, direct communication with an audience. How many records do the big acts sell? For that matter, who are the big acts?"

This was exactly the sort of thing that Harold Stone could not tell him.

Russell explained that rock and roll had in his opinion been subverted by commercial imperatives and that hits were now created by studio producers using canned formulas. "There's so much money at stake they've oligopolized the industry. It's all product, Victor. That's what's good about books. There's hardly any money involved."

"John Irving makes money, Doctorow makes money."

"Not compared to Madonna."

Victor persisted, wanting to know what music Russell listened to. When he mentioned Dire Straits, who performed a song called "Money for

Nothing," Victor's eyes lit up. He asked Russell to recite the lyrics—a handy little text—and took out his notebook to write them down under the *No Free Lunch* heading, failing to note, however, that the band was British.

"What if I gave a reading," Victor asked, stroking his strong, cleft chin contemplatively. "Do you think we could purvey it as a major literary event? I haven't given one in New York in seven years."

"I think there'd be a lot of interest," Russell said. "Do it up at the East Side Y. Could be big."

"What if Jeff introduced me?"

"Jeff? That wouldn't have been my first pick."

"It's precisely the unexpectedness of it that appeals to me, the disjunctive conjunction. Pierce and Propp. What if we were to do a joint reading? Combining our constituencies, so to speak?"

"I'll see what I can do."

"But do you really think it's a good idea?" Victor demanded, as if Russell had been responsible for generating the notion, and proceeded to enumerate the drawbacks and potential dangers of the plan. After fifteen minutes of solo dialectic he agreed with himself that they would proceed cautiously. In the meantime he had spread out in front of his plate a battery of pills and capsules—nine in all, to be taken in a predetermined sequence. "Bellow put me onto these," Victor explained, popping two. "Saved his love life," he confided. "Lowered my cholesterol twenty points. You send away to this company in Connecticut."

"You should talk to Jeff," Russell muttered. "He has a keen interest in pharmacology."

"What does your wife say about the market," Victor asked later, upon the arrival of his cuttlefish risotto—a dish associative, he suggested, of Ionic poets and scribes: white rice stained in a broth of black ink. Victor had his own broker, but he second-guessed him as he second-guessed the weatherman and the conventional wisdom, as he would second-guess Russell Calloway. Nothing was simple, nothing what it seemed to be.

"She's cautious."

"Women *are* cautious," Victor said, cutting, in his trademark fashion, from this highly specific observation directly to the realm of the universal. "Men are the great romantics, the dreamers and fools. Women are realists. Like Jane Austen."

"What about *Jane Eyre?*"

Victor waved a large, definitive hand as if at an invisible buzz. "A product of sexual repression," he said impatiently. "Brontë me no Brontës, that's kid stuff. But I'm interested in Corrine's perspective. This could be the first business cycle in history where we have a female perspective, a feminine influence in the financial community. Will it introduce moderation, flatten out the testosterone surges of the market, as the introduction of girls at an old New England prep school reduces the incidence of broken glass and food fights . . . overlay some other kind of lunar, tidal, menstrual rhythm? Somebody should be working on a computer model for this, or at least a monograph."

"The market hasn't shown much restraint the last couple years. Even though there are plenty of women around."

"Everybody's getting rich, Russell," Victor confided, leaning forward and engaging him with that toilet-plunger gaze, which was unsettling and flattering in equal measure. "Every remotely sentient being except for you and me. If you were in any other business right now, you'd be making twice, ten times what you do now. You're clever. And I know what they pay you. . . ."

This was Russell's cue to blush. He probably did know, the son of a bitch.

"A mind like yours, at the top of your field for your age. Look at the books you published last year. You're practically famous. And me. It gives me more pain than pleasure to contemplate the fact that I am perhaps the only writer of my era who has the capacity to reinvent the novel. Do you realize the kind of responsibility that entails? All the while thinking—I don't have to tell you—that if I'd gone into business I would be a millionaire many times over. Why should I live in poverty? I understand the stock market better than my broker. But I don't have capital. I need more money. I deserve more. So do you."

"Are you telling me you want to renegotiate your contract?"

"I think we should both renegotiate our contracts," Propp said flatly, popping down three orange pills in quick succession.

"I don't think Master Harold and Company are going to appreciate that idea," Russell said, not unhappily.

"I want more money. You know I can get more if I go elsewhere. You want to publish this book. It's going to make our reputations, yours as well as mine. I flatter myself that you're my natural ally, Russell. Harold is the, if you will forgive the cliché, stumbling block. I want to go around Harold. Harold's tired, for him everything has already happened. He believes he is at the end of the whole Hegelian daisy chain of history. He seems to think he *is* the end. The old bastard can't get it up for anything new."

"I wouldn't go quite that far," Russell said, recalling Harold on the couch with Carlton. But he was pleased to hear Victor expressing the same doubts that he'd been eager but unable to introduce into the conversation.

"You should be running the house."

"If wishes were Porsches, poor boys would drive."

"My dear boy, at this point in American history I daresay that wishes are Porsches. I feel that we in this insane city are living in an era in which anything can happen. Do you remember what Nick Carraway said as he was driving into Manhattan in Gatsby's big car and the skyline of the city came into view over the Queensboro Bridge? As they cross into the city, Nick says, 'Anything can happen now that we've slid over this bridge . . . anything at all.' "

Russell nodded on cue, though he wasn't sure he *exactly* remembered, word for word; but "sort of" was not a phrase one wanted to use with Propp. One presumably had Gatsby and other key texts committed to memory.

Victor rubbed his chin in contemplation. "My sources tell me that your star is falling at Corbin, Dern. Perhaps it's time for a youthful coup d'état," he said, his dark eyebrows rising like the shadows of twin hawks on the sheer cliff of his forehead.

"As someone once said about the pope—I have no army."

"Do you have a banker?"

"Only a cash machine."

"Why don't you buy the company?" Propp said suddenly, as if it were the obvious solution, which had inexplicably eluded them till now.

"I can't even afford to buy an apartment, Victor."

"That doesn't matter. Look around you, Russell. All you need is ambition, imagination and leverage."

"So far as I know, the laws of nature have yet to be revoked."

"You haven't been reading the papers recently."

In fact, the idea was not so wild or remote that it had not occurred to Russell, but he was surprised, almost embarrassed, to hear the older man describe his fantasy.

Victor leaned across the table and put his huge hand on top of Russell's. "Credit, Russell, the philosophers' stone of our era. You can turn the lead of wage slavery into golden destiny—if you have the courage."

"Could I count on you, Victor?"

"My dear boy, haven't I made that clear already?" said the older man, the sharp blades of his lips pressed together in a conspiratorial smile.

8

"I always dream about winning the lottery, man, but I don't never buy no ticket."

"That's like the ad says—you gotta play to win."

"I know I gotta play to win. All you need's a dollar and a dream, like the man says. Well, I got the dream, all right. Now I just need the damn dollar."

" 'Sall I'm saying. Got to lay down your one dollar."

Waiting in line outside the mission, the two conversants exhibited the moist camaraderie of new drinking buddies, temporarily at ease after jointly solving a conundrum of logic. Both were underdressed for the cold, hunched into themselves as if around the embers of fading internal combustion. One sported a knit hat with a tassel and the legend "Ski Mad River Glen," the other a baseball cap inscribed "Drexel Burnham Lambert Bond Conference '86," which he had insulated and waterproofed with an inner lining fashioned from a green plastic garbage bag.

A voice down the line said, "The lottery's a regressive tax foisted on the classes that can least afford it by the fascist state."

Like athletes conserving energy, the two winos turned slowly and economically to regard the speaker—a pimpled face and neck sprouting from a fringed buckskin jacket with an "Eat the Rich" button on the lapel; the long hair, drawn back in a ponytail, conveyed the impression of a coonskin cap.

"It's a trick of the ruling classes to hide the economic realities of the fascist state from the paling masses. You think rich people play the lottery? You think Donald Trump buys lotto tickets?"

"He don't need to," said the man in the Drexel cap. "His ship already come in."

"That's right," his buddy agreed. "I'm just saying, Where's my ship? That's all I'm saying, Dan'l Boone. I want my piece the fuckin' pie."

"Goddamn right you do. That's what my friend's saying, Mr. Hillbilly. He wants to know, Where's his damn ship?"

"Whoa, there she blows, man. Lookit there."

"That ain't your ship. That Miss Corrine. She a married lady."

"I've had me plenty married ladies. You trying to say I can't get me no married lady?"

Hurrying down the Bowery from Cooper Union in her Belgian loafers, Corrine assessed the line outside the mission. Like restaurants, the missions and soup kitchens each had their distinct clientele, the patronage here mainly male, divided equally between black and white, the majority wearing their Sunday manners because the food was decent and the space limited. A few, most of whom she recognized, talked loudly, complaining, bragging, challenging their neighbors on small points of etiquette or credulity—"You don't think I could get a job with the city just like that if I wanted to, you calling me a goddamn liar? I'm talking about a *good* job"—preserving in their mendicant state something of the air of boxers before a fight, the demeanor of hustlers about to scam a free meal from an unsuspecting authority, this stance answering the needs of their residual dignity. Others waited quietly to accept whatever might be given. A few were drunk, trying not to show it. Some, whacked out on their own internal chemicals, barely knew where they were: schizophrenics with eyes shuttered against the outer world, an autistic man in a white jumpsuit who compulsively paced out four steps that might have been a foxtrot. The queens coveyed up near the front of the line, shrill and animate as tropical birds, plumed with elaborate coiffures and gaudy scarves—the dandies of the street life.

"Hey girlfrien'!"

"Co-reen!"

"Our lady of perpetual dee-light."

Corrine waved generally and slipped in the door, where the smell of food mingled with the heavy institutional odor of disinfectant on linoleum. The other volunteers were setting the tables with plastic utensils, bowls of grape jelly and baskets of fluffy white bread.

"You want to scatter the manna," asked Irene Goldblum, handing Corrine a roll of yellow tickets. A harried social worker with salt-and-pepper hair, she had tended to the poor, tired and huddled misfits of the Lower East Side since graduating from Barnard in 1969; the exhaustion of the effort showed on her face. To Corrine she seemed cynical about her chosen calling—but Corrine visited the Lower East Side only twice a week, and that for just the past year.

"You're a wet one, bubeleh," Irene had said after, on her first day, Corrine had given away all her cash to the patrons of the mission, instigating a riot in the process. "You'll be more help to them and us if you don't feel too sorry for them. Two-thirds of these men are substance abusers and ninety percent of them are con artists, so watch out your heart doesn't bleed too freely."

Maybe she was wet, but Corrine believed her compassion had a logical foundation. Living in the city, she felt bound up in a delicate, complex web of interdependence and she was determined to play her part. The misery as well as the vitality of the metropolis seeped into her psyche. After all these years in the city she had yet to develop a nonporous shell.

The line tensed and shifted as Corrine appeared outside the door. Grimy, cracked palms were extended. This was the moment that fights broke out, although the line tended to police itself when one of the female volunteers handled the tickets. Corrine was especially popular with the regulars.

The queens slapped each other's hands away and examined Corrine's wardrobe with professional disinterest.

"That a Chanel suit, girl?"

"I wish."

"Who does your hair, honey—I got to come uptown and get me some of that."

"Girl goes to that fancy Gore Vidal salon."

Farther down the line, a handsome, streetworn man said: "My hostess with the mostest." This was Ace, Corrine's recent party guest. For several weeks now he had been telling the other men in line about the party in increasingly fanciful detail, lately conveying the impression of an intimate acquaintance with Corrine and her stylish uptown friends. The VCR was never mentioned. "Got my appetite with me today. I'm off the crack and off the juice and I'm in God's hands and that's the truth."

The mention of the deity seemed to set off a chain reaction. Intimates of weather and natural disasters, the men of the streets inclined strongly toward religion, particularly the fateful, fundamentalist strains of Christianity.

"You people don't eat no pork, does you," asked the next man, walleyed and angry. "Just once I'd like me some nice pork chops." The mission was run by a yeshiva, and many of the men felt obliged to bite the hand that fed them, particularly since it was Jewish.

"Them Jews didn't recognize our savior," said the next man in line, who clutched his shopping cart as if he suspected Corrine of intending to steal it. "They failed to recognize him yea even like the woman who anointed his feet with oil and they put him to death."

"Her name's Calloway," insisted Big George, a stately old black man who was also called the Mayor in deference to his long tenure on the Bowery. "That's a Catholic name."

"My husband's, actually," said Corrine.

"You—you're what they call an Aryan from Darien," George said.

"Where are you living, George," Corrine asked.

"Oh, I got my mobile home. Sleeping on the E train."

"Catholics just as bad," said the walleye. "You know why's the delay in the New Jerusalem? It's because of the pope and his troops, they robbed the streets of gold and ransacked the city of glass. It's all inside the Vatican now—and he built hisself a throne of gold, saith the Lord. Now they waiting for the reimbursement on the insurance policy for the New Jerusalem. But the day is coming when the righteous they shall be lifted up into God's bosom and the unrighteous shall be cast into the outer darkness."

"It's the people have to rise up for themselves and overthrow the bankers and the lawyers and the real estate interests," insisted the ponytail. "This city, this neighborhood, belongs to the people, but the sushi eaters are gobbling it up with their designer—"

"The who eaters?"

"You mean the Japs?"

"No, man, not them . . ."

Corrine pressed a ticket on the foxtrot man, whose feet traced an invisible set of instructions on the sidewalk. Farther down the line a debate was in progress about the existence of a rogue leopard, at large in the streets of Manhattan. Several men claimed to have seen the beast, and one said a friend of his had been attacked and mauled.

Reaching the end of the line Corrine saw a familiar tall figure hunched in conversation with two bikers down the street. In his ragged prep surplus he looked like a scarecrow planted on the Bowery to frighten off the pigeons. The bikers sat sidesaddle on their Harleys, parked at rakish, fuck-you angles against the curb; the Manhattan headquarters of the Hell's Angels was just around the corner and Jeff lived a few blocks away in a loft on Great Jones Street. As she watched, one of the Angels reached up and poked his finger into Jeff's chest. Her first instinct was to rush over, but she held back. Jeff eventually exchanged the brothers' handshake with both men and shambled away up the street, almost passing before he recognized her.

"Corrine! Christ . . . what are you . . ." He swept his limp blond bangs away from his surprised face. "How are you?"

"I'm fine. You all right?"

"As right as usual. What, this is your day to expiate?"

"Yup, I've brought my teaspoon down to bail the ocean of human misery." She nodded toward the Angels. "What are you doing—research?"

They drifted along the sidewalk back toward the mission. Looking down at her feet, Corrine saw a graffito she had seen elsewhere, a martini glass with a slash through it.

"I'm abandoning the New England family novel for gritty urban realism." He looked at her with an almost bashful smile.

"That you boyfriend, Krin?" someone called from the line.

"I seen his picture somewhere. He's that actor."

"Hey, brotherman, I seen you over to Reagantown, ain't I?" said Ace, shivering in a hooded Columbia University sweatshirt worn under a shiny tuxedo jacket.

"One of my doubles," Jeff said.

"Hey, if I can tell you exactly where you got them gloves, will you give 'em to me?"

"*Exactly* where," Jeff asked, looking at his pigskinned hands, trying to remember himself where they had come from.

Ace was slapping his arms for warmth. "The exact very place."

"You're on," said Jeff.

"You got 'em on you hands, sucka. Am I right, or am I right?"

"You gotta admit, he's right," said the man beside Ace. The crowd seemed to agree.

Jeff immediately removed his gloves and handed them over. The recipient looked almost as surprised as Corrine.

"You didn't have to do that," said Corrine.

"A bet's a bet."

"You're weird, Jeff. Where are you going?"

"Nowhere special," he said. "See a man about a dog."

"You want to have a drink afterward?"

He seemed to hesitate. "Okay, I'll meet you at Great Jones."

He kissed her at the door. The queens howled as he slouched away. "Hey there, long and slim. Come on back here."

Jeff seemed even thinner than usual, Corrine thought, as she brought another half-loaf of bread to one of the tables; he could almost pass in a soup line.

"More bread, please, miss." Especially in winter, they asked for bread until they were cut off, loading carbohydrates against the cold. And jelly—they layered Smucker's on everything, for the sugar.

At table three a fight broke out over extra sugar packets, one man trying to strangle Ace with his scarf. They toppled to the floor. Here near the bottom of the food chain, sugar was the basis of a primitive system of exchange. Mrs. Goldblum swooped down and scared the combatants into a truce. Ace managed to keep two extra packets of sugar in the articles of agreement that ended the scuffle.

Ace felt hot, the mojo was on him tonight for certain. Feinting at shadows with his new gloves, he paused on the Bowery, trying to feel his luck. Like many men on the street, Ace was a fatalist. Whatever was going to be would be. You just had to try not to get in the way of it. Coming up on a dude in a suit, he asked for a quarter. The man passed him by like he was the Invisible Man, but Ace was used to that, people not hearing him and not seeing him, the normal citizenry equipped with that streamlined New York tunnel vision—eyes straight ahead and fo-

cused on the next stop lest the gaze get snagged on something ugly—
equipped with radar that registered his presence as an obstacle to be
avoided like a rock or a pile of dog shit. It could be such a bitch that
sometimes you almost yearned for the straight thing, and yet he found
a certain romance in this business of pure subsistence, foraging and
hunting like the early pioneers in a hostile landscape, that was far more
exciting than flipping burgers, humping furniture, riding his ass all over
the city on a bike delivering messages.

He drifted over to the bandstand at Tompkins Square Park and found
some of the boys smoking that crack, but he had no green, so he moved
right along, cruising down Avenue C to the big lot in which a squatter's
camp had sprouted in the rubble of a demolished tenement block, a
makeshift urban encampment of tepees constructed after a truck carrying
bolts of fabric had overturned on Houston. The members of an ad hoc
drinking club which had formed around a bottle of Night Train, having
discovered the driver unconscious, pried open the back and found bolts
of silk and cotton tapestry depicting scenes of knights on horseback in
pursuit of unicorns, which looked much too valuable to leave in the
gutter, so the men had rolled the cargo up to the empty lot in which
they'd been sleeping. The next day the first tepee went up. Now there
were a dozen, the once scarlet material bedraggled and fading in the rain
and sun and snow, covered over with plastic garbage bags and aluminum
foil. Shanties of plywood and sheet metal had risen among the tepees,
and other settlers had squatted the abandoned tenement next door. A
huge mural painted on the exposed, windowless side of the building
portrayed an idealized, Edenic version of the community under the title
THE NEW JERUSALEM, but most people called it Reagantown. Altogether several hundred citizens had taken refuge here, among them families with children and pets; many more, such as Ace, passed through,
looking for food, parties and shelter. A giant Vietnam veteran named
Rostenkowski informally ruled the community, doling out the donated
food, selling lean-to space for a buck a night and overseeing the drug
trade.

The night air was smudged with smoke and heavily freighted with
smells of food, sweat and urine. Campers were huddled around the
burning trashcans, sharing bottles and cigarettes. Looking over at Rostenkowski's tepee Ace saw Corrine's friend, the tall dude who'd given

him the gloves, step out and gaze up at the sky as if he were trying to get his bearings from the stars. Ace, he was looking for a girl named Sally Sweet.

"Gone visit the oval office," asked a man called Sixtoe, who actually had eleven toes in all.

"Just like the president," said Ace.

Then someone told him that Rostenkowski had thrown her out, told her not to come back, because her arms broke out all purple and Rostenkowski said it was the AIDS.

"How come the white man always get to be the fucking landlord?"

"You better go get yourself a test, brother."

"If you gonna go, you gonna go," Ace observed, tautologically, but he felt bad about Sally, she was only sixteen.

After cleanup at the mission Corrine met Jeff at the Great Jones Café, a small crowded juke-joint that was one of his hangouts.

"If I can tell you exactly where you bought that shirt, will you take it off," he asked the bartender, a bleached blonde in a tight black camisole.

"My girlfriend stole it from this place she used to work."

"That's *exactly* what I was going to say. Off with it—now!"

The bartender sauntered away. Jeff seemed almost relaxed here. Never easy to locate, in recent years he'd become more distracted and elusive than ever. There must have been a moment, she thought, after he finished his book, when he unwound, but his contentment seemed to diminish in proportion to its success. Russell said that as an elitist and a misanthrope, Jeff couldn't help hating himself after so many people had liked his book. After sticking with him for three years through the hard times, his girlfriend, Caitlin, packed it in once he finally succeeded. She didn't like all the new competition, she said. "Do you hear anything from Caitlin," Corrine asked.

"I hear she's engaged to an investment banker. You don't think it will ever happen to someone you actually know, and then—wham! Just like that. A lesson for us all. I guess it's a reaction to three years of me."

"Well, I'm a *stockbroker*, as you so kindly reminded me on my birthday."

The bartender, who might have moonlighted as a female wrestler, directed at her one of those feminine surveys of suspicious appraisal.

"You're not really a broker. Some people turn into their jobs. Not you."

"Does that make me a hypocrite, doing something I don't believe in?"

"You're like . . . a missionary to the dark continent of Wall Street, bringing a little sweetness and light to the financial sector. What do you want, a beer?"

"Just a diet something."

"*Diet something*," the blonde simpered, clutching the pistol grip of the soda gun fiercely. She managed to convey the impression that it was beneath her professional dignity to serve soft drinks, let alone *diet* soft drinks, and that she was doing so only because Corrine was, inexplicably, a friend of Jeff's.

"You given up drinking? Manhattan social life will be revealed in all its tawdry horror and you'll come to despise us all."

"Maybe we should all move."

"We should. But where is there?"

"We have to live here but you could live anywhere. I like to think of you on a New England campus, smoking a pipe and fly-fishing."

"I'm a fisher of women."

"Have you ever slept with her?" she whispered, once the bartender had finally rolled out of earshot. "She looks at me as if she'd like to stick me in the blender headfirst."

"Actually, I think she'd like to put you in feet first and work down very slowly for maximum pain."

"You didn't answer my question."

"You're right, I didn't." He stared her down.

She sipped, licked the carbonation sting from her lips. "Do you ever wish you'd married Caitlin?"

"We were as married as anybody—I liked to think of it as a marriage of inconvenience. We fought as much as any married couple . . . made ourselves expert on each other's weaknesses. . . . I think that counts as marriage, doesn't it?"

"You know I know you just pretend to be cynic."

"*We are what we pretend to be, so we must be careful about what we pretend to be.*"

"—Vonnegut."

"Yes, very good. Though I think Aristotle said it first."

"Well, you seemed like a good couple."

"It's easy to *seem* like a good couple," Jeff said ruefully. "I was always waiting for you."

"I don't feel like I've really talked to you lately." Corrine didn't want to encourage this line of speculation. "Don't you ever want to settle down?"

"That's your job. Someone's got to drink these drinks and fuck these sleazy girls so you can live a normal life."

"You used to talk about your feelings, Jeff. Not just joke about them."

"Basically," he said, "I think men talk to women so they can sleep with them and women sleep with men so they can talk to them."

"Where does that leave us," she asked lightly.

"In a Zen garden. Green and yellow mosses, raked gravel. Silence."

She nodded in frustration, and looked away. "Come have dinner with us," she said, finally.

"Sorry. Booked."

"Walking the dog?"

"Something like that." He fired up a cigarette.

"Try not to forget the old friends," she said coyly.

He cocked his head, seeming to hear a tune at the back of his mind. "Ah yes, 'the old friends.' Sounds familiar. So it *was* you who sent me that Yeats poem."

"What poem is that?" She affected an expression of innocence.

He recited:

> "Though you are in your shining days,
> Voices among the crowd
> And new friends busy with your praise,
> Be not unkind or proud,
> But think about old friends the most:
> Blah de blah iamb anapest . . .

"I forget the rest. Either you or Crash. Worried about a few good reviews going to the Jeffer's head. Well, I became an asshole in spite of your best efforts."

"But you *always* were an asshole," she said, wishing she had a cigarette.

When she was around the boys she started to talk like them—arch and tough.

"I think I screwed up that joke, I should've said 'where you *got* that shirt,' not 'where you *bought* that shirt.' The curse of precise grammar . . ."

Jeff would not let her take the subway, inserting her in a cab with a smoky kiss. "There's something I've been wanting to ask you for a long time," he said as he hunched down to her ear.

She looked up almost fearfully. "What?"

"What was Salinger really like?"

9

FAME
by Juan Baptiste

. . . Your penis gets bigger, of course. Or your breasts. And generally you change your name. You start with a name like Norma Jean or Archie Leach or James Gatz. It's not required, of course. But here in America, it's good to remember we like people to start from scratch (KENNEDYs *excepted). We like inventors. And creativity begins at home—self-invention is the national birthright. You were born in some dumb 'burb? Tired of the same old meat loaf on the table, the same old face in the mirror day after day? No problem, move to New York—the city that enshrines the concept of novelty right in its name. Nose too big, tits too small? Get thee to a plastic surgeon. Be a model, or just look like one. Get with the program. Catch the buzz. Life and liberty you got, now get happy. Get hip. Get laid. Get rich. Think big.*

Look at JOHNNY MONIKER, *six months ago the guy was working in a pizza joint, a year ago he was living in the* Midwest. *How about* BERNIE MELMAN, *you think he was born a billionaire? And* MADONNA *started life in Detroit with some unpronounceable name. Even yours truly,* JUAN BAPTISTE, *could tell you a thing or two about humble origins. And also about the surgery, the perjury, the forgery and the orgiery behind the big names.*

As for instance when I crashed a black-tie dinner at the TEMPLE OF DENDUR *in the Met, where my slumlord was receiving an award for his services to humanity and the advancement of culture. I cabbed all the* way uptown to ask him how come there's no hot water in my building. His wife the movie star in her CHRISTIAN LACROIX bubble-assed gown rises to lead the applause—listen, flap flap flap, it's the sound of modern prayer, the gesture of inverted envy, hands pressed together in hero worship. And while she's standing there, look at my landlord's famous wife, take a good look, small-town girl who rose from her knees to become a great star—remember, boys and girls, Juan says that nothing succeeds like sucking seed. And my slumlord's best friend in the whole world, billionaire Bernie Melman, is up at the microphone saying that my slumlord is probably, without exaggeration, the greatest human being that ever lived. . . .

. . . Can you imagine if the walls of the Temple of Dendur had ears, this ancient thing that was standing around the desert of Egypt for a few thousand years listening in on all the pharaoh dish before it was scooped up stone by numbered stone and reassembled inside its own wing of the Met? . . . Were they telling the same kind of lies back then? I don't know, I like to think the lies we tell here in the new, improved capital of the entire late-twentieth-century world are the biggest, baddest, most shameless lies of all time. . . .

Everybody was at the party, although somehow they neglected to invite yours truly . . . an oversight, no doubt. . . .

Earlier I'd been to a screening of Fatal Attraction, starring MICHAEL DOUGLAS and GLENN CLOSE, a movie about what happens to you and your bunny rabbit if you screw around on your wife. . . . Juan says two stars for good elevator sex and bad bathtub ring. This town is brutal on monogamy. Then, speaking of marriage—and finding myself uncharacteristically on the Upper East Side—I stumbled up to Russell and Corrine Calloway's Saturday-night salon. He's an editor at Corbin, Dern and she's the Waspy beauty who reminds us just a wee bit of the young KATHARINE HEPBURN, or of that recent ALEX KATZ painting Alba in Black at the MARLBOROUGH GALLERY. My downtown companions TONY DUPLEX, LETICIA CORBIN (coincidentally of the Corbin, Dern Corbins) and Johnny Moniker mixed with the people who ask "What do you do?" when they meet you. Remember, boys and girls, Juan Baptiste says it's not what you do—it's who you do. . . .

Flash! Juan's fashion tips of the week: For men—I predict a vogue for codpieces. . . . As for you girls—don't forget that party tits, aka silicone *breast implants, tend to explode on the Concorde . . . something about the sound barrier. . . .*

Part of Russell's morning mail, this essay was at the top of a stack of tearsheets from a downtown magazine called *Down Under*, with a letter from Juan Baptiste, presumably the author, reminding him of their meeting, pointing out "the plug" and proposing that his columns might make an interesting book, a chronicle of the nightlife of the city.

Russell's assistant, Donna, had attached a yellow Post-it note to the submission: "Didn't know you knew Juan—this seems like kind of a cool idea to me."

He called out to Donna, who appeared in the doorway wearing a "Die Yuppie Scum" T-shirt.

"You interested in this?"

"Sure. I think it would be excellent if we could just for once maybe publish something interesting for a change."

"Sorry the list has been such a disappointment to you, Donna. Look, how about if you look hard at this and give me a report when I get back from vacation?"

She nodded, cracked her gum. Clearly overwhelmed with gratitude, he thought.

Near the bottom of his mail pile was a letter from a credit card company. *Congratulations, you have been pre-approved for a gold card.* This was a surprise. So far as he knew, he was overdrawn and overdue on all the others. He was about to chuck the letter, when he saw that, because of his excellent professional standing, he'd also been *pre-approved for a credit line of fifty thousand dollars.* All he had to do was sign the form and return it in thirty days. There had to be some mistake, and yet there was his name on the card and again on the cardholder's agreement. He quickly signed the agreement, sealed the envelope and dropped it in his out box. He couldn't wait to tell Corrine.

On his way out the door, he took a call from Tim Calhoun, who sounded drunk. Tim said he was nearly finished with the new book and invited Russell to come fishing down in Georgia to celebrate. Russell begged off—"Vacation with the wife, good buddy." But he was happier about this call than the last, when Tim was in urgent need of bail money.

On his way to lunch, Russell encountered Harold in the men's room. "Hi, Harold," he said as he swung up to the urinal. Standing at the next urinal, Harold glanced at him and made an indistinguishable sound.

"I'll take it," Russell said. Donna had Zac Solomon on the phone from Los Angeles. Russell hadn't spoken to him since the party more than a month before.

"Mr. Calloway? Please hold for Mr. Solomon."

"Fine." Thinking, God, I hate that "hold for" shit. Russell supposed he could have Donna do it, "Hold for Mr. Calloway." Plenty of the assholes around the office did.

"Russ-*ell*. That you, guy? Do I hear a little Russell in the bushes? A rustle of *leaves*, possibly." Then, in falsetto, "Oh God, look at that over there, in the woods, that naked couple—they're *russell*ing the leaves, they're forni . . . fornic . . . God, I can't say it."

This was probably funnier when it was someone else's name. But maybe I'm just tired, Russell thought. When it was over he said, "What is it you're auditioning for, Zachary?"

"The question is, what are *you* auditioning for, guy? In fact I'll tell you what you're auditioning for. I want to talk to you about a job."

"Why me? I don't know anything about movies."

"Neither does anybody else. That's the beauty of this business. Three years ago I was crunching numbers for Manny Hanny. Then I helped put together a finance package for United Artists. Two years ago I get a stupid idea for a movie, come out and set up my own production company. Now I get all my phone calls returned yesterday, I've got more money than I know what to do with, and I'm fucking a different actress every night of the week. God, I love this country."

"Why share the booty with me?"

"Say I'm feeling generous. I need some help here, guy. I need some brains. I also need product. You know the book world, you could help me get a jump on print material coming out of New York. You know how to spell your own fucking name, which puts you way out ahead of the pack, L.A.-wise. You could help me work with Jeff, who's a genius but also a total pain in the ass if you know what I mean. Can I just between you and me ask since we're on this subject—and needless to say, this is absolutely in strictest confidence—if maybe he doesn't have a, you know, bit of a substance abuse problem."

"No," said Russell, "he doesn't." Jeff might get fucked up more than was good for him, get a little wired up sometimes, but that was part of who he was. These people out in L.A., Russell thought, were all temperance freaks after that snowstorm blew through a few years before. But even if Jeff had been a stone junkie, Russell wasn't about to tell Zac Solomon, or any other relative stranger. As he understood the concept of friendship, that's what it entailed.

"Yeah, well, whatever," Zac said. "Still, you might look into it. People out here are a little jumpy these days, I mean even a rumor can stop a career dead in its tracks. What I'm mainly saying is, you're hot—Jeff's book and that novel by what's-his-name you did last year. We got heat, we got fit, we've got *synergy*."

"Seriously, Zac."

"Why should I be serious? Look where I live. I don't get paid to be serious."

Dave Whitlock drifted into the office, sat down on the arm of Russell's couch and picked up a magazine from the end table. Russell held up a single finger.

"Fly you out here, put you up. Hey, you can come out with Jeff on Thursday. Or else I can meet you in New York next month."

"Zac, I like movies enough to know I don't understand how they're made. Books is what I know."

"What are you making, seventy-five, a hundred?"

Out of embarrassment, Russell remained silent. He wished.

"Whatever it is, I can double it, guy."

Whitlock stood up to leave but Russell signaled him to wait. He wanted him to hear this.

"I'm pretty happy where I am, Zac. Plus I'm about to go into a meeting. Let me think about it, all right?"

"We'll get you sooner or later," Zac said. "There's money falling out of the fucking palm trees out here. *Sayonara*."

"Job offer," Whitlock asked, after Russell hung up.

"I'm in demand," Russell said. "Let them know that upstairs."

"I'll try to remember," he said gloomily, dropping the magazine back on the table as if it, too, had failed to yield answers to the meaning of life or higher corporate profits.

"This Rappaport book of yours is going to lose us a shitload of money."

"It's not going to lose a shitload of money," Russell said irritably. "It may not hit the list . . ."

Whitlock snorted derisively. "Nobody wants to know about Nicaragua and nobody wants to know bad things about the nice old man in the White House."

"If Harold would get behind the fucker, it would do fine."

"What'd you do to piss him off," Whit asked.

"I turned thirty. I changed offices. I don't know." Hearing Whitlock ask about his disfavor as if it were a confirmed fact rattled him, especially on top of the call from Solomon, which reminded him of how little money he was making.

As Whit waved a morose good-bye, Russell recalled his father's rules to live by, imparted the day before he drove off to college: Never endanger a woman's reputation, never climb on another man's back, never talk about what you make or what things cost. Amidst the rakes, bags of weed killer and turf builder in the garage in Michigan, packing the car with stereo, books and clothes, his dad suddenly turned patriarchal; this phenomenon always left both of them embarrassed, as when the old man had explained sex to him many years before. Russell stood awkwardly, a box of records in his arms, as his father recited the golden rules. Later, he repeated these maxims for the amusement of friends, but he was stuck with them. He tried to savor a feeling of condescension toward Zac, but he felt more keenly ashamed of his salary, and depressed that the Zacs of this world were getting rich.

If he was going to make any money, Russell decided, it was probably going to be in the market. He needed to start playing Duane's instruments—futures and options. If only he had some capital . . . and then he remembered the brand-new credit line—fifty big ones. He could invest it in short-term instruments. Why not?

Donna steamed in, blackly. "Do I have to listen to that preppy bitch Carlton? I mean, I thought *you* were my boss. If she's supposed to be my boss, too, then I quit."

"What," he said, "are you talking about?"

A high degree of color burned through her white makeup. She paced back and forth, two steps in each direction as she spoke. "She told me to get rid of this—" Pointing to her "Eat the Rich" button. "She said you knew about it. What is this, fucking *high school* or something? Did you know about this?" Stopping directly in front of him, defiantly crossing her arms.

Russell nodded. "I was asked to tell you to lose the button."

"By that blonde cunt?"

"Please. By Harold, actually."

"So?"

"So, obviously I ignored the request."

"So, who's my boss is what I want to know."

"I am for the moment. And as your boss I order you to continue wearing the button."

10

"Now I'm really going to quit drinking," Corrine announced.

Russell was fooling with the radio knob with one hand while he clutched the wheel of the rental car in the other, dialing through static as he strained to see into the white cone of the headlights.

"I think there's a good station out of Manchester," he said. "Hey, maybe while we're in the general neighborhood we should visit your old friend Salinger."

"Russell, did you hear me? I said I'm going to quit drinking."

"I heard you." Tacking in on a series of harsh chords, he said, "What do you mean?"

"I mean what I said."

"You mean you're going to quit drinking? As in *stop*?"

"Why won't you acknowledge what I'm saying here?"

"I didn't think you were serious." He looked over at her for the first time since her announcement, squinting quizzically.

"Why wouldn't I be serious?"

"You always say that."

"Well, I mean it this time."

"Okay."

Sunday night, driving back to the city from Vermont. After a weekend of skiing she felt less healthy than ever. The night before, a big dinner with friends who lived near Middlebury, a couple they knew from school. Both worked for the state government in Burlington, Jeannie as an environmental biologist and Chip as a consumer advocate. They were trying to adopt a kid. On weekends they went rock climbing, whitewater rafting, cross-country skiing.

"What is this music?" Corrine said. "Sounds like something Jeff would like."

"The Cure," Russell answered.

"Cure for what?"

"That's the name of the band, Corrine."

"How do you know that?"

"I just do."

"Well, I don't." It upset her when she discovered these discrepancies in their knowledge of the quotidian world, as if in going through his pockets she had come across tricornered napkin scraps inscribed with lipsticked numbers and cryptic notes. Married five years, dating on and off five before that . . . how did he get to know these new things without her? Didn't they have the same lives? Did they?

The night before, sitting in the big, drafty house drinking wine and playing Trivial Pursuit, Corrine had been filled with admiration and envy for life as practiced by their host and hostess, yet at the same time it didn't seem quite real to her. If she was not entirely happy with her existence in the city, she didn't think that this one—woodstoves and vegetable gardens—was available to her anymore. Two roads diverged in the wood, and I . . . I didn't even notice until just now. Russell reciting Frost last night. Out Far and In Deep. Then two more roads diverging, and two more, and suddenly here you are in the middle of . . . *somewhere*, pretending you know where you're going.

Waking this morning at six-thirty in the killingly white guest room without curtains, sick with vegetarian chili and cheap red wine. Russell insisting the Bloody Mary would help. Nothing red, please God. Better dead than red. So she had a screwdriver.

"Why," asked Russell, emerging from miles of silence.

"Why what? Why am I quitting drinking?"

"Yeah."

Something important lurked behind the decision, but the thought of trying to explain it was exhausting. "I don't know. Just a health thing, mainly."

After another ten miles, the salt-blanched road unspooling like gray ribbon between walls of dirty beige snow, she turned to him. "Don't worry. I won't get righteous on you. Okay?"

"Good," he said. "And try not to be boring, either."

Sunday nights were the worst, he thought. Driving in wet ski clothes, Corrine asleep now beside him, he felt the familiar dread closing in on him—hurtling toward the city, the office, the stifling sense of enclosure, abetted by a new sense of anxiety about his standing with Harold. He knew it was a matter of time. He'd lost his momentum at Corbin, Dern, probably even before he opened that door on Harold and Carlton. He had to make a move before he turned into the sort of lame-duck editor whose career was moribund at forty.

It used to be school he dreaded. After the Sunday tortures of itchy gray pants for church and the visiting of relatives, the specter of unfinished homework and some kid who promised to beat you up. Spend your childhood wanting to be an adult and the rest of your life idealizing your childhood. Mondays. Every week cold-starting the engine again. That song about the kid who brought a rifle to school, blazed away at his classmates, said he didn't like Mondays when they asked him why. I hear you, man. Radical, though. Corrine a little radical, too—this new temperance. They'd already quit smoking, for Christ's sake. Two summers before, a nightmare. Everybody leaving the inconvenient vices behind. The new puritanism. Sloth, gluttony, recreational drugs were out. Narcissism, blind ambition and greed by contrast were free of side- or after-effects, at least in this life, and who was counting on the other anymore?

Corrine lifted her head, looked out at the featureless road. "Where are we?"

"The Taconic."

"Do you still love me?" she said sleepily.

"Let me think about it."

"Russ."

Why she required a verbal confirmation every few days he didn't understand. A girl thing, or a Corrine thing? By now he had trouble making the distinction.

"Yes, I believe I do."

"How much?"

This was a game between them, but it was not unserious. He wedged his legs up against the steering wheel and held his hands apart as far as they would go within the car. "About this much."

"Okay." She lay down in his lap and fell asleep again, then woke up with a policeman's flashlight in her eyes and blue light pulsing in the rearview mirror—Russell's second speeding ticket in three days.

"Russell, why are you always in such a hurry?"

"Because at my rear I always hear time's fuel-injected, turbo-charged hearse hurrying near."

"You do not. You don't even *believe* in your own mortality. You act like you're going to live forever." He'd been skiing like that all weekend, flat-out, crashing spectacularly once—splayed across a mogul, the snow he'd churned up settling like a cloud of smoke over his colorful corpse. The blue light continued to flash ominously behind them.

"You have to fool yourself into believing you're not going die. Otherwise you'd be miserable."

"If you don't realize it could end at any minute you won't value it properly. Sometimes I worry that you don't feel things very deeply."

"Division of labor. You do it for me." He squeezed her knee and kissed her as the policeman slammed his car door and tromped back toward them on the shoulder of the highway. "Try not to be quite so serious all the time."

"Why don't you give it a try," she countered. "Just once."

It seemed only minutes later that she was in the office, Monday morning, hand on the phone receiver. For a moment she'd gone completely blank—she couldn't remember whom she was going to call, what she'd been doing before—and then she heard Duane Peters's voice a few feet away:

"I'm predicting this stock could double before the end of the year. . . . No, forget that. Biotech you don't want to know from. Thank your lucky stars I got you out of that in time. That was a Dunkirk. Bodies all over the beach. What's happening now is health and leisure. I'm calling you first on this one. . . ."

Listening to Duane made her feel even gloomier. Her face green in the glow of her Quotron, she looked down at a list of names in front of her: certified public accountants in the greater metropolitan area. Accountants were a hard sell—conservative, tight and inconveniently knowledgeable.

She started with Ablomsky, Leon. A woman answered, her voice scratchy and querulous.

"May I please speak to Mr. Ablomsky?"

On the other end there was silence.

"Hello, is Mr. Ablomsky there?" When there was still no response she said, "This is Corrine Calloway from Wayne, Duehn. Do you expect him back?"

"No." A choked syllable.

"No, you don't expect him soon?"

"He died two weeks ago."

She felt herself go all cold along her spine and at the tips of her ears, as if a wind had poured out of the receiver from Brooklyn. "Oh God, I'm sorry," she said, but after that she felt powerless to speak, or to hang up.

The silence on the other end gave way to a rising intake of breath, which finally broke into a sob. When Mrs. Ablomsky began to speak, her voice was dry and brittle, like an old letter recovered and preserved after a season of rain and snow.

"He's gone. Murdered. We come into the city once a month . . . once a month we dressed up and took the train . . . he was wearing his brown jacket . . . we went to Macy's . . . and then a boy came up behind and grabbed my purse. . . . It was too much for Leon. He'd already had one coronary. Keeled over in the street . . ."

"I'm . . . I'm so . . ."

"Thirty-two years. I'm sorry, I shouldn't, I just thought . . . your voice, a girl's voice but serious. I mean, you don't sound silly. Do you smoke? You sound like a smoker."

"I used to. I quit."

"That's good," she said. "I'm glad. Don't smoke."

She started to weep again.

What could Corrine possibly say? "Did the police . . ."

"The police! What do they know?"

"Are you . . . all right? Is there anything I can do for you?"

"He was a good husband, a good provider. He'd just bought me a new pair of gloves at Macy's, I'd put them on in the store. We used to go to Gimbels before it . . . before it closed. . . . Leon was very upset when they closed Gimbels, he took it hard. . . ."

Trailing shirttails and shoelaces, Jeff appeared in Russell's office as if from bed, his shirt more frayed than usual, the button-down collar unbuttoned and upturned, knees showing through his ripped chinos. Only the blue blazer imparted a precarious note of formality. Adjusting the bill of his cap, inscribed with the motto "Save Me from What I Want," he disheveled himself onto Russell's couch and plucked the *Post* from Russell's desk.

" 'Wild Cat Terrorizes City,' " he read.

"Who is this person," Russell asked Donna.

"Your lunch date."

"Your meal ticket, actually," Jeff said.

Washington Lee was just sliding out to lunch with an agent when his assistant announced a call from Donald Parker. The lunch hour, or rather the lunch two and a half hours, had already begun, in Washington's opinion, and normally he considered the institution sacrosanct; but Donald Parker did not call every day. Fortunately. "I'll take it," he said, warily retreating to his office.

"Donald. What can I do for you, my man?"

"Washington, it's like this—I thought we should have this little talk about how come you're not getting with the program, not taking care of your own people."

"What you talking about?"

"Talking about your company not publishing Afro-American literature. Talking about a respected Afro-American author being insulted and assaulted in your very own office, bro'."

"Don't give me that shit, that nigger's a headcase. Came in my office and threatened me."

"Not the way I heard the story."

"You're hearing jive." Indignant as he was, Washington was also nervous. Parker was an activist with a hyperactive sense of racial injustice, the bald black avenger. He and Washington had a nodding acquaintance, and though he didn't make a point of saying so in front of his white friends, Washington occasionally admired the lawyer's guerrilla media theatrics. Whenever one of his own ran spectacularly afoul of the system, Parker's picture was in the tabloids the next day, his naked forehead wrinkled with concern, a furious scowl emerging from his beard, surrounded by a posse of angry supporters. If the accused was black, he was counsel for the defense, scourge of police and prosecution, skeptical of the legal system; whenever a black appeared to be the victim of white violence he unequivocally demanded swift, harsh justice. Parker was capable of summoning a thousand supporters into the street at the drop of a racial epithet. Even if you didn't like him, there was no percentage in saying so. Washington sent a check to his youth organization every year.

"This is not a big thing," Washington said calmly, "and it's not a color thing."

"Everything's about color, Lee. For example, if you happened *not* to be black, Jamal would be suing your ass for assault with a deadly weapon, but I convinced him that it would just cloud the issue going after the brother."

"It was a squirt gun. *Gray* in color, as I recall."

"Says you."

"The brother can't write, Donald. A disability he shares with most of the fucking populace. That's all. End of story. Sad but true."

"Maybe your judgment's been a little colored—or should I say, bleached—hanging out around all those tweedy white folks. Way I hear, you don't have any time for people of color. Seems like you're forgetting your obligations."

"I didn't get elected to this fucking job. I was hired my own self. I didn't see you there cheerleading at my job interview."

"Maybe not. But if not for Malcolm and Martin and a thousand others, they wouldn't let you in the motherfucking door. As it is, you got hired as house nigger. And you got to answer to your people. We have a list of demands," Parker said.

"I thought editors were supposed to take successful authors out to The Four Seasons or something," Jeff observed, looking around the saloon on 18th Street.

"They wouldn't let you in. But I'm sure your movie friends will take you to the Russian Tea Room if you ask them nicely."

Jeff's long, thin gaze finally speared the waitress; he ordered a Bloody Mary, in which Russell declined to join him. Thinking about what Solomon said, looking at Jeff's—was he imagining it?—haggard face.

"I hear you're going to L.A. this week," Russell said, hearing also a note of irritation in his own voice. Was he annoyed that he'd learned about it from someone else, or annoyed at the actual idea? He liked to think he was bigger than those literary fundamentalists for whom working in the movies was equivalent to damnation.

"Call me Faust," Jeff said.

"Hey, I didn't say it was a bad idea. It does get you out of New York. You could use a little sun."

"Would you buy a book from an author with a tan?"

"Hemingway," Russell said.

"Hemingway doesn't count."

"So how's it going," Russell asked, casting a large net, the holes of which were big enough to let anything unpleasant slip through. It was a principle with Russell not to ask Jeff about his work; when he was ready he would show it. They both believed that books could be talked away. Russell was afraid that Jeff wasn't writing, but he couldn't come out and ask.

"Shining days."

Between them there was a delicate etiquette of masculine stoicism which was suspended only under extreme emotional duress or drunkenness, two conditions that were often coincident. Russell did what he could, which was to observe the forms of the ritual that insulated them from extremes of emotion.

"I think I will have that drink," Russell said.

"You *animal*, you."

Thirty blocks south, Corrine was sitting in a booth at a Greek coffee shop with Mrs. Leon Ablomsky. Corrine had arrived early—lest Mrs. Ablomsky get there before she did and confirm her belief that their appointment was a whim Corrine would repent, that a young girl with such a refined voice who worked for a big brokerage house would probably have a million other engagements, that something would surely come up in the interval between Corrine's inviting an elderly widow like herself to lunch and the time it took her to take the subway in from Brooklyn, though she would understand perfectly, she'd just have her cup of soup and some cottage cheese and maybe subway up to see the skaters at Rockefeller Center, which Leon used to enjoy doing so much.

And indeed, Corrine had second thoughts, as soon as she hung up; she couldn't imagine telling anyone that she was going off to have lunch with a keening widow she'd inadvertently surprised on a cold call. Before eleven-thirty she started to call the number three times to cancel, but she didn't think she could bear to hear that voice say, "It's all right, I understand."

When Corrine arrived she scanned the coffee shop, in which at least five candidates fit her notion of widowhood. Then the door opened behind her, and a woman who wasn't nearly old or decrepit enough cocked her head and whispered, "Are you Corrine?" She wore a hazel mink, which if not of the latest cut or color—younger women including Corrine were buying the rich, dark colors, cut below the knee—was of obvious quality and fit her beautifully. Her face was lined, but not unattractive, her eyes bright and only a little sunken. Corrine almost said, You must have been very beautiful.

They shook hands awkwardly and eventually seated themselves at a booth where each of them elaborately removed and folded her coat, adjusted her skirt and checked her purse. When Corrine patted her purse a second time, just as Mrs. Ablomsky was doing the same, they both acknowledged their discomfort with a laugh and a shrug.

"You can call me Muriel," she said. "You're probably thinking this is the craziest thing you ever let yourself in for."

"No, no . . ."

"I understand. It's all right. But for me, sitting around that house . . . Well, I had nothing to lose."

"It must be—"

Muriel nodded. "It is." Her gaze turned inward, and Corrine felt constrained to be silent until she reappeared from the depths of her reverie.

"Shall we order?" she said, looking up and forming a deliberate smile.

"Great, yeah, let's order," Corrine said, opening the huge vinyl-jacketed menu as though it were something she'd been dying to read since college.

"What are you reading," Russell asked, chewing beef as ketchup dripped between his fingers.

"Catalogues. I subscribe to all of them. It's just amazing what you can buy in this country, an alarm clock that projects a beam of light onto the ceiling so you can see the time without lifting your head. Orthopedic pet beds, crocodile golf bags." Jeff's lamb chops were chilling on his plate while he finished his drink. "Reading some Cheever, actually."

"Angst in the suburbs," Russell said dismissively. Once, he might have liked Cheever, but since the writer had been canonized he considered it his job to defy the conventional wisdom. As a member of the white educated middle class he felt condescending toward his own kind whenever he encountered them in fiction.

"You think truth and beauty are exclusive to the foul slums and the frozen wind-scoured steppes, the bazaars and the trenches? The gates of heaven and hell are yawning right out there in the backyard, Jack."

This sounded to Russell like Jeff making a case for his own stories.

"Other than that, I don't know. I have trouble reading these days. There's something so . . . You have to sit in one place, right? It all seems so inauthentic, and I don't just mean the bad stuff. The artifice of sitting down, the way language implicates you in the lie right off. 'April is the cruelest month.' Yeah? Bullshit. How about February? But once you start, you're inside the thing; the rhetoric has you, do you know what I mean?" He picked up a lamb chop by the bone and shook it three times in Russell's direction like a baton.

"Actually, I haven't got a fucking clue."

"I once heard a story about a lecture by J. L. Austin," he said, after he'd dropped the chop back on his plate and wiped his hands. "The language philosopher. Austin was speaking somewhere, yammering away and then he says, 'It is interesting to note that while in most languages two negatives make a positive, it is never the case that two positives make a negative.' And then, from the very back of the room, this guy says, in a sneering tone, 'Yeah, yeah.' I'm with him—I'm with that guy. I say, *Yeah, yeah.*"

* * *

Sipping a Bloody Mary in the Grill Room at The Four Seasons, Washington pretended to listen to the agent pitch a book. Though this was hardly his scene, he was none too thrilled with his table position in the middle of the room, right about where Nebraska would appear on the map—the power tables being the banquettes that lined the room, facing in so that all the players could see one another. Harold Stone and all the other big publishing dicks.

Not a whole lot of brothers here in the Grill Room, it went without saying—a soaring rosewood-paneled stage with no distracting props or *décor* to detract from the entrances and exits of notable white boys. A clean, well-lighted place for doing biz, but Washington couldn't concentrate on biz—or the wine list for that matter—with Donald Parker hanging over his head. Parker was going to jam up his shit in a serious way, and it was infuriating. Nobody was on Russell's case to advance the cause of white people. Parker wanted a quota of books by and about black Americans, and he wanted more personnel; he'd decided to target Corbin, Dern because of its prestige, and because of the alleged mistreatment of the lunatic who'd invaded Washington's office. Now Washington had the choice of trying to convince management that Parker's demands were reasonable or maybe having the son of a bitch get way out in front of him and leave him looking like a lackey. Even in the lily-white publishing world—especially in the lily-white publishing world—Washington could not afford to lose his cred and cachet. His colleagues in publishing counted on him to be right-thinking *and* fabulously cool. What he really didn't need was to have his program called into question. If the brothers started hollering Oreo he might actually have to start coming to work on time.

"Girls today, I guess you didn't have to go through what we did. I used to hate it, and then when I finally got to where I loved it he wasn't interested anymore. I felt gypped, I can tell you. You never stop missing it. But after a while a marriage is about something else."

The conversation had shifted in the middle of Muriel's chicken cutlet, Corrine's attempts at commiseration yielding to Muriel's advice on marriage.

"I wish we could've had children," Muriel said. "Are you planning to?"

"I hope so."

"Don't wait too long, honey."

"I'm ready, but he isn't."

"So surprise him."

She definitely couldn't tell Russell about this lunch. It would only confirm certain ideas he had of her—what he called her Mother Teresa syndrome.

Observing the waitress as she shimmied off toward the kitchen, Russell asked, "What happened to that girl you brought to our place on Corrine's birthday. The model, the one with the—"

"She went the way of all flesh."

"She *died?*"

"No, she just paled. Had to trade her in for a new model."

"God, I hate you," Russell said admiringly. "Could I borrow your life for a while?"

"You want to trade?"

"Would you?"

Jeff issued a wavering ring of smoke from his pursed lips. "Sure thing." This was just one of the things Russell missed about smoking, the way it could be used for italics and punctuation. "I always thought you'd be the writer," Jeff said. "You were better than me."

"I'm not enough of a gambler. Plus we got married." Russell thought about it, shook his head. "Sometimes I wish I'd waited a little longer, taken a chance." Russell felt that Jeff would understand he was conflating several yearnings—the notion of the writer's vocation being tied up with a certain attitude of going for broke, a categorical refusal to admit or accept the conventions. Whenever he thought of the road not taken he imagined himself as Dylan Thomas or Scott Fitzgerald or Hunter Thompson, never as a college professor with car payments, though the latter was the more likely form of a contemporary American literary career.

"You wait too long, you spoil," Jeff said. It sounded like something they'd said in college, but they were both past thirty now, and Russell, at least, was having to discard some of his more extravagant youthful conceits. The tragic view, the rebellious posture became less tenable. Lately he thought Jeff was taking himself a little too seriously as a *figure* and not seriously enough as a writer, but he didn't want to piss him off by saying so. And he dimly suspected that Jeff performed a vital role in his own ecosystem, following the road Russell hadn't taken and thereby saving his best friend the trip.

Back at the office, Russell took a call from Corrine.

"What's up?" he said.

"Just wanted to say hi. Are you all right?"

"Fine, I guess."

"Russ, I'd just die if anything happened to you."

"What brought this on?"

"I don't know—I just suddenly got a scared feeling."

"Nothing to be scared about, Corrine."

"That's not true—look around you."

Her parents' divorce, Russell thought, had made Corrine a little apocalyptic. After he'd calmed her down and hung up, Donna came in with the afternoon mail and dumped it on his desk.

"You see Harold shot down your genius poet?" She pointed to a manuscript on the pile with a note from Harold attached. Though in abandoning his own poetry Russell was required to devalue its importance in the larger scheme of things, he retained a sense of affection, a guilty admiration as though for the noble little woman he'd left behind to come to the big city. The collection in question struck him as the best he'd seen in years, and he had an unspoken understanding with Harold that he could publish a volume every year or so. Or at least he thought he did.

Harold's note said: "This is probably good enough to be published somewhere but I don't see why we need to do it."

Later that night Russell quoted the note for Corrine. "I'm going to have to find a new job," he said.

"You'll get a better job."

"And then there's Jeff," Russell said, refusing to be consoled. "He's in a very weird frame of mind." They were sitting on the floor in front of the television with their plates on the coffee table.

"Why? About what?"

"I don't know."

"You don't know?" She laid down the fork on which she had just twirled a mouthful of pasta and looked at him. "You had lunch with your best friend and you don't know what's wrong with him?"

"I said he was in a weird mood. You don't necessarily pry into somebody's moods, Corrine." He poured more wine into his glass and looked at the level in the bottle. "If you're really serious about not drinking, I'll end up having the whole bottle myself every night."

"The cork works both ways." She picked it up and held it for his inspection. "You can put it back in and save the rest for another night."

"It doesn't taste the same."

"What about Jeff? What did he say?"

"He complained about how cheap I am. Very sensitive and poetic of him."

"I can't believe your best friend's having a nervous breakdown practically and you don't even talk about it."

"He's not having a nervous breakdown. He's just tired. His work's not going well. Mine's not either, and I'm not making half the money he is. Do you realize he made a couple hundred thousand last year? I don't always like going to work but I do it. Jeff's eventually going to have to go back to work, too."

"God, I don't believe it." She was holding her fork halfway to her mouth, leaning away from him as if to get a better look. "At that moment you know who you sounded like, exactly? I mean down to the last inflection?"

"Who?"

"Your father."

He knew she was right, though he was not any happier with her for seeing the justice of the observation.

She thought it was cute; what really scared her was when he reminded her of *her* father. "Getting a little pot there, too," she said, patting his rounding belly.

He brushed her hand away. "Just because I'm sitting down."

"Yeah, and if I were suspended from the ceiling facedown my boobs would stick out more." Then she said, "I have a job, too, you know, and I had a hard day. Plus I just made this big decision about my health that I'm trying to stick with, and you might be a little more supportive about it."

He put his arm around her, pulling her in close against his ribs. "We both need a vacation. Another week and we'll be on Colombier beach." He nodded toward the television set. "What is this shit we're watching?"

"I got a video. *Hannah and Her Sisters.*"

Russell grimaced. "Angst in the penthouse."

Corrine set up the VCR. "It got great reviews."

"Exactly. What's wrong with *Blue Velvet*?"

"You've seen it five times."

Halfway through the movie she said, "If you slept with my sister—"

"It's just a movie, Corrine." Whenever they saw a film dealing with adultery, Corrine became gloomy and suspicious, anticipating the eventuality. Partly to divert her, Russell complained about the great apartments in the movie. "This is what I really hate about Woody Allen," he said. "Look at this, everybody lives in two-million-dollar apartments with no credible means of support. Here's a starving artist—right?—with a loft in SoHo the size of Shea Stadium." He viewed the screen, as was his sometimes habit, one-eyed through a tube that had once lived inside a roll of paper towels.

"Russell, don't do that, you're going to ruin your eyes or something. You know that drives me crazy, but you still do it."

"It makes it more challenging," he explained.

"Retarded development," she countered; he had, she decided, a ten-year-old boy's appreciation of props. If there was anything remotely hat-shaped in the room, Russell would sooner or later put it on his head. Corrine either loved this or hated it, depending. At first you loved all the idiosyncrasies of the one you loved; then, one by one, they became slightly annoying.

An hour later, having finished the bottle of wine, he was asleep, his head back against the couch, his mouth open, like a baby bird trying to suck nourishment from the sky. Unfortunately, this reminded her of her own father, a man also prone to fall asleep in front of the television set

—leaving the women behind with all of the things they wished to say. He had finally moved out after Corrine went off to college, but he'd already been gone for years.

Like the city around her, Corrine was wide awake. Turning off the VCR, she heard a siren on Second, car horns, voices and music. She went to the window and looked out at the lights, like stars, each one a different world. If, down the avenue, someone in that big new tower were looking north and saw this light, what would they think? They wouldn't think anything. She felt a slow ooze of panic, uncertain whether she had a place in this frozen galaxy, whether she even existed at this moment.

"Russ, wake up," she said, shaking his arm. He yawned, shook his head and stood up.

"What?" he said. "What is it?"

She felt foolish now, but a moment before, she had felt that she was about to disappear. "Nothing," she said, squeezing his hand, looking for herself in his eyes.

II

"So how's the weather," Zac Solomon asked, with morbid relish, phoning Russell in Manhattan to renew his offer of a job.

Producers, agents, lawyers, managers, promoters and account executives in California, when calling their counterparts, clients, lovers and victims in New York in wintertime, would inevitably work around to this question of weather, which they imagined to be a long, arduous struggle against hostile, arctic elements—as if they'd never heard of central heating or woolen clothing, picturing their poor northeastern cousins shivering around fires in smoky caves, gnawing frozen bones for marrow. All statistics confirmed that the ranks of those living at this elemental level of survival were indeed swelling, but for Russell and Corrine and their tribe the New York seasons were somewhat abstract, having more to do with the cycle of holidays, fiscal year and fashion than with nature.

Still, there came a moment in February when the gray sky seemed to drop so low it brushed the top of one's hair, while the slush reached over the tops of shoes and the dry skin on one's face felt as if it were being stretched on a rack and cured for glove leather. Love itself seemed old and worn-out, like the shoes bleached white and brittle from the salt. This was the day that newcomers to the city called a travel agent, the old hands already holding tickets to warm islands.

Russell and Corrine had their own favorite island, where they rented a house for a week. Corrine's grandfather once had a villa there, and though he'd sold it years before, Russell and Corrine had returned every year since their honeymoon. For most of its history the island was a casual secret: inhabited first by Swedes and then by Bretons, refuge of pirates, smugglers and sail bums, a soccer field serving as landing strip for infrequent charter planes. They liked the fact that there were few Americans, that the French colonists and visitors were not *too* French, the rock stars not *too* numerous, that there were no big hotels and no casino. For their honeymoon they had rented a one-bedroom cottage. Later they started bringing their friends and renting bigger places; the year before, it had begun to feel way too much like New York for Corrine, with nine of them and a big bag of mushrooms in what had suddenly become the high season, and she made Russell promise they would go alone this year.

Toward the middle of March—and not a moment too soon, for either of them, they boarded a 747 at Kennedy, wearing light clothing under winter coats. While passing a cargo terminal they observed two police cars racing after a red van that sideswiped a forklift and fishtailed out of sight behind a hangar—or rather, Corrine observed it, for Russell was, as usual, reading; the van had disappeared before she got him to look up. A few hours later they were in St. Maarten, where the heat and sunlight as they stepped onto the runway seemed to burn off the filmy residue of anxiety they'd carried from New York. They boarded a small twin-engine plane, holding hands as they looked out the window at the blue-green water mottled with dark green patches of reef, Corrine watching as the smaller island came into view, a jagged green dinosaur back poking up out of the blue water. Below the shuddering wing a huge vanilla yacht was anchored outside the harbor, the scale provided by the smaller sailboats tacking respectfully around it. A satellite dish cupped skyward from the topmost deck, which bristled with electronic antennae. "Look at that," she said to Russell, but suddenly the plane dove precipitously like a gaming falcon for the short runway painted on a patch of sand between a sharp, rocky ridge and the ocean.

Everything was unchanged, including the comical little jeeps, which were the principal transportation; they rented one at the airport and drove out to the house in which they'd spent their honeymoon—three rooms and a terrace cantilevered out from a steep hillside overlooking a shallow bay and the Caribbean beyond.

"I'd forgotten how steep the hills are," Corrine said.

"It's a volcanic island," Russell explained, as they wound around the last hairpin bend toward the driveway. She liked the fact that he knew things like that.

"Why can't we live here," she asked that night as they sat in a familiar restaurant in town. Their waiter was an American about their own age who had first arrived as crew on a motor sailer and had married a French-woman he met in a dockside bar. Although once a New Yorker, he now manifested a bronzed, tropical serenity.

"Because neither one of us was born rich," Russell said, very happy with his second piña colada, feeling a little naked being in a restaurant in a short-sleeve shirt without a jacket. Not a natural man of leisure, he made an obscure principle out of the idea that dining out at night called for a sports coat if not necessarily a tie, and it was a victory for Corrine that he had come out tonight without one. "At least *I* wasn't born rich, and your damn grandfather gave all the money away. I still don't un-derstand why he had to give it *all* away." They had passed the old Makepeace compound earlier and Russell was feeling the loss as if it were fresh.

"I told you—he was mad at my dad for marrying my mom. And he hated his southern in-laws. When George Wallace tried to keep that black guy out of the University of Alabama, he decided to give it all to this black college which just happened to be a mile away from Grand-mom's ancestral home."

Despite Corrine's preference for this colorful version, which made her grandfather sound merely cranky, Russell knew that Corrine's family, on her father's side, had a tradition of patrician philanthropy, and he was vicariously proud of it. Still, he didn't see why Gramps couldn't have just hung on to the vacation house on the mountainside.

"We could get jobs here," Corrine said. "New York seems so awful when I think about it right now."

"Bored out of our minds inside a month."

Even if her notion was impractical, she didn't see why he had to be so brutally realistic. Why wouldn't her company be enough for him to thrive on forever? But Russell seemed to miss the buzz of New York, the friends and shoptalk; it had been her idea to come alone this year, without Jeff and Washington, et al.

Corrine asked the waiter about the big yacht anchored outside the harbor.

"That's J. P. Haddad's two-hundred-six-foot Feadship. Been anchored out there for two weeks. Never comes ashore."

"J. P. who," asked Russell.

"You've heard of him," Corrine said. "He only owns about half the world."

"Hasn't touched dry land in three years," the waiter insisted. "Just cruises between the islands buying and selling companies over the radiophone. One of his men was in here a few nights ago, says he never leaves his cabin, ever. Got a crew of nineteen, not one of them's ever laid eyes on him. Weighs about eighty pounds, they say, and white as a corpse."

Over the following week they would hear more about Mr. J. P. Haddad, little of it probable or verifiable. The only thing that was certain about Haddad was what he owned—great chunks of corporate America. Corrine remembered hearing that his nautical seclusion had been reinforced by the arrest of Ivan Boesky, and that the feds had a warrant for him if he ever set foot in the States. On the island, it was said that he stole ashore at night in disguise. They heard that a very famous female movie star lived on board with him. A young gay couple they met on the beach one afternoon assured them that a very close male friend of theirs was his lover and that they had seen him in a gay bar in the port. Corrine nodded credulously, overearnestly, as one of these two naked strangers, a sort of perfect male android whom she recognized as a model, described Haddad as tall, muscular, sailorly. There was very little to worry about on the island, and the presence of J. P. Haddad's yacht provided a conversational theme with which to hail naked strangers.

Their first morning they awoke early to the dissonant music of testosterone-crazed roosters, with which the island was infested. They breakfasted on their terrace in the warm turquoise light, looking down on the sea, the salt air laced with floral essences. Lizards stirred the dry leaves in the garden, reminding Corrine of their honeymoon, when they'd found one in the bed. She had cried the first morning after the wedding, without really knowing why, poor Russell baffled and chagrined, asking what was wrong.

After breakfast they drove out to the beach. Corrine insisted that Russell not bring any manuscripts along, at least for the first day. Neither would she approve the two novels he'd brought along—both serious, *New York Review of Books*-approved—or a dense exposé of CIA malfeasance, in galleys. "This is vacation," she said. "You should read something really trashy." They combed through the musty-smelling, swollen paperbacks and Reader's Digest Condensed novels on the living room shelves, the discards of a thousand vacations, compromising on a James M. Cain thriller for him and for her a fat best-seller that had been on all the beaches a few summers back, a tale of sisters screwing and clawing their way to great heights of power and glamour while secretly yearning for Mr. Right.

"You slut," Russell said, holding the book at a distance.

"I'll read you the wet parts."

"My wife reads S-and-F novels," he said mournfully.

She looked at him quizzically.

"Shopping and fucking," he explained.

Almost alone when they arrived at the crescent-shaped beach, they set out their towels and arranged their lotions, bottles of sunscreen numbered according to degree of protection, a tube of sunblock for nose and lips. Corrine, particularly fair and thin-skinned, spent ten minutes on her preparations for sun worship, calling for Russell's assistance on her back.

"Should I leave my top on," she asked.

Russell shrugged inconclusively; at times he seemed possessive on this score and at other times he seemed almost to want to show her off—as when he encouraged her to wear sleazy low-cut dresses in the city. Now she wondered if he was indifferent. Had he ceased to see her as a sexual creature? Maybe she hadn't been at her sexiest recently. . . . She removed her top. . . .

"Let's make it a really romantic vacation," she said.

Russell grunted, turning a page of his book.

She whispered in his ear: "I'm going to give you the blow job of your life when we get back to the house."

He looked up, appearing confused, and nodded sheepishly, then re-turned to his book, already absorbed. Replenishing her sunscreen, she examined her body against the evidence of those passing by. Sometimes she thought he used reading as an escape from her and her attentions.

"Do you think our being gone from New York has a tangible effect?" she said abruptly, in a tone Russell recognized as being devoted to loopy metaphysical speculation. "I mean, I was just thinking that the city's a huge system of infinitely complex relationships, even if it's too complex for us to figure out. Our not being there is part of the equation of what happens. For instance, if I *were* in New York right now, and if I happened to be standing on a sidewalk on my way to lunch, waiting for the light to change, and if a car happened to jump the curb, I might be struck dead. By not being there, I may have freed that space on the sidewalk for someone else who might be standing there and get run over. And in that event you might say that I'm partially responsible for that death. In a weak sense I'd be responsible at the end of a long causal chain. We're all linked by these causal chains to everyone around us. But especially in the city." She tried to visualize tangled skeins of fate and conspiracy raveling together and diverging like the network of pipes and tunnels and wires under the city, invisible yet linking them all.

"Pretty soon," Russell said, "we'll all be linked by AIDS."

"Not us," Corrine said quickly, feeling fortunate to be insulated inside the walls of marriage at the same time that she felt guilty for feeling safe while the plague raged outside. But maybe she wasn't safe at all; suddenly she wondered what had been behind Russell's remark. "Will we?"

"Maybe not." He continued to read, as he had throughout this exchange, and all at once the other women on the beach seemed potentially menacing.

Corrine searched in vain for a flaw in the shape of the bronzed body crossing in front of them. Suddenly, the body stopped and the blond head swiveled in their direction.

" 'Allo."

"Uh, hi."

Corrine turned to look at her husband, wondering if the catch in his throat was guilt, and if so what kind.

"This is Corrine," Russell gurgled.

"I am Simone," the body said helpfully. "Did you just arrive," she asked, in what seemed to Corrine a condescending reference to her paleness.

Russell nodded. "Where are you staying?"

"With friends," she said. "Maybe I'll see you around."

The banality of this exchange seemed to Corrine indicative of acute sexual tension. She lifted her husband's sunglasses from his face.

"Just someone I met somewhere. She had an idea for a book."

"A *book*? You expect me to believe that?"

"Corrine, I barely know her."

"She seems very comfortable being naked around you."

"*Corrine.*" He reached over to touch her as if to ground the negative charge building within her. She recoiled at his touch, jumped up and stormed off down the beach. Men were not to be trusted, not even Russell; her father had proved that. She would move into her own apartment, a little studio somewhere, with sad plants, sprung wicker furniture. She would have to give up her dream of children, but at least she wouldn't have to wonder anymore when he stayed out late, when he traveled on business. What she had seen in Russell's eyes was that, at the very least, he *wanted* that body. Some night after three margaritas he would betray her, and she didn't think she could stand it.

As if to escape these anxieties by ignoring them, she began hunting for shells in the rocks at the far end of the crescent of sand. She came upon a conch, still pink and opalescent inside, which she grudgingly allowed Russell to examine when he came to retrieve her.

Accustomed to the flash floods of Corrine's emotional landscape, Russell gave her a few minutes to calm down. While technically innocent, he was guilty in principle. He wanted to fuck Simone a hundred different ways, immediately. And yet he had been slightly abashed when Corrine talked about giving him head. Their sex life together marked the apogee of his experience and yet lately he found his lust directed toward strangers. Walking down the beach to fetch his wife, he decided it was just a phase.

After they had taken a swim Russell wanted to go snorkeling. They walked over to the edge of the beach where the reef started, and swam out, Corrine suppressing her fear, not of anything in particular but of something unknown in the depths. Suddenly they were surrounded by the brilliant, oddly shaped fish and she forgot to worry.

After a while she told him she was going in. He said he'd stay out a little longer. As she lay on the sand reading, a French guy tried to pick her up. Cute, very wiry and tan, muscles like knots, and a thin Gallic face. When he asked her where she was staying and whether he could see her, she laughed and told him she was married, her earlier jealousy almost forgotten.

"So are many people," he said, letting sand sift from a small opening in his fist as he squatted beside her.

"But some of us," she said, "are happy."

Unfazed, he smiled and said he'd see her around.

"Who was that," Russell asked, tossing his wet snorkel and fins down beside her.

"One good Frog deserves another," she answered coolly.

"You should see your back," he said.

She could already feel the heat building under her skin, the burn rising up from within.

"I saw a shark," he said happily. It was important to him in some deep masculine way to imagine there was danger in the vicinity.

"I wanted the first night to be romantic," she complained, feeling the burn.

"Last night was our first night," Russell said.

"Not really. This is our first full day and night."

"Anyway, we've got seven more," he said.

"Only six," she corrected, sounding miserable.

The next morning Corrine was still a little sun sick, so they stayed around the house. Russell was sweet, spraying her with Solarcaine and reading to her from her smutty book, but she could see he was still in New York, part of him anyway.

"Did you ever ask Harold about the raise," she asked over lunch.

"He said we'd taken some heavy losses last year on big books that flopped, and pointed out that the company stock was way down, as if I didn't know. I own some of the shit."

"Your books did great," Corrine said. "Didn't you tell him that?" A lizard shot up the wall behind Russell's head. He was reading again, book flattened beside his plate. When he failed to answer she said, "Well, I don't know how the company's doing overall, but their price-to-earnings ratio looks great. I've been looking into it. I think they're way undervalued. In fact, Whitlock told me they were."

He looked up from his plate, having mutilated a piece of grouper. "When?"

"At my birthday party."

Nodding reflectively, he said, "Let's go to Gustavia."

In town, they bought T-shirts that said "Sorry, No Phone." Devotees of the island were proud of this technology gap, which kept away the worst people from Hollywood and Wall Street.

Coming out of the T-shirt shop they ran into Simone, her body partially covered up for a change. She walked the street as if it had been family property for generations. There was also something proprietorial about the way she greeted Russell. She languidly introduced them to a friend, recommended a bar in town. Corrine didn't like her any better with her clothes.

"This place is getting a little too fashionable for me," Corrine observed later that night, after they'd been seated next to a very loud Neo-Expressionist painter and his entourage. But Russell failed to acknowledge her complaint. Proximity to the glamorous, it seemed to Corrine, confirmed in Russell some sense of his own entitlement.

"Russ? Why couldn't we—not right away but sometime—have, you know, a baby." She'd been waiting for an hour to find the moment to say this, and now, having blurted it out over dessert, when she received no immediate response from Russell, she wondered if she had once again only imagined saying it. He was studying the wine label and she couldn't even be sure he was listening. Finally he looked up at her.

"Just because Tom and Casey are having a baby—"

"Russell, this has nothing to do with Tom and Casey."

"They can afford a baby."

"You think only rich people have babies?"

"Where would we put it?"

"We'd put it in a cardboard box beside our bed. I don't know. What does that matter? Why are you always such a jerk about this? You always focus on these irrelevant side issues. Is it possible there are other apartments in New York besides ours—bigger apartments, for instance?"

"They cost more money."

"We could get a two-bedroom in a less fancy building. You're always saying you want to live downtown, we could look down there. Find a loft, maybe."

"I hate lofts."

"God, you're so—"

"You know how much I make, Corrine. Without your salary and with one extra mouth—"

"So we do without some things. It's a question of priorities. I thought you *wanted* children."

"I do. Just not . . . now."

"When, with your second wife?"

Corrine seemed more startled than Russell by what she'd said. Looking at her, he could see what was happening in her mind; already her words were becoming fleshed in imagination—the dissolution of their marriage taking place, the lonely nights of the divorcee.

He grabbed both of her hands in his and shook her out of her reverie. "Listen, just let me think about it a little, okay? Maybe I'll go talk to Kleinfeld about the raise."

"I'm getting old, Russell," she said mournfully.

"You've still got a couple years before we have to shoot you."

Over the next few days they established a routine of beach and lunch, beach and dinner, which seemed by the end of the week, even to Russell, to be a birthright, along with the rented house and the brilliant weather and the rooster calls entwined with the thinner music of seldom seen birds which at moments brought them back, like certain songs, to the dawn of their marriage and filled them both with sudden desire. Later they would both look back on those few days with a sense of wonder and regret—timeless afternoons of long lunches and naps, dreaming and making love on chaises longues. Then, just as they had rediscovered the basic principles of pleasure, it was time to pack and go home.

12

The inhabitants of Manhattan tended to become inured to street demonstrations. Blue police barricades would sprout overnight in front of embassies and corporate headquarters. Aggrieved Irish or union members, angry Arabs or Jews—marching, chanting slogans, waving placards—were a feature of the landscape, like the invisible homeless. Such an environment dictated a degree of willful obliviousness, and Russell Calloway could be even more oblivious than most in the course of moving about the city. He frequently navigated the crowded sidewalks reading a book or magazine, occasionally bumping into signposts or other pedestrians. When he returned from the islands, however, he was fleetingly sensitized to the peculiarities of urban life, briefly conscious of the fantastic web of mundane conventions composing this outlandishly complex organism: the system of signs whereby, for instance, he raised his arm toward an approaching yellow car on Second Avenue which then stopped beside him, or the interplay of signals regulating the dynamic mesh of human and vehicular traffic at rush hour as several million people flowed to or from places of work. Even the kamikaze bicycle messengers tracing anarchic paths through the grid were part of the design. These millions on their unconscious individual tracks through the maze—after a week of white sand and blue-green water, the density of humanity seemed overwhelming. Likewise Russell was intrigued by the chanting, picketing crowd on the street as he approached the office, though not quite so alert as to notice that these efforts were directed at his own employer.

Several dozen protesters, mostly black, marched within the police barricades on the sidewalk in front of his office building, carrying signs: Russell recognized the notorious black activist whose name he could never remember among them, his head an inversion of the average male's, his full beard ending right where the sideburns might normally begin, his head shaved smooth and shiny black. He dressed like a lawyer, which he was, an impeccable chesterfield on his back at the moment. Emoting fiercely into a reporter's outstretched microphone. The great sacramental pose of the era—a reverse image of the king knighting subject with his sword.

"Hold on," called a technician, "I need a level on sound."

"Why don't we change the battery while we're at it," said the reporter—a briskly attractive, demographically correct blonde.

Suddenly the protesters relaxed, like actors on a break, and Russell slipped into the building.

The receptionist appeared surprised when Russell stepped out of the elevator, as if the idea of a device that ascended a hundred feet in seconds and dispensed a human being into the eighth-floor reception area were entirely new to her.

"Maureen, I've only been gone ten days," he said.

"Your messages are on your desk," she answered, as though apologizing for not having them waiting on a silver salver.

So where else would they be? he thought. "What's going on outside?"

"A demonstration," she answered helpfully.

Donna's desk was unoccupied and inexplicably neat. It usually looked like a sidewalk on the Lower East Side, covered with scraps of paper, periodicals and empty beverage containers. Odd piles of books and correspondence had sprung up all over his own desk. He called upstairs and asked Kleinfeld's assistant if he could come up in ten minutes; after making him hold, she announced Kleinfeld would expect him at four-thirty. Unready to face the mail, Russell wandered off to the coffee station. An editorial assistant named Kate something-or-other seemed to recoil at his approach.

"What's been happening around here," he asked. They were between pots, Kate having started a new batch. "Who's sleeping with whom?"

"I guess, uh, you know about Donna," she said.

"Who's *she* sleeping with," he asked enthusiastically, watching the pot fill—the thin stream of brown water.

"I mean *about* her. Maybe you didn't hear."

"About *what*?"

Harold wasn't in his office. Russell didn't bother to greet Carlton or even pretend he wanted her permission to go in.

"He'll be in at eleven," she said, in an even, neutral tone.

"Be so fucking good as to tell him I stopped by," Russell said.

Washington had yet to come in—it was only ten—so Russell backtracked to Whitlock's office.

"What do you know about Harold's firing my assistant?"

After taking one last look at the amber numbers on his computer screen, Whitlock spun his chair around to face the door. "If we didn't own the damn building I don't think we'd even have a net worth." He rolled his chair away from the desk—a rare indication that he could spare a few minutes away from the burden of having to account for the lavish expenditures of flaky editors. "So how do you like our protesters," he asked.

"What's that about?"

"Washington rejected some guy's book, I don't know. Everybody's going crazy around here."

Russell sank into the gray leather couch: Whit's office was the second biggest on the floor—the publisher and big corporate suits residing upstairs—and looked more like the center of power than Harold's, with tastefully framed posters from MoMA and a matching Italian leather couch and chair. "So—Donna. Not a pleasant scene," Whit said, a certain morbid pleasure flickering through his concerned expression, like silver through worn vermeil. "Harold sent Carlton over to tell Donna to take that button of hers off. Apparently she spit on her."

"Who, Donna spit on Carlton?"

"Yeah. Something of a cat fight ensued."

"Jesus." Russell leaned his head back on the cold leather and stared at the ceiling. "What are the chances that—"

"Forget it, Russ. Harold's not real pleased about this. I heard he told you to take care of it."

"He did."

"And?"

"I didn't."

"This is a corporation, Russell."

"Oh, is that what it is? This is a fucking publishing house. If I wanted to work for a *real* corporation I would've gone to business school for Christ's sake." He stopped and sighed. "Sorry, but you know what I mean."

"Yeah, I know, I know." Whitlock stood up and walked to the window. "It meant a lot to me getting this office. But sometimes it doesn't mean shit, you can see through the whole thing. Sometimes when Donna walked by in her black leather I'd feel silly wearing this suit. Maybe that was the problem—she was one of those people who made the grown-ups feel like they were faking it."

"Nice suit," Russell said, trying to lighten the mood. When Whit got personal, it was a little like seeing your father cry. Stiff as Whit could be, it seemed to Russell that he might just possibly melt into a puddle at your feet if you didn't watch the conversational temperature.

"Paul Stuart."

"You *are* making more than me."

"Not that much," Whit said, and he would know, being the financial officer. "And I'm still paying off loans from school." He got that personal look again. "Guess who just got turned down for a raise?"

"You too?"

Whit nodded. "My building's going co-op. I'd like to buy my place, but right now I couldn't buy the bathroom."

Russell stood up. "I don't understand this. I had three six-figure paperback sales last year and I know of about ten others—so how come we supposedly had such a bad year?"

"Those are receivables," Whit said. "They won't show up for a year or two. The bad year we're seeing now actually happened about two years ago, when we were the B-One squadron of the industry, dropping all those big dud bombs into the stores."

"Is that why my profit-sharing plan's worth squat?"

"Basically." When Russell turned to leave, Whitlock added, "Don't make it a showdown—this thing with Harold. It's not worth it."

Back in his office, Russell took a call from Leticia Corbin, the weird sister of the company's chairman. He couldn't remember exactly how it was she'd turned up at his place a couple of months before; it seemed she was part of Jeff's entourage.

"I have a proposal that might interest you," she said. "I wonder, could you come by my house tomorrow to discuss it with me?" Russell was not in the habit of dropping by the houses of prospective authors at their express convenience, but Leticia Corbin owned thirteen percent of the company and anyway it was right around the corner. She was a satellite of the late Andy Warhol, and it was remotely possible she was peddling a memoir. He'd died just a few weeks before, and the vultures were all landing. It was also possible that her brother somehow figured in this request, though Russell gathered they didn't get along.

Washington slouched in, smoking meditatively. "Man, that girl of yours had some mouth. Some of the shit she was screaming when she got the boot—it was like to turn me white. Meantime I have to figure out a way to chill that Parker."

"What's *that* shit all about," Russell asked, although his mind was elsewhere, his purview already narrowing around his own immediate concerns within an hour of returning to the office.

By the time Harold arrived, Russell had tamed his anger to the point of calculating the most he could salvage from his loss. He had transferred the engraving of the great horned owl from his east wall to the dartboard, but without the prospect of Donna's coming in, he realized, at least half the point was lost.

He had also called Corrine in full rage, and she'd pointed out that there wasn't much to be gained by confrontation. All Russell could hope was that, having cut him, Harold might throw a bandage his way in the form of help on the Rappaport book. By late afternoon that hope had diminished, when Russell learned that even before he had left for vacation the print run had been cut by another twenty-five hundred copies.

At four twenty-five Russell ascended the interior staircase, which linked disparate realms. Topside was corporate, the putative brain that animated the bodies on the floors below. The cubicles of the editorial, production and design departments combined, in various ratios, aspects of garage sale and office furniture showroom decor; on the ninth floor, by contrast, certain strict zoning laws seemed to have been on the books since the twenties, when the company had been founded. Framed dust jackets of ancient best-sellers and Pulitzer winners competed for wall space with hunting prints in the chestnut-paneled reception area, the latter reflecting the equestrian tastes of Whitney Corbin, Sr., the founding genius of Corbin, Dern and Company. These hunting prints were distributed throughout the hallways on the floor, although the chestnut paneling extended only into the generous office of Whitney "Trip" Corbin III, grandson of the founder, fiftyish and seldom seen on the premises, preferring golf clubs and cocktail shakers to Dictaphones and computers. Since the company had gone public back in the go-go years of the late sixties, the value of the Corbin family holdings had substantially increased, while the responsibilities of the eponymous "chairman" had correspondingly decreased. It happened that he was in today and, staring out the door with his feet on his desk, was in a perfect position to spot Russell passing in the hallway.

"Calloway," he bellowed, as if calling across the fairway. "Get in here."

Russell framed himself in the doorway, hoping he wouldn't need to go farther. "Hello, Whitney. You're looking industrious."

Corbin was holding the butt of a fly rod in his hand, winding line onto the reel from a spool, which leaped and danced on the carpet as he cranked.

"Shit, hold this damn thing for me, will you." He handed Russell a pencil and directed him to stick it through the spool of fly line as an axle. "And tell me what's going on downstairs."

"We're just sort of acquiring manuscripts and trying to sell them as books." The spool of fly line spun rapidly on the pencil as Corbin reeled.

" 'Trying' is a good word—definitely the right word in this case. Been a shit season. You fish?"

"Only for compliments."

The line snagged somewhere on the spool; Russell untangled it while Corbin waited patiently, rod in hand.

"How's your friend who wrote that marvelous book of stories for us? Pierce, that's the one. His father went to St. Paul's with me—did I ever tell you that? When are we going to see his follow-up?"

"Soon, I hope."

"So, what brings you up here," he asked, once the bird's nest was finally untangled and the fly line safely spooled onto the reel.

"Meeting with Jerry."

"Good man. Plays a very fair game of golf. Three handicap. You don't play, do you?"

Whitney Corbin, offshoot of a midwestern dry-goods fortune, and Frederick Dern, the son of a Columbia history professor, had started the company in the spring of 1925 after the twenty-three-year-old Corbin returned from a *Wanderjahr* in Europe with a nasty venereal infection and, not unrelatedly, many new contacts in the expatriate literary community. Dern, his former Princeton classmate, was working as a junior editor at Scribner's. They started on a modest stake from Corbin's father. The company carved out a niche specializing in European modernist texts, surviving from year to year and eventually thriving, on the modest scale of publishing success, as some of their authors and titles became classics; and the Corbin, Dern name became an imprimatur, a kind of brand name for serious literature. If Corbin, Dern had been a car it would have been a Bentley; if a fish, as Whitney Corbin sometimes liked to imagine, it would have been the brown trout: aloof and sulky, with European manners, not the biggest or toughest fish in the water, but perhaps the hardest to get on the line.

Corbin bought out his childless partner in the forties and passed the enterprise along to Whitney Jr., who expanded into children's books and started a profitable line of travel guides just as the American middle class began to travel. He brought the company public in the sixties, retaining forty-one percent of the stock in the family. Whitney Jr. was more interested in the financial side of the enterprise than the literary, hiring others, among them Harold Stone, to take care of what he called proesy and pose. Junior's heirs had taken little interest in the business; Leticia was interested, it seemed to her father, mainly in male homosexuals, including "that son of a bitch who painted soup cans," while her sister, Candace, was devoted to squandering his money in the conventional manner. The son, Whitney III, was most concerned with the sporting life—golf, fly fishing and waterfowl hunting being his primary occupations. After his father's death, he appeared in the office at intervals, leaving the business side in the hands of his publisher, Jerry Kleinfeld, the proesy and pose to the legendary Harold Stone.

Kleinfeld had worked his way up through the sales force and prided himself on being approachable and more or less one of the guys. In contrast to Harold's, his office contained a photographic history of the occupant's life and career, including scores of chummy photographs of Kleinfeld with celebrities from the worlds of politics, show business and sports—any one of whom, you got the impression, might be about to call on business more important than you were bringing into the office.

"What's up, fella?" he said by way of greeting. In his late forties, extensively bald, Jerry Kleinfeld had the impatient, almost manic air of a younger man—or of someone who had realized long before that he wasn't young anymore and therefore didn't have a second to waste. In the relatively slow-motion world of book publishing he was considered a gadfly.

Before Russell could answer, he said, "Can you believe this shit outside? We do more third-world crap than anybody in the fucking business, we pay not only Washington's exorbitant salary but his goddamned monumental world-record expense account, and now we're supposed to form an Afro-American imprint, hire more blacks and pay blackmail to Parker's Committee for Lining the Pockets of Media-Savvy Niggers. Jesus Christ!"

"Listen, Jerry, I'm worried about the Rappaport book," Russell said, despairing in advance of the other subject. "We're sending the wrong signals cutting the print run. I know this book can break out if we get behind it."

"I'm gonna tell you something I wish it wasn't true," Kleinfeld said, leaning back in his chair and lifting one leg in the air to inspect his loafer briefly, distorting, ethnicizing his syntax as if to certify his artlessness. "I think that book ought to shake the government to its fucking foundations. That's the first thing. The second thing is, it's obvious nobody gives a shit, Russ. We're not getting the newsbreaks, we're not getting bubkes. I'm sorry, but that's the way it looks from here. I'm not gonna bullshit you, buddy. And I have to go with Harold on this one. Can you believe I get these fucking shoes custom-made for me in Italy by Artioli and the damn things don't fit right." He lowered his leg. "What else?"

"Case closed on the Nicaragua book?"

"You drum up some press and we'll print more books. Case closed till then. What else?"

As economically and pragmatically as he could, Russell introduced the subject of poetry, emphasizing the intangible benefits that resulted from the publication of serious literature, important writers such as X, Y and Z—the kind of great authors who had put Corbin, Dern on . . .

Kleinfeld waved this hot air away with his stubby, three-ringed hand. "I know that fucking speech, Russell. I hear it from all you guys. Cut to the chase."

Russell performed a short, tough pitch for his poetry manuscript, while Kleinfeld looked off into space and flogged the surface of his desk with a length of telephone cord. After half a minute he interrupted.

"Tell you what, I'll read it myself, okay? Personally. Meanwhile you get me some blurbs from the heavy-hitters, all right? I can't do better than that."

"Okay," Russell agreed, not satisfied but aware that his time was up. By now he was too demoralized even to bring up the subject of his raise.

"You're doing a good job for us, fella," Kleinfeld said, rising and planting a hand on Russell's shoulder, then escorting him out into the hall. "We all lose a few now and then. But I'll see what I can do for you on these poems. I like your commitment. Half of those deadbeats down there are so busy trying to find the next best-selling exercise book they wouldn't recognize Ernest Hemingway if he unzipped his fly and plunked his big dick right down on their desks."

When he arrived home Russell was distracted, though he didn't seem as upset as Corrine was afraid he might be—just very far away, like a saint undergoing a vision. He flipped on the news while she went through the mail. In the evolution of a marital division of labor, mail duty had devolved to Corrine. Tonight there were two credit card bills, which she opened first, then two credit card offers—it seemed like every day they were invited to open another Visa or MasterCard account.

Invitations to a benefit for the American Museum of Natural History and an opening for an artist she hadn't heard of, and a heavily engraved invitation to a party at Minky Rijstaefel's house in honor of Count Eurotrash.

"Do we know Minky something?"

"We've met her somewhere," Russell said. "I think Jeff slept with her once." He had become morose again.

"Want to go to her party?"

"Could be good. Weird, anyway. Why not?"

Corrine reached for her datebook and wrote it in. "How about dinner at the Museum of Natural History?" She didn't tell him the invitation came with a note from Casey Reynes, who was on the junior committee.

"How much?"

"Hundred and fifty a head."

"Unless we're *out* of our heads let's be busy that night."

Corrine ripped that one up. Since neither of them had heard of the artist she noted the event with a question mark.

After that the real mail, always meager by comparison—tonight only a postcard from Jeff, which showed an armored Spaceman standing at a urinal, captioned: *Rest Break, New World Pictures*. Corrine read it for Russell, skipping "Dear Corruss,"—his acronym for a couple he thought of as being just a little *too* married.

Everything you've heard about the movie biz & the weather is true so I'll skip that. Which doesn't leave much to tell except everybody's in bed by ten o'clock—but not with me. Written 6 script pages in two weeks. & that's mostly white space. Told Solomon I'd write faster if he rents me a Ferrari.

    Tic tac toe—Jeff

When she finished, Corrine read it again silently. "I'm going to call him," she said. "Don't you think? He doesn't sound good. Russell?" He held up a finger, poring over his legal pad. She went into the bedroom to call Jeff, but there was no answer.

When she came back out Russell looked up. "Do you know how to read profit-and-loss statements?"

"Yeah, I read a pretty good P and L." And then she proceeded to prove it, walking him through a stack of papers as well as a basic history of corporate finance. Hours later, sensing his agitation from inside her own sleep, Corrine woke up and massaged the stiff muscles in his neck.

"Russell?"

"What?"

"Did you sleep with her?"

"Who?"

"Donna. Is that what this is about?"

"Hell, no." His voice carried a fairly convincing degree of indignation.

"So this isn't some nookie competition between you and Harold?"

"I can't *believe* you'd think that."

"I'm just trying to figure out why you're acting so strange. Talk to me, Russell."

"I don't want you to worry."

"You don't think I know when you're upset?" For several minutes she listened to his breathing.

"Sometimes I think I'm the smartest guy in the world, the best in the business. Then some mornings I wake up and I know I'm a complete fraud, that everything I've done is pure dumb luck and I've just lost the luck. I'm sitting here with bad cards and I can't even remember the rules. Harold's just calling my bluff. I thought I was the hottest thing going for a while, and now . . . Have you ever heard that thing somebody, some critic said—Not only does the emperor have no clothes, he has bad skin. Well, that's how I've been feeling lately. Like a naked eczema case."

She rubbed the back of his head. "Hey, Harold's just being an asshole. You've just got to stand up for—"

"I know, I know. That's what's bothering me. I've either got to leave, or fight."

"How can you fight?"

"I can buy the company."

"Go to sleep, Russell."

13

If her brother looked exactly like someone who was at least the third of his kind, the spawn of gentrified, self-perpetuating capital, Leticia Corbin appeared to have sprung from different loins altogether, seeming to have invented herself several times over with an eye toward erasing the trail of her pedigree along the way. Where Trip Corbin was bibulously ruddy beneath a perpetual tan, Tish's cultivated ghoulishness was accentuated by white pancake makeup, the ancestral country-club pinks and greens abandoned for bohemian noir, with the odd touch of crimson showing in, say, a slash of makeup.

The other sister, Candace Corbin van Duyn, of Palm Beach and Southampton and New York, was much more in the Corbin mold, if somewhat more publicly visible than the run of her breed, a well-married horsewoman and hostess whose moves between houses and between parties were authoritatively reported by *Town & Country* and *Women's Wear Daily*. Tish, on the other hand, was frequently seen in what passed for the demimonde press, usually in harshly lit nighttime group photos with thrash rockers, performance artists and East Village fashion designers, always managing to convey the impression of yawning widely with her mouth stoically closed. She was rumored to be a junkie.

A quick walk from Russell's office, her townhouse was on Gramercy Park, in one of Manhattan's last romantic precincts. Encrusted with woody vines, the Italianate mansion was shedding an old coat of mustard-colored paint. Russell pressed the buzzer and waited. He was about to ring again when the door was opened by a young light-skinned black man in a waistcoat. "Please follow me," he said in a chiseled, vaguely

British accent. Trailing him up a long, musty staircase from the parlor floor to the second floor, Russell had a good chance to take in the laced knee-high boots and the jodhpur pants that bloomed above them. Led into a dark salon in the front of the house, he was invited to take a seat. "I'll tell Miss Corbin that you're here," he was told.

The room was lugubrious. Opaque brocaded draperies sealed off the front windows; much of the scarce light within was provided by candles. Issuing from an invisible source, Mozart's Requiem pervaded the room, like incense, with its funereal pomp. The decor was a mélange of Oriental, Art Deco and SoHo contemporary, with an overall aspect of Opium Den. A huge Warhol portrait of Leticia had the place of honor over the carved marble fireplace. A moment later the original entered, wearing a black kimono and red slippers. The long, pale face seemed too suggestive of the skull underneath, and the dark rings under her eyes appeared to have been painted there. Her unnaturally black hair was severely cut, reminiscent of Louise Brooks and the Chinese Red Guard.

"Hello, Russell Calloway."

"Hello . . ."

"Call me Tish. In the sixties I called myself Serenity but I got tired of that—like everybody else. It wouldn't be much of a name for the eighties, would it? Sit down, Claude will get us some refreshments. I don't suppose you'd remember the sixties, would you, Russell Calloway?"

"I gather they came right before the seventies." Scanning the room for seating, Russell noticed an iron chair that might have been inspired by the Crown of Thorns, a spiky affair one could only hope wasn't meant to be functional.

"Fun, isn't it," she said, observing the direction of his gaze. "That's for my brother, should he ever come to visit."

Russell sat on the edge of an upholstered chaise while Tish sank into an armchair across from him, lighting up a long brown cigarette.

"Smoke," she asked.

"Quit."

"God, how boring. I don't want to hear about it. I suppose you exercise, too. Belong to a gym and all that. Wear condoms and brush after every meal."

"Actually, I'm a bisexual junkie with bad hygiene and a strong interest in bondage."

"Smile when you say that, darling, or I shall have to insist that you marry me."

Russell had to wonder which qualification interested her the most.

"Though I must say, please don't take offense, but you do look terribly predictable, fashionwise."

"Thomas Mann said, Dress like a bourgeois, think like a revolutionary." Who was Morticia Addams here, Russell wondered, to be giving him a fashion critique, even as he felt uncool.

"Did he really? Did he actually *say* it, darling, or did he simply write it down? I always wonder about all these wonderful things people supposedly said. I think you should get extra credit if you actually say them at the dinner table instead of after, sitting at a desk in some stuffy room with all the time in the world to think. Truman would just blurt those things right out, and Andy, well, he did, too, not that he was *terribly* verbal. Poor Andy." She sighed. "So, we can see how you're dressed. Do you think like a revolutionary, is the obvious question. And if so, how can you possibly work for my brother, *Mortmain* Corbin, at that excruciatingly dreary publishing house?"

"I find myself faced with the drab necessity of making a living."

"Do you *like* your job?"

Russell was not sure if candor was prudent, but there was something very purposeful about the question. "I can't say I'm entirely happy with the way things are being run."

Leticia squinted at him through a great cloud of smoke. "Go on."

"There are things I'd do diff—"

"Let me tell you a story," Leticia interrupted. She went on to describe a friend who was a poet and an artist and a photographer, a Berliner and "one of the most fascinating creative minds in all of New York." Russell nodded when he heard the vaguely familiar name. "A real poet in the *largest* sense of the word. The man was a genius. Andy said so. To the ends of his fingertips, and he had extremely long fingernails. Well, I sent him to Trip. What do you suppose happened?"

"What?" said Russell, fixating on her cigarette, fighting the sudden urge to bum one.

"Trip turned down his proposal. Can you imagine how embarrassing that was for me? I own thirteen and two-thirds percent of the house. And Trip says he doesn't quite see the potential. Well, I can't say I was surprised. Trip couldn't see the end of his nose if he didn't paint it red every night. It's such a waste. Corbin, Dern meant something once. When my grandfather founded it, his model was the Crosbys' Black Sun Press. Harry Crosby was a friend of his, did you know that? Till he killed himself, of course, in that delicious double love suicide. In any event, Gramps wanted to bring the avant-garde home to America. Did you know the first person he published was André Breton? Not to mention that he can't even keep the price of the stock up where it should be. Between us, darling, I doubt he can keep anything up anymore."

It took Russell a moment to figure out that the last two sentences referred to Whitney Corbin III and that they had moved back to the present. Or at least to that region of the present where Tish Corbin lived.

"Why is it, Mr. Russell Calloway, that in the middle of what I am told is the greatest bull market in history, my Corbin, Dern stock has declined in value? I hear doormen at clubs talking about the money they're making in the market."

"You should ask your brother."

When she lifted the cigarette to her lips, the sleeve of her kimono slid back on her arms; without being too obvious about it, Russell inconclusively scanned her arm for tracks.

"I despise my brother. We have not spoken in three years."

The knee-booted Claude returned, bearing a tray with a heavy Georgian tea service and assorted pastries.

"My brother was eleven when I was born. When I was a year old he tried to suffocate me with a pillow, a memory which I finally unearthed after many expensive years in analysis. When I was four my father bought me a llama, which was my dearest companion for two years, until my brother shot and killed it."

"Will there be anything else," Claude asked, after laying out the tea.

A llama?

"My feet."

"Yes, ma'am."

Claude knelt down in front of her, removed one of her slippers and began massaging her foot. Russell tried not to appear startled. In his inner ear the theme from *The Twilight Zone* started up.

"My brother is a killer, Russell Calloway. He would like to kill me, no doubt. But for the laws, which make it difficult, he would.

Candace—my older sister—is just like him, a bimbo, and she doesn't give him any trouble, but they'd love to get rid of me. I have reason to believe a nearly fatal car wreck I was involved in some years ago was not . . ." As her voice trailed into a whisper, Leticia Corbin appeared to be concentrating on some deep, primal experience. Finally, she looked up, her expression mournful. "The spirits of the animals he slaughters will probably haunt my family for generations to come. I see you wear leather shoes," she said, this theme of feet becoming general. "There are many attractive alternatives to animal products. I'd like to give you some literature before you leave."

"You said you had a proposal for me." This was all getting a little too weird for Russell.

"A proposal? Perhaps. Perhaps that's what you'd call it." Claude had switched feet now. "What I had in mind is something larger than a book proposal. I wonder if I can trust you?"

Russell spread his hands wide and shrugged to indicate that this was entirely up to her and of rapidly decreasing interest to him.

"I'm thinking of starting my own press. Something small and tasteful. But also crazy and daring. Philosophy, fashion, aesthetics, some of Andy's unrealized projects . . ."

Russell could just imagine.

"Is that better," Claude asked.

"A tiny bit, thank you, Claude. It's just something I have to live with. Unless those idiotic doctors finally locate the source of the pain. I lie awake half the night in pain and they say it's imaginary. Of course, I have no experience in the technical side of the publishing business. My brother never let me near the company. So I would need help."

"Do you have capital?"

"I intend to sell my shares in Corbin, Dern."

"Your brother won't like that. The family holdings significantly reduced—it might even lead to somebody else taking over."

"That's one of the things I like best about the idea, Russell Calloway. Sticking it to big brother."

Maybe the flakiness was infectious, but suddenly Russell's interest was fully engaged.

"You've got to be careful how you sell a big block of stock like that. A company as small as this—you can't just throw thirteen-odd percent of it on the over-the-counter market. You'd probably want a single buyer."

"You seem to know a lot about these things," she said, with an arch smile.

"I'm just beginning to learn. But I like to think I'm a quick study."

"Are you? You look too innocent to me."

"I guess we'll just have to see about that, won't we?"

"Do you know someone who could buy my stock?"

Russell stayed for another hour, Claude dispensing Lapsang souchong from the elaborate sterling tea service as they discovered, for all their fashion differences, a patch of common turf. By the time he left, Russell had convinced himself that she had some excellent instincts and Leticia had come to the conclusion that despite the dull wardrobe this was a quite brilliant young man.

They had a dinner date for the following week.

14

Trina just barely made the nine-twenty Concorde out of Heathrow, which would put her in New York by eight-thirty the same morning and at her desk just an hour later than usual, virtually without loss of workday. She handed her hanging bag to the stewardess, slid past a beautiful Eurasian-looking woman she thought she recognized from the fashion magazines, and dropped into her seat beside a male blue-suit approximately her own age. Hermès tie, pinstripes, face meticulously reproduced from a recent Dartmouth yearbook.

He looked at his watch, a butter-and-sugar Cartier tank, and sighed. "If this plane is just about one minute late it could definitely screw me up but good," he said, seeming to address the pink pages of his *Financial Times*.

Trina nodded noncommittally.

"If I had all the goddamned time in the world I'd fly Air-India or something."

He seemed eager to talk—albeit in brusque, self-important bursts—which was entirely against the rules of serious business flying. But then, she was wearing her Giorgio Sant'Angelo dress, suitable for late nights at Tramps and Annabel's, so she wouldn't totally wrinkle the business suit she'd change into in the limo from Kennedy. So of course, he probably didn't think she *was* a business flyer. Thought she was an airborne international slut.

"Bradley Seaver," he said, suddenly turning as if he had just that moment noticed her.

"Trina Cox."

"Pleasure," he said. He shook his head savagely, looked at his watch again as if it were a very badly behaved personal accessory indeed. When she continued to ignore him, he muttered theatrically, "Christ, I better make this meeting."

Trina started to look through her bag for an annual report.

"I'm an investment banker at Morgan," he said. "M and A. That's mergers and acquisitions."

"Sounds very interesting," said Trina, sliding the annual report back into the bag and dripping a little southern honey into her voice.

"You'd be surprised. It *is* really interesting."

"Actually—" she began, but he was caught up in his globe-altering vision.

"I buy and sell billion-dollar companies practically every day, and hardly anybody in the whole damn country understands the magnitude of what's going on. The government doesn't even understand. They don't have a clue. Which is actually just fine with us." He went on to explain how he and his colleagues were attacking bloated corporations, over-throwing corrupt and sybaritic management, slaying the dragons of inefficiency and complacency, carving up the slothful kingdoms into streamlined pieces and selling them off in the marketplace.

After years of inflation someone had noticed that the equity of corporate America, as reflected in stock prices, was undervalued. A new, pro-business president said it was morning in America, inflation subsided, and smart shoppers began to wake up and call their brokers. The financial-services industry grew like an oil town in full boom. And if buying stocks on margin in a rising market could double your rate of return, buying companies outright with borrowed money and reselling the parts seemed to be the fastest way anybody had ever thought of to get fabulously rich. Interest payments were tax-deductible, so it was just dumb not to borrow as much as possible and buy everything in sight. Debt was good, equity boring. He toiled, said Bradley Seaver, in the most lucrative field of his era.

"What do you do?" he paused to ask, after about twenty minutes.

"I'm in M and A at Silverman," she said, her own firm being a far more significant player in the field than his.

Flushing deep pink, Bradley Seaver donned his headphones and fiercely ignored her for the rest of the flight.

An hour out of New York, Trina walked back to the restroom. The model she'd recognized earlier was waiting for a "Vacant" sign, peering nervously down the front of her blouse. "Do you know anything about implants," she asked Trina. "Because they feel kind of funny, like they're kind of expanding or something." The woman reached up and squeezed one of her own breasts, wincing piquantly.

She looked up with an expression that seemed to invite Trina to feel for herself, an experiment Trina chose not to perform.

"I don't know, I just got them last week and I just remembered this guy telling me a couple months ago about some girl whose implants like exploded on the Concorde. So I'm kind of worried."

"I didn't see any warnings on my ticket," Trina said.

"Really?" Appearing somewhat reassured, she glanced down at Trina's chest. "Are *they* real?"

A few hours later, Trina was getting the paisley tan in her midtown Manhattan office, soaking up radiation from her computer screen as she pored over a spread sheet. Hunched over the keyboard, she leaned into the monitor as though preparing to plunge into the emerald labyrinth of numbers. Since she'd hit the Street her eyesight had gone from twenty-twenty to something that sounded like her blood pressure, and now her eyes were watering behind her contacts, but given what had happened to her income over the same period she wasn't looking for sympathy. Just trying, at this moment, to figure out the cash flow on a division of a sportswear empire that management was taking private. Since the announcement of the tender offer, two other bidders had jumped in, driving up the price and effectively depriving Trina of another week of sleep. She leaned back and stretched her neck, stole a gulp of caffeinated primordial slime from her Harvard Business School mug.

Her assistant, Christopher, knocked and entered, bearing several garment bags draped over his outstretched arms with almost ceremonial delicacy. Christopher had excellent taste and a semiprofessional expertise in clothing, courtesy of the Fashion Institute of Technology, so she sent him out every season to pick some new suits. "I think you're really going to love these," he said, laying the bags out on Trina's couch and stroking them flat. "The new lines are fabulous. The Chanel especially."

"I'm sure they're terrific," Trina said as the phone buzzed. "Can you get that?"

Christopher walked stiffly over to the desk and picked up the receiver. He was still sulking when he said, unexpectedly, "Russell Calloway?"

It had been years since she'd seen him. Besieged as she felt, she was intrigued enough to take the call. "Hello, Russell? Is this a time warp, or what?"

"It has been a while," he agreed. "Gene Fisher's wedding a couple years back?"

"You're making me feel very old, but at least you'll always be older than me. Fat and balding yet?" *And are you drumming up money for the alumni fund?* she speculated. But Russell wasn't the alumni-fund type.

"I'm told I'm well preserved. I was wondering if I could buy you lunch."

This sounded like a come-on. Was it possible that he had split up with the beautiful and perfect Corrine Makepeace?

"Love to," she said, the doubtful sincerity of this statement accompanied by a reflexive surge of native southern intonation. "But I'm kind of busy for the next three or four years. I've had to cancel like six of my last seven nonbusiness dinner dates, which makes me real popular, as you can imagine. . . ."

But she was curious enough to flip through her datebook, searching the end of April for an open day. Normally Christopher would tell her if she had a lunch free, but he had retreated in a bit of a huff.

"How about next Tuesday? It'll have to be somewhere close. You know Smith and Wollensky? If I don't call to cancel I'll see you at twelve-thirty."

He must have seen the article puffing her as one of the top women in M&A, Trina decided, though he didn't seem the type to read *Fortune*. But she didn't have time to speculate right now. She didn't have time for a love life right now, either, but it was important to feel the buzz of sexual tension once in a while, keep the frequency open just in case she met somebody really wonderful on a plane when her laptop was down and the bathroom happened to be vacant.

Russell had been a year ahead of her. They hadn't known each other well, and if memory served, she disliked him almost as much as she sort of liked him. She ran with the jocks and the kids whose last names were on the dorms and the classroom buildings. He seemed scornful of all that—a midwesterner determined to be arty and political. She remembered him smoking those French cigarettes that smelled like asphalt, sitting over coffee in the snack bar conspiring about literature with Jeff Pierce, that slouching bad boy whose grandfather had built the gym, with whom Trina would've liked to have gotten sweaty.

Never very bohemian, Trina Cox had gone into investment banking on graduating, just as a frenzy was beginning. As a trainee, she had fortunately found herself in mergers and acquisitions at First Boston, where the new game was being invented. Her department advised corporate clients on takeovers and helped arrange financing in exchange for fees in the millions; soon it was clear that the bank was missing out on the big action by merely serving as bridesmaid for these multimillion-dollar unions. First Boston started to put its own cash into the deals. Bliss it was in that dawn to be in finance, but to be in M&A was heaven.

After two years as an analyst she did the mandatory MBA; from business school, Cox took her nascent expertise to a white-shoe investment bank that was itching to get in on the new M&A action, but which, much to her irritation, remained reluctant to dirty its hands with hostile takeovers. She was trying to get them to loosen up.

Being a girl had not made it easier; the *Fortune* piece was sort of a joke, since Trina was one of about three women in M&A. The locker-room, dick-waving ethos of Wall Street had as much to do with the fact that half the guys were former nerds and dweebs as with the fact that the other half had actually *played* contact sports and belonged to fraternities. Knowing this gave a woman leverage. Trina herself was far from being a nerd, and had the kind of feminine self-confidence that can instantly pierce the armor of male posturing. Her voice, perennially hoarse and raspy, had the authority of money and breeding; and in the manner of men who are said to undress women with their eyes, Trina had the ability to make certain men recall every instance of sexual dysfunction they'd ever experienced. Her sexual appeal was more a function of vitality than of raw beauty, her cheeks having a fullness that made her look too much younger than she was, her hair an inconspicuous shade of brown; she was seldom the most attractive woman in a crowded room, but she was usually in the running.

Born in Virginia of what is still called, without irony, a good family, she might have married well and ridden to foxes, as her mother and her older sister had done. Reacting against the trust-funded languor of her father, a gentleman ornithologist who tripped off to the Amazon to look for new parrots and grebes, she followed earlier generations of empire-building male Coxes to Wall Street. It didn't hurt that she was a better rider, skier, wing shot and tennis player than most of the men she worked with—accomplishments that mattered more to them than to her. A man had a harder time treating you like a bimbo if you'd hammered him at squash the week before. He might hate you, or he might want to marry you, but he would surely stop asking you to fetch him a cup of coffee.

After another hour of cash-flow analysis she looked up and saw the garment bags lying on the couch.

"Christopher," she called out. "Let's see the new wardrobe. Show me what you've got."

"There's no hurry," he said, still petulant.

"No, really, I'm dying to see."

The following Tuesday she was fifteen minutes late and Russell was waiting at the bar. He had filled out since she'd last seen him, but was still very collegiate. Boyish face, blue blazer over jeans, and—cute touch, this—a bow tie. Seemed like years since she had seen a man less than fully pin-striped.

Theirs was an acquaintance just tenuous and faded enough to make the kiss on the cheek slightly awkward, both tilting heads to the same side, both simultaneously correcting to the other side.

"Been up to Providence, recently," he asked after they were seated.

"Haven't had the time." He looked nervous, increasing her suspicions that this was a date. The waiter came over and greeted them in a thick mid-European accent, plunking down the heavy flatware.

"Cutlery for the men who carve up America's big corporations," Trina said, picking up a formidable steak knife. "This is sort of a midtown outpost of the Street," she added, explaining that her first boss had always taken her here with clients. "There's some kind of sumptuary law that requires investment bankers to eat prime beef surrounded by mahogany paneling and brass rails."

She looked out at the room. A fat man two tables over waved at her. His companions were shouting for the waiter, pointing at empty glasses, hacking away at giant lobsters and prime ribs that spilled over the edges of their plates.

"Friends of yours?"

She shook her head. "Traders," she said, "the Neanderthals of the financial world. Oral compulsives. They scream and cuss into the phone all day, fueled on martinis and beef and cigars."

"You people in M and A aren't exactly shy and retiring."

"Naw, we kick some serious butt," she said in a deep, masculine voice. "But I doubt you're interested in any of this stuff, Mr. Calloway."

"Curiously, I am."

"Russell Calloway, class poet? Admit it, you feel this vast superiority to us money-grubbers."

"On the contrary, I think it's fascinating what you do. Especially now. Which is part of the reason I asked you to lunch."

This didn't sound promising, she thought. "I was hoping you remembered I had a great ass."

"Actually, I'm more of a breast man," he said, with a bad-boy grin, keeping his eyes fixed scrupulously on hers.

"I met a girl on the Concorde you might like."

"Just what I need."

"What *do* you need?"

"I recently got a submission, a novel, I think it's good. The protagonist works for a medium-sized company. He thinks he's about to get fired, and he gets this crazy idea to buy the company."

"That isn't crazy."

"Well, that's what I wanted to know. I was hoping you could listen to this thing and tell me if it's realistic. This guy doesn't have any money. He borrows like seventy million."

"Lunch money," Trina said, buttering a slab of bread. "Why don't you make it seven hundred—just to keep from falling asleep."

"Let's work with what we have for a minute. This character isn't rich."

"Not yet he isn't, but that's the whole point of leverage. Big corporations used to acquire smaller corporations, but now we're seeing minnows swallow whales on practically a daily basis. The minnow goes to the bank and borrows money to buy Moby-Dick. You need collateral for a loan, so the little old minnow pledges the whale, which he doesn't yet own, as collateral. Then when the deal is done he pays off the loan with pieces of blubber."

"Sounds perfectly reasonable," Russell said facetiously.

"Who was it said, 'Give me a big enough lever and I'll move the world'? Well, you give me enough leverage and I'll buy General Motors."

"Personally, I wouldn't want it," he said. "My father's a GM man."

"You're from Grosse Pointe, right? I like the Pistons for the playoffs." She turned toward the waiter, who was standing lumpishly beside their table. "Shrimp cocktail, sirloin medium rare, creamed spinach and more of this diet caffeine. Are you ready to order?"

After scanning the menu, Russell ordered the sole and a salad.

"So what industry are we talking about here?"

Russell hesitated. She raised her palms interrogatively. "Hog farming, software?"

"Publishing, basically."

"Basically?"

Shrugging his shoulders, he drew his lips into a tight, pensive grin and glanced up at her with eyes that seemed to plead for some kind of understanding: he had to go to the bathroom immediately, or else he was about to make some declaration of love. She reached across the table and put her hand on top of one of his. "What is it, honey?" She didn't remember him as the shy type at all. In fact, what she had just remembered was a drunken grope with him on someone's couch after a kegger. But there was another possibility.

"I'm not a mind reader, but offhand I'd say that either you want to fuck me or you want to buy a company."

Russell actually blushed.

She shook her head and laughed. "You sly dog. So you want to buy out your publishing house, am I right?"

He shrugged ruefully.

"And you don't have any money. So what do you have, big guy? You know, there are a hundred boys and girls like me out there hunched over computer screens searching for takeover prospects. It's open season, Russ, and publishing's hot lately. How come nobody's nailed Corbin, Dern before now? Why hasn't it been put into play? And keep your voice down, will you, because if you don't, the company *will* be in play. This afternoon."

"I have information that doesn't show up on the balance sheets."

"Wait a minute, doesn't the family control the stock?"

"Forty-one percent."

"That makes it almost impossible." She watched him during this interrogation, leaning close enough to feel his coffee-scented breath. His eyes were a very inviting, light cerulean shade of blue. Easier to read than dark eyes. "—Unless you've got someone in the family behind you."

"If I tell you everything now, what do I have left?"

"Maybe you have a deal. You're Mr. Inside."

"That's a beautiful suit," Russell said, looking obliquely down the front.

"Someone bought it for me."

"He's got good taste."

"And he types."

"Keep him."

"I will." She dipped a large pink crescent of prawn into the cocktail sauce and bit it in half, perfectly content to leave a false impression about the male in question.

"What else have you got, Russell?"

"Real estate. The office building is paid off and it disappeared from the books years ago. It's worth ten at least."

"We could sell it and lease back a few floors. That's good, but you wouldn't be the first to have picked that up. Any hidden receivables?"

"Half a dozen big paperback sales that won't show up on the books till next year, year after."

The waiter arrived with platters of meat.

"You'd have to sell off some of your divisions to pay down the debt."

"I've got the figures here for you," he said, lifting a leather portfolio and dumping his water glass all over the table.

"It's fine," she said. "I'm barely wet."

"Now you know why my family called me Crash."

"Not everybody's favorite word in my line of work. Anyway, what about this racial stuff? This protest?"

"I think it could work to our advantage," he said, mopping up the mess with his napkin. "Depresses the price of the stock."

"Maybe we can rock & roll," Trina said, half an hour later, dropping the steak knife on her empty plate. "It's beginning to sound doable."

"You're a very dainty eater," Russell observed facetiously, having given up halfway through his sole.

"I work it off."

"In the gym?"

"The office. My exercise routine involves sleep deprivation and adrenaline production."

"Seems to work for you."

"So how about Corrine? You two still together?"

"We're hanging in there. She's fine. She's a broker for Wayne, Duehn."

"Is she really? Well, that's nice," Trina said in her thickest southern accent. She'd never liked Corrine Makepeace, and the fact that she was a retail broker did nothing to improve her opinion. Retail was chickenshit. Cold-calling rubes. You might as well sell Amway door to door. "Have you told her about this?"

"Yeah, of course. She helped me with the numbers."

"She wouldn't pass on any of this information to her clients, would she?"

"Trina, she's my wife."

"My boss, Nicholas Aldridge, has been married for five years—don't ask me how he found time for the ceremony. He's on the road about two hundred days a year. And when he calls his wife from the road he doesn't say where he is or who he's seen or when he'll be back. That's the nature of the business."

"Corrine already knows."

"Be a little circumspect, even with Corrine. If we go ahead you simply can't tell her everything. I like secure, leakproof channels of communication on a deal." She was laying it on a bit thick, but she wasn't about to have Corrine Makepeace looking over her shoulder. She smiled at Russell. "All I'm saying is, you don't have to tell her everything, do you?"

"I guess not."

The waiter came to tell her there was a phone call. She excused herself and took the call at the captain's stand, handing her credit card to the waiter. Aldridge needed her immediately. She signed the check and hurried back to the table.

"Sorry, gotta fly. Let me look this over and we'll get together next week to talk about it, okay?" She kissed him on both cheeks and bolted for the door.

Trina met with Russell and Leticia Corbin the following Saturday. She put together a proposal for her boss, but it was almost a week later before she finally had a chance to discuss it with Aldridge. Having slept an average of three hours a night between Monday and Thursday, when she finally sat down in Aldridge's office Saturday afternoon she felt the righteous, energizing exhaustion of accomplishment. Sleep deprivation had become a fix, like runner's high, like the high-yield junk bonds in an investment portfolio. She was ready for another deal.

Although the offices occupied the top floor of a brand-new glass tower in midtown, Aldridge's lair resembled the headmaster's study at an old New England prep school such as the one Aldridge himself had attended. The most conspicuous feature of the decor was his collection of model ships. An incredibly detailed scale replica of the USS *Constitution* circa 1812 was drydocked on his Hepplewhite desk; miniature clipper ships, sloops and galleons were becalmed on the polished mahogany Sargasso of an Early American sideboard. Some of the models were gifts from clients, inscribed with the date and name of the deal they commemorated as well as the name of the ship.

In his association with old wood, sail canvas, Moroccan leather and Cuban tobacco, Aldridge declared his descent from the merchant bankers of the old school. Trina's admiration for his style was compromised by a certain impatience. His caution would prevent him from ever being the biggest player on the street.

Trina had brought Chip Rockaby, a junior associate who'd helped with the numbers, along to the meeting. He was a real bird dog, even looked like a golden retriever—big blond head and dumb, happy blue eyes. Once he sniffed a deal he wouldn't let go until you ripped it out of his mouth and slapped him silly.

"I can see why you like this deal," Aldridge said, sucking air, head tilted skyward as he fired up a Montecristo, cheeks puffed out like Dizzy Gillespie's.

Trina braced herself for the antistrophe.

"The numbers are pretty good . . ." He paused and removed the cigar from his mouth, and examined it as if he was pleased to know there were some things in life you could still count on. "Even if they aren't very big."

"We think this could be a no-brainer," Chip offered. "A slam dunk."

Go get him, boy. Woof woof. Find the birds, Chipper.

The phone buzzed. "Hold on a sec."

Grunting monosyllables into the receiver cradled on his shoulder, Aldridge began to twirl his cuff links, tasteful gold lozenges with monograms. The boys around the office considered Aldridge a sartorial role model. His shirts and suits, handmade in England, had a limp, fluid quality that reminded Trina of much-handled dollar bills. His cuffs were French, his collars spread or fastened with stickpins. The patterns on his ties, when patterns they had, were nearly invisible to the naked eye. Rockaby wore the junior version of the company outfit: Brooks Brothers button-down shirt in white or blue, single-breasted wool suit in blue or gray, and rep ties from the same source. Today was a blue shirt and gray suit day. No one ever said so, as far as Trina knew, but it would be unseemly for Chip, who was only twenty-five, to show up at the office in a bespoke suit or with a pair of cuff links. That would have to wait until he made partner. With the internationalization of the business you saw some guys at other firms going in for the braces and those clownish Turnbull & Asser striped shirts with high white collars, but you'd never make partner here with that kind of wardrobe. Trina herself stuck with tailored suits from the more conservative designers and kept the hemline around the knee, showing just enough leg to remind them which restroom she patronized.

Having reinserted the cigar between his teeth after he hung up, Aldridge invigorated himself with a lungful of smoke and sighed.

"You think this is doable," he asked Trina.

"Absolutely."

"I grant you it looks fine on paper. But it's not just a question of financials. This kid Calloway is totally unproven as a manager. We'd be losing senior management."

"Deadwood," Chip said.

"He's good," Trina said. "They've been grooming him for editor in chief."

"Maybe. But this is a relationship kind of business. We could capture the town only to find that the gold and the grain and the girls have disappeared."

Here it comes, Trina thought. Parable time.

"In this case let's call the authors the girls. Let's call the business relationships with other publishers and agents . . . the grain, and let's call the good name of the firm the gold. All those things could disappear overnight if we undertake a hostile takeover."

Aldridge drew extra hard on his cigar, like a reluctant diver preparing to submerge. "I've talked with the executive committee. We're going to have to pass on this one, Trina. I know you like it. You could be right. And we appreciate you bringing it in. But you know how we feel about hostiles. We don't want to jeopardize our relations with clients . . . particularly for such a small deal."

He unmoored his cigar and examined his watch. "Cripes, I'm getting out of here, go have a drink at the Racquet Club."

"When are you going to put me up for membership?" Trina demanded.

Aldridge smiled lamely. It was an old joke, but one that still unsettled him; women weren't allowed to join the Racquet Club. He laughed sheepishly, muttered, "Sorry . . ."

"You will be sorry," Trina opined, a few minutes later, in the safety of the ladies' room. "Old fart."

15

"What exactly does this fellow Parker want," Trip Corbin asked, his tan brow furrowed in puzzlement, as far out of his element as the salmon mounted on the wall above his head.

Steal your car and rape your women, Washington wanted to say, but he saw that his white audience was extremely uptight. And so was he, for that matter. Here in Corbin's office, under the accusing glass eyes of stuffed birds and beasts, Washington shared the tufted, cracked leather sofa with Harold and Kleinfeld, desperately trying to smother an incipient fart, hoping to sound more confident than he was feeling.

"First thing, he wants publicity. Dude's like a plant, heliotropic, he gets bigger every time a flash bulb goes off. This is political theater, okay? He needs to slap us around some. He needs his people to *see* him slap us around. Eventually he'd love patronage—a few jobs for the brothers, a little money for his organization. But the exposure's the sure thing."

Although press coverage of the protest against Corbin, Dern had subsided for the moment, and Parker himself appeared infrequently, a small contingent of his followers maintained a vigil with placards behind the police barricades outside the building. Rasheed Jamal, wearing a neck brace, had filed a civil suit against the two security guards who had ejected him, and against the publishing house. Partly as a result, Corbin, Dern stock had dropped from fifteen to twelve and a half in over-the-counter trading.

"How do we get rid of the asshole?" Kleinfeld demanded.

As the only black person in the room, Washington was apparently supposed to know these things—to interpret the drumbeats coming from the jungle for the white sahibs. But right now he was preoccupied with the idea that none of them would say anything if he cut one; they'd be thinking, Yeah, those Negroes, they eat a lot of black-eyed peas and shit.

"We wait him out," Washington proposed, "or we sit down to talk with an open checkbook."

"Why don't we just tell him to fuck himself," suggested Kleinfeld.

"Because we have a tremendously valuable reputation to protect," Harold said testily. Though not a complete idiot along the lines of Whitney III, Kleinfeld could be, in Harold's view, a flaming philistine.

"And Parker knows it," Washington said loudly, clenching his lower abdominal muscles. "Which is one of the reasons he picked us. He figured out we'd hate to lose our liberal intellectual cred."

"What do we know about Parker's private life?" Kleinfeld wondered out loud. "I mean, is he vulnerable? Can we get anything on him?"

"Jesus Christ, Jerry," Harold snapped. "Let's just schedule a meeting to hear them out."

"We'll have to shake a few bills at them," Washington said.

"Well, that's what it costs to play nice," Kleinfeld explained, glaring at Harold. "Washington, you wanna set this up?"

"It's got to come from one of you. Sending me on the errand is exactly the wrong way to go."

"All right, all right," Kleinfeld agreed.

"For Christ's sake," said Corbin, in the tone of a man whose patience, and attention span, have been sorely tried. "Granddad used to have Ralph Ellison out to the Connecticut house when I was a kid."

Washington could contain himself no longer.

It being nearly noon already, Washington decided to drift off toward his lunch date at Lola, allowing time to stop at a cash machine since he hadn't done his expense report in several months, hence hadn't been reimbursed, hence might not be fully paid up and operational on his plastic.

At the cash machine he was trapped in a long line. When it was finally his turn, Washington slipped his card into the slot and punched in his code. Waiting for the computer, he felt everybody else waiting behind him, all the white bodies pressing toward him. He could read their minds:

Hope this colored boy doesn't hold us up. Not that I'm prejudiced but it's like they always walk slow on the sidewalks when you're in a hurry— something left over from slave days when they didn't get paid for working, or from Africa, because it was so hot, but right now I don't care, I'm in a hurry, goddamnit, us white people have work to do.

WE ARE UNABLE TO PROCESS YOUR TRANSACTION AT THIS TIME.

"Bullshit," he said aloud. Nothing wrong with his account, should be two grand in there easy. He pressed the BALANCE INQUIRY button, hearing the shuffling of feet and impatient moans from the back of the line, feeling the eyes drilling into his back. Whenever this had happened before, he had usually been prepared for possible failure, but now he was certain that some kind of mistake had been made and it wasn't his fault, goddamnit, and he wasn't some ghetto nigger who kept a negative balance, though the numbers on the machine said he was considerably overdrawn. If this had been his bank he would have stomped inside and demanded justice. He tried one more time to make a withdrawal while attempting to block out the sounds of pissed-off white people, finally ripping his card from the machine and storming out to the anonymity of the crowded sidewalk.

By the time he showed up in Russell's office a few hours later, Washington had converted his compounded humiliation into amusing anecdotes. He told Russell how he'd wandered off to the men's room as the check was arriving and hung out for a while, leaving a notoriously cheap Dutch publisher to pick up the tab, and then evinced surprise and indignation when he finally returned to find the check paid. And his morning's attack of flatulence—whoa, what a hoot, a deliberate *épatement* of the bourgeoisie. After a few minutes he realized, to his amazement, that he felt marginally better.

If anyone asked, he could truthfully say Russell was his man—one of his best friends—but he'd sooner jump out the window than appear too vulnerable in front of him. He believed Russell counted on him to stay cool and keep up appearances. He was not particularly conscious of dissimulation; it was ingrained for him to be one way with Russell and another way with Harold and somebody completely different in black company.

Even if Washington had wanted to confide, Russell would not have really grasped the racial element, the way in which for him it was always like being the only woman in the room when a Tampax commercial came on TV. When he fucked up, somehow he always felt the scarlet N light up across his chest. Russell was completely out to lunch on the Racial *Thang*. Sometimes he forgot Washington was black, and other times he thought it was just swell even though it didn't really make any difference—all of that was solved by the civil rights movement, bro', and we intelligent, educated, right-thinking white folks are just tickled to death to have black pals. Yeah, slap me five on that one! Occasionally, Russell figured he got a few extra style points for hanging out with the blood. But Crash was all right, not like the white people who *tried* so fucking hard—who just casually happened to say, "You know, I actually really like the new Michael Jackson album," and, "I see Jessie Jackson made an interesting speech in Chicago the other day." Oh, yeah? Well, gosh, thank you, white guy. And I just love old Jackson Browne.

Just now Russell appeared to be far away; he wore a troubled expression which was, to Washington's suspicious eye, freighted with guilt. "I'm fine," he insisted lamely when asked.

"Problems at home?" Washington had never believed in the perfection of the Calloway union, if only because everyone else did. And he didn't believe monogamy was a viable condition.

In response Russell shook his head pensively. "Did you know that rich bitch Casey Reynes is pregnant?" he said, out of nowhere.

"Jesus, no."

"Now Corrine's all eager to spawn."

"I hope that baby's white."

"What? Wait a minute . . ." Russell examined his friend's face closely. "You didn't. No *way*."

"Okay, have it your way, I didn't . . ."

"I don't believe you," Russell said, clearly hoping to be convinced. "Casey Reynes? Her majesty, Queen of Wilmington, Southampton, Park Avenue and Belgravia? You fucked her?"

"A gentleman doesn't discuss these things."

"You're not a gentleman."

"Okay, I fucked her."

"When?"

"I don't have the dates handy."

"You dog," Russell said happily.

"Speaking of fucking, what do you think about Jeff's new story?"

"What new story?"

"New issue of *Granta*," he said casually. Washington liked to deliver the news personally, and he could see that this was a scoop, Russell's expression modulating from blank to black. Even if Jeff's story had been harmless it would have hurt Russell to learn of its existence from someone else.

"About a glamorous, happening young New York couple. Not a bad story, a little racier than his early stuff. I was going to ask you if it's part of the novel, but I guess . . ." He left Russell to complete the thought, knowing he was too proud or angry to ask for his copy and suddenly feeling he'd been semicruel in mentioning it. But he'd been curious; the story was clearly based on Russell and Corrine. Washington stood up. "Maybe you got time to sit around and shoot the shit, but I got work to do." Sotto voce he added: "That fine new assistant of yours, you don't mind if I ask her out for a friendly drink, do you?"

The protesters were gone by the time Washington left for the day, the mangy bastards. Trying to jam up his action. But here he was, striding into a crisp evening, inhaling the smell of thawing concrete, party spoor and female hormones in the air, having dodged the bullet for yet another day. He had been meaning to get busy on the Fanon book, but even inside his hermetically sealed office he could feel the wild call of the spring night. He could hear the scratching at his heart's door of a dog that needed to be walked.

16

At six-fifteen on a May morning crisp as fresh currency, a gray stretch limousine rolled up to the curb in front of a limestone Beaux-Arts mansion in the East Seventies, trailing—like an infant of its species—a gray town car in its wake. Four steroid abusers, armed and decorous in dark three-piece suits, debarked from this fleet, two of them to guard the sidewalk outside the door while the other two staked out positions on either end of the block.

At six-thirty the principal resident of the townhouse emerged at the top of the steps, towered over by another bodyguard. Verging on the plump, his pinkish head hatless and semihairless, his dapper figure snugly wrapped in a charcoal double-breasted suit too rakish in cut for a banker and not quite dramatic enough for a gangster, he stood five-foot-three in his shoeless state, five-six-and-a-half in his custom loafers with elevator instep. The men waited below, taut in their gabardine as their leader looked up and down the street, popped a finger in his mouth and held it up to the wind. "Like Bobby Dylan says, you don't need a weatherman to know which way the wind blows. Right?"

A cheerful chorus of assent rose from the troops.

"And you don't need a detective to know who blows who. Excuse me, *whom*. That's my free advice for today, boys. Now let's walk."

Every weekday morning Bernard Melman departed for work in this fashion. His house, built by an offspring of financial vampire Jay Gould, was one of the largest private residences in the city, and currently shared a block between Fifth and Madison with a men's club, a CIA safe house,

several mansions subdivided into cooperative apartments, and the con-
sulates of two troubled foreign powers.

If the weather was inclement, Melman might step into the waiting
limo, where two of the men would join him while the others jumped
into the idling sedan, and thus the caravan would proceed down Fifth
Avenue. But today he set off on foot toward Madison, and the bodyguards
rapidly deployed themselves around him in a flying wedge formation
while the vehicles pulled off in the other direction and turned south on
Fifth, as blaring taxis swerved into the middle lanes and barreled past,
the lugubrious fleet driving at walking pace down the Avenue, parallel
to the pedestrian group on Madison, connected by walkie-talkie. Until
recently these cars had been black, but then someone wrote in a magazine
that it looked like a funeral procession every morning and Melman had
immediately traded in for the lighter-colored cars, commenting that it
was not so much that he was superstitious, but he hated the idea people
might think some anonymous corpse was paying the tab for cars that *he*
owned.

Meanwhile, on Madison, early-morning joggers and dog-walkers
yielded the sidewalk to this black gabardine juggernaut. Melman delighted
in creating havoc among his troops, stopping abruptly or veering off on
a whim, testing his men like a coach.

The pulling guard on the left side this May morning, entirely ignorant
of his boss's interest in King Charles spaniels, was clipped when he failed
to open ranks in order to allow Melman to admire a pair of them leading
an elegantly thin blue-haired matron down the street.

"Give me some room here, boys." Bending over to pat the cowering
brown-and-white spaniels, he practically barked himself. "Good little
guys. We have five of them at home," he informed the owner.

"Don't you just adore them," she said nervously. "I don't know what
I'd do without Paolo and Reggie."

Whether this man was someone terribly important whom she should
know or simply a mobster, which was her first guess, it seemed wise to
humor him, and the fact of his five King Charleses certainly spoke in
his favor, this being the dog owned by all the right sort of people—Pat
Buckley and all that crowd. Among the young striving professional set it
was currently the thing to own a sharpei or two—hairless, wrinkled
Chinese grotesques that looked like pigs wrapped in blankets of half-dried

pie dough, which in the opinion of this matron only those seriously tyrannized by fashion could covet. King Charleses, on the other hand, were cute and lap-sized, like most of the dogs favored by the mature, cultivated woman, and relatively quiet and low-strung compared with Yorkshire terriers or toy poodles; she couldn't help thinking there must be some good in a man who had five of them.

"You be good boys. And a good morning to you, madam," Melman said in parting, wincing a little as he straightened up—he suffered chronic lower back pain—and the defense closed around him again.

Melman's elaborate security system was, his detractors would say, unnecessary—serving essentially the same purpose as his Tintoretto or his wife's rubies. Not that there weren't some who would be happy to receive news of Bernard Melman's demise. In the course of a dozen corporate takeovers, four of them hostile, he had made enemies, though none of them was likely to gun him down on the street. And while his name and picture were frequently in the press, it was equally unlikely that he would be mobbed by adoring fans. His rivals ridiculed his entourage, as well as the regal scale on which he lived and consumed; periodically, certain voices in the press and the business community questioned his methods.

Not a man to beg for approval, Melman attributed the animosity he inspired in some quarters to jealousy, to anti-Semitism and to the fear and loathing of the clubby old-boys of corporate America. He was the dark outsider who'd barged in to ask for their daughters' fair hands, corporately speaking—with the understanding that if denied he would elope. He had started with a frumpy little furniture-manufacturing concern owned by an uncle of his first wife and used it as a vehicle to acquire other, larger companies. He was a guppy swallowing tuna; the big fish always laughed at him until the lights suddenly went out. Then they called him a shark. Usually he sold off parts of the new companies, keeping those with giant transferable tax losses or other useful assets and merging them with the rest of his empire. He saw value no one else saw—in food processing, toy and cement manufacturing, discount retail chains and auto parts. Again and again he outsmarted the stock analysts, not only in buying but in selling short at the brink.

Melman had withdrawn from college for a year after suffering a breakdown. He was eventually diagnosed as manic-depressive, and his mood swings had been partially tamed by medication. His subsequent buying sprees were punctuated by periods of retrenchment which, as only his closest associates were aware, often coincided with his own periods of depression. On this rhythm he had acquired a fortune that would any day now exceed a billion dollars, and abruptly he had developed a historical sense. He began to read biographies of empire builders like Alexander the Great and Julius Caesar and of the mercantile masters of America's first gilded age, a century before, delightedly conscious of the fact that from that time to this, no private citizen anywhere had made nearly as much money as fast as Melman and a handful of the other men who lived within a five-block radius of his house. A few of the new plutocrats were based in Los Angeles or London, but the financial markets from which these new fortunes derived, insofar as they had a physical location, were based in New York, and all the new titans kept a residence somewhere within half a mile of Park Avenue and 72nd Street, decorated by the same two or three decorators.

Bernard Melman did not lack for friends and admirers. No reporter ever had trouble finding quotable testimony to his graciousness and generosity. His second wife, a stunning Amazonian blonde who had been the decorator's assistant when Melman had had one of his apartments redone five years before, was devoted to him. An orphan from an obscure Appalachian background, she was judged by many to be the most beautiful of the trophy wives of New York nouvelle society and was rumored to be entirely faithful to her husband.

Melman's bankers and lawyers loved him; the trustees of the Metropolitan Museum, in front of which institution he was currently dangling a donation of ten million dollars, were lavish in their praise. Many of the arbitrageurs who speculated on the movement of takeover stocks were profoundly grateful. And there were very few of the old Social Register Wasps and Our Crowd Jews who weren't delighted to attend his parties; what was left of old New York society was not nearly vital enough, after the democratizing blitzkrieg of the sixties, to resist the transfusion of this bright new money of the eighties. And why should it, some of its members suggested. If it had taken a generation for the Rockefellers to gain admittance to the parlors of the Astors, it took only a hundred million or so 1987 dollars for the current crop of financial wizards to purchase a guest list of sterling old names and high-voltage celebrities.

Some Jewish members of the financial community harbored a seldom whispered fear that Melman and other financial buccaneers were giving them all a bad name. Melman's high profile was a little galling to the old crowd, whose families had lived demurely on Fifth Avenue for a century and founded the great Jewish investment-banking houses that Melman had circumvented in his impatient parvenu binge of acquisition, and who were proud to say they couldn't find Cleveland—Melman's birthplace—on a map. But most turned up at his dinners on time.

Melman and his gang rejoined the motorcade at the intersection of 59th Street and Fifth Avenue, and arrived at the office just before seven. He bowed to kiss the hand of his personal secretary, Denise, who giggled nervously, flattered and flustered anew as she was every morning.

Inside his office one of the two remaining bodyguards helped him remove his jacket and hung it in a closet. Then both retreated discreetly. As Melman picked up *The Wall Street Journal*, laid neatly on his desk, a frail-looking man limped into the office, dragging his right leg with each step, his right arm held to his side at a peculiar angle.

"I was talking to London," the man said, taking a seat across from Melman's desk.

"They ought to make you a fucking citizen over there," Melman said cheerfully. "You practically got an accent. Always talking to London when I need you. Goddamned teabags. It's hard to believe those people ever ran the world. The only way they coulda pulled it off was everybody else was intimidated by the accent. *I say, excuse me, but we really must insist on taking over your country. Be good chaps and carry our kit, will you?*"

"We've got an ailing division over there. It wouldn't hurt if you'd concentrate on it for a while, Bernie."

"Next thing I know you'll start talking that way," Melman said, although no one else listening to Linder would consider this likely. Melman himself seemed hugely amused by the idea. "Come limping in here in a fucking kilt."

"You need to talk to them today."

"What am I supposed to do, spend my whole day *running* things? I do deals."

"I know this."

"I haven't done a deal in *weeks*, Carl. It's like not getting laid."

"I know this also." The sex-and-deal analogy was Melman's favorite, though Carl Linder often wondered idly when his boss had last been laid and whether he found it nearly as interesting as making a deal.

"I'm thinking I'm going to buy this publishing house."

"I don't see why."

"I like books."

"This I *didn't* know."

Melman gestured toward the rosewood shelves, filled with rows of leather-bound volumes. He stood up and walked over, pulled one out and held it aloft, hefting it to demonstrate its solidity. "A lot of guys, they buy fake books for their offices, just these long strips of instant so-called books—strips of leather stuck on a board."

"This is me you're talking to, Bernie. Your decorator ordered those books by the yard."

Melman rolled his eyes and shook his head sadly. "That doesn't mean I don't like them. I have my own books at home. Have you read Plutarch?" Melman demanded. "Plutarch on Caesar? Well, you should. You might learn something besides numbers." Although he had graduated from Denison and the Wharton School of Business, Melman had something of the autodidact's innocent enthusiasm when it came to the liberal arts, to which he had come only recently. People didn't understand how hard you had to work, he often reflected, after single-mindedly succeeding in business, to acquire the habits and hobbies and interests of a rich man.

Bernie Melman's right-hand man and chief number-cruncher was worried about this latest scheme. Never predictable, Melman was increasingly liberated from quotidian restraints and notions of common sense with the exponential increase in his wealth and power. And his illness, tamed though it might be by lithium sulfate, always threatened to assert itself. Carl Linder feared that Bernie had been building up to a major manic phase for the past year and a half. He was increasingly imperial. The recent purchase of the giant fashion empire whose offices they now occupied had seemed to Linder and others to be motivated by extrafinancial considerations. The board of the old company rebuffed Melman's advances and wooed other bidders, and the eventual price Melman paid exceeded even the most optimistic assessment of the company's value and seemed to reflect Melman's desire to own a big, glamorous corporation after years of cement and discount retail. The day after pulling the ripcord on his seven-million-dollar golden parachute, the departing CEO commented scornfully to *The New York Times* that it was the highest price ever paid for a good table at '21.' Linder himself thought it was fine to buy Picassos and Légers for image-enhancing purposes. And for that matter they turned out to be excellent investments. Himself, he did not particularly like the Modigliani nude, the Picasso Blue Period saltimbanque, or the Braque collage that hung in the office. But that was one thing. He figured Bernie was competing with all those other guys and their wives. Even the ten million Melman was thinking of giving to the Metropolitan—the terms were clear. You buy prestige, good press, then take the tax write-off. But buying a company was something else. Linder believed in details and numbers, which, along with tax laws that favored debt over equity, were the basis of the Melman empire.

Melman was orbiting his desk now, pacing madly, doing what Linder, not normally given to metaphor, called his gerbil walk. His young daughter had once owned a pair of gerbils that ran obsessively in place on the exercise wheel, and Bernie, when he was in the middle of a deal, could scarcely sit down, even when he was on the phone. He always moved clockwise. At the end of each business day one of his secretaries would untwist the cords of the phones in his office, twirling counterclockwise.

Bernie Melman had his own reasons for wanting to buy Corbin, Dern, but he got a kick out of exasperating Linder. Mystifying your functionaries and followers was one of the secrets of leadership. Corbin, Dern was small change and didn't promise much immediate cash even if he busted up the company, but publishing had a certain cachet and strategically the acquisition fit into his long-range program, giving him a wedge into an industry he wanted to enter. Media was the coming thing, no question. Besides, he was intrigued by the kid who'd brought him the deal. He had a lot of baby bankers breaking down his doors but this one was something different.

Melman was lighting his first cigar when his secretary announced Trina Cox. "You stay," he said to Linder as he sat down behind his desk. Trina was shown in and directed to a leather armchair. She was wearing a snugly fitted bright red suit.

"Nice threads—Donna Karan, am I right?"

Trina looked down at her skirt and shrugged. "Ask Christopher." The chair had a slung leather seat which dropped the butt and thrust the knees up, making it awkward to lean forward or keep a skirt closed.

"You guys've met, right? Trina, Carl, et cetera . . . Carl can't stay long—he's got a fox-hunting date with Princess Di." Watching Trina fix her skirt as she settled into her chair, he added, "Saw your man Aldridge at Mortimer's the other night. What's his story? Kind of a tight-ass, isn't he?" Melman was curious to test both her loyalty and her powers of observation.

"He's of the old school. A little conservative, yes."

"A little too wimpy for your tastes, right?"

"I think we're missing out on some exceptional opportunities."

"Like Corbin, Dern?"

"That's one example."

"So let's look at it. Tell me about your man Calloway. He can really deliver one of the family? What, the junkie sister? It's gotta be her. I've met the other one at Palm Beach, a real Eva Braun—this ice-queen socialite with a riding crop up her ass. So it's the junkie, right?"

"Let's say we're dealing on a need-to-know basis here."

"Come on, honey, are we doing business here or yanking each other's chains?"

"We're deciding whether we can do business, Bernard."

Melman raised his eyebrows at this unexpected and possibly disrespectful use of his given name. Like many powerful men, he got a kick out of going by his nickname. He leaned back in his chair, looked up at the ceiling and sighed a huge cloud of smoke, which hung over him like a troubled thought. Scorning the big marble ashtray in the center of the desk, he tapped his ashes into a half-full Spode coffee cup. "You're a real Wasp, aren't you," he said.

She shrugged. "We Coxes missed the *Mayflower*, but we caught pretty much the next boat over."

"Is Calloway fucking the junkie?"

"I'd be extremely surprised."

"You would, would you? But you don't know for sure? Listen, honey, first thing—you do business with me, right?—first thing is you know your shit backwards and forwards, you become the world's leading authority on your target, right? You find out whose name the CEO's wife moans in her sleep, who she meets for lunch at Le Cirque, and what's *his* favorite position. You learn everything there is to know. Knowledge is power, right?"

"Calloway's not fucking the sister."

"Is he fucking you?"

"Only in his dreams."

Melman smiled. "Only in his dreams, right. I like that."

"Russell is happily married. His wife's a stockbroker. And my intelligence says neither one of them screws around."

"Either they belong in a museum or something's wrong with your information." Leaning forward, Melman tapped and shaped his cigar ash on the edge of the coffee cup. "Fidelity—this day and age, Fidelity's just the name of a discount brokerage house."

Trina was aware that her skirt slid up her thigh each time she shifted, and was nearly convinced that the chair was designed especially for this purpose. "You don't believe there's such a thing as a happy marriage?"

"Sure, I believe in happy marriages. I have one, right? Carl here has one—" Carl issued a grunt of what might have been protest at this description of his own marriage. "I just don't believe there's such a thing as fidelity. What do you think?"

"I wouldn't know, I'm not married."

Nodding glibly, he tried to stare her down but she held his gaze with bemused concentration. "How tall are you?" he said.

"Pardon me?"

"How tall are you? You know, your height?"

"Five-seven."

"You're not five-seven."

"Last time I checked."

"Stand up."

Trina hesitated.

"Go on, I want to see how tall you are."

Seizing the opportunity to fix her skirt before it disappeared up around her waist, she stood up, not without difficulty. The chair was like a swamp.

Melman came out from behind his desk. "Carl, you measure."

They kicked off their shoes and stood back to back. Trina could feel

Melman raising himself up on the balls of his feet. He was at least two inches shorter.

"Carl, what do you say?"

The lame man limped over wearily. "I call it a draw," he said. "And now, Bernie, I've got to call London. Morning, miss."

Melman winked at Trina as Linder pulled the door closed behind him. "I try to use every advantage I've got. Like owning the judge." He slipped on his loafers and sat on his desk.

"I can be short if I need to be," Trina said.

"I kid Carl, but without him I couldn't—" Suddenly he grimaced and reached for his hip. Groaning loudly he moved his head slowly from side to side, his expression gradually relaxing. "You know anything about back pain?"

"Only where it's located."

"I got a bitch of a lower back." He eased himself from the desktop and hobbled slowly back to the orthopedic chair behind the desk. Reluctantly Trina resumed her seat. "Backs are this mysterious thing, right? I've had the best chiropractors in the country working on me and they can't do shit. But that's my problem. So, what about this protest I've been reading about? This Parker character?"

"One, it's driven the price of the stock down. Two, old management's stuck with this, not us. New-broom kind of deal, we pay Mr. Parker a few out of goodwill." She paused. "Particularly since I know you are quietly involved in some substantial charities serving the black community."

Melman smiled appreciatively, hunched up his shoulders and spread his hands. Inserting a pen in the corner of his mouth he said, "And Calloway? I should meet him. Smart guy?"

"He's good. Maybe one of the best editors in New York, and I think he's got the CFO on his team, which gives us managerial talent. With guidance he could handle the core division. We'll sell off the rest immediately."

"Ambitious?"

She nodded.

"But not *too* smart and ambitious, I hope. Right? Do you know what I'm saying?"

"I think I'm picking up your signal, captain. He's manageable."

"And if he doesn't work out?"

"That would be up to whoever put up the money."

"So, what about you? You're smart, ambitious, pretty. What do you want out of life?"

"Set up my own firm, do deals."

"You like doing deals?"

"I love doing deals."

"I mean, do you *really* like doing deals. You better, okay? You better like it more than anything. Some of you yuppie kids with MBAs, you want to get rich. You want to *buy* shit, right? Your BMWs and your fucking houses in the Hamptons. Sure, everybody wants to be rich, but you gotta love the deal, you gotta love winning. Money's just the way you keep score."

Trina's skirt was sliding up her thighs again. On top of the lecture it was really pissing her off. She fought her way up out of the chair. "This trick peekaboo chair is bullshit, Bernie. You want to see my stuff? Be a man about it. You want to see it?" Trina lifted her skirt up over her hips. Holding the skirt up above her waist with one hand and tugging her panty hose down to thigh level with the other, she twirled like a model, displaying the view in the round. Bernie found himself unable to look away or speak.

After a suitably indecent interval she tugged up her hose and dropped her skirt. "Now could you please get me a real fucking chair, please?"

Bernie recovered from his trance, flashing a big toothy smile. "You're gutsy," he said, as if she'd passed a test of his conscious devising. "Maybe I can help you do some business."

He came out from behind his desk rolling his own chair, holding it for her. "Try this, most comfortable chair in the world, custom-made for me in Milan."

17

"Bernard Melman?" Corrine said. "Are you kidding? The guy's a pirate." She was trying to find her other pearl stud in the chaos of her jewelry box. They were running late for a dinner party, and the only pairs of earrings she could find were old hippie things from junior high. Sterling hoops and hammered copper disks. If they ever really needed money she could always pawn her jewels for twenty or thirty bucks.

"For my purposes he's an angel of mercy. Christ, does this tie look all right?"

"Wear the burgundy with the little fleurs-de-lis."

"What does he want with a seventy-million-dollar publishing house? That's petty cash for him."

"He probably wants the cachet. Think of it as money-laundering."

This term, with its associations of gangsters and drug dealers, rang true in Corrine's secret estimation. Disloyally, she hoped that this scheme of Russell's would die of its own accord. She had been so busy lately she hadn't had the energy really to challenge him.

"Can we please stay home tomorrow night?"

"God, yes. I don't know. Check the datebook."

"I hate this dress," she shouted. "I look huge. I'm like the queen of the cholesterol festival. I can't go looking like this." She walked to her closet and flung back the door, then thumbed through the rows of fabric shoulders, past the sensible business suits and colorful prints from Laura Ashley to her inadequate selection of evening and cocktail dresses in black and red and green and black again.

"Corrine, if you were any skinnier the dress would fall right off. Besides, we're late."

"Don't sigh like that."

"Like what?"

"In that condescending way you have like you're dealing with a child or a household pet."

"Sorry," Russell said, holding his breath. With Corrine, dressing for a party could be a traumatic event. She became violently critical of her own appearance and her wardrobe. The process could end in tears and threats of violence.

"You're still doing it."

"Doing what?"

"Looking at me that way." She took a deep breath. "Okay, I'll go like this. If you want you can tell people I'm your fat, ugly cousin from out of town."

"I've been doing that for years."

When they were in the cab she said, "Are you going to meet with Melman?"

"I'm seeing him tomorrow."

"You wanted to publish more poetry and political books. Now you're meeting with Bernie Melman, the man who gave greed a bad name. Do you see anything ironic about this?"

But Russell was perfectly able, at this juncture, to suppress his sense of irony.

Early the next afternoon Bernard Melman pointed a fork at Russell's sternum as he ventilated some of his ideas about money. With his balding pink head, fierce eyes and well-cut black suit he put Russell in mind of a turkey vulture (Falconiformes Cathartidae, Audubon, plate 87).

"J. P. Morgan used to say the only thing he considered when he was loaning money was the character of the applicant."

Russell Calloway considered this notion. "Would he have backed St. Francis of Assisi on a chain of animal hospitals?"

The reference either escaped Melman or failed to engage him. "The vet my wife takes her spaniels to over on Lex, the guy grosses three or four million a year. I'd lend this guy money whatever his name is. So what are you, Catholic?"

"Lapsed."

"How tall are you?"

"Six-one."

"Get outta here. You know what the average height is for men in this country? The average height is five-six. You thought it was more, didn't you? But that's average. Five-six. If you factor in the rest of the world it's much shorter. In some countries I could play professional hoop. So you're sticking to this six-one story, huh? Okay, fine. I gotta tell you, though, it's my experience that tall guys generally have smaller dicks, bigger the guy, smaller the tool, it's kind of an inverse-ratio sort of thing, don't you think?"

"I haven't made a real *study* of it, myself."

"Ouch, I think I just got zinged," Melman said. "Carl, did I just get zinged, or what. I think this ex–altar boy is calling me a homo."

Carl Linder grunted incoherently.

"Forgive Carl, he's kind of distracted. Waiting on a phone call from the Queen of England announcing his fucking knighthood. *Sir Carl.* Sounds nice, doesn't it?" Melman summoned the maître d' and explained that if the Queen of England called she was to be told that Carl was busy eating shepherd's pie and couldn't come to the phone.

"So don't worry," he told Russell after Carl had failed to fight back. "I don't hold a man's height against him. But I tell a lot about him from the way he walks. Just watching you walk over from the office, I said, Here's a guy who's awfully sure of himself. You've got this wide-open, confident stride, and you don't carry yourself defensively, like a guy expecting a shot from an unexpected corner, or for the ground to open up at his feet and swallow him. You've obviously never been kicked in the balls, am I right? You can see it even in the way you're sitting."

Melman's own posture, it seemed to Russell, reflected a precarious triumph of stasis; he seemed ready to spring into the air at any moment.

"I've been going over your list," Melman said. "You've published some great books."

"I publish what I like," Russell answered coolly, determined not to kiss Melman's ass.

"You've got taste. I admire taste," Melman enthused, as though he were far too successful on the only scale that truly mattered to deny other men their particular virtues.

They were dining at '21,' the world's most expensive former speakeasy.

The man whose job it was to welcome people at the door had greeted Melman in an ecstatic manner and led him to another greeter, who in turn escorted the party into the dining room, where they were handed off to the maître d', who lubricated the last few steps of their progress into the banquette immediately inside the front door of the saloon. The two bodyguards were given a place at the bar.

The restaurant kept an orthopedically customized chair standing by for Melman's use, fitted with a coccyx-level pad to support the lower back. Another corporate raider whose weight fluctuated between four hundred and five hundred pounds had a double-wide model waiting for him—Bernie dubbed it a self-love seat—whenever he flew in from Los Angeles. Hanging from the rafters of the first-floor saloon was a collection of toys, models and pennants suggestive of a prosperous thirteen-year-old boy's bedroom, each signifying the ascent of a regular to a top corporate position—a football for the customer who bought himself an NFL team, an airplane for the patron named chairman of an airline. Melman pointed out his own trophies, including a pennant inscribed with the name of his fashion empire and a plastic butcher knife signifying his capture of a meat-packing concern.

"If we go ahead with this thing we'll hang a book from the rafters, put your name on the cover," Melman suggested. He then identified for Russell a couple of other corporate chieftains with inferior table positions. "All along the front wall here is the gold coast. Over there"—he pointed to the two other rooms—"that's Siberia."

Visibility was the single desirable quality in a table. At this time in the history of dining this was true generally, though in the speakeasy days, when gamblers and bootleggers had been among the elect and the aura was one of illegal commerce and clandestine pleasures, the desirable tables at '21' had been in the remotest corners of the far room. Movie stars conducting extramarital affairs, under the influence of long-abandoned codes of conduct and primitive, Manichaean notions of publicity, once chose their tables on the same principle. But this was an era of exhibitionism.

"If you ever come here without me, you make sure they remember you—use my name. Don't let them send you to the salt mines."

If this concern with the pecking order might have seemed obsessive and parvenu to the clinical gaze, Bernie's boyish enthusiasm was disarming, and Russell's critical faculties were somewhat dulled in this shrine to the masculine romance of old New York, where sacramental cocktails with names like Manhattan and Sidecar were still served by uniformed old men who had never attended an acting class, and cigar smoke rose like incense on the altar of power and money.

For Russell the restaurant had naively romantic connotations courtesy of his father, who had traveled to New York on business and brought back to Michigan tall tales about the metropolis in the East, not the shortest being an account of the fancy tavern with a number for a name where a hamburger cost nine dollars. This, in Russell's mind, took its place alongside giant alligators in the sewers and sidewalk-fried eggs among the primary legends of the city that he gradually came to identify as the setting of his dreams.

Russell ordered the hamburger, which cost twenty one-fifty now and lacked a top bun. Linder ate chicken hash and said little. "He always has the chicken hash," Melman observed.

"You got a problem with my chicken hash?"

"You should diversify your intake of protein, for Christ's sake. Eat some fish."

"I don't like fish."

"It's good for you."

"If it doesn't have at least two legs I don't want to eat it."

"How's that for a principle?" Bernard Melman declared. "Anybody says Carl Linder isn't an honorable man, you tell him the guy has scruples, he won't eat anything with less than two legs, right? No poor fucking defenseless one-legged creatures, no amputee chickens. So what do you think—" he said to Russell. "You think I don't have principles?"

His mouth full of ground beef, Russell suddenly realized that the banter had given way to substance.

"Why would I think that?"

"You're a good liberal intellectual, you probably think I'm the devil incarnate." He reached down, lifted a shoeless foot up to the table. "Look, no cloven hoof."

"Some of us are trying to eat," Linder complained.

"A lot of people don't understand what I do. And it's easy to despise what you don't understand, especially when the rewards are so great. Capital is supposed to flow where it's most needed, like water. But our economy is full of bottlenecks and dams and stagnant backwaters that nobody's visited recently. I'm like the Army Corps of Engineers. I dredge the silt out of the waterways."

Given the environmental record of that agency, Russell thought this an unfortunate metaphor, but he did not want to interrupt a speech to say so.

"Most corporations are run by salaried managers with no ownership stake, right? Do they look out for the stockholders? No. Do they stay innovative, develop new products and services to serve the public? Some do, the good ones. But a lot of them stagnate. Management gets lazy, falls into habits, looks at the short-term earnings to cover their asses, instead of the long term. What do they care about the long term? They don't own stock, they've got their retirement plans. They protect their own interests and salaries, and the shareholders get screwed. That's when I put them on notice. I go in and offer the shareholders an instant premium. I say, 'Five'll get you ten,' and I bet you I'll still make a profit in the end. I'm the guy who hikes in from another village and says, 'What, you're only getting ten cents for your coconuts? Over in my village they're worth twenty. So I'll give you fifteen.' "

"You give them ten and a half," Linder said.

"I give 'em ten and three-quarters, and they're happy to take it. So I go to another fucking village where they got wampum sitting around idle, right? So I borrow a few belts to buy up the coconut plantation. I say, 'What are you getting, eight-percent interest from the old established planters and their banks? I'll give you twelve percent.' Okay, ten, maybe. But everybody wins, right? Capital flows where it's needed. I rationalize the process and everything works better. Overthrow the oppressive old regimes. What I really am, I'm a corporate revolutionary. I'm the Che Guevara of the boardroom."

Melman had asked him earlier, as they were walking over from his office, not to speak about the potential deal in public. As they waited for coffee he leaned forward and said quietly, "If anybody asks, you and I met at a party, and I wanted your advice about a book I'm thinking about writing. Because, believe me, when I go out to lunch with somebody, a stock can go through the ceiling before the closing bell."

He leaned even closer, his genial lunchtime expression having disappeared. "I think you've got the junkie sister in your pocket. That's just a guess—nobody's told me anything. Am I right, Carl?"

"We have not received any information regarding the disposition of shares in any corporation."

"So maybe I could take her out to dinner myself, buy her some heroin or cocaine or whatever. And maybe she likes me for one reason or another, decides to sell her shares to me. Meantime, I've bought up four-point-nine percent on the open market. So what do I need with you?"

"With all due respect," Russell said, "books aren't air conditioners or carburetors."

"Not from where you sit, maybe."

Melman's turkey-vulture gaze was obscured in a great cloud of cigar smoke, and when the smoke cleared he was smiling pleasantly.

Back at his office, Russell inserted a piece of company stationery in his old IBM and composed a letter.

"Dear Jeff," he wrote:

I have just finished reading the *Granta* story and I wish I could say I loved it. I always told you your best stories were the ones fully *imagined*, in which you had departed furthest from the actual circumstances of your immediate experience. So I don't think it's being hypocritical to say I don't appreciate your casual appropriation of *my* experience. And I would be lying if I said I didn't feel betrayed.

Your embellishments seem uniformly unflattering and hurtful, particularly in ascribing an act of betrayal to "Connie." Which is, I take it, what the elliptical ending of the story is intended to reveal.

Am I meant to infer that you know something I don't—i.e., that Corrine slept with Duane Peters—or simply that you are resentful of what you so clearly believe to be our fool's paradise? I don't think we ever hung out a sign billing ourselves as the world's perfect couple. God knows we have our problems, but they're *our* problems. I don't recall asking you to comment on them in print. . . .

For some reason he hadn't told Corrine about the story, perhaps because he was bothered by the implications. He didn't really believe Jeff knew something he didn't know, and simply to raise the subject at home would be unpleasant.

* * *

"It's for you," Corrine said, a few nights later, holding the receiver out to him as if it were one of his nasty-smelling tennis shoes. Russell was prone on the couch, reading a manuscript.

"Melman's going to back us," Trina announced.

When Russell whooped, Corrine glanced up from the book she was reading with calculatedly restrained irritation.

"I don't want to say any more over the phone," Trina said.

"What are we, spies?"

"Meet me for a drink."

Russell looked over at Corrine, who was watching, book in her lap, from the armchair. "It's practically eleven," he said.

"If we're going to go ahead with this thing you better give up any ideas you have about normal business hours. And ditto for your wife."

Indeed, Corrine didn't understand why she couldn't come. "Haven't I been helping you all along," she asked.

"Trina's got this big thing about security," Russell explained.

"I think she's got this big thing about you."

"It's business, Corrine." He was irritated at her for his own guilty sense that it *wasn't*, in fact, just business. "Look, I'll be back soon and I'll tell you all about it."

"Don't do me any favors," she said, turning away. "I'll probably be asleep. Unless I'm out with one of my attractive male associates." That set Russell to brooding again, as he descended in the elevator, on the subject of Jeff's story.

Packaged in a tight pink coatdress, Trina was gobbling mixed nuts at a table in the Oak Bar. "They asked me in this very snotty way if anyone was joining me," she said. "Apparently they decided I was a hooker. They used to have a rule against unescorted women at the bar. What are you drinking?"

Russell tried to order a glass of white wine but Trina insisted he drink a real drink. "We're about to enter another dimension. Soon we'll be living in deal time. And only the tough survive."

"You have a peanut skin on your lip," he said.

"Where, here?" She brushed at the wrong side of her lip. "Show me."

Russell reached over and nudged the brown speck from her pink lip. She puckered and then kissed the air between them.

"Thanks, hon'. So aren't you excited?"

"I think so."

"Come *on.*" She reached down and squeezed Russell's thigh. "Melman's going to raise a war chest of a hundred mill' for us. And he's setting me up in my own firm."

The waiter arrived to inform Trina that she had a telephone call. While she was gone Russell tried to survey the spongy tundra of his feelings. He wasn't sure he wouldn't prefer to leave everything as it was before, tell Trina he was just kidding. Who did he think he was, taking over a publishing house? A stranger was going to lend him a hundred million dollars. The whole concept was a lethal cocktail of hubris and temporary insanity. He could see that now, and he was scared silly, prematurely nostalgic for the scale and the texture of his current life, the one that was just about to end, with its mundane certainties and decencies. The idea of Corrine sitting at home made him sad, as if he were flirting with a destiny that might somehow eventually exclude her. He could stand up right now and walk out before Trina returned, throw down a twenty and leave his unfinished drink sweating beside hers on the table. If he stayed here and finished this drink, he was afraid he would commit himself to an inexorable progression of events.

A head-turning, heart-stopping redhead appeared in the door, snug in a tiny black strapless dress. She scanned the room purposefully and at that moment Russell would have considered trading his kingdom to be the man she was seeking. She caught him staring and suddenly smiled and waved, as if he *was,* in fact, the very person she'd been searching for all along. With mounting exhilaration and fear he watched her walk toward him.

"Hi."

"Hello."

"I wouldn't mind a glass of champagne."

"Do I know you?" Although he imagined himself passably good-looking, he was not so accustomed to the attentions of beautiful strangers as to be jaded.

She leaned forward, looking into his eyes, unnerving him. "Do you want to?"

Russell found himself unable to articulate an answer.

She leaned still closer, put her lips against his ear, and whispered, "I'll do absolutely anything you want for three hundred dollars."

Finally understanding, he blushed at his own naive vanity at the same time that he found his imagination wandering into the dizzying space opened up by the word "anything."

She wet her pursed lips with the tip of her tongue.

His own lips were dry, his throat constricted and parched. "Actually I'm with somebody," he croaked. "She's just making a phone call."

"Too bad," she said, sliding gracefully to the adjacent stool and turning her attention to a pinkly balding man who was thoughtfully stirring the cubes in his scotch. He nodded and smiled politely when she said hello.

"*Anything*," he asked a moment later, loudly enough for Russell to overhear.

Her red hair rose and fell across her bare back as she nodded, licking the back of her dress like an inverted flame.

The pink man reached inside his jacket for his wallet. He mouthed the question again and she nodded, this time with her chest as well as her head. He slid some money across the bar and placed her hand on top of it. Then, clearly and distinctly, pausing between each word, he commanded: "Paint . . . my . . . house!"

"I want to go dancing, celebrate," Trina said, on her return. "Finish your drink, already."

"You won't believe what just happened," he whispered.

"I know, you got hit on by a hooker. Congratulations. Now take a real woman dancing."

"I can't go out dancing," he said, though the idea did seem appealing, suddenly; after his brief encounter with the redhead he was worked up, his hormones boiling.

She reached over and palmed his cheek. "Russell, we're going to be spending a lot of time together from now on. You can't be afraid of little old me."

"I'm not afraid. I could beat you up with one hand tied behind my back."

"Show me."

Somehow this sounded to him very much like the word "anything" as it had been uttered a few moments before.

"Take me to Au Bar. One drink."

He looked at his watch: midnight. Russell's sense of gallantry prevailed over domestic loyalty. They had a drink at the bar and then sat down with some friends of Trina's. By the time he got home it was nearly two o'clock. He could tell from Corrine's breathing on the other side of the bed that she was awake, but since she was pretending to be asleep he decided to collaborate in the fiction, though it was possible that she might know that he knew she was only pretending and might thereby become even angrier. He felt guilty for coming in so late, and indignant at being made to feel guilty. Corrine, he told himself as he fell asleep, was going to have to loosen up a little.

18

Minky Rijstaefel acquired her nickname shortly after coming out, at age seventeen, when *Town & Country* announced that she owned twenty-three furs. Minky was one of the young transatlantic set, which, in its more expansive moments, brushed up against some of the indigenous population groups—like one of the kisses with which members greeted each other. The kiss was actually two kisses, one on each cheek, or rather, two simulated kisses, actual physical contact being avoided in the interest of makeup preservation and of easing the strain of performance in the case of those who actually couldn't stand the sight of each other. The kiss had come via the continent, as had a third of the guest list for Minky's party. About ten percent were English, while the American contingent was divided between social young Upper East Siders, and downtown freaks and personalities for piquancy.

Corrine wore a black Calvin Klein that she was afraid required more *pour le décolleté* than she could give it, maybe right before her period she could pull it off, but Russell insisted it looked good—in a tone that really meant, Hurry up and get dressed. Russell wore his tux. She loved him in the tux, which she'd helped pick out four years earlier—a Christmas present financed by his father. Russell had been thrilled and pretended not to be as he first debated the store—Brooks Brothers, Paul Stuart, Barneys—then wrestled with the thorny issue of notched versus shawl lapel with the salesman at Barneys, Russell trying to convey the impression of a man who had already worn out three or four tuxes in his life.

"Oh, Russell, you're such a nut," she said, turning away from the vanity mirror and looking over at him sitting on the bed struggling with his suspenders. And very handsome, she thought. Accustomed to these inexplicable exclamations, Russell stood and asked her if she would insert his cuff links—a request that inevitably followed his struggle to do it himself. He used to put them in first, before donning his shirt, but his hands had grown too big. She always savored this moment in their joint toilet, amused at Russell's frustrated helplessness.

Twenty minutes later they stepped out of a cab in front of a mansion on East 72nd Street. On the sidewalk an informal reunion was taking place as blonde women in dark raiment embraced and kissed air while their escorts pumped hands. Inside, an aging vassal took their wraps and then pointed out both the staircase and an elevator.

"Oh yes, by all means let's take the elevator," said Corrine, suddenly breaking into a limp and giggling.

Another uniformed retainer ushered them into the elevator, modest in size but lavishly paneled in rich, burled wood, trimmed in brass, where they were joined by an Italian-speaking group whose competing fragrances made the elevator seem very close. The elevator man slid the gate shut. With a barely perceptible hum they ascended one floor and emerged into a ballroom rife with chilly blondes with high-rise cheekbones and bobbed noses, and dark men, trim in their cummerbunds. The Italians began waving as soon as the elevator door opened.

"God, this looks awful," Corrine whispered.

They headed for a bar across the room, where they heard the bartender tell one of the guests, "I think the Dow has at least another five hundred points in it." Jesus, Corrine thought, when the bartenders become experts you know it's time to get out.

Their hostess suddenly materialized, a blonde of middle height who would have looked teenaged with her round cheeks and cute, tumescent mouth if not for the fierce green eyes, which appeared to have previously belonged to some antique Borgia assassin. She had a full, rounded body that men seemed to like, though Corrine was inclined to apply the word "chubby." And in her opinion somebody ought to tell Minky she should *not* be wearing that pouf skirt which was so very hot right now, half the women here in them. Get thee to a spa, honey. Big bubble around the ass.

Minky greeted Russell, Corrine and several others in succession and

Corrine was certain she had no idea who any of them were. Then Minky slipped away and Russell said, "Oh, damn, there's Harold." Now approaching with his young escort, Harold had hesitated when he first saw them but apparently concluded it would be more awkward to change directions.

"Corrine, you know Harold," Russell said. "And this is Carlton . . ." He suddenly couldn't remember her last name.

Both men acted flustered, though Harold always seemed uncomfortable in social situations.

"We were just going to get a drink," Harold said, pointing and retreating to the bar.

Corrine saw Casey Reynes across the room and left Russell to talk to some Englishmen he seemed to know.

The Englishmen were speculating on the authenticity of the breasts of an actress who'd just passed. "A mate of mine was on the Concorde last week, said this girl's tits exploded from the pressure."

"How extraordinary."

"Have you seen Jeff Pierce," Russell asked, remembering one of the Englishmen as a journalist who'd written about Jeff recently. Russell hadn't seen Jeff since he'd fired off the letter, which had served to drain most of his bile: now he was concerned that he'd been too harsh.

"He's here with that model, Nikki something, the bastard."

"I've heard she's involved in a cult that kills babies," said the other Englishman.

"You don't say?"

"Sort of a Ponce de Léon Fountain of Youth type of thing. Her agency has to pay off the parents."

"I should think so."

The hostess had suddenly spotted a new arrival. "Johnny, how sweet of you to come," she said, though she had never actually met the man whose cheek she kissed, bumping up against his black sunglasses. The recipient of this greeting seemed confused. He introduced his companion, a slight blond ghost in a black turtleneck. "This is Juan Baptiste, the, uh, gossip, uh, columnist."

"I just love the way you wear your tie, Johnny," Minky screeched, tugging his bow tie, knotted like a ribbon around his exposed white neck, beneath an open formal shirt and an ill-fitting gray suit. Minky tugged Johnny Moniker off to meet some people. A few minutes later, when Juan ordered a drink, the bartender asked, "Was that Johnny of Monaco."

"An impostor," Juan answered, as he noticed Russell at the bar. "Presumably," he said, by way of greeting, "I can take it as a sign of acute interest that you have not yet returned my manuscript, or otherwise responded to my proposal."

Russell had no idea who this person was, so he stalled. "I'm showing it around to some of my colleagues."

Fortunately Juan flourished a business card with the logo of a major tabloid. "I've moved uptown myself, but I think the downtown pieces have a historical validity."

"Absolutely, Juan," Russell said brightly, placing him. "You know, my assistant's a big fan of yours, actually." Suddenly he wondered what Donna, who after all was no longer his assistant, had done with the damn manuscript, and reminded himself that he had to help her find a new job. And respond to thirty-nine other submissions, write a letter of recommendation to the Guggenheim committee, get Colin and Anne a wedding present, pay the Visa bill . . . and get another drink immediately. . . .

When Corrine looked over at Russell again, he was talking to a woman she was almost sure was that trollop they'd seen in St. Barts, leaning close to hear, or more likely to look down her dress. Suddenly he looked up and saw Corrine and—was it her imagination, or was that a guilty look spreading across his face? Talking to her friend Casey, who was abstemiously pregnant, Corrine realized that everyone else around her was in some stage of intoxication and that it wasn't really fun looking in from the outside. She had a small revelation, on the order of realizing that the weather was getting warmer every day: The social world of Manhattan was a machine lubricated with alcohol. And one felt very squeaky and cranky without it. Even Casey, abstaining for her final months, sounded foolish, babbling about some minor social intrigue. Russell would want to stay till the bitter end, of course.

A new entrance seemed to have excited the general interest, a big ponytailed man in army surplus togs standing in the doorway of the ballroom, flanked by two muscular black men in T-shirts.

"Hey, that's Paul Rostenkowski, the homeless guy," exclaimed a female voice behind her. "He lives in this tepee downtown, I saw him on TV the other day."

Minky swept over to congratulate this new guest on his arrival.

It was a curiously self-referential affair. People kept asking each other their opinion of the party, comparing it with past events, querying each other on future invitations. Looking for Corrine, Russell spotted Jeff across the room, but Russell's path was blocked by two young social lions.

"Were you at Pablo's dinner on Tuesday," asked one.

"I was at Constantine's and then we went to Club A."

"Why is Minky having a party for Uri?"

"He had one for her wisdom teeth last year."

"*Wisdom* teeth? *Minky?*"

"Wasn't that the actor—the one with the funny tie. What's his name, Johnny something."

"Actually, he's a look-alike Minky hired for the party. The bartender told me."

"Is she getting *that* desperate?"

"Johnny Mannequin."

"That's it."

Buzzed, and a little bored, Russell saw Jeff slip into a bathroom at the back of the parlor floor and made his move to follow. He collided with a model. "Do I know you," she asked. He knew she was a model because she had *model* written in tall, thin letters stretching from the toes of her highly arched feet to the thrusting blades of her clavicles. Beneath an open leather jacket, the lace of her black bra winked at him. The long, straight hair breaking on her shoulders; the unlined, angular face. Only models wore blue jeans to black-tie events. She was the perfect example of her type, and his heart suddenly ached at the thought that he was wedlocked, that this girl and all the other girls in the world in their incredible variety and identity would forever remain strange.

"I mean," she added, "aren't you somebody?"

"I'm a self in the limited, Humean sense," Russell proposed.

It was established that Marina, although in fact a model, was in the poetry program at NYU, which nearly provided a slender justification for the ensuing exchange of phone numbers.

"I'll take you out for lunch sometime," he said in parting, immediately wondering why he had offered. Suddenly he wanted to see Jeff, with whom, at least, he could share the dilemma of being a male *Homo sapiens*.

The bathroom door was closed. Russell knocked once and then pushed the door, which unexpectedly yielded. Jeff was sitting on the sink. Swiveling slowly at the neck, he turned on Russell a milky, distant look that betrayed faint recognition. His bow tie was cinched around his bare left arm, and a drop of blood had run from its source just below his bicep to the hollow inside his crooked elbow. In his other hand a syringe dangled lightly between two fingers like a cigarette.

"Christ, Jeff."

A dazed smile gradually bloomed on Jeff's face. "Russell," he said. Russell locked the door and watched, transfixed, as Jeff untied the bow tie and rolled down his sleeve. "You used to do drugs in bathrooms with me," Jeff said, a note of reproach in his voice.

"Not . . . like this."

"No, it was all just good, clean recreation." Jeff tilted his head back and closed his eyes, exhaling a sigh of animal contentment. He mumbled, "Day tripper." Eventually he lowered his head and opened his eyes, as if performing a languid perceptual experiment. He seemed mildly surprised to see Russell. "Would you, uh, believe me if I said I was a diabetic? Not enough sweetness in my life, a dearth and deficiency of sweetness. Or is it too much? And you? What's your excuse? What are you? Let's see—how about *dilettante?*"

"Are you all right?" Russell felt stupid as soon as he asked, not even sure what he meant.

"Just peachy. At this exact moment I am absolutely right with the world."

"Let's get out of here," Russell said, coming up behind Corrine.

And suddenly, remembering she was angry with him, she said, "Who was that brunette you found so fascinating?"

"Some poet I met somewhere," he said, his manner a little too studied, it seemed to her, as he steered her down the stairs.

"*Poet?*" She didn't want to let this pass unchallenged, but Russell seemed distracted, upset. "You okay," she asked.

He nodded unconvincingly.

"God, that was Eurotrash hell," she said as they stepped into the street.

"Some kind of hell," Russell muttered.

"Are you all right?"

"I just need some air."

She was happy, and surprised, that he was ready to go. Usually she needed a block and tackle to haul him out of a good party, but he seemed played out.

Behind them, the party was still going strong. An hour later the English journalist discovered a woman in the bathroom with her wrists slashed. An ambulance arrived. Eventually everyone learned that it was Delia, no last name, who had been the girl of the moment a few years before. The English journalist would write about her. His article would appear several months later in *Vanity Fair*. And Minky Rijstaefel would have a party celebrating the publication of the issue.

19

At Detroit Metro, Russell rented a car, one of the local products, which nowadays seemed as generic and bland as the mechanical walkways that had conveyed him from his gate to the baggage claim. The big automakers displayed their sexiest models in the terminal, mounted on squat pedestals in the middle of the floor like taxidermied specimens of an endangered species, this being the hometown of American transportation. At the rental counter it had not occurred to him to ask for a General Motors car, although this had been the policy of his family since before he was born, at a hospital heavily endowed by that company—bundled home in a Chevy convertible, with fins, to a house in Birmingham whose mortgage was paid for by his father's GM salary. Not till he was out on I-94 did he notice that he was driving the competition.

This was the first time home since Labor Day, eight months before. The featureless sprawl of the roadside landscape reminded him of the comment of a New York/Exeter kid in his Freshman dorm: "I visited the Midwest once. There was nothing to see and nothing to keep you from seeing it." At that moment he hated all New Yorkers and all snobs. So he tried to imitate them, telling Corrine when he first met her that he was from Grosse Pointe—the expensive, pedigreed suburb of Detroit, which even the eastern preppies had heard about. Thank God, she didn't seem to remember, not that she would've cared. In the car he grunted loudly and shook his head at the memory of this earlier self, then flipped on the radio, trying to remember the call numbers for the university station, looking at the landscape through eastern, urban eyes almost fifteen years after he'd left, and finding it wanting in interest and beauty.

Turning north on 24, he tried to imagine the ruins of the city to his right. When he was very young they'd go in once in a while to Hudson's, to a ball game, before the riots of '68, which they'd watched on the local and national news. He couldn't remember being downtown after that until he went in with his high school friends to buy pot and get drunk in Greektown. He thought of Stein's remark on—what was it? Oakland? No there there. Or Chrissie Hynde on Akron. My city was gone. Except it had never been his city. He'd grown up about as close to Motown as any other white kid who had ever listened to Marvin Gaye and the Supremes.

He took the Birmingham exit, and stopped at a liquor store to buy a bottle of Glenfiddich. His father was a scotch drinker but bought himself the cheap stuff, a habit that seemed absurd to his son, as did the practice of driving to the next town to save three cents a gallon on unleaded premium. These little tics of false economy provided a great deal of satisfaction to the old man and drove both Russell and his brother up the wall. Browsing through the wines he found a surprising bottle of '79 Lynch-Bages and picked it up for dinner, which would certainly be some cut of red meat his father had picked up at Price Chopper on sale several months before, pulled out of the freezer and thawed under the broiler.

After turning off the commercial highway he passed through neighborhoods green with shrubbery, four- and five-bedroom homes on acre lots subdivided out of farms after the war. He turned into a dead-end lane. The white colonial in which he had lived for much of his life came into view behind the spiky red leaves of the Japanese maples he and his father had planted in a row along the street. Russell working the hose, filling the deep holes with water, his father wrestling the burlap-wrapped packages of roots into position.

Today his father was watching the street, and he came to the door as Russell climbed out of the rental car. They embraced on the driveway, an awkward male hug, uttering words of greeting. When they stepped apart his father looked at the car, while Russell looked his father over— grayer, thinner of face. But Russell was relieved that he didn't see an old man. He still retained the basic features of a handsome middle age.

"What's with the Plymouth, young man?"

"Is that what it is?" Russell said. "How can you tell? I thought it was a Chevy."

"Still a smart aleck, I see." He tried to cuff Russell playfully on the back of the head, but he wasn't quick enough.

"Still driving that Buick," Russell asked.

"Yeah, and just between you and me I wish to hell I could drive a Mercedes."

"Go for it," Russell said.

"I just might do that," he said grimly, as Russell retrieved his overnight bag from the shotgun seat. "Traveling light," he observed, Russell hearing a trace of disappointment in his voice. In fact, he'd planned to spend only one night, though he had been vague with his father over the phone. Maybe he could manage one more night, he thought.

"Corrine's well," his father asked as they proceeded automatically to the kitchen at the back of the house.

"Great. She had a friend coming in from Denver, or she would've joined me," Russell said.

"So it's not trouble between you?" his father said, alluding to the purpose of Russell's sudden visit.

"No, I told you, nothing bad. Quite the opposite."

"That's a relief. She's a great gal."

He handed his father the bottle of Glenfiddich.

"My wealthy son."

"A simple thank you is the traditional polite response," Russell observed, thinking perhaps the scotch had been a tactical mistake.

"Join me in a cocktail," asked his father, already reaching in the freezer for the ice.

This was one of the things Russell loved about his father, the slightly formal way in which he delivered these ritual incantations, *Join me in a cocktail?* or *What's your pleasure, young man?* Nodding his acceptance, Russell scrutinized his surroundings with a vague air of suspicion. "Why does the kitchen seem so much smaller?"

"You don't notice any change," his father asked coyly.

"Something's different."

"New floor and cabinets," his father said proudly. "The wood's darker than before. That's what you noticed. Scotch?"

"Sure. Why'd you do that?"

"We've had the same kitchen since we moved here."

"Seems like kind of a waste," Russell said.

"I happen to live here, young man."

"Sorry, I forgot."

"I noticed."

"I've been incredibly busy, Dad. And it's not like you haven't seen us in the city."

They both sipped their drinks experimentally, and then his father hoisted his in conciliatory manner. They touched glasses.

"I thought we'd stay in, thaw a couple of steaks."

"Sounds good."

"We should be eating fish," his father said, and Russell thought he was alluding to calories and cholesterol. "Remember Fish Stick Fridays," he asked, referring to the ancient Catholic practice of abstaining from meat every Friday, until the immutable laws of the Church had changed.

"It sounds pretty crazy to me," his father said, after they had finished dinner and Russell had revealed his plan. He wanted not so much his father's capital as his blessing.

"I know. I mean, it must. New business ideas always sound wild." Russell hadn't expected it to go down easy. His father had grown up during the Depression, worked on salary for the same company all of his life, risen steadily through the corporate ranks and invested in blue-chip stocks which had over the years rewarded his patience. The idea of buying out one's own employer had to seem radical.

His father smiled. "I never thought I'd hear my left-wing son lecturing me about new business ideas. I remember arguing in this room about Watergate, young man. You thought Nixon should have been escorted directly to the guillotine."

"I still think so," Russell said, but now they were both grinning. Several times in the past they had nearly come to blows over politics, Russell's mother intervening to preserve some semblance of peace.

Returning to his earlier tack, Russell said, "So what have you got? Two hundred thousand in GM stock that's not going to go anywhere in your lifetime. It's a dog. I'll double it for you in three months."

"There's absolutely no guarantee you can pull this off."

"Even if we fail, the stock will shoot up as soon as we declare intent. At worst we walk away from the table with a big pile of chips."

"At least GM *makes* something. Maybe it's not the most efficiently managed company in the world. Maybe we're dinosaurs. But there's something wrong with the economy when it rewards the speculators and lawyers and bankers without producing anything. No wonder the Japs are killing us."

Scowling fiercely, his father lit a cigarette. Russell remembered how that scowl used to terrify his friends. And Russell himself at one time. Now he felt solicitous—almost, it occurred to him, as if he were the concerned parent. And in the familiar setting of the den, as he sat on the old couch, which had grown softer over the years, he became infected with some of his father's doubt. He had grown up here, and even as he struggled against it, he had absorbed something of his father's worldview as unconsciously as he had inhaled his cigarette smoke.

"What do you suppose your mother would say," Russell's father suddenly asked.

"She'd see that I had to do this," Russell said. "She'd trust us both to do what we had to do."

His father nodded, looking up at the ceiling, cigarette smoke pluming from his nostrils. "You know," he said, his voice a little wobbly, "it wasn't because I was mean that I made you kids earn all your spending money. She used to think I was too hard on you. Especially that summer in college when you wanted to go to Europe with Jeff."

"God, I was mad at you."

"I just wanted you to know that . . . I wanted you to be able to take care of yourself."

"I understand," Russell said a little curtly, for he had heard this before.

"Do you know what I mean," his father asked, as if he hadn't heard.

"Yeah, I know. Don't worry. I'm not going to hate you if you don't invest any money. We've got a commitment from this guy Melman. I just wanted you to know what I was going to do, and I thought you might want an opportunity to buy into the deal."

"And there's your brother to consider. It wouldn't be fair to just hand the estate over to you."

"I'd cut him in, too." As soon as he had said this, Russell cringed at his own grand manner. "What a guy, huh?"

His father watched the smoke unfurl from the tip of the cigarette. That was one of the harder things for Russell about giving up smoking, the pleasant distraction of having a toy at your disposal, something to do with your hands. "I'm not telling you to be like your old man and collect your salary from a big corporation all your life. Because you know what?" He suddenly lowered his gaze and looked hard at Russell. "They're bastards. They don't really give a goddamn about human beings in the end. That's what my father told me, a UAW man all the way, working the line, seeing from the bottom up, and I thought I was a lot smarter than him. But he was right."

Russell was afraid he was about to see his father cry. And so he said, as lightly as he could, "Trouble at the office, Dad?" As much as he wanted to understand his father, he was afraid that real intimacy after all the years of cautious proximity would reveal some frightening genetic secret in himself.

"I'm taking early retirement. Their decision, not mine."

"You have no choice?"

He shook his head.

"Shit."

"Nicely put," his father said after a moment, the spell of gloom dissipating. He pushed the TV tray forward and walked to the kitchen with their plates.

"I can see how you might want to be conservative with your assets now," Russell said, trailing behind.

"Maybe. Either that or go for broke. Let's have a nightcap."

20

Sleeping alone was like death. Even from inside her dreams she could sometimes feel Russell's body or its absence. As if something terrible had once happened that she'd forgotten, she had dreams of being chased, dreams of being cut with razory metal, and when she awoke from such dreams, being alone was like a second injury. All the years with Russell hadn't entirely eased her sense that she might be abandoned at any moment. Her mother used to disappear, the first time when Corrine was six—Corrine and her sister, Hilary, playing in their room, suddenly the door flung open and her mother with a fierce red look in her eyes screaming at them, they were terrible girls, they had ruined her life, tearing the pictures off the wall and scattering toys and clothes. Corrine and Hilary huddled in the corner until she disappeared, as suddenly as she had come. That time they didn't see her for three days. Their father, who didn't like little girls who asked too many questions, said nothing. When she reappeared she was fine, the good mother who played cards and watched TV with them. And every morning Corrine would leap from bed and race downstairs to see if her mother was still among them.

Waking up on a Saturday morning without Russell, she wondered if he missed her when they were apart. Somehow she imagined it was almost a relief to him, a break from her constant presence, her smothering attention.

She lay in the warm cocoon beneath the quilt staring at the thin slice of dusty sunlight that entered the room where the curtains joined, heavy chintz drapes she had bought when the English-country look took over Manhattan a few years back. Russell thought they were girlish but he conceded the bedroom to her, and she had made it into a nest lined with white wicker and floral fabrics, while the living and dining rooms had a dark, masculine feeling of leather couches and sturdy chairs. Lying in bed she noticed the peeling paint on the ceiling. The whole place needed painting.

In the living room she turned on the TV for company, made coffee and read the *Times*. Saturday paper—no big horror shows on the front page. Jim and Tammy Bakker scandal. Gary Hart momentum. Bush eating pork rinds to atone for Andover and Yale. Just plain folks—who summer in Kennebunkport. Cautious optimism in the business section. Foresee continued growth and stable interest rates in the blah blah . . . Crossword puzzle, God, she thought, why does 4 down have to be "adulterous"? At least nobody trying to force-feed her this morning. She hated to eat breakfast, but Russell was always after her to choke something down, as if he wanted her to blimp up or something, just because she'd had a little problem when she was a teenager a few thousand years before. All the girls she knew went through that stage, practically. A prep school thing, like Fair Isle sweaters and silly nicknames. Miss Anorexia Nervosa 1972—Corrine Makepeace. Fighting against the body's sudden ripening. When only the year before prep school she'd chanted with the other girls in the junior high locker room, rhythmically squeezing palms together to work the chest muscles the way the boys did to make farting sounds:

> We must, we must,
> we must increase our bust.
> The bigger the better,
> the tighter the sweater . . .

Katie Petrowski already with big ones and Corrine with her training bra. Clearing the table, last night's Chinese cookie fortune: "If wishes are modest they will come true." Save to show Russell. Reality check. Earth to wheeler-dealer Calloway.

She returned *Jules and Jim* to the video store and walked over to Madison to meet Casey Reynes at Marigold, where they lunched on Diet Cokes, Casey big with heir. Corrine thought she looked wonderful and said so.

"Please. If I just *survive* I'll be happy. They had the most gorgeous suits at Armani, and me big as a townhouse. Don't you think it would be thoughtful of Tom the Fourth to vacate the premises a few weeks early so Mom could get on with redecorating?"

Corrine would have gladly traded places. Sucking on her lemon slice, she said, "I think it would be a relief to not have to be glamorous. You have this dispensation. I'm so tired of picking an outfit in the morning. I'm tired of *dressing*. I think I just want to be barefoot and pregnant."

"I'll show you a dress at Valentino that will change your mind about that."

Despite her condition Casey had already been shopping, and she displayed some linen sheets she'd bought at Pratesi for her guest room. "So much better for you than cotton," Casey claimed. "Don't even talk to me about blends." Casey's husband was a trader and seemed to make more money than even she could spend, though she tried very hard. Commerce aside, he was worth millions the day he was born. Shopping was Casey's primary occupation. After lunch they went to Valentino and Versace, where Casey bought a suit and a belt and Corrine restrained herself. Vicarious shopping. Casey bought and Corrine watched. A blouse she admired was almost a month's rent. If they had not been former roommates, Corrine would have judged Casey superficial and decadent, but she retained a historical impression of a fat girl with a beautiful singing voice whose idol was Sylvia Plath, which made the Madison Avenue Casey seem more substantial than she could possibly appear to a recent acquaintance.

They stopped in at the Whitney, and the visit might have seemed to indicate a remission of Casey's acquisitive fever, but after only a few minutes she turned to Corrine and said, "Tom and I are thinking of buying a Fischl," as if the procession of canvases on the walls reminded her of nothing so much as shop windows.

"Let's have tea at the Plaza," Casey said suddenly, turning away from a Hopper painting.

They took a cab there, sliding along the border of the park past the line of idled horse-drawn carriages waiting, the blinkered horses chewing blindly in their feed bags. Like many other inhabitants of the city the horses looked more attractive from a distance—Corrine loved the *idea* of a romantic carriage ride through the park, the moon and the turrets of apartment buildings around the park appearing and disappearing above the feathery treetops.

With her socially correct shopping bags, Casey marched through the dazed tourists in the Plaza lobby, leading Corrine up an aisle of potted greens and Easter lilies to the clearing in the greenery where the thin strains of a string quartet competed with the clatter of silverware and the mostly feminine voices of those seated at tables—women of a certain age, with chemically lightened hair and sun-darkened skin, older versions of Casey.

Tea at the Plaza—this was one of the things Corrine had always wanted to do but never gotten around to. Always too busy. It would be a wonderful city to live in if you had three different bodies. One to work like a fiend, getting ahead, the second to lunch at Café des Artistes and take in auctions at Sotheby's and exhibitions at the Met and poetry readings at the Y. The third body to wake up late in the afternoon and stay out till dawn. Work, play and live: with just one body it's impossible, except when you're very young and you first come here and then it's magical for a short period when you get your first job and discover the city like an explorer and you never need to sleep, but suddenly you find you're older and you realize you don't have any money compared with everyone else in the city, or maybe when you get a few dollars you become older and by then you've lost the ability to be three people at once. Or else you're rich, like Casey, and all the rules are suspended.

Freeing her serviette from its ring, Casey said, "You will absolutely not believe what the father-to-be did the other day. You know the Goodharts, don't you? He's English, practically grew up at Blenheim. Anyway, they're off to Kenya for a month and they were afraid they'd miss the baby, I guess, so they come over for dinner with two little Tiffany boxes. So I put one of them on Tom's plate. And he opens the box and says, 'Hey, I've always wanted one of these.' And we all look at him and finally I say, 'Tom, darling, it's not for you. It's a rattle for the baby.' 'A rattle?' he says, blushing. Well, it turns out my darling husband thought the baby's rattle was a cock ring."

The waitress arrived and deposited a tea service and a sort of silver shelf of little pastries and crustless sandwiches that looked too pretty to eat.

"It's terrible, always wanting to eat," Casey said. "And my doctor keeps telling me I need to put on more weight. And then there's sex. You start to feel so unattractive. . . ."

"Has Tom lost interest," Corrine asked, opening a tiny sandwich like a book to check the contents, prepared to be indignant at the perfidy of the other sex. Patres unfamilias.

"Actually, I wasn't really thinking of Tom."

Corrine looked up from her slim volume of buttered cucumber, a little bit shocked, a reaction that Casey, despite her artfully jaded tone, seemed to have anticipated.

"Well, don't tell me in all these years you've never . . . I mean, Tom *is* away half the time and it's not like I don't have a sex drive. Marriage isn't about sex, anyway. The Europeans know that."

Fascinated, Corrine leaned forward. "Aren't you worried about—"

"That AIDS thing is so overhyped," Casey said, taking a smug swallow of tea. "Honestly now, how many heterosexuals do you see splotched up with Kaposi's sarcoma?"

"I meant, about the baby?"

"Well, it's safe right up to the last month, and believe it or not, some men find it kind of a turn-on."

"But what if . . . what if it's not Tom's?"

"It's his. If I'd had any doubts about that, I wouldn't have even told him. I already had two Hooverings when I wasn't sure."

Corrine felt wicked just listening to this. "I can't believe . . . I mean, how do you manage?"

"Simple. Pay for the room in cash, and by all means don't take home any of those telltale little shampoos."

21

After work Trina walked the few blocks down Park to the Racquet Club, a pink stone fortress that squatted in the Bauhaus glass thickets of lower Park Avenue like a waistcoated Edwardian banker waiting patiently amidst the rabble in a bus terminal.

Arriving at the office that morning she had found that Aldridge was in Cincinnati for the day; but he'd left word for one of the senior partners that he would be in the grill at the Racquet Club at seven, and despite the rule barring women from the club, or perhaps because of it, Trina decided to call on him. She'd planned to ask for him, but the flinty-faced Irishman at the front desk disappeared into the cloakroom with a large package as she walked in; she slipped past the desk and ducked into the elevator before he returned. While she was trying to decide which floor to push, the elevator began to ascend, slowly and noisily. As if of their own volition, the doors opened on the third floor; just beyond the door nude men loitered on benches, drifted through the steam, hailing each other in unnaturally hearty voices. No one noticed her as she punched the "Close Door" button, but a gray flannel voice commanded, "Hold that elevator," as the doors began to close, while from the other side of the damp hallway a young, classically proportioned athlete/banker whom Trina had been eyeing turned suddenly, catching just a peripheral glimpse of her, which at the time he would dismiss, and which later, after the sighting was confirmed, he would recall for the benefit of his friends in the grill room: *I feel like someone's watching me—you know that feeling?—and I look toward the elevator, the doors are just closing, and I swear I see this girl, and I mean a damn good-looking girl, in the elevator, but I say, Naw, can't be.*

Stepping out on the second floor, Trina found herself in a cavernous world of dark wood, old varnish and cracked leather upholstery that seemed to be perfumed with the essence of some long-extinct masculine hair tonic. The walls were hung with sporting prints, ancient wooden rackets and mounted brass plaques inscribed with the names of tournament winners and dates stretching into the last century, the names of several of Nicky Aldridge's forebears among them. A number of the plaques were devoted to competitions in an obscure form of indoor tennis that survived here and in a handful of places in the Old World. A sepulchral hush prevailed, the common rooms being unpopulated. It occurred to Trina, who lived in a one-bedroom condo in a five-year-old skyscraper on Second Avenue, that if Aldridge's great-grandfather were to be time-transported to Manhattan in 1987, this was one of the few places in the city he would recognize, and feel at home in.

She followed the sound of voices to the grill room. Aldridge was sitting alone at a table, transferring a large dollop of soft cheddar cheese out of a crock onto a cracker, one of seven or eight men lounging in a room that could have accommodated a large wedding.

Looking up, he seemed pleasantly surprised for a moment, and then, realizing where he was, he said, "Trina, what the hell—"

"Just wanted to see your secret male tree house. Very nice."

Silence fell across the room as the men at the other tables noticed the intruder.

"How'd it go in Cincinnati?" She reached over and removed the cigar case from Aldridge's breast pocket, extracted a torpedo and bit a slot in the tip.

"They're holding out for half a point." He looked around nervously. "Look, you probably better leave."

"I am leaving," Trina said. "In fact I'm leaving the firm."

Nicky nodded slowly, inserting into his mouth a pale orange cracker spread with bright orange cheese. Suddenly his interest in Trina's move exceeded his concern for club rules. "You took the Corbin, Dern deal somewhere else?"

"Yeah."

"Where you going?"

"I'm setting up on my own. You know Peter Risch, my friend from First Boston? He's coming with me. And I'm taking Rockaby with me. Cox, Rockaby and Risch."

"Sounds propitious."

"Thanks." Finding matches in her purse, she lit the cigar with a show of great pleasure.

"Can't say I'm *really* happy about this. I'd rather have you around. Rockaby, too."

Trina shrugged. It was the way of the world, and Aldridge knew it. He could choose to be a bastard about it or not.

The bartender, a short man in a mauve uniform, appeared at the table. "May I remind you, sir, that club rules prohibit women from all areas of the club except the downstairs waiting room."

Aldridge nodded. "Trina, you heard the man. Have to continue this discussion elsewhere."

"Get her out of here!" boomed a voice from across the room.

"No," Trina said. "I'd rather stay." She smiled and raised her eyebrows at Aldridge, to show him that there were no hard feelings, but she was committed to seeing this adventure through to the end.

"Evan here will have to call . . . God, I don't know, do we even *have* security here," he asked, demonstrating the happy ignorance of the fully serviced class.

Evan nodded.

Trina shrugged again.

"Well, do whatever you have to do," Aldridge said to the bartender, spreading his hands helplessly.

"Who'd you take the deal to," he asked Trina.

Trina puffed on her cigar. "Bernie Melman."

Aldridge raised his eyebrows and whistled. "When you said you were leaving I didn't know just how far you were going."

She had expected this. The gentleman thing. "There's billions of dollars out there we're turning up our noses at. 'The times they are a-changin',' Nicky."

Aldridge munched thoughtfully on a cracker. Cox's last phrase amused him. He had been at Columbia when the Dylan song of that name came out, had participated in the protests there in 1968 and been knocked cold by a billy club. Maybe Cox wasn't even thinking of the Dylan song, but the phrase and the perspective it yielded Aldridge made him feel curiously solicitous of this young woman, so smart and so ignorant.

"You may be right," he said. "I'm not going to bust your, uh, balls on this. But I like you and I want you to be careful out there. Maybe we're a little behind the times. Or maybe other people have gotten too far out in front of themselves. Some things never change. Death, taxes —and somebody always pays for lunch."

Aldridge took his cigar case from the table and selected a smoke. He examined it fondly and lit up. "Ever heard of Jimmy Ling?"

"No." She could feel a story coming on. God, was she glad she wasn't going to have to hear any more of these stories.

"Jimmy Ling was the Mike Milken slash Bernie Melman of his time, which was basically the early seventies. Sounds Chinese but he was actually Texan. . . ."

While he paused to puff his cigar, Trina picked up an orange cracker and spread it with orange cheddar spread; it seemed appropriate that in this place they served a kind of cheese and a kind of cracker that hadn't been seen elsewhere in the city for years.

A uniformed security man steamed into the grill room. "Are you all right, sir," he asked, staring at Trina.

"Do I look endangered?" Aldridge's withering scorn communicated itself to the guard. "Please escort my friend here to the lobby if you think you can manage it."

"Do I get a final request," Trina asked.

"Sure."

"Finish the story."

"Well, briefly, Jimmy Ling started out of his garage with three thousand dollars, and within a couple years Ling-Temco-Vought had become I think the fourteenth largest corporation in the country. Bought up a lot of companies, and he did it all with leverage. Invented this special one-stop process where instead of borrowing the money and then going after the company he'd offer the stockholders paper. Soft money. He'd trade bonds—subordinated debentures—in exchange for their stock. People started calling the bonds Chinese paper. Some of us think of it as the original junk bond. Face value looked good. But then interest rates shot up and there was nothing behind the paper. Ling-Temco-Vought collapsed like a ton of fool's-gold bricks. It was basically a house of cards in the first place."

He drew deeply on the cigar, blew out a great gout of smoke. Melman, Trina noted, continued to speak while he was smoking his cigar. Not that she was quite sure what that might mean. The security guard, after Aldridge's dressing-down, stood at attention throughout this recitation.

"Chinese paper, huh?"

Aldridge shrugged. "Just a story. Only fifteen years ago, but nobody remembers it."

"I'll keep it in mind." She stood up, holding out her hands as if for cuffs, which gesture served to increase the embarrassment of the men.

"For what it's worth," Aldridge concluded.

Trina handed her cigar to the security man, who took it instinctively without knowing what to do with it, then marched out of the grill room ahead of him.

Aldridge hoisted another orange-smeared cracker and called out to the barman for one more drink. Basically, kids like Cox scared the hell out of him. He and many of his peers had more or less drifted into investment banking and finance; they had come from schools and families where it was a respectable option, like the ministry for genteel British families of the nineteenth century or the military for a certain type of southern family. And like career officers who dutifully march off to war, he and his fellow bankers soldiered on through the mud and gore of the seventies when the stock market took heavy losses and interest rates climbed sickeningly like casualty figures in a losing battle. Hard times. They'd held enough ground to counterattack when the battle turned around in the eighties, and suddenly they had to run to keep up with the front. But these new kids, the class of '80 or whatever it was, they were carpetbaggers. Opportunists without a sense of history, or of allegiance to institutions. Terrifying when you thought about it, kids in suspenders who believed they were entitled to make millions, as scary in their way as the remorseless child murderers who inhabited the ghettos to the north, who'd pull the trigger on anyone who stood between them and their momentary desires.

"Fucking kids," Aldridge was heard to mutter as the barman brought him his drink. It would be time to get out soon, retire with his legally sanctioned, criminally excessive gains. He would be forty-four in a few days.

Bull Soames, old pal of his from Salomon Brothers, waddled over, Chivas in fist.

"What the hell was all that about, Nick?"

"Brief glimpse of the future, Bull."

22

"What's the deal here—you don't let minority-type people sit at your front booths?"

The hostess's brittle carapace of attitude was visibly pierced by this remark, although she herself was Asian. She glanced nervously between the row of front booths and her appointment book. "Julian always saves a booth for me up front," Washington added, appealing almost simultaneously to the mutually exclusive notions of an elitist social hierarchy and a democratic standard of fairness. This contradiction seemed to escape their hostess, who, after a moment's tortured hesitation led them to the table Washington requested.

In his opinion, life was too short to eat a meal in an unfashionable restaurant, and this was the most talked-about downtown establishment of the season. It was remarkable not so much for its fixed as for its transient decor, their fellow diners appearing to have been selected by an interior decorator. A sleek feline prettiness prevailed. The movie actors and columnar fashion models wore ripped jeans and T-shirts, and everyone else wore black. The lighting was brilliant, as if to facilitate photography. Russell would normally be happy to be here, though he had what he considered to be larger issues on his mind.

In his blue business suit, Whitlock was conspicuously out of place. "How's the food here," he asked, after they were seated.

"We don't come here for the food," Washington said. "In fact, it's hip to say you hate the food."

"So why *do* we come?"

"We come here so we can be abused by that hot little Asian piece and then beg for attention from these arrogant mannequins slumming as waiters and waitresses. Because it's happening. Because at any given moment there is one single place which is the dead center of hip consciousness and at nine-thirty on a Wednesday night in May of 1987, this is it. So dig it, Whit. And try not to look like you just got off the fucking bus."

Whitlock did not appear convinced. "It's a little early to celebrate," he said, after Washington waved to the waiter and ordered a bottle of champagne.

"We're not celebrating yet," Washington said. "We're just drinking. Once we start celebrating, you'll know it, chief."

Russell had confided his plan earlier in the week. Washington had extracted a series of concessions and promises and then brought a lawyer to lunch for a final discussion, wheedling and negotiating to the point that Russell was nearly sorry he had ever approached him at all. But he was a good editor and he had superb political instincts. It was David Whitlock, though, whom Russell really needed. He knew all the numbers, was as intimate with the financial details of the company as anyone they would be up against. And if there was something wrong with Melman's campaign, Whit would spot it.

"I feel more than a little uncomfortable about all this," Whitlock began. "I was sitting in front of the computer last night running numbers and projections and models, and I suddenly realized I was trafficking in inside information. I have access to stuff that someone outside couldn't get at."

"That's true of any management buyout situation."

"Well, maybe it's not illegal, but is it ethical? We're going to buy stock out from under people who don't know what we know. Is that fair?"

"It's the nature of markets," Russell said. "Nobody has to sell."

"Fuck fair," Washington said, "I want to know if this is going to work. What does your computer tell you about that, Whit?"

"It's feasible. Russell's right that the company's undervalued. Shit, so is Exxon. I'd still like to know where you're getting the rest of this cash."

"It's there," Russell said. He did not particularly want either of them to know that Melman was giving him almost ten percent of the equity, subject to future performance goals. As sort of a side bet, Russell had purchased a hundred thousand dollars' worth of the stock, taking the full fifty thousand dollars of his brand-new credit line and doubling it with a margin from his broker—shares that would leap in value at the announcement of a tender offer. Trina Cox was getting a small piece of the action; Melman, who was raising most of the capital through the banks and keeping most of the equity for himself, had authorized Russell to shave off a thin slice for Whitlock, if necessary.

"Where's *there?*"

"For now we see through a glass, darkly; but then—"

"The other side can raise money, too. Harold and Kleinfeld and the rest. If they mount a successful defense, we're out on the streets. And what about loyalty?"

"How do you spell it," asked Washington.

"Harold's done a lot for you two. He's done a lot for publishing."

Washington rolled his eyes, and then a silence fell as they all seemed to contemplate the figure they were reluctant to cast as antagonist in the proposed drama.

"What's he done for me lately?" Washington said, breaking the spell. "Besides shooting down my last two books? Harold's mainly been jamming me up."

"Ditto."

As if witnessing something unseemly, Whitlock turned away while Washington and Russell slapped hands and clinked glasses. "Is that who I think it is?" Whitlock said suddenly, nodding sideways toward the next booth at a screen actress with frizzy blond tresses and lips almost pneumatic in their fullness.

Leaning forward, Washington said, "If you come in with us, we'll make this the official company cantina, we'll have her in our booth, we'll have her sitting in your lap, Whit, because we'll be such bad motherfuckers every girl in town will want to know us. To know us is to blow us, you hear what I'm saying? Once we hit the big money, I personally guarantee you'll have to have the pants of your suits let out in the crotch. We'll make you an honorary Negro. Shit, you can buy new suits—we'll have old Paul Stuart himself come down to the office and measure you personally. We'll be too busy and important—"

"Is that why we're doing this?"

"That's why anybody does anything."

"I thought I heard Russell just yesterday talking about Literature and socially conscious publishing."

"That's because he's a repressed white boy, he has to say that shit to fool himself. You're too smart for that, Whit. You're a businessman, right? You went to bidness school, not like this turkey here, this culture vulture. You live in the real world, you know what makes it go 'round. This is America, land of opportunism."

Russell was pleased to see that Washington was already on the job. Explicitly disingenuous—speech for him was always to some extent a performance—Washington nevertheless had the ability to convince, if only to the point that you felt it would be very stuffy to believe completely in your own position, or for that matter in anything. It would be so uncool. In this fashion he often managed to conquer. Nobody wanted to be left out. Like Hamlet, Whitlock would always find sound reasons for both sides of the argument; ultimately it would take an appeal to his emotions to win him. Now, with Washington on Russell's side, it came to this: Did he want to be one of the boys?

After Whitlock ventured off in search of the men's room, Washington asked Russell if he'd told Jeff what was afoot.

"Not yet."

"I wouldn't let him hear it from anyone else," he said, as Whitlock reappeared.

A tiny elfin figure passed in front of their booth, a young blond man dressed entirely in black, his long, pale face bisected by heavy dark glasses. He fluttered a hand at Washington.

"Aren't *we* important tonight," he said.

"Every night," Washington said.

To Russell: "Still looking over my book proposal?"

"We're looking hard at it," said Russell. Who *was* this guy?

"I'm thrilled."

"Who was that," Whitlock asked. "I thought Truman Capote was dead."

"Got reincarnated as a gossip columnist," said Washington.

"What," asked Whit.

"That's Johnny the Baptist. Chronicler of quips that pass in the night."

"Shit—*that* guy," Russell muttered. "I think I lost his proposal."

"Is he going to write about us," Whit asked. "What if Harold hears about this?"

Washington rolled his eyes. "About what? Three guys nobody's ever heard of who work together having dinner? Stop the presses. Anyway, don't worry, he never writes about anybody who dresses like you."

Fearing that Whit was becoming isolated, Russell took the black linen sleeve of Washington's Versace jacket between his fingers and said, "Speaking of dress, did they let you wear clothes like this up at Harvard? Didn't they teach you about oxford cloth and tweed?"

"They tried. And I tried to teach them how to dance."

"Obviously a standoff."

"Yeah, but we always had girls from Brown to console us," Washington countered. "They used to cruise up from Providence just desperate for real male companionship."

"You were welcome to most of them," Russell said.

"Very chivalrous of you."

When Washington excused himself, Russell leaned closer to Whitlock. "Listen, on top of everything else we've talked about, I can promise you one percent of equity if the deal goes through and a flat hundred thousand if it doesn't. I'm making it real easy for you, Whit. You're getting a free ride."

"It doesn't feel easy."

But as dinner progressed, Whitlock relaxed. He warmed to the role of innocent abroad, refusing to take his surroundings for granted, complaining about the brightness of the light and the delicate size of the portions. He kept asking the waitress for a pair of sunglasses and an electron microscope; for dessert he facetiously requested three and a half grams of sorbet. But he snapped to attention and earnestly pumped the hand of Julian Heath when the elegant, distracted owner of the restaurant came over to say hello. Whitlock understood, despite his relative social innocence, that the owner of a fashionable restaurant was a personage whose importance was roughly equivalent to that of a magazine editor, a symphony conductor or a painter with a one-man show at the Whitney, although as it happened this one wished to be known for his sculpture and bitterly resented having to be civil to sculptors and painters who did not own restaurants, as well as filmmakers, rock stars, novelists and the fashion lemmings who followed them around. Doing a restaurant was something Heath had backed into, practically, a way of paying the rent until his sculpture took off, but now the place he'd opened a few years back for the SoHo art crowd had become so successful that he was stuck with it, stuck with a five-year lease and the label of restaurateur. This, his second restaurant, was even hotter than the first. It didn't seem fair to him: if it had failed he'd have been in his studio right now hammering steel instead of stopping here to schmooze with Washington Lee, though Washington was okay, he had spent a lot of money in Julian's restaurants, was good-looking and amusing and a spade to boot, and he usually brought the same kind of people with him—at least until tonight. It was policy at the restaurant to hide the suits in the back corner. What the hell was this crew doing at the front booth?

"Okay, okay," Whitlock said as Heath escaped, having succeeded in igniting small fires of self-satisfaction in the breasts of the three publishing colleagues. "I surrender. Order champagne. You knew I'd say yes, so let's get it over with."

23

The buzz enters through his lungs and spreads like an electric current
into the bloodstream, passes Go and collects two million dollars, rockets
up the spine, deposits it at the back of the skull, where it explodes in a
burst of white phosphorescence—that prickly feeling in the scalp is what
it feels like to step onstage in front of the screaming people, plugged into
the main source, tapping into power absolute and burning with that pure,
white light. . . .

But the light fades. The light always fades, the buzz modulating into
raspy static; the tingle that started on the inside of his skull has moved
deep into the folds of his brain. Ace leaned back and rubbed his head
against the wall as if that might soothe the sudden itch—a fiery, sub-
cutaneous rash which must at all costs be scratched.

Holding a blackened glass pipe, he was sitting on a warped linoleum
floor in a room with five other people, three men and two women. There
was an old bathtub in the middle of the room, painted green long before
and flaking now, filled with soda and beer cans, cigarette butts, plastic
wrappers, glass vials and organic refuse. From within came the rustle of
paper, sounds of scratching and mastication. Claws.

Oh, *man*, he thought. *Ugly*.

At one end of the dim, narrow room, a fat man in a distended Billy
Idol T-shirt perched on a tall chrome stool that appeared to have been
uprooted from an old luncheonette, filling the doorway with his bulk.
At the other end of the room was a second, closed door. The steel had
been crudely blowtorched at chest level and fitted with a sliding panel.
Behind the door a sweating homeboy huddled like an astronaut inside

an armored capsule, a former bedroom also paneled in steel; a shoulder-wide triple-bolted steel hatch opened to a hole punched through the brick wall of the adjoining tenement, providing a handy escape route.

Two brothers in fishnet shirts slouched in the corner, looking psychotic—Ace glanced away real quick, lest they think he was dissing them. A white boy gazed longingly at the oracular glass pipe in his hand; in his football jersey he looked as if he'd just driven in from the suburbs, a boy who was going to be late for geography class the next day. After staring for several minutes at the blackened, empty tube, he stood up, tacked over to the rear door and, with all the dignity he could muster, knocked on the little steel panel. The panel slid back and a voice barked, "Yeah?"

"You take checks?"

"Get out my face, Jack."

The panel slammed shut. The boy slumped back against the wall with his hands over his face.

Ace could relate to that, having just finished his last, having run through forty bucks. Six left, which was as good as nothing, unless he split a dime with one of these disgusting dope fiends. Looking down at his feet he wondered what anybody might pay for a pair of reasonably new high-top Ponys.

The sounds coming from the bathtub were really getting under his skin. Was he imagining it, or was there really a rat or some other beast in there? Either way it was nasty. He glanced at the foot of the bathtub, a claw wrapped around a ball, squeezing the ball, crushing the life out of the poor helpless fucking ball.

A skinny white girl with raccoon eyes crawled over in Ace's direction. "I'll do you for twenty," she said.

Ace shook his head carefully, economically, not wanting to feel it coming loose from his neck.

"Ten."

"Fuck off," he said, the head-shaking having proved painful, trying to think how he could score. Last thing he didn't need was no trip to no oval office, anyways.

She crawled over to the fat man at the door. "How 'bout you?"

"I'm working," he said.

Looking up at his overstuffed rock star T-shirt, she said, "I spent three days with Billy Idol in Nassau." She'd said this several times already in Ace's hearing. It was definitely the high point of her life, getting done by Billy Idol, even though it was a total lie for sure.

"Yeah?" said the fat man. "He came into this bar where my cousin used to work at. Drank vodka and tonic."

"That's what he drinks," the girl said with solemn conviction.

"He just walked in, you know, like he could be anybody, and just kind of sat down. You know?"

"That's what he's like," the girl said.

They meditated silently for a moment on their separate, coincident visions of Billy Idol, she sprawled on the floor and he perched on the stool that had every right to collapse underneath him, while Ace tried to figure how to get some money to scratch this maddening itch.

"What's your cousin, a bartender?"

"Dishwasher. But he got fired."

"Oh, that's too bad."

Ace wanted to scream. Either he was completely losing his mind, or he had heard this conversation twenty minutes before, or maybe it was the day before. Maybe it was some other fun couple.

"Listen, I'll do you real good for twenty bucks."

"You already did me for ten, you stupid slut."

"I did? When?"

Nodding toward the bathtub, the fat man said, "Catch that rat I'll give you ten bucks. But you got to do it with your hands. And kill it," he added, his eyes disappearing into the fat horizontals of his face as he smiled.

The girl crawled gamely for the bathtub.

Seeing in her desperation an acute version of his own, Ace was suddenly overcome with disgust. The buzz was gone, replaced by an insatiable void. He stood up and lurched past the fat man and down the stairs. On the way out he passed a ravaged cowboy staggering on the staircase, carrying in his arms a VCR wrapped up in its own outlet cords, looking down at his burden warily, as if it were a roped calf that might suddenly explode into motion.

In the open air, the dead buzz sputtered into a rage that hissed and crackled within the clouds of his brain, like an incipient lightning bolt ready to blast the highest object on the landscape. But nothing was moving on Avenue D, except for Ace and the bugs under his skin. He told himself they weren't really there; last time he binged, he ripped his arms all up trying to scratch them out.

It was dark, probably early morning; he'd traded his Swatch for a vial hours before. Couldn't even get a scam going at this time of night.

Spotting a seriously fucked-up white man in a tuxedo shambling toward him, he considered rolling the guy, though as the dude approached his height began to look formidable. Ace was still considering a move when he recognized Corrine's friend, the writer. All things considered, Ace decided to appeal formally.

"Hey, man, met you up to Corrine's place. You shouldn't be wandering around down here, not this time of night."

Jeff stared down on him. "Is that a threat?"

"No, man, no way." Though the tall man could hardly stand up, Ace sensed a reckless menace in the dark, glassy stare. He shuffled off again before Ace had found the words to hit him up for money.

Ace didn't want to cope with the shantytown hustlers, so he headed for an empty lot over on 3rd Street, then ducked through a hole in the wire-mesh fence and plunged through the garbage toward the back of the lot. Something was moving in the brush against the building back there, like a flashback to the fucking bathtub with the rat—or maybe it was somebody else crashing out in his spot. He kicked a piece of plywood experimentally and it seemed to explode. A snarling fur coat materialized from the mess—a big spotted cat, which rocketed over the debris and disappeared through the hole in the fence.

Astonishment and fear soon modulated to economic speculation. If he'd been quicker he might have picked something up and whacked the fucker over the head. Hey, somebody'd pay thirty, forty dollars for the skin, easy.

24

Harold Stone received the news in Washington, D.C. He was at National Airport, on his way back to New York after lunching with a senator who wanted to do a book. The lamb chops in the Senate dining room were better than the proposal: confessions of a reformed liberal, a genre stretching back at least to St. Augustine, which had enjoyed a spectacular revival in the past seven or eight years, during which time liberals had had nothing much to do except reform and write books about the process. Still, he might have to publish it, Harold had decided, if only as part of a publishing gestalt that kept the channels of information and power open between Washington and New York and Cambridge. The senator's book would lose money, but it might pay off in other ways, although Harold would have felt better about the proposition if this self-professed statesman had not looked baffled at a conversational reference to Metternich.

With fifteen minutes until the next shuttle departure, he called the office, wondering as he punched the number what he was going to do about Carlton, who had outlived her bloom as a lover but remained his assistant. The relationship would continue on for a while, lingering like a patient on life support, but essentially it was over. Probably he would have to promote her to get rid of her, shuffle her off to another floor or at least to the other side of the eighth. Of course, some were gracious enough to seek employment elsewhere, and he was always good for a reference. But the last, Judy Setsenbaum, had made noises about legal action and they'd had to kick her upstairs at a substantial increase in salary, which prompted Kleinfeld, the little bastard, to lecture him about shitting where he ate.

He was remembering what Judy Setsenbaum looked like, when he finally connected with Carlton.

"Harold," she said. "I've been trying—"

Kleinfeld was suddenly on the line. "Harold, your goddamn little protégés down the hall have put the goddamn company into play. They've got six percent of the stock. They filed a Thirteen-D today. The little pricks are trying to buy our asses out."

"Who is?" As astonishing as this sounded, Harold couldn't help wondering how a man who barely cleared the dashboard of his Mercedes could be so free with the diminutives.

"Calloway, Washington and Whitlock."

"Whitlock? Jesus."

"That's right, they got our CFO. But Calloway's the ringleader."

"They're *kids*, for Christ's sake."

"Tell it to their bankers, Harold. They've got Bernie Melman and probably Drexel behind them. Can you fucking believe this?"

"I'm just getting on the shuttle. Where's Corbin?"

"He's fishing in Belize or some goddamn place. We're trying to find him."

By the time Harold got to the office the young conspirators had gone home.

"First thing, we'll have their offices cleared and locked," Kleinfeld said. "If they have the balls to show up tomorrow morning they'll find themselves shut out. I called security and made sure they didn't take anything out but the clothes on their backs. If I had my way, they'd have walked out naked."

"I'm sure they already have whatever they need, Jerry. They didn't hatch this up yesterday over lunch."

They were in Kleinfeld's office surrounded by pictures of his famous friends. Of the less recognizable faces Harold had always suspected that one or two were probably mobsters.

"I warn you now, I'm not going to let this happen," Kleinfeld said, as if he suspected Harold's determination. Hours after he had first heard the news he was still deranged and bitter, like a man who has just discovered his wife's infidelity. "Can you believe what Calloway said to me this afternoon? He says, 'Nothing personal.' I told him, 'You better believe it's personal, you little cocksucker. Before this is over I'm going to *personally* fucking demolish you.' "

"How'd they get to Bernie Melman, anyway?" In recent years Harold had devoted much effort to studying the ways of a system he'd made his reputation knocking, and he was well aware of Melman's position and power.

"How the fuck do I know? Maybe they met him at Le Cirque."

"Do we pay them enough to eat at Le Cirque?"

"Nobody *pays* for anything anymore, that's the fucking problem. They're totally leveraged. Bridge loans, junk bonds, whatever. The money's out there. Money's cheap. The banks used to be like convent girls, you couldn't get a feel without a marriage license. Then Drexel started to practically give it away, and now they've all got red lights on over the door."

Harold was weary of Kleinfeld's simpleminded, ahistorical views on capitalism, not to mention his proclivity for carnal similes. He had long before concluded that if figures of speech based on sports and fornication were suddenly banned, American corporate communication would be reduced to pure mathematics.

Partly out of strategic habit and partly to meditate, Harold looked out the window and let the silence build, absently calculating the span of Kleinfeld's patience. Through a window across the street he watched the fat hindsection of a woman in a babushka pushing a vacuum—Eastern European, probably Polish. He thought of Isaac Babel, Victor Propp's putative forebear, shot by Bolsheviks; wondered how as a young Stalinist he had been able to wish away all those brutal facts, though even in his youthful folly he felt superior to the Kleinfelds of the world, who'd never possessed the imagination to be that callow. While Harold was sitting in Greenwich Village cafés prepping for the revolution, Kleinfeld was schlepping around the Midwest with a trunkful of books as a college rep. Theirs had been an uneasy alliance, since Kleinfeld came in as publisher to stanch the company's chronic hemorrhage of cash. But the former marketing manager and the former radical intellectual wunderkind had managed to accommodate each other. Now they would have to strengthen the alliance.

"I don't think we need to panic," Harold said finally. "If they can raise fifty we can raise a hundred. To these fresh-faced world-beaters like Russell, everything's ad hoc. They don't see that this is a city of nets— if you don't know the ropes you're likely to trip."

"Yeah, yeah. All I know is they're halfway there already, Harold. They didn't storm the Bastille—they called Bernie Melman."

"So we hire Wasserstein and Perella at First Boston."

"How about the Gambino family?"

"Careful," Harold said, absently putting a finger to his lips, half of his attention focused on the Carlton situation. A student of history, of Gibbon and Carlyle and for that matter of Ecclesiastes, he could already see that this, too, would pass. Somehow he knew they weren't going to lose the company.

Kleinfeld, in his taut corporate commando mode, spun his head in both directions in a gesture of reconnaissance. "You think they bugged the place?"

"Don't be ridiculous, Jerry." Harold hated using Kleinfeld's first name, but sometimes it was unavoidable. "I meant, in general let's be circumspect. But no, I don't think electronic surveillance is exactly Calloway's style. Whitlock's the biggest problem. Does he have an employment contract? We can throw a bunch of legal motions at him straight off about violating the terms of his contract. We'll bury them in motions."

"I'm surprised at Washington. I thought he'd be savvy enough to come to us first looking for a better offer."

"Well, maybe we should go to him."

Harold nodded thoughtfully, appreciating for the first time how useful his colleague, basically a street fighter, might be in this kind of battle.

They talked about lawyers and investment bankers for another half-hour. Between them they were acquainted with many of the best in the city, and this knowledge calmed both of them. The lawyer who had invented the poison-pill defense against hostile takeovers was a lunch partner of Jerry's. They put together a list of calls for Carlton, who was waiting eagerly outside Harold's office when the two men emerged.

"Are you going to the Whitney tonight," Kleinfeld asked.

"I don't know," Harold said, for Carlton's ears, because he really didn't want to take her along. Tonight he felt like being with the grown-ups.

"I just can't believe those guys," Carlton whined, putting a hand on

Harold's shoulder after Kleinfeld was gone. "I mean, who do they think they are?"

"Oh, do shut up," Harold said.

"The Whitney Biennial is a periodic attempt to irritate everyone in the art world and confuse those outside of it," Victor Propp announced to Juan Baptiste—hoping to be quoted, the two of them swaying like buoys as the crowd surged around them in the museum lobby.

The show had been open for a month, but the publishing world was only now taking it in, at a party hosted by *The New York Review of Books*. Everyone was talking about the video installations, the basketballs-floating-in-the-aquarium, and the photo collages done by a pair of twins, the *new* new work framed between familiar names, and speculating about whether the de Koonings were "appropriations" or outright forgeries, which would at least have invested them with novelty.

Up on the third floor, Russell was mesmerized in front of a painting that consisted entirely of obscene words stenciled at different angles across the canvas. He was fascinated because the "artist" had submitted a novel to him a year or two before, a thriller set in Berlin in the thirties. "And now here he is in the Whitney?" he complained to Corrine. "Pull a few words—granted, colorful words—out of your manuscript, paint them on a canvas, and bingo, you're a famous painter."

"It's kind of funny," Corrine said.

"It's scary, is what it is. And you're a philistine if you say so. *Look* at these people."

"Shhh."

"Ever since the twenties nobody wants to be one of the boors who booed Stravinsky or Duchamp. That's the great legacy of modernism—the fear of being a rube."

"Calm down," she said, though she could see he was having a good time in his own fashion, working off the anxiety of the day.

She reached over and straightened his black bow tie, tucking it under the wing collar of his shirt. "If you're going to be a captain of the publishing industry you've got to look the part." She was immediately sorry she'd said anything; Russell's posture became rigid again as he remembered after a few moments of amnesia everything that had been making him intolerably anxious over the last few weeks. She could see that he was expecting someone to come up and acknowledge today's announcement of intent to buy the company, the stock running up three and a half points. The night before, he'd been unable to sleep. She had tried to talk him out of proceeding, but now that it was too late to turn back she just wanted him to relax.

The perennially single Nancy Tanner swam into their vicinity, kissing Russell, tossing her head in such a way as to lash the man behind her with her abundant blond hair.

"Isn't that Johnny Moniker," she asked, "over there by the Julian Schnabel? I'm dying to meet him, I haven't had a date in weeks. Ever since I quit drinking I can actually *see* these mutts I meet at midnight and it's so—"

"I quit drinking too," Corrine said.

"Oh, yeah? Which meeting do you go to?"

"I, uh, I don't actually go to meetings. I just quit."

"You're not in the program?" She looked at Corrine as if she weren't sure it counted if you quit on your own. "I go to the one in the basement at this church over between Park and Madison, it's really cool. You've got to come. The guys are to die for."

Russell had drifted away; when Corrine caught up with him he was standing in front of a huge color photograph of a group that looked as if it might be IBM's board of directors.

"You know," he said, "I really think we should consider buying some photographs."

"I think you're really silly." Ever since he'd contemplated the purchase of a seventy-million-dollar company Russell had been acting like a man undaunted by lesser purchases. Contemplating these negative millions, he had become very chummy with the four- and five-digit numbers. The week before, he'd proposed they take a summer house in Southampton that went for ten thousand a month, when, as far as she knew, they didn't have a liquid nickel. "Anyway, I came to give you a Harold alert. Recent sighting in the vicinity."

"Where?"

"Over by the wire sculpture."

"Maybe I should get this over with."

"Maybe we should just get out of here. We're going to be late for dinner."

Moving with the prevailing tide, they had almost reached the elevator when a cross-current brought Harold and Carlton within inches of them, Harold suddenly so close that Russell could smell his breath, his eyes as they focused on Russell's like talons sinking into flesh, filling the younger man with fear and shame. If the contest between them had been an ancient dispute over leadership of the clan, Russell might have lost it in that moment, facing the older chieftain. He would have turned and fled into the woods beyond the circle of firelight.

"I'm surprised you'd show yourself in public," Carlton said, breaking the spell.

"I don't think Russell has anything to be ashamed of," Corrine said. "After all Harold's done for you."

"It's not personal, Carlton," Russell said, avoiding Harold's eyes. "Some of us keep the lines between our personal and our business lives quite distinct, actually."

Carlton threw her glass of wine in his face, dousing several bystanders in the process. Temporarily blinded, Russell felt Corrine tug him toward the elevator.

The next morning's *New York Times* noted the bid in a short item in the business section: "Melman Group in Hostile Bid for Publisher."

That same morning, aboard a fifty-four-foot Bertram sportfisherman several miles off Costa Rica, Whitney Corbin III was watching bait dance from the outriggers on the turquoise water and dreaming of blue sailfish taildancing at the end of the line, when he received a call on the radiophone.

At first he was filled with indignation at the idea that a bunch of kids would take over the company his grandfather had built up out of thin air. Nevertheless, he told the bait boy to put out the lines and fixed himself a drink. By the time the glass was empty he'd calculated the immediate cash value of his shares on the basis of the current bid and considered the advantages of retirement. New blood might be just the thing for the old house, after all. And this thing with the black people was terribly disheartening. Corbin thought that his grandfather, once a fiery young entrepreneur himself, might agree with him. Harold Stone and Jerry Kleinfeld, holding little stock themselves, were not apt to see these advantages, but the older board members might. If anything, he thought the bid rather too low. As he fixed himself another drink, his indignation rose again at the idea that anyone would try to get the company on the cheap, just because the stock was underperforming lately. Anyone who wanted to buy the Corbin, Dern name had better appreciate that they weren't just picking up some real estate and a back list, goddamnit. The name alone was worth twenty million.

In the meantime, it looked like an auspicious day for sailfish.

Two days after the Whitney benefit, Juan Baptiste took note of related events in the society column of a leading tabloid:

Arguments about the merits of the art on the walls at the *New York Review* snore—yes, at the Whitney!—were overshadowed by a real-life brawl. The fur—and the wine—started flying in earnest when hotshot young editor RUSSELL CALLOWAY bumped into Corbin, Dern publishing czar HAROLD STONE just hours after the announcement of Calloway's hostile takeover bid for the prestigious publishing firm. Just so you know, Calloway's being backed by BERNIE MELMAN, the diminutive billionaire corporate raider.

Encountering young Calloway and his lovely wife, CORRINE, as they admired the much-discussed BRUCE WEBER photo-collage, Stone threw a glass of red wine at his former protégé as *tout le monde* looked on in horror. Who says literature is dull? Certainly not *moi*. The glamorous young Calloways retreated after an exchange of remarks too spicy for a family newspaper, Russell's tuxedo and wife Corrine's CALVIN KLEIN strapless somewhat wetter for the wear. And you wonder why the beautiful people wear black? Stay tuned —this is clearly a story destined to overflow the staid columns of the business pages.

25

After Jeff failed to appear for a dinner party one Friday night, Russell went to look for him the next morning. He waited till eleven, took the subway downtown, got off at Astor Place and lingered over the would-be merchandise spread out on the sidewalks—an extensive selection of unwanted books, records, magazines, clothes, household appliances and unidentified objects including a nearly complete set of *TV Guides* for the year 1984.

"Who buys those," Russell asked.

"Collectors," said the proprietor of this display, squatting on the sidewalk smoking a joint.

"People collect them?"

The vendor sucked a final hit out of the roach and snubbed it out between his fingers. "Shit, I hope so."

Down the Bowery, near Corrine's mission, an army in uniform black leathers occupied the sidewalk in front of CBGB, armed with beer cans and jagged haircuts, temporarily displacing the winos.

It was nearly noon when he arrived at Jeff's loft on Great Jones Street and pressed the button labeled "Sweetness & Lite, Inc.," among the cluster of jury-rigged buzzers beside the door. He rang several times. Eventually Jeff projected himself horizontally from a third-floor window—a disheveled gargoyle. Not so shortly after he disappeared, Russell was buzzed in.

The elevator was a relic from the Industrial Revolution. It made you wonder how the machines had won, Jeff said; it also made you nostalgic for stairs. Russell uncaged himself on the third floor and knocked on the door. Taped at eye level was an old cookie fortune: "You will attract cultivated and artistic people to your home."

Hair akimbo, white limbs comically overflowing the apertures of a black kimono, Jeff eventually held the door open.

"We're going to the baths," Russell said, his voice echoing in the sepulchral space.

Jeff rubbed his eyes with a droopy sleeve. "I don't actually *feel* like going to the baths."

"Why not?"

"Call me hydrophobic."

"It's been months. Come on, it'll wake you up. What are you going to do, go back to bed?"

"Why should I go to the baths if I don't want to?"

"Because I'm asking."

Jeff surveyed the immediate area like a man who has awoken into strange surroundings. Sighing, he said, "All right," and shuffled off to the bathroom.

The open floor of the loft suggested a campground recently worked over by bears. Just beyond the kitchen was a long picnic table with benches. Cans, bottles, butts and the odd shred of clothing were visible on the wide plank floor; at the far end a wrecked bed. Leaning against the wall was a life-sized painting of a man in a suit, frozen in a racked, unnatural posture suggestive of a falling heart-attack or gunshot victim —a picture worth Russell's annual salary. He wandered over to Jeff's work space with vague intentions of spying. A wall of books rose fifteen feet to the ceiling. An amber monitor glowed blankly on the steel fire door that served as Jeff's desk, and Russell took as a hopeful sign the fact that books and paper were piled everywhere, as if in use.

"Okay, let's go," said Jeff, emerging brightly from the bathroom.

"You could sell the painting and endow a maid," Russell suggested.

"I just sold it," Jeff said, "and endowed a lost weekend."

As they started along Great Jones, Jeff pointed to a sign in the window of the building next door: DANGER HOLLOW SIDEWALK. "Now that's a good title," he said. "Sort of confirms the vague suspicion you get wandering the streets. Treacherous surfaces."

"That last would be a good title for your recent *Granta* offering," Russell said. "Treacherous surfaces indeed." Jeff didn't exactly flinch, but neither, for a change, did he have a smart-ass retort.

They walked over to 10th Street, where the old "Russian Baths" sign was still hanging, peeling and faded, a relic encroached upon by incipient art galleries. "The trouble with art," Jeff told Russell, "is the kind of company it attracts. Art tending to be sluttish, inevitably inviting Money up to see its etchings."

They hadn't been to the bathhouse in months; Jeff had wondered if it would still be there. Buildings disappeared overnight in the city, like black rhinos from the African savanna. In the morning only a smoking pile of brick and mortar would be left, the skin and bones; the next day a Pasta Fasta, or a Younique Boutique.

They paid at the door, stashed their keys and wallets in the safe and picked up locker keys. Old men with proud bellies and withered muscles hanging from their limbs strutted between the locker room and the deli counter, slapping their thighs and chests, moving with exaggerated unconcern, speaking through various tongues and accents with the same stagy gruffness, in accordance with the international rules of fraternal male nudity. Jeff and Russell undressed and walked downstairs, wearing beltless green robes and oversized flip-flops. Outside the steam room the masseur pounded a body lying prostrate on a wooden catafalque, obscured beneath a mound of Ivory soap lather. "Hey, boys," bellowed Sidney the masseur, his voice wobbling in the humid air. "Any takers for a wash and a rubdown later?"

"Can't afford you, Sid," said Jeff.

"Be a lot more expensive you end up at the doctor's office with hypertension, or at the shrink for nerves." Sidney believed himself to be engaged in a venerable branch of preventive medicine; indeed, many of his customers seemed to have lived far beyond the biblical threescore and ten, or whatever passed for a natural life span these days.

"You take Blue Cross," asked Jeff, to which the masseur answered:

"I take the long green."

As they stripped to shower Russell glanced at Jeff's arms, unable to see much except that the left was mottled near the crook of his elbow. They plunged into the steam amidst six or seven of the regulars, who fell silent as they entered, appeared to be melting into the wooden benches. The young men were reconnoitered and soon the conversation resumed.

"So the driver of this vehicle is a paraplegic. Doesn't even have a license. He shouldn't have been in that car." This was Abe, a senior citizen with blotchy pink-and-white flesh who was the unofficial patriarch of the steam.

"What happened to the other guy," someone asked.

"What, the bus driver?"

"No, the guy that got hit." There were several grunts of assent, as if many were confused on this point.

"Like I was saying," Abe said, "the paraplegic, who has no business driving that car, he hits the pedestrian, hits him pretty good, and he goes flying across the street. Then he gets run over by the bus."

Abe stood up, doused himself with a bucket of cold water.

"Who got run over by the bus, the paramedic?"

"Paraplegic. That means he's paralyzed."

After a long pause, someone asked, "How'd he get out of the car if he's paralyzed."

Abe groaned. "No, it was the guy he hit that got run over by the bus. The paraplegic was driving."

The steamers fell silent, looking at Abe through the mists to see if there would be a moral, some edifying coda to this story. After a few minutes he started to talk about a Brooklyn school superintendent who was discovered in a closet with an eight-year-old girl. "Said he was playing hide-and-seek."

"How about that panther's been attacking people?" said another, seeking to seize the news initiative.

"Not a panther," snorted Abe. "It's got spots."

"Well, whatever it is. Tiger, leopard, whatever."

The damp, lolling bodies noticeably stiffened and shrank as three burly figures swaggered into the steam room. Where there had been no room on the benches a moment before, a long stretch of empty wood suddenly manifested itself. The new arrivals claimed their territory, the smallest of them sprawling, on the bench while the other two sat formally on either side. The small one resembled a keg of beer with hair. He let out a large, self-satisfied sigh and began to sing a song in Russian. The melody, if any, was obscure, but the audience was rapt, and anyone who might have been thinking about leaving the steam room postponed his departure until the performance was over.

Russell lay back in the breath-tightening steam and found himself thinking about sex with women who weren't his wife. From imagining the Frenchwoman at the museum he found his thoughts sliding concupiscently toward Trina Cox. When the song was over and his body warm he stood up and left the room, and plunged himself into the ice-cold pool outside the door, mortifying the flesh. The organ that would offend, if it could, retreating and shrinking.

"That was Ivan Matlovich," Jeff said, once they had dressed and taken a table at the snack bar. "Emigrated from Odessa seven years ago and made his first million in eighteen months. In Little Russia, over in Brighton Beach, the guy's a legend. Started with protection and extortion rackets, moved into chop shops that strip stolen cars down to their component parts in a matter of hours, eventually branched out into hijacking and gasoline-tax skimming."

Jeff often surprised Russell with these detailed accounts of the back alleys of New York, drawing on what seemed an inexhaustible store of anecdotal lore of the low life. Russell chalked it up to *nostalgie de la boue.*

"These chop shops in Brooklyn, they cut cars up with blowtorches and sell the innards to an auto-parts wholesaler in North Carolina, who eventually sells them back to a Chevy dealership in Queens. The junkie thief gets a hundred and fifty dollars, but through the agency of some loaves-and-fishes kind of economic-miracle deal the parts are worth three times what the vehicle itself is worth. With that kind of math operating it seems amazing that there are any automobiles left intact on the streets. Cars are obviously inefficient, economically nonviable. Sort of like what's happening on Wall Street. Ivan Matlovich being the unpolished version of your new pal Bernard Melman, the well-known corporate chop-shop king."

So there *was* a moral to this story, Russell discovered. "I wanted to tell you," he said.

"But you didn't," Jeff reminded him, sharpening the tip of his cigarette against the lip of an ashtray.

"I couldn't."

"Somebody tied you up and gagged you?"

"More or less. There was a lot at stake here. I couldn't just follow my own inclinations. The whole deal could've gone down the tubes."

"What did you think, I'd call the press? Time was, you would've told me the moment you thought of it. You would have asked me what I thought before you decided what to do."

"Life gets more complicated as we get older, Jeff."

"I liked it better when you just followed your inclinations. Pretty soon, Crash, you're just going to be a job title in a fucking suit."

Not wanting to unscroll his own list of grievances, Russell sipped his coffee.

"Did it occur to you that I have something at stake here, too?"

"Hey—I'm sorry."

"So I get to read about it in the newspapers, like everybody else?"

"I tried to call you before the announcement. You haven't exactly been available recently."

"Washington managed to find me."

"He told you?"

"Let's say he tried to prepare me."

Russell stored this item away while Jeff drained his beer.

"I don't understand why you're doing this. Tell me how Bernie Melman is different from our singing gangster friend Ivan Matlovich."

"Grow up, Jeff."

"I think you're getting old enough for both of us."

"What's your great plan: Shoot smack, die young, stay pretty?"

Russell knew he should pursue this line—that lurid scene in the bathroom still vivid in every particular—but he was afraid of pushing Jeff out of reach, and uncertain of his rights. He didn't know how to weigh Jeff's transgression of the rules of health and clean living against his own betrayal of the adolescent verities of Romantic poetry and rock-and-roll. And for all of the excellent reasons he could muster for not having confided his plans, he recognized the validity of Jeff's complaint. He should have told his best friend. But he'd been faced with two conflicting imperatives, and honoring one trust seemed to entail violating another. What did Kant have to say about a situation like that?

Russell ordered a beer and bummed a cigarette—indirect gestures of comradeship. He hadn't smoked a cigarette in two years. Jeff handed over a Marlboro, lit it from his Bic. Smoking was once one of their shared avocations—endless discussions of sex and literature, wreathed in smoke. When they first met, Jeff was besotted with Joyce, infatuated with Ireland

and Catholicism. Russell, an Irish Catholic from the Midwest come to a rich man's college, secretly wanted to be a preppy from an old family so he could afford to be as careless and cynical as Jeff. They shared a dissatisfaction with their native clay and a belief in the metamorphic agency of literature.

Russell felt high after three drags, groping for articles of truce.

"Have you decided what you're going to read next week at the Y?"

"I thought I might read your recent letter."

"Not one of my best efforts. Written in haste."

"Point taken."

They both puffed, pacifically, on their cigarettes. "Victor's been driving me crazy," Russell said, "calling up to try out passages on me. Reading over the phone."

"And when does he plan on finishing the great masterpiece?"

Russell shrugged, thinking he might well turn the question around. Like alcoholics, blocked writers were always morbidly curious about their peers. It had been more than three years since Jeff finished his first book, and Russell had no idea at all how far he was into his second.

Switching to casual acquaintances and celebrity scandals, they ordered two more beers, abandoning their duel without further comment, on the understanding that old friendships require mutual undeclared acts of amnesty and a certain stoic willingness to bear wounds. They drifted out into the street, the warm viscous air of the early-summer afternoon draining them of ambition. It was a day for drinking beer. They decided to buy a six-pack and shoot pool at Julian's, a ritual that went back to the days before Russell got married, when they had briefly shared Jeff's old apartment on the Bowery after Russell returned from Oxford. Later, after Jeff's book hit, they'd swagger into the pool hall with a gram of coke and play for hours between trips to the bathroom. Straight pool, eight ball, nine ball and cowboy . . . Pool was something he'd picked up from Jeff, who'd grown up with a table in his house, though he pursued the game, Russell believed, for its lowlife ambience and associations.

"Remember when we were broke," Russell said, his memory triggered by the stench of garbage and urine fermenting on First Avenue. "Saturdays we'd sneak up to Corbin, Dern and raid the out boxes for books, haul them to the Strand. Twenty-five cents on the dollar, some days it seemed like a fucking fortune."

"Talk about raiding—now you've *really* figured out a way to rip them off." He paused. "Not that I didn't do pretty well myself."

The sense that life was changing rapidly and his chagrin at failing Jeff combined to make Russell nostalgic; Jeff wasn't quite buying it, though Russell was grateful for his apparent acknowledgment that his agent had extracted ten times what either of them had expected for the second, unwritten book. Walking past the Palladium on 14th, Russell reflected that they'd both done better than they'd had any right to expect, though no better than they'd always believed was their due. Still, he would have supposed it would feel better than this.

26

Sasha Melman and her social secretary were attending to the place cards when Bernie arrived home. He crept up from behind and stood on his toes like a ballerina to kiss his wife's long, cool neck.

"Who is this Washington Lee," she asked, stooping to offer her cheek.

For a moment he was baffled. "Who?"

"That's what I want to know. He's on the guest list, and I certainly didn't put him there."

"He's our extra man," said the social secretary, a corpulent blonde in a caftan. "Mr. Melman suggested him after Cappie Raymond canceled."

"Oh, him. He's an editor."

"Why are we having him?"

"It's business."

"Well, who should I put him next to? Is he old, young?"

"Actually, he's black."

"Really? How interesting," she said, in a bemused tone that seemed to suggest she had more social experience with Tibetans.

"Yes, I thought it might be," Melman said, rather pleased with himself now. And it was just a small dinner party, anyway, not a major event.

"What if I put him next to Minky," she suggested to the secretary. "She's the youngest single girl we've got, and I'm not sure I trust her next to the ambassador after that stunt she pulled in Southampton. . . ."

Greeted at the front door by a tuxedoed attendant, Washington was admitted to a vast entry hall, marble underfoot and ormolu overhead, where he surrendered his umbrella under the suspicious gaze of two security thugs. One did not need to interview them to understand they did not quite approve, securitywise, of young black male guests. A more accommodating attendant bowed him toward the staircase and seemed prepared to carry him up the stairs, if required. Washington managed the ascent under his own power, eventually attaining level ground in what looked very much like a museum—ancient mummies standing at attention with champagne flutes in hand; high walls encrusted with paintings in elaborate gilt frames, each bearing a lozenge or plaque inscribed with artist, title and date. While the paintings in Melman's office were stridently modernist, the domestic collection, like the furnishings, was from earlier centuries—a full-length Sargent portrait of a stern female Bostonian being the painting nearest to the present day.

His hostess disengaged herself from a group of sleek, brightly plumed women, all of whom seemed to have medium-length domes of blond hair. She greeted Washington as if they were old friends. He recognized her from her pictures in W; she recognized him by his color. "How nice to *see* you. Let me introduce you."

She took his elbow, her hand surprisingly large. A legendary beauty, close up Sasha Melman looked, to Washington, rather like something fashioned from a new synthetic, a permanent-press version of the human epidermis. As if she were meant to be seen not in person but in photographs.

Washington had heard of many of the guests, rich and accomplished people who were perfectly willing to deposit a certain amount of credit to his general account simply because he was here among *them*. The Melmans didn't have just *anybody*. Mainly, it seemed to Washington, they had tall, thin women with cleavage and short, pudgy men with leverage. He moved cautiously around the room, which seemed over-furnished with gilt and upholstered antiques, trying not to upend anything, and made a point of drinking far less than he wanted to, lest he find himself engaging in some faux pas. He would have been much happier if he'd known someone. Finally Minky Rijstaefel appeared, breathlessly kissing everyone in the room, in Washington's case actually making contact, and on the *lips* no less, providing a goal for the evening. He'd had his eye on her for a while. If he could just survive this fucking dinner, then he would invite her out later for some *live* fun.

He listened politely while a knot of New York plutocrats made fun of rich Texans: "So Joe Bob says, 'What do you want for Christmas, Sally Sue?' and Sally Sue says, 'Actually, I was thinking this Christmas I'd like a divorce.' And after a long pause Joe Bob says, 'Actually, darling, I wasn't planning on spending *that* much.' " Washington considered telling them the joke about the black Mother Hubbard whose kids all have the same first names, but then Melman took him aside and led him into a book-lined den. On inspection the books proved to be leather-bound collected-works editions of nineteenth-century authors; Washington would not have been surprised if Bernie, who seemed, for a moment, to be examining the collection of titles fondly, had pulled one from its shelf to say, "See, *real* books," to distinguish himself from those home decorators who bought false spines to order.

"Just wanted to tell you I'm glad to have you aboard, right?" he said, but in fact, he also wanted to ask Washington to work as a go-between, one black fellow to another, and find out what it would take to make Donald Parker happy. "Everybody's going to make out on this deal, and we like to start out with goodwill. You know what I'm saying?"

Washington was powerfully inclined to tell Melman to go fuck himself, but he found himself unexpectedly docile here in Melman's own house, in the presence of the artwork and the servants and the Frankenstein wife. Melman himself seemed perfectly at ease with his surroundings while not seeming to belong to them at all. Imagining him as an accountant in New Rochelle made it possible, for a moment, for Washington to be direct: "I can tell you right now, sending me to carry messages is going to piss him right off."

"What, you two don't get along?"

"That's not the problem. I just think that sending your only, uh, black employee would smack of, how you say in English—"

"What is he, prejudiced? Fucking guy screams racism whenever anybody in Harlem catches a fucking cold, and you're telling me he doesn't want to talk to you because you're black? This is bullshit." Bernie rested a hand on Washington's shoulder, winked at him and whispered, as if the preceding tirade had been delivered for hidden microphones of dubious quality. "Look, I know what you're saying. All *I'm* saying is, set up a meeting. Tell Parker I'm a real asshole. Really run me down, say whatever you can think of. Then see if he opens up at all, see if you can find out anything for me in advance, okay."

"I'll see what I can do," Washington said doubtfully, acutely aware of his own capacity for avoiding unpleasant duties but eager to show some goodwill. Meantime, Bernie's arm, draped on his shoulder, required him to stoop as they paced around the room.

At dinner Washington sat at one of four tables, between Minky Rijstaefel and a fat woman whose husband was on the board of the Met. Normally, Minky whispered, really fat people wouldn't be invited to dine at the Melmans', but Bernie was dying to get on the board of the museum. "He's dangling ten million, which was basically what the last seat cost you know who, but what with the bull market he might have to come up with a couple more. . . ."

Having indulged liberally of the Taittinger and the Pétrus, Washington needed to relieve himself; he'd been reluctant to do so when dinner was announced, and now his need had increased, but he couldn't very well leap up from the table between courses. He stayed away from his wine and water glasses and pretended to be interested in the fat lady's discussion of Jean Michel Basquiat and other Afro-American artists. Finally, after he'd eaten the two thin wafers of veal that constituted his main course, he could stand it no longer.

"Are you holding?" Minky whispered in his ear, when he asked to be excused for a moment. Though he wasn't, he suddenly worried that this was precisely what his host and hostess would think, seeing him race to the bathroom before dessert. The wild-eyed Negro drug addict. But he didn't suppose pissing on the Persian carpet would make him outlandishly popular, either.

He shook his head, negative on possession, but Minky gave him a look which, if he was any reader of the feminine countenance, combined skepticism and lust.

Walking stiffly out of the dining room he encountered a tall, bald retainer standing at attention, Jeeves-like, just outside the door.

"Men's room?" he inquired succinctly.

"There is a *rest* room just around the corner, to your left, sir." Carrying a hint of accent, his voice conveyed a firm core of delegated authority, as if he were the majordomo rather than just another flunky.

"Just wanted to steal the fixtures, man."

Rounding the corner, he collided with a body, painfully jarring his bladder and knocking the body, that of a teenaged girl, to the floor.

"I'm sorry," he said, reaching down to take the girl's hand. She was worse than deadweight, giggling and thrashing as he attempted to right her before anyone could witness this. She was, he saw, very drunk.

"Who are *you*?" she demanded, as he held her shoulders and pinned her upright against the wall.

"A guest."

"A. Guest. Nice name. What's the A stand for?" She found this a marvelous joke; he had to hold her as she went limp with laughter.

"Who are you?"

"C. Melman. The C stands for 'Caroline.' Or . . ." The thought was so hilarious that she was unable to complete it. Something slipped off her wrist; she reached down and picked up her watch, rocking back on her heels and nearly tipping over backward as she righted herself. She held up the watch, a Cartier Panther, the clasp of which had broken in their collision. "Ten-thirty curfew. Three minutes to spare."

"Congratulations. Now, if you'll excuse me," he explained, "I've got to, uh, go to the restroom."

"Me too."

"Not with me."

"Can go by yourself s'long's you promise come back."

They were alone in the hallway, but it seemed likely that at any moment one of the slaves would march into view and witness this sordid scene, in which he was implicated.

In the bathroom, he took his time, hoping she would stumble off down one of the endless corridors. There was much to occupy his attention; a set of Jasper Johns prints, gold-plated fixtures, toilet paper neatly folded at the end to point, hotel style. He yanked on the roll gratuitously, vowing to come back later and check up on the housekeeping.

The girl was still leaning against the wall where he had left her. "I'm, like, a little dizzy," she admitted. "I think I better lie down for a little while, I'm feeling a little . . . Will you walk me to my room?"

"I better get back to the grown-ups." Watching her, he began to feel dizzy himself.

"I want to show you something," she said archly.

He waved and started to leave, but she leaped across the hall and seized his arm.

"Okay, I'll come with you," she proposed. "Say night-night to Dad and dear old Stepmother."

Washington wasn't about to reenter the dining room with his host's drunken daughter draped all over him. Innocence was no longer the issue.

Giggling, she raised her eyebrows luridly, an operation that seemed to disorient her. She collapsed into his arms, dropping her watch on the floor. "Let's go see Dad and the dyke," she suggested dreamily.

He bent down to retrieve the brilliant timepiece, known in certain circles as the mistress watch, lowering himself slowly while supporting her weight on his shoulder. "Have you got a pocket?" She shook her head many more times than was necessary.

"You hold for me. Hold me."

"Why don't you just go upstairs to your room," he suggested desperately, stashing the watch for the moment in his jacket pocket.

"Take me."

Suddenly another Jeeves impersonator appeared from around the corner. "Is everything all right?"

"I think Ms. Melman needs to go to her room," Washington said innocently.

"You promised a bedtime story," Caroline whined, as Washington attempted to hand her off to the butler.

"Thanks very much," he said to Jeeves, who viewed him coldly, after they had broken Caroline Melman's grip on Washington's neck and transferred her to the butler's arms.

Washington's instincts, as opposed to his reason, dictated flight. Though he hadn't done anything wrong, the ancient wisdom of his race told him that he'd be blamed, and perhaps in anticipation, he felt guilty. He didn't think he could deal with the fallout, the explanations, the stiffs back there in the dining room.

Rapidly descending a staircase intended for grand, cinematic entrances and exits rather than tawdry escapes, he attained the marble entry hall, and thought he was home free, until he saw the two bodyguards huddled in consultation with the majordomo who had first steered him, so disastrously, toward the bathroom. All three of them turned to regard him as he descended. He tried to suppress the feeling of guilty terror that spread from his brain to his face, to convince himself he was guilty of nothing worse than a breach of manners in leaving without a formal farewell—etiquette not being an area in which the domestic staff had any enforceable authority. Attempting to summon a little hauteur for these underlings—*My umbrella, man, the hundred-and-fifty-dollar stick from Sulka with the burled malacca crook, thank you so much.* Under the evil eyes of the bodyguards, Washington felt the righteous indignation of the holy innocent: How *dare* you even *think* of harassing one of Mr. Melman's guests, in violation of the most fundamental precepts of hospitality? Patting down his pockets, reflexively, to demonstrate that he had not in fact unscrewed and pocketed the eighteen-carat-gold bathroom fixtures, he felt a suspicious lump in his jacket and realized with maximum horror that he was in possession of his host's daughter's ten-thousand-dollar gold watch. His hands and knees began to shake as he approached the vigilant triumvirate stationed between him and the front door.

Lurching like a drunk in his terror, he nearly collapsed on the pale peach runner stretched between door and stairs. To minimize the potential for further indignity, he scooped the watch from his pocket and handed it to the bald man, muttered something about finding it on the carpet and fled into the welcoming night.

27

By show time the house was nearly, if heterogeneously, full: students in blue jeans and practical cottons surreptitiously studied the downtown aesthetes in black leather, who were unhappy to find themselves among so many suits, those hip real estate lawyers and media execs who hadn't had time to change after work, including one young free-lance social critic in blue pinstripes who stood in the ticket line and complained, "This place is full of yuppies." There were also widows who lived on Sutton Place and in Bar Harbor who came to all of the readings and contributed generously to the support of poetry magazines and experimental theaters; gaunt twenty-two-year-olds who worked at bookstores and publishing houses and ad agencies when not laboring on their first novels. Harold Stone was here—with one of the young literature students—as were the chiefs of half a dozen publishing houses and magazines. The press was present to verify the reality of the occasion. Juan Baptiste, happily settled into his uptown gossip column in one of the tabloids; a stringer from the Cleveland *Plain Dealer*; a feature writer from the *Times*.

Defying the summer heat, a man in a giant hooded green parka was camped out amidst a sprawl of books, papers and bags in the front row. A correspondent of Victor Propp's, he possessed a complete collection of the author's periodical publications and many related and marginal materials, stacked in cardboard boxes inside his tiny walk-up apartment in Jamaica, Queens. Others with a similarly hungry if less proprietorial air loitered in the aisles—those wild-eyed men and women who haunt literary events hoping to receive some impossible, healing message from the laureate, the wise man in whose words they have discovered the unique private significance, or whose words they may not have read yet but fully intend to, in the meantime seeking a sign—a word, a blessing, the telephone number of a good agent. Bernie Melman arrived late, with Sasha towering blondly at his side, along with two of his bodyguards, and took his reserved seat in the front row beside the man with the green parka, who defensively rearranged his own empire of paper.

Russell had primed the pump by inducing a friendly journalist to write a short piece titled "Who the Hell Is Victor Propp?" for the front section of *New York* magazine. Bernie Melman's wife had planned a "little supper" at their home after the reading, which the *Post*'s society column had that morning declared the "hottest invite in town."

Russell and Corrine were waiting backstage with Victor and his companion, Camille Donner, a celebrated lover of litterateurs. A thirtyish beauty with famous red hair, she had lived with two other novelists before moving in with Propp. In addition to her amuletic function, she attended to the quotidian details of life, which Victor found impossible, serving as housekeeper, secretary and treasurer—though it was difficult for most observers to envision Camille with a mop in her hands. She, too, was said to be writing a novel. Harold Stone had introduced her to Russell years before at a publication party; as she looked through him, his body at that time having the low-density, transparent quality common to editorial assistants and others of negligible position, she had nevertheless taken the time to ask him who he thought was the best novelist in America. When, partly out of a young man's desire to purvey unconventional opinions, Russell had proposed dark horse Victor Propp, she'd been surprised enough to focus her green eyes on her interlocutor for a moment and size up his conviction. "Who," she'd asked, scribbling a mental note to double-check this seemingly eccentric opinion with higher authorities. Pleased to have captured her attention, Russell had ardently described the work of his cultishly obscure hero while trying to cope with waves of mind-scrambling lust—a conversation that he doubted she would wish to be reminded of, and that he had never mentioned to Victor. Now she stood beside the great man, her lover, serene with the conviction of the beautiful woman who has no need to make strident claims on the notice of any gathering.

Victor was pacing the floor of the hospitality room, increasingly nervous. Only slightly less agitated was Mathilde Fortenbrau, the benevolently schoolmarmish representative of the Y, who began tugging on her steel-gray pigtails at seven forty-five. "Perhaps we should call him again," she murmured over and over. Russell had planned to meet Jeff for a drink downtown first, but when he called to confirm a woman with a Spanish accent had answered and announced he was busy and would come directly to the reading instead.

Corrine tried to reassure Victor about Jeff's reliability. Russell was not so sanguine. He kept meaning to do something or say something, while systematically avoiding the issue of drug abuse even in the privacy of his own mind.

"Frankly, I imagined this bad-boy thing was just a literary persona," Victor protested. "I mean, he comes from a respectable New England family, doesn't he?"

Russell called Jeff's number and shouted at the answering machine, to no avail. Mathilde pulled hard on alternate ponytails, tipping from side to side. "This has never happened before," she said. "Even with Dylan Thomas." Her associates hopped like sparrows between backstage and the auditorium. At eight-twenty everyone agreed there was no choice but to begin without Jeff. Russell offered to give the introduction in his place.

"I can't go out there," Victor insisted. "I'm not going to make a fool of myself." His long forehead creasing with worry, he plucked at the hairs in his beard.

"John Berryman called from a bar on Third Avenue a few minutes before he was scheduled to read," Mathilde recalled. "We sent a delegation to fetch him."

"What should I do?" Propp demanded of Camille, who was sitting browsing through a copy of *TriQuarterly*, rather, it struck Russell, as if shopping through a catalogue for a new companion.

"You'll either have to go on or cancel the reading," she answered sensibly. Her response drove Victor to despair.

Russell massaged his shoulders. "Calm down, Victor. They're your fans," he said. "This isn't really Jeff's crowd."

"I don't have any fans, there are only ten people in the country who *understand* what I'm doing." Victor was nearly in tears. "They've turned out for some kind of freak show, to see the Boo Radley of American letters. . . . I won't even consider going through with this . . . this *disaster*."

Propp ripped himself out from under Russell's grip and ran, bolting out the backstage door through a tunnel that bypassed the auditorium. Russell gave chase and reached the sidewalk in time to see him disappear in a cab.

Moments after the announcement of cancellation, Bernie Melman charmed his way backstage with the assistance of his bodyguards.

"What is this shit?" he barked at Russell. "We're going to pay this asshole . . . how much? and he can't even get up and read out of his own fucking book? Now I've got fifty people coming to my house for dinner, right, to celebrate this fucking calamity. What the hell am I supposed to tell them?"

"Artists are temperamental," Russell offered.

"Well, so am I temperamental. And right now I'm in a real bad temper. Hey, I wonder," he said, turning to the two bodyguards. "Do you think that makes me an artist? Christ, what kind of fucking business is this?"

"Have you met my wife," Russell asked, thrusting Corrine forward in the spirit of throwing oil on raging waters.

"How do you do?" Bernie said, suddenly calm, looking her up and down with an air of thorough appraisal. "I'm very pleased to meet you."

"Russell," Corrine demanded, refusing to play her role, "we've got to find Jeff."

"And this is Camille Donner," Russell said. Camille was more obliging than Corrine, postponing her flight to her lover's side. When Russell and Corrine exited, she was deep in conversation with the tycoon.

"Let's just go down there," Corrine said, when they had returned to their apartment. She'd already called three times.

Russell was not so certain, afraid of what they might find.

"We still have a key," she said. "Don't we?"

"I'll go."

"I'm coming," she said, reaching for the portable phone, pressing the redial button.

"Corrine, there's something you—"

A shriek from Corrine abbreviated this thought.

"Can you believe it, he fell asleep," Corrine said, after she finally hung up, her exasperation leavened with relief. Looking at Corrine, Russell could imagine the justice of the charge she would make when he told her what he'd seen at Minky Rijstaefel's party. The next time Jeff didn't show up somewhere he might not be able to answer the phone. He wanted to tell her, but he couldn't shake the indefensible notion that in his silence he was protecting both of the people he loved best.

The reaction to the nonevent at the Y was curiously mixed and ultimately satisfied those who initially had the most reason to be unhappy. Victor Propp's dusty, enigmatic legend grew immeasurably, burnished with a shiny coat of scandal, while Jeff's performance was in persona. In the absence of an official explanation, the rumors that circulated were much more interesting than any possible response to an actual reading. The two were alleged to have duked it out backstage. The teetotaling Propp was supposed to have passed out in the classic novelist's manner. Many sympathized with the reports of the sensitive artist and recluse, palsied backstage with agoraphobic terror or overcome with stage fright. Others considered the cancellation a deliberate piece of strategy on the part of the notoriously strategic Propp, the nonreading an extension of his policy of nonpublishing. In his new column, Juan Baptiste subscribed to this theory, concluding: "Also a no-show was best-selling novelist JEFF PIERCE, who later in the evening was healthy enough, if not necessarily *compos mentis*, to attend the after-opening party for TONY DUPLEX at Nell's." A week later, in an essay published in a downtown weekly, a fashionable critic was uncharacteristically fulsome in his appreciation of Propp as "the quark and the black hole of contemporary American literature, a nearly theoretical entity whose size and shape and importance can be deduced only partly from visible manifestations," and concluded that "Derrida having made the author obsolete in favor of an endless scrim of *écriture* and intertextuality, Propp apparently means to erase even the text with his long silences, punctuated by glimpses of dazzling prose—the silence itself assuming legendary proportions, the long-unfulfilled promise of the novel, which we register in pieces, like glimpses of flesh beneath a hem, this deferred gratification perhaps the very point of the enterprise."

Victor Propp himself particularly liked this essay, and he carefully clipped it and added it to the heavy leather-bound scrapbook he had purchased in Florence some years before in anticipation of the reviews that would greet his novel, which scrapbook now was nearly filled with articles in anticipation of that blessed event.

28

Jessie Makepeace had always gotten along well with her son-in-law—better, it sometimes seemed to Corrine, than with her older daughter. The first time she and Russell had met they stayed up together half the night in the kitchen in Stockbridge, killing a bottle of vodka while Corrine slept in her old bedroom. Russell said she was ballsy, intending it as a compliment. "Like a house on fire" was the phrase Jessie used to describe their happy conspiracy . . . though as an idiom for amity it seemed pretty inexplicable to Corrine, who could always spare a little worry for the strange lumps embedded in the language, as if, like nodes in the breast, they might bode ill or conceal dangerous truths.

"She was the little girl who always asked why. Used to drive me crazy," Jessie said, rattling the cubes in her drink. " 'Why, why, why' . . . You were the most curious little girl anybody ever did see."

Jessie was sitting cross-legged on the living room floor with her back against the fold-out couch that was her bed when she visited Russell and Corrine in New York. "Drove her teachers crazy, didn't know what to do with her. And when they tested her IQ it went right off the chart."

Why did it seem to Corrine that her mother made this fact sound like a defect, a genetic mutation that had fortunately proved relatively harmless, Corrine having, by general consensus, turned attractive after a homely childhood and having managed to get married? Her mother had been here only ten minutes but already Corrine could feel herself becoming brittle and humorless.

"What's so bad about being curious? Or smart?"

"We're just teasing you, honey," Jessie said, lighting up a Pall Mall.

We? Corrine thought, while Russell went to the kitchen for an ashtray.

"I'm dying to hear your news, Russell," said Jessie. "When's my son-in-law going to take over his own publishing house? Did I tell you we even read about it in our *Berkshire Eagle*? I've got the clipping in my suitcase, remind me."

With his usual enthusiasm Russell was happy to summarize and even embellish recent events in the drama, making it sound like a cross between *High Noon* and *Paradise Lost*: the staggering amounts of money, the night of the wine hurling, capsule biographies of the various contestants.

"I don't think you're being really fair to Harold," Corrine interrupted. "He's done an awful lot for you."

"And I've given a lot back to him, and to the company," Russell said. "Doesn't mean I have to stand by and watch Harold and the others run it into the ground, strangle new ideas and new talent. The question is, What's Harold doing for the shareholders and the reading public?"

Russell's manner of speaking had changed in the last month. Resorting to phrases like "the reading public," he'd gone pontifical, talking about the rights of shareholders and the stagnation of American business. Of course, he'd picked a lot of it up from Bernie Melman and that twit Trina Cox. Corrine had noticed it in some of their college friends—the way they started talking like their jobs. Men more than women. Speech was the early-warning sign, the canary in the mine. Over dinner you're having a perfectly reasonable conversation about art or the sex lives of celebrities and suddenly the word "prioritize" would come out of someone's mouth like a wad of gristle coughed up onto the tablecloth. Educated people started using nouns as verbs—"access" and "impact." The ideas and the politics soon followed. "Say what you want about Reagan, but . . ." Maybe there was something wrong with her, that she hadn't been able to turn into an actual stockbroker with a stockbroker's haircut and wardrobe and way of looking at the world. Some childish recalcitrance. There were days when she almost believed she was doing something useful—helping her people get a decent return on their money. Then she'd go into a sales meeting where they would talk about customers like lambs to the slaughter, to be loaded up with a lot of high-commission packaged junk, and she would realize she actually *was* a sleazebucket.

Russell was explaining the gospel of the LBO to Jessie as though he were reciting the Declaration of Independence.

"And you do this all on borrowed money?" Jessie said with guileless admiration, getting right to the heart of the matter.

Russell winked. "That's the beauty of it. Buy now, pay later."

"You know, I wanted to ask you—now that the house is mine, I've been thinking of taking out a second mortgage."

"There are definite advantages."

Wait a minute, Corrine wanted to scream, who is it that actually *works* in the financial sector in this household? She also wanted to bum a cigarette, two years later. Instead she asked, "Have you talked to Dad since . . . recently."

"We talk through lawyers," Jessie said. "It's more hygienic. Why, has Mr. Second Youth been in touch with you? I didn't think so. Man's got the paternal instincts of a reptile. You know that two hours after you were born he played a round of golf? Did I ever tell you that story, Russell?"

"You look like you could use another drink before we head out," said Russell, who was now aware of the precariousness of Corrine's mood.

"And when I asked him—sure, if we've got time I'd *love* another—I asked him what we should name Corrine, he said, 'It's up to you.' Can you believe that? The proud father. Up to me. Thanks very much."

Corrine stood up and stalked into the bedroom. Just before the door slammed shut behind her she heard her mother ask, "What'd I say."

She knew her father was a neglectful bastard who seemed incapable of love, but she didn't necessarily want to hear it said aloud. It wasn't as if Jessie had been Mother of the Year. Sometimes her childhood seemed to Corrine like one long wound, the recent divorce a knife that had laid the scar wide open again.

She lay facedown on the bed, too angry to realize that she was crying. A few minutes later she heard the door open and felt Russell sit on the bed.

"She doesn't mean to—"

"That's the trouble, she's so goddamn insensitive."

He stroked her hair. "We've got to get going, Corrine."

"You go."

"I don't want to go without you."

"You two, you'll have a great time. She'd rather be with you anyway."

"Corrine . . ." He said this in the adult way that was supposed to recall her to her senses and remind her of her responsibilities. "I don't want to see *Cats* again." He ran his finger behind her ear. "I'm a *dog* person." He was trying to get her to laugh now. "Here I lower my snotty aesthetic standards because your mom wants to go see this furry Muzak-al spectacle, and you won't even come along to ease the burden. What if someone I know sees me going into the theater?"

"Tell them you're thinking of buying it. That won't surprise anyone who knows you."

"Come on, we're going to be late." Impatient now.

"I'm not going."

He exhaled violently, in exasperation. A minute later he rose from the bed. The bedroom door opened and closed, and then a few minutes later the outer door. She heard faint laughter in the hall, the shudder and squeak of cable and pulleys from the adjacent elevator shaft, and then she was alone.

"Always had that temper," Jessie said in the elevator. "When she was good, she was very, very good, but when she was bad she was awful. She'd fall into these black moods for days and then she'd suddenly be so happy you'd want to strangle her. What's with this teetotaler bit, anyway?"

"I don't know, she sure didn't get it from me." Then, feeling disloyal, Russell said, "I think the divorce has been tough on her."

"Hey, tell me about it," Jessie said, taking his arm as they walked past the doorman into the street. "Love your building, but don't you think you kids need a bigger place? Now that you practically own a company."

"Actually, we're just starting to look," Russell said.

"You kids are so lucky. Got the world by the tail, haven't you?"

"Maybe just a little piece of it," Russell said, though he didn't think she was half wrong. If Corrine would just cheer up and get with the program. She was in one of her troughs—her inner barometer down and dropping, like her weight—just when he felt he'd reached the Memorial Day weekend of his own life's calendar. But she just got that way sometimes; her mother was right about that. A year after they moved to New York she'd had a bad spell, and quit law school abruptly. A crisis of conscience or confidence which she'd never been able to articulate. She stayed home watching old movies, sleeping half the day, reading Kierkegaard, eating chocolate ice cream and potato chips, somehow losing weight. The turnaround was gradual, its trigger as inexplicable to Russell as the cause of her depression. One evening when he arrived home she announced, "You know, I've been trying to decide why we need to be physical entities. I mean, why do we have to be in these bodies that half the time don't really feel like they belong to us, anyway, and I finally decided—well, how else am I going to be able to wear all my clothes?" She did not go back to law school; though she had excelled, she hadn't enjoyed it, and Russell encouraged her to do something less stressful, the job at Sotheby's being a sort of educational convalescence.

Corrine kept listening for his return. Surely he would not be able to sit through a play, knowing how insensitive and cruel he'd been, knowing she was back here all alone, as she had always feared she would be ever since the first time her mother in an incomprehensible rage had driven off into the trackless night. For weeks on end Jessie would pack the lunches and read bedtime stories; then suddenly one night she would appear in the bedroom to rip the pictures off the walls and tell Corrine she was a terrible, awful girl, before driving away. The morning after, her father was silent behind the newspaper as she and her sister ate their cereal.

Not only did Russell sit through the play—he took Jessie out for a drink afterward. By the time they returned, Corrine was miserably asleep.

The next morning Russell announced that they were going shopping, with the air of a despot declaring a national holiday. Corrine needed a sexy new bathing suit for the Hamptons, he suggested, and maybe a new summer dress. "And I think I need me an ole Big Daddy white linen suit on account of it being so hot and me being impo'tant, and maybe some nice crocodile loafers, and Jessie will surely find something she just can't live without."

A guest at the breakfast table would have found a mother and daughter almost excessively chummy and affectionate. Russell, who had some experience in this area, was still a little amazed at the way Corrine started in, giving her mother an impromptu neck rub while they exchanged gossip about friends and neighbors back in Stockbridge, clearly more accomplished than Russell at this kind of willful amnesia. The acute critic might have detected some overacting, three people projecting to the last row in the house.

For her part, Corrine woke up repentant, determined to harmonize with her mother and her husband, and in this spirit was able almost immediately to suppress her skepticism about Russell's plan of therapeutic shopping, and about the larger program of which this was a part. She wanted to lighten up; she really did. She had decided to try to be enthusiastic about the Corbin, Dern takeover, and the summer house and everything else, if only on the principle that if her husband was marching over a cliff she didn't particularly want to be left standing alone on a smug precipice.

So they went shopping, strolling over to Madison, beginning at the new Ralph Lauren store, which looked, Russell said, like the world according to Whitney Corbin III, a fantasyland for would-be Anglo-Saxons of all ages, races and creeds. But Russell proved no more immune to the fantasy than dozens of other Saturday shoppers competing for sale items and the attention of clerks, even as he remarked knowingly that everything in the place was plagiarized from Brooks Brothers and Savile Row. With less hesitation than he usually brought to a purchase, as if warming up for bigger things to come, Russell bought the desired loafers with the encouragement of the two women, smart crocodile mocs that looked so expensively casual.

Then they perilously navigated the siren straits of expensive Italian-dressed windows—Pratesi, Valentino, Armani and Versace—Russell yielding again to the tug of desire at Sherry-Lehmann, a habit he had acquired from Harold Stone, purchasing a bottle of Les Amoureuses and a bottle of champagne, which exercise seemed to give him a buzz and sharpen his acquisitive instincts.

The last stop was Bergdorf Goodman, where they immediately—and in Russell's view, predictably—ran into Casey Reynes, who was *thrilled* to see Mrs. Makepeace again and who told them all about the new baby, spreading the pictures out on the perfume counter. From the detailed descriptions of its amazing habits and foibles, Russell thought, one might imagine that it was the first infantus *Homo sapiens*.

"He's quite pale," Russell said, smiling at Casey. "I would've thought he'd have a little more color."

For a moment Casey looked baffled, then went slightly pale herself, scrutinizing Russell's face; but she recovered quickly. "I'm refurbishing my wardrobe after all those months of maternity dressing," she told the women. "Tom told me just to get absolutely whatever I want after what I went through, the sweetie. He's in Minneapolis on a deal."

Russell detected here an implied comparison of husbands and credit limits. "Casey still can't quite believe you can't just pay somebody to carry your child," he sneered after she'd buzzed off to the Chanel boutique to look for a pair of those divine velvet stretch pants.

"She's not so bad," Jessie said.

"What was that about the baby's complexion," Corrine asked.

Corrine bought a couple of Diptyque candles; Russell bought them both perfume, Shalimar for Jessie, and Joy for Corrine. While they were downstairs Corrine thought she might need stockings, and the new Donna Karan black hose had those 1940s seams up the back; but she also needed nude, and Russell said get both. Then Russell insisted that Corrine buy a little black dress by Azzedine Alaïa, though she thought it was just a little too clingy and a lot too expensive for about a half a yard of fabric. Russell said, "Every good girl deserves LBDs," explaining to Jessie, who looked puzzled, that it meant little black dresses, and Jessie said she thought it had something to do with LBOs, and Russell said, not really, but in this case maybe. Corrine dutifully reminded him she hadn't exactly been a *good* girl lately, but once she tried it on she liked it, and as she walked around she began to love it even though it was racier and more *fashiony* than she usually preferred, which was probably what made it exciting, like the Tina Turner wig, like a costume that turned her into a different person, someone sexier than Corrine Calloway.

In the dressing room, she was just unzipping the back when the door opened and Russell slipped in. He ran his finger from her bared shoulder all the way down her arm to her wrist, then lifted up her hand and kissed the wrist and nipped at it with his teeth. When he sucked two of her fingers into his mouth, the inside of her thighs began to tingle and her knees to tremble. She asked where Jessie was and Russell said she'd gone off to look for the ladies' room. "But what about the salesclerk?" she whispered. Then she didn't really care, as Russell pulled the dress away from her shoulders, looking at her with his glassy, dilating blue eyes before he ran his tongue up along her underarm, his legs shaking as she reached for his zipper; she didn't know how he could stand up. In the next booth two women conferred nasally about a skirt, one saying she thought it was too big. It certainly *was* big, Corrine thought, stifling a laugh as he forced her back against the wall . . . and fucked her till she had to bite his shoulder so she wouldn't cry out, although by that time the salesclerk had already inquired twice if anybody was in there, in a tone that made it quite clear she already knew the answer, and the voices in the next dressing room had dropped to scandalized whispers.

29

Summer had come to the city like a youth gang appearing suddenly on the corner: sullen, physical, odorous and exciting, charged up with ungrounded electricity. Anything could happen. There were mirages, heat devils of rumor, an increased susceptibility to soft entertainment and murder.

Escape was on the minds of most residents, but there was a certain caustic pleasure to be had in the melting streets. The viscous air seemed to superconduct sexual currents among a million steaming pedestrians, the blunt glances of languorously interested parties, like the days, lasting longer than in other seasons. Despite signs of plague, the thick reek of renegade lust was in the air; at night married couples and the might-as-well-be-marrieds lay on damp sheets as if precariously balanced, trying not to fall out of love.

By day, business was conducted inside the air-conditioned towers. After they had been locked out of their offices at Corbin, Dern, the Calloway–Whitlock–Lee triumvirate had taken an office on the West Side in the Brill Building. This was called headquarters. The language had become distinctly martial, even as life became more expansive and luxurious. Trina Cox's new firm occupied a suite in Rockefeller Center. Their midtown canteen was '21.' Here, under Trina's supervision, Russell and Whitlock wooed bankers and brokers and shareholders in their new tropical-weight suits. The man whose job it was to stand and welcome customers as they walked in the door greeted them by name now. The bills were charged to the shell company that Bernie had set up to swallow Corbin, Dern. Russell, who had always been careful with his expense account, relished the new prodigality.

Authors were courted downtown at The White Room with Washington, an activity of almost equal importance, since agents were exploiting the situation and neither Russell nor Harold wanted to see writers defecting to the other side. It did not occur to anyone that the men in gray suits might have been happy with the novelty of what they imagined to be the stylishly raffish downtown restaurant or that authors, who as a class are envious of and dependent on the expense accounts of others, might prefer to dine at the more venerable and expensive establishment. Harold Stone, Jerry Kleinfeld and the old management were conducting their own campaign at The Four Seasons, a few blocks east of '21' on 52nd Street. Board members who broke bread with Russell and Whit on Monday frequently dined with Harold and Jerry on Tuesday. Harold abhorred this politicking, but he took some enjoyment from the campaign by making a serious run on the oldest and best bottles in the wine cellar at The Four Seasons. Those authors who were not currently in AA tended to be thrilled when a twenty-year-old bottle of Petrus or Romanée-Conti arrived at the table, and grateful later. And Harold reasoned that if, in spite of this hospitality, he lost the fight for control of the company, the new owners would have to pick up the tab.

Victor Propp, still working on his second book, was among the prizes being contested. He was critically sniffing a honey-colored glass of Montrachet at The Four Seasons one afternoon when Harold Stone said, "I assume we can count on you, Victor. We've had our differences, but I can't believe you . . . Let's face it—Russell's relatively unproven and Bernie Melman is a ruthless philistine, for all his Post-Impressionists."

"He does own a Cézanne I'd dearly love to see."

"How's the book," Harold asked curtly.

"It develops new layers almost seasonally," Victor confessed, sucking through his teeth to aerate the wine. "I've come to think of it as a palimpsest, but not without linear narrative. I even dare to think it could be a contribution to our literature. Of course, I'd like to think that my publisher, whoever that might be, shares my guarded optimism."

"We do. We always have. That's why we have a *contract* with you, Victor."

Propp cited the case of a literary rival who had recently extracted a seven-figure advance from another publisher, which amount struck Victor as an authentic vote of confidence.

"Be realistic, Victor."

"The times have outstripped realism, Harold. Try to cultivate a touch of absurdity. It might help you to catch up. Do you think the Montrachet is a bit acidic?"

Two days later Victor lunched with Russell, Trina and Washington at The White Room.

"Is that a rock-and-roller," he asked about a greasy-haired diner at the next table.

"Hair model," said Washington.

"What's Harold's pitch," Russell asked.

"He gave me a nice lunch."

"What did he offer," Trina asked.

"It was my understanding that he would give me a million to stay with him." Victor put his hand on Trina's thigh in token of something or other. Whatever the attractions of the other side, he clearly liked Russell's investment banker.

"We'll give you a million and a quarter," Trina proposed. "Half cash, half paper."

"Nice high-yield, low-calorie paper," observed Washington.

"Junk bonds? I hardly think so, ladies and gentlemen. I'm a writer, after all, and I daresay I know all about worthless paper."

"It's called risk," Trina said. "Like we're taking with you and your invisible novel."

"I want equity."

"The guy's meshugge," Trina said, turning to Russell. "Where'd you find him?"

Late into the warm weekday nights, Trina, Chip Rockaby and Dave Whitlock huddled in her new office suite in Rockefeller Center, consulting green figures under Russell's anxious gaze, seeking to justify a higher tender offer, in case their first was rejected by the board. Melman checked in by phone, as did Victor Propp, who had no formal role in the takeover but couldn't bear to be left out or, apparently, to face the blank screen of his word processor. Fascinated by the financial arcana, Russell wanted to observe everything, although when Corrine complained about his hours he conveyed—without quite intending to deceive—the sober air of a man weary and burdened by new responsibilities.

For the number crunchers, a spirit of necessary optimism prevailed in calculating future earnings, and the value of the individual divisions on the auction block. The more bullish the projections, the higher the price they could offer. It was essential to look on the bright side, which suited Russell's temperament as well as the times. Prices had been going up for years; what looked expensive today would be cheap by next week. Whitlock was something of a drag in this regard. He kept objecting to rosy prognostications, pointing out the cyclical nature of the business, but Russell was impressed with the manner in which Trina coaxed him along.

It was ten o'clock one summer night when they finally quit. Sustaining energy had become such a habit that Russell knew he wouldn't wind down for hours. He suggested dinner. The lawyers had already gone home. Outside on the sidewalk, Chip decided he was too exhausted to go anywhere. He collapsed into a taxi. Which left the, to Russell's mind, somewhat ungainly troika of Whitlock, Trina and himself.

"Where do you want to go," Trina asked.

"The White Room?"

"It's such a production," Trina said.

Whitlock followed the exchange with interest, sweating eagerly in the heat radiating up from the sidewalk, while Russell groped for a channel of communication to which he wouldn't be tuned.

"I'm pretty beat, anyway," said Trina, glancing ruefully at Russell, who nodded.

"Come on, you guys," Whitlock urged. "Let's grab a bite."

"I should get home," said Russell.

Over Whitlock's protests he flagged a cab for Trina, and kissed her cheek, reading a friendly challenge in her raised eyebrows.

Climbing into another cab, Russell gave his own address. A clouded bulletproof Lexan barrier separated him from the driver, and also from the life-giving air conditioning, which leaked feebly through the tiny holes theoretically allowing him to communicate with the driver—if indeed he spoke English. The presence of the barrier was justified by a perfect circle of logic; steaming in the malodorous backseat, Russell certainly felt the urge to strangle the chilled and insulated cabbie.

He felt himself in the grip of one of those extreme moods that come upon city dwellers, his spirit hemmed in by walls as it was agitated with the static charge of the desperate social and mercenary activity around him. He needed to expel this nervous energy from his body, talk it out or shake it out on, say, a loud, crowded dance floor.

Corrine would be worn-out from her day, perhaps already asleep. Full of schemes, he wanted to talk about the deal that had absorbed all of his attention for weeks. But she was tired of hearing about it. He didn't suppose he blamed her, but she shouldn't blame him. He would settle down again soon enough, but at the moment he wanted to stake a claim on the attention of the larger world, beyond the private realm of his family and friends. If he were to die at this moment, in this miserable steaming coffin of a cab, he would leave nothing behind: he'd published some books, on the sufferance of Harold Stone, most of which would have been published anyway, marginally improving them with his blue pencil. The thought that only his friends, his father and Corrine would miss him made him angry. He had great faith in his own abilities, but he did not have the power to exercise them.

Sometimes he wondered if he had blunted his ambition in marrying so early. Corrine accepted and loved him as he was. By not demanding more of him, perhaps she'd held him back. He had never developed that predatory, competitive edge. Sexual appetite suddenly seemed like a corollary of the will to power and creation; he pictured himself as a housebroken creature, lulled into slippered complacency. Why should he go home, goddamnit, when he didn't feel like it?

Two blocks away from his house, he leaned forward and barked a change of address at the ventilated plexiglass; a few minutes later he was deposited in front of Trina's building, a new luxury tower on Second Avenue. He had dropped her off here a few weeks before. Now he followed a red carpet through a green grove of potted foliage and announced himself to the doorman, who asked, "Is she expecting you."

This routine question discomfited him, implying a certain level of conspiracy in Russell's ostensibly whimsical decision to stop by: the ethical dimension threatening to assert itself.

"Quite possibly," he said.

"I'm so glad you came over," Trina said southernly. "I just couldn't quite handle old Whitlock tonight, but I'm definitely not ready to crash. God, excuse the mess. . . ."

Although the apartment was by no means neat, it was essentially empty. The living room was devoid of furniture except for a single director's chair, a stationary bicycle, and an old Vuitton trunk stacked with magazines, newspapers, annual reports and empty food cartons. A collection of Perrier and Diet Coke bottles nested in a corner outside the open kitchen area. Russell walked over to the picture window, which looked out over the East River to the semiurban sprawl of Queens.

"How long have you lived here?"

"I don't know. A year? Maybe two, actually. I know, I know—I've got to get some furniture. You want to go out somewhere?"

"Sure."

"Or we can have a drink here."

"Okay."

"I think I've got a bottle of Dom some client gave me."

She retrieved the bottle and then looked around for a suitable place to drink it. "The bed's the only real furniture. You don't mind, do you? We can sit in there and be comfortable."

Russell thought it would be priggish to object, two colleagues having a drink. So what if it was the bedroom? The limited decor was gender-neutral—a pair of skis leaning against the wall, a framed poster from the van Gogh show at the Met. They sprawled out on the bed, Russell asking about the financing, the soft-money options of a higher bid.

"So the beta factor," Trina explained, "is the risk factor of a given investment. It's the multiple, beyond the T-bill rate, that you use to calculate the required return on equity. Is this incredibly boring?"

"No, absolutely not."

"I know—I'm like the investment banker from hell. Shut up, Trina, for Christ's sake."

"No, really."

"Well, anyway, a beta of one is the market rate. Oops, little spillage, here." Licking her wet wrist, she said, "A high beta, like two, indicates high risk and a higher required rate of return. See?"

Russell nodded earnestly, grasping a small portion of the concept. A bottle of Möet appeared suddenly on the bedside table. Trina was easy to talk to, and it seemed to him she talked like a man, relating war stories from her days at Silverman, sketching grotesque portraits of her colleagues. He felt more and more relaxed. That Corrine could object to this—sitting around shooting the shit, hanging out, like the guys—was absurd, though he should call her soon. Christ, it was already eleven-thirty. But they were just sitting here, side by side on a piece of furniture that just happened to be a bed.

Even when she twisted over on top of Russell to pour him another glass and kissed him instead, as if merely because she chanced to be in the immediate vicinity—this was harmless enough. Why should anybody object to this pressing together of lips, which felt so good, after all? Why should pleasure be a zero-sum commodity, when the store of it could be so easily expanded, the wealth increased by sharing?

Everything seemed perfectly natural up to a certain point, but eventually, at about the moment that his hand almost inadvertently discovered a breast, his conscience began to awaken from its champagne daze.

"I've got to go," he said, pulling himself free and rolling to the far edge of the queen-sized bed. This attempt at an assertion had a quavering, experimental ring to it; if she'd attacked him at that very moment he might have surrendered.

But instead she simply said, "Are you *sure*?"

In another half-minute he was sure, or at least sufficiently convinced to stand up and say good night.

"Don't tell me you've been faithful to Corrine all these years," she asked, as he was leaving.

Actually, he had, but this confession would sound unbelievable, and slightly shameful, so he merely winked as he waved good-bye. Maybe he was a low-beta kind of guy, after all. In the elevator, plummeting downward, he felt a flutter of guilt. But once he was out of the building in the warm night air, he decided that the salient and final point was that he *hadn't* done anything, and he strode briskly along the avenue toward home.

30

The weather was a leveling element: all seemed equal under its sway, although the homeless proliferated that summer like tropical greenery pressing up through the cracks in the sidewalk, while immigrants camped till long after nightfall on tenement stoops outside purgatorial rooms, playing dominoes and percussive dance music from home on new portable stereos. The only sound that emanated from inside the insulated towers of money was the constant, ubiquitous hum and drip of air conditioning. The wealthy stayed walled inside thermal fortresses, or they went to the beach.

For the first time, the Calloways had taken a house of their own for the summer: a wood-shingled nineteenth-century farmhouse on the edge of a potato field near the ocean. From their bedroom at night they heard the waves, and when on cloudy days the sea was not visible there was the compensation of the sunset, spread out over the flat horizon like a cooling ingot of molten gold glowing rosily through the cumulus. Mature hedgerows and several well-placed maples shielded them from most of the million-dollar vacation homes that sprouted brazenly amidst the spuds, the fruit of new fortunes made on Wall Street and Madison Avenue. Reckless experiments in solid geometry vied with gargantuan imitations of indigenous Shingle Style cottages. Situated between the traditionally fashionable towns of Southampton and East Hampton, the potato fields had become reversely chic in recent years. When Russell joked that the location made him feel closer to his Irish roots, Corrine pointed out that they could *buy* a house in Ireland for twenty thousand dollars—the tariff for the ten-week season in the Hamptons. Despite her reservations she liked the farmhouse, which in contrast to its self-conscious new neighbors had a certain ramshackle charm.

David Whitlock and Washington Lee were frequent guests, sharing a bathroom with the occasional midwestern novelist recuperating from a semester's teaching, or East Village poet deeply suspicious of sunlight and physical recreation. Tim Calhoun, who had once said that the only good poet was a dead poet, had come up from Georgia to deliver his new novel, pledge allegiance to Russell's new enterprise and drink some bourbon; one Saturday night he'd started shooting rabbits in the front yard with an unregistered .44 Magnum revolver. Victor Propp lasted nearly a day before he leaped up in the middle of dinner, tormented by sudden inspiration, and commanded the smoldering, compliant Camille Donner to drive him back to his desk in the city. Despite repeated invitations Jeff remained in the city, and when Corrine pressed him he said, "The devil's in the Hamptons."

To get to their summer house and back they acquired a Jeep, this being the requisite transport for youthful urban warriors that year, taking its place alongside the already cliché BMWs and Saabs in East Side garages—and also on the meaner streets of The Bronx and Queens, where it was the ride favored by the better-heeled crack dealers and where its martial pedigree and rugged-terrain capabilities made more sense. The Calloways had never been able to afford a car before, much less the three-hundred-dollar monthly garage fee standard in their neighborhood. But given the seventy- or eighty-odd million dollars of debt that Russell was about to partake in—and a large advance on salary from Melman—the car loan seemed, like the cost of the rented house, proportionally minuscule.

After the car stereo was stolen one night when they left the Jeep outside their building for five minutes, they installed a removable model and Russell hand-lettered onto a piece of Chinese-laundry shirt cardboard the words NO RADIO. This practice served only to remind Corrine of the disparities around her. To her it seemed like the smug slogan of a club to which she didn't want to belong, a mantra of frightened privilege. When she drove by herself she didn't put the sign in the window.

On one occasion they made the trip out to the Island in Bernard Melman's helicopter, after lifting off from the bank of the East River and watching the skyline, spiky as a bed of nails, fade behind them in the haze. Everything felt so heavy, Corrine didn't see how the helicopter could possibly get them aloft and keep them there. Her body was like a bladder full of some dense, foul-smelling substance. She hadn't felt like eating at all, lately. But once they were out of sight of the city she usually began to feel better.

They entertained frequently in the country—"country" being the term applied by Manhattan dwellers to the region of densely populated villages at the eastern tip of Long Island. Their parties acquired a small reputation because they were an attractive new couple in the Hamptons, because they were younger than most of the people who took houses east of Westhampton, because Russell was on the verge of becoming important in the sphere of which this spit of sand was the summer outpost, because in their innocence they mixed people in unexpected configurations.

Within days, it seemed, Russell's circle of acquaintance had grown exponentially. Having spent a few moments in the press, he found himself neighborly with the people who actually lived there—on the pages of magazines. Pop stars, literary lions and business moguls were occasionally among those at the dinner table. Russell didn't question his new social position, and he became annoyed with Corrine if she referred to the sudden change in circumstances, which she suspected was partly a function of the relaxed social conditions of the season and the place, or of the patronage of Bernard Melman, who summered nearby at a huge waterfront house in Southampton that everyone wanted to see from the inside, if only to share in the indignation that swept the Hamptons after he had gutted the ninety-year-old Stanford White mansion in order to seal and insulate it for central air conditioning.

When Corrine worried about the extravagance of their socializing Russell insisted that he was surreptitiously conducting business; many summering writers had, in fact, signed the Villa Pommes de Terre guest book. One night at the Calloways', after seven vodka martinis and a bottle of Chardonnay, a six-foot-four Pulitzer-winning novelist, who looked like a great blue heron with Albert Einstein's hair, offered to leave his wife for Corrine, his manner so lugubriously courtly that she had to try very hard not to burst out laughing. Russell mentioned to a second visiting literary totem, a compact athlete of fifty who wrote best-selling comic epics, that he'd played some baseball in college, and was promptly invited to play shortstop in the annual writers' and artists' softball game, in spite of intense competition from many of the local elite who neither wrote nor painted—the owners of media empires, galleries and movie studios whining, pleading and threatening the respective coaches for a turn at the plate.

While Corrine and several hundred vacationers watched, Russell hit two doubles and a triple, caught three flies and tagged two runners, his workaday awkwardness banished. He was actually an athlete, Corrine recalled proudly, watching him, almost graceful when he narrowed his concentration to the physical realm. A gallery owner in right field who was being sued for fifteen million by the widow of a dead Abstract Expressionist was heard to bitch about the ringer on the writers' team.

There was a legend about a hot novelist, the toast of the literary season one previous autumn, who had disgraced himself in his sole appearance at this game. Thereafter his career had foundered—a series of bad breaks and bad reviews in a spiral of increasing obscurity—and most of the literati attributed this fate to his hapless performance on the field. Superstitiously, Russell took his own game to bode well for the future.

Tan and triumphant, sitting on the porch back at the shingled house with a gin and tonic on his knee, Russell said, "Baseball, she been bery, bery good to me." It was hard not to share his good spirits, but when he added, "Life is good," Corrine feared he'd jinxed them and she rapped her knuckles on the door frame, which proved to be metal rather than wood.

Russell watched the Iran-contra hearings on TV, bellowing with indignation at what he took to be the perfidy of the Reagan administration. Washington watched with him for several hours one Friday afternoon. Far from being indignant, he seemed pleased to have his sense of endemic official skulduggery confirmed. "This shit goes on all the time," he explained to Russell. "They just got caught this time." Washington had been particularly pleased when Russell's candidate, Gary Hart, tripped over his own pantlegs, which happened to be down around his ankles, and had to withdraw from the race. Joseph Biden, too, would later drop out, when he was caught with someone else's words in his mouth.

In town and country, Bernard Melman entertained on an imperial scale, and the Calloways attended several of his parties at the beach house, which they, like many of the guests, secretly found a little *too* overblown, and even more secretly enjoyed.

As he walked to work in the city one morning in July, cocooned in his scrum of sweating bodyguards in black suits, Bernie Melman was considering his upcoming party, the centerpiece of his season. Among the respondents to the hand-delivered invitations were three senators, three cabinet members, five movie stars, two network anchormen, a former quarterback, two princesses, a baron, two dukes and a marchioness, three gossip columnists, innumerable fashion models, a pop singer and seventeen of the Forbes Four Hundred. The usual suspects. Among those who had sent regrets, once again, were his parents.

Melman *père* owned a carpet-cleaning service; Bernie's older brother was a surgeon, his younger brother a patent attorney. The three of them together didn't make half a million a year, but the brothers had gone into respected professions, whereas Bernie, no matter how much money he made, could not allay his parents' suspicion that he was some kind of con man. In fact, they almost disapproved of his wealth. Just the week before, his father had sent along a clipping from *The Plain Dealer* sharply critical of leveraged buyouts. Moreover, Bernie's parents had yet to forgive him for divorcing his first wife, whom they loved and who spent holidays with them, and were barely civil to the new one, whom they referred to as "the Queen." *Divorce* was not a word in their vocabulary, except insofar as it referred to a lurid Gentile practice.

Only recently had they shown any interest in his acquisitions. When he told them he was buying a publishing company, his father asked if he was going to publish Saul Bellow. "Not yet," Bernie responded.

"Hmmm," said his father, an absent hum that indicated to his son his mind had just stepped out for a long, solitary walk.

"There's no reason why I can't publish him in the future," Bernie said, adding, "Have you heard of Victor Propp?"

"What's he published?"

The old man had him there. "I'll find Saul Bellow, all right?" And indeed Bernie had tried, approaching the Nobel laureate through official and private channels, so far without success. Meantime, he'd offered to send his private jet to Cleveland—his parents could come to the party and be back home in Chagrin Falls that night. The social, political and business elite of the country were coming to Bernie Melman's summer house, some of them flying from as far away as Los Angeles, but his mother was unwilling to miss her bridge club.

One humid Saturday evening a few weeks after Russell's group had made the first tender offer, Corrine found herself on a back porch of the Melman summer house, scanning the lawn for Russell after having disengaged herself from a trio of younger Kennedys down from Cape Cod for the party. Fifty yards away, the ocean throbbed against the beach; on the lawn, waiters in tuxedos darted like pilot fish around CEOs in jeans and polo shirts. She caught sight of Sasha Melman, a head taller than most of the company. Corrine had talked to her earlier in the afternoon. She was like something constructed on specifications for a rich man, encased in jewelry, dermatologically taut. As Corrine pondered the mysteries of tall, rich women, she spotted something—was it the blow spout of a whale?—out just beyond the surf.

Retreating inside in search of a bathroom, Corrine ascended a back staircase to avoid the crush downstairs. After the sun and the noise outside, the cool upstairs hallway was sepulchral and eerie. Hearing music and voices behind a door on the second floor, she crept forward and listened, recognizing Jeff's voice above the lugubrious rock. When she knocked, the conversation stopped abruptly. "Shit," said the other voice.

It was too late to retreat gracefully, so Corrine identified herself and eventually Jeff opened the door.

She stepped cautiously into the room. The initial ambience was that of a bar at closing time, the air heavy with smoke, sweat and beer, although the room faced the ocean and was bright with tropical fabrics and white wood. But, the shades were down and the air hadn't been stirred in hours. Tony Duplex, the neo-expressionist painter, was sprawled on the unmade bed.

"Yeah, I remember," he said, in answer to her nervous greeting, with that reflexive solipsism of the famous.

"You didn't tell us you were coming out," she said to Jeff.

"Tony made me come along." Jeff looked like he always did, boyishly aging, his lanky frame draped in jeans and oxford cloth and, in honor of the season, a badly rumpled off-white linen jacket.

"My fucking dealer made me come, and I wasn't about to face this alone," Duplex explained. Hair pulled back in a ponytail, he was wearing shades and a black T-shirt, his face an important new shade of white.

"Your dealer?"

"Yeah. That asshole Melman owns about half of my work, so I have to go to his parties. My dealer's afraid he'll start selling short if my attitude doesn't improve. So here I am in the fucking Hamptons for the fucking weekend. I dragged Jeff along."

"The devil's in the Hamptons," Jeff observed.

Tony reached over and cranked up the volume on the boom box on the bedside table, from which an adenoidal voice whined: "If you ask me why I hate you, I'll try to explain. . . ."

"You like the Cure?" Tony shouted to Corrine, suddenly hospitable now that he was sure she was leaving.

"Cure for what?"

"The cure for fucking Phil Collins," Jeff said.

"Are you coming down," she asked Jeff.

"I'll be down."

"Why don't you stay at our place tonight?"

"I'm probably going back in. But I'll call you."

Outside the door, Corrine turned to Jeff. "Please come." She stood on her toes and threw her arms around his neck. "Don't push us away."

"I'll try," he said.

Back on the porch, she was about to walk down the steps and plunge into the crowd, when she realized Bernie Melman was standing next to her. To Corrine's eyes he looked a little ridiculous in casual attire, with his hairy arms and his belly swelling out over a pair of kelly green trousers. Some people were simply not meant to be seen out of uniform. Feeling she was being unfair to him, she said, "It's a nice party. Thanks for having us."

"Having a good time?"

She nodded.

"How can you tell?"

Corrine shrugged helplessly.

"You should get out there and mingle, meet your second husband," he said, smiling impishly. "Some of the richest men in America are out on that lawn in their Bermuda shorts, and at least three of them have already asked about you. I said you were married, but these guys, they think when they see something they like they can have it. They wanna open charge accounts for you at Bulgari and Bendel's, you name it. Personally, I can't vouch for any of these mutts," he said, seeing she was just *barely* amused. "In fact, if you want I'll have them hauled off the premises immediately. Just say the word. One word. Whoosh. Into the fucking ocean, right? You met my man, Ralph, over there," he asked, indicating a dark shadow on the corner of the veranda. "Ralph's way beyond black belt, he's got a fucking platinum belt in some Korean martial art you never even heard of, it's so secret. Hey, hey, Ralphie boy . . . what's the name of that kung fu you do?"

"Tae kwon do, Mr. Melman," the adept called back.

"Right, whatever. Listen, he could get killed for even saying that out loud. Secret stuff. Once some moron actually tried to mug me, and Ralph threw him all the way across Fifth Avenue, all four lanes, right into a fucking pushcart. Pretzels flying everywhere. So say the word, he'll put these guys into orbit. Or anybody you want. Like that little number down there hitting on your husband. Boom! She's outta here."

Down on the lawn, Russell was indeed engaged in conversation with a distressingly thin brunette with the coltish features and theatrical gestures standard to models.

"Or *him*, maybe," Melman added, winking.

"I should think you'd be a little more loyal to your new business partner."

"Russell, hey, I love Russell. He's a great guy. Smart, good-looking. But I wouldn't exactly call him a business partner. For him it's business, for me it's more like charity."

There was some kind of disturbance out on the lawn and beyond, a noisy riptide of agitation that seemed to be drawing bodies down toward the sea. Registering danger, Ralph moved in closer to Melman, who looked up toward the newly excited pitch of voices coming from the ocean.

They walked down to the beach together, following what was left of the crowd down the lawn. Shouts and squeals were drifting back from the water's edge over the roar of the surf, and some of the people up front were now surging backward, creating an undertow to the predominant beachward trend. Corrine kept pressing forward and suddenly found herself thrown against Russell, who took her hand.

"Can you see it," she asked, just as a great silvery-blue crescent rose over the tops of heads like a streaming sliver of moon and they were almost knocked backward in the general retreat.

"Come on," said Russell, his face boyish with excitement. He tugged her forward until they broke out of the crowd at the edge of the high-tide shelf of sand on the beach.

The creature was thrashing in the shallows, half out of the water, a man-sized fin standing almost upright on its exposed flank, dwarfing the humans submerged to their waists in the surf. Churning the foam and sand, it was trying to swim onto the shore, as if it had given up on its watery life and hoped to emulate the remote ancestor it shared with these puny, agitated terrestrials. A powerful stench filled the air—something ancient, retrieved from the bottom of the ocean. "Go back," Corrine whispered. Looking into the huge black eye, above the gray furrows of the belly flesh, she felt herself drawn into an abyss of sadness.

Russell stripped off his shirt and plunged into the water to join the men who were trying to push the whale back, away from the shore.

"Watch the tail!" someone screamed.

Several times they managed to nudge the animal out a few yards, but the incoming waves and the animal's own struggle to beach itself were relentless. Russell was up to his waist in the water shouting directions and throwing his weight against the slippery doomed bulk. As darkness fell, a Coast Guard cutter appeared a hundred yards offshore. Nine or ten policemen were shifting around helplessly in the sand when Russell finally emerged from the water.

The party had achieved an acute focus; all of the guests were veterans of the charity fund-raising circuit, and now a crisis had been laid right at their feet. No one knew what to do. A man from First Boston was already taking up a collection to save the whale, walking along the beach with a silver champagne bucket.

"It's horrible," Corrine said.

"I know." Russell was less ebullient now, winded and shivering. "You want to take the car?" he said. "I'm going to stay."

"Jeff's here."

"He is? I thought he melted in sunlight."

"Try to get him to come to the house tonight, okay? He's holed up in a dark room with that creepy Tony Duplex."

"I'll try. But don't hold your breath. He's got a lot in common with this goddamn fish."

She'd guessed Russell would stay to the end, do what he could do. He couldn't bear to think something exciting was happening without his participation, and the sunny, pragmatic tint of his character allowed him to believe that he would have some positive effect on the outcome. But she had seen the doomed look in the whale's eye, and she didn't want to see any more.

The man taking up the collection, red-faced and glassy-eyed under his Mets cap, thrust the champagne bucket under her nose.

"Say the whale, say the whale."

"How?"

"*How?*"

"What are you planning to do with the money?"

His jaw slowly worked loose from the rest of his face and hung slack. The question, evidently, had not occurred to him before.

31

On Sunday nights a hundred-mile strand of red tail- and brakelights unspooled between Montauk and Manhattan, like a string of melancholy beads signifying the end of the weekend, Russell and Corrine's among them.

The night after Bernie Melman's party they were listening to WINS news radio for progress reports on the beached whale as they motored slowly toward the city. By eleven it was pronounced dead. The music stations, meanwhile, all played the same lugubrious U2 songs over and over—"With or Without You" and "I Still Haven't Found What I'm Looking for," real Save the Whales music. Phil Collins was bound to whine into earshot any minute now. It seemed to Corrine that rock and roll was more fun when they had first come to New York, when they used to stay out half the night dancing. Whatever happened to Blondie, the Cars, the Clash?

"I wonder," she said, "whose job it is to pronounce whales dead?"

Russell was taking this defeat personally. There was little fatalism in his makeup, scant suspicion that animal flesh was merely the helpless vessel of tyrannical amino acids, that human destinies were written indelibly by a capricious deity. Corrine thought he lacked a sense of evil and for this reason was ill equipped to go into business.

As if to demonstrate his inability to read her mind, Russell suddenly said, "I like Bernie. He's turned out to be a really decent guy."

"You think everybody's a really decent guy." For all of his intelligence, Russell had always been a little dumb about people, always erring on the side of trusting the guy with the waxed mustaches.

She told him about her conversation on the veranda with Bernie. "I don't know how far you can trust him. He's funny and everything, but it was almost like he was propositioning me."

"Well," Russell resumed, after a short, air-conditioned silence, "I can't say I blame him."

"That's all you have to say?"

"What do you want me to say?"

It wasn't until that moment that Corrine admitted to herself what she really wanted was for him to give it all up—renounce his dealings with Melman, forget about buying the company. They were in over their heads. That's what she'd been feeling at the party. And so, though she hadn't particularly been offended at the time by Melman, she persisted in exaggerating the offense.

"You'd do business with a man who wants to sleep with your wife?"

"Jesus, Corrine, lighten up. Some of my best friends want to sleep with you." He thought this a witty compliment, but when he looked across at her she was staring into the glare of the windshield, shaken, wondering which best friends he had in mind.

Suspended between the red lights in front and the white lights behind, they rode in silence the rest of the way into Manhattan. On his side, Russell brooded on what he took to be Corrine's Manichaean nature: she was so goddamn extreme that anything she couldn't love she feared. The extremes were becoming more pronounced of late. And she was getting too thin, her eating habits verging on the anorexic—a problem that had recurred intermittently with her since prep school. When she didn't feel she could satisfactorily control other aspects of her existence she decided to chastise her body.

He tried to resume the conversation several times, as if nothing had happened, but she answered in clipped monosyllables.

The *Daily News* headline read: "Whale Crashes Shark's Party." The *Post*: "Whale of Guest at Hampton Beach Bash." The humpback whale was thought to be the largest leviathan to wash up on Long Island in this century. A day later, the *Times* ran two column inches beneath the headline "Whale Beached in L.I." A *Village Voice* columnist charged that Melman had dumped several gallons of whale pheromone off his beach the day before the party, a claim that a Melman spokesman called "ridiculous," citing the evidence of several marine biologists who derided the concept. Much later, in a valedictory essay about the eighties published in *Harper's*, the party at which Bernie Melman had exhibited a captured whale was cited as a signal instance of the decade's egregious excesses.

That summer Corrine still took the subway downtown to her office and back from Monday to Friday, but everything else had changed. Russell had always had too much of a desire to please, in her opinion, and his campaign to take over Corbin, Dern had almost transformed him into a politician. He needed to be collegial with Dave Whitlock, Washington Lee and Leticia Corbin; he needed to smile for the stockholders and the outside members of the board, to feed and stroke the writers. No one but Corrine's husband, apparently, could do it. He also needed to spend an inordinate amount of time with Trina Cox. And apparently he had to drink a lot of liquor in order to take care of everyone, because he usually came home all flushed and slurry, having first called from a telephone booth to say the group had moved from one location to another and did she want to join them. Not being a drinker anymore, she didn't like those all-night dinners quite so much; it was like being a foreigner at the table, and anyway it was usually shoptalk, so she mostly stayed home waiting for him to roll in.

In the early part of the summer he would arrive home amorously charged, as if he'd undergone some kind of testosterone transfusion, and at times she wondered just whom he was fucking. . . . He seemed to be taking over the world through the vessel of her body. By July he seldom had the energy even to kiss her good night. The wife, apparently, was the one who didn't need any extra attention, perhaps on the principle that she would always be there.

The first tender offer had been rejected by the board of directors after weeks of acrimonious debate. To ward off the Melman group, a poison pill was adopted by the board; Melman's lawyers filed suit in Delaware, asking the court to declare the poison pill measures "invalid and unlawful." Corbin, Dern filed a countersuit. Jerry Kleinfeld found a white knight, a German publisher who agreed to back them and who sweetened the pot by two dollars a share. Then J. P. Haddad, the offshore investor whose boat Russell and Corrine had seen in the Caribbean that March, called in an offer almost identical to that of the German-backed management group. Because of the difficulty of comparing the bids, which combined hard and soft money in varying proportions, the board called for one more round of bidding. Russell was dejected but Trina was sanguine. After taking the call from Whitney Corbin in the offices of Melman's lawyers, Trina called Melman in Southampton and put him on the speaker phone. He had known about the Germans but not about Haddad. "That prick. He beat me out on the last deal, and no way I'm going to let that lunatic have this one. Let's go sudden death. How high can we go, Trina?"

"I don't see how we can justify more than another buck a share."

"Let's think about bumping it up two-fifty a share, and make it a two-tier offer."

A day later Trina and the number crunchers had put together a bid that would add four million to the cost of the company, on the basis of a somewhat optimistic assumption about what they could get for spinning off the textbook division. Melman returned to the city in his helicopter. Over drinks with Russell, Washington came in with a valuable piece of information: The Germans were prepared to go to twenty-one.

"How do you know this," Russell asked.

"I've got my sources."

"That's not good enough. I have to know for sure."

"Pillow talk, my man."

Demonstrating one of his occasional bouts of obtuseness, Russell held up his hands in bafflement.

"The name Carlton ring any bells?"

"You're doing Carlton? Harold's squeeze?"

"Hey, chief, we all got to do our part."

"Jesus. Can we trust her?"

"This is the revenge scenario, all right? Harold's dating some new bimbo, and Carlton's still sitting right outside the door when he meets with his boys to discuss business."

"I don't *believe* you, Washington."

"Sometimes even *I'm* amazed."

* * *

The deadline for the final bids had passed six hours before, and the Melman group was waiting to hear from the law firm representing the Corbin, Dern board. Upon returning to the city, Bernie had graciously insisted that the negotiating team camp out in his offices. They had been hanging out now for thirteen hours, talking, ordering food in from '21,' periodically taking calls from lawyers and wives, knocking pink golf balls across the lush gold-and-peach-hued expanse of the Aubusson carpets of the main conference room into upended wineglasses.

They were living in deal time, where an adrenaline camaraderie prevailed. Each of them seemed smarter and funnier than usual to the others. Two topics predominated: the deal and sex. There was the joke about the lion and the monkey; about the shipwrecked sailor, the Doberman and the sheep; the Frenchman, the Englishman and the Jew. The Jews told Jewish jokes, Russell Irish jokes, the lawyers lawyer jokes.

Trina told the one about Dennis Levine, the investment banker convicted of insider trading: "Guy must be a retard, took him eleven trades to make a lousy eight million." Melman's repertoire was encyclopedic, and he always got the biggest laughs. Russell was half delirious with exhaustion and passive smoke inhalation. "I used to stay up half the night just for fun," he said to Rockaby.

"It's more fun to do it for money," Rockaby answered.

Melman's bankers seemed to thrive on this ritualized, heightened form of sleeplessness, but Russell was impressed that Trina could more than hold her own against this expensive crew.

Although his presence was neither required nor entirely appropriate, Washington had stopped by after his dinner to catch some of the deal buzz. He arrived on the fifth floor with his disposition slightly ruffled beneath his Comme des Garçons suit; the security men in the lobby— one of whom he was almost certain he recognized from the night of his ignominious retreat from Casa Melman—had given him a hard time, at first refusing to call upstairs, threatening instead to call the police.

"I'm thinking of filing a suit against your thugs," he told Melman, "for incivility against my civil rights." Washington had never explained his disappearance from Melman's dinner, fearing that the subject, once raised, might prove endlessly embarrassing. He sent a conventional thank-you note to Sasha Melman and arranged the meeting with Donald Parker as instructed, something he might not have done otherwise.

"Have a brandy," said Bernie. "You want a brandy? You want a cigar? Carl, get the man a brandy, for Christ's sake. You like art," he asked as Washington surveyed the paintings on the wall.

"The Dubuffet's boring, but I like the Duplex."

"I've got the biggest collection of that asshole's stuff in the country. At least for another day or two. He almost burned up my summer house a couple weeks ago. Look around, I gotta make some calls here."

Russell was schmoozing some suits in the outer office. Washington found it impossible to distinguish their names or faces. This, Russell said, was the law team. Three pink-faced guys in blue suits, one of them holding a putter. Not straight white bread, a touch of rye—slightly balder, and shorter, than the average member of the Harvard Club. How did these boys tell themselves apart, anyway? Would their wives notice if they switched cars at the train station in Chappaqua and drove to the wrong houses? Honey, you look shorter tonight—tough day at the office?

"How does it look," Washington asked.

"It's a slam dunk," said Russell.

"Is it that good," Washington asked, half ingenuously.

"Yeah, it means, you know . . ."

"When do we know if we got our fucking jobs?"

"Should be sometime tonight."

"I'll check back," Washington said. "Meantime I want you white boys to keep working on your long putts."

Emerging from the elevator downstairs, he called, "Later, Guido," to the no-neck who'd given him shit. Seven limousines of various lengths were docked at the sidewalk, idling. Washington climbed into a black Lincoln.

He looked at the startled driver in the rearview mirror. "You're on account for Fried, Flotte and Cadwallader, right?"

The driver nodded.

"Let's roll, then. Fifty-eighth between Park and Madison."

"You got a voucher," the driver asked.

"I'll need one, thank you."

The car slipped into gear and angled out of its berth into Fifth Avenue.

"I'll take the chopper back," Washington said, when they pulled up in front of Au Bar, where the doorman said hello and lifted the velvet rope to let him pass. No great triumph—the place was half deserted, a sprinkling of Greek shipping-money scions and last year's debutantes. He had a drink and picked up a girl who claimed she'd met him in the spring. He wondered, in this case, about the extension of the verb "to meet." He didn't remember her, but he should have; she was definitely doable, an English girl busting out of her gold-sequined bustier. Said her name was Samantha. "Let's go somewhere, Sam," he said. "This place is beat."

She said she was waiting for some friends, an answer he hated.

"Let's meet them downtown," he suggested, needing to purge himself of something he'd picked up in Melman's office, the odor of polite white greed that clung like a bad after-shave. You just can't shake that stench on the Upper East Side.

"There's a party over on Seventy-seventh and Park."

These negotiations did not look promising. Lack of enthusiasm on the part of the principals: he didn't want to stay and she didn't want to go. In the final analysis, he didn't feel that he absolutely had to have it. So he cabbed solo to Nell's and ran into a few acquaintances there, but not the person who would seem, if only for a few hours, like the reason he'd launched himself out when he could have been home banging away on the Frantz Fanon book.

Waiting at home for word on the offer, Corrine resented her absentee role. Before Russell had acquired a team of advisors, she'd walked him through the numbers. They'd stayed up late every night for a week. She had been the first to tell him it was theoretically possible to buy the company, to work out how much it might actually be worth, to map out a possible scenario. Which didn't mean she thought he *should*. She thought it was crazy.

Just because something could be done didn't require that you do it. Russell had no sense of the fragility of life, of the boundaries that might be crossed if you reached too far. Growing up for Russell had been as smooth as a series of promotions, and his mother's death ten years before had seemed to him a cruel exception to the general bounty of nature.

For several days Corrine tried to talk some sense into him. "This is just some dumb male thing between you and Harold. Why don't you guys just go to the men's room tomorrow and measure each other, declare a winner."

"So maybe all of history is some dumb male thing."

"Russell, listen to yourself. Stop while you still have a sense of humor."

"Since when is ambition a crime?"

"When it's excessive."

"You're the one that wants to have kids," he said.

"Whoa! Time out for non sequitur."

"Well, do you want to raise your kid in a one-bedroom apartment?"

"I can't believe your shamelessness." Countering the disparagement of his own sex with an appeal to what he took to be a feminine susceptibility. "You mean, if I go along with your crazy project, you'll condescend to get me pregnant?"

When it was clear that he wouldn't be talked out of it, she had surrendered and tried to support him. Maybe people who didn't know that they couldn't accomplish certain tasks sometimes succeeded out of sheer naiveté, like bumblebees, which had never heard they were aerodynamically incapable of flight. Besides, he was so excited it was like watching him bloom again after a long, loveless winter. Aware of her reservations, he would often woo her with flowers and impromptu gifts. She wanted to encourage that, though it sometimes seemed sad to her that what he wanted from life was so different. She wanted the kind of home she'd never known as a child, the delicate illusion of which had been finally shattered with her parents' divorce. She couldn't understand why Russell needed to rule the world, or why he thought it was a big deal when they got their picture in a magazine.

After one of those long, coded, largely silent contract negotiations that constitute married life, they came to an implicit agreement that seemed lopsided in his favor: She'd be quiet and he'd be nice. She would go along with him in return for future consideration. It was like one of those corporate debt restructuring deals where you had to accept unredeemable paper in the hope that it might be worth something someday and because you had no choice.

Corrine had advised against pursuing the deal, but that didn't mean she was immune to the thrill of the attempt, or happy about being left out. Home alone again, she flipped through magazines, too restless to read a book. In an hour she had run through a pile consisting of *Architectural Digest*, *Self*, *Vanity Fair*, *Vogue*, *Elle*, *Details* and *Manhattan, inc*. She felt exhausted. Reading magazines was like going to a cocktail party, a series of three-minute conversations. Having skipped dinner, she'd gone on to eat an entire bag of potato chips, which was really disgusting. She now weighed nine hundred thirteen pounds.

Eleven o'clock. Corrine turned on the TV, turned up the air conditioner. In the kitchen she found a Snickers bar. Soak up some of that disgusting oil and salt from the chips . . . it felt as if a supertanker had run aground on her duodenum.

She wondered if she should call again. Why didn't he call?

The Odd Couple on TV, Felix cooking dinner for Oscar. Corrine realized she wouldn't be so hungry if she had eaten a proper dinner. Back in the kitchen she found a Lean Cuisine lasagna dinner. Less than three hundred calories—that was sensible. But tomorrow, she decided, she would go on a real diet. Fast. Really starve herself. Being fat in the summer was horrible. Nuking the lasagna, she observed its progress through the door of the microwave as the *Honeymooners* theme drifted in from the living room. "Chef of the Future." Russell's favorite show. Corrine didn't like it so much, she thought all the poverty and bickering was sad. But sometimes she watched when Russell wasn't home, imagining him slapping his palms against the coffee table and hooting as she tried to figure out what was so funny.

Somebody she knew, she forgot who, once said that missing people was a way of spending time with them.

After *The Honeymooners* she snooped around in the freezer for something sweet and turned up a DoveBar, feeling herself getting fatter with every bite. It was twelve-thirty. She watched *Star Trek*, trying to remember her Platonic theory from college. What was it? Spock was intellect, McCoy was emotion, and Kirk the integrating, ruling factor, what Plato called the Spirited Element. The importance of a liberal education demonstrated, QED.

When the show was over she ate the other DoveBar because it was there, sitting in its perfect wrapper in the freezer, calling out to her, shivering her name. At one-thirty she went into the bathroom, put a finger down her throat and threw up.

* * *

At three-thirty Washington found himself down on the Lower East Side, on a street of burned-out, boarded-up tenements. Nothing was happening anywhere in the city so far as he could discover. A white Toyota with Jersey plates rounded the corner and slowed in front of him. A white face efflorescent with acne called out, "You selling?"

"Not even holding, goddamnit," Washington yelled back.

A few doors away a couple of kids who had been huddled in a doorway rushed into the street and waved the car forward. Washington crouched down and knocked on a rusty freight door set into the sidewalk. A minute later the door opened up, and a head popped out and nodded at Washington, who descended the treacherous iron stairs underground. He walked uncertainly along a dank, vaulted passageway and pounded on a steel door.

When his eyes had adjusted to the smoky dimness of the cellar, he descried Juan Baptiste and Leticia Corbin among the wounded bodies and twisted faces at the bar. He waved in slow motion. You knew you were really hurting when you were glad to see these underworld shades. "Good to see you, my man," he said to Juan, kissing the frigid white cheek of Leticia, who said she was celebrating her brother's imminent downfall. Washington raised an eyebrow and hinted that there were wheels within wheels, that it wasn't over till it was over, that he was in fact an integral part of top-secret negotiations which were in progress at this very moment, watching with interest the couple who were silently fucking in the corner.

Near dawn, he was in a cab headed uptown. He was reluctant to inspect his suit too closely, having ridden on the back of a garbage truck from Delancey up to 14th, that being the only vehicle moving in the early-morning wasteland of the Lower East Side. Then two cabs had sped past him, a young black man on a deserted street, one cabbie shouting, "Fucking walk!" from the window.

Inside the lobby of Melman's office building a couple of uniformed goons impeded his inexorable progress toward the elevators. Weren't these the same assholes he'd dealt with earlier? Always hard to tell with white people. They certainly didn't seem to recognize him.

"May I help you?" A wide guy in a badly tailored suit, neckless and virtually lipless, was doing an imitation of a defensive line, stepping between Washington and the elevator.

"Not unless you got a cigarette."

"Sorry. Authorized personnel only."

All this hassle was making Washington tired and thirsty. Hoping he had a squirt or two left, he reached in his jacket pocket. . . .

"Watch out! He's got a gun!"

Suddenly there were real guns everywhere, a big .45 right in his face and another coming upside his head . . .

Near dawn the phone rang.

"Say hello to the new editor in chief," Russell said.

"What?" She had been asleep, dreaming that she was asleep and waiting for him to come home from a date with the vampire Leticia Corbin.

"We got it. We won."

32

"I can't believe I'm up and walking around at seven-thirty on a Saturday morning. Do I have any clean socks?"

"Russell, don't sniff your socks. It's gross."

"Gotta do that sniff test when the drawer's empty. Maybe I'll prep out and skip socks. As a member of a lynch mob, do you suppose it's bad form to be sockless?"

"It's not a lynch mob, Russell. You're trying to save his life. Why can't you get straight on this—instead of identifying with his problem?"

"Is that a coy allusion to the fact that I have a hangover?"

"I didn't—"

"I wouldn't wish this on my . . . I wouldn't even wish this on Harold."

When Zac Solomon called from California to say that Jeff had nodded off in the middle of a pitch to studio execs, Russell had finally decided to share with Corrine his suspicions about Jeff's drug consumption. Furious with him for not telling her sooner, she quickly turned practical, investigating detox programs and hospitals, calling Jeff's parents. Jeff was back in New York, and Zac had flown in the night before to supervise the intervention. He was a veteran of these missions, being a reformed abuser of substances and having recently intervened on a screen star who was freebasing his way into the John Belushi Hall of Fame. He also had a professional interest in Jeff's rehabilitation, having bought screen rights to two stories from Jeff's book.

At eight a.m. the group convened at a coffee shop on Lafayette. The gruffness of the Greek counterman, the sullen resentment of the early-morning working people, the jaded resignation of a couple in matching black leathers and black-dyed, spiked-out coifs seeking sanctuary from the sudden daylight—everything contributed to Russell's air of gloom. He kept putting himself in Jeff's shoes, imagining how he would feel. He could picture the signs and the forks in the road that had led Jeff to the bathroom at Minky's. Russell had read the same books, listened to the same music. If he hadn't married Corrine he might have been the one who made a laboratory of himself, mixing all the chemicals together. Opening doors marked DO NOT ENTER.

But Christ, he thought, you weren't supposed to take it so literally. They'd grown up with drugs, just close enough to the sixties almost to believe in pot and acid as the sacraments of a vague liberation theology but not so close that they didn't soon take them for granted. Not long ago, as putative adults, they were doing coke together at parties and imagining they'd discovered the pleasure principle. Not so long before that they were editing the college literary magazine, going to keg parties, reading Baudelaire.

Jeff's parents arrived, anomalously together, though they had the easy fit of people who have come to dislike each other over the years and who derive great pleasure from their fighting—after all these years their aim and timing were perfect. Jeff's mother, Bev, was a tall, tan, elegant brunette with the look of a wealthy sportswoman—a habitué of tennis courts and marinas. She'd flown in from Santa Fe, where she had recently opened a crafts shop.

Tears in her eyes, she embraced Russell, then kissed Corrine on one cheek; she had once explained to Russell, with the solemn air of one for whom these things mattered, that only pretentious arrivistes and Europeans kissed both. Wiping her eyes, she said, "I brought you two a little prez," and handed Russell a gift-wrapped package about the size and shape of a collapsed fly rod. Emitting a sibilant, tinkling sound, it seemed to involve some kind of liquid. "It's a rain stick," she explained, as Russell cautiously peeled away the wrapping on a fat, varnished stick. "It's filled with little shells and beans and pebbles, and when you turn it over it sounds like rain."

"What an extremely useful and tasteful gift," said Wick Pierce.

"Wick is upset because we haven't yet been able to mimic the sound of scotch splashing on ice," she said, not missing a beat.

"I've changed, Bev. It's been years since I bothered with ice."

"I get them made for me in Mexico," she explained to Corrine, who was trying out the stick. "I tested it out in the lobby of the hotel as I was leaving, and a little boy standing there with his father said, 'Daddy, I have to go to the bathroom.' Isn't that too cute?"

"No home complete without one," said Wick, whose handsome, once chiseled features were slightly smudged with the bloat and flush of drinking. After graduating from Amherst, Wick had moved to Greenwich Village to be a Stanislavskian actor until Bev, a senior at Smith, had become pregnant, prompting him to move back to Massachusetts and take a job teaching English at Deerfield. It was supposed to be a temporary thing while Wick wrote his play, but the play never got written and Wick had come into his trust fund at the age of twenty-five. Wick came from an old New England textile family, and while the fortune had been subdivided many times before it reached him, his own share was just large enough to smother ambition. He embarked on the curious but not unprecedented life of the casual New England academic whose salary barely covers the liquor bills. Bev, who came from a moderately prosperous middle-class family, rose to this life of faculty club and country club, keeping horses and lording it over the less fortunate teachers and spouses. Jeff had grown up with art and tennis lessons and a live-in cook, in a style that Russell had much admired when he first visited, freshman year, the year Jeff's parents were divorced. Wick still lived in Deerfield, with his second wife, a Jennifer—Jeff having once remarked that all young second wives were named Jennifer. To a degree that seemed excessive to Russell, he acted contemptuous of this background and of his family, which had served as the basis for the eccentric clan portrayed in his stories, though he liked to imply in interviews that he'd been born on the streets and raised by mad dogs.

Russell had been afraid, before the collection was published, that Jeff's parents would never speak to him again—not that there was a lot of communication taking place at that time. Insofar as they recognized themselves, each seemed to think the other came off worse, and any residual hard feelings faded when people began to ask them if they were related to Jeff Pierce, the writer.

"Can you believe it," said Bev, shaking her hair out from her scarf. "I catch this one drinking a Bloody Mary in the hotel bar this morning. Of all mornings."

"I told you, goddamnit, it was a virgin."

"Of course, Wick. And so was Jennifer."

Zac Solomon arrived a moment later, tan and robust.

"I just want you to know," he said after introductions, "I think your son is a genius. He's got a great future ahead of him—once he cleans himself up."

"We certainly appreciate your help," Bev said. "Russell tells us you've done this before. You know, I was reading in *People* about this young actor who freebased right before he shot the antidrug commer—"

"Jesus *Christ*, Bev."

"For your information this actor happens to be someone Jeff met while he was out in Hollywood, in fact I believe they actually spent some time together, and I just thought it was an interesting point of comparison."

"My ex-wife once fancied herself an actress," Wick explained apologetically.

"And my ex-husband is a failed writer, unlike his talented son."

Corrine put her arm around Bev. "We're all a little tense, Bev."

"I just want Mr. Solomon to know that Jeff's father is an alcoholic. I think it's like, what do you call it? Carrying coals to Newcastle. I mean, Jeff probably wouldn't even have this problem if he'd learned moderation from his father. It seems a little hypocritical—"

"The main thing here," Zac said, "is that Jeff sees that the people who love him are aware of his problem and willing to help him. So let's start there. I want you to know this is definitely not going to be a day at the beach. He's going to be angry and wounded and strung out. He's going to lash out at all of us. We can't be offended by anything he says or does in the next few hours. So are we ready, guys?"

No one said anything.

"This is where he *lives*?" said Bev, as they turned on Great Jones Street, her tone of voice implying that the neighborhood might be the cause of his problem, or that at the very least it was an appropriate setting for drug addiction. To Russell it seemed only slightly rattier than the average Manhattan street, certainly better than some. A bum asleep in a doorway, garbage in the street, the building fronts peeling and crumbling. But there were million-dollar lofts behind these dirty windows. He felt obliged to explain this to Bev, almost adding that a famous artist lived in the building next door to Jeff's, before he remembered that the artist was also a notorious junkie.

"Why anyone would choose to live in this city is beyond me."

Nobody, this morning, was in the mood to enlighten her on this point.

"Here we are." Russell was not entirely happy to find that his key still fit the front door lock. It just seemed brutal to corner a man in his lair this way, at this hour of the morning. The group piled into the antique steel cage of the elevator. "Isn't this supposed to have an inspection sticker," Corrine asked nervously. Everyone listened intently to the tinkle of the rain stick Russell was carrying. They stepped into the dimly lit third-floor hallway. Beside Jeff's door stood the front fork and handlebars of a Harley-Davidson motorcycle, like a cyclopean sentry, the headlight staring squarely at them. The brown fedora wedged between the handlebars atop the headlight accentuated the effect of anthropomorphism. Russell bowed deferentially to this talisman and tried the key in the Medeco lock.

"Are we ready," he asked.

The loft was dark, except for the amber glow of a computer screen on the other side of the room. The air was acrid and stale, residual tobacco smoke mingling with laundry rot and a sharp, medicinal odor. Russell found the light switch.

The landscape confirmed them in their mission. It was much worse than it had been on Russell's last visit, even worse than anyone expected—the wide-planked floors strewn with clothes, paper cups, food cartons, cigarette butts—at the same time that it exactly answered the notion of a junkie's apartment. Which is what it was, Russell realized, finally accepting what he had been unable quite to believe about his friend.

"My God," said Bev.

"Let's confront," said Zac, nodding to the bed at the far end. "Ladies, you sure you can do this?"

Bev shook her head but joined the group sneaking through the wreckage to the bed, where Jeff was knotted into the sheets, lying on his right side, breathing laboriously through his nose. A used syringe and a bloodstained washcloth lay on the milk crate that served as a bedside table.

Russell called his name in a voice that sounded to its owner false, high and stilted.

Jeff opened his eyes. After surveying the scene he closed them and turned his head into the pillow. He burrowed deep into the mattress.

"Jeff, we're not going to go away." Zac tapped his shoulder.

"This is a fucking nightmare," Jeff said. "Tell me this is a nightmare."

"You know why we're here, son," said Wick, who had been rehearsed.

"You've got a problem, guy," Zac said.

Russell was speechless.

"I don't fucking believe this is happening," said Jeff.

"We're here to help you," said Wick.

"We're here because we love you," said Bev.

"Hold the fucking violins," Jeff said. "I think I'm going to be sick."

Corrine said, "We're going to take you somewhere where you can beat this."

"Go away!" he screamed.

"We're not leaving without you," Zac said.

Looking up again, Jeff said, "If I'd known you were coming I would've dusted."

Zac persisted. "You know what we're talking about, big guy."

Unthinkingly, Russell twirled the rain stick in his hand. At that moment it sounded like an entire waterfall.

"What the fuck is that?" Jeff said.

"It's a rain stick," explained Bev.

Jeff sat up in bed, glaring at the object in Russell's hands as though it were responsible for this horrible wake-up call. "I can't handle this without a fix." In a temporary gesture of modesty he raised the sheet around his waist. Then he threw it aside, saying, "What the hell, you've all seen it before," and walked naked to the bathroom.

Russell looked up at Corrine, who avoided his eyes, wiping her own.

The five of them stood helplessly around the bed, frozen in position. "Isn't somebody going to stop him," Bev asked.

"The doctor said to let him maintain till we get him to the hospital," Wick reminded her.

"Well, I'm not going to just stand here like an idiot." Bev knelt down and began picking up the clothes around the bed. Corrine joined in eagerly.

"I think he's going to come with us," Zac said. He walked out to the front of the loft and raised the blinds.

Jeff emerged from the bathroom, a towel around his waist.

"You all right?"

"Great. I *love* waking up this way." He seemed normal, looked no worse than Russell had two hours before.

Hugging his fouled laundry, Bev sobbed, "Oh, Jeff."

"I mean it. Really wonderful to see you all."

"Are you going to come to the hospital, guy?"

"Do I have a choice?"

Half an hour later Jeff and Russell were walking east on 4th Street, deep into Alphabet City. At the corner of Avenue C, Jeff told Russell to wait while he ducked into a *bodega*. The doctor had advised them to let Jeff self-prescribe whatever he required for the drive to the hospital in Connecticut. The fact that he needed to score almost immediately after shooting up indicated to Russell a fairly remarkable habit.

Two Hispanic men loitered enigmatically under the red plastic awning. A third sat on the sidewalk, his head lolling on his shoulders, a strand of saliva connecting his open mouth to one shoulder. The buildings on either side of the *bodega* were bombed out. A bedsheet that said SQUAT NOW hung from one of the unboarded windows. STOP GENTRIFICA- TION was sprayed beside the chained door. A community of tepees, tents and shacks had sprung up in a nearby empty lot.

Jeff emerged from the *bodega* shaking his head. "We'll have to go over to the reservation," Jeff said, indicating the Hooverville, an edge of panic in his voice. "The quality's not steady. It's crapshooting, you might be spiking up four percent pure, or ten."

"Do you enjoy all . . . *this*?"

"It's nice to have friends in low places." Jeff sighed. "Wait here," he said, leaving Russell at the curb to contemplate the corpse of a rat splayed on the spokes of a tireless bicycle wheel. A heavy septic stench hung in the air. Jeff was in conference with a man in camouflage pants whom Russell recognized as Paul Rostenkowski, the homeless activist whose picture was often in the paper. They disappeared inside a tepee. A group clustered around an open-pit cooking fire regarded Russell with uncon- cealed suspicion. Staring, a white man wrapped in a bedspread lifted a baseball bat from the ground and whacked it experimentally across his palm. A young black man detached himself from the group and picked his way across the lot toward Russell, who tensed for a confrontation and scanned the area for possible weapons.

"Yo, Russell, what's happening? I was at your house once for a party. How's the wife?"

"She's fine, she's good." Russell didn't recall having seen this man before in his life, but he was happy at this moment to pretend that he did. "So what are you up to?" he said.

"Same ole same ole. I got some stuff in the works, some job possibilities. . . ."

"Yeah? Excellent."

"Couple irons in the fire, so to speak."

"All *right*."

"So like tell Corrine Ace says hi," he said, shaking Russell's hand, as Jeff emerged from the tepee.

Wick was waiting in his car outside Jeff's building. Russell and Jeff went upstairs, where Bev had cleaned up and packed some clothes and toiletries. Zac was gone. "One for the road," Jeff said, disappearing into the bathroom for five minutes.

He allowed Corrine to hug him and limply shook hands with Russell. To Russell, he looked almost relieved finally to surrender his fate to others. Folded into the backseat of the Jaguar, he stared straight ahead as the car pulled away, taking his crisis with him, thereby depriving Russell and Corrine of one crucial layer of distraction from themselves.

33

It was still dark outside when Russell awoke, alert as a sentry. He rose at six and showered, spinning hot and cold water knobs in futile attempts to regulate the temperature of the water, scalding one hand, then numbing his lathered scalp as he rinsed out the shampoo under an icy torrent. This apparent divorce between cause and effect in the plumbing failed to stifle his brisk sense of well-being.

Corrine was dozing strenuously between snooze alarms when he left the apartment at six-thirty. Lately she was showing less of her usual enthusiasm for rising and shining. As Russell had become increasingly involved in his work, she had grown less and less interested in her own. When he kissed her good-bye she mumbled something about a baby present for Casey.

Outside, autumn had arrived on the city streets. The noxious gases of the summer had dissipated and the chilly morning air carried an olfactory hint of new leather. This was Russell's favorite season, the season of beginnings in New York, social springtime on the metropolitan calendar. Having nothing but time, he walked across the park to the West Side. A squirrel was hauling a slice of pizza up a maple tree. A band of schoolboys, commanding a rise above the bike path, lobbed stones at passing joggers.

A sleepy guard nodded to him in the lobby of the Brill Building, where they were keeping offices until all the papers were signed. Which was not a bad thing, according to Trina: "You'll have an easier time figuring out who gets fired without having them standing next to you in the little boys' room." The erstwhile editorial director and publisher had not proven to be good losers, but Russell was relieved to discover that most of his colleagues had come around to the idea of a fresh regime; there had been only a couple of immediate resignations. During his exile Russell had been barred from having anything further to do with the books he had in production; he was, after all, fired. Now he picked up his old duties while courting and rating the staff in concert with Washington and Whitlock. He resurrected a few of his projects that Harold, whom he now referred to as "the lame owl," had seen fit to bury. At the same time, Russell and Trina were shopping the textbook division. Another plan under discussion was to sell the old building off for a quick twelve to fifteen million and lease back a few floors for office space. In the meantime Harold and Company could dream on in Corbin, Dern's ancestral home.

Entering the barren sixth-floor suite of the Brill Building, Russell encountered two janitors emerging from his office. One looked sheepishly guilty, as if caught in the act of stealing; the other smirked defiantly.

"Just finishing up here," said the former.

"This your office," asked the latter, pointing his thumb at Russell's door. "I think you mighta left something in there by mistake," he said, barely able to contain his mirth.

They slipped past him with their mops as he went to investigate. Inside his office, a body lay sprawled on the couch, as naked as the beige walls.

She was lying facedown in a pool of blond hair, her face burrowed in the corner of the sofa. No major wounds were visible, although the broad expanse of her back was striated with fresh pink scratches. One leg sloped down from the couch and trailed off into a pile of clothes on the floor. The other tapered down toward a thin gold ankle bracelet. From the doorway Russell could see more than enough to make him doubt she was naturally blond.

He crept forward, and stopped when he was close enough to touch her, then leaped into the air when a hand casually launched itself from the couch and attacked an itch in the vicinity of her ear. Russell's first impulse was to run and hide before his presence was registered. His second reminded him that this was his office and that this girl was the anomaly. But he felt guilty and convicted in the presence of this live, naked woman, who, on examination, was extremely well formed—for he recognized among his other emotions the incorrigible buzz of outlaw desire.

The blond hair stirred and issued a moan. Suddenly she lifted her head, which had been buried in the crevice at the back of the couch. "Warren?"

"Warren?" Russell repeated, now even more puzzled.

She turned abruptly, cleared the hair from her face, took Russell in, then herself. She dove for the tangle of garments on the floor and pulled them around herself as best she could. Her face looked much younger than the rest of her, the small upturned nose dusted with freckles, and the big smudged lips. "Who the fuck are you?"

"I'm, uh, the person whose office this is."

"Where's Warren?" She was angry and frightened.

"I don't even know *who* he is." Despite his moral and tactical advantage, he felt much more embarrassed than he was trying to sound. His voice was shuttling between octaves. This made *him* angry. "Nice tan," he said maliciously.

She lashed out with a kick that just grazed his retreating calf.

"Tell me who Warren is."

"This is his office," she hissed, "and you better get the hell out." And then, "He brought me here last night to . . . he wanted to show me his . . . I guess I fell asleep." Hearing her own failed account seemed to dispirit her and drain her of anger. Indeed, it was difficult to imagine a dignified explanation of the present circumstances. She buried her face in something white and crocheted.

Russell had an inspiration. "Is Warren a black guy?"

She nodded without looking up.

"Fresh bandage on his forehead?"

She looked up at Russell with gratitude and hope, as if, having solved this mystery, he might also tell her who *she* was. Then her gaze slid across his shoulder and darted behind him as a new wave of panic seized her face. He looked around and saw Whitlock standing in the doorway. Rolling his eyes, the chief financial officer retreated down the hall.

"So what's *your* name," Russell asked his guest.

At eight a.m. Bernie Melman checked in with a phone call. Normally Russell would just be climbing out of bed at this hour, but today, as editor in chief elect and part owner of the company, he had already written three letters and disposed of a naked woman.

"Please hold for Mr. Melman. . . ." Russell picked up his own phone, since Donna, newly rehired, had yet to arrive for work.

"Hey, is this the new boss? I've cornered four million shares of a company in London this morning. So how many books have you signed up today?"

"I regret to inform you I am the only person in publishing who's awake yet."

"That's the trouble with publishing. You gotta get in there and kick some ass."

"I'm ashamed of my colleagues. But we'll do it."

"So what about this what's-his-name thing?"

"Washington Lee is his name, *n'est-ce pas?*"

"I'm sorry about what happened, right? But I'll be goddamned if I'm going to let some . . . let him blackmail me."

"I think it would help if you fired the guy who roughed him up. In fact, I think that's all he wants."

"It was an honest mistake, for Christ's sake. Guy pulled a fucking gun."

"A squirt gun, Bernie."

"Chill him out, will you? I don't have time for this chickenshit."

Victor Propp's daily call came in at ten-thirty. Now that the excitement of the deal had passed, he was having second thoughts about the outcome. "Did you see your stock lost a quarter-point yesterday? What's going on over there? They accepted a tender offer for twenty-one and a half and the stock is trading at twenty."

"Everything's golden, Victor."

"I don't trust Melman. I have reason to believe he intends to use Corbin, Dern as a vehicle. All of these corporate pirates are moving into communications and media because that's where the power and the glory ultimately reside. . . ."

Holding the phone lightly to his ear, Russell rummaged among the packing boxes for his infantry helmet.

"You're a midwestern Gentile, Russell. You don't understand these Jews."

"Speaking of Gentiles," Russell said, "how's Camille?"

"I'm too old for her," Victor said mournfully. "It's only a matter of time before she leaves me. I envy you your marriage. You have a soulmate and a helpmeet. I know, I know—what did I expect? But I once believed . . ." His voice trailed off. "I think she's corresponding—secretly, of course—with Kundera. . . ."

As he sorted through a box on his desk, Russell was jolted back to consciousness when Victor announced that he was thinking of going to Simon & Schuster. "They've made an offer, pardon the cliché, that I can hardly refuse. You know I want to publish with you, Russell, but the new Corbin, Dern is something of an unproven commodity."

Russell thought this a bit rich coming from the author of a largely hypothetical masterpiece, but he earnestly appealed to friendship and loyalty, asking Propp to wait until he had approval to match the offer.

Feeling deflated and nervous, suddenly uncertain of this new order and his own place in it, Russell put in a call to Melman, who was tied up in a meeting. Russell was prepared to argue the case for keeping Propp at virtually any cost. Erring ever on the side of credulity, he had long believed in Propp's genius, won over as much by the force of the writer's personality as by the sporadic fragments of the work. In an era in which literary greatness was in short supply, Propp's novel seemed to him, as faith in the deity had to Pascal, worth the wager of belief. But as he sat alone in the empty office, he began to question his own judgment, to wonder if he might be wrong about Victor and about a hundred other things. This feeling was aggravated by a phone call from the author of the Nicaragua book, which had been published in the midst of the takeover and which disappeared without a trace. The embittered author blamed Russell. For the first time in his life Russell experienced severe doubt about his own tastes and abilities. He called Corrine at her office; her voice arrested the free-fall of his panic, locating him within a set of familiar coordinates. He asked her what time she'd gotten to work, what was happening with the market; when she asked, he said he was fine, not quite so punctured as to leak.

Sprawling across the recently vacated couch across from Russell, Washington fingered the bandage on his pistol-whipped forehead as he listened with less than perfect attention to Russell's speech.

"I come in here on the morning of my first official day—you know, we could've ended up without *jobs*, Washington—and what do I—"

"Hey, I said I was sorry. You want it in writing?"

Two painters were unfurling a noisy tarp on the floor under one wall.

Washington stretched out familiarly on the couch. "Want her *phone* number?" He sucked the last inch of tobacco from his cigarette, examined the filter critically, took his plastic Walther from his pocket and fired at the glowing tip till it sizzled and blackened.

"I want to know when you're going to get with the program and act like a fucking responsible adult."

"How about a responsible *fucking* adult. What are you, celibate? This is *me* you're talking to, Russell. Don't pull this 'mature' shit on me. I used to scrape you off the floor and carry the remains home to your hot little wife, Crash. And I always had the decency not to slip her the old forked tongue when I kissed her good night. Understand what I'm saying? Get in touch with yourself, Jack." He tossed his cigarette butt into the basket at Russell's feet and moistened his lips with the tip of the squirt gun.

Russell was looking out the window at the giant yellow cat's eyes across the street, a billboard hovering above the Winter Garden Theatre, wondering if T. S. Eliot was perhaps spinning in his grave. "This is a whole new game, Wash, except it's not a game anymore."

"And what is this jive biz-school talk? Just 'cause you got a title now, it don't make you a book."

The painters rattled and stomped around as if they were paid specifically to make noise. Sitting still for a scolding in front of the help was definitely not Washington's idea of a good time.

"We have this company, and even if we don't feel like actual adults we've got to pretend our asses off. We can't stay out all night anymore and drag preteens up to our corporate offices for a few more lines and a hot beef injection."

"Then let's give the company back to the old farts. I guess I didn't read the fucking fine print, chief."

"Excuse me, but we gotta move this desk back," one of the painters said to Russell, who stood up and walked over to a window looking out on a porno marquee on Broadway.

Washington sighed. "You know what this is about, man? This is about you and it's about Jeff. This nigger ain't even in the fucking foreground of this picture. It's about you being pissed off that you're married and can't have a little taste of the stuff you see walking down the street and leaning against the bar and winking at you in the subway. It's about you wanting to poke your investment banker."

The painters had suddenly become very quiet and dainty in their work.

Washington lit up another cigarette. "Well, sorry, Jack, but you took out the marriage license, not me. And it's not my fault Jeff's a junkie. Going to church for somebody else's sins isn't my thing. So get off my case. Lighten up. Lighten up on Jeff, for Christ's sake. So he went all the way down that nasty road—what fucking skin is that off your ass? Let him fuck up on his own and forgive him your own self. Let me fuck who I want. It isn't about you, asshole. It basically doesn't have shit to do with you."

Russell was looking out the window. "Okay, *Warren*."

Washington shrugged. "So hey, I'm sorry. My *nom d'amour*. Girl passed out and this boy had to get home for his beauty rest."

"Why'd you come here? I'm just curious. You don't have a room with a bed in it?"

"It was close, man. I didn't want to lose the moment. I needed to visit that oval office."

"Times have changed, Wash. We have to be more righteous than the righteous. I don't need this shit anymore. I can't use it."

Washington stood up and stretched. "You just tell me what kind you do want, and that's just the kind I'll give you."

"Tell me what you want from Melman."

"You his messenger boy now?"

"I just want this over with."

"I asked him to fire the storm troopers who pistol-whipped me, and so far I can't get no satisfaction. From now on he can talk to my lawyer."

"This could make things very awkward, Wash. I mean, Bernie's our finance."

"Bernie's our asshole. Tell Bernie he can paint my fucking house."

Russell spent the rest of the morning on the telephone wooing skittish agents.

"Of course the financing's in place," was his refrain. "Don't worry about it, the money's there."

Between calls he stared from his window down Broadway, where the marquee of the Circus Cinema advertised PICK OF THE CHICKS and BOOBACIOUS.

Next door, Washington took a call from Bernie Melman.

"Please hold for Mr. Melman," said the secretary.

And that, Washington said to himself, was his second mistake.

"Washington, Bernie Melman here. I just wanted to tell you how sorry I am about that misunderstanding the other day."

"A week ago, actually."

"Russell tells me you're doing okay."

"The stitches are out, if that's what you mean."

"I'd hate to have this sour our relationship. So if there's anything I can—"

"It might behoove you to dismiss that racist who beat me up."

"Listen, you don't know how hard it is to fire somebody these days. You need a dispensation from the ACLU, practically. I got you on one side and this guy who's been with me four years on the other. But I think we can arrange something amicable here, right?"

"Anything's possible. You tell me."

"Let's get together next week and talk about it."

"I'd hate to see a guy like Parker get hold of this thing. You never can tell—he might really run with it."

"I know you wouldn't let that happen," Melman said, the amiability draining from his voice.

"Shit happens, Bernie."

"Not to me, it doesn't."

At the end of the day—after a stressful meeting with Jerry Kleinfeld at the Corbin, Dern offices to discuss details of the transition—Russell met Trina Cox for a drink at a Japanese restaurant. In greeting she slipped him several inches of tongue, which somehow put him in mind of the red, white and pink slabs of fish behind the glass of the sushi bar. Trina herself seemed particularly corporeal, red-cheeked and fleshy—as if she'd just ridden in on horseback, English saddle of course—her hair barely tamed with one of those black velvet hairbands that only girls who went to prep school knew how to wear. Russell's resistance to her dental probe was somewhat lax. "I'm in the mood for something raw," she said, sliding her eyes across the glass case before returning them to Russell.

"The *toro* is good," Russell suggested, disingenuously.

"When I did a deal in Tokyo I had this great dish called *odori ebi*— dancing shrimp. They have these prawns swimming in a fish tank behind the sushi bar and they dip them out and peel the shells off right in front of you, the shrimp are twitching like mad, and then they pop a little *wasabi* on their tails to keep them twitching. You eat them," she said, "while they're still alive."

"What's got *you* so cranked," Russell asked, feeling invigorated himself, unconsciously leaning forward when she did, dropping his gaze into the shadows below the lacy edge of her silk top.

"I've got a possible new deal going, a hostile. Makes me feel kind of carnivorous."

Russell described his own day. To be able to admit the almost physical pleasure he was taking in his work, in his new position in the world, was a great relief. At home, with Corrine, he felt he had to hide his enthusiasm, pretend he had not become one of those people whose actions have consequences in the world beyond their apartment walls, pretend to be interested in new curtains.

"Let's celebrate, Russell. We deserve a little something."

' I can't, not tonight," he said, absently admiring the slope of her bust.

She flagged the counterman and ordered sake. "When are you going to Frankfurt?"

"I don't know. Early October?"

"I might be in Brussels. Maybe I'll hop over and say hi."

"That would be nice," he said, looking away as if to disavow any excessive personal interest in the travel plans of this particular business associate.

34

Corrine dreams that she is flying, clinging to a powerful winged back, but she can't see the human face. She is a child. Beneath her the East River sparkles kaleidoscopically; septic microorganisms waiting like piranhas to devour anything that falls into their ken. Now she is buffeted by violent thermals, losing altitude, falling . . .

"Your alarm went off half an hour ago." Russell shaking her awake. "I need a forklift to get you up these days."

It was true. She never wanted to wake up anymore. Let me sleep all day.

Russell playing his shaving tune in the bathroom—a long whistle of hot water, then the clunk of the valve in the tap, followed by another screech—his head full of business and power. He woke early these days.

"Are you up?" he sang above the whine of the hot-water pipe.

When he finally emerged in the paisley robe she had bought him for his birthday the year before, she said, "I was flying in my dream."

"Sex," he said, bending close enough for her to smell the almond scent of his shaving soap.

"No, that wasn't—"

"Something about airline stocks. Takeover rumors at Pan Am."

"I was flying over the East River."

"Buy Eastern Airlines."

"But I was about to fall."

Russell stood in front of the closet studying the row of shirts. "Buy insurance."

"When did you get that tie?" Yellow with a tiny print.

"I don't know. A while ago."

"You look like all the guys at my office."

"You really know how to draw blood, don't you?" He was smiling.

"It was a man with wings but I couldn't see his face," she said, once again demonstrating, it seemed to Russell, her random-access memory.

"Now we're back to sex." He walked toward the bed holding a blue shirt with floppy French cuffs and a yellow tie. "Who was this winged man? You catch his name?"

"Icarus, maybe."

He held two barbell cuff links in his palm; she took them and pinioned one cuff, then the other, decided not to ask when he'd adopted French cuffs.

"You sure it wasn't Duane Peters?" he said.

"Duane? Duane from the office? Why would you think that?"

"That story Jeff wrote. The character based on you seems to have an affair with a character not unlike your pal Duane."

"He's *your* broker," Corrine reminded him. "And it was a *story*, as you like to say."

"A lot of it was pretty real."

"Not that," she said nervously.

But Russell seemed merely perfunctory in his suspicions, checking himself now in the mirror. "Kiss, kiss. Gotta go."

The falling dream was still with her at the office; the market had been bumpy, gliding and dipping on wings of wax. Outside, the leaves were beginning to turn and fall as interest rates rose ominously. Yet the new *Business Week* was bullish as ever. "The economy is strengthening, inflation is modest, corporate profits are exploding, the three-year binge of corporate takeovers is still in full force, and the U.S. stock market remains the cheapest in the world." So no problem, apparently. After five losing days the Dow was soaring again. Corrine was making money for her clients, but she felt a sense of vertigo. Sick, actually. Between phone calls she tried to remember when her period was due. Duane Peters raced past, his yellow tie flipped insouciantly over his shoulder, patting hers and humming "We're in the Money."

When she'd come in the week before, Duane had congratulated her on Russell's victory. "How are you going to celebrate?"

"I'm buying the very best in sackcloth and ashes."

"In *what?*"

"In token of my new widowhood."

"I'm getting a boat," Duane said.

"You?"

Duane winked and put a finger to his lips.

"Did Russell tell you?" He shook his head. She mouthed the words *You could go to jail.*

"All very discreet," he said, as she spun and walked away.

Since then he'd avoided her, but in the elevator at the end of the day, he invited her for a drink at Harry's. The Dow had closed up seventy-five on 210 million shares. Once they were on the sidewalk she stopped. "Did Russell tell you he was making a run on the company?"

"Don't worry, he didn't tell me anything."

"I think I ought to know if my husband's a felon."

"Let's not be *real* obvious about this, shall we?" They were caught up in a surge of ambulatory bodies, the evening drainage of humanity from the great ziggurats of the Financial District.

After several blocks they detached themselves from the flow and Duane clapped his hand on her shoulder. "Two months ago Russell placed an order for a hundred thousand dollars' worth of stock. He didn't tell me anything. I just thought he must have known what he was doing, particularly since he worked for the damn company and I knew he didn't have any money of his own. I copied the trade, but not in my own account. A friend bought some shares. Okay?" They were standing in a peaceful alley lined with three-story brick houses that had once been the tiny Jewish ghetto of New Amsterdam.

"It's not okay. I should report you."

"Corrine, let's not get radical about this."

"But Russell didn't buy any stock himself, right? Melman did all the buying. We don't have any money. We certainly don't have a hundred grand."

"Just between you and me, he borrowed fifty thousand on some credit card and I leveraged it up to a hundred on margin."

"You're both out of your minds."

"We're both players, babe. Forget about it. We never had this conversation. New topic. Like, who was it was telling me you had lunch once with J. D. Salinger? So what did he talk about?"

"It was years ago, I don't even remember."

"He must've talked about something, for Chrissake."

"He talked about vitamins."

An hour later Corrine was serving chili to the men at the mission, and the contrast served only to increase her loathing for the world of arbitrage and copied trades and bullish yellow ties. Although autumn seemed to quicken the pulse of most city dwellers, the homeless became glum and apprehensive as the nights grew colder.

Two hours later, at a bistro in SoHo, she looked at Russell over a bottle of Veuve Clicquot.

"On our credit card, Russell?"

"The stock's up forty percent. That's forty thou'. Don't worry about it."

"What if you'd lost the bid?"

"I didn't." He winked. "Which is what we are celebrating here. I wish you'd eat something, maybe even break down and have a glass of champers. . . ."

"The deal isn't closed yet. It's still contingent on the financing, Russell. What if that falls through?"

"It won't."

"Promise me you'll sell all the stock and pay off the credit line."

"I will."

"What you did was just crazy, but what Duane did was illegal."

"He's your friend, not mine," Russell said pointedly. Not really threatened, he was only too happy to deflect attention from his own shortcomings.

"Don't be ridiculous," she said. "So he's got a crush."

They were out alone for what seemed to her the first time in months. Russell was irrepressible, full of himself and his plans for the company. She just wished she felt a little better so she could appreciate his mood.

When they got home he became very gentle and amorous, coming up behind her in the bathroom and rubbing her back as she brushed her teeth and watched his face in the mirror while trying to suppress the squirrelly weirdness in her abdomen, because she wanted to make love to her husband, to do the mystery dance. Was it just them, or were men and women on such different schedules? Had Russell's ardor slackened as hers grew inexorably more acute? She pictured a nocturnal future in which she was propped sleepless on fluffed pillows cradling a dull hardcover under a book light, while Russell's back rose like a cliff from the middle of the bed.

Her orgasm obliterated the nausea, but only for a while. Check tomorrow and see when you're due, she thought, remembering how—when was it, three weeks, a month ago?—Russell had come home from a business dinner in one of these passionate moods that she had learned to seize upon, how he'd steered her down the hall into the bedroom, unzipping the back of her dress as he went, and how she had thought about her diaphragm sitting in its little plastic clamshell on the shelf of the medicine cabinet, and then decided that her need for him was greater than her caution and wouldn't wait, that his need might not survive the interruption, and would it be so bad, after all?

It was noontime the following day before she remembered to look at her checkbook, where she kept a fairly accurate record of her cycles, marking off the days of her period on the calendar in the back. July 31 through August 5 were crossed off. It didn't take much math; as something like giddiness swelled up within her she saw that the pattern of marks on the rows of weeks showed her late by about two rows. The pattern hardly varied through 1986 and most of 1987.

In the ladies' room, Corrine examined her face carefully in the mirror. She reached up to cup her sore breasts in her palms. Bigger, definitely bigger. Russell would like that part, wouldn't he? As she studied herself in the mirror her eyes swelled with tears. She wasn't sure why. For the past few days, she realized, she had not felt at all in command of her own emotions; it seemed as if some powerful new force was struggling to assert itself, demanding her attention, letting her know that for the rest of her life her tears and her smiles would be subject to a new authority.

After a long meeting in which he and Whitlock had studied P&Ls on all outstanding contracts, Russell was informed by Donna that Corrine had called again.

"New button," Russell asked, pointing to her left breast, which invariably displayed an inspirational message; it was her signature, just as Russell's was a silk pocket square. The new one read: "I Kill When I Come—Robert E. Chambers": a reference to the current case of a teenager who claimed he'd inadvertently strangled his date during an alleged sexual encounter in Central Park. "Very tasteful, Donna," Russell remarked.

"We can't all be yuppies," she said.

After retreating into his office, he called Corrine's office.

"What's up?"

"Nothing. I just wanted to say hi. Are you all right?"

"I'm fine, kind of going out of my mind here. These books don't show much profit, most of them. Are you sure you're all right?"

"I'm fine. I guess I just wanted to hear your voice."

Corrine left work right after the market closed, and stopped at a pharmacy. Half an hour later, having peed into a paper cup and emptied it into a test tube, she awaited the results of her home pregnancy test. What if it came out positive? Was she going to tell him? Maybe not right away. He'd just delivered a lecture about how they couldn't afford to have her quit her job.

Too nervous to read or think, she turned on *Live at Five* and paced the floor of the living room, checking the bathroom every few minutes. What does it mean, she wondered, that old thing about the rabbit dying? She scrutinized the test tube. If a sort of clot precipitated out from the solution, then chances were good they'd need a second bedroom in about eight months.

Arriving home after drinks with a neurotic but important agent, Russell found Corrine in one of her buoyant moods. She asked him brightly how his day had been, and he replied that it started off with the news that the old Corbin, Dern management was suing him on seventeen counts. "And Washington's threatening to sue Bernie Melman. Then Bernie told me absolutely no way will we pay a fucking penny more, as he nicely put it, for Propp's book until he delivers the merchandise. One of the all-time great days, a real salad, not to say halcyon, day. Remind me, how and why did I get into this mess?"

"Let's go out to dinner," Corrine suggested, moving around the apartment like a trapped fly, landing for a moment to straighten a picture or move an ashtray before taking off for another part of the room.

"I'm beat. Let's order in."

"We could eat at home by candlelight. We haven't done that in ages, Russ. And then maybe take a bath."

"Whatever," Russell said, but when he saw the look on her face he got up from the chair he'd collapsed into and took her in his arms, pressing her cheek against his collarbone, where it had been so many times before.

"It's just work," he said.

"Oh, Russell," she whispered, "I'm pregnant."

"I was so afraid you'd be angry," she said later.

"Why would I be angry?"

"Well, unhappy, anyway." They were lying on top of the bed, their clothes scattered on the floor and the bedspread.

"God, I've been such a jerk lately, haven't I?"

"Maybe just a tiny bit of a jerk."

"I've been a pig."

"But now you're cured." She giggled. "A cured pig. A ham, I guess that makes you."

"You're going to be an extremely silly mother."

For several minutes they lay there in silence. Russell waited for the first glimmer of doubt to qualify his happiness; he imagined it would come, and if so it should come and go immediately in order that he could continue to feel this way, as if he were the first man in history to have conceived a baby with his wife. A muscled patriarch, holding a club in the light of a huge fire, standing guard over the woman and child within the cave. At first he'd been shocked. But the next thing was a huge wave of excitement, which brought in its wake an overwhelming desire to make love to Corrine, to bring himself into contact with this mystery.

"What are you thinking," Corrine asked, propping herself up on one elbow and looking down into Russell's eyes. "Are you okay? Tell me."

"There's something worrying me, a big question," Russell said, looking grim, almost hating himself when he saw the panic in her eyes. "Andover or Exeter?"

At four a.m., Russell woke in a cold sweat. He got up and walked into the living room, his hands trembling, wishing he had a cigarette, though he had quit them more than two years back. He had never been so scared in his life as now.

Who the hell was he to be a father? Still practically a kid himself, thirty-one years old, about nineteen and a half emotionally. Up till the night before it seemed that a trip up the Amazon or in the Himalayas, a life in Paris or Kyoto, a stint in the Peace Corps or as a ski bum— these things were still hypothetically possible; he and Corrine had talked recently about a year in Florence. And what about that little episode with Trina, he hadn't actually *done* anything . . . anything much, a little tongue, a little tit . . . but still, goddamnit, what kind of father was he going to make if he was so easily tempted to fuck around? *Screw* around. With a kid he had to stop saying "fuck" all the time, too, and that was highly fucking likely. And money. What if the deal failed? He wondered if his own father had entertained any of these fears, imagined his own generation was spawned with less forethought. Coming of age in the wake of an alleged sexual revolution, in the brief heyday of the pill and legalized abortion, his was perhaps the first generation to view reproduction as a strictly voluntary bodily function. Was he ready to volunteer? Uncle Stork wants *you*.

Outside the windows, the eastern sky went from pewter to pink to pale blue. *Baby blue*, he said to himself, experimentally.

As the Dow dipped on news of a falling dollar, Corrine wondered if the life growing within her could possibly be unmarked by the turmoil of the past few weeks. Between job and marriage, her anxiety level was running at an all-time high: working fourteen-hour days, fights with Russell. And didn't she smoke part of a joint at that party in Steve Kopek's loft? Tears came to her eyes as she thought of all the joints she had smoked in college; she imagined singed and twisted chromosomes. And then, in the summer—she panicked, remembering the summer, and phoned Russell, insisting that Donna break in on his other call, her voice so high and quavering that he could hardly understand her at first.

"Remember," she said, "we took all that ecstasy out on Fishers Island."

"We took it maybe three times, Corrine."

"Oh, Russ, why did we do it?"

"Because it was fun. I'm amazed you didn't get pregnant back then," he said, recalling those sensual molten exed-out nights.

"So you're not worried?"

"I didn't say that."

"You *are* worried, I can tell by your voice. I can tell you're really worried and disappointed."

"Let's face it, babe, it's hell being married to a junkie."

"Russell!"

"I didn't mean it." Clearly he needed to attune himself, he thought, to this new superliteral frame of mind. When he heard her sniffling on the other end he said, "Why are you crying?"

"I was just thinking of Jeff when you said that word."

"He'll survive."

"Maybe we shouldn't have a baby."

"I thought you wanted to be pregnant." He realized immediately that his voice betrayed his exasperation and wondered if it would be like this for the next eight months. "Corrine?" When she didn't respond he said, "Look, we'll talk to the doctor about it, okay? Have you made the appointment yet?"

"I go in on Monday."

"Fine, till then drop a Valium and relax."

"Russell!"

"Whoops, not funny. Just try to chill out, and I'll be home early."

Russell next took a call from a literary agent who had once been his coke dealer, who had transferred his sales activity to the taxable sector after marrying. He still tried to maintain a sense of clandestine activity in his new profession, to invest his literary products with an aura of contraband.

"I have something you might like to taste," he said, after the preliminaries had been dispensed with. "Great stuff. Fiction. Some would call it roman à clef, but in my view that's selling it way short. Of course, I don't know if you can handle it or not, given your association with a certain novelist who some people may—mind you, I'm just saying *may*—identify with a certain less than sympathetic character in this book. But I hear he's dumped you for Simon and Schuster."

"What the hell are you trying to say, Irwin?"

"Can I trust you absolutely to keep this to yourself?"

"Yeah, sure," Russell said.

"Camille Donner."

It took Russell a moment to contextualize the name. "Propp's girlfriend."

"Everybody's girlfriend. She's finally written the book."

"And Victor's in it?"

"We're talking dignity in tatters. We're talking leave town in the middle of the night with bag over head. Make that two bags. The auction's next week. I'm looking for six figures to open."

"Deal me out." Although he might have lost Victor's book, because of Bernie's caution and Propp's manipulation, he didn't want any part of this.

"I understand. But just between you and me, if you're waiting for Victor's big novel, word I hear—it's a fictional entity. A mere figment of our imaginations. Straight from the lady's mouth. There's nothing there."

It did not take Russell long to get over his promise to Irwin, for whom secrets were a thoroughly liquid commodity. But when he called Victor there was no answer, and then he had a meeting with the bankers.

Shakier for Russell's reassurances, Corrine stared blindly at her Quotron. The sins and carelessness of the parents, she knew, were visited on the fetus. She had seen the movies and read the books, had watched the transgressing expectant mother tumble down the staircase, had heard the doctor say, *I'm sorry we couldn't save the child.*

Corrine was superstitious. Although her mind was disciplined and scientifically inclined, she believed in correspondences between things seen and things unseen that had not yet been unveiled by science; she believed in the power of words to stir and shape events in the world, so for much of the afternoon she tried to block out a word that described her worst fear, scrambling it when it raced up on her, mouthing other words and phrases like *mismanage, misnomer, mystery dance.*

That night, she dreamed she was skiing. The ski slope in her dream is peculiar in that it goes up and down like a roller-coaster track. Corrine, bulging huge with child, schusses down and up a chain of hills. Russell passes overhead on a chairlift, shouts down to her, but with the wind in her ears she can't hear what he's saying. She comes to the top of two parallel slalom courses. Jeff is at the top of one of them. Let's race, he says. What about the baby? Corrine says. Don't worry, Jeff says. They shoot side by side down the parallel slalom courses, and after that they go to the lodge, where the bartender gives them some ecstasy and Corrine realizes she isn't pregnant anymore. Where's the baby? she screams, and Jeff says, I think you left it back there.

On the other side of the bed Russell performed erratic swim strokes sleeplessly. Biology was not working for him as it was for Corrine; he wanted to catch up with her, become physically transformed into a father. While making love to her the night before, he felt the ancient imperatives of blood and the race, but now he was locked out again and he knew nothing but anxiety. Debating whether he had the courage to ask Corrine if she was sure the time was right, he felt guilty for even thinking such a thing. He knows that once asked, the question could never be taken back, that no matter how she responded Corrine would remember it forever. . . .

But the long night exhausted his doubts and fears, and in the morning he was strong and eager for his new role, full of love for the woman asleep beside him. He rose shortly after dawn and imagined himself in future fatherly postures as he prepared a breakfast tray and woke her a few minutes before her alarm.

It made perfect sense to Russell, confirmed his sense of Corrine's superb eccentricity, that she got morning-sick at night. The Sunday night before her examination was particularly bad. She threw up during *60 Minutes* and again during *Murder, She Wrote;* in between she complained that Diane Sawyer changed outfits three times during one segment, and then asked Russell if he thought Diane was prettier than she was. In the morning, still feeling awful, she called in sick to work, deciding to rest before her afternoon appointment.

Shortly after lunch, Corrine called Russell at the office. Her voice was weak and raspy.

"Are you all right," he asked.

"I lost it, Russell."

"What do you mean, you lost it?" he said, although from the tone of her voice and the sinking dive of his heart he knew exactly what she meant. And though she sounded too weary and sad to bother with the details, he had to hear everything in order to try to understand how just at the moment when he had begun to believe in a miracle it was suddenly rescinded.

In the aftermath Russell treated her with extreme solicitude. Corrine took the week off from work, and he stayed home with her the first two days, feeding her, coddling her as one would a privileged invalid. She had lost a lot of blood and her hormones were in a state of chaos; the doctor told her it would be a couple of months before her body was back to normal. Although he also said that this was a common event, that many pregnancies terminated in the first trimester, she could not help feeling guilty. Somehow Russell understood this and tried to convince her that she was blameless, that this was nature's way of telling you. At first she was angry with him, too, reminding him of the many times he'd said they weren't ready for a child, but eventually she saw how deeply he also felt the loss. And when he told her that he felt guilty because he had briefly wondered whether they could afford the baby, and had considered the alternative, she was able to reassure him and put her own sense of blame in perspective.

That Saturday, Russell took her for a walk; he tied a scarf around her neck, although it was relatively warm even for September. Walking over to the park, Corrine was a little shaky on her legs; she held Russell's arm for support, and suddenly she had a vision of the two of them creeping along together as an ancient couple, wizened and bent with the years, holding each other up, and for a moment she felt better.

But the park was full of babies, babies in strollers, babies in those backpack rigs, babies on their father's shoulders. She was the only one, it seemed, without a baby.

That night Russell took her to Raoul's, where she drank a glass of wine and laughed when he described his assistant's latest outfit, her latest button and her latest telephone conversations with her latest boyfriends.

A fine drizzle was falling as they left the restaurant, Corrine carrying a doggie bag with the remains of her steak—the doctor had prescribed red meat for her iron deficiency. The hunched, hooded figure rooting through the garbage can at the curb almost bolted when she touched his arm, but she held out the bag and said, "Please, take it, it's practically a whole steak." He cautiously accepted the bag and slipped off down Prince Street, like a dog, Russell thought, who does not want to tempt fortune by remaining at the scene of the windfall.

Back uptown, they prepared for bed. Corrine put on a nightgown, an infrequent event, but one he understood and accepted. She was deeply preoccupied.

"I'm going to quit my job," she said, her voice strident, after the lights were out. "I've been thinking about it all week. I know it's going to be tough, but I'm sorry, I want to do something useful with my life."

"It's all right." He wrapped his arm under her shoulders and pulled her toward him.

A few minutes later, in a voice filled with sleep, she said, "We can try again, can't we?"

"Of course," he answered, feeling beneficent in this abstract promise at the same time that he was troubled with a twinge of guilt over the fact that he really didn't mind waiting.

35

The limousine rolled up the long hedge-lined driveway and stopped in the cul-de-sac in front of the administration building. Before the driver had a chance to walk all the way around, the far passenger door popped open. Like a groggy pupa struggling to awaken, falling back, failing to free itself from its clinging shell in its initial attempt, a man in tuxedo emerged, holding a magnum of champagne by its neck.

Smoking his first cigarette of the day, Jeff watched from the window of his room as the man listed from one foot to the other, dazed in the brassy morning light. From this distance he looked almost familiar in his comic dishevelment. As the driver approached him he darted away and began to twirl and dip like someone who wished to finish the dance which had been so rudely interrupted by an unexpected car trip. His arms open in a posture of yearning, he glided toward a blue spruce tree at the edge of the driveway, waltzed straight into the branches and fell backward onto the pavement. A figure in white emerged from the administration building and, in concert with the driver, coaxed the failed dancer to his feet.

The fat nurse rapped on Jeff's door and called, "Time for your breakfast, honey."

Always the same old shit, he thought. Every morning breakfast. Then it's time for lunch. Then dinner. It all tasted like cardboard and cigarettes, and it didn't satisfy, because it wasn't what you really wanted. You wanted something else and you thought about it all the time, and these other, approved channels of desire and fulfillment seemed hopelessly second-rate. At night, every night, he dreamed of white powder deliquescing in a spoon, turning milky clear above an ice-blue flame. Going downtown in his dreams.

This, apparently, was the way it was going to be for the rest of his life, the fucking diurnal shuffle. Ella, the nurse, though—there was a girl who enjoyed her pancakes and eggs. Three hundred pounds, give or take, and the white uniform made her look even bigger. An improvement if they would dress the help in black, perhaps. Little black uniforms. Slim them down a little.

"Couldn't we change the order, at least. Start with dinner, say?"

"You being silly, now."

"*Silly?* Is that a technical term?" he called after Ella's retreating bulk. "Are you trying to confuse me with that psychological jargon?"

The impeccably groomed lawn had turned silvery-gray overnight, dusted with the first frost of the season. *Winter is icumen in, lhude sing goddamn.* Going outside was still a shock, the world appearing new, not quite real, like something wrapped in an invisible layer of plastic, or possibly like a brand-new yet inexplicably stale planet from which the plastic had just been removed. He hadn't been straight in a year, and now, with his pupils at normal size and his brain stem detoxified, everything looked different.

For those not restricted to their rooms, meals were taken in the dining room of the big house, which resembled a cheerful country inn—a white Georgian colonial sitting on a hill amidst acres of lawn and satellite buildings. Jeff trudged up the footpath from Glover House, his residence for the past two weeks. Just like being back in prep school, except that it wasn't. Different curriculum: group therapy, AA, biofeedback, arts and crafts, individual therapy and more AA.

Warily passing Carlyle House, from which he had recently graduated—the setting of his hellish withdrawal, where the tuxedoed new arrival would wake up sweating tomorrow. Abandon dope, all ye who enter here. Jeff dubbed it the Wildlife Refuge. New inmates often arrived at the end of long benders, still drunk and stoned from the party, whacked out when they started the tests, drawing blood, checking blood pressure, separating out the pill and scag freaks from the coke and booze people.

Pharmaceutical downs were allegedly the hardest, but downtown was none too fucking easy. When Jeff really started to get sick they kept waking him up to check his pulse, the handy green plastic bucket always there beside his bed in anticipation of the violent revolution of his outraged cells. A real sickness unto death, walking between two nurses up and down the hall to keep the heart moving, that beat-up old heart. DTs, of course, and the taste like living metal at the back of the mouth. Phenobarbitol for seizures and Clonidine to get rid of cramps. At one point he suffered a vision of Russell and Corrine coming after him with Henckel's kitchen knives, slicing his guts into pink and blue ribbons—the cause of this horrible pain.

For forty years a discreetly famous dry-out tank for Park Avenue drunks, Carlyle House had been a small, lucrative colony of the main psychiatric facility. But detox admissions had doubled and trebled in recent years; depression was showing steady growth, but substance abuse was *booming*. Some of the inmates were double threats—depressed addicts. Jeff admired the manic-depressives, believing that they were most closely attuned to the roller-coaster spirit of the age/state of the nation.

Depressives and addicts mixed freely at meals. Jeff had his little group of misfit toy friends. Dropping his tray of rubber eggs and cellulose toast this morning between Delia and Mickey. Beautiful, skinny Delia with her insane raccoon eye makeup sat motionless in front of her tray, the former cover girl of the year, looking out the bay window while her nurse exhorted her to eat. Delia fit every category of pathology covered by the establishment.

"Want to hear my dream?" Mickey said, lighting a cigarette and dropping the match in his orange juice. Mickey was a seventeen-year-old crack addict. Though he had been in for three months and was presumably clean, he always arrived at breakfast dressed for the nightlife, his long, stringy hair unwashed, his black linen jacket wrinkled and stained, reminding Jeff of the bad old mornings of his recent past.

"I'm in my car—I don't even have my driver's license yet, right?—but anyway, I'm in a car cruising down the West Side Highway way down in the Village. Around the Meat District, you know where that is? I can tell that's where it is, too, because there are these, like, sides of beef hanging on hooks all over the place. And I'm cruising in my car. So like I see this transvestite hooker, you know, one of those horrible creatures that work the orifices between Manhattan and its colonies, you know, I mean, isn't that what a tunnel is—it's like a hole, think of what that does to you, driving into a hole every day to go to your shitty little work cubicle in the city and then driving back out the hole to return to this aluminum-sided box where your wife is waiting. The really hilarious thing is, a lot of these transvestite hookers are saving up for operations so they can be *real* women and get married and live in some shitty little subdivision in Jersey. Do you know that most transsexuals get married and more than half don't tell their husbands?"

Jeff suddenly recalled a rumor he'd heard, that Bernie Melman's wife was a transsexual. He couldn't remember where he'd heard it.

"So anyway, I cruise past one of these fake chicks and then I'm slowing down my car but I'm kind of looking in from outside my dream and saying, Whoa, wait a minute, this is a dude, as in a male-type person. And then I wave the guy over—he's still dressed like a girl, right?—and he gets in the car and starts going for my zipper. I notice his makeup's melting. It falls away from his face like skin and I'm expecting to see this guy and instead it's my mother, man. My mother disguised as a guy disguised as a hooker. I mean, how twisted can you get? Taylor's gonna love it."

Mickey tapped his ashes carefully into his eggs, making two gray nipples on the glistening yellow aureoles of the yokes, and looked sideways at Jeff. "What do you think? You're speechless? Personally, I think it's got everything, big analytic box office—sexual ambiguity, homoeroticism, explicit Oedipal scene. Everything except the cigar. She didn't actually go down on me or anything, I woke up before that. But the transvestite thing raises some interesting issues for me. Like, when I was twelve or thirteen I started dressing up as a girl so I could get into the clubs. No way could I look old enough as a guy, but I could always get in as a cute girl. I got in everywhere, the Milk Bar, Area—even the after-hours clubs, A.M. P.M., Save the Robots. Then I'd slip into the men's room and change back into a boy. Dr. T thinks it had to be more than a matter of convenience, of course, a cigar is never just a cigar in this fucking place, is it? He thinks my adventures in cross-dressing were deeply significant. So hey, I admit, sometimes I got into being a chick. Once in a while I forgot to change my clothes. My mom found my makeup kit one time. I was like fourteen by then. Want to know what she said?"

He looked around the table, soliciting curiosity.

"I'll tell you. She didn't say a thing."

"You want a cigarette, Delia?" Having mangled a piece of toast he had painted with jam, Jeff felt entitled to light up.

She was still looking out the window. Jeff was about to repeat the question when she turned her head toward him and met his eyes. He tapped out another Marlboro and placed it between her full, chapped lips, smeared unevenly with red lipstick. He lit the cigarette from his lighter. Delia had not spoken in two weeks. Without really having known her, Jeff had seen her around for years. Born of hillbillies in Arkansas, she was a hot model in the early eighties. He would see her out all the time, and one of his favorite rock singers had been her consort for a year or two. She was only twenty-seven, and the life she had lived in Hotel Manhattan had seriously abraded her; she hadn't modeled in several years, and she'd been here about four months, having arrived after slitting her wrists at Minky Rijstaefel's party. Jeff seemed to recall having been there himself. Maybe. That line from *Vile Bodies*—"Oh, Nina, what a lot of parties." He didn't seem to remember much of the last year—fortunately. Delia's medical bills were allegedly paid by her last patron, a wealthy and titled European. Even in this sanctuary for the twisted and the broken, Delia was considered deeply weird.

Mickey's cigarette hissed and died in his coffee cup. "It's been unreal," he said, standing up and reaching behind his head to touch his ponytail. It was a habit he had, as if he thought the fashionable appendage would disappear. Or maybe he did it for luck. People here were superstitious, readers of signs and omens, susceptible to peripheral visions and invisible currents of airborne malevolence. Standing beside the table, Mickey looked like a crooked little flagpole trailing a thin pennant of hair. He'd been on the cocaine diet for five years, freebasing his way to that slim boyish figure.

"See you at basket weaving."

Everybody smoked. They were all addictive personalities and this was the only permissible compulsion. In group or AA, you looked around the room and smoke was pouring from lips as if from internal conflagrations, everybody burning up inside. In group last week they'd set off the smoke alarm. Alarm shrieking, the dazed and confused looking more so, hunched in their chairs holding their hands over their ears.

It was like prison or the army, where you had so little control over your own destiny that you seized every opportunity to mark time in your own manner, to gratify yourself independently of the people who controlled the keys and the passes and the med cabinet. So you smoked.

Pale from detoxification, the dancing fool whose arrival Jeff had witnessed a few mornings before smoked Gauloises, from the blue package Robert Motherwell had stuck in that famous collage. Well, if you were going to die, why not get on with it, and the hell with low-tar sticks? After all, half the people in the room had tried to do it. Self-inflicted razor tracks trickling out from under shirt cuffs. The druggies did it on the installment plan, although they denied it at first.

While they all fired up their cigarettes, Beverly, the MSW, was asking the new guy to introduce himself. His name, he said, was Brad Balfour.

"Why are you here, Brad?"

"I've always wanted to visit Connecticut."

"Tell us a little about yourself."

"I'm a venture capitalist from New York City, capital capital of the world."

"Anything else?"

"Five-eleven, one-fifty, blue eyes, and yes—I'm single."

"What else?"

He exhaled a cloud of smoke that would have done a blast furnace proud, looked out the window and sighed archly. Jeff wondered how he could possibly be so feisty after detox, and decided, a little scornfully, that the guy had a minor coke habit. For all his insouciance, though, his hands trembled and his eyes were ringed with the unflattering mascara of sleep deprivation.

"I'm a drug addict."

"Good." She nodded and let him off with this admission.

"Jeff, do you want to talk today?"

"Not really," he said.

"I've got a problem with that," said Fran, the alcoholic editor whose magazine, *Woman Today*, had published, as threatened, an unflattering profile of him after he turned down its request for an interview. Jeff didn't know if she had anything to do with this sordid transaction, but he disliked her instinctively and suspected her of being here to research an article.

"Why don't you tell us about that?" said Beverly.

"It's like, Jeff has this superior attitude. He doesn't share with us. He thinks he's too famous or something."

Beverly swiveled her head to Jeff. "What do think about that?"

"When I can think of something intelligent to say I'll *share* it with you."

"See? It's like he's saying the rest of us aren't intelligent."

"I don't think Jeff means that, do you, Jeff?"

Jeff sucked a big ball of smoke into his lungs and blew it out. "I keep seeing this glossy magazine page with an article by Fran called 'How to Get the Most out of Rehab.' "

"That's not very kind, Jeff."

"Or maybe, 'GroupSpeak: How to Sound Smart (and Look Good) in Therapy.' "

Beverly frowned. "I think Fran has a valid point here, Jeff. Perhaps you should reexamine your attitude toward the group."

In arts and crafts Delia stenciled pink bells on the handle of a basket as her special nurse, who was charged to stay within arm's length, stood by and watched. It was her fourth basket. They were manufactured elsewhere and the hospital bought them in bulk. Woodworking entailed sharp tools—clearly out of the question. Old Evelyn Salmon dithered past, supported by her cane on one side and a nurse on the other, followed closely by blue-haired Babs Osterlick.

"That's a lovely basket, dear."

Delia continued to paint.

"She's such a pretty girl," said Babs, puffing as she came to a stop beside her friend, her coif shining bluely like a polished sapphire.

"Lovely, but so thin," said Evelyn. "It would be all right if she just had a little more up top." Evelyn herself was endowed with a massive outcrop of bust, to which she often alluded in the presence of the younger men at the institution. Evelyn and Babs were approaching seventy. There was nothing particularly wrong with them—a touch of geriatric flakiness—but both had become lonely when their husbands died. Both husbands leaving behind piles of money, they had decided to spend their latter days here rather than in a nursing home, making generous contributions to the capital fund and paying full hospital rates for their lodging. The company amused them. They referred to detox patients as "the drunks" and the rest as "the loonies."

"Why bells, Evie?"

"Probably wedding bells. Poor girl's cooped up here while all the other little girls are getting a jump on the nice young men."

"If she puts on a little weight and buys a padded bra she'll do fine."

"Ding dong," said Babs, her upper body moving metronomically as she tottered away, shifting from her good leg to her stiff one. Making no sign that she was aware of them, Delia continued to paint.

"So how are we feeling today, Mr. Pierce? . . ."

The shrink's professional shtick was the genial, fatherly manner tinged with authority. Bejowled, he had a fleshy bulldog face that reminded Jeff of the late Dylan Thomas, a nearly comic juxtaposition of appearance and reality. Dr. Taylor wore cardigans and brown brogues that appeared to be made out of some petroleum-based synthetic, and he somehow conveyed the impression of smoking a pipe, though he did not. His office was immaculate, like the model unit of a condominium complex. Issues of the *Journal of Psychopharmacology* formed a perfect fan across the coffee table.

"Like shit." Jeff lifted his right foot and disheveled the arrangement of magazines on the coffee table with his toe. "Not an original metaphor for a negative emotional state, but I think it fits the case."

Dr. Taylor nodded, his jowls shaking. "That's understandable. Your body is still recovering from addiction. But we've got to try to identify your issues—"

"I'm worried about the rain forests."

"Tell me more about Caitlin, Jeff. She left you two years ago. Why do you think she left?"

"Why not ask her?"

"All that need concern us here is why *you* think she left."

"Because I couldn't commit?" This answer had an experimental, interrogative rise.

"That sounds like something she would say."

"It's true. I wanted everybody in the world to love me, and her ambitions for me were narrower. She just wanted me to love her."

"And did you?"

"Yes. But it didn't seem like enough. Ideally she would've been a blonde, brunette redhead who was whippet-thin and also voluptuous, tall and petite, nurturing and independent, fiery and complacent, whorish and motherly."

"You expected a lot from her."

"I suffer from gross expectations. This may be the only sense in which I'm a somewhat representative figure."

"Did writing a book give you a sense of fulfillment?"

"The day I finished it I suppose it did."

"Then?"

"Then an absolute conviction that the book wasn't very good—segue to more yearning, restlessness, insatiable, undiagnosable desire."

"Let's try and break that down, shall we?"

"You and what wrecking crew?"

Mail call. More books from good old Russell, the fucking dope; Jeff had been unable to read since he arrived, his concentration shot to hell. And a separate package from Corrine, which included a new copy of *Charlotte's Web*, a secret shared favorite, which Jeff had once read aloud to her in a frigid farmhouse near Middlebury, Vermont, while she nursed an ankle twisted on the slopes of Killington. Russell was off in Oxford being scholarly and all that. The nurse flipped to the end of the book and read aloud the last lines, underlined by the subtle Corrine: "It is not often that someone comes along who is a true friend and a good writer. Charlotte was both." She looked up at Jeff to see if these lines had some special, encoded significance.

"Sounds like drug lingo to me," Jeff said.

He had to open the other books in front of the head nurse, who checked for narcotics and sharp instruments. She held the books upside down and fanned the pages, ran a letter opener up the spine of the hardcover *The Stories of John Cheever*. The late St. John, the country husband half drowning in alcohol, trying to be someone for whom the garden and the family and the holy smell of new wood in the basement workshop were enough, unable to resist the baby-sitter or the paper boy or the midmorning drink. And here am I, thought Jeff—a blue-blooded junkie in suburban Connecticut.

A buddy had been assigned to Jeff when, upon graduating from detox, he'd enrolled in group. Tony had missed this morning's session because he had a pass to go into town on a job interview. Tony Del Vecchio once managed a chain of bar/restaurants based in New Haven. A tough guy, he'd started dealing coke; a natural fit, pure synergy, he explained, alcohol and drugs. Eventually he couldn't keep his nose out of the bag. Then he'd started going downtown, first chasing the dragon just to come down from the coke. Before he knew it, he was skin-popping, which led effortlessly to mainlining speed balls. After losing his job, house, wife and kids, he'd finally chosen to come here as an alternative to jail. He related this story at the first AA meeting Jeff attended, his confession tinged like all of them with the perverse pride of the survivor.

"Hey, buddy, what's this I hear about you in group," he asked, taking the chair beside Jeff's bed and turning it around, sitting down with his arms folded on the back.

"What can I say? I've never been good in groups."

"I'm just trying to help here." Tony was an unlikely-looking Samaritan, tattoos staining his forearms. "What have you got against Fran?"

"Right now I hate everybody."

"Tell me about it, buddy." He clapped a hairy hand on Jeff's knee. "I been there. Huh? It's like there's this big fucking hole in you screaming to get filled up, and everything else is just boring and stupid. Am I right?"

Jeff read the homemade tattoo on the back of Tony's hand: "Born to Party."

"I especially hate Fran."

"How's that?" Tony offered him a Camel filter, which he accepted.

"She's a fucking phony. People like Fran are the reason you start doing drugs. So you won't be like them. I don't care if she claims she's an alcoholic, she's one of the straights, one of the anal rule followers. She's a *group* person, the original happy camper."

"Bullshit. You take drugs to get high."

"She did something nasty to me," Jeff said, realizing how petty it would sound if he tried to explain it.

"Are you sure?" Tony removed his hand from Jeff's knee and slicked back his hair repeatedly as though massaging his thinking apparatus. "You probably did a lot of shitty things under the influence. Am I right? Huh?" He slapped Jeff's shoulder. "Why don't you think about that. Why don't you start by forgiving her. Then think about Step Eight in the program, that's the one where you think about the persons you failed. Make up a list of all the people you hurt because of your substance dependence. Then in Step Nine you try to make amends."

"I'm still stuck on Step Two," said Jeff. "The one where we come to believe that a Power greater than ourselves can restore us to sanity."

"That's the big one," said Tony. "Give it time."

"The entire history of civilization has been directed at freeing us from God and other arbitrary and bogus authority figures. And now, just because you crash the station wagon into a telephone pole you're supposed to say, 'Sorry, Dad, I'll eat my spinach and go to church this Sunday'?"

After dinner Corrine called. Jeff was in the TV room watching *Jeopardy* with the other burnouts when he was summoned to the phone.

"Just wanted to say I've been thinking about you."

"Been thinking about you, too."

Neither one of them seemed able to add anything. Jeff could imagine her embarrassment, her fear of saying the wrong thing.

"How's Crash?"

"Boring. All he ever does is work, and when he pops in for a second to change his clothes that's all he can talk about. He hardly even knocks anything over anymore."

"Divorce him and marry me."

"You're a real safe bet."

"That's just the point." He tried to sound chipper. "Would you rather be safe, or happy?"

"We were thinking of coming up this weekend."

"Neato."

"Try to feign some enthusiasm."

He couldn't imagine being enthusiastic about anything, much less a Sunday brunch with America's sweethearts. Somewhere in some sealed-off compartment of his heart was the knowledge that he loved these people, but he couldn't actually feel it. Mostly what he felt was angry.

They were out there in the world, and here he was, stuck in the fucking nuthouse.

"I don't think I'm ready for that," he said.

"You must need something. We could bring—"

"How about you bring me about twenty balloons of junk."

"Not funny."

"Gosh, I guess I must've lost my sense of humor in detox."

"We love you, Jeff."

"We? What's this 'we' stuff? Love's not a group activity, goddamnit. Even though the mental hygienists here act like it is. Group fucking therapy. Do you know—we're encouraged to share and hug a lot. The word 'share,' that's a goddamn intransitive verb up here. We're supposed to write little journals where we say, 'I shared with Tony today. . . . Fran shared with us about not being able to share with her family.' I know you and Russell like to do everything together, but in this case why don't you just speak for yourself." He paused, picturing Corrine's pained, beautiful face on the other end. "I love you, too," he said angrily. "Just give me some time to stop hating you."

36

"Do you want to talk about why we don't have a sex life anymore?"

"No."

"Well, I do." She knew, of course, but she wanted to hear him say it.

Lying beside her in the darkness, he sighed emphatically. "Corrine, I have to wake up and go to work in five hours."

"Is it that you find me repulsive after . . . after what happened?"

"Of course not, that's ridiculous."

"What am I supposed to think? It's been weeks since you touched me. You think I'm disgusting."

"You're supposed to understand I've got a truckload of shit on my mind right now, that I'm under a *lot* of pressure at work."

"What about what I've been through?"

Russell could hear those little tearful catches seeping into her voice.

She turned toward him and burrowed into his side. "We sound so *old*. Could you ever have imagined when we first started seeing each other that we'd have this conversation?"

"We *are* older, Corrine."

"I don't want to be an old married couple already. I'm too young to be old."

Russell sat up in bed with a furious heave of his shoulders. "Look," he shouted. "I don't have time for this right now. Everything's all fucked up."

"So tell me about it," she shouted back. "I'm your wife, Russell."

"All right, all right, I'm getting weird signals from Bernie, for one thing, and we're hemorrhaging staff and authors. People are saying they hear the deal is shaky. Well, that becomes self-fulfilling. And I don't know if I really have a job yet, not until the papers are all signed."

"But you own part of the company," Corrine said soothingly. "That's something."

"Melman has controlling interest. And he's got his own agenda, which doesn't necessarily include me."

"Isn't it possible," she said quietly, "that you're overreacting?"

"I don't think so."

After a long silence she said, "I'm sorry. I didn't know."

He lay back down. "You were right. About the deal. I wish I'd never thought of it."

"It'll work out." She reached over and stroked the furrows in his forehead, which reminded her suddenly of the blubbery striations on the beached whale at Bernie Melman's summer house. That was the day she'd known that everything would go wrong.

"Wait a minute—aren't we sort of rich now?"

"We may have a couple million in stock if everything goes through," he said gloomily.

"My God, listen to yourself. You could retire and write poetry."

"It's a little late for that, Corrine."

"You're thirty-one years old, Russ."

"Almost thirty-two."

"I'll buy you a cane. Come on! It's not too late for anything. You've done what everybody wants to do—make a pile of money and do what they want."

"I'm not ignorant enough to start over from scratch. When you're twenty you don't know how hard it is to be a poet or whatever, and if you can fool yourself long enough and work hard enough you may have a shot at becoming what you were pretending to be. It's not just a question of time and money. It's a question of being able to fool yourself."

"Just a couple of months ago you fooled yourself into thinking you could buy a whole company."

"Maybe I used up my capacity for faking myself out. Anyway, it's easier buying a company than writing a significant poem."

Although she believed much of what he'd said, Corrine would have been sad to think *he* really believed it. If she lacked his general optimism, she recognized his tendency toward self-dramatization.

"Why didn't you tell me all of this earlier?"

"I don't like to leak."

"Talking's not leaking, for God's sake."

"Can I say something, then? Can I, like, be really honest for a change?"

"Of course."

Corrine raised herself up on one elbow and looked down into his face. In the darkness she could just make out the outline of his head on the pillow and the glint of his eyes. He took her hand in his own.

"I'm worried about you. You're too thin. You're disappearing in front of my eyes. You know this has been a problem for you in the past. I think you should get some help."

She turned her back to him and pulled the sheets and blankets up around her shoulders. Couldn't he see how big she was? All he had to do was look at her. She felt his hand measuring her hip.

"It's because I'm too fat that you won't sleep with me, isn't it?" she said. "That's what you really mean."

"Corrine, don't do this."

"I don't blame you for thinking I'm gross," she said.

"Are we even speaking the same fucking language?"

"Don't yell."

What made him angrier still was that at the most fundamental level she was right about one thing. They didn't make love as much anymore and he was angry that he had lost some of his desire, a thing he never could have imagined ten years before. He was angry because she had come near a truth he could not bear to admit even to himself, which was that passion cannot be sustained forever, though other compensations might replace it. The tragedy of monogamy. To acknowledge this seemed disloyal. It also seemed to him a failure of manhood; having for a long time wanted his wife as often as he could get her, he feared that his own vitality was waning now that this was no longer true.

Russell turned on the bedside lamp, rolled out of bed, flipped off the covers and scooped Corrine up in his arms.

"You'll hurt your back," she protested as he carried her like a baby across the room and lowered her legs to the floor.

"Look at yourself!" he shouted, standing her in front of the full-length mirror and ripping her nightgown open from the neck with both hands, peeling it away from her body as she struggled against him. She dug her fingers into his cheek as he yanked one of her arms from its sleeve. When he twisted her arm so far she thought it would break, she sank her teeth into his shoulder, drawing blood. Though in all her fury Corrine was no match for him.

"Look." The pink nightgown lay shredded on the carpet at her feet, her arms pinned behind her back. One hand encircling her wrists, he grabbed the back of her head with the other and forced her to face the mirror. She tried to shake her head free.

"What do you see?"

She closed her eyes tightly, opalescent flashes of color swelling in the darkness behind the lids like globules of fat floating slickly on the water in a saucepan.

"What do you see? Go on, look at yourself."

She was spinning. She held her eyes shut until she felt herself disappearing into a pit of nausea and blackness.

"What do you see, goddamnit?"

"A monster," she said, facing her own reflection at last, seeing in Russell's grasp an anonymous form that resembled a supermarket turkey, plump and white and plucked.

"There's hardly anything to see," he said.

"An unlovable monster."

Russell released her then. He picked her up again and carried her gently back to the bed. Suddenly she felt weightless and insubstantial in his arms, as if he were not so much lifting her up as holding her down, keeping her from drifting up and dissolving into the night like a snowflake caught in a thermal.

"One of us has to get smaller," she whispered. "You take up more and more room in the house, so much space. I feel like there's none left for me."

As he lay her down on her own side of the bed, the right side, which had always been hers since they started sharing a bed years before, the sensation of heaviness reasserted itself and she sank through the coiled-spring whirlpools of her mattress into a dreamless sleep.

Russell woke at seven twenty-seven, oversleeping by nearly an hour. After starting the coffee in the kitchen, he hurriedly showered and shaved. At eight he tried to wake Corrine. He kissed her cheek, shook her warm, bony shoulder gently for fear it would break off in his hands. A thick strand of blond hair encircled her neck like a gold choker. "Corrine?"

He continued to shake her. She issued a faint syllable of protest and tried to turn away from him.

Finally he succeeded in getting her to open her eyes. She scanned his face fearfully. "Rise and shine."

She closed her eyes and shook her head.

"Please."

"I don't feel shiny."

He stroked the hair away from her forehead. "Well, even if you don't, you still have to go to work."

"I don't ever want to go to work again."

"That's a little extreme, isn't it?"

She opened her eyes to glare up at him. Russell had seen this look before and it frightened him. "I never wanted to be a stupid stockbroker anyway. You made me do it."

"I *made* you do it?"

"You let me know in your own none too subtle way that we needed to bring in more money. I wanted to get my certificate and teach. I hate my job. I hate the people I work with. I feel like a con artist. I hate the whole—"

"I didn't know you felt this way."

"You didn't want to know. You wanted me to keep bringing home a stupid paycheck."

"I'm not that venal, am I?"

"No, you went into a noble profession. You didn't want to dirty your soul grubbing after money. You're a sensitive soul. Fucking Maxwell Perkins, that's you. Russell Calloway, friend and patron of literature. But you didn't mind turning your wife into a capitalist, sending her out into the marketplace. Whoring her out to the yuppies."

"In case you haven't noticed, I've been doing a little money-grubbing myself lately."

"You bet I've noticed. And it's not very becoming, honey."

"Neither is this mood of yours. You do what you want. I'm going to work."

"I gave notice last week," she said as his pin-striped back disappeared out the door. She thought he hadn't heard, hoped he hadn't heard, till he reappeared in the bedroom doorway.

"You did?"

"I told you I was going to," she said contritely. "You said you understood."

He sat down on the bed beside her, ran his hands repeatedly through his already slicked-back hair, brushing it off his forehead. He nodded. "That's okay," he said. "If that's what you want."

"It is?"

"I don't want you doing something you hate."

She lifted herself on her elbow and kissed him. "I just couldn't do it a minute longer. Life's too short."

He nodded. "Don't worry about it. You're absolutely right."

"I didn't know who I was anymore. And I felt like our marriage was falling apart, too, like it was going to die if somebody didn't start paying attention."

Russell shook his head. "Don't worry about that. So when do you finish?"

"The ninth. You're sure you're not angry?"

"I'm sure. I'll take you out to dinner to celebrate when I get back from Frankfurt."

"I forgot about Frankfurt."

"I'll be gone less than a week," he said.

"Who's going with you?"

"Just me, Washington and the sub-rights director."

"Not Trina?" She watched his eyes. He always turned away from her gaze when he told a lie.

"Why would Trina come?" Not until he had finished the sentence did his eyes cut away. Did that mean he was telling the truth, or that he was getting better at lying? But he seemed innocent enough, checking his pocket for keys and then hunting through his top drawer for the dry-cleaning slip, knocking his stud box to the floor. As she speculated about Russell's sexual waywardness, Corrine was somehow reassured to see the shaving soap on his earlobe.

37

Russell and Corrine drove up on the Saturday of the last softball game. Jeff had moved to the main house at the top of the hill—progress of a sort. The administration presumably wanted inmates to know that it was all uphill. From this modest summit he watched them pull up in their Jeep, Delia sitting beside him, her nurse standing at a discreet distance. Russell had the top down and Corrine was riding with her hand on top of her head as if to keep her hair from flying away. After he parked, Russell loped around the front of the Jeep and offered his arm to Corrine, who bounced out of her seat and shook out her wind-tossed hair like a golden retriever emerging from water. Jeff didn't know if he was ready to face their frisky cheer. America's fun couple visits the funny farm. He had yet to forgive them for landing him in this place, and it didn't necessarily make him feel any better that they looked so good. "Here's the Prince and Princess in their six-horse carriage," Delia said.

As they always did when they were tense from fighting, Russell and Corrine tended to become broad and vaudevillian in their attempts to put on a good show and to spare others their unhappiness. After fixing her hair, Corrine curtsied archly and locked her arm in Russell's. She hadn't particularly wanted to ride all the way to Connecticut with the top down, not on a chilly morning in early October. "We shall not," he'd said, "be tyrannized by the calendar." Well, bully for us, she thought, wondering all the way up why with Russell she could never just come right out and say what she meant, ask for what she wanted, in this case to put the top up. But what she really wondered was why after all these years Russell couldn't be more sensitive to her moods and desires, more adept at picking up hints. Why did she have to take out a damn billboard every time she needed something? Russell blurted out his whims and desires as they occurred to him. It wouldn't occur to him that she might communicate less directly.

By the time they got lost outside of Darien she was seething. And Russell simply would *not* stop to ask for directions, reminding her exactly of her father, who would drive in circles for hours rather than reveal ignorance in front of a stranger. Then when she'd suggested that Jeff might still be a little upset with them, Russell responded, "No shit." She didn't like his implication that they hadn't done the right thing, so she had asked him straight out if he would rather have let Jeff go on killing himself, and he came out with, "It's his life." He'd actually gone on to say that there were worse things than being a junkie, that maybe Jeff couldn't be like everybody else. She burst out of the Jeep at a red light and crossed three lanes of traffic to ask for directions at a gas station, which she then conveyed to him in terse snippets, and otherwise they did not speak again until they pulled up in the parking lot of the hospital.

Jeff started down the hill to meet them. Corrine ran the last twenty yards and leaped on him. It was the rare visitor who wasn't self-conscious here; Russell's ruddy vitality made him seem especially out of place, his awareness of this fact making him even more awkward. As soon as he saw Jeff he began to smile like a child who has been commanded to do so for a camera or a frightening relative. What remained of his midwestern Catholicism was embarrassed by the very idea of a mental hospital, and he still felt culpable for Jeff's rude incarceration. Recently he'd been troubled with memories of small betrayals and abdications. He saw that as the world had come knocking on Jeff's door he had gradually drawn away and slipped out the back, out of some perverse sense of emotional economy if not outright jealousy. At first Jeff's triumph had been his own—the respectful reviews, the best-seller lists. His star had risen with his best friend's. But at some point he grew tired of being referred to as Jeff Pierce's editor and annoyed by what he imagined to be the perception that his success was the lucky strike of his friendship with a talented writer. To the degree that he had stifled and domesticated his own appetites, he resented Jeff's sudden license to gratify his wishes almost indiscriminately. He hadn't just walked the dog, he'd let it run free to gorge and fight and fuck the bitches.

It wasn't his fault that Jeff was an addict, but he knew he hadn't helped.

The two men shook hands.

"Welcome to Bedlam," Jeff said.

"We brought you a few things," Corrine said, rustling the Bergdorf bag on her arm.

Jeff raised his hands to fend her off. "I'm afraid this merchandise will have to be submitted for a Good Nuthousekeeping seal of approval," he said, beckoning them inside, where he presented them with arch ceremony to the people on duty at the nurses' station. "Are you approved for chocolate," asked the nurse, holding a foot-long Toblerone bar aloft. Jeff nodded. "I'm just a junkie," he explained cheerfully. Some of the depressed patients were on medication that virtually exploded in combination with certain enzymes in chocolate. The books and cigarettes passed inspection, but the bottle of Geo. F. Trumper Extract-of-Lime aftershave was confiscated. "Glass," explained the nurse, shaking her head. "And *alcohol*," she added, reading the label.

"There goes my chance," Jeff said, "to smell like a gin and tonic."

Stifling her dismay, Corrine asked to see his room. There wasn't much to see, but she commented favorably on the view and on the light from the two windows. With its private bathroom and stained pine furniture verging on the antique, the room would have made a perfectly decent single at a New England bed-and-breakfast.

"It's lovely," Corrine said.

"Neither bars on the windows, nor straps on the bed," Jeff said, knowing that Corrine was relieved not to find any hint of the clinical, semipenal nature of the institution reflected in the interior decor. "They had both at Carlyle House, where I detoxed."

Corrine linked arms with Russell and Jeff as they walked down the big lawn through the fecund smell of a recent mowing, the leafy tang of autumn in the air. "I love the fall," Corrine said. "Taking your sweaters out of mothballs, raking leaves and college football games—all that stuff. Summer is overrated. I was the weirdo who couldn't wait for school to start again. Had my pencils all sharpened in my pencil box and my notebooks labeled."

"We hated girls like you," said Russell.

Jeff saw Delia lurking in the shadow of the big elm. When he waved, she disappeared behind the tree.

"Corrine actually *liked* math," Russell added.

"I know," Jeff said.

"Can you imagine?"

"That's Carlyle House," he said, pointing at what appeared to be a handsome white Georgian mansion. "Scene of fiendish tortures supervised by Medical Inquisitors and Latter-Day Puritan Clerics disguised as nurses."

"Well," she said, "thank God you're through with that." They walked in silence down a shaded path. Corrine sniffed the air dramatically and squeezed the arms of her escorts. "You know what this reminds me of? That gorgeous day at the beginning of senior year when the three of us skipped Transcendentalism seminar and smoked a joint on top of the observatory."

"Very transcendent," Russell said. Jeff was about to say he didn't remember, when he looked over at Corrine and saw that she was crying. Neither of the men could think of an appropriate reaction, so they continued walking.

Wiping her eyes with the back of her hand, she asked, "Why does it seem like just yesterday when it was really such a horribly long time ago."

They drifted toward the softball field, where the athletic director, a bearded young intern from the state hospital, was racing around blowing his whistle. The players themselves seemed unnaturally subdued, leaving the coach to do the pep talk for both sides: "Hey, hey, pitcher's got a rubber arm. . . . Knock it out of the park. . . . Heads up in the outfield. . . ."

"Why aren't you playing," Corrine asked.

"The worst moments of my youth," Jeff said, "were associated with baseball. The smell of leather and bubble gum still makes me nauseous. My father dragged the happy family off to England on an exchange program, and when we got back all the kids were playing baseball. I struck out my first seventeen at bats and after that I only got worse. One time in junior high I got on first base with a walk, so I decided to distinguish myself by stealing second. Which I did. Trouble was, one of my teammates was already *on* second. He had to go for third and we both got thrown out."

"Russell's dying to get out there and play. He was the big hero at the artists' and writers' game in East Hampton."

Russell shook his head in an approximation of modesty. They were standing behind the backstop, watching a young man being coaxed into the batter's box by his nurse and several teammates. A thirty-five-year-old who looked sixteen, Rick had tufts of hair that conjured up a palsied barber, and eyes like cloudy liquid within the fishbowl lenses of his glasses. Rick was a severe case of something, Jeff told them under his breath, and was, in fact, about to be transferred to a more appropriate facility. When Jeff first met him he'd introduced himself as the president of the United States. His identity changed frequently, particularly when he was watching TV. "That's me," he'd say, when an actor caught his fancy. "I'm that guy."

The bearded doctor showed him how to hold the bat in front of his body for the bunt. Making no concession to athletic fashion, Jeff's friend Mickey was on the mound for the addicts, funereally chic in his black suit and pointy King's Road shoes. He underhanded a pitch, which struck Rick's bat and dribbled to a stop a few feet from the plate. The depressives huddling on the sidelines suddenly cheered and screamed, urging him toward first base.

Rick took off. As he neared the base he veered off into foul territory and kept going. His attendant, a strapping matron built for power rather than speed, waddled after him. Rick broke to the right and bolted for the road, a well-traveled rural highway that curved blindly into the woods just beyond the main driveway. The depressives were still cheering, while the bearded doctor-coach scuttled back and forth, rodentlike, between home plate and the edge of the batting cage, uncertain of what to do. Rick ran without grace, like a toddler, stumbling twice, losing one of his sneakers, but his enthusiasm was unbounded and he easily outstripped the nurse.

Russell launched into a run and raced across the grass toward the road. Though he ran fast, Rick did not run straight, his somewhat erratic trajectory tending to arc toward the point where the road looped back into the trees, and Russell cut him off at the curve just after a red Volvo station wagon had swerved past, horn blaring. Russell spun Rick back onto the lawn, held him around the waist while he flailed and cackled with laughter, and finally turned him over to the winded nurse.

Both teams had fallen silent as the two runners converged at the road.

"Another save for Calloway," said Jeff. "One more and we can put him up for canonization."

As they walked back, Rick and Russell were greeted with equal enthusiasm, as if they constituted a winning team. Jeff had disappeared. Up at the main house, the nurse told them that he had retreated to his room with a headache and that he would call them later.

38

Corrine had always loved autumn, and nowhere more than in New York. Exiles returned from their weekend and summer refuges, and the half-melted skyline snapped to attention in the breeze as the limp, fetid city regenerated itself.

When Corrine was at prep school this was the season of cotillions and balls and boys with hip flasks in the pockets of their first tuxedos. And later, of triumphal urban reunions with old friends newly hatched from New England campuses, and the evolution of new alliances, all of which seemed, on the old academic rhythm, to begin in the crisp leafy air of September. Far from conjuring thoughts of mortality, the falling leaves seemed like confetti pouring down on the festivities. Autumn was one long Advent season leading inevitably to the Christmas tree at Rockefeller Center and holiday parties and robin's-egg-blue gift boxes with red bows from Tiffany.

This year, though, the equinox provided no lift. The city seemed to her to have lost its poetry. The headlines were ugly, the party invitations looked like tickets to limbo or worse, and the leaves were aptly dying. The men at the soup kitchen added new layers of old clothing, grimly anticipating the cold; every week there were more of them. Her depression felt symptomatic of a general malaise, and she resented it when Russell implied it was the miscarriage, resenting at the same time how little it seemed to have affected him.

The week after visting Jeff, Russell flew to Frankfurt, where the international publishing tribe gathered once a year; he'd been revved up about the trip for weeks. She hoped, without grounds, that he would calm down upon his return. Among their friends and class, single-minded devotion to one's career was considered the cardinal virtue, but in Corrine's view fanaticism was heavy upon the land. Broadly construed so as to include eating, drinking and talking on the phone with authors, agents and editors, work claimed all of Russell's energies, and it was making him a dull boy with respect to his wife, though no doubt Trina Cox thought he was just mahvelous. Maybe it was a function of her new sobriety or her impending unemployment, but increasingly Corrine sensed that—gossip aside—most of what passed for conversation in this noisy city was only shoptalk.

Her last week of work, Corrine watched the stock market drift downward. She called all of her clients and explained that she was leaving, advising them to move some of their capital into cash. Many she turned over to Duane's care, but she advised Mrs. Leon Ablomsky, the widow, to move totally into cash. "The market's getting strange," she explained. "I'd be worried about you if you stayed in."

Mrs. Ablomsky was more worried about her new friendship than her money. "I suppose I'll never hear from you again."

"I promise I'll stay in touch."

"You young people have your own busy lives. Pretty soon you'll be having a family, God willing, and you won't have time for me."

God willing, Corrine thought with a pang.

On Tuesday morning, October 6, some kind of panic broke out like subterranean fire and suddenly everybody was selling. By the end of the day, the market had lost a record ninety-two points on 176 million shares and Corrine's colleagues were dazed by the rout. Everyone retreated to Harry's for a postmortem, blaming higher German rates, program trading, looming budget and trade deficits. Although Corrine had been as frantic as anyone during the day, she now felt detached. The next day the Dow dipped thirty and then caught a thermal to close up two points. Nobody had a clue about what was going on.

On Thursday the market dropped thirty-four points. Bearish humor prevailed at Corrine's farewell party the following day, where she was complimented for her sense of timing. Among the parting gifts were two teddy bears. Her boss, who'd given her a pack of tarot cards in token of her renowned superstitions, suggested that the market was falling in anticipation of her departure and that she owed it to the rest of them to stay. Duane's gift of *The Interpretation of Dreams* was inscribed "To a Dream Girl, with Love, Duane." As the party was breaking up he asked her to dinner, knowing that Russell was in Frankfurt. She lied and said she had plans, and invited him over to the apartment for dinner the following week.

She was planning a surprise dinner party for Russell's birthday. She had been resisting the idea of inviting Trina Cox, but she realized it would look deliberate and peevish. From her desk she called Trina's office. A male secretary answered, told her Trina was out of the country for a few days.

"Out of the country," she asked, barely able to speak.

"Brussels," the secretary said. "To be precise."

Corrine felt herself go limp with relief. Brussels was okay.

"Hold on a moment. . . . Sorry, she *was* in Brussels yesterday but today she's in Frankfurt."

"Oh, God."

"Do you have that number?"

"Is it the Frankfurter Hof?"

"I beg your pardon. I didn't hear you."

"Is she staying at the Frankfurter Hof?"

"Let me . . . yes, that's right. Would you like to leave a message here in the meantime?"

A howling storm of wind and noise seemed to wash over her, and when it receded she was holding the receiver to her face and a voice was saying, "Would you like to leave a message?"

"No message."

She misdialed twice before successfully completing the second sequence of numbers. There was no answer in Russell's room, which didn't really surprise her; she was almost relieved. After all, he might have a satisfactory explanation as to what Trina Cox was doing in Frankfurt, at his hotel, though he had specifically denied that she would be going. Irrationally, she imagined that this grace period would give him a chance to come to his senses and undo whatever damage he might have done. The desk clerk came back on the line asking if she would like to leave a message.

"Yes, I would."

"You will be leaving this message for Mr. or Mrs. Calloway?"

"Mrs. Calloway? You have a Mrs. Calloway?"

"You wish to leave her a message?"

"No. A message for Mister. From Corrine. From Mrs. Calloway . . . the real Mrs. Calloway . . . Tell him . . . The message is . . . Oh, Jesus . . ."

She didn't think she would make it to the ladies' room, past all the work stations, past the wide bodies of strangers and the white faces that swiveled like gun turrets tracking her flight.

In the bathroom she sat huddled in a stall with her face against the cold metal partition, clutching the toilet paper dispenser, trying to ride out the alternate waves of anguish and nausea.

She had no idea how much time had passed before the door opened, admitting a gust of shrill conversation accompanied by the ticking of high heels across the tiled floors.

"She calls your house?"

"She calls my house and says, 'This is Mrs. Townsend. Harlan's wife.' She really emphasizes the word 'wife,' big fucking deal, like this'll impress me. You know? What's she want, a medal? Just 'cause she managed to let herself get knocked up ten years ago. So, I'm like, 'Who?'"

"No. You said that?"

"I say, 'Who?' Just like that. Just like I'm saying it to you now. Playing it totally cool, you know. Like I'm not going to give her the satisfaction. Keep my dignity, you know, let her make a fool out of herself. I go, 'Who?' And she goes, 'I know who you are.' I mean, *really*. Like she's caught me in the act or something."

"She can't prove anything."

"That's what I say. It's not like she's got photographs or anything. So I say, 'I don't know what you're implying here, but I don't have anything to feel ashamed of, and anyway, if you're unhappy at home, then don't go blaming it on me, and furthermore—'"

"I do blame you," Corrine said, emerging violently from the stall.

"So who are you," asked the frightened woman who had handled Mrs. Townsend so deftly, as Corrine approached like the avenger of matrimony.

39

Trina arrived in Frankfurt at noon, having finished business in Brussels early. Neither of them had exactly planned a meeting in Frankfurt—a plan inferred a contract—but when she suggested she might stop off for a day, Russell said it might be fun, full of admiration for the fact that she casually hopped planes between European cities, for the generous purview and reach that this implied. It was difficult, lately, to get Corrine to take a taxi downtown.

Certainly Trina had not intended to stay with Russell, but when she arrived she discovered there was not a single room to be had in the entire city, let alone in Russell's grand hotel, one of the few prewar structures left downtown and currently the humming center of the European book world. Mr. Calloway was not in his room, and the red-jacketed desk clerk, martial in bearing, had no idea when he was expected. Trina was sweaty and tired and there was this incredibly annoying piece of gristle stuck in her back teeth from the sausage she'd eaten for breakfast. Hanging around the lobby—however sprawlingly replete with overstuffed arm-chairs and couches—was not Trina's idea of fun, and she was not the kind of girl who meekly submitted to fate.

"I'm Mrs. Calloway," she said. "Could you please show me to our room?"

If the clerk was skeptical, Trina's hauteur carried the encounter. He summoned a bellhop with a guttural bark. As she turned away he said, "May I record your passport number, Mrs. Calloway?"

"Certainly." She dipped into her shoulder bag and produced the document. As he opened it, she added, "My maiden name, of course."

*   *   *

When Russell returned to his hotel room to dress for dinner, he discovered Trina doing sit-ups on the floor, ankles hooked beneath the footboard of the bed. "I bought you some chocolates in Brussels," she said, "but then I decided to deliver them myself."

After back-to-back drink appointments, Russell was disoriented by the sight of his investment banker in filmy gym shorts and clingy T-shirt with a fresh patina of sweat over her limbs and face. Her kiss was relatively restrained, merely a greeting, perhaps to compensate for the presumption of commandeering his room. But the animal scent of her body permeated the air in such a way as to make the outcome of the evening seem, for Russell, almost a foregone conclusion—even before she complained that she'd never before failed to get a goddamned hotel room. For months he'd imagined and rehearsed this encounter; now he drew back and looked for a reprieve from his desire at the very moment that its consummation had become inevitable. Uneager to confront his impending dilemma, Russell uncorked a bottle of champagne from the minibar and entertained Trina with gossip from the fair: Harold Stone was haunting the event as minister without portfolio and Ghost of Frankfurts Past. "Poisoning my well, no doubt." Washington was juggling three different women. Camille Donner, Victor Propp's former squeeze, had turned up, flogging the foreign rights of her roman à clef and incidentally shopping for a new mate. A bootlegged chapter of the book circulating at the fair sketched a portrait of a certain middle-aged contender to the Great American Novelist title as being impotent in bed and at his writing desk. "Poor devil," Russell concluded loyally, regretting a certain zest in his account of the gossip.

"We are all strong enough to bear the misfortunes of our friends."

"What a terrible thing to say," said Russell, who admired her toughness but couldn't help thinking of Jeff.

"I think I stole it from Montaigne." Trina had not been made privy to what Washington called the perils of Pierce.

"So what are your plans?" Russell was suddenly anxious, calculating that he had ten minutes to shower and change if he allowed twenty minutes for the cab queue and half an hour for the ride to the castle west of town where the dinner would be held.

"I've got a ticket for New York tomorrow," she said, adding coyly, "I thought maybe I could avail myself of your couch tonight." Russell hadn't asked Trina how she talked her way into the room; she was nothing if not resourceful.

"If this is a problem for you, I can maybe fly out tonight."

"No, no. You're . . . here. It's no problem. I mean, I'm glad you came." Of course it was a problem, but for some reason he wasn't able to say so. Men were not supposed to admit, it seemed to Russell, that there were ever any circumstances under which they did not necessarily wish to get laid.

She accompanied him to the dinner, an important event sponsored this year as every year on the Friday night of the fair by a German publisher who called it his own '21' dinner—dinner for twenty of his favorite colleagues and himself, though the ranks often swelled according to the enthusiasms of the invited guests. Russell saw no alternative to asking Trina to accompany him. But he was happy to have her beside him as the cab passed through the gates and ascended the steep, winding drive, the Gothic windows of the *Schloss* glowing yellow above them. When they pulled into the porte cochère, Russell said, "It always reminds me of something out of Wagner."

"God," said Trina, looking down. "I don't know if my tits are big enough for Wagner."

"I think they'll do nicely," Russell said.

By the time drinks at the bar were concluded, Trina had so captivated their host, the seventy-five-year-old publisher, that he deftly rearranged the seating plan in order to place Trina on his right, where, when she leaned forward and lifted her knife hand, he was able to command a nearly unimpeded view of her unfettered right breast. He was impressed, too, as was the company at large, by her bulletins from the martial front of big finance, and by the fact that she had once shot grouse on the same Scottish estate he visited every November. Getting outside a bottle of '61 Château Palmer, which had followed close on the Krug, Russell allowed himself to feel proud of his escort. Beneath the vaulted thirty-foot ceilings and Baroque chandeliers, against a backdrop of medieval tapestries, sitting beside the streaky-blonde young wife of a famous Italian novelist, he was willing to concede that even the illusion of the good life might occasionally be enough.

Russell was happy to be here with old Hoffman, who was the kind of publisher he wished to be: a man of principle as well as a man of the world, who during the war had gone into self-imposed exile in New York. Like Whitney Corbin, Hoffman was born to the business, but unlike Corbin he had taken to it with passion and extended his father's literary and intellectual empire. Brecht and Mann and Hemingway were among his friends, and when he had taken notice of Russell at the book fair two years back, the young American editor was thrilled to be a part of that extended circle. The year before, Hoffman had published a translation of Jeff's book, and in celebration they had spent the last night of the book fair drinking together till four in the morning. The thing that had impressed Hemingway when they had first met, Hoffman told Russell, was that the young Hoffman could hold his liquor. The year his father had published *Death in the Afternoon*, Hoffman had gone drink for drink with the famous writer without visible effect—and Hoffman was glad to see that young Calloway could hold his liquor, too.

The older man's regard meant much to him, and without stopping to examine the implications too closely, Russell decided that his admiration for Trina was another sort of benediction, a shared masculine enthusiasm. Meanwhile he was talking with the Italian novelist's wife about the Red Brigades and speculating on why so little fiction had come out of the sixties. Approaching forty herself, she had once been the lover of a famous terrorist. Her history as the lover of famous men dwarfed Camille Donner's and gave her an aura as palpable as her ancient husband's intellect. "It's an extremely complex business," Russell said, out loud, "balancing the need for social organization against the anarchic demands of the heart."

"Back then, we thought it was very simple, very black and white," she said, thinking he was still talking politics.

Pouring another glass of claret, he said, "I mean that I love my wife, but I sometimes wonder if it's . . . ungenerous not to love other women." He felt that she, as a seasoned mistress and a European, would know exactly what he meant.

"Americans are like children," she said. "You believe this fantasy of true love, yes? You think marriage is only about love and it means you only must sleep with one person forever. No wonder you are having so many divorces."

Looking over at her seventy-year-old husband, Russell could imagine that she probably had broader views of the motives for marriage. Was it a coincidence that she took this moment to smile sweetly and say that she would be visiting New York next month?

Sitting on his other side, Trina squeezed his thigh. "Thanks for bringing me," she said, leaning into his ear and dipping to kiss the nape of his neck. It occurred to Russell that he should get to a phone to call Corrine; it would be awkward to call her from the room later, even more so if she called him. Hoffman changed places with Trina. He dropped a fatherly arm around Russell's shoulder and proffered a cigar. He asked Russell about plans for the new company. Russell began to explain the state of publishing in America, with hand gestures. One of these gestures intersected an inconveniently placed glass of red wine, which emptied itself across the table. "Yes, yes, you're quite right," Hoffman shouted. "This is no time for wine. Bring on the Armagnac!"

The party continued in town at the Lipizzaner, the hotel piano bar. They were sitting at a table with some boisterous Scandinavians. A bottle of aquavit disappeared rapidly. One of the Swedes said, "The Finns, they drink like fish." Why fish? Russell wondered. The scaly, finny Finns.

Moments later he was on his way to the men's room, which Trina, never one to wait in line, was about to exit. Instead she pulled him inside and pushed him against the sink, wrapping her face around his, her tongue probing the depths of Russell's throat, while her hands performed cartographic operations on his surface. So engaged, they were discovered by Harold Stone, who appeared suddenly in the doorway. In a moment he was gone, and Russell could almost believe he had imagined the encounter, except that Harold's expression of contempt seemed so unpleasantly real. Trina, however, neither recognized nor even noticed the intruder; her ardor was unabated. But Russell felt caught out and diminished under that gaze, however brief. He saw himself as foolish and weak, easily led by others, far too secure in his belief in his own decency. He feared, suddenly, that he was not *serious*, that while he shared their weaknesses, he lacked the *gravitas* of men such as Harold Stone and Hoffman. He didn't belong at the big table; he never would.

Back in the bar, it took another drink to blur this perception. When he sent a bottle of champagne to the table where Stone was holding court with a group from Gallimard, it was returned. In defiance, he turned his full attention to Trina in her breathtakingly low-cut dress, his partner in youthful insurrection. As she leaned forward to whisper in his ear, he eagerly damned all rules and conventions to hell.

Upstairs, lying on the bed, peeling silk from flesh, he saw a red light blinking across the room, reminding him of that line from "Love in Vain"—was it "the *red* light was my baby"? But it seemed to be far away across a body of water, and then Trina crashed over him like a wave that carried his scruples away. . . .

Several hours later the aquatic sensations had yielded to desert conditions, an acute drought having developed in Russell's mouth. A desolate gray light filtered through the white gauze drapes. Waking abruptly, he sensed instantly that something was wrong, although it took many seconds to assemble and weigh the evidence. He felt the body beside him, and hoped against hope that he was home, but the surroundings were unfamiliar and the body, for the first time in many years, proved not to be Corrine's.

The blinking message light served to focus his senses and to unleash the hounds of guilt. The message that had been waiting through the night was undoubtedly from Corrine. The red light continued to blink waspishly, as the red digits on the bedside alarm clock became 6:55 a.m. Almost two a.m. in New York.

Apparently carved out of clammy, pinkish stone, Trina didn't stir as he slipped out of bed, picked up the message envelopes under the door and retreated to the phone-equipped bathroom, where he first swallowed several liters of water directly from the tap.

Although he wasn't sure exactly how he'd been caught, he wasn't really surprised. *Bigamy still illegal here. See you in court.* Sitting naked on the floor with his face pressed against the tiled wall, he considered his options. He had to call, certainly. Of all the things he might have been required to do at this moment, feeling the way he did, calling Corrine was about the last task he would have chosen to perform. It occurred to him that she might not even be there. Maybe she'd already left him.

The machine picked up; he heard his own voice across the ocean telling him no one was home right now. After the beep he croaked into the machine, halfheartedly asking her to pick up. The tape stopped and the connection was broken. A second call produced similar results.

He was scheduled to fly the following day and had five or six appointments scheduled in the meantime, appointments that, he decided, he could not afford to keep. He called the concierge and requested a seat on the next plane to New York. He wanted to get out of this room immediately.

Lying on her stomach with her arms spread and her ass slightly aloft, Trina stirred eventually, lifted her head and looked around briefly before collapsing again. "What are you doing? Come back to bed. Ouch."

"I'm packing."

"Come back to bed and fuck me."

"It's a nice offer, but—"

"Wait a minute." She rolled over onto her back. "I thought you were staying till tomorrow."

"Corrine called."

"Ah. The palpable click of the wedlock."

He went into the bathroom to pack his shaving kit. When he came out she looked defiant. "So what's the big deal? She doesn't know anything."

"She knows."

"Well, so long as you're already convicted, you might just as well relive your crime."

Russell decided not to ask for details, but the fact was, he couldn't remember the actual commission.

Was it just German formality, he wondered, or did he sense a certain chilliness at the desk? Russell left-handed the assistant manager an envelope containing two hundred dollars, a bribe intended to ensure a room for the following year. The assistant manager inclined his head several millimeters in acknowledgment of the gift.

Russell had never blacked out in his life. The lost pieces of the night before were all the more frightening because they seemed to signal a betrayal on the part of his body. Having since college enjoyed an extraordinary tolerance for alcohol, he could not understand this betrayal, nor did he think he had drunk so much more than on other occasions when he'd suffered no more than a hangover.

In the cab to the airport he contemplated the wreckage he'd left behind as he compulsively patted himself down—the instinctive, panicked gesture of the befuddled traveler—and was unable to find his keys in any of his pockets. He feared that Corrine would not be home to let him in. At the airport he tore down all of his luggage and still couldn't find them. Sitting amidst the debris of his luggage he might have cried, but his tear ducts were dried out, his eyes parched.

It was only with some difficulty that he convinced the hotel operator to ring his vacated room, explaining that although Mr. Calloway had checked out, he had left a sleeping body belonging to the alleged Mrs. Calloway behind. After ten rings the operator came back on the line to tell him there was no answer; he asked her to keep trying. Finally Trina picked up. There was scant welcome in her voice.

He explained about the keys.

After several minutes she came back on the line to say she couldn't find them. "Losing everything, aren't we?" she observed. "Our keys, our nerve . . ."

"Why did the staff treat me like the Antichrist when I checked out. What did I do?"

"I don't know. You *did* threaten to buy the hotel when they asked us to leave the Lipizzaner after last call."

It seemed entirely meet and right that business class was overbooked, that the plane sat for three hours on the runway after the passengers had finally boarded, that Russell sat in coach next to a colicky baby.

40

"Do you think literature can save you?"

These were the first words Jeff had heard Delia utter in weeks. They were at the supper table in Glover House, talking about suicide. Mac, a fat depressive who taught history at the University of Connecticut, was explaining how the rope broke when he tried to hang himself. Delia, however, seemed to be addressing Jeff.

"Me in particular," Jeff asked, speaking softly, afraid that his voice might scare her back into herself. "Are you asking if it can save me?"

"Anyone. Can it help people?"

"It can't save you, but it can kill you." He saw that his reflexive archness had disappointed her, and was sorry when she retreated back into silence.

Having decided that Delia was no longer dangerous to herself, the authorities had finally dropped her down from Level Three, in which she was attended by special nurses twenty-four hours a day. And on this chilly October evening she was eating, or rather, failing to eat, her first unchaperoned meal.

"What is this foulness," Mickey asked, holding a piece of meat impaled on his fork.

"It's called veal," Jeff snapped. "Milk-fed baby cow."

"I can't eat this. Do you know what they do to these animals? They like suspend them in slings in dark barns. . . ."

"Cruel food," said Delia.

Jeff reached over and held her hand steady as she lit a cigarette. All the campers' hands shook because of the medications they were on, or the ones they were coming off.

Mickey then explained that he was going to patent a slingshot-shaped stick designed for use in institutions such as this one. Designed to support the unsteady wrist, the crotch of the Y-shaped stick would be upholstered with fabric in a psychologically neutral color.

"I'll make millions. And I'll fly my private helicopter over my father's terrace and piss on him while he's sunbathing."

Dr. Taylor appeared in the food line, a rare public appearance, reminding Jeff of his absurd session this afternoon.

"You think Caitlin left you because she didn't like your dog?" he'd said. "That seems a little simplistic."

" 'Any man that loveth me must also loveth my hound.' Sir Francis Bacon. *Not* the painter."

"You're speaking metaphorically?"

"Woof woof."

Out in the sitting room amidst the other antiques, blue-haired Babs Osterlick and busty Evelyn Salmon sat at their usual stations observing the exodus from dinner.

"There's that nice tall boy."

"Jeffrey."

"Hello, Jeffrey."

Jeff waved.

"That one comes from a good family," Babs said. "His people have a place next to ours on Mount Desert Island."

"A lot of the drunks are from good people. Is he a drunk or a nut?"

"Drugs, I think."

"I like a tall man."

"Such a pretty girl," said Babs as Delia wandered out a moment later. "Lovely hair."

"But skinny," observed Evelyn. "The boys like more up top."

"Where's everybody going," Babs asked presently. "Is it time for the movie yet?"

"The drunks have to have their meeting first."

"What is the movie?"

"I hope it has that young actor . . . what's his name?"

"Warren Beatty."

"No, the other one. The naughty one."

"Jack something."

"That's it."

Delia joined Jeff on the porch, where he was smoking a solitary cigarette before the evening AA session.

"Do you hear voices," she asked.

"Now?"

"I've heard that writers hear voices."

"I try to," he said. "Lately I don't hear much of anything."

"I do."

"What do the voices say?"

"They tell me I'm a bad person. They tell me to do things."

"What things?"

"Sometimes they tell me to hurt myself."

"I have a voice like that. The junk monster. *Feed me, feed me.*"

"Is it a boy or a girl voice?"

"It's sort of a growl now, but it started out as this torchy feminine whisper that used to sing outside my window, lure me out into the night. Desire calling."

"I like you," she said, with the unabashed directness of insanity.

"I like you, too."

"I like your friends Russell and Corrine, too. I didn't used to think so but now I do. They have a bright green aura."

Jeff took a long drag from his cigarette, then looked into her eyes. "They're *nifty*," he said after a while. "Ah, yes."

"There's somebody else inside my body," Delia said.

Jeff nodded, as if to say that this was often the case.

Then it was time for AA.

After supper the depressives received their second meds: particolored pills in a Dixie cup. Delia got lithium, Nardil and Thorazine, plus a multiple vitamin. Hers was one of the heavier meds. The people in substance abuse, who were denied medication, envied her. The doctors were still tinkering with the balance on her meds. The week before, she'd almost gone through the roof of Glover House when the Nardil finally kicked in after eight days. When she failed to respond the first week they kept upping the dosage until finally she woke up at five one morning declaring that she was the handmaiden of the Lord, and she had to be kept under restraint for two days.

The AA meetings were held in Carlyle House. Jeff, Delia and Mickey traditionally occupied the same chairs in the back right corner. It seemed important to observe a routine.

Halfway through the hour Mickey elbowed Jeff's ribs. "Did he actually say his name was Brit Hardy?"

The newcomer looked like a Brit, with his chinos, button-down pink oxford shirt, thick blond hair that looked as if it had been walked through by the athletic, unringed fingers of girls named Sloan and Kelsey.

"There was one night that sort of nutshelled the whole thing," he was saying.

"Nutshelled," Jeff queried.

"I'd just done a huge deal where I brokered the sale of a bauxite mine and I realize I've made like a couple hundred in one day, and so of course I buy an eight ball to celebrate. So I'm sitting around my loft with my girlfriend, who happens to be Miss Brazil 1985 . . ."

Confession as another form of self-assertion, Jeff thought, indistinguishable from bragging. Each time the alcoholics recounted their war stories the bottles multiplied and the mounds of cocaine grew until the entire process seemed an extension of the intemperance and excess that had brought them here in the first place. It was bullshit just like therapy was bullshit just like everything else. We're all drowning in it, Jeff thought, and choking on it.

That night, the day before he left for Frankfurt, Washington took the train up to visit, overcoming, he insisted, a profound fear of self-improvement and the philosophy of abstinence. "Do the visitors got to take a drug test," he asked on the phone. He and Jeff shot pool in the game room, talked about what a pain in the ass Russell had become. Jeff felt at ease for the first time in months. The mutual feeling was that he'd been busted.

* * *

Delia took a walk, her first unescorted stroll in weeks. Suspecting that her privileges would be revoked at any moment, she wanted to test her liberty more than savor it. She was not used to being alone, and she was not entirely sure she liked the idea.

Half an hour before curfew she walked from Glover House up to the main house, taking the long way around, past the tennis court and the chapel. The air was cold and sharp, and the moon was nearly full. Little needles of frostiness pricked the insides of her nostrils and her lungs; the black metal posts of the lanterns that marked the footpath were glazed with white. The lanterns were spaced at ten-foot intervals, and when she half closed her eyes they seemed to shoot off rays of light, like picture-book stars in a long curving constellation that marked the bridge into another galaxy. She opened her eyes and continued up the path, passing a lantern in which the glass was broken. She walked by the tennis court and had almost reached the chapel before she turned back, without understanding exactly *why*, drawn almost against her will, telling herself she wanted just another look and imagining a purely theoretical aspect to her interest—curious that in an institution where such care was taken to banish sharp edges, here in plain sight was a potentially deadly weapon—thinking that she would take a look and make sure of what she had seen and of course if you tell someone they can't have something they will become fascinated by the proscribed object, even obsessed. She could feel a tingle of illicit anticipation as she approached the broken torchère, checking behind herself to make sure she was unobserved, feeling the rhythm of her steps to be inexorable now, as if she no longer had anything to do with her motion or direction. Something was guiding her. She could hear a voice calling her back. It was the sweet, seductive voice. The one that was nice to her.

Still there: framed in black metal, two whiskery slivers of glass flanking a long, flamelike shard. Her breath became labored as she stared . . . a hot flush rising to her face. For a moment she was paralyzed, as the attraction to this object was counterbalanced by everything else she could feel. *Take it.* She stepped forward and pulled the piece of glass out of the metal frame, bending back the wire crosspiece and wiggling it back and forth till it came loose. She held it up to the light of the moon. A

beautiful object, the shape organic like a teardrop or a flame. *Go ahead.*
She tested the tip of the flame on her fingertip, drawing a tiny red blossom
to the surface. She heard a chorus of voices whispering in her ear, swelling
toward a weird crescendo of morbid affirmation. She'd heard them before,
the last time. She was supposed to tell Dr. Taylor the next time.

Slipping the glass into the pocket of her parka, she looked into the
whispering shadows that surrounded her.

Back in her room, Delia buried the shard deep in the soft soil of the
jade plant on her windowsill. While she slept that night, the crystal she
had planted in the soil grew into a perfect red rose. The rose shed a tear,
which turned to glass and tinkled as it hit the floor. The blossom began
to speak to her in a smoky, throaty voice. The rose wanted to be picked.
Delia knew it was against the rules, and she shivered with excitement as
her hand moved through space toward the trembling petals, but the fat
nurse woke her up and it was morning, again.

"We used to have this expression."

"Who?"

"Me, Crash, Wash."

"Crash is your friend Russell?"

"Right, we'd say we had to feed the dog, which meant getting high,
getting drunk, getting laid—all the lower appetites. When we first came
to the city we used to think we could do anything, we used to stay up
all night feeding the dog."

"You used cocaine?"

"Of course. The fun was never going to stop. Even Corrine had her
own feisty little dog, sort of a schnauzer. I think it died. Russell had a
big one, we had the big old hounds that used to run and hunt together.
Russell's has gotten fat and happy, I guess, sprawled on the rug in front
of the fireplace whacking its tail on the floor once in a while when
Corrine calls its name or rubs its head."

"So the cocaine led to the heroin."

"I don't know, what the fuck does that mean? You try to fill the big
empty. You find a name for your yearning—call it God or money or
Corrine. You call it literature. Call it heroin—or junk, smack, downtown, scag. Heroin most of all, because it swallows all the others. You

don't hurt, you don't even feel. It simplifies and incarnates your need, and it becomes everything. You fall into the arms of Venus de Milo."

"You'd compare God to drugs?"

"I don't think I can explain this to a man who flower-arranges the medical magazines on the coffee table."

The doctor gazed benignly into Jeff's face. "Why did you say Corrine?"

Jeff shrugged.

"How are you coming on Step Eight," Tony asked one night at dinner, playing the AA sponsor. "You made your list of the people you hurt?"

"Who needs a list? I have perfect recall."

"No addict's got perfect recall."

"I hurt everybody."

"Make a list. You're going to feel a lot better when you ask their forgiveness."

"I doubt it." Lord, Jeff thought, let this cup pass from me.

"I guarantee there will come a moment when you feel nearly overwhelmed with shame and grief for what you've done to yourself and the folks around you. And when it does, you're about to feel better. Count on it. But first you got to ask for understanding and forgiveness. Check with me, though, before you do anything drastic. Your head is going to be twisted for a while longer."

"Will you read me a story tonight," Delia asked after dinner.

"I'd like to," Jeff said, "but I'm afraid I can't."

"Please."

The childish simplicity of the request touched him, but he hadn't been able to concentrate on a page of print since detox.

"I keep hearing the voices."

"Okay, I'll try. No promises, though."

That night after meds and evening AA, he carried several books to Delia's room. While most of the inmates tried to personalize their cells, hers was bare except for several plants, obviously gifts, and a spray of red roses wilting in a plastic vase on the floor near the bathroom.

She sat on the bed, rigidly vertical, poised as only a model with ballet training could be, her feet tucked up under her thighs. Jeff pulled a chair near the bed, feeling self-conscious about the whole thing. He would have preferred to close the door to passersby in the hallway, but this was against the rules.

" 'To begin with the beginning,' " he read, forcing himself to concentrate on the dense lines of print, unsure if he would be able to keep sorting out the letters, forming the words, following the sense. It was the story of a man named Francis Weed, whose airborne brush with death precipitated a loss of faith in the diurnal verities of his life. From time to time Jeff looked up as much to rest his eyes as to check on Delia, who was staring straight ahead, toward the windows. Would she identify, he wondered, with Julia, the wife, "whose love of parties sprang from a most natural dread of chaos and loneliness." He read on through a Westchester cocktail party in which Francis recognized the maid as a prisoner, an accused collaborator, he'd seen after the war; later he embraced the baby-sitter and fell in love with her. Jeff lifted his eyes up to Delia, but she seemed impassive, enthralled by something far away outside the window.

Then Francis Weed struck Julia, and Jeff worried that he was reminding Delia of her own suffering at the hands of men. But she was either completely absorbed or completely oblivious. He read on through as Francis insulted his neighbors, yearning for the girl and through her for some other life: " 'The feeling of bleakness was intolerable, and he saw clearly that he had reached the point where he would have to make a choice.' " Sickened with love, Francis Weed went to the psychiatrist, took up woodworking and tried to make peace with himself and with the single, hedged green acre of life he had been given in which to live.

"Do you think we could ever be married," Delia asked, several minutes after he had closed the book. "I don't mean to each other, necessarily. I just wonder if we're excluded from all that, people like us. It's like you want to believe in that and you can't. You want to have this nice life, but you just see right through it even if you wish you didn't."

"I'd like to go back and try."

"Your friends Russell and Corrine are made for it."

"I don't think it's always so easy for them."

"I once played Ophelia," she said. People like Delia elided the connective tissue of their thoughts the way others dropped consonants, though Jeff found he understood her more and more. "Do you think other people feel the things we do?"

"I don't know."

"I thought you were smart."

"I used to think so."

"My mom gave me her wedding dress, the only thing she ever gave me. I'll show it to you sometime."

She unfolded her legs, climbed off the bed and walked over to the window almost stealthily, as if she were stalking a bird on the windowsill. She dug with her fingers in the soil of a potted jade plant.

"Will you take this for me," she asked, handing him with no little sense of ceremony a long sliver of glass.

Jeff held the shard in his hand, looking at it without at first comprehending what it was. He stroked his right index finger across the sharp crescent, then lifted a tiny flap of white skin from the neat incision, which slowly filled with blood. He looked up at Delia, tears welling in his eyes. He could not identify the source of the sadness he felt rising within him and overflowing. Imagining Delia's grief, he had inadvertently tapped his own.

He began to sob. It seemed impossible that he could have contained this sadness for so long without bursting, without even recognizing the pressure of it for what it was. All the sealed-off cells of pain and remorse were suddenly exposed; he felt the cumulative pain of all his hurts, all of the slights, indignities, embarrassments, insults and rejections he had ever suffered, which he thought he had forgotten—none of which could yet begin to account for this sorrow he was feeling, which was far too vast to be merely his own, but which connected him with the bottomless reservoir of human suffering, most of all with the people *he* had hurt in his short, reckless life. All the harm he'd visited on others came back to him; he felt the shame of a hundred cruel, arrogant, careless things he had thought or said or written. Every word he'd written was false, puffed with conceit and elegant malice. And he could hardly bear to think of Caitlin, her long, failed struggle to love him as she suffered his silences and lies and his fierce resistance to love, her grief at their parting. He thought of poor Russell, and he looked up through cloudy eyes at Delia, who felt so terrible she thought of killing herself. Sobbing violently, he wondered how the race had survived so much grief.

Unperturbed, Delia sat beside him on the bed, lifting his injured finger and inserting it in her mouth, licking away the blood, calmly sucking his finger as he cried.

41

The apartment was empty. Nothing was immediately noticeably missing, but to Russell the rooms had the ominous resonance of a crime scene once the chatty assistant super with his jangling, hip-slung key ring had disappeared. A search of the premises failed to yield a note; Corrine's drawers and closet were partially empty. The doorman observed that it was a wonder the young couples these days ever saw each other—alluding to the fact that Corrine had left with her bags late the night before and here was Russell just returning from his trip.

Over Chinese food and television, surrounded by photographs of the life they'd made together and the artifacts they had assembled, he tried to imagine where she would go, postponing the search in the hope that he might outlive his hangover and his jet lag, or that he might not. On the flight he had drafted versions of what he was going to say, the truth seeming, as usual in such cases, too potent. In the face of overwhelming evidence to the contrary, he still clung to a ragged conviction about the purity of his intentions, but he did not expect his wife to share his faith.

His heart seized up when the phone rang. He waited through three rings before answering. It was Washington, calling from Germany, ostensibly reporting on the day's business but in fact avid for details about the disaster of Russell's personal life, recent events that confirmed all of Washington's basic assumptions about human nature. His enthusiastic sympathy implied a bond that Russell was not necessarily eager to acknowledge; on the other hand, his emphasis on tactics over ethics was, at this moment, quite helpful.

"It's simple, Crash, you say Trina blew into town unexpectedly so you chivalrously let her stay in your room and you stayed with me in mine."

"She's not going to believe that."

"What choice does she have? She can't afford not to forgive you."

When Russell called Jeff at the hospital, he was sympathetic but utterly devoid of advice. The story Russell told him had been lightly edited, though he wasn't entirely aware of the process—the automatic flick of the pencil deleting an adjective here, a comma there, although the essential nouns and verbs remained intact.

"So did you or didn't you? The way you tell it, we're somewhere between the idea and the act."

"I did, but I don't actually remember much."

"And you want *me* to tell you that doesn't *count*?"

"What should I do, Jeff?"

"The field of monogamy is not exactly my specialty. I flunked that class."

After a long silence, Jeff suddenly blurted, "Did you hear about Propp? I just saw it today in the *Times*. Evidently the cleaning lady found him slumped over his Macintosh. The computer was still running."

"Jesus! What happened?"

"I don't think they know yet."

Russell was dumbfounded, this tragedy seeming to add its weight to his own.

"Wait a second," Jeff said, "aren't you the executor?"

Where *would* she go? More of a man's woman, Corrine didn't have that many girlfriends. He called her sister in Philadelphia, then her friends in New York. Eventually he tried Casey and Tom Reynes, the only friends he could think of who had an apartment big enough for boarders. A member of the household staff eventually summoned Casey, whose manner was suspiciously colder than usual although she claimed not to know Corrine's whereabouts.

He wanted to get the *Times*, for Victor's obituary, but he was afraid to leave the phone. He fell into a leaden but unrestful sleep on the couch in front of the TV, and was awakened in the middle of the night by the explosion of the phone.

"I'd just like to hear your story."

"Corrine, I didn't know she was coming to Frankfurt."

"I don't believe you."

Russell tried for something between the truth and his own best version of himself. His story included unexpected last-minute business in Frankfurt for Trina and concluded with a false image of Russell sleeping on the other twin bed.

"How dare you," Corrine said.

"How dare I what," he asked.

"I'm staying at Casey and Tom's place for now. I'm going to look for an apartment. I'll be drawing on our checking account until I find another job. I wouldn't have quit my fucking job if I'd known you were—"

"Corrine—"

"Don't say anything, you bastard. I don't think I can stand to hear you lie again. This is just the culmination of everything you've been wanting to do. You've been playing on the power-and-money team for a while now, and Trina fits right into the agenda. I kept thinking once this deal was over I'd get you back, that you'd start being a husband again, that you'd remember my existence, even. And then, after . . . after . . . ." She didn't complete the thought but he knew what that was in reference to. If she attributed their troubles to his absorption in business, it seemed to him that the miscarriage had blighted their happiness. "You obviously want your freedom, so I'm giving it to you. Good-bye. And good fucking luck."

Moments later the phone rang again.

"Corrine?"

At first he heard only the transatlantic static, then: "Hey, brother, is that you?" The voice weird and slurry.

"Wash?" Russell looked over at the clock in the kitchen. It was five a.m. in Frankfurt. "Are you all right?" Not that he was too worried, a five-a.m. phone call from Washington Lee being not unheard-of in Russell's circle.

"Just wanted to say hi, man. You hear about Propp?"

The apartment that weekend was a monument to everything he had forgotten he loved, an echo chamber of recrimination. He couldn't sleep in their bed, redolent of Corrine and domestic carnality. Leaving the TV on for company and distraction, he slept for a few hours on the couch.

All of Sunday stretched out endlessly in front of him into a bleak and companionless future. Driven from one end of the apartment to another by the prickling eczema of guilt, he found that he could not sit still or read so much as a magazine. Finding it impossible to work it out in his mind, he sat down and wrote a long letter to Corrine in which he begged for another chance. After three drafts he didn't know whether to mail it immediately or burn it in the fireplace.

He went out and saw that the leisured city was now composed of couples, where only days before it had been populated largely by sleek, predatory women. Like a man with a hangover, Russell had lost the layers of skin and shell that protected him from his environment; now everything—the chilly air and the raspy light of October, the voices and the traffic, as well as the casual glances of strangers—rubbed against the exposed ganglia of his nervous system. Cut off from the glib social order disporting itself around him, he felt disowned by the great city he thought had adopted him.

He eventually located a copy of the previous day's paper and took a stool in a coffee shop. Peering at the captive pastries beneath plexiglass, he imagined a future of solitary meals and coffee refills among the ageless ladies asking "What's the soup?" and picking suspiciously at their chicken salad, the remains of which they would have wrapped to take home for the Yorkie. The waiter, a young Greek with girl troubles, worried the toothpick in his mouth and refused to take geriatric conversational bait, ignoring, for the moment, the old girl with the red tam signaling from the back booth who left a quarter tip every day.

Propp was eulogized in several columns notable for the scrupulous balance of their accountancy: testimony to his greatness was weighed against the reservations of those who suggested he was the slick purveyor of the cultural equivalent of a pyramid scheme. Harold Stone, identified as his friend and editor, split the difference, calling Propp, "one of our great literary eccentrics." The crucial piece of evidence, the manuscript of the novel, was at present unaccounted for. The cause of death was said to be unknown.

Russell stopped at a florist's on Madison and bought two dozen red roses, then dragged over to Casey and Tom's apartment on 72nd and left the flowers and his letter for Corrine after the doorman informed him no one was home *chez* Reynes.

In his bereavement he invested every vista with gratuitous symbolism and tragic import. The merchandise in the store windows seemed point-less and grotesque—fur and feathers of the mating ritual, the smug equip-ment of domestic life. On 57th and Madison he passed three young ballerinas in leotards, on the cusp of adolescence, their hair pulled back into fierce buns so that it seemed to stretch the already taut, unlined flesh of their faces back over their skulls—as if they were rehearsing, far in advance, the face-lifts inevitably to come.

Walking through Central Park, he passed a well-groomed old woman in a tailored suit sitting on a bench, her skirt hiked up, a stream of urine coursing audibly through the dust between her sensible loafers. She looked straight ahead. Farther along, a group of tiny children were heav-ing sticks at a terrified squirrel trapped in the upper branches of a small tree. "How would you like it if I threw sticks at you," Russell asked the little boy who was leading the attack.

"Fuck you," said the boy, a four-foot tyke in a Ghostbusters jacket.

"Yeah," his little girlfriend said.

"Nice mouth," Russell muttered, walking on.

Moments later a parent materialized beside Russell, a fit, prosperous specimen in a pink and gray warm-up suit. "Did you threaten to hit my kid?"

"I suggested," Russell said reasonably, "that he stop throwing sticks at defenseless animals."

"Pick on someone your own size."

"Yeah, you big jerk," said the son, standing at a safe distance, eager for spectacle and vengeance.

"Instead of a six-year-old kid."

Fearless with self-loathing, Russell said, "How about I pick on you?"

"Just try it," the man answered, forming a fist with his right hand and slapping it rhythmically, like a ball, into the open mitt of his left.

Without pausing to think, Russell smashed his own fist straight into the man's face. The boy howled as his father sank to his knees, tenaciously grasping Russell's thigh, and a screaming band of reinforcements assem-bled on the asphalt trail. Desperate to free himself, Russell launched his knee into the man's chin and knocked him backward, feeling in his kneecap the violent collision of upper and lower teeth.

"Stop him!" shouted a wifely ponytailed blonde in chinos and pink cardigan. "Hit him."

"Kill him!" howled the little boy.

Three others, two men and a woman, rushed up and hovered indignantly above the fallen champion of the nuclear family. "Let's get him," said one of the men, but something in Russell's face gave them pause. Bent over the downed man, the wife let out a piercing, pitiful scream, which sounded like the death cry of a small animal.

Russell turned, almost colliding with a fat man wearing headphones, and ran past a mother with two preschoolers in a twin stroller, up an incline and over a rocky outcropping. He dodged through a wooded grove, followed a bike path down through an underpass, skirted the woods around the edge of the great pond past Strawberry Fields and emerged onto West 72nd Street.

After turning south on Columbus, he threaded the languid pedestrians drugged with brunch and shopping, ducked into a bar and ordered a shot of Jack Daniel's, his hands trembling with adrenaline and rage. Standing at the bar he had two drinks, chewed his ice cubes and savored his bleak isolation. He couldn't think of anyplace he wanted to go, or anything he wanted to do, without Corrine. He wanted to tell her about the indignity he had suffered. To whom would he narrate the events of his life, if she were to disappear from it? Who would listen to his stories? As the whiskey soaked in, it occurred to him that a spouse was the person who listened to the story of your life and who, making certain allowances, chose to believe you.

Sunday night she called again. Russell was microwaving frozen pizza and watching sports, afraid to miss her.

"I got your letter," she said.

"Please come back."

"I don't know." She paused. "You've wrecked something. It's going to take me a while to figure out what's left."

"We love each other," he insisted.

"If we didn't," she said, "we wouldn't be speaking. I'm going to my mom's house in a few days. I have some thinking to do. You do, too. I don't know if you even want to be married to me anymore."

"Of course I want—"

"Russell, you wouldn't be able to admit it to yourself even if it was true. You're loyal in your own way and you wouldn't let yourself think it, but I think you want excitement and freedom and glamour and action more than you ever wanted me. Think about it while I'm gone."

"What about dinner with the Shermans tomorrow night?" he said plaintively, hoping that the maintenance of social appearances would seem as important to her as it suddenly did to him. A week before, Russell would have blown the Shermans off at the slightest excuse, but now it seemed grossly irresponsible to cancel on a mere twenty-four hours' notice. "And then there's the museum benefit, isn't that Wednesday night? We can't just . . ." All at once he felt he understood the purpose of decorum, manners and hypocrisy. From the outside, marriage was merely a set of habits; going through the motions was sometimes the only way to keep going.

"The four hundred other people at the museum will just have to take up the slack, Russell." Her tone of voice was hard and faceted.

"I got in a fight in the park today," he said. "I almost got killed by a mob."

"I've got to go. I don't know what I'm going to do, Russell. But remember, if I hear anything about you, if you're so much as seen in the same room with Trina, I'm calling a lawyer. In the meantime, try not to drink too much."

After a dreadful sleep he dragged himself to the office Monday morning, forgetting until he was in the elevator that his office keys were somewhere in Frankfurt. He browsed through the papers in the Greek coffee shop downstairs, finding nothing more on Propp, then sat in the hall with a manuscript and waited for Donna, who arrived after an hour.

Carl Linder called a few minutes later.

"We tried to get hold of you in Frankfurt on Friday."

"Some domestic problems developed."

"So you just hop on a plane and leave things hanging at the book fair?"

"Washington took care of things."

"Mr. Lee's not running the company, and he does not enjoy Bernie's full confidence. He's been threatening to sue, you know, which for his sake I hope he doesn't. So what Bernie wants to know is, are you on the team, or not?"

"Which team is that?"

"Think about it. Meantime he was asking about this guy Propp's manuscript. As far as we know, he died before he signed with Simon and Schuster, which leaves us publisher of record. If there's something there, it's ours, lock, stock and barrel. But before we make a stink, Bernie thought it would be nice to know if quote it's any fucking good unquote. Get back to us on this."

Russell had already made an appointment with Victor's lawyer to visit the West Village apartment and go over the writer's effects, but he found the vulturish interest of Carl's call off-putting enough that he didn't mention any of this.

Juan Baptiste called a few minutes later. "I've got this zany idea for an item: Jeff Pierce in detox. Call me silly, but I think it has wheels. What do you think?"

"Sounds too easy," Russell managed to say, his headache *really* kicking in.

"You're denying?"

"I don't confirm or deny. Never have."

"You don't confirm. You *do* deny."

"All right," Russell said uneasily. "Of course I deny."

"Jeff's not in detox?"

"Where do you get this shit?" Russell said, uneager to continue lying.

"You know I don't give sources."

"In lieu of ethics—*professional* ethics."

"Let's keep it mercantile," Juan said. "Let's trade. Hey, I'm not even asking about your friend Propp. But a little bird did say there *was* a big empty bottle of Tuinals in the bathroom."

"I've got nothing to swap." Russell didn't know what else to say.

"Where *is* Jeff?"

"He disappears to write. New York is very distracting, you know. He doesn't like people to know where he is." If Juan had anything solid, Russell thought, he would have tried it by now. "Fishing season's over."

"Let's go back to this idea of a trade," Juan proposed. "I hear you're in trouble. Authors abandoning ship in droves, horrified that a grand old publishing house has been sacked by the understudies for the cast from *The Young and the Restless*."

"We've lost a couple writers. It's been amply noted in the press."

"But I'm not talking flesh wounds, I'm talking cerebral hemorrhage.

In the same way I hear Jeff is in rehab, a little bird is telling me Bernie Melman's considering a pullout, et cetera. The common law of buzz, or rumor, which after all is commonly known as half-truth, declares that fifty percent of the smut and innuendo that reaches my ears is true. So in this case I calculate that half of my current dish is bankable. One: Jeff is in rehab. Two: Corbin, Dern and Kids is on the skids. If you don't confirm one, I will have to assume, mathematically, that the other is entirely true."

He paused. Russell wasn't biting. "I'll give you one for free," Juan said. "Bernie Melman has canceled all his social engagements for the past two weeks because he is under a doctor's care at his home on Long Island, suffering from acute depression."

Russell realized that he hadn't talked to Melman since before the fair, but he didn't need to tell Baptiste this.

"What about this persistent rumor that Mrs. Melman is a transsexual?"

"Sounds extremely plausible, but I told you, I've got nothing to swap."

"The corollary to the notion that any rumor is at least half true, is that any half-truth, repeated often enough, becomes entirely true. If I write that a nightclub's dying, it sometimes happens that it's up for sale the next week. Cause and effect? You be the judge. I'd hate to be the one to say that you're stretched out on a slab with a sheet over your body. So tell me about Jeff."

"Jeff is hard at work on his next book."

"One can only hope he will have a publisher when it's finished."

In retrospect, Russell could see that rejecting Juan Baptiste's book might have been an error in judgment.

The next night he was sitting in front of the TV when the doorman buzzed, announcing Colin and Anne Becker. "Send them up," Russell said without enthusiasm. He was not eager for company.

"Happy Birthday!" they shrieked when he opened the door.

"My birthday's tomorrow."

"The party's tonight," Anne said uncertainly, as she surveyed the eerie apartment. "Are we the first?"

"Corrine organized it for tonight because of the museum thing tomorrow," Colin insisted, barging right in. "We just got in from the airport from Santa Fe."

"Probably there's a message on your machine," Russell said.

Colin placed Russell's hand around the neck of a bottle wrapped in silver paper, while Anne presented him with a large coffee-table book titled *Mushrooms of the World*. "I hope you don't have it," she said. "It's hard to buy books for you." Russell opened the book to a glossy color close-up of a giant morel. Suddenly he remembered that he and Corrine still owed the Beckers a wedding present; the oversight at this moment seemed terribly poignant.

"Corrine's mom is sick," he said. "Nothing serious, but we had to postpone the party." He assured them it was nothing serious, thanked them for the gifts.

"We're not about to let you stay home on your birthday," Colin said. "We'll take you out to dinner." Russell begged off, claiming he wasn't feeling well himself. An hour later, after they had finished the champagne and he had trundled the tenacious Beckers out the door, Washington appeared, direct from Frankfurt.

"As long as nobody's waiting up for you," he said, "you might as well come join me for a cocktail." He looked as if he hadn't slept in days, and his hands were shaking.

"I don't feel like going out. And you don't look like you *should*."

"Give yourself a break. You'll go crazy hanging around here."

"Are you all right?"

Weaving from side to side as he did so, Washington nodded his head emphatically.

"We could go to Heaven," Russell said.

"*Nobody* goes to Heaven, man."

"What do you mean? I thought it was the new place." Russell didn't keep up the way he used to, but two weeks before this particular club had been the dead center of hip consciousness, at least according to Juan Baptiste's column. "I thought everybody went."

"Only the meek, the halt and the lame, child. Heaven turned bad real quick, quicker than I've ever seen it happen. Used to be it took a few months, sometimes six months. But this was like, Monday the hordes were throwing themselves at the door, begging to be chosen, Tuesday the badmouth had started going around, and by Thursday they were hiring barkers from Times Square to drag people in off the streets, free admission, free drinks, free drugs, free love. Friday you couldn't give away the lease on the place, and the owners turned down an offer of three mill' right after it opened. Feature that, I mean, where did that three million disappear to?"

They went to a new club that didn't have a name, which to Russell's dismay occupied the premises of the former bathhouse patronized by him and Jeff. Little had changed; most of the fixtures remained intact. No one was waiting at the ropes to get in, and those inside had the air of tourists furious to discover themselves among others of their kind. The former changing room served as a dance floor. Washington tried hard to find trouble, but the smart and interesting people were somewhere else —most likely home, thought Russell, who recalled many happier nights of this sort spent in Jeff's company—and the two young women who asked them to dance looked like a high-risk group unto themselves, with their lace bustiers and leather miniskirts.

"What are you—in school," Russell asked the brunette, having declined to dance, watching Washington shake it up with the blonde.

"I'm an actress now, I guess. Why not? I was an investment analyst at Salomon Brothers until last week, when they laid me off."

Washington caught up with Russell at the door as he was leaving. "What's your problem, Jack?"

"I can't do this. I'm leaving."

"No problem. We'll take our show on the road."

They made it back to Russell's apartment shortly after four, by which time the conversation had turned to mush, although the two friends remained upright for another hour, pledging eternal friendship and solving the Corrine problem and puzzling over Propp, though the next morning Russell couldn't recall the fine print.

In a lucid interval Russell asked, "Whatever happened with the meeting you were supposed to set up between Parker and Melman."

Trying to hold the tip of his cigarette still while introducing it to the flame from his lighter, Washington said, "Watch for a new, high salary, low-stress job title on the payroll. Something like Minority Affairs Consultant."

Russell's father called him promptly at seven-thirty to wish him a happy birthday. Russell could never be certain whether it was an innocent habit or a perverse desire to impose his own schedule on his older son, but he inevitably called at this hour. Waking up with the sun seemed to be, in his eyes, a necessary if not a sufficient condition of responsible adult life. While fending off his father's curiosity Russell tottered around the apartment clasping the portable phone to his head like an ice pack, discovering Washington fully clothed and inert on the bed.

"The big three-two," his father said.

"The big three-two," Russell repeated.

"I'm very pleased with the way everything's coming together for you."

"Everything coming together."

"When do you sign the papers?"

"Papers?" At that moment in the history of his mental associations the phrase suggested divorce. Then he realized his father was talking about the deal.

"Uh, probably within a couple weeks."

"I'm very proud, son."

"Thanks, Dad."

"So how does it feel?"

"Feel?"

"Did you celebrate?"

"Sure. Yeah. Celebrated. Little hung over."

His father chuckled knowingly. "You take care of yourself, son. And keep up the good work."

He slept for another hour on the couch, phone in hand, until it chirped again.

"I wanted to do this before I lost my fucking nerve," Jeff said.

"Do what?"

"Apologize."

"What, for waking me up? Where are you?"

"Still at the hospital." There ensued a long pause, which Russell did not feel capable of filling. Finally Jeff said, "Part of the program here is, you know . . . admitting your mistakes and owning up to them. I've done a lot of things I'm not proud of."

"Join the club. Forget it."

"You have to acknowledge your mistakes and ask forgiveness of the people you've hurt," Jeff said, in a language that was not quite his own; you could almost hear the rustle of semislick inspirational brochure paper. Russell was glad Jeff had stopped shooting heroin, but he was unnerved to hear him talk this way.

"Consider yourself forgiven. What are friends for?"

"I feel like I have to say this. It's about me and Corrine."

Russell was instantly, dreadfully alert, as though he had slept all night and never had a drink in his life. "Corrine?"

"It was a long time ago."

"What are you saying, Jeff?"

"Basically, it was when you were in England on that fellowship, before you guys got married. . . ."

42

Finally Russell staggered to work, while Washington crawled home to change. Russell did not have the slightest interest in going to the office, but the apartment, which earlier had been merely haunted, now seemed thoroughly fouled. Like a suburbanite who has learned, after years of rich domesticity, that his home is situated on a toxic waste dump, he felt retroactively poisoned, memories wrecked along with his future.

Walking across town he felt ill, liable to vomit at any moment. At a newsstand he bought a pack of cigarettes for the first time in more than two years. The blind vendor asked him the denomination of the bill, a ten in fact—But what if it had been a single? Russell thought. The blind man would never know. Indeed, the vendor's weathered face seemed to display an expression of wounded skepticism. The notion that he could pick up a magazine and walk off with it made Russell furious at the man's vulnerability. Didn't he know they stole everything in this city? *Trust* was just a word sometimes conjoined to *Bank*.

Tiny shards of glass embedded in the sidewalk ignited as he passed, walking west. Russell believed that he was as aware of his own weaknesses as one could be without systematically attacking them or profoundly disliking oneself, and it had never been that difficult for him to imagine himself as the potential villain, the adulterer, the quitter in the marriage. To comprehend Corrine in this role was staggering. Standing beside a sign that said NO STANDING ANYTIME, he slipped a cigarette between his parched lips and stared down at the matchbook the vendor had given him. Imprinted with a pair of splayed female thighs and genitalia, it bore the legend "Dial 990-FUCK."

As he stepped out of the elevator, Russell nearly tripped over two fat orange cords running from his office to the utility closet in the common hallway. Dance music throbbed from the open door. During the night, it seemed, his office suite had been transformed into a nightclub; it was now bristling with hip young men and women in black clothing, and high-tech lights.

"I've been trying to call you," Donna said, seeing his puzzlement. "You didn't forget about the photo shoot?"

Glenda Banes emerged from a thicket of telescoped aluminum saplings. "I hate shooting on location," she said. "I certainly hope you're getting a bigger office once your deal is finished."

He kissed her proffered cheek.

"My goodness, had a hard night, did we?" She held him by the shoulders and examined his face, then said cheerfully, "You look like shit. Carlotta—have we got a fucking makeup job for you!"

Violently nauseated, Russell fled for the bathroom, passing Whitlock, who stood at the door of his own office shaking his head at the spectacle.

Russell leaned against the tiled wall with his eyes closed; there was a knock on the door.

"Are you okay in there," Donna asked nervously.

"Not really."

"You want coffee?"

When he didn't answer she said, "If you're *really* hung over I can get you a chocolate shake."

"Do you have anything for pain?"

"I got some Percodan in my desk. And maybe a Darvocet."

She returned with a yellow pill, which he swallowed, sucking water from the sink to wash it down.

Russell sat in a chair as he was powdered, combed, brushed and moussed. After half an hour of this he was handed over to the stylist, a young man with a crisp brush-cut who wished to dress him.

"Couldn't I just wear my own clothes?" Russell said.

The stylist regarded him with pity, his blue blazer with contempt.

"We want people to think you're hip," Glenda said.

From the rack of startling clothing they'd brought along Russell finally selected a suit and shirt that were not so bold as to further aggravate his queasy stomach.

"What's the matter, you don't like the Replacements? We can change the music. You go for hip-hop?"

Finally they placed him behind his desk and turned on the lights. With great difficulty Russell was able to keep his eyes open in the glare. Simply to pretend that he was not physically ill and emotionally wrecked required a heroic effort; to smile was beyond his overtaxed capabilities. Glenda screamed orders at her staff and wooed Russell with honeyed suggestions. "Think about something that makes you happy. Think about sex."

Russell suppressed a bitter laugh at this suggestion.

After an hour she was exasperated. "Jesus, Russell, you look like you just lost your best friend."

The assistants fluttered, tugging and pulling at his clothing, patting his clammy face dry and adjusting his hair. He had sweated through three shirts by the time Glenda stopped shooting.

After two hours, which seemed like eight, the crew began to fold up camp, and Russell fled the office for lunch. In the lobby, he met Washington coming in.

"Have some lunch?" Russell said, happy to see someone who might feel, at least physically, as bad as he did.

"You're the boss."

Once they were seated at the Japanese place across the street Washington said, "You want to talk about it?"

"I don't know." It was not their habit to talk about the things that mattered most.

"That's cool, it's up to you."

Russell lit a cigarette while Washington ordered two beers.

"Jeff slept with Corrine."

Nodding his head gravely, Washington spewed Delphic plumes of smoke from his nostrils.

"What, you knew about this?"

"No, it just makes sense in retrospect. There's always that thing between friends and lovers. Taboo and jealousy crossed with the desire to share everything. A blind dude could see the chemistry between them."

"I'm glad it seems so unremarkable to you."

"When did it happen?"

"Five, six years ago. I don't know."

"Before the holy bonds of wedlock?"

"I think so."

"Let it go then."

"The major calamity of my life, and you want me to shine it on?"

"I'm just saying it happened a long time ago. There are worse things. You think the good marriages are the ones where everybody's all faithful to the end? I think maybe the best ones, if there are any, survive the big shit. The bard say, 'When the sea was calm, all boats alike showed mastership in floating.' "

"*You're* telling *me* about marriage?"

"Just telling you about life."

"It's a measure of how low I've sunk that I'm listening to you." Like everything, the cigarette was starting to taste really bad.

"I don't think I can stomach raw fish right now," Washington said, examining the menu. "Don't forget," he added, allowing himself a smile, "you did the nasty thing to her, too."

"I'm scared, Wash."

"That's what it's like being single, chief."

"I wonder if Jeff's told her he told me."

"Probably."

"Why doesn't she call, then?"

"Why do you think? She's ashamed. You both need some time."

"I don't know if there's enough time in the world," Russell said, shuffling together the packets of sugar and Sweet 'n Low in the sugar jar. Wondering if things could get any worse, he recalled a line from Lichtenberg, that you can't really say conditions are going to truly improve, but they certainly have to if they're going to be any good.

Back at the office, Donna was reading *Blitz*, her black work boots up on the desk. She informed Russell that both Carl Linder and *The Wall Street Journal* were trying to reach him. He shoveled the piles of books and manuscripts off the couch and onto the floor, and stretched out full length. With his marriage in ruins, all that tethered him to the planet was his work; and the fate of a company was more or less in his hands. But right now he couldn't face so much as his mail.

Donna barged in, bearing a gift. "Happy Birthday," she said, humming a few notes of the song through her nose. "Et cetera, et cetera." Suddenly she was blushing; sentiment and ceremony flustered her. "I never know what to get you," she said defensively as he tore open the silver paper. Russell prepared to feign enthusiasm.

He lifted up a length of soft red and black rope in his hand. "A tie?" There were three other pieces of tasseled cord in the package.

Then he noticed the brochure, "Love Ties," which featured a photograph of a nude woman tied spread-eagle to a four-poster bed.

"For you and Corrine," Donna chirped. "I figure married life might get a little dull sometimes, so I thought . . ."

Perhaps these, he thought, were the famed bonds of matrimony.

"My boyfriend, Gus, he loves them."

"I can imagine." Russell leaned forward and kissed her awkwardly. "Thanks a lot."

"I didn't figure anybody else would think of that."

"Only you, Donna."

Later Russell asked Donna if she had heard any rumors about the company.

"Nothing specific," she said, "but according to the graffiti downtown, the whole capitalist system's going to collapse pretty soon and be replaced by an anarchist utopia."

"That's good news," Russell said.

At five o'clock Russell called Casey and Tom's and got their answering service—"Reynes residence"—a snotty voice informing him no one was home.

He imagined that Jeff had talked to Corrine and that she was avoiding him. He still hoped she would deny everything in some convincing way, that Jeff would plead temporary insanity, or wishful thinking, with regard to his confession. A few weeks before, he had complained to Russell over the phone about the propensity of his fellows in the program to invent and exaggerate past crimes.

The phone rang intermittently, but Donna took care of it, informing him among other things that the *Times* wanted to talk to him about Propp. "Tell them to talk to his friend and editor Harold Stone," he called out. When, eventually, he lifted his arm from the couch to look at his watch, it was six-twenty. He stood up and walked to the window; outside, the big yellow cat's eyes were coolly surveying the street.

That night he had dinner with Tim Calhoun at The White Room. Much as he wished to entertain the man, who expected his semiannual night on the town, Russell could barely summon the energy for conversation. When the novelist went off to the men's room Russell called for the check. Nancy Tanner waved to him from a big table on the other side of the room as a thin pair of arms faintly redolent of Shalimar and cigarettes wrapped themselves around his neck, and a tongue belonging, like the arms, to Trina Cox probed his left ear, bringing back sense memories that were all the more unwelcome for being extremely arousing. All at once pieces of their night together came back to him. Brimming with champagne, Trina declared that she forgave him for his cruel mistreatment and insisted he go out dancing with her party. She climbed into his lap and tried to resume her exploration of his ear. When Calhoun returned, Russell managed to palm him off on Trina, who was more than willing to show him the town.

"Package for you, Mr. Calloway," the doorman said, bringing a fat, squishy garment bag out of the package room—Corrine's mink. Apparently the fur vault in which it spent the summer returned it on a prearranged schedule, unaware of any interruption in the Calloway domestic calendar.

Russell and Corrine had purchased the coat two or three years before, when they couldn't afford it; they had gone to the store just to look, lured by an ad in the paper. Outside it was August, but the furrier's showroom was chilly, sepulchral, haunted by small skinless ghosts, faintly tinged with musk and the coniferous tang of northern forests. Gliding out of the underbrush as if on figure skates, a salesman had given them an introductory course on furs, starting Corrine out in Russian sable. She giggled nervously at the feel of the satin lining slipping over her bare arms. After that, of course, the advertised special was a bit of a letdown—male skins sewn together by palsied, half-blind, underpaid sweatshop apprentices, apparently. When they finally found a coat that looked as if it had been tailored for Corrine, it cost twice as much as they'd planned to spend. She had just begun her job as a broker and Russell was making less than almost everyone they knew. They couldn't possibly. But goddamnit, Russell had decided, that was why they were going to. His mouth was dry, his tongue sticking to the roof of his mouth as he said, "We'll take it." Corrine protested, already removing the coat, shaking her head, but Russell insisted in spite of, or perhaps precisely because of, the syncopated flutter of his heartbeat, the hollow vertiginous feeling in his stomach, the sweat on the palms of his hands.

He threw the garment bag on the dining room table and fixed himself a large birthday vodka. Once upon a time he would have considered it romantic to try to drink away his grief. Now it seemed just analgesic.

Bernie Melman was not returning Russell's calls. On Friday the price of Corbin, Dern over the counter dropped from nineteen to eighteen, which was odd, given the outstanding tender offer of twenty-one and a half. Nearly everything dropped on Friday, the Dow losing a record 108 points, and Juan Baptiste's Friday-morning item certainly didn't help the price of Corbin, Dern.

That *was* boy-wonder publisher RUSSELL CALLOWAY dancing his cares away on the floor of Jonestown the other night. He has *beaucoups de* worries these days, what with rumors of shaky financing for his buyout of Corbin, Dern, the veddy distinguished old-boy publishing house—not to mention the suspicious demise of CD author Victor Propp. But who was the blonde, in conference on Russell's lap? Not wife CORRINE. An aspiring editorial assistant, no doubt . . .

P.S. Anybody seen New Englandy author JEFF PIERCE? Sources report he is brushing up on his arts and crafts at an exclusive Connecticut hospital.

For almost a week he'd kept himself awake at night rehearsing angry interrogations interspersed with self-rebukes, but when Corrine finally called Sunday night from her mother's house, Russell was temporarily depleted, as if the many practice conversations had exhausted the possibilities of her actual response. "How do you *think* I am?" he said, in answer to her nervous inquiry.

"I'm sorry."

"Jeff's excuse is he was drunk, which apparently passes for an explanation in AA. What's yours?"

"It was years ago, Russ, before we were married. You were in England and we were arguing all the time over the phone. It was like you asked me to marry you just so I'd wait for you, and then I didn't really think you wanted to and I was so scared. I thought you'd met someone over there and Jeff just tried to comfort me."

"Comfort is not an emotion that needs to be administered vaginally."

"It was a mistake I've regretted ever since, and I always prayed you wouldn't find out, Russ, and I've tried in so many ways to make it up to you even when you didn't know."

"How many times did this comforting ceremony take place?"

"Russell, don't."

They talked for an hour. Frigid with scorn at first, Russell became angry; later he cried. Corrine cried, too, and for a time they seemed to be trying to console each other, as if they were old friends who had suffered separate, unrelated tragedies.

"I have your mink," he said at one point, when he couldn't think of anything else.

"Keep it. Maybe you can sell it."

"It's yours."

"I don't want it. It suddenly seems like a ridiculous thing to have."

"Thanks," he said.

"I'm sorry. I just mean almost everything about my life has been so frivolous and stupid. A mink coat. Jesus. I don't know, it's like, what were we thinking of?"

After a long pause he said, "I still can't believe it." But what made it worse, finally, was that he could. At the time, years before, he couldn't have believed it, but evidently his convictions had gradually become more sophisticated. He wanted to say he couldn't live without her, but he was afraid that somewhere along the line he might have lost the romantic fanaticism of innocence which allowed him to host such absolute beliefs. Suddenly that loss seemed almost as large as the other. By the time she hung up he felt dull and heavy, uncertain of anything except, perhaps, that his heart would never be as simple again.

43

The big, rolling lawn was ratty with the neglected growth of Indian summer and littered with the curled, browning shrapnel of exploded oak and maple leaves, the season changing as Corrine watched, nature pressing on with its heartless agenda. The last of the elm trees by the front gate looked sick, having finally succumbed to the plague that had wiped out its family. Corrine walked down to the pond over the wet morning lawn and spooked a flock of migrant mallards. Though it was only the middle of October she could feel the sharp chill on the morning air. Winter in New England, a season of confinement, darkness and incest.

Almost from the moment she arrived, Corrine regretted going home. If it seemed natural to return to the nest after a fall, this particular nest was broken and nothing was quite the way it should have been. Her mother wanted to help and comfort her, but she also required company in her own chronic misery.

Corrine had grown up in this house, a white Greek Revival with black shutters, peeling paint and sagging roof, impregnated with familiar smells and memories. And yet now it seemed as if someone had moved all the furniture almost imperceptibly and fiddled with the dimensions of the rooms. Instead of shrinking, as she'd heard the settings of childhood usually did, it had grown larger in the absence of the family. Her father's absence, especially, opened space in the middle of the drafty rooms. Though Corrine had been coming back throughout the five years since her father left, she noticed it all over again now.

The homing instinct that drew her here was accompanied by an equal and opposite reaction that made her resent the intended source of comfort.

Almost from the start she was testy with her mother. Having come for a sympathetic ear, she found herself reluctant to confide all. When she looked at her mother she saw too much of herself, and this made her frightened and angry. She did not want to commiserate on the awfulness of men, or share in the sisterhood of failure. This she imagined to be her mother's perspective, and so it was what she responded to, unable to see that her mother's position was tinged with nobler motives. Refusing to identify with anyone else, Corrine insisted on the uniqueness of her own marital problems. As bad as things might appear to her now, she clung to the belief that her marriage to Russell was a special case.

Chain-smoking at the kitchen table with *Jeopardy* on the television set on the far counter, Jessie Makepeace was trying to get the story straight for perhaps the fifth time, going over the ground again as if, it seemed to Corrine, to savor someone else's unhappiness. Over the phone, the week before, Corrine had told her about calling Frankfurt and discovering another Mrs. Calloway registered to Russell's room. Since arriving home she hadn't divulged much, and she had yet to tell her mother about her recently revealed history with Jeff. Deeply remorseful and ashamed, she wanted only sympathy at the time.

Jessie said, "I never pegged Russell as the type."

"I wouldn't say he was the *type*," Corrine said, a note of defensiveness creeping into her voice as she straddled separate loyalties. "It just happened."

She was still angry with Russell, but she felt that in his absence she had to present his side of the case. It was time to tell her mother the rest.

When Corrine had finished confessing her own transgressions, Jessie whistled theatrically, like an old broad in a black-and-white movie, smoke escaping from between her pursed, cracked lips. "Of all the people you could've picked, honey." Jessie liked Jeff nearly as much as she liked Russell. He had been here to the house, had been Russell's best man at the wedding. Jessie clipped out reviews and articles about him and renewed a long-lapsed subscription to *The New Yorker* after it published one of his stories. She had never felt that Caitlin was good enough for Jeff, in the years they were together, and several times she had banteringly suggested that Corrine picked the wrong friend.

"It was a long time ago," Corrine said, eyeing her mother's cigarettes longingly.

"Corrine, there's no statute of limitations on sleeping with a man's best friend. Men are about forty percent testosterone and the rest is all pride, and you really kicked him right in the old pride when you slept with Jeff."

"I know."

"Boy, you really did it!"

"Thanks for that confirmation, Mom."

At least now, Corrine had the satisfaction of knowing that her mother couldn't say that it was just like what had happened to her, or that men were all alike.

"So how *is* Jeff," Jessie asked.

"I wish you wouldn't ask like that."

"Like what?"

"As if you're secretly enjoying the soap opera."

"Corrine, I was only asking how he was. You know I'm crazy about Jeff."

"He's still in the hospital. They let him out in another week. I don't know, I don't imagine these are the best times of his life."

"I don't understand," Jessie said. "Jeff had everything going for him. How does somebody like that get hooked on drugs?"

If Corrine hadn't solved this mystery, it was not for lack of trying. At different moments she believed that Jeff's unhappiness stemmed from guilt about his success, such as it was, guilt about his feelings for her, sadness about his breakup with Caitlin. And yet she'd sensed there was something doomed about Jeff when she'd first met him. Like hers, his family history was not reassuring; for all of their diluted class entitlement they recognized that sense of loss in each other. But Jeff's adolescent unhappiness, more acute than her own, seemed to her to have some grand, universal component. Life *was* insupportably sad, and gazing at Jessie's scotch glass sweating on the windowsill she could almost understand Jeff's search for oblivion, if that's what it was.

"I remember Jeff saying once," she said, "that what really separates us from the other animals is an instinct for self-destruction."

"You know, you're always quoting Jeff." Jessie sucked hard on the last half-inch of her cigarette and stubbed it out in a corner of the overflowing ashtray. "So are you in love with him?"

"I've always been a little," Corrine said. "Maybe a lot."

"Why do we all like the bad boys, I wonder?"

"Not so much bad as wounded. Russell's so open and strong, Jeff's sort of dark and tortured." Russell had been in England and Jeff seemed to need her; there was a brief moment when she'd almost convinced herself to believe that loving Jeff was another way of loving Russell. It happened more than once, though not for long. "But now it's over."

"Then go back to Russell."

"I don't know if he'll have me. I don't even know what I want."

"Why don't you stay here for a while?" Jessie said.

"I don't know."

"I was thinking we could open a business together. Antiques, maybe."

"I've applied for a job with the District Attorney's Office. There's an internship on the task force investigating insider trading."

"You only have one year of law school, honey," her mother said, putting her drink down. "Isn't that a problem?"

"They've got plenty of lawyers, but they need people who know securities."

"Muckraking, huh? Your father's father would be pleased, the old bleeding heart." Though she could have used a slice of the family money that this old gentleman had given away, Jessie had a soft spot for the man who had disliked his son, her ex-husband, enough to deprive him of an inheritance.

Over the weekend Corrine had raked leaves and read *Franny and Zooey* for about the seventeenth time. She thought about the day she'd unwittingly had lunch with an older man she met in the stacks at the Dartmouth library. She was a freshman at Brown, visiting a boy whose name she could no longer remember, who'd been completely drunk and obnoxious from the moment she arrived Friday night. Saturday morning, after sleeping on his couch, she retreated to the library, and this nice old guy named Jerome had started to talk to her about the book she was reading—D. T. Suzuki on Zen—and then invited her to lunch, and for some reason she had trusted him. They drove out to the country to his house, which had a high chain-link fence around it. They lunched on grains and beans and vegetables, and all he talked about was vitamins and herbs and macrobiotics. He said he'd been working on a book about diet and spiritual health for years. After lunch he showed her the cinder-block bunker where he did his writing, and only then did she realize it was Salinger. He dropped her back at the library and never once mentioned fiction. Jeff and Russell had often tried to wring more out of her, but that was it. A man obsessed with vitamins.

Corrine was raking leaves again on Monday when her mother came out on the back porch with a mug of coffee and a cigarette.

"You picked a good time to leave your job. I was just listening to the news—the stock market's going completely down the drain."

Corrine rushed inside and turned on the TV in the family room. Flipping among channels she learned that the market was down three to four hundred points, no one knew for certain; the tape was running at least an hour behind the market because of the huge number of transactions.

She called Russell at his office.

"I know, I know," he said. "I've been trying to get Duane on the phone to see what I can sell, but the lines are jammed. I can't find out what's happening on NASDAQ. It's total fucking chaos."

"How much do you have in?" she demanded.

"You don't want to know."

"Did you sell that block you bought with your credit card?"

"I was going to. This week, in fact."

"Jesus, Russell. You could end up owing more money than we have."

"I'm acutely aware of this, Corrine. Anyway, Corbin, Dern should hold its value. The tender offer's in place."

"If the market collapses, the deal goes right along with it. Your financing will evaporate. You don't get this stuff at all, do you?"

Then Corrine tried to reach Duane, but without success. Eventually there was nothing to do except watch the news and count the bodies. It felt absurd, after more than two years on the Street, to be watching this apocalypse on television in the family room in Stockbridge. Two hours or so after the market closed, the damage was finally tallied. It was 1929, no matter what channel you turned to. One of the broadcasts was live outside a crowded Harry's bar, brokers shaking their heads and acting stricken for the cameras. Feeling left out, Corrine watched eagerly for familiar faces. The satisfaction she might have been entitled to, having anticipated disaster, was diluted by the sense that she'd been cheated of a ringside seat on a historical event, and by guilt about having left her former colleagues holding the bag.

"I hope your father lost his goddamn shirt," said Jessie, stirring the fresh ice in her glass of scotch with her pinkie. "My lawyers couldn't find it, but I know he had a big trading account somewhere."

Corrine thought about her conversation with Russell and suddenly wondered if he wasn't positioning himself for the future. She really had no idea what kind of money he'd been playing around with in recent months. Maybe he'd already sold that stock. For all she knew, he might have a bank account offshore. It didn't seem like Russell—secrecy being alien to his nature—but neither did it seem like Russell to check into a hotel with another woman. And Trina Cox would be more than capable of hiding money, she might have seen the crash coming—the two of them planning all along for an eventual divorce. Corrine had always trusted Russell in everything; now that trust was fractured and she didn't know if she could believe anything. It suddenly seemed that even the stock market crash was part of the intricate conspiracy against her happiness, and the feeling was confirmed when Nancy Tanner called later that night from New York. She didn't mean to butt in, Nancy said, and it really wasn't any of her business, but she thought Corrine ought to know that she had seen Russell and Trina Cox having dinner a few nights before.

"It was really embarrassing, she was like, all over him. I mean, I didn't know what to do, I think you guys are such a great couple and all, I feel terrible, but I just thought you deserved to know."

"That's really nice of you, Nancy. I've always admired your desire to share information."

"I just thought . . ."

"Think again, Nancy. Next time you have this impulse to pick up the phone, don't. Okay?"

Though she did not give Nancy the satisfaction of seeing it, her worst fears were now confirmed. Finally it was all over. She had specifically forbidden him to see Trina. The fact that he'd immediately returned to her, and done it so flagrantly, demonstrated that Trina was more than just a fling, that they *had* planned everything, that Corrine was a complete fool.

Later that night she talked to Casey, who had just gotten back to the city from her house in Millbrook. "Tom is absolutely frantic about the market, he says we've probably lost half a million." Casey's tone indicated that, in fact, this sum was hardly worth a *giant* fuss.

"Did you *see* the *Post*? Russell is such a pig," said Casey, who had never liked him, feeling that Corrine deserved someone rather better and correctly suspecting that Russell despised her. With very little prompting she read Corrine the gossip-column sighting of Russell in the company of an unidentified blonde at a low-rent nightclub.

44

On Tuesday, October 20, 1987, a gray stretch Mercedes rolled slowly down Fifth Avenue, sliding past the mist-shrouded foliage of the park, followed by a smaller version of itself. The cars turned left, away from the park, and stopped in front of a limestone townhouse. Men in dark suits leaped out to reconnoiter the street. Two of them took up stations on either side of the front steps, their vigil slightly more tense than usual, both wondering if their jobs were secure. Although none of the men was intimate with the financial markets, it was nearly impossible not to be aware of the previous day's catastrophe. Half a trillion dollars had allegedly vanished in a day, leaving behind neither smoke nor rubble. So far as one could see, the buildings of the metropolis were still standing, and as the sun moved westward one imagined that the postmen would find the factories and farms outside the city in their usual locations, about to resume business. And yet this morning's headlines were funereal. The mysterious event was referred to as a "meltdown," a term evoking in many viewers disturbing associations of nuclear disaster.

As if in anticipation, Bernard Melman had become increasingly glum and testy through the early part of the fall, a phenomenon that longer-tenured members of his staff had seen before; he had retreated to South-ampton for several weeks with doctors in tow, and had remained in his room while his security force lingered on the porches. Just a few days before now, Melman had returned to Manhattan, more subdued than usual.

At precisely six-thirty, the heavy front door of the townhouse opened and Melman appeared. He walked out to the edge of the steps wearing a severe frown above his customary double-breasted suit.

"Well, boys . . ." Pausing for effect, he suddenly produced a stagy smile, with the air of an amateur magician pulling a dove out of a hat. "Let's go to the office."

The men laughed with relief, and not only because they were paid to do so.

"Are we walking or riding," he asked no one in particular, cocking his head in a broad imitation of a quizzical pose. "I think we'll walk."

The bodyguards nodded eagerly, imbibing the boss's good humor. Apparently the world hadn't ended.

Halfway up the street he stopped abruptly. "Boys," he said. "I want you to be extra vigilant today." He pointed up to the sky. "Watch out for falling stockbrokers."

As they strolled down Madison, Bernie Melman's step was sprightly, his pace aerobic. Like a sports fan who is happiest when players try to kill one another with hockey sticks or when stock cars kiss the wall and burst into flames, he seemed invigorated by catastrophe. He believed he had the common touch, which indeed he had with everyone in his employ, and when he was in an especially good mood he liked to share his views on life.

"This is a great day for shopping," he announced, halting to look in the window of Sherry-Lehmann, the wine merchants. "The smart shoppers wait for prices to fall. America's having a fire sale today. Whoa, let 'em pass," he said, gesturing for his men to make way for an elderly couple tottering up the avenue.

"What some people fail to realize," he resumed, back on the march, "is that wherever there are losers there are also winners, right?" He slowed his pace dramatically, nearly bringing the procession to a halt. "The trick," he concluded, "is to be among the fucking winners."

As expected, Carl Linder did not quite share his employer's optimism. Melman sometimes thought he kept Linder around only because his basset-hound mien always made him feel happier by contrast. "Why the long face, Carl," he asked when Linder limped into his office for their breakfast conference, though his expression was no gloomier than usual.

"I'm fine," he muttered.

"You're not worried, are you?"

"Not especially, but I do think we should be careful. The economy's staggering. People are worried. Even if you came out okay yesterday, you don't operate outside of that context. We've got to be worried about the long-term prices of all those bonds you're holding."

This said, Linder was still happy to see that Melman had risen out of his colossal psychochemical funk. He was also pleased that Melman, in his depression, had anticipated every form of doom and disaster for himself and the planet and had ordered a big selloff of assets.

"This isn't 'twenty-nine," Bernie said. "Everybody's bank accounts are guaranteed by the FDIC, basic indicators are sound. This should scare some sense into those boneheads in Washington about the fucking deficit. And we shorted the market two weeks ago. So smile."

"What about Corbin, Dern?"

"I'm about to take care of that." He asked his secretary to get the banker responsible for the bridge loan on the phone.

The credit officer sounded extremely nervous and harassed. "Jesus, Bernie, this is one hell of a mess. How do you stand?"

"Not a care in the world, pal. You sound a little frantic, though."

"I'm about to go into a meeting," the banker said, adding significantly, "We're going to have to reevaluate some of our loan commitments in light of what's happened."

"That's exactly what I wanted to talk to you about."

"I'm afraid we may have to reconsider the Corbin, Dern."

"I agree one hundred percent."

"You do?"

"I want you to withdraw the financing."

"You *do?*"

"No, I'm joking, what do you think? Of course I do, and I want a letter from you to that effect this afternoon."

"Sure. You got it," the banker said happily. "Can I ask why?"

"Just get me that letter. And I'm sure you can understand why we never actually had this conversation."

"Let's just say I want to renegotiate," Bernie explained to Linder after he'd hung up. "The tender offer is subject to financing. No financing, no deal." He had decided to submit a new, bargain-basement offer once the bank pulled out of the old deal, then presell the textbook and children's divisions, trim half of the staff away and possibly tap Harold Stone to run the new, leaner operation.

"Very brassy," Linder observed.

"Just reacting to the new business conditions, Carl."

Pacing her office in Rockefeller Center, Trina Cox was not nearly so sanguine. She hadn't been hit directly—working in M&A, she had scrupulously shunned the market in order to avoid conflicts of interest—but it was the aftershocks she was worried about. Whether the market recovered or continued to plunge, it was a hell of a time to be opening a business. And she also worried about her new rabbi, Bernie Melman, who suddenly had become unavailable to take her calls. Up to this moment, her timing had been impeccable. If she'd remained at Silverman she would at least have been a little less exposed. On the other hand, if Bernie stayed behind her she was as secure as anyone on the street.

Trina's secretary arrived at seven with coffee and doughnuts looking hung over and frightened. "Do I still get paid to be your slave," he asked.

She shrugged.

He scooped up the phone as it rang. "Bernie Melman calling for Trina Cox," he squawked, deftly imitating the accent of Melman's secretary.

"You'll know in a few minutes," she said, taking the phone.

"The thing is, Trina, whenever there are losers there are also winners. I backed you because you strike me as a fucking winner."

After the chitchat Trina sensed they were coming to the point.

"I like to think I'm a winner, Bernie."

"I want us to continue our business relationship. Let me just lay out a hypothetical situation for you. Given the stock market situation, I think it's quite possible that our lenders may not want to back the current offer for Corbin, Dern. They may not think the company is worth what we offered for it, and they may be right. Which could give us a clean slate to go in and make a lower bid."

"Sounds good."

Bernie cleared his throat. "When I say clean slate, I mean clean, right?

I'm afraid I've lost confidence in our management team. Calloway's a bright kid, but I don't need a fucking literary Eagle Scout to run this company. We need a fucking grown-up. Do you have a problem with that?"

With a slight, quickly suppressed pang, Trina said, "Nope."

On Wednesday, Russell took three calls before attending the memorial service for Victor Propp—whose official cause of death, he'd learned the day before, was "massive coronary." The first was from Trina Cox, who informed him that the financing on the Corbin, Dern deal had fallen through in light of Monday's events and that therefore, effectively, the deal was off, although it was possible that certain parties might make another offer, subject to the new financial conditions and possibly with new personnel arrangements.

"Any possibility I'd be part of the new deal," he asked.

"Just between you and me, Russell, not a fucking chance."

"It was fun," he said, trying for a conclusion.

"Could've been a lot more fun, if you'd really gone with it."

"Probably."

"Let me tell you a secret, Russell. It's them against us."

"Them?"

"The short, unattractive men who run the world."

"That's the secret?"

"Absolutely. Winning is never going to matter to you as much as it does to them. So—you lose."

"Thanks for the insight."

"Do you mind if I ask you a question? When we were in Frankfurt that night—I'm just curious—I asked you what I consider to be a nice question, a very selfless proposition, as it were. Do you remember your answer? You said, 'Paint my house.' And you laughed like it was the funniest thing you ever said. What the hell was that supposed to mean, anyway?"

The second call was a margin call from Duane Peters, his elusive broker, asking Russell to cover losses on his stock holdings, in particular the massive hit he'd taken on his leveraged block of Corbin, Dern.

"Where were you for the last two days, you bastard?"

"I was on the phone."

"Not my phone, you weren't."

"Do you have any cash?"

"Of course not."

"We'll have to sell off stock. I'm trying to get a quotation on Corbin, Dern. I'll call you back." When Duane did call back, Russell learned that CD had lost forty percent, leaving him, after the margin call, with an eighty-percent loss on borrowed money.

The third call was from a lawyer, a Weston Strickley, informing Mr. Calloway that he represented Mrs. Calloway, who wished to have copies of the records of all of his financial transactions for the year 1987, with particular reference to securities transactions in the past month, as well as the names and numbers of any and all offshore accounts. If Mr. Calloway failed to provide these, a court order would be forthcoming.

An hour later a scrofulous, red-faced man handed Russell a smudged subpoena that barred him from liquidating, transferring or in any other way disposing of marital assets, including securities.

45

Born in the Midwest, an adoptive easterner, Russell harbored the traditional suspicions about southern California. He imagined it to be the headquarters of cult religions, health fads and Babylonian decadence—the last being the substantial attraction. He didn't see how you could really be serious about anything when the sun was always shining idiotically. Nevertheless he hoped the West Coast might represent an evolutionary step up from the bad faith, bad conscience and smug sophistication of New York—the outer edge of the whole migration away from history, culture, Europe.

Stepping out of the terminal at LAX two days after Thanksgiving, he felt a charge of erotic potential in the hot, smoky air. It was a radical transition from Michigan, where he had just spent a gloomy bachelor Thanksgiving with his father and recently engaged brother. From the limo, courtesy of his new partner, Zac Solomon, he spotted a sign that said NUDE COCKTAILS over a squat bunker on the edge of a field rhythmic with oil wells—a flock of prehistoric birds pecking the earth blindly.

La Cienega ran in a straight line to the Hollywood Hills, although the landscape faded and blanched out after a mile or so and they drove fifteen minutes before Russell saw the dark line of the hills emerging through the smog directly in front of them. Parched and sharp against the sprawling, populous flats—like the backbone of a starving hound—this long ridge did not look particularly hospitable, but up along the switchbacks the world below disappeared; brilliant gardens and blue-green pools flourished in the rock crevices. Russell's hotel stood on the edge of the hills, just off Sunset—a literal translation of a Loire Valley castle towering above the palm trees, a fantasy realized, Russell was told, in 1929.

In the midst of all the sunshine and newness, he was happy to find his hotel comfortably tattered, run-down and full of cool, stale shadows. Increasingly, the residential suite—with its mismatched veneer furniture, ancient kitchen appliances and atrociously orange, perpetually damp carpet on which grew an as yet unclassified strain of moss or lichen—was a refuge from the dazzling brilliance outside. Years before, he'd moved to New York believing himself to be penetrating to the center of the world, and all of the time he lived there the illusion of a center had held: the sense of there always being a door behind which further mysteries were available, a ballroom at the top of the sky from which the irresistible music wafted, a secret power source from which the mad energy of the metropolis emanated. But Los Angeles had no discernible center and was also without edges and corners. Russell didn't get it—this riotously overgrown suburb of his unmourned Midwest, plunked down on Cap d'Antibes. He was grateful to be lodged up against a hill, even if only his back was resting against something solid.

Though lost, Russell was not unwilling to learn, to admit that the old principles had failed him, to try to suspend judgment until he could exercise it again—the sun and the apparent formlessness of life here at the edgeless edge of the continent reminding him of lines from Stevens: "You must become an ignorant man again / And see the sun again with an ignorant eye / And see it clearly in the idea of it." He had an ignorant eye and the sun was certainly shining, but even after several months it was still just glare.

Work had the virtue, at least, of shiny novelty, and Russell had always been an enthusiastic starter. He optioned two books in the first week, and began to talk to directors and actors. The directors were easy to tell from the actors—they all wore beards, conceiving themselves the intellectuals of the community. Russell arrived in town trailing a vague legend of success from the East, and Zac amplified it considerably; everyone wanted to have lunch with him. The fact that his attempt to take over a publishing company had failed did not, finally, register as much as the fact that he had done *something*. His days were full, and the notion of the movie business as a languid affair conducted mainly at poolside was quickly discarded. The day began at seven-thirty with a breakfast meeting at one of the big hotels and proceeded unabated through a business dinner at seven-thirty. At times it occurred to Russell that his schedule reflected the illusion of activity rather than accomplishment, but he was grateful it didn't allow him too much time to think.

For all the hours of work, the community was infused with a sense of its own glamour. The end product of all their labors cast a reflected glow back onto the meanest laborers in the industry. The typist was animated by the consciousness that her drudgery transmitted lines that might be spoken by stars on screen, while agents and producers, driving their expensive cars to important meetings, were understandably tempted to believe *they* were the stars of the real drama, of which the public saw only the puppet version.

Having once pictured the enterprise as a shark tank churning with blood, Russell was surprised at how much free-floating goodwill and bonhomie he encountered. A childlike glee prevailed at having discovered not just an unlocked candy store but the actual factory where all of the sweets were produced. Like children, the inside players were capable of sudden cruelty and violence to their own, but there was so much wealth to go around that the predominant spirit seemed generous, the politics gentler than those in a graduate English department, where there was so much less plunder to be divvied up. A lucrative, unofficial socialism was practiced; if you lost one job, another would be offered elsewhere at a higher salary.

There were rules, of course. In the wake of a hedonistic binge earlier in the decade, a curious puritanism held sway in Babylon West. Zac had run Russell through the drill at one of their early lunches at a casual expensive restaurant on Melrose. The tented dining room was like a shrine to healthful simplicity, with pastel-colored patrons and menu offerings of grilled fishes and raw vegetables.

Zac had been reverentially cataloguing the sexual malpractices of those at neighboring tables. Suddenly he asked, "How was your dinner with Packard the other night."

"We got on fine. He was eager to let me know that he'd read several books in his life, and I tried to assure him that I liked movies."

Zac nodded thoughtfully. "He said you were pounding drinks."

"Jesus Christ. I had a martini and two glasses of wine, for God's sake."

"A lot of people did too much of everything in the early eighties, and now there's a kind of collective hangover. In the fifties they had the Red Scare, now we got the White Scare. That's how Jeff really queered himself out here. And you being associated with Jeff, you know . . ."

"I'm guilty by association?"

"I'm just trying to explain, guy. There's this competitive health thing now. So your lunch partner waits for you to order the tuna and then he'll order three pieces of arugula and call it a meal, giving you to believe that you are a monstrous glutton and therefore not spiritually streamlined. When you order a glass of white wine he'll tell you about his personal trainer, who drives to the house every morning at five in a semi full of Nautilus equipment for a private workout before his breakfast of three strawberries and one piece of dry whole wheat toast. Anyway, one thing about AA, it's the best pickup scene in town."

Solomon encouraged him to look for a house, offering to guarantee the financing, but Russell remained in the hotel, clinging to his transience for security. After almost two months alone in the New York apartment, he was becoming accustomed to a life without cozy domestic touches and to the blandly reassuring babble of an unwatched TV set.

Zac lived several hundred feet above him, up the canyon, in a house of indeterminate style that clung to its quarter-acre of the hillside; behind the house, set into a cliff like a flat gem, a redwood deck framed a shimmering oval of turquoise that seemed to defy the antique notion of water seeking its own level. Zac threw a party at the house a week after Russell's arrival to introduce him to the local fauna. These included producers, studio executives, agents and lawyers, as well as a smattering of actors and actresses. The women were of two types, industry professional and strictly ornamental. In terms of a contemporary standard of female beauty, the process of natural selection of the species, reinforced by cosmetic surgery, had reached in Los Angeles an acute level of refinement. There was an obvious surplus of young blonde women in jeans and breathtaking stretch tops who identified themselves as actresses, all of whom *acted* very glad to have Russell in town. One of these women became his companion.

Katrina Ostrom was an aspiring actress from Denver, sweet-natured beneath the fresh, still wet lacquer of apprentice professional glamour, not yet twisted and deformed by the hard lessons she was learning in this profession. So far she had played a dead body in a made-for-TV movie and had two lines in an upcoming feature. Just a few months more acclimated than Russell, she took him to parties and drove up to Santa Barbara with him on the weekends, but he would not let her spend the night in his room. He knew it was a flimsy scruple at best, but he could not bear the possibility that Corrine might call in the middle of the night while someone else slept beside him. Curiously, Katrina didn't find this fastidiousness particularly offensive or surprising. Although he didn't inquire too closely, he gathered that the recent men in her life had treated her as a minor accessory.

If he was not as cynical as Zac, who referred approvingly to their liaison as a low-maintenance relationship, Russell was certainly not looking for a soulmate. At first, he'd been astonished and grateful that he was able to perform the act with anyone else, let alone a beautiful girl of twenty. After more than a decade with Corrine it seemed nothing short of miraculous; and now for the first time in his life he was conscious of being older than the twenty-year-olds. But as pleasant as it might be, he couldn't help comparing, and at times the idea of making love was unbearably sad and he would find himself unable to go through with it. When this happened he would become short-tempered and impatient. One night at Katrina's tiny, messy studio in a converted motel in east Hollywood, he had begun to kiss her until suddenly overcome with a wave of revulsion, perhaps brought on by the tang of onion on her breath. "This place is a pigsty," he said.

She rose from the bed and started to pick up the clothing scattered around the bedroom. Suddenly, the sight of a flimsy silk teddy held up to the light between her long fingers filled him with remorse.

"I'm sorry," he said. "I'm absolutely unbearable. I don't know how you can stand me." He jumped from the bed and held her close against him.

"You're not so bad. In fact, you're the nicest guy I've met out here."

But he could become only worse, like the others, faced with such meager expectations. In what he took to be a gesture of noble renunciation, he told her they shouldn't see each other anymore; he subsequently broke his resolution twice in the course of three weeks, calling her late at night and asking if he could come over. The third time he called she said, "I'm sorry, Russell."

"Is somebody there," he asked.

In an exasperated whisper she said, "I can't just sit around hoping you'll call."

He was almost relieved that the opportunity for further damage had been removed, knowing that he had behaved badly. Drifting like a leaf on the current, Russell felt incapable of making hard decisions on his own.

46

Corrine's New Year's resolution was to date. She knew she owed it to herself to get over Russell, or at least her friends insisted she did—but every time a stranger tried to put his tongue in her mouth it seemed either comic or tragic. Duane Peters got as far as the hook on her bra before she started to laugh. Casey Reynes fixed her up with a blind date. Her friend was a Makepeace, after all, and her candidate for Corrine's bed, and hand, was Christian Howorth, of the Memphis Howorths, Yale '77, whose endowments and accomplishments took Casey fifteen minutes to relate, the most pertinent being that he had inherited money, had made a great deal more in arbitrage and had bailed out before the market collapsed. When he arrived at her door on a run-down street in Chelsea in a tastefully understated town car with driver, he was as handsome as billed. At the theater and later at Lutèce he proved an engaging and fertile raconteur. He was a three-time member of the U.S. equestrian team, a skier and a gentleman, standing to hold her chair when she returned from the ladies' room, leaving her at her door that night with a delicate kiss. His taste seemed impeccable insofar as women were concerned: he sent roses with a sweet note the following morning and called for another date that afternoon. She went out with him twice more, the last time to the Reyneses' ski house in Vermont. He was great in every way except that he wasn't Russell. When she finally told him she really wasn't ready to date yet, Casey was furious. "God knows I tried to help her," Casey told friends, in a tone that suggested Corrine was now fornicating with German shepherds and shooting heroin like her friend Jeff Pierce.

Jeff took her to dinner on her birthday. Though they had talked on the phone frequently, she hadn't seen him since he'd been released from the hospital a few months before. He looked too thin and tired, and there was a new awkwardness between them. The conversation was strained until she reminded him of her last birthday, when he had brought that teenager with the tits to their apartment, and Corrine had thrown water on him, and he and Crash had knocked over the vase.

"Jesus, was that only a year ago?" he said. "Everything before the hospital seems like old black-and-white television. I was ripped that night. In fact, I shot up in your bathroom."

"God, Jeff," was all Corrine could say.

Jeff told her that later, when he'd returned to his loft with the model, she had suddenly lifted her head up from the pillow and told him, caveat emptor, that her tits were *enhanced*—just so he wouldn't, like, be all *shocked* or anything—and he'd been so surprised by this earnest, urgent revelation that he was unable to stop laughing, much less to perform. Hearing him tell it, Corrine laughed herself, a lately unaccustomed exercise of facial muscles.

"Story of my life. Nothing turned out to be real," he said, grinning sheepishly until he saw that Corrine was crying.

"Please don't say that, Jeff."

Offering up his napkin, he observed that it was stained with marinara sauce. After patting down his pockets in search of a handkerchief, he ripped the pocket from his shirt and handed her the piece of blue oxford cloth.

"You're not eating," she chided, when she'd regained her composure. "You look like a skeleton."

"Look who's talking."

"I've gained weight," she insisted.

"How is he," Jeff asked as she dipped a fork ostentatiously into her angel-hair.

"I think he's seeing someone. He hasn't told me but I feel it."

"And you?"

"I can't picture being with anyone else. I keep *trying*, goddamnit, but I just can't feature it."

He fired up a cigarette and scratched at his wrist, which, she saw, was splotched with some kind of plum-colored rash. She wondered if he was back on the needle. "I still love you," he said.

"What's that on your arm?" she said abruptly, then laughed nervously at her own non sequitur. Pulling on a strand of hair draped over her shoulder, she said, "Sorry. I love you too, but it's no use to either of us."

"Utility be damned. I've never exactly been the practical type."

"No. But I suppose when it comes right down to it, I am." She reached over and touched his mottled hand. "Aren't I?"

One night, looking for her birth certificate to verify her existence to her new employer, she came upon a limp, folded piece of lined paper, with a poem written in Russell's backward-leaning hand:

> Let the Muses sing and the Graces dance
> Not at their wedding only but all their days long
> So couple their hearts that no ill ever befall them.
> Let him never call her other than my Joy! My Light!
> And she never call him other than Sweetheart.
> And when they must depart this earth
> Because they have sweetly lived together
> Let one die not a day before the other
> But he bury her, she him, with even fate
> One heart let jointly separate
> O happy both!

Russell had chosen the poem, one of his grad school Elizabethan treasures, that best man Jeff had read at their wedding in Stockbridge more than six years before. So perfect then, it was almost unbearable now, bringing home for the first time the possibility that they might not end their days together.

Between crying jags she went to work at the DA's Office downtown, sifting through mind-numbing mountains of documents in search of evidence of securities fraud, twice a week taking the number 6 train up to Bleecker to work at the mission.

One night she was clearing dishes when news began to circulate among the men that the police were massing in an empty lot on Avenue D for an assault on the shantytown where many of them slept. A forcible eviction had been threatened for weeks, the winter cold having failed to depopulate the future site of middle-income condominiums. Many of the men hurriedly bolted the last of their food.

"They got bulldozers and tanks and shit," Ace told Corrine, hyperbolically, wiping his mouth with the back of his hand and stashing an apple in the pocket of Russell's old parka.

Corrine stripped off her apron. "I'm coming too," she said.

"It's gonna get ugly," he warned, but Corrine thought it might be less ugly if people like herself were on hand, hoping that her business suit and general appearance would offer some small measure of protection. She followed Ace and a dozen others out into the street, shivering in a wind that carried the smell of acrid smoke, the smudged night sky glowing to the east.

The shantytown was brilliantly illuminated from within and without: dozens of fires burning among the tepees and lean-tos; fierce spotlights trained on the camp from across the street. The bulldozers, four in all, were backing down from two flatbed trucks, diesels drowning the shouts of the squatters, who waved lumber and bricks at the blue phalanx of riot-helmeted policemen. Ace and Corrine pressed through the crowd of spectators. The yellow bulldozers lurched and wheeled around, turning their implacable blank faces toward the mob. A brick arced across the night sky and struck the helmet of one of the policemen, knocking him backward.

As Corrine's group approached, a detachment of cops broke away at a right angle to cut them off from the camp; the rest of the force moved forward behind shields, their billy clubs held aloft. The idling bulldozers rumbled and belched smoke. Half of the squatters melted away as the police advanced into a volley of projectiles. Corrine watched three cops run toward her. One in particular seemed to have singled her out; his lips were drawn tight beneath a dark mustache, and he fixed her with a look of simple hatred. She was frozen by that look, unable to believe it was directed at her. Ace grabbed her hand and yanked as the billy club descended, grazing the edge of her hip, sending an electric current of pain into the bone. She might have screamed, but the air was full of the noise of pain and anger and she could not distinguish her own voice.

Looking back over her shoulder she saw cops flailing wildly at the crowd.

They fled west, Ace towing her by the hand, hurting her arm as he raced through the streets. "In here," he said, pulling her through a hole in a chain-link fence, her dress catching on a hook of wire before ripping free. The lot was strewn with garbage and the debris of deconstruction. Hands on Corrine's hips, Ace shoved her down behind a discarded Christmas tree. Lying on the cold littered ground she could hear the clatter of flight, the heavy jangling pursuit of the police, screams and curses. She pressed her face into the earth. Ace lay close, breathing rapidly.

As she lay in the dirt staring at the limbless torso of a plastic doll, Corrine envisioned the violence spreading and consuming the entire city, an orgy of rage and destruction. There was nothing left to stop it—no compassion, no law, no common purpose. "It's a fucking war, man," Ace said, more excited than afraid, after a detachment of helmeted policemen had clattered past. She was so cold that her hands and feet were beginning to go numb. "Let's blow," Ace said, when she told him.

After ducking back through the fence, they encountered a mob of ragged men wielding sticks, pipes and bottles. For a moment Corrine thought they were about to charge, but some of them recognized Ace.

"The pigs clubbed my lady, man. Can you believe this shit?"

The mob roared and suddenly she found herself absorbed into the group, the men seeming to accept her protection as part of their mission.

"Let's get out of here," Corrine said.

"It's a lot safer with these dudes," Ace said. "Situation like this—you on your own, you're just meat."

The would-be juggernaut lurched west in search of a target, competing voices calling out prospective destinations and plans. Corrine was so cold and dazed she could hardly interpret the noise around her. She kept smelling gasoline. Suddenly there was a focused burst of energy, a hush falling over the group as they arrived in front of a seemingly abandoned building, the door of which had been replaced by a crude steel panel. One of the men walked up and pounded on it; the man who opened it was knocked down, and within a moment the group was surging up the dark, narrow staircase.

She found herself in a small room furnished only with a filthy bathtub and loose cushions. A sharp medicinal odor made her eyes tear. Three of the men had pinioned a fat white man wearing a Billy Idol T-shirt against the wall, while two black teenagers stood cowering beside another steel door. As Corrine watched, a panel on the door slid open. The leader of their merry band rushed forward and slammed a pipe into the opening. Others surged forward, obscuring her view, the smell of gasoline overpowering the other, unfamiliar smell. A flame sprouted from the neck of a wine bottle, and then, suddenly, the flow of movement was reversed as she heard a hollow thump that sent them tumbling back down the stairs and out into the street, the men howling and whooping as they ran, Ace still pulling her along, his eyes glazed.

After that she saw a pink-haired kid in a black leather jacket knocked to the ground and kicked silly, a car set on fire, starbursts of shattering glass. As they looted a *bodega*, someone shouted that he had cornered a mountain lion in the adjacent lot. The mob flowed toward this promising rumor. Ace drew her up near the front of the pack; standing on her toes she saw a feline cowering in the corner between the brick wall and the chain-link fence, emaciated and filthy, its spots just barely visible in the torchlight. "It's an ocelot," she said, not certain how she knew. For a moment all were silent. Then someone hurled a stick, and the men raced after the cat with their clubs, Corrine screaming.

Ace carried her off as someone shouted "Cops!" The two of them broke into a run down Avenue C to Houston, where Corrine flagged a cab, almost unable to believe that this minor article of the social contract had survived intact.

"My God, we were almost killed," she said to the cabbie. She needed a witness, someone from the real world to tell her she was not crazy.

"Where to," he inquired blandly.

Corrine gave the address of her building. Ace put his arm around her, but she could not stop shivering. There was blood on the sleeve of her shirt. She was afraid to be alone after what she'd seen, and afraid that no one else would believe her if she tried to describe it.

Ace followed her up to her apartment and watched TV while she took a shower. When she came out of the bathroom he stood up and put his arms around her. She hugged him briefly but tried to extract herself when he forced his knee between her legs.

"What's the matter?" he said. "You can't deal with a black man?"

Corrine was unable to speak. Fear had made her mute, but she was determined not to show it.

"A black *homeless* man. You come down the Bowery twice a week and serve up some fucking stew doing that charity thing, then get on back to your nice little white girl life?"

"It's not—" she managed to blurt, but he cut her off.

"I'm tired of white motherfuckers telling me color's got nothing to do with the shit. 'Hey, you negroes, we be keeping you down and killing you with dope and locking you up and shit. But it ain't 'cause you a nigger, nigger. Ain't nothing personal.' "

"It's just . . . I miss my husband," Corrine said.

Ace pushed her away. She was almost certain he was going to strike her, but suddenly he looked down at the floor and shook his head. "Just for once I want somethin' nice. You know what I mean?"

He turned and left, slamming the door behind him.

Corrine was astonished to find no mention of the events on the Lower East Side in any of the papers either the next day or the day after, when she noticed, buried in the *Post*, an item about the murder of an alleged crack dealer on East 3rd Street. A mob of disgruntled customers had reportedly poured gasoline in the slot of the reinforced door through which he conducted business, and then matched it, the steel fortress behind the door becoming an oven in which the dealer was incinerated. Three hours later, according to the police, the walls were still glowing red in spots.

She went to the mission a few nights later, but Ace didn't appear. The following night he was standing across the street from her apartment when she returned from work. She started to walk toward him, but something in his expression made her retreat. He did not attempt to follow her inside or speak to her, and she was too frightened to say anything herself. He was still there an hour later. She called Jeff, but by the time he showed up Ace was gone. Several months later someone at the mission claimed he was dead. "It was the AIDS got him," the man said; at any rate she never saw him again.

47

Russell and Corrine talked almost every night, though he was careful not to inquire too closely into her affairs or her feelings. Still angry, he didn't know what he wanted from her or how the damage to their marriage might be repaired, and so he waited for something to happen, as if for a new drug to be invented that would heal this particular disease of the heart, in the meantime treating their marriage as one would treat a patient in critical condition, for whom any strenuous exertion might prove fatal.

He sensed that she was angry, too. Usually they confined their conversation to the concrete details of financial and minor social matters. They had to decide whether to sublet the apartment; Corrine had taken the studio in Chelsea and refused to move back into the old place with its memories. She and her lawyer had finally been reasonably satisfied that Russell had not stashed away heaps of loot, but the legal expenses entailed in proving that he was broke had pushed him even further into debt and added an entirely new constraint to their communication; suddenly there was a structure of official censorship between the damaged channels of their hearts. And Russell, when he stopped to think about it—when he received a lawyer's bill, for instance—was furious at Corrine for having put things on this legal footing.

He was making more money than before, but Corrine's new internship paid a token salary and he still faced litigation with regard to the collapsed Corbin, Dern deal. Bernard Melman had come back with a lower, re-financed offer; he had sold off several divisions in advance and enlisted Harold and some of the old management to run the firm. Donald Parker was an editorial consultant. The upshot of Russell's takeover attempt was that Corbin, Dern had been cut up into pieces, thirty or forty people had lost their jobs, and a man who was already too rich had turned a ridiculous profit. Whitlock had taken a job at Random House, and Trina was said to be specializing in something called turnaround—restructuring deals that had gone sour.

For Russell and Corrine, the apparatus of a joint life remained intact until they were prepared to dismantle it actively; forwarded bills, invitations and postcards from those corners of the world to which news of their domestic strife had not penetrated continued to require their attention. Their joint checking and savings accounts needed to be fed. Almost daily they were confronted with small questions that required consultation and allowed them to avoid the larger ones. They had to decide what to do about the house in St. Barts, on which they had made a deposit for the first week of March.

"I don't think I can get away," said Russell. "Maybe we should just swallow the loss."

"I sent my sister a birthday present from both of us," Corrine said one night in February, a week before Valentine's Day. "A little brooch from the twenties I found in that thrift shop on First Avenue. It was only twenty dollars," she said, as if concerned that he would think her unthrifty. "I signed the card from both of us."

Russell had heard about the brooch two nights before, and though he still was not sure what a brooch was, he said, "How is Hilary?"

"She's fine. She sends her love. How's your dad?"

"He's all right, I guess. I'm a little worried. As far as I can tell he just sits around the house all day. I don't think this retirement deal is his idea of fun."

"You know, we still haven't gotten Colin and Anne a wedding present."

In this way they took pains to assure each other that nothing had really changed, that it was perfectly normal to be conducting a marriage at a distance of three thousand miles.

Like a diligent student, Russell attempted to learn everything he could about the business. Where he might once have believed that this discipline was not worthy of serious study, he now found satisfaction in the very notion of humbling himself. Old habits dying hard, he read screen-plays and books about cinema. He also attended every screening to which he was invited, and haunted the theaters in Westwood, where he could watch new movies in the company of the youthful audiences for whom they were intended.

On the one hand he felt he had no right to his snobbery, and on the other he never let go of it, telling himself that, having failed at a higher calling, he deserved no better. Like so many before him, he had come to Los Angeles to start fresh, to reinvent himself, but he carried his past with him in such a way that he could not help sometimes revealing himself not as the eager immigrant but as a jaded exile.

If occasionally he couldn't help disparaging his environment, he was often embarrassed by the large salary he received despite his relative ignorance. Then there were days when he would drive to a meeting with the top down believing himself lucky to be where he was and even lucky to be alive.

At lunch with a famous young actor, he could feel jadedly superior to the gawking diners—not, he told himself, because he was impressed with himself for lunching with the actor, but because he believed that unlike them he could take it or leave it. It was just business. And it was something to tell Corrine, for a hoot, precisely because she wouldn't be impressed, either, and they could both look down on the culture at large.

Something must have been wrong with his delivery, when he tossed it off that night, because she was silent on the other end of the phone, on the other side of the continent.

"Hello, are you there? Tune in, Rangoon."

"I'm here," she said.

"Is it cold there? I feel a certain chill coming over the wire."

"I just don't feel like hearing about what a wonderful time you're having with all the beautiful and famous people."

When Russell explained that he had dropped the name tongue in cheek, she laughed bitterly.

"It's even worse when you name-drop and then pretend you're not."

Feeling the justice of her charge, he curtly said good night.

The next night she called back and apologized. "Oh, Russell, how did it ever come down to this?"

"I don't know," he said grimly.

"I want us to be together again."

"We will be," he said, not knowing exactly why he said it, except to comfort her. Having both expressed this vague desire, they left the details hanging.

One evening, among the messages the desk clerk had given him, Russell found a note that read: *I'm in room 34. Please call.—Blazes Boylan.* Upstairs in his own room, Russell's eyes moved between the television news and the telephone. He and Zac had a dinner date at The Ivy with a VP of production. He was gathering his things, searching for his keys, when someone knocked.

They stood in the doorway, looking each other over, Russell taken aback at Jeff's appearance, the way his skin seemed to hang on his frame like his clothes. "You want to come in?"

Jeff glanced around the suite, coughing into his hand. "I think I had this room once." He looked up. "The ceiling definitely seems familiar. You going somewhere?"

"Dinner."

Jeff nodded, weighing this information. "I came out here to see you. That's why I'm here. I wanted to talk."

Russell checked his watch. "I've got a few minutes."

"I might need longer than that."

"For someone who's supposed to have kicked his bad habits you don't look very healthy." Jeff was skinnier than ever, his skin as chalky as it had ever been in his downtown days.

"You, on the other hand, look like a fucking surfer."

Russell called the restaurant and left a message for Zac saying that he would not be able to make it. He would think of the excuse later. Death in the family, dog ate the homework.

"You want to get a drink," he asked, before he remembered. "Sorry, force of habit."

"Actually," said Jeff, "I do."

They drove out to the Santa Monica beach, where the sun was just beginning to drop over the steely convexity of the ocean toward Asia, and sat down in the sand twenty yards from the surf. A large, intelligent-looking sea gull circled and landed a few yards away, swaying back and forth on its thin legs like a man standing on the deck of a wave-tossed ship, facing off at an angle away from them as if to convey the idea that it was in the neighborhood on other business but would be happy to accept a dinner invitation.

Jeff winked at the sea gull, then gazed out over the water. Detaching a can of beer from a six-pack, he opened his mouth to speak, faltered and sighed.

"The writer at a loss for words," he mused. "Sometimes I think words are like girlfriends—can't find a good one to save your life when you're actually looking, but when you don't need any they're falling out of the goddamned trees."

Suddenly he appeared self-conscious, as if in alluding to *amour* he had glimpsed the ugly thing between them. He took a deep, raspy breath and said, "Look, my list of regrets is longer than my first book. But I've nearly made a vocation of hating myself. For hurting you most of all. And for compounding it with my ham-handed apology. Misapplication of Step Eight. Or Nine. Whatever. I pretended even to myself I was asking your forgiveness, but what I was actually saying was, Fuck you, Crash, because I was furious with you for sticking me in that place. Among other things. Actually I'm still mad, even though you thought you were saving my life. Maybe I didn't want my life saved. It's my fucking life, right?"

Jeff scooped up a rock and heaved it toward the surf, then lit another cigarette. "And I was angry with you for slowly abandoning me before that, letting friendship slip away while you were taking care of business."

Russell nodded. "I know."

"I was even mad at you for being married to Corrine. I could tell you that what happened with Corrine and me was addictive behavior or something. It's this big relief to say you've been helpless against alcohol and drugs, to have an excuse for all the rotten things you've done." He cupped his hand over the cigarette to protect it from the wind, then took a long, reflective drag.

"Did it ever happen when we were married?"

"Once," Jeff said.

"When?"

"You don't want all the sordid details, do you?"

"Maybe not."

"I've been in love with Corrine since the beginning. I could hardly help that. We've always loved the same things, Crash. I remember at school everyone was always telling me I had to meet you, how you and I were so much alike. Which of course made me hate you. Then later, after you suddenly had Corrine Makepeace living in your room, that almost made me want to hate you all over again."

"I didn't know you were that interested."

"From the beginning it was too late to tell you. God, I was jealous. Especially in New York."

"*You?*"

"No, my fucking doppelgänger. Who do you think?" Laughing mirthlessly through his nose, he scooped up a handful of sand and let it trickle through his fist onto his sneakers. "I sometimes think of everything I've done since college as an inverse image of your life. Parallel lives. You settled down with Corrine, became the editor. So I did the other thing. *All* the other things."

"You're blaming me?" Russell had meant this lightly, but he could hear the accusation in his voice.

"Sometimes I thought that if I'd married Corrine I would have lived your life and you would have done some of the awful shit I ended up doing." He took a deep breath and clenched his fist around a ball of sand. "I think we both convinced ourselves it was a weird way of being closer to you—I know that sounds like the worst kind of rationalization. So okay, it is. It was. But you were in England and we were both lonely. Or Corrine was lonely and I'd always wanted her."

"Where does Caitlin fit into this?"

"Caitlin knew—I think that's why she finally left. Not that I didn't give her some other reasons. In the end, though, Corrine loved you and she stayed, right? And she did the right thing. I couldn't have been what you were for her. It turns out we're not interchangeable at all."

Jeff coughed violently, scattering sand as he raised his hand to his face. When the attack had subsided he wiped his lips with the back of his arm and shook his head violently. Russell wondered if he was supposed to be drinking.

When he regained his voice, Jeff said, "I felt entitled to take anything

I wanted, do anything I wanted. I was a *writer*, right? The rules didn't apply. Anyway, I'd like to go back and do everything differently. But I can't. *We* can't."

Before Jeff had even started this speech Russell discovered he wasn't angry anymore. Unimaginable things happen and we are forced to comprehend them. Before your best friend sleeps with your wife, you would say that it is the unforgivable crime, but only when you're faced with it do you learn what you can live with.

"Are you asking for forgiveness?"

"No, actually I was really hoping you'd keep hating me."

Russell extended his hand and Jeff clasped it. Later he would wish that he had hugged him, for it was his move to make, but it seemed then that there would be time, and at that moment on the beach his sense of holding back was overshadowed by a vast surge of relief, which accompanied the realization of how much trying to hate Jeff had taken out of him.

"What's that shit on your wrist?" Russell said.

"Age spots." Jeff lit another cigarette, cupping his hands over the beleaguered flame of the lighter. "Forgive her, Russell."

"I want to," he said, though he wondered why this seemed more problematic. Sitting there in the cold sand, it made him sad to realize that he understood Jeff far better than he ever would understand Corrine, that the one kind of love was ruled by a different set of laws from those that ruled the other. Because no matter how much you pretended, one kind was exclusive and the other was not. And it made him sad, too, to realize that in spite of this, something was lost between them. "I see us," he said, as if to compensate himself for this insight, "as cranky old men in stained cardigans playing cribbage and silently cursing the pretty nurses."

"No, I see *you* as the old fart on the front porch, in a rocking chair next to Corrine. Despite your little lapse in Frankfurt, you're basically the guy who asks the hooker to paint his house."

"Who does that make you," Russell asked, as Jeff collapsed in a fit of violent coughing. He held one hand over his mouth and propped himself up with the other.

"I'm the guy," he croaked, then cleared his throat, "who can't help believing that getting the hooker to do something else will lead me to an ecstatic merger with the raw stuff of the universe. And who ends up with the clap."

"Aren't you supposed to be healthy now," Russell asked when the coughing jag finally subsided.

"It takes a body a long time to recover from what I did to mine," Jeff said, looking out over the ocean.

"You *are* clean?"

He nodded, poked his cigarette out in the sand.

"You know, I was jealous of you and your nasty, freewheeling life. All the way, right up to the hospital door, part of me wanted to go along for the ride."

"It wasn't that much fun."

The last light was draining into the ocean now.

"At least Washington landed on his feet," Jeff said. "You heard he's back at Corbin, Dern, working for Harold and that corporate pirate of yours?"

"Yeah, he called me. He seems so predictable, and then he always manages to surprise you."

"What really happened with Victor's book," Jeff asked. "Someone told me last week there were thousands of pages of gibberish."

As darkness settled around them, Russell explained how before leaving New York he'd gone to Victor's apartment in the Village, accompanied by a suspicious and proprietorial Corbin, Dern attorney. They spent two days going through Victor's file cabinets, uncovering multiple copies of the pages published in magazines and journals, annotated over and over again in different-colored inks, most of the pages so dense with longhand scrawl as to be entirely illegible. Some of them were nearly black, and fragile as ancient parchment. Apparently Victor had been reworking the same half-dozen chapters for some twenty years. His safety deposit box contained a birth certificate and three thousand in cash. That was it, as Russell had reported back to Corbin, Dern in a stiff, unpleasant meeting with Harold. But Camille Donner, who had previously hinted that the book was a myth, had lately assumed the mantle of grieving widow. In her new version of their life together, she had left his side only temporarily, to attend the Frankfurt Book Fair. Since then, she had hastily rewritten the last chapters of her roman à clef and had opined in an interview that the masterwork, which she had seen with her own eyes, was hidden in a cellar or vault. Conspiracy theorists reported that Corbin, Dern actually had the manuscript and was hyping it with mystery. But the majority concluded that there was nothing there, and that there never had been. Smart New York buzzed with the judgment of fraud, the news humming across the same wires that years before had carried the early rumors of Propp's genius. He became a symbol of false promise and hyped expectations, though Russell chose to consider this a case of noble failure. Failure being something Russell believed he was beginning to understand.

48

Like a man inside a dream who sees himself lying asleep on the bed, Russell felt for a long time that he was waiting to be awakened from the melancholy coma of his days. When, a few weeks after Jeff's visit, the phone rang into the stillness of five in the morning, Sunset Boulevard eerily silent outside the windows of his hotel room, he knew that a summons was at hand.

"Corrine," he said, sitting up in bed, "what's the matter?"

"It's Jeff."

Russell seemed already to know what she was going to tell him, though he'd begun to hope that this particular doom had passed by somehow, dispersed harmlessly into the atmosphere like a storm that breaks up before reaching land.

"What happened?"

"He was in the hospital. Nobody knew. I didn't know until I read in the paper this morning that he'd checked into St. Vincent's. It was pneumonia. I'm at the hospital." Russell waited. On her end Corrine seemed unable to continue, and he was willing to wait indefinitely rather than hear her finish.

"He died fifteen minutes ago."

"You don't die of pneumonia," Russell said, even as he realized that many, many people did die of pneumonia these days, like characters in nineteenth-century novels. Lately it was in all the obituaries.

"I think . . . I think he was very sick. He'd been sick for a while."

"Did he tell you?" Neither of them seemed willing to name the disease. "Did the doctors say anything?"

"He knew he was dying," she said. "I should've known. He looked terrible when I saw him—we had dinner. . . . I should have done something."

"There's nothing you could've done."

"I feel like this is *all* my fault," she sobbed.

"I'll get there as soon as I can."

"Come home," she said.

In the will he'd made out a week before he died, Jeff asked to be cremated. He did not want a funeral. After the various hospitalizations the estate was modest, but royalties and what money he had left were to be divided equally between medical and cultural charities. In his loft, which was neat and scrubbed, a manuscript addressed to Russell lay on the desk beside the word processor. For the second time in less than six months Russell found himself the literary executor of a dead friend.

Though he briefly considered honoring Jeff's prohibition against a memorial service, Russell decided that those who were left behind required some sort of farewell. Corrine strongly disagreed, but in light of recent history she decided not to press her claims on Jeff's memory.

Caitlin sat in the second row, having flown back from London for the memorial, stoic beside her banker fiancé. Walking up the aisle, Corrine was taken aback, like nearly everyone else, at the sight of a beautiful girl with big lemur eyes, wearing what appeared to be a wedding dress, sitting alone with a potted jade plant in her lap. Corrine wondered if she herself could have been that thin, back when she had almost stopped eating, when eating seemed to be the only thing she could control.

Sitting in the front beside Bev and Wick Pierce, Corrine was only intermittently aware of what anyone, including Russell, was saying. He was speaking now, trying to maintain his composure. Russell and the other men—they were all men up there at the altar, as usual—were talking in their imperial masculine way about what Jeff had accomplished in the world, how he had left his words behind. And Russell had solemnly informed her that the new book, written in the last few months, "was Jeff's *Ivan Illyich*." As if that alleviated the sting and made everything okay. "It's sort of about all of us," Russell said, when she asked. She didn't know if she was ready for that.

Listening to all of the fulsome eulogizing, Corrine became more and more annoyed at this secular consolation, this idea that leaving behind a stack of pages or a pile of stones with your name on it redeemed the life that no longer was being lived. Russell had almost left their marriage behind in *his* quest to build some kind of monument. Piling up stones, he had forgotten all about mortar. Concerned with everything except the most important thing, like the man in the joke who lost his arm and mourned his Rolex.

When they talked about what had gone wrong during the past year, Russell and Corrine were always telling two different stories. In his history of their world, the battle for control of a publishing company and the stock market crash of 1987 would feature prominently, stirringly; in hers these were footnotes in tiny print. These public events—like the death of a loved one from a communicable disease, like a financial collapse— revealed like a lightning flash, for a split second, how connected and interdependent each of them was at all times, their well-being intimately bound up with the fate of those around them.

She didn't think she could remotely explain what she was thinking to Russell, and for a moment she almost despised him again. But she loved him in spite of this, and that was the whole point. She once dreamed of a perfect communion between souls, believed she had achieved it with Russell. Now she was willing to fight for something less.

Finally an old poet, bearded and calm, a friend from one of Jeff's other lives, one of the lives Corrine was not familiar with, was reading Nashe's "A Litany in Time of Plague" in a voice both sonorous and nasal.

> Rich men, trust not in wealth,
> Gold cannot buy you health;
> Physic himself must fade,
> All things to end are made.
> The plague full swift goes by. . . .

Russell had read her the poem years before, when he still read poetry aloud to her.

> Beauty is but a flower
> Which wrinkles will devour;

> Brightness falls from the air;
> Queens have died young and fair;
> Dust hath closed Helen's eye.
> I am sick, I must die.
>   Lord, have mercy on us!

She had asked Russell what the line "Brightness falls from the air" actually *meant*. She'd always been more comfortable with math and science, with their relative certainties. Russell had told her a scholar proposed that the word was "hair," and that the *h* had disappeared as the result of an Elizabethan printer's error. But he preferred "air." And when she pressed him he just said, "Think about it." And now, suddenly, she could picture it clearly: brightness and beauty and youth falling like snow out of the sky all around them, gold dust falling to the streets and washing away in the rain outside the church, down the gutters into the sea.

And yet for her own tribute she would have taken a more modest sentiment, from a children's book. "It is not often that someone comes along who is a true friend and a good writer."

And then it was over. The mourners shuffled out into the drizzle outside St. Mark's, posing or refusing to pose for the several photographers, talking about Jeff, about mutual friends and about the details of lives that they were about to resume now that this encounter with death was over, the panhandlers who lived in the churchyard working the well-dressed and ¬piritually tenderized crowd. Russell shook hands with Washington and then they embraced, slapping each other's backs.

"Did we do something wrong," Russell asked.

"Undoubtedly."

"Still, it's hard to believe you're working for Melman."

"Hey, chief, it's simple: he needs a guy like me, and I need a job. It's the perfect basis for a relationship."

Russell smiled ruefully, as if he finally understood a joke that he was the last to get. He nodded when Washington put an arm around his shoulder and suggested they go somewhere for a drink.

Russell spent the first night back in New York in Corrine's studio, the old apartment having been sublet. After that he stayed on, although it was only after a week that they dared talk about the future and acknowledge this new arrangement. He didn't know what he wanted to do, Russell told Zac, but he didn't think he would be returning to Los Angeles; Zac told him to take a month to think about it. Although they couldn't really afford it, Russell and Corrine had decided to take their vacation after all, to give themselves a chance to get to know each other again.

They left New York in a snowstorm, after sliding in a school of filthy yellow fishtailing cabs up the FDR Drive along the East River. Five hours later they were in the tropics. It was a commonplace of life in the age of air travel, but the transition seemed miraculous to them both as they walked off the plane in St. Maarten holding hands. Soon they were riding bumpy thermals above the multicolored, lightly corrugated Caribbean. "There it is," said Corrine, as she always did, when the island came into view.

Looking down at the water, she saw a ghostly shape against the dark green background of a reef, a huge blue lozenge on the sea floor, which appeared to be the hull of a large boat. Several buoys on the surface marked the location of the wreck. She tried to point it out to Russell, on the aisle seat, but by the time he looked out the tiny window they were over the ridge above the airstrip.

There were phones on the island now, and it seemed to them more crowded and noisy than they remembered. The restaurants were prohibitively expensive, though probably no more expensive than before, and after their second night they bought groceries in town so they could economize on meals. Their third night they made love again for the first time in half a year. Both of them were shy and awkward; each experiencing a kind of double vision, as if they were watching themselves making love in a dream, knowing the other's body so intimately and yet finding it new and strange. In the morning they were taken for newlyweds by shopkeepers and waiters.

Later they heard that the wreck Corrine had seen was J. P. Haddad's yacht, lost in a big storm earlier in the winter, now eighty feet down. It had taken eight hours for it to sink. The crew had successfully reached shore, but some claimed that Haddad himself had gone down with the ship. Certainly no one knew his whereabouts. A voluble American told them, one night in a bar, that all the sea cocks had been opened, the intake tubes slashed. "You know," the man confided, "he lost everything in the crash." The blue hull was still out there under the water when they flew back to New York, and sometimes in later years the image would bob up into Corrine's consciousness—when she first heard, more than a year later, about the collapse of Melman's empire, for instance —an enigma somehow associated with that time of their lives, just as men in yellow ties conjured the preceding period.

New York is chilly and curiously quiet when they return. Feeling cramped and restless in the small studio the first night back, they go out to eat at a bistro in SoHo. When they leave the restaurant, a fine snow is falling.

Walking over to West Broadway for a cab they pass a young boy sitting huddled in a shadowed doorway. Russell exerts coaxing pressure on Corrine's arm as she slows; he feels her missionary impulse kicking in, imagines the look of concern crossing her face, which is turned toward the boy.

"Wait," she says, disengaging her arm and walking over to the boy, then crouching down beside him. "Are you okay," she asks him. Russell's instinct is to protect her from the con, but coming closer, he can see what she sees. So young, barely a teenager, the pale face frightened and pathetic.

"I'm cold," the boy whispers.

Corrine takes off her scarf and wraps it around him, then turns to look imploringly at Russell. He reaches into his coat pocket, extracts the three dollars' change from the coat check, hands it to her. She gives it to the boy, then lingers. Russell has to exert gentle pressure on her arm to move her away. In the cab, she wonders aloud how such a young boy would come to be shivering in a doorway and what might be done to help. She is still brooding as they go up the stairs, as they undress for bed. Although he knows he will be able to forget the boy's face and sleep tonight, he understands that Corrine cannot, and he is almost proud of her for it. He looks out the window at the falling snow, then turns and takes his wife in his arms, feeling grateful to be here even as he wonders what he is going to do with his life in strictly practical terms. For years he had trained himself to do one thing, and he did it well, but he doesn't know whether he wants to keep doing it for the rest of his life, or even, for that matter, whether anyone will let him. He is still worrying when they go to bed.

As Corrine drifts off to sleep, she rolls toward him in the bed and mumbles, "Thanks." Russell isn't sure if she means for tonight, or for coming home.

Feeling his wife's head nesting in the pillow below his shoulder, he is almost certain that they will find ways to manage. They've been learning to get by with less, and they'll keep learning. It seems to him as if they're taking a course in loss lately. And as he feels himself falling asleep he has an insight he believes is important, which he hopes he will remember in the morning, although it is one of those thoughts that seldom survive translation to the language of daylight hours: knowing that whatever plenty befalls them together or separately in the future, they will become more and more intimate with loss as the years accumulate, friends dying or slipping away undramatically into the crowded past, memory itself finally flickering and growing treacherous toward the end; knowing that even the children who may be in their future will eventually school them in the pain of growth and separation, as their own parents and mentors die off and leave them alone in the world, shivering at the dark threshold.

STORY OF MY LIFE

FOR GARY

CONTENTS

The age of Cronos was in general characterized as the age of anarchy, the time before the institution of property, the establishment of cities, or the framing of laws. We may fairly infer that it was not gods, but humans, who first became dissatisfied with the blessings of anarchy.

— Philip Velacott, introduction to The Oresteian Trilogy

STORY OF MY LIFE

1

GETTING IN TOUCH WITH
YOUR CHILD

'm like, I don't believe this shit.

I'm totally pissed at my old man who's somewhere in the Virgin Islands, I don't know where. The check wasn't in the mailbox today which means I can't go to school Monday morning. I'm on the monthly payment program because Dad says wanting to be an actress is some flaky whim and I never stick to anything—this from a guy who's been married five times—and this way if I drop out in the middle of the semester he won't get burned for the full tuition. Meanwhile he buys his new bimbo Tanya who's a year younger than me a 450 SL convertible—always gone for the young ones, haven't we, Dad?—plus her own condo so she can have some privacy to do her writing. Like she can even *read*. He actually believes her when she says she's writing a novel but when I want to spend eight hours a day busting ass at Lee Strasberg it's like, *another one of Alison's crazy ideas.* Story of my life. My old man is fifty-two going on twelve. And then there's Skip Pendleton, which is another reason I'm pissed.

So I'm on the phone screaming at my father's secretary when there's a call on my other line. I go hello and this guy goes, hi, I'm whatever-his-name-is, I'm a friend of Skip's and I say yeah? and he says, I thought maybe we could go out sometime.

And I say, what am I, dial-a-date?

Skip Pendleton's this jerk I was in lust with once for about three minutes. He hasn't called me in like three weeks which is fine, okay, I can deal with that, but suddenly I'm like a baseball card he trades with his friends? Give me a break. So I go to this guy, what makes you think I'd want to go out with you, I don't even know you? and he says, Skip told me about you. Right. So I'm like, what did he tell you? and the guy goes—Skip said you were hot. I say, great, I'm totally honored that the great Skip Pendleton thinks I'm hot. I'm just a jalapeño pepper waiting for some strange burrito, honey. I mean, *really.*

And this guy says to me, we were sitting around at Skip's place about five in the morning the other night wired out of our minds and I say—this is the guy talking—I wish we had some women and Skip is like, I could always call Alison, she'd be over like a shot.

He said that? I say. I can hear his voice exactly, it's not like I'm totally amazed, but still I can't believe even *he* would be such a pig and suddenly I feel like a cheap slut and I want

2

to scream at this asshole but instead I say, where are you? He's on West Eighty-ninth, it figures, so I give him an address on Avenue C, a rathole where a friend of mine lived last year until her place was broken into for the seventeenth time and which is about as far away from the Upper West Side as you can get without crossing water, so I tell him to meet me there in an hour and at least I have the satisfaction of thinking of him spending about twenty bucks for a cab and then hanging around the doorway of this tenement and maybe getting beat up by some drug dealers. But the one I'm really pissed at is Skip Pendleton. Nothing my father does surprises me anymore. I'm twenty going on gray.

Skip is thirty-one and he's so smart and so educated—just ask him, he'll tell you. A legend in his own mind. Did I forget to mention he's *so* mature? Unlike me. He was always telling me I don't know anything. I'll tell you one thing I don't know—I don't know what I saw in him. He seemed older and sophisticated and we had great sex, so why not? I met him in a club, naturally. I never thought he was very good-looking, but you could tell *he* thought he was. He believed it so much he could actually sell other people on the idea. He has that confidence everybody wants a piece of. This blond hair that looks like he has it trimmed about three times a day. Nice clothes, shirts custom-made on Jermyn Street, which he might just casually tell you some night in case you didn't know is in London, England. (That's in Europe, which is across the Atlantic Ocean—oh, really Skip, is that where it is? Wow!) Went to the right schools. And he's rich, of course, owns his own company. Commodities trader. Story of Skip's life, trading commodities.

3

So basically, he has it all. Should be a Dewar's Profile, I'm like amazed they haven't asked him yet. But when the sun hit him in the morning he was a shivering wreck.

From the first night, bending over the silver picture frame in his apartment with a rolled fifty up his nose, all he can talk about is his ex, and how if he could only get her back he'd give up all of this forever—coke, staying out partying all night, young bimbos like me. And I'm thinking, poor guy just lost his main squeeze, feeling real sympathetic and so like I go, when did this happen, Skip? and it turns out it was ten years ago! He lived with this chick for four years at Harvard and then after they come to New York together she dumps him. And I'm like, give me a break, Skip. Give yourself a break. This is ten years after. This is nineteen eighty-what-ever.

Skip's so smart, right? My parents never gave a shit whether I went to school or not, they were off chasing lovers and bottles, leaving us kids with the cars and the credit cards, and I never did get much of an education. Is that my fault? I mean, if someone told you back then that you could either go to school or not, what do you think you would have done? Pass the trigonometry, please. Right. So I'm not as educated as the great Skip Pendleton, but let me tell you—I know that when you're hitting on someone you don't spend the whole night whining about your ex, especially after like a decade. And you don't need a Ph.D. in psychology to figure out why Skip can't go out with anybody his own age. He keeps trying to find Diana, the beautiful, perfect Diana who was twenty-one when she said sayonara. And he wants us, the young stuff, because we're like Diana was in the good old days. And he hates us because we're not Diana. And he thinks it will make him feel better if he fucks us over and makes us hurt the way he was hurt, because that's what it's all about if you ask me—we're all sitting around here on earth working through our hurts, trying to pass them along to other people and make things even. Chain of pain.

Old Skip kept telling me how dumb I was. You wish, Jack. Funny thing is, dumb is his type. He doesn't want to go out with anybody who might see through him, so he picks up girls like me. Girls he thinks will believe everything he says and fuck him the first night and not be real surprised when he never calls again.

If you're so smart, Skip, how come you don't know these things? If you're so mature, what were you doing with me?

Men. I've never met any. They're all boys. I wish I didn't want them so much. I've had a few dreams about making it with girls, but it's kind of like—sure, I'd love to visit Norway sometime. My roommate Jeannie and I sleep in the same bed and it's great. We've got a one-bedroom and this way the living room is free for partying and whatever. I hate being alone, but when I wake up in some guy's bed with dry come on the sheets and he's snoring like a garbage truck, I go—let me out of here. I slip out and crawl around the floor groping for my clothes, trying to untangle his blue jeans from mine, my bra from his Jockeys—Skip wears boxers, of course—without making any noise, out the door and home to where Jeannie has been warming the bed all night. Jumping in between the sheets and she wakes up and goes, I want details, Alison—length and width.

I love Jeannie. She cracks me up. She's an assistant editor at a fashion magazine but what she really wants to do is get married. It might work for her but I don't believe in it. My parents have seven marriages between them and any time I've been with a guy for more than a few weeks I find myself looking out the window during sex.

I call up my friend Didi to see if she can lend me the money. Didi's father's rich and he gives her this huge allowance, but she spends it all on blow. She used to buy clothes but now she wears the same outfit for four or five days in a row and it's pretty gross, let me tell you. Sometimes we have to send the health department over to her apartment to open the windows and burn the sheets.

I get Didi's machine, which means she's not home. If she's home she unplugs the phone and if she's not home she turns on the answering machine. Either way it's pretty impossible to get hold of her. She sleeps from about noon till like 9:00 P.M. or so. If Didi made a list of her favorite things I guess cocaine would be at the top and sunlight wouldn't even make the cut.

My friends and I spend half our lives leaving messages for each other. Luckily I know Didi's message access code so I dial again and listen to her messages to see if I can figure out from the messages where she is. Okay, maybe I'm just nosy.

The first message is from Wick and from his voice I can tell that he's doing Didi, which really blows me away, since Wick is Jeannie's old boyfriend. Except that Didi is less interested in sex than anybody I know so I'm not really sure. Maybe Wick is just starting to make his move. A message from her mom—call me, sweetie, I'm in Aspen. Then Emile, saying he wants his three hundred and fifty dollars or else. Which is when I go—what am I, crazy? I'm never going to get a cent out of Didi. If I even try she'll talk me into getting wired with her and I'm trying to stay away from that. I'm about to hang up when I get a call on the other line. It's my school telling me that my tuition hasn't arrived and that I can't come back to class until it does. Like, what do you think I've been frantic about for the last twenty-four hours? It's Saturday afternoon. Jeannie will be home soon and then it's all over.

By this time I'm getting pretty bitter. You could say I am not a happy unit. Acting is the first thing I've ever really wanted to do. Except for riding. When I was a kid I spent most of my time on horseback. I went around the country, showing my horses and jumping, until Dangerous Dan dropped dead. I loved Dan more than just about any living thing since and that was it for me and horses. That's what happens, basically, when you love something. It's like, you can't get rid of the shit you don't like, I have this rotten crinoline dress that's been following me from apartment to apartment for years, but every time I find something I really love one of my sisters or girlfriends disappears with it the next day. Actually, we all trade clothes, hardly anybody I know would think of leaving the house without wearing something borrowed or stolen, if it was just clothes I'd be like, no problem, but that's another story.

So anyway, after horses I got into drugs. But acting, I don't know, I just love it, getting up there and turning myself inside out. Being somebody else for a change. It's like being a child again, playing at something, making believe, laughing and crying all over the place, ever since I can remember

7

people have been trying to get me to stifle my emotions but forget it—I'm an emotional kind of girl. My drama teacher has this great thing he always says—get in touch with your child, which is supposed to be the raw, uncensored part of yourself. Acting is about being true to your feelings, which is great since real life seems to be about being a liar and a hypocrite.

Acting is the first thing that's made me get up in the morning. The first year I was in New York I didn't do anything but guys and blow. Staying out all night at the Surf Club and Zulu, waking up at five in the afternoon with plugged sinuses and sticky hair. Some kind of white stuff in every opening. Story of my life. My friends are still pretty much that way which is why I'm so desperate to get this check because if I don't then there's no reason to wake up early Monday morning and Jeannie will get home and somebody will call up and the next thing I know it'll be three days from now with no sleep in between, brain in orbit, nose in traction. I call my father's secretary again and she says she's still trying to reach him.

I decide to do some of my homework before Jeannie gets home—my sense-memory exercise. Don't ask me why, since I won't be able to go to school. But it chills me out. I sit down in the folding chair and relax, empty my mind of all the crap. Then I begin to imagine an orange. I try to see it in front of me. I take it in my hand. A big old round one veined with rust, like the ones you get down in Florida straight from the tree. (Those Clearasil spotless ones you buy in the Safeway are dusted with cyanide or some such shit so you can imagine how good they are for you.) So I start to peel it real slow, smelling the little geysers of spray that break

8

from the squeezed peel, feeling the juice stinging around the edges of my fingernails where I've bitten them. . . .

So of course the phone rings. A guy's voice, Barry something, says, may I please speak to Alison Poole?

And I'm like, you're doing it.

I'm a friend of Skip's, he says.

I go, if this is some kind of joke I'm like really not amused.

Hey, no joke, he goes. I'm just, you know, Skip told me you guys weren't going out anymore and I saw you once at Indochine and I thought maybe we could do dinner sometime.

I'm like, I don't believe this. What am I?—the York Avenue Escort Service?

I go, did Skip also tell you about the disease he gave me? That shrinks this Barry's equipment pretty quick. Suddenly he's got a call on his other line. Sure you do.

It's true—that was Skip's little going-away present. Morning after the last night I slept with him I was really sore and itchy and then I get this weird rash so I finally go to the doctor who gives me this big lecture on AIDS—yada yada yada—then says the rash is a sexually transmitted thing that won't kill me but I have to take these antibiotics for two weeks and not sleep with anybody in the meantime. I go, two weeks, who do you think I am, the Virgin Mary? and she goes, as your doctor I think I know your habits well enough to know what a sacrifice this will be for you, Alison. Then she gives me the usual about why don't I make them wear condoms and I'm like, for the same reason I don't fuck with my clothes on, you can't beat flesh on flesh. I want contact, right? Just give me direct contact and you can keep true love.

9

Anyway I never did tell Skip, I don't know why, I guess I just didn't want to talk to him, the son of a bitch.

So I'm smoking a cigarette, thumbing through my *Actors' Scenebook,* sort of looking for a monologue, I've got to get one for next week but I haven't found anything I like, I start browsing around the other sections, Monologues for Men, Scenes for Two Women—no thanks—Scenes for One Man and One Woman. Which is about the worst scene there is.

The phone rings again and it's Didi. Unbelievable! Live—in person, practically. And it's daylight outside.

I just went to my nose doctor, she goes. He was horrified. Told me that if I had to keep doing blow I should start shooting up, then the damage would be some other doctor's responsibility.

What's with you and Wick? I say.

I don't know, she goes, I went home with him a couple of weeks ago. I woke up in his bed. I'm not even sure we did anything. But he's definitely in lust with me. Meanwhile, my period's late. So maybe we did.

Didi has another call. While she takes it, I'm thinking. The wheels are turning—wheels within wheels. Didi comes back on and tells me it's her mom, who's having a major breakdown, she'll call me back. I tell her no problem. She's already been a big help.

I get Skip at his office. He doesn't sound too thrilled to hear from me. He says he's in a meeting, can he call me back?

I say no, I have to talk now.

What's up? he says.

10

I go, I'm pregnant.

Total silence.

Before he can ask I tell him I haven't slept with anybody else in six weeks. Which is totally true, almost. Close off that little escape hatch in his mind. Wham, bam, thank you ma'am.

He goes, you're sure? He sounds like he's just swallowed a bunch of sand.

I'm sure, I say.

He's like, what do you want to do?

The thing about Skip is that even though he's an asshole, he's also a gentleman. Actually a lot of the assholes I know are gentlemen. Or vice versa. Dickheads with a family crest and a prep-school code of honor.

When I say I need money he asks how much.

A thousand, I say. I can't believe I ask him for that much, I was thinking five hundred just a minute ago, but hearing his voice pisses me off.

He asks if I want him to go with me and I say no, definitely not. Then he tries to do this number about making out the check directly to the clinic and I say, Skip, don't give me that shit. I need five hundred in cash to make the appointment, I tell him, and I don't want to wait six business days for the stupid check to clear, okay? Acting my ass off. My teacher would be proud.

Two hours later a messenger arrives with the money. Cash. I give him a ten-dollar tip.

Saturday night Jeannie and Didi go out. Didi comes over, wearing this same horrible surfer shirt she's had on all week

11

and her blond rastafarian hair. Really gross. But she's still incredibly beautiful, even after four days without sleep, and guys make total asses of themselves trying to pick her up. Her mother was this really big model in the fifties, Swedish. Didi was supposed to be the Revlon Girl or something but she couldn't be bothered to wake up for the shoot.

Jeannie's wearing my black cashmere sweater, a couple yards of pearls, jeans and Maude Frizon pumps.

How do I look? she goes, checking herself out in the mirror.

Terrific, I say. You'll be lucky if you make it through cocktails without getting raped.

Can't rape the willing, Jeannie says, which is what we always say.

They try to get me to come along, but I'm doing my scene for class Monday morning. They can't believe it. They say it won't last. I go, this is my life. I'm like trying to do something constructive with it, you know? Jeannie and Didi think this is hilarious. They do this choirgirl thing where they both fold their hands like they're praying and hum "Amazing Grace," which is what we do when somebody starts to get religious on us. Then, just to be complete assholes, they sing, *Alison, we know this world is killing you . . .* et cetera, which is kind of like my theme song when I'm being a drag.

So I go:

> *They say you're nothing but party girls*
> *Just like a million more all over the world*

They crack up. We all love Costello.
After they finally leave, I open up my script but I'm

12

having trouble concentrating, it's this play called *Mourning Becomes Electra,* so I call up my little sister at home. Of course the line is busy and they don't have call waiting so I call the operator and request an emergency breakthrough on the line. I listen while the operator cuts in. I hear Carol's voice and then the operator says there's an emergency call from Vanna White in New York. Carol immediately says Alison, in this moaning, grown-up voice even though she's three years younger than me.

What's new? I go when she gets rid of the other call.

Same old stuff, she says. Mom's drunk. My car's in the shop. Mickey's out on bail. He's drunk, too.

Listen, do you know where Dad is? I go and she says, Virgin Islands last she heard, maybe St. Croix but she doesn't have a number either. So I tell her about my school thing and then maybe because I'm feeling a little weird about it I tell her about Skip, except I say five hundred dollars instead of a thousand, and she says it sounds like he totally deserved it. He's such a prick, I go, and Carol says, yeah, he sounds just like Dad.

And I go, yeah, just like.

Jeannie comes back Sunday morning at 9:00 A.M. She's a shivering wreck. For a change I'm just waking up instead of just going to sleep. I give Jeannie a Valium and put her to bed. It's sort of a righteous feeling, being on this end of the whole experience—I feel like a doctor or something.

She lies in bed stiff as a mannequin and says, I'm so afraid, Alison. She is not a happy unit.

We're all afraid, I go.

In half an hour she's making these horrible chainsaw sleep noises.

Thanks to Skip, Monday morning I'm at school doing dance and voice. Paid my bill in cash. Now I'm feeling great. Really good. In the afternoon I've got acting class. We start with sense-memory work. I sit down in class and my teacher tells me I'm at a beach. He wants me to see the sand and the water and feel the sun on my bare skin. Hear the volleyballs whizzing past. No problem. First I have to clear myself out. That's part of the process. All around me people are making strange noises, stretching, getting their yayas out, preparing for their own exercises. Some people I swear, even though this is supposed to be totally spontaneous, you can always tell some of these people are acting for the teacher even in warm-up, laughing or crying so dramatically, like, *look at me, I'm so spontaneous.* There's a lot of phonies in this profession. Anyway, I don't know—I'm just letting myself go limp in the head, then I'm laughing hysterically and next thing I'm bawling like a baby, really out of control, falling out of my chair and thrashing all over the floor . . . a real basket case . . . epileptic apocalypse, sobbing and flailing around, trying to take a bite out of the linoleum . . . they're used to some pretty radical emoting in here, but this is way over the top, apparently. I kind of lose it, and the nurse says I'm overtired and tells me to go home and rest. . . .

That night my old man finally calls. I'm like, I must be dreaming.

Pissed at you, I go, when he asks how I am.

I'm sorry, honey, he says, about the tuition. I screwed up.

You're goddamn right you did, I say.

Oh, baby, he goes, I'm a mess.

You're telling me, I go.

He says, she left me.

Don't come crying to me about what's-her-name, I say. Then he starts to whine and I go, when are you going to grow up, for Christ's sake?

I bitch him out for a while and then I tell him I'm sorry, it's okay, he's well rid of her, there's lots of women who would love a sweet man like him. Not to mention his money. Story of his life. But I don't say that of course. He's fifty-two years old and it's a little late to teach him the facts of life. From what I've seen nobody changes much after a certain age. Like about four years old, maybe. Anyway, I hold his hand and cool him out and almost forget to hit him up for money.

He promises to send me the tuition and the rent and something extra. I'm not holding my breath.

I should hate my father, sometimes I think I do. There was a girl in the news the last few weeks, she hired her boyfriend to shoot her old man. Families, Jesus. At least with lovers you can break up. These old novels and plays that always start out with orphans, in the end they find their parents—I want to say, don't look for them, you're better off without. Believe me. Get a dog instead. That's one of my big ambitions in life—to be an orphan. With a trust fund, of course. And a harem of men to come and go as I command, guys as beautiful and faceless as the men who lay you down in your dreams.

2

SCENES FOR ONE MAN AND
ONE WOMAN

Watch out! Rebecca's coming to town, and I'm definitely not talking about the one from Sunnybrook Farm. This is my maniac sister. She's flying in from Palm Beach with her latest squeeze, staying at the Stanhope. If I was the management at that establishment I'd hide all the valuables, tie everything else down and stretch a tarp over it. Last time she was in New York they actually threw her out of the Sherry Netherland, and Rod Stewart and his band used to practically live at that dump. Like, I'm sure those guys behaved themselves, right?—TVs out the windows, groupies out the wazoo. . . . So you can imagine what my sister can do to a room. Becca uses things up quickly—cars, credit cards, men, drugs, horses, you name it. The men and the credit cards are sort of mixed up together—after she's totally burned out some guy she usually asks if she can have a credit card which he'll wait for five days and then report stolen. I don't know, she must give great head is all I can say because these guys always say yes, even when she's done something really horrible like sleep with their best friend. The best way I can think of to describe Rebecca is to say she's like the Tasmanian Devil, that character in the Bugs Bunny cartoons that moves around inside a tornado and demolishes everything in his path. Or else she's like an entire heavy metal band on tour—all wrapped up in this cute little hundred-and-ten-pound package.

What really worries me is the combination of Becca and Didi. When those two get together it's like—what were the two things you were never supposed to mix in chemistry class or you'd like blow up the whole school? You know what I mean. Not oil and water—something else. So much for my education. Blanks that never got filled in. None of the above. Story of my life. Anyway, I know several drug dealers who are going to open bottles of Cristal and buy new Ferraris when they hear that Becca's back in town—I'm talking about guys who bought their *first* Ferraris out of profits from Didi's trust fund—but for the rest of us it's basically like hearing that a hurricane's cruising across the Gulf toward your brand-new uninsured beach house. Just when I was getting my acting together.

But the main thing is I've met a guy and I'm totally in lust, so who cares about Rebecca? What's really amazing is that his mind is what I was attracted to first, and I wasn't even thinking about the other thing.

I'm at Nell's, as usual, hanging out. Me, Didi, Jeannie, Rebecca and my friend Francesca, who I haven't mentioned yet—she's practically my best friend, we used to show horses together, no one else could stand her because she was Super-JAP, her Dad's a big movie producer and her mother is some sort of Rockefeller, so she had a stableful of the best hunters and jumpers in the country, she was always throwing tantrums and screaming at the judges and the other girls but we got along great from the word go, and now she supposedly works for William Morris although I've never been able to reach her there. She has one of those incredible jobs that you just hate the people who luck into them, the kind of job I'd have to have if I was ever going to become a member of the work force. So she works for William Morris, but when I say *works* I'm being a major philanthropist. I mean, she gets this job as an assistant to a high-powered agent and the next week her boss gets diagnosed with AIDS and of course everyone is totally sympathetic and enlightened—I mean, come on— so of course the agency keeps him on even though he's in the hospital half of the time and three-quarters of his clients bail out for ICM and CAA and Triad, so all Francesca has to do is show up once in a while and answer letters of condolence. But meantime she's got this sort of credibility and access from being with William Morris, not to mention being her father's daughter.

So Francesca, she knows everyone, right? Partly because of her family and also because that's her great passion in life, meeting rich and famous people. A lot of people think she's a snob or a starfucker because all she can talk about is lunch with Jack Nicholson and drinks with Sting, but she's so up front about it you can't hold it against her, really. She's totally wide-eyed, which is pretty amazing given her background: all these famous people always coming over to the house for dinner, you'd think she'd get jaded, but she'll walk across the room to meet a guy who had a walk-on in "The Young and the Restless," congratulate him on his career. Granted, it's a little bit *too* much sometimes—like, Francesca, I'd like you to meet Adolf Hitler, and she'd be like—oh, wow, I just loved your last war. Her ambition in life is to get invited to Mick and Jerry's house for dinner. She keeps cultivating people who know them and saying nice things in public about Mick's music and Jerry's legs and even *I* want to puke sometimes when I'm around her. But basically she's totally cool and would do anything for me or any of her friends.

So we're sitting on one of those supposedly antique couches at Nell's and I have to go to the bathroom—no, honestly. It's wall-to-wall people so while I'm waiting for this path to clear this guy says to me, didn't I see you on stage in Williamstown last summer?

And I'm like, sure.

He goes, in *The Seagull,* right? Wasn't that you?

And I go, I wish.

He looks real young—I mean he looks my age, boyish. Blondish hair that needs a trim, white sneakers, blue jeans, white shirt, this old ratty blazer that fits him like a bathrobe. Eyes like the Caribbean, warm and blue green.

So I go, if you want to meet me, just say so.

And he says, you are an actress, aren't you?

And I say, how can you tell?

I don't know, he says, the way you carry yourself.

It's called a Maidenform underwire, I go, because that's where he's looking.

God bless the manufacturer, he says. I'll buy some of their stock tomorrow.

I like the way he raises his eyebrows and the corners of his lips when he says this.

So I look down at his crotch and say, you'd be better off buying stock in Levi Strauss. Looks like it's going up.

I kind of hope they might come down, actually, he says.

And I go, suit yourself, there's no law against self-abuse.

He doesn't have a snappy comeback for that one. Most guys can't really go the distance. But still, he's cute.

So really, I say, how'd you know I'm an actress? I'm thinking, maybe my training is starting to show, I know my voice is a lot less nasal than it used to be, at least some of the time, my voice teacher says I've got to work my voice down into my chest—it'll have a lot more room down there, he goes, he's sort of a dirty old man, but cool. Plus I'm working on my posture. My mom used to actually try to get us to walk around the house balancing a book on the top of our heads, that's so typical of her, we'd be like, right, sure Mom, pass the Doritos and turn up the volume on your way out—that's probably the only thing anybody in my house ever thought of doing with a book so naturally I'm impressed by guys who actually read some. But I kind of wish I'd listened to my mom about posture, I'm like the hunchback of Seventy-eighth Street and now I have to improve my posture for my acting career. Anyway, I'm asking him how he knew I was an actress.

I guess I'm just incredibly perceptive, he says.

I go, am I supposed to believe that?

Also I overheard you talking to your friends, he says.

You've been eavesdropping, I say. Actually, I'm kind of

flattered. Usually when I'm out with Didi it's hard to get any attention. Plus I like the fact that he's honest enough to admit the real story—if there's one thing I hate it's the usual bull-shit.

He tells me his name is Dean Chasen and I tell him mine is Alison Poole. I mean, that's a sign right there—if I have any doubts about a guy I just give him a bogus name.

Dean's waiting for me when I come out of the bath-room, so I let him buy me a drink. Francesca and Didi are waving and pointing from the other end of the room but I ignore them, I'm into what Dean is saying, it turns out he knows everything about theater, even though he's a Wall Streeter, sells bonds or something. We start talking about all the plays around town and he asks me about my classes and then we have this debate about method versus other kinds of training, when he first came to New York he studied at the Neighborhood Playhouse for a while under Meisner. He's thirty-two, it turns out, but he seems a lot younger. He says he wants to retire at the age of thirty-five and write plays, maybe novels.

It's a funny thing but I've noticed when I'm with cre-ative guys like artists and actors, they hardly ever talk about their work, they're always talking about the stock market or something like they're trying to convince you they under-stand the real world, then you get with stockbrokers and bankers and all they want to talk about is art and the thea-ter and they practically apologize for making a lot of money.

Usually when I meet a guy it takes me about three seconds to wonder how big his dick is. Didi and Jeannie swear by the hand method—you know: big hands, big dick—

but I was so into just talking to Dean and listening to him that it was like hours before it even occurred to me to notice he had these long, delicate hands, and after the first night I slept with him I called Didi up right away and said thin fingers don't always mean what you think.

We just start talking like we've known each other all our lives. Dean notices a lot of stuff, he has this really interesting way of looking at the world—for instance, they have this real good DJ at Nell's and he was spinning some weird oldies in with the new stuff and suddenly Dean says, you know, 'Lightning Striking Again' is the only song that actually *features* the backup vocals.

So I say, I like the line, *I can't stop now, I can't stop,* that could be my theme.

Anyway, Dean just notices these funny little things. I like that. In some ways he's like a five-year-old boy practically. When I told him he was like a little kid he says, Alison, we're a nation of children. I love the way he comes up with stuff like that. I mean, I was just talking about him but he turns it into something about the world.

The next thing I know we're at his apartment, still talking. It's like we're a dialogue machine or something. I tell him about my old boyfriends and that I've slept with thirty-six guys and I go, how about you?

He goes, none, totally deadpan.

And I go, don't give me that.

And he goes, honest, no guys. Cracked me up.

He tells me about Patty, this girl he just broke up with after two years. He still loves her, he says, but basically he doesn't like her, she wants to get married and move to the suburbs and he's not ready for that. So they broke up about a month ago. I tell him he doesn't seem like the suburban type and he says, really.

Sometimes I feel like I'm stuck between being my father and being some kind of animal, he goes. What I do for a living—don't get me wrong, I like it and it's challenging as hell, but it's so conventional I feel like I have stay up all night and beat myself up just so I know I'm still alive. He says, in a few years I'm going to quit and just do what I want to do.

So fine, I say, who's stopping you?

I'm afraid I'll stop myself, he goes. I'm afraid I'll get fat and complacent in the meantime.

I'll call you in three years and remind you, I say.

If the markets hold up, he says, I'll have a million and then some by then. This starving artist thing, I don't think it's entirely necessary, you know? If I can put some money away I think I'll be able to really concentrate on writing a lot better than if I'm working as a messenger, he says.

Absolutely, I go, but I'm thinking, I don't know, how many great writers worked on Wall Street for half their lives then suddenly started cranking out the old masterpieces? I mean, I like this guy a lot, but my brain is still functioning, okay?

So then we talk all about drama and he keeps jumping up to pull books off the shelves and read me bits, he's got like about eight walls of books, his living room looks like the public library or something.

Finally when the birds start squawking outside he says, you want to stay over? and I'm, like, sure, why not? Here we are having this great conversation, but I'm also thinking, here's this guy I really like and respect, maybe I shouldn't fuck him. You know, it's been so long since I've met a guy who isn't a total asshole that I forget what the rules are. Then I remember about Skip's little present. The doctor told me two weeks and it's only been about a week since I started taking the pills and I still feel a little itchy. And it's weird but all of sudden now that I can't fuck him I really want to, and for a minute I consider taking my chances. But that would be a really shitty thing to do, so I explain the situation and he's really sweet about it. We'll just have to wait, he says.

Easier said than done. First we're just kissing, and then he touches my breast, and that's the road to trouble. My left nipple in particular. If you want to get Alison all hot and bothered that's the button to press. After an hour of touching and kissing and rubbing I'm going out of my mind. Dean brings me off with his hand but it's just not the same, I want more, I don't want to stop.

Poor Dean is like, dying of a monster hard-on. After a couple of hours it feels like something carved out of stone and heated over the fire. I'm wondering if maybe I should help him out a little but I think oral sex on the first date is pretty rude, like I'm almost always turned off when some guy I hardly know goes down on me. Under the circumstances I should do something for Dean but the thing is, I really want him inside me.

Please, I go. Please. He's on top of me, kissing and dry humping.

Alison, he moans. Don't.

I can't stand it, I go.

I can't either.

Goddamn Skip Pendleton, I go.

Skip Pendleton? he says, lifting his head from my shoulder.

You know him? I say.

He's like, he's a friend of mine.

Small world, I say.

Dean goes, he was the one who gave you this . . . disease?

I think so.

You *think* so?

I can tell Dean's a little bummed out about this. He kind of rolls away, and even though he tells me it's fine, he didn't know me then, I can tell he has that whole male competitive thing. Men don't want women unless they've been wanted by other men, they're not interested if you're not desirable to their friends. But then they expect you to have resisted all the interest until they came along. I guess it's because he knows Skip. The idea of the other thirty-five didn't seem to bother him too much.

Suddenly, out of the blue, he says, don't you ever worry about, you know, AIDS?

I say, sure, I worry, but I think it's been blown out of proportion. I try to be careful who I sleep with.

Like Skip? he says. That fucking guy is a walking petri dish.

I'm like, I thought you said he was your friend.

The next day, actually the same day, I wake up at one in the afternoon. I try to remember if I have class, what day is it. Dean isn't in bed. I smell coffee but I don't hear anything. I figure maybe he's gone to work, but then I hear him moving around out in the next room. There's a phone next to the bed so I dial Francesca.

Tell me everything, she goes. I want details. Length, width, position and duration.

I go, you got your computer booted?

Francesca enters all of her conquests on her computer with detailed notes about their performance plus she has separate files for the sex adventures of her friends.

I explain the problem to her. She's already heard about my social disease, must be everybody's favorite subject this week.

Well, she says, at least you gave him a blow job, I hope.

I go, actually I didn't.

Alison! What's the matter with you? Don't you like him? It's the least you can do after getting the poor guy all hot and then telling him you caught some slimy social disease from his best friend. You're really slipping.

After that I call my apartment to talk to Jeannie. My sister Rebecca answers the phone. She sounds crazed, which is a big surprise.

What are you doing there? I go and she goes, after we left Nell's we went over to Emile's house and bought a quarter and we're just trying to finish it up.

I'm like, it's two in the afternoon, for Christ's sake. Most normal people have already been to sleep at least once already.

Did you get laid? Rebecca wants to know.

Then Didi comes on the line. She screams, you better have since you ditched your best friends. Then in a pretty normal voice, if anybody who's been up all night drinking, smoking and doing coke can have a normal voice, she says, come over and help us finish this quarter ounce.

Where's Jeannie? I go, and Didi says, Jeannie passed

out in the bedroom around five and went in to work at nine.

I'm worried about Jeannie because she's the only one of us who actually has a job and at this rate she won't have it long. It's hard to concentrate when you hang around with us.

After trying unsuccessfully to find my old man, who still hasn't come through with a check, the son of a bitch, I get up and go into the other room, but first I look around for something to wear, being the incredibly modest girl that I am. In his closet he's got about twenty shirts and I pick out a blue Oxford from Brooks Brothers. I approve. When I was thirteen I started wearing my father's Brooks Brothers and now my standard outfit is one of those big old fat business-men's shirts—sixteen and a half thirty-four, untucked of course—leggings, white socks and sneakers or loafers.

The door to the bathroom is open and the water's running. I kind of peek in. I'm a little worried about what kind of mood he'll be in. Dean's shaving, so cute in his plaid boxer shorts, and he's using one of those old-fashioned safety razors, the kind I remember Pops using—that's my grandfather. He has one of those shaving brushes all lathered up beside the sink and it's weird, I have this kind of déjà vu of being a really tiny girl and waking up real early one morning in Gran and Pop's house in Palm Beach and following the sound of running water to Pop's bathroom where he was shaving just like this. He let me watch and I was so impressed, like I was witnessing some religious ceremony. This was like, prehistoric times, before Mom and Dad got divorced.

28

Good morning, I go, and Dean looks over, says good morning. He's smiling even though you can tell he doesn't want to. He tries to swallow the smile, remember that he's mad at me.

So how are you this morning, I go, and he says fine.

Did you blow off work, I ask, and he says he called in and said he was taking the day off, he had one coming. He says it like he wants me to think he was planning all along to take the day off, as if it had nothing to do with me or staying up all night.

And I go, I didn't know people still used those kind of razors.

And he says, I guess I'm an old-fashioned guy.

And I go, that's cool, I like that.

And he goes, oh yeah? I'm surprised.

Why are you so surprised, I say.

And he says, I think of you as a postmodern girl.

I don't know if this is a compliment or what, it doesn't really sound like it, but just to clear the air I go, sorry about last night.

And he says, what's to be sorry for?

And I say, you're probably a little horny.

I'll live, he goes.

Jesus, men can be so silly when they think they're being macho and tough. Sometimes I think there must be some kind of secret ritual like circumcision where all boys have three-quarters of their brain removed at adolescence, or else they just have to promise that they'll act and talk like they've been lobotomized, grunt in monosyllables like cavemen, and limit their emotions to the range between A and B. Still, they're the only other sex we've got. And they can make you

29

feel so good sometimes you want to scream like the house-wife who's just won the big prize on "Wheel of Fortune" and generally forgive them for being men.

So Dean finishes shaving, wipes himself off and walks out into the kitchen, ignoring me. I follow him in. Cute butt. He sits down at the table and picks up the *Times*.

I'm thinking about firing up the first cigarette of the day but then I get another idea.

Poor baby didn't get no satisfaction, I say, coming up behind him and rubbing the back of his neck. I start singing, I can't get no . . . I can't get no . . .

He resists for a while, keeping the muscles tense as I work my way down, pretending he's reading, but gradually he starts to slump in his chair and when I kneel down in front of him and start to massage the inside of his legs he lets out this big moan. He reaches out to stroke my hair, leans his head back, closes his eyes, his breath catching in his throat when I reach for the little opening in his boxers.

He gasps when I take him inside my mouth, and that's just the beginning. I mean, I haven't met too many guys who say *no thanks, honey, I'd rather watch the game* when you suggest a blow job. But still, I never heard anything like the chorus of weird satisfied sounds coming from Dean while I'm going down on him. It makes me feel really good, like a nurse or maybe an angel, doing my good deed for the day. I mean, this boy is appreciative and that really inspires me.

What can I say? I'm an actress.

Let me just say that in general my feeling about blow jobs is, I can take them or leave them. In fact, mainly I could

30

leave them. Guys, of course, won't let you and I suppose you can't blame them. I mean, if it's anything like having a guy you really like go down on you, particularly if he's shaved recently, then who can hold it against them, really? God knows I'd rather lose my left arm than go without that for the rest of my life. So, like, I usually figure its kind of a trade-off. You know, the I'll-lick-yours-if-you'll-lick-mine kind of thing. Except one thing that really grosses me out—somebody ought to write a book about modern etiquette that covers this sort of thing—one thing I hate, right? is some guy going down on me the first date. I think that's incredibly presumptuous and rude. Fucking is one thing. But sticking your face in someone's crotch—I mean, that's really intimate. And I get really uncomfortable and weirded out when it's some guy whose name I never did catch over the music on the dance floor. I think you should put some talking and kissing mileage on your lips before you put them on my, uh, lips. Okay, guys? Just in case anybody out there wants to know.

And another thing I don't like, as long as we're on the subject, is when some guy is going down on you, and you're like—wow, even if there isn't a God it's okay, I can deal with it no problem, like, I could give a shit—and you're floating in some kind of warm liquid trance when you suddenly feel the old pivot. You know what I mean, the old swivel where he's still got his tongue in your southern cleavage but it's rotating, swinging the hips northward and suddenly there's this dick banging against your teeth. I don't know, I suppose trading favors is what it's all about. I mean sometimes I think we're all just masturbating each other any way you look at it. If we're not jerking each other around, we're jerking each other off. But still, do we have to be so blatant about it? I mean, *really*.

Actually, my last real boyfriend, Alex—the only real boyfriend I ever had in my life, we went out for five years—he was blatant about it. He'd make deals. Like, for instance, I'd be looking through the new Saks catalogue that just arrived in the mail and I'd point to a sweater or something and say, I love that, and he'd go, I'll get it for you and I'd go, really? and he'd be like raising his eyebrows and winking. And I'd be like, oh, yeah, I get it.

So I'd get tough and make him fill out the order form with his credit card number and seal the envelope before I'd go down on him. And when I was really being a hard-ass I'd make him walk it out to the post office with his hard-on. I don't know, I think it turned him on even more. The harder a time I'd give him, the harder he'd be.

Alex was really pissed when I read in *Vogue* or somewhere that there's like twelve hundred calories or something like that in an average load of come. Because at the time I was kind of anorexic and the last thing I was looking for was a way to swallow an extra thousand-plus calories. So I got kind of reluctant after that. Because, really, it seems to me it's kind of rude and insulting not to swallow. Like inviting someone to your house for a dinner party and then making them eat in the kitchen with the help. Anyway, God was Alex pissed. I think he even wrote a letter to the editor of *Vogue*. Or maybe it was *Cosmo*. Whatever. He got paranoid and started talking about feminist dykes taking over the media and stuff. And when he wanted it he'd whine and squirm like a hound with his nose in a foxhole, because as I say I wasn't that hot on the whole operation to begin with. When you love someone, okay. I loved Alex, and there is some kind of special thing about doing something for someone you love that's a better feeling than anything else in the world, even if it's something you normally wouldn't do at all. Or maybe especially if it's something you normally wouldn't do.

Did I say love? Wash my mouth out with soap. Dean said this great thing last night, we were talking about drama, and Dean quotes this line, it goes, men have died from time to time and worms have eaten them, but not for love. And I'm like, absolutely. It's from Shakespeare, a girl called Rosalind says it. Dean says I remind him of Rosalind, says she's a great character. So maybe I'll check out this play, see if it's got a monologue I can use.

Anyway . . . I wonder sometimes if it would have lasted with Alex if he hadn't fucked me over. Then I say—what are you, soft in the head? It never lasts. I haven't seen one example yet. But there's still this ideal in your head, you know, like a vision of a place you've never visited, but that you've dreamed about or seen in a movie you've forgotten the title of, and you know you'd recognize it immediately if you ever saw it in real life. It would be like going home, tired and whipped after a really long time on the road, if home was like it's supposed to be, instead of the disaster area it actually is.

3

SENSE-MEMORY

So I kiss Dean good-bye about three in the afternoon.

Can you taste yourself? I go, and he blushes. I swear, these older guys are so straight. Cracks me up. You'd think growing up in the sixties when everybody was balling at rock festivals and doing acid would've made them pretty wild, but most of the guys I know who are around thirty—they shock pretty easily. I don't know, maybe it's just me. Am I so outspoken? All my friends are like this, so how weird can I be? But I think with a little work we might be able to loosen old Dean up. He's definitely got potential.

Anyway, Dean, he's wearing this shit-eating grin on his face which he's had ever since I came up for air, which is a good thing, I'm glad he's happy, since I have to ask him for cab money because I've got to get back to my apartment to change and pick up my script and then downtown to Strasberg within the hour. I hate to start right in hitting him up for money but he's real sweet about it and gives me a twenty and I kiss him again and before we know it we're both getting into it again and it looks like school may be out the window, but then I remember my little problem, plus the phone rings so we both step back gasping for air and he goes, I'll call you—his voice all sexy like it's been smoked and sandpapered, then doused in hot pepper sauce—and I go, you better.

Not that I wouldn't call him. I will if I want, when I want. I hate waiting for anything, including for the phone to ring. Why wait? is my motto. I don't understand these girls who think the guy has to call them, like its some kind of deviant behavior for females to touch the push buttons on a phone. *Ooh, icky. I couldn't possibly!* My mother was always like that. Even after I know she's screwing the pool man, she has these little formulas for ladylike behavior she picked up at Miss Porter's or someplace—*a lady never calls a gentleman.* Probably wears white gloves when she gives a hand job.

My mother. She called last night just before I went out to dinner wanting to talk about her boyfriend. Carl owns a construction company supposedly and she's trying to decide whether she should break up with him since he's shiftless and lazy—those are her words, she talks like a plantation belle—but she's been trying to decide for five years. Anyway, it gives her something to think about besides Dad. She used to do charity work and paint watercolors, really beautiful landscapes, at least I thought they were really beautiful when I was a kid, I used to love to watch her paint out on the sunporch, we had this great house on Long Island when I was a kid and my parents were still married, I loved all the shades of blue in her paint set, these blue disks that between them contained all the moods of the sky and the ocean. But the pictures got smaller and smaller until they were about the size of postage stamps, she was using these brushes with one bristle, painting transparent mountains the size of pimples, then she stopped completely. I think it was Dad making fun of her that did it. Every time she tried to do something it was a joke. From what I can tell, now she just watches the religious shows on TV and drinks wine all day. This is someone who wouldn't think of carrying a handbag that wasn't made out of alligator or wearing a party dress twice but she's buying Gallo Chablis by the gallon. Finally I got sick of hearing about Carl so I told her I'd call her later. My opinion of Carl, if you really want to know, is that the best thing that could happen to Mom is if some of his nice associates in the so-called construction business would dress him up in a cement wet suit and send him scuba diving without a tank.

Down on the street I get a cab driven by a crazy Russian. He wants to tell me the story of his life, starting with the fact that he's Caucasian.

I White Russian, he says. White!

Hey, I can see that already. It's kind of racist to keep insisting on it, if you ask me. I don't know, maybe he wants me to think they named the drink after him or something. Every ten seconds or so he rolls down the window to spit whenever he wants to show what he thinks of Communism. At least I think that's the idea. I kind of hug the right side of the cab so I don't catch any of the spray.

In America, he goes, you eat caviar for breakfast every morning if you are wanting. (I bet this is news to the girls in the typing pool.) He goes, not so Russia. (Window down—hock, spit!)

Then he goes, what do you do, fashion model?

I go, I'm an actress.

Oh yes, he goes. Movies. I know. *The West Side Story.* That's a good one, I go.

You ever come to Brighton Beach, you look up me, the Russian says when he lets me off in front of my apartment.

And I'm like, is that in the Hamptons, or what? Never heard of it. Then I ask him if he'll wait and he goes sure.

In the elevator I'm hoping Didi and Rebecca won't be there, or at least that they'll be asleep. It's kind of hard to get started on your day when a couple of vampires have taken over your apartment. At the door I hear these weird Oriental voices coming from inside. It sounds like group therapy for giant insects.

I almost gag on the cigarette smoke and cocaine sweat when I open the door. When my eyes adjust to the dark I see them huddled on the couch, Rebecca in her leopard body stocking and Didi in the same leggings and sweatshirt she's been sporting for the last couple of weeks.

You scared the shit out of us, Little Sis, Rebecca goes.

Did you bring any beer? Didi says.

How about cigarettes? says Rebecca. We *need* cigarettes.

You need professional help, I go.

Didi goes, you bring any blow?

There's still about a gram here, Rebecca says to Didi. And Didi goes, that's good. Are you sure?

So Rebecca says, I think so. I don't know. Maybe it's

only about seven-eighths of a gram. Or three-quarters. I don't know.

God, that's not very much, Didi goes.

And Becca goes, well, maybe nine-tenths.

And I'm like, fun with fractions. Actually, Becca was really good in school, not that she ever went, but one time they tied her down long enough to give her an IQ test and then told Mom and Dad she was a genius. Becca never let us forget it. She decided it meant that she didn't have to bother going to school or do anything that required any effort at all, ever again.

We have to call Emile and get more, says Didi, suddenly panicked.

I love coke conversations. They're so enlightening. I mean, do I sound like that? It's almost enough to make you swear off drugs forever.

The place is a real sty, beer and wine bottles all over the place, and for some reason about half of Jeannie's wardrobe is scattered around the room, plus there's like this residue of cigarette ash and cocaine on everything. The air reminds me of Mexico City, totally unbreathable. I go into my room to change.

Tell us about your new stud, Rebecca shouts from the living room.

We want details, Didi says. Length and width.

The next minute, Rebecca says, Alison, do you have any Valium? That's the good part about dealing with coke monsters. If you don't like the topic of conversation, just wait a minute and you'll get a new one. On the other hand, it never really changes at all. It's like a perpetual motion thing. The topic is always drugs.

When I leave they're calling the deli to order beer and cigarettes, Becca holding the receiver between her shoulder and her cheek while she goes down on the mirror.

Do they sell Valium? Didi goes.

Does who sell Valium? says Becca and then she goes, hello, who is this?

And Didi goes, who are you talking to? Then she seems to realize that I'm leaving. She gets real indignant. Sit down, she says. You have to help us finish this coke. You can't go anywhere until it's gone.

Didi is so bossy when she's wired. She insists that everybody else get fucked up too, plus she directs the conversation. Usually she gets away with it since she's the one who paid for the coke, plus everybody has this kind of awe of her, she's sort of a prodigy, like a crazy person. But I'm not buying it today.

Alison, she screams. Come back here. You can't go.

So then I remember this thing in my purse, it's like a business card from this drug counseling program, Jeannie gave it to me as a joke one night, actually one morning after we'd been up all night—somebody at work gave it to her and they weren't kidding. So I open my purse, fish through my wallet, all these scraps of paper, napkins with guys' phone numbers, and I find this thing, it says, MESSED UP? STRUNG OUT? NEED HELP? DIAL 555-HELP.

I go, Didi, I got a present for you. And I give her the card.

And she's like, Alison, you bitch, come back here, as I'm cruising out the door.

I'll visit you in the hospital, I say.

* * *

Didi would make a really good dictator of a Third World country. She absolutely has to be the boss and the center of attention. If someone's talking about something she's not interested in she shouts, boring! and changes the subject to something more interesting, like herself for instance. Somehow she pulls it off. Partly because she's gorgeous. Partly because at most social events she's the one with the most blow, and she uses it like a carrot and a stick. She'll sit there in the middle of the floor with her big white bag and she'll let people drool while she chops really painstaking lines or just yaks on and on as if she's oblivious to what everyone's really concentrating on, except of course she's not. She just likes to torture people. That's the carrot part. If she thinks you want it she'll keep you hanging on, like the Supremes say. But at the end of the night when your nose is bleeding and you're dying to go home and sleep, she'll demand that you do these huge lines that would choke an industrial-strength vacuum cleaner. And when you say, no way Didi, I gotta split, she'll get real indignant and go, after all this free blow I gave you, you're just going to walk out on me?

The classic story about Didi is that she makes her boyfriends change the channels when they're having sex.

I've totally forgotten about the Russian, who's been sitting there in the cab for about fifteen minutes. I feel really bad about it, poor guy probably had his fill of waiting in Russia, standing in those incredible lines for his ration of rotten

41

groceries and stuff, actually it sounds like New York now that I think about it, but still, I have to get cigarettes, we're talking absolute necessities here, so I tell him two more minutes and I zip around the corner to the deli.

Pack of Merits, I say to the old fart behind the counter.

Hard or soft? he says, smirking.

Hard, I tell him. You know I like it hard.

The old guy cracks up. He never gets enough of this joke.

Coming out of the store I get caught in this horrible preteen pedestrian traffic jam from the school down the street. Gremlins. I practically get run over by this tiny kid with a T-shirt that says REALITY IS AN ILLUSION PRODUCED BY ALCOHOL DEFICIENCY.

Where was Planned Parenthood when we really needed them? is what I want to know.

The cabbie is cool. He's been grooving on some funky ethnic-type music on the radio—dueling balalaikas or something. You never know how many kinds of music there are in the world until you move to New York and start taking cabs. It's like, from your apartment to Trader Vic's you get Cuban music, and then from Trader Vic's to Canal Bar you've got Zorba the Greek music and then Indian ragas from Canal Bar to Nell's, Scandinavian heavy metal on the way from Nell's up to Emile's apartment. After that you start singing the Colombian national anthem.

I ask him if I can smoke and he says, not problem. And I'm like, this cab should be a national historic landmark or something, the last taxi in New York City without a No Smoking sign.

So we're cruising downtown and the Russian's telling

me the story of his life, the short version. I can't understand all of it, with the music and his accent and all, but the climax of the story is his first visit to an American supermarket after he's finally gotten an exit visa and split the Motherland. Or is it the Fatherland? Anyway, whichever, according to what this guy tells me, having Russia for your parentland proves my theory that it's better to be an orphan. So when he first gets to the old U S of A he goes to this supermarket in Brooklyn and can't believe what he sees, all the aisles of food and stuff. What really flips him out is the meat counter. He looks at all this red meat under plastic and he goes to his cousin—*Who for is all this meat?* (That's how he says it.) *Is for high officials?* he goes and his cousin goes, *It is for anyone who wants.*

I break into crying right there, the cabbie goes, to think how wonderful it is, all that meat in nice plastic for all the people who want.

I don't know, I'm going to ask him if there was a special sale that day, free meat for the masses, but I feel like a cynic. So then I feel sort of guilty and touched, you know, I'm so spoiled and this guy can weep at the sight of a pork chop. So when he asks me for my phone number as he's dropping me off I almost give it to him, but then I say, sorry, I've got a boyfriend, which is sort of true in a way. Maybe. I hope. But I like this guy, he's nice, so I don't do what I usually do which is to give him the number of the Midnite Escort Service. I just say, maybe next time.

My first class is dance, then voice. My voice teacher gets ticked off at me because I'm not concentrating. I keep talking through my nose, it's a big problem with me, and he says, what are you thinking about?

I don't say anything, but I'm thinking about Dean. And it kind of pisses me off—one night with this guy and he's distracting me from my acting. This is one of the reasons I don't believe in relationships. Who needs the distraction? But probably it's just lack of sleep. Being tired always makes me sentimental. Like when I'm really hung over I can turn on the radio and start bawling at the lyrics to some stupid song, even if it's a song I really hate. Or, you know, after a really hard night I'll pick up the *Post* and read about some hero who saved a puppy from drowning and I'll want to write him a letter and offer to marry him or have his children or something. Not that I actually do it, you know, but I think about it.

I've got this theory that the brain is sort of like H_2O— it's got a bunch of states. When you've been exercising and going to class and generally being a good girl the brain is a solid and it makes the right decisions. But when you've been out all night trashing yourself with alcohol and controlled substances, or sometimes when you're having really great sex, your gray matter turns to mush and your judgment turns to shit. You know, right in the middle of a good orgasm you'll go completely liquid and for a while afterward you'll think about true love and marriage and other, like, ancient myths.

Finally voice is over and I go to my acting class, which is usually my best. The sensory exercise for the week is sharp taste. Our teacher, Rob, gives us a little pep talk first about how we really have to taste it, and it should be clear to anybody watching us, say, from across a restaurant, that we're experiencing this sharp taste. So I decide on jalapeño peppers. I'm a fiend for Mexican food, and I like it hot. I always order extra jalapeños on the side. I sometimes think I must have some kind of chemical deficiency that can only be filled with Mexican food. Not to mention margaritas. The trouble is, when you start drinking frozen margaritas, there's no telling where you'll end up, or with who.

So I start thinking about jalapeños, and everybody else in the class goes off into their thing while the teacher walks around checking us out. After ten minutes I'm like bored out of my gourd. My cheeks hurt, and my eyes feel like they're starting to grow mold they've been watery so long. The teacher asks Burt, the guy next to me, what he's tasting and he says gorgonzola cheese.

I can't see that, Rob says.

I say, thank God we can't smell it.

And Rob goes, Alison, if you were concentrating you wouldn't have even heard my remark, which is true.

Finally he can see we're all really bored with sensory so he says try something psychological over that, which is cool because that's when it gets interesting.

For example, he goes, think of something good you did for someone else that made you feel good about yourself. And put that together with sharp taste. Okay, people, he says, let's really reach down and use our instrument.

The instrument is like, all your acting skills and knowledge and talent put together, your body too but more than your body, it's not an actual thing but kind of a concept. Anyway, I think about it for a minute and then I just about die. Something good you did for someone . . . sharp taste.

They told me later that within two minutes I had the

teacher watching me and that pretty soon he told everyone else to knock off what they were doing and watch me. I don't know, I was off in my own world, acting. I'm doing something true, I know I'm not just faking it this time and even though it's acting something I'm not really experiencing it's absolutely honest, my reaction, the sensations I'm feeling and I'm completely in my own reality, it's like dreaming, you know, or like riding when you feel almost like you and your horse are the same animal, taking your best jumper over a hard course and hitting everything perfectly. . . .

Something good that I did for someone . . . sharp taste. I was combining these two incredible sensations. And I knew it was the best I had ever done. It was taking me to a place I'd never been. When I finally came out of it, everybody was looking at me.

That was wonderful, the teacher says. Very very good. You were completely in tune with your instrument. Tell us what your sensory was, Alison.

Jalapeño peppers, I say.

And he goes, what about your psychological?

You really want to know? I go.

Yes, of course, he goes.

Well, I was thinking about giving my boyfriend a blow job.

That cracks everyone up.

And I'm thinking, boyfriend? Why did I say boyfriend? What's the matter with me? I'm totally in lust. I know it will pass so I don't worry about it too much and in the meantime I got this incredible acting experience out of it. I figured out real early on that the bad stuff—all the shitty things that ever happened to you—feeds your work, I mean, the teacher says the more bad things that happen to you the better for your art, and I'm like—hey, I could be a fucking genius, but anyway, this is the first time I've made something enjoyable really work for my art, pardon the A word.

When the laughter dies down my teacher says, were you thinking of a specific instance, or just in general?

Specific, I go. Very specific. In fact it was this morning. This cracks them all up again.

Then we get down to acting. I'm glad he liked my sense-memory because I don't have anything ready to perform. Luckily there's some eager beavers ready to strut their stuff. I don't know, you've got to be a bit of masochist to be in this class because Rob can be brutal. First this girl Janet who used to write her own material until Rob finally put a stop to that. It was pretty horrible. She gets up and says she's going to do Blanche from *Streetcar.*

Rob goes, not the kindness of strangers. I thought I told the class I didn't want anybody doing that monologue ever again.

Old Janet's standing in front of the class looking like— oh, God, why does he hate me? And I'm feeling nice and safe in my wobbly little classroom chair, thinking, better you than me, Janet.

Rob sighs and tells Janet to go ahead so she does, yada yada yada, really bad, I mean, bring back Vivien Leigh, please.

Finally Rob shouts, she's in the attic.

I don't know what it means but he always hollers this whenever he really hates something. He'll tell us the story some day, or so he says.

Janet asks, do you want me to stop?

Please, Rob says, cease and desist. Then he launches into this thing where he tears her performance apart and goes on to talk about her sex life—Rob should have been a psychotherapist. You just broke up with your boyfriend, didn't you? Rob shouts. Janet squeaks yes and then starts bawling. He gets really personal in his criticism. The roles we choose and how we perform them show a lot about us, Rob says.

And while I'm supposed to be paying attention I'm wondering what Dean is doing, if he's thinking of me. Then I think I may have to go out and screw somebody else or something just to get my sense of perspective back.

4

TRUTH OR DARE

After class I stop off at the tanning salon. I'm hoping Mark will be there because I'm flat broke and I used my last tanning coupon a few days ago. Luckily Mark's behind the counter but he has to give me a bunch of shit first and say if his boss catches him giving out free tans he'll be shit-canned and I have to remind him about some favors I've done for him, so he gives me my usual bed but I have to wait five minutes so I decide to call Francesca from the pay phone after I borrow a quarter from Mark.

Alison, he goes, have you ever thought of getting a job?

Not really, I go. Have you?

I've got a job, he goes.

And I go, you call this working?

If I really gave a shit what Mark thinks I could tell him I had a job once. I was a waitress for about three seconds. I don't know, it was pretty terrible, these businessmen thinking the price of their filet included a handful of ass and the manager wanted to sleep with me, plus the other waitresses weren't too keen on me since Jeannie's father owned the restaurant. Sorry, I just wasn't raised to work. I mean, you take an indoor cat eating smoked salmon and lying around in the sunny spots all its life—you can't suddenly chuck it out into the cold and expect it to feed itself and fight like an alley cat. I should start a clinic for former rich girls. Deprived Debs Anonymous.

Francesca picks up on the second ring. Tell me all, she goes. I want to know everything about Dean. I need details. Length and width, the works. Did you take my advice?

Francesca likes to pile up the questions, mainly because she hates to stop talking, she's like scared she'll have to let someone else talk the way kids are afraid of the moment when somebody notices it's their bedtime. I don't know, that sounds too negative, what it really is, she's like a force of nature, Niagara Falls or something.

I go, I took it.

And she's like, tell me all.

And I'm like, I'm not going to tell you everything. It was good, it was great, I like him. I'm in lust.

And she goes, I can't believe you're not going to tell me every little thing, your best friend, I'm so upset, at least tell me how big.

So I go, big.

And she goes, oh God, let me sit down, I'm getting dizzy, it's been so long since I've been laid two inches would feel big to me. Four inches would feel like a baseball bat. This is no fair, I have to live vicariously through your lust life and now you're holding out on me. Listen, do you know Bobby Cayman? Real dark, craggy. Looks like he just stepped off a Harley Davidson? I ran into him at Nell's after you left with what's-his-face and he is a total hunk.

Forget it, I tell her. Used to be a junkie.

Shit, why do I always go for men in the high risk categories?

It's true. Francesca only seems to like guys who look like heavy-metal lead guitarists or bikers, hunks in leather with needle tracks and dubious sexual histories, the kind of guys who are like, what is it that Dean says?—walking petri dishes for sexually transmitted diseases. Francesca could get laid a lot more often if her tastes weren't so narrow. She's real picky, but she picks badly. It's like, choosy mothers would never choose the kind of guys Francesca likes for son-in-law material. Sometimes I think she looks at a guy and goes, oh, wow! my mom would really be horrified by this stud.

It was so depressing at Nell's last night, Francesca says. There were absolutely no celebs. Plus I heard that Mick and Jerry had a dinner party and I wasn't invited again. I'm really upset at Caroline because she knows them like really well and she was there last night and she still won't introduce me.

Did I already say this is Francesca's big goal in life, to get invited to Mick and Jerry's house for dinner? I don't know what she'd have to live for if the invitation ever came. She goes on and on about this dinner party she wasn't invited to while I'm thinking I should probably get a bikini wax except I don't have any money. Plus I'm not a glutton for that kind of pain. It's not easy to bring tears to my eyes, but the old bikini wax does it every time. Underarm waxing is the worst, though. These places should hand out Demerol free of charge.

Mark tells me my bed's ready so I tell Francesca I gotta go and I'll call after I finish tanning. Then I call Jeannie collect at work.

Did you get any sleep? I go.

Hardly, she goes, and then she makes me tell her the whole story about Dean. Finally I ask her if she's checked the messages and she hasn't so I dial in and hear Francesca's voice again, plus some crazy guy named Mannie looking for Rebecca, he sounds deranged, not a stable unit, there's always some crazy guy looking for Rebecca. But no Dean.

When we went to L.A. last summer, Francesca and me, we'd catch this air-quality index on the radio. We were supposedly out there looking for jobs, right? We had this little house in Santa Monica on Second Street which was Party Central—but anyway, what was I talking about? Oh yeah, there was this radio station we listened to, and between Madonna and the Beastie Boys the DJ would be like—the air really sucks today, don't go out unless it's absolutely necessary kind of thing. I really hate Madonna but that's another story. So anyway, coming back to my apartment made me think about the air-quality index . . . don't go inside unless really you have to. Heavy smog, hydrocarbons and BO. I mean, it's never exactly a rose garden, but this is radical. Rebecca and Didi are really disgusting is all I can say. I have to open up all the windows and run the fan in the air conditioner for cross-ventilation. I don't even want to think about dealing with the ashtrays. If I'd bought stock in Philip Morris yesterday I'd probably be a rich girl today.

So I clear some space on the bed and lie down with my script for a half an hour or so but the next thing I know the phone is ringing and I've been asleep and I'm listening to my message going—hi, this is Alison, Jeannie and I aren't home right now, so leave the data and we'll call you lata.

So I pick up and it's Dean.

He goes, hey, how's my little postmodern girl?

I'm spacey, I go.

By definition, he goes. So what are you doing? he says.

I think I was just having an erotic dream, I tell him, because it's just coming back to me.

Was I in it? he goes and I'm thinking, for a supposedly smart guy Dean can be pretty predictable. I could lie, of course, and say he was but I feel really strongly about always being honest no matter what. That's my personal code, basically— do anything you'd be willing to admit, and always tell the truth. I don't know, though, that thing about Skip, telling him I was preggers, it's been bugging me. It's the first time in years I can remember that I've lied, but we were talking survival. And revenge, which is a girl's best friend.

So when Dean wants to know is he in my stupid dream, I go, I'm not sure, because I'm not. I don't think it was any guy in particular. Maybe if I went right back to sleep I could find out. But I can tell he's kind of hurt that it wasn't him in the dream. Jesus! What a baby. So I tell him about my sense-memory exercise in class, how I had to think of something good I'd done for somebody. . . .

You *told* the class that?

Sure, I say. I mean, why not?

He goes, you didn't tell them my name, did you?

Of course not, I go. Like it would mean anything to them anyway. Dean the Famous Bond Salesman.

Dean keeps saying over and over that he still can't believe that I told them. But I think secretly he's really flattered, you know?

Finally he asks me if I want to go to dinner and I say yeah, definitely, and he asks if I have any preference and I say Mexican, I don't know, I just suddenly have this craving for hot salsa and margaritas. Love that spicy food. Must be my southern blood, did I mention my mom's from Georgia? Anyway Dean says cool, he knows a place.

Are you sure that's okay? I go. I'm like suddenly thinking maybe he had some big plan that I spoiled. The last time I went out on an actual date this guy sent a limo around and we ate at Le Bernardin and he was all upset that all I wanted was a salad because he'd gone to all this trouble and I guess he had these visions of us feeding each other oysters and snails and lusting across the meat like Albert Finney and that chick in *Tom Jones,* but I felt like I'd done my bit spending about five hours on makeup and borrowing an Alaïa evening dress from Didi and emerald earrings from Jeannie. Granted, a salad's not very sexy but it's results that count, right? And any girl who gets invited out with any regularity and scarfs the paté and the tournedos and the mousse is eventually going to kill the goose that laid the golden egg, you know? Sure, there are fetishists who write letters to *Penthouse* about lusting after the fat girls, but let's face it . . . I mean, Alaïa doesn't make those sexy dresses in size fourteen. Which I've gotta say is Francesca's problem. That girl loves eating the way I love . . . well, let's just say the way Didi loves blow. We're talking addiction. It's sort of funny that they're friends, now that I think about it. Didi hasn't eaten in about eight months and Francesca never stops. Being in a restaurant with those two is a really weird experience. Didi jumping up to go to the Ladies every three minutes and Francesca screaming at the waitress to bring more bread. And butter. Luckily it doesn't happen too often since Didi can never get it together to show up anywhere.

Anyway, I'm talking about dinner plans, right? and I'm suddenly worried that Dean had some big romantic idea that I'd just blown, but he says Mex is fine, dress casual and he'll come by at eight-thirty.

Jeannie comes home a few minutes later. She throws herself down on the bed and says, God, I can't wait to get married so I can quit working and lie around the house all day.

Jeannie is engaged to this guy Frank Salton who's a tennis pro on Hilton Head. She flies down to see him every weekend, which is the main reason she has to have a job — that and a few other bad habits—since the allowance her parents give her only covers the rent plus one or two outfits a week. I was going to mention food but Jeannie doesn't really eat. They're supposed to get married this fall. I don't know. Frank's a decent guy—I know, because I introduced him to Jeannie. Actually that's kind of a problem. I went out with him before Jeannie. For about five minutes. But still. Anyway, she could definitely do better. Frank's got a decent body, but he's no brain surgeon. One time he broke his index finger and he couldn't read for six weeks, right? Had to skip the Sunday funnies till his pointer got better. Plus Jeannie is used to a lot of money and Frank's never going to make a ton of it. Not to be a snob. I don't think it's a reason not to get married, but it's kind of stupid, if you ask me, to pretend that these things don't make a difference.

Don't you ever just want somebody to take care of you? Jeannie says.

I go, I miss having a maid, if that's what you mean.

You know what I mean, she goes.

I'd get bored, I say. Having the same guy around all the time.

Not me, Jeannie says. I can't wait. I'm going to sit around and watch the soaps, eat bonbons, cook dinner, the whole thing.

I'm like, since when did you ever cook anything?

I can learn, she says.

You'd better, I go. On Frank's salary I don't think you're going to be able to afford help.

She goes, fuck you, Alison.

Hey, I go, I'm just being realistic.

I mean, really. I'm trying to tell her what life is really like. Wake up and smell the espresso, babe.

So Dean comes by and picks me up, looking good, casual and sexy in chinos and a cotton sweater. Even though she's not going out, Jeannie brushes her hair and touches up her eyes before he comes over. She gives him the eye and I can tell what she's thinking. It kills her that I went out with Frank, and she develops these weird physical crushes on any guy I go out with but I doubt she even realizes it. I think she'd like to sleep with all my boyfriends. Partly it's like a revenge fantasy, but also its because she loves me and looks up to me and sympathizes totally with me, you know, and automatically likes a guy if he's passed my selection process. Reminds me of my sister Carol, who never liked the clothes she bought for herself and only wanted to wear stuff from my closet. I guess it's a compliment. With Jeannie, it's kind of like, we share sweaters and shoes and dresses so why not men? At least, I sometimes think that's what's going on in her head when she starts flirting with my guys, though probably not consciously. It's sort of a great idea, sharing a lover with someone you love. But it's too weird, really.

Did I mention about Jeannie and Alex, my old boyfriend? Somewhere in Jeannie's mind there's this doubt about marriage and domestic bliss with Frank, this little cloud floating around—it's like, picture a perfectly clear sky and that's probably a pretty good picture of Jeannie's mind—I love her but I definitely wouldn't let her take my law boards for me. Anyway there's this little thing she has going over the phone with Alex, he calls up for me but sometimes she picks up or else I'm not home and they've developed this incredible flirtation where they're talking about sex and teasing each other and they've never even met. I told you about Jeannie and my boyfriends. In a way I'm kind of irritated but in another way I'm like, great, I hope Jeannie sleeps with Alex because if she does she'll have a hard time settling for the notion of a lifetime of sleeping with Frank, who is not exactly Valentino in bed. I think it would be good for her, and anyway, this marriage idea is kind of bogus. . . .

* * *

So Dean and I are in this frantic place on Second Avenue packed with well-groomed gringos getting sloppy on margaritas.

Popular place, I go.

Dean says, these people are all bankers trying to improve the balance of payments with Mexico and prevent default. That's the only way I can think of, he goes, to explain the popularity of Third World food on the Upper East Side.

Most of them look like they could use some spice, I say. Not that Dean is exactly the hairy barbarian himself. I mean, it seems like his idea of wild is argyle socks. But it's okay, I like straight guys, I'd never go out with anybody who's as irresponsible as me. Most of the guys I know have really high-powered jobs and make up for lost time when they're not in the office. The Berserk After Work Club. I seem to attract them in a big way, all these boys in Paul Stuart suits with six-figure salaries and hellfire on a dimmer switch in their eyes.

The waiter knows Dean and he keeps bringing us free maragaritas so I get really blasted. Not blasted exactly. I just get really horny. Story of my life, right? I mean, who needs tequila? But then I remember my little problem, which makes me a mondo unhappy unit.

Dean's like, you want to come over? and I'm like, sure, yeah, but basically I'm still out of commission. He says that's okay, sex isn't the only thing he ever thinks about, and I'm like, well, I hope it's near the top of the list, anyway. He cracks up.

So we get to Dean's house and the phone is ringing. I don't know why I say house, it's an apartment. It's like, living in New York never really seems normal, you keep thinking of the world as a place where people live in houses and drive cars to the 7-Eleven.

Somebody called Didi for you, Dean goes, handing me the phone.

Didi's just bought her stash for the night and she wants to come over. God, I don't know. A couple of lines would be nice, but I've got class in the morning, plus it's Dean's apartment and it's not really up to me. So I go, you don't really want this beautiful maniac friend of mine coming over here and wiggling her cute little tail all over the place and forcing nonprescription drugs up your nose, do you?

And he says, sounds terrible, ask her how soon she can get here, and I go, really, you don't mind? and he goes, why not? And I figure, well, I tried, right? but just to be safe I check my watch—it's a little after eleven—and I say to Dean, we definitely kick her out at one, right? If not sooner.

Absolutely, he says.

And suddenly Dean goes, wait a minute, this isn't Didi Spence, is it? Well, it turns out Dean knows Didi's cousin Phil. And of course he's heard stories. I don't think there's anybody in New York who hasn't heard about Didi.

Listen, I go, you better not start drooling all over Didi in front of me.

And he goes, Alison, I only have eyes for you.

I'm like, right, Dean. If you think I believe that I've got some swampland in Florida I'll sell you real cheap.

* * *

Didi shows up a little after midnight.

By this time I'm chewing my fingernails off thinking about getting a line, right? If she hadn't called at all that would've suited me just fine. We're watching Carson, I'm kind of giving Dean a backrub. It must be bimbo night. I can't believe some of the so-called actresses who are making a killing out there in videoland. You can see, when they get live on Johnny, these starlets without stage training, that they don't even know how to talk. Doing a TV series they can shoot five hundred takes while some dimwit walking talking inflatable doll who the producer slept with tries to learn how to say Gesundheit! Or they can just change the script and say, bless you! and the prompter gives the lines word by word offscreen and then the editor cuts away just before she starts to pick her nose. I'm sorry, but the stage is where real actors and actresses live and die. You can't fake it up there. We're talking truth in advertising. My teacher says acting is about truth, and I finally figured out what he means, you know what real acting is when you see this fake shit on television. I'm not saying I'd turn down a role in a movie or even a TV series. But there's a lot of bimbos making huge bucks. I can't stand watching Johnny pimp for NBC's latest sitcom, so we switch to Channel J to check out "Midnight Blue," that cable show that's all T and A and hand-held cameras and ads for escort services . . . which is like a blast of honesty and fresh air after this horrible network cosmetology.

So finally the buzzer rings in the middle of the nude talk show. Didi breezes in wearing the same clothes she had on before she went to bed this afternoon. Still, I can see that

Dean thinks she's all right. Any minute the saliva will start trickling down his chin. Sometimes I wonder why all my friends are good-looking. I must be an idiot.

Mirror, says Didi, before she's even inside the door.

I know your cousin Phil, Dean drools.

Didi ignores Dean and walks over to draw the living room curtains. Dean gets her a picture from the wall, a framed poster for a play called *Zoo Story,* sounds like something I could relate to. Didi sits down on the floor in front of the coffee table and dumps out a mound of blow.

I'm so mad at Whitney, Didi says, launching into a story about a friend of ours who's supposedly spreading rumors about Didi. I don't know why Whitney would want to spread rumors about Didi, the truth's kinky enough. Dean is a little stunned. This chick has just walked in and taken over his apartment, like an army commander or something. She chops and folds the stuff endlessly until I'm about ready to hit her over the head with the brass lamp. Dean rolls up a bill, probably just trying to be helpful, although I think he's a little impatient too. Didi doesn't even look at Dean's bill. I don't know, she is rude, but it's kind of like what do you call it, a parachuter who won't let anyone else pack his parachute. Didi's into the ritual and the equipment. It's what she does. When she's good and ready, she rolls her own bill, does a couple of monster lines—what Didi calls lines other people call grams—and then tortures us for a few more minutes holding the rolled bill in the air and waving it around while she bitches some more about Whitney. Finally the spoiled little brat lets us play with her toys and she looks around for the first time.

This your place? she says to Dean.

Dean looks up from the mirror and nods his head so hard I'm afraid he's going to break his neck.

You own or rent? Didi asks, lighting up a Merit.

Rent, Dean says.

The buzzer rings and Didi goes, that's probably Francesca. And I'm like, Didi, what's the deal here? and Didi goes relax. Dean goes to the door and comes back with Francesca and Jeannie. Naturally we hear Francesca's voice even before Dean gets the door open, and I'm sure his neighbors do too. And isn't it interesting that Jeannie's dressed to kill? A few hours ago she's all set to go to bed, and now she's in black cashmere and hose. Plus we should've bought stock in Chanel before she started in on her face tonight. Didi and me usually just wear leggings under a shirt or something, except I change mine every day, but Jeannie and Francesca wouldn't think of going out of the house without a thousand bucks worth of fabric on their backs. Jeannie has this expensive WASP look and Francesca's dressed as usual, sort of the expensive-flooze chic—sequins and cleavage—which actually does suit her. I mean, if you're pushing size 12 and headed for a D cup, you might as well go for it. She gives me a huge hug while she finishes this urgent story that she's right in the middle of, which has something to do with some rock singer.

Do a line, Didi demands. Everybody do a line. House rules.

Didi can't stand it, of course, that someone else has center stage when she's the one who brought the drugs. Plus it bugs her that Francesca doesn't do drugs—for someone like Didi, health, sanity and moderation are like a personal affront.

Jeannie doesn't have to be asked twice, she dives right in.

Francesca ignores her and says, I'm so upset, there's the ugliest picture of me in *Women's Wear* at Nan Kempner's party and I look so fat, the caption says, Francesca Green, also known as the Goodyear Blintz, wearing a waterproof canvas tent by L. L. Bean. I swear to God that's what it looks like in the picture. I've got to go on a diet. Even I'm grossed out by myself and I don't scare easy. No wonder I haven't been laid since boarding school. Not that there are any men out there worth breaking a sweat with. They're all jerks, basically. Present company excluded, Dean honey. Ooh, he's so cute isn't he? (She goes over and hugs Dean, gives him a big kiss. She just totally cracks me up.) Not my type though, she says. Too clean-cut. I like them mean and nasty-looking. I want guitar heroes and boys who were raised on the streets by wolves. Attila the Hun is my basic dream lover. Oh, God, did I tell you guys I met David Lee Roth the other night at Raoul's? That boy is to die for. . . .

Will you stop babbling and let somebody else talk for a change? Didi says. She's furiously chopping up more blow, after Jeannie did the last four lines. Jeannie's sitting demurely on the couch with her legs crossed and her hands folded on her knees in her finishing school manner, posing for Dean while she pretends to listen to Francesca. Sometimes I think the only good thing you can say about cocaine is that it affects Jeannie the exact opposite way it affects everyone else, she clams up for the whole night, lockjaw, so we don't have to listen to her flirt.

Meanwhile, Dean's like the cock of the walk, looking every which way. I think he likes having four young girls in his apartment, even if he doesn't quite know how to handle all this estrogen in the air. Looking over at him nodding and beaming at Francesca and then Didi makes me want to grab him and drag him off to the bedroom. He's got those swimming-pool eyes, you want to dive right in.

Did you hear about Kristin? Francesca says.

Didi shouts, boring, boring. New rule, she goes. No talking about boring subjects.

Francesca goes, so what shall we talk about? Your drug habit?

I don't have a drug habit, Didi says. I do drugs because I love them. Habits are boring routines.

We all kind of roll our eyes while Didi goes down on the mirror. Even my guy looks a little skeptical and he's only known Didi for an hour.

I'm certainly glad to hear that, Dean says. Otherwise I'm afraid I'd have to ask you to leave the premises immediately.

I know, says Didi when she comes up for air.

What? I go.

Truth or Dare, she says.

Oh, no, says Jeannie.

We can't subject Dean to Truth or Dare the first night, Francesca goes.

Didi goes, it's not the first night. Alison went down on him last night.

Thanks for reminding us of that, Didi. Jesus.

Dean's got instant sunburn. He's like, is there anything else that you all would like to know about me? I'd hate to think I was holding anything back.

Jeannie says, do you have a brother?

He shakes his head, then he says, what's Truth or Dare?

64

I don't know—I'm a little dubious. I mean, I did just meet him and Truth or Dare can get pretty heavy. Plus I want to be in bed in about twenty minutes. I check my watch—definitely no more than half an hour for sure.

Didi explains the rules. You've got to be into it, she says. Everybody has to swear at the beginning to tell the truth, because otherwise there's no point. When it's your turn you say either truth or dare. If you say truth, you have to answer whatever question you're asked. And if you say dare, then you have to do whatever somebody dares you to do.

Whatever? says Dean, with this big grin on his face.

Within reason, Didi says. No physical violence and no sexual contact, but anything else.

Didi just likes this game because she's an exhibitionist, Francesca says. She can't wait to take her clothes off.

Shut up, says Didi. Now, everybody has to do two big lines to start out. Then I'll go first.

Didi starts with me, which figures.

Alison, she goes. Were you physically attracted to Dean when you first saw him?

For Didi that's pretty tame. I kind of wish she hadn't asked me, but I have to answer no. Then I look over at Dean and add, not at first, but Didi waves her arm and says, no, no explanations, no excuses. I want a simple yes-or-no answer.

Then it's my turn. So I turn to Jeannie and say truth or dare and she says truth, so I say, are you physically attracted to Dean? Partly because I want her to admit it and partly because it will cheer Dean up to hear it.

Jeannie nods. Dean smiles. So now it's Jeannie's turn. Jeannie asks Francesca if she ever slept with this hunky guy who worked the stables at this fairground in Harrisburg and

Francesca says they actually did go to this motel room and everything but this guy brought a bottle of tequila and he got so drunk he passed out.

And Jeannie mentioning Harrisburg reminds me of this big trip we all made out there to look at Dangerous Dan, the whole nuclear family, actually driving down the interstate in a station wagon like normal people. Dad had come back for a trial reconciliation and I desperately wanted this horse Dangerous Dan so Dad decides we'll make a family expedition out of it. Me and Rebecca and Carol squabbling in the back and playing license plate games, Mom and Dad up front being seriously polite to each other. Wow, that's as weird as it gets—the American family.

Anyway, after that station break it's back to Truth or Dare, which so far is pretty harmless. I can see Didi getting restless already, chopping more lines. Francesca says, Didi, truth or dare, and then when Didi looks up Cesca says, and don't say dare, because I have no desire to see your body.

Okay, Didi goes, truth.

And Francesca asks her if she was the one who started this rumor about Francesca which is too complicated and boring to explain, but Didi says no, it wasn't her, and Francesca says she's glad, and then Didi looks at me and I'm like, uh-oh, I can see trouble coming here, and she goes, Alison, on a scale of one to ten, how would you rate Skip Pendleton in bed?

Didi is such a bitch sometimes. She really knows how to cause trouble, which is probably the whole point of this game, to hit where it hurts, but I know Dean is pretty sensitive about the whole Skip Pendleton thing. But what can I do? I'd give him an eight, I go. Eight, eight and a half.

Dean's wincing but hey, once you start lying it's hard to stop and I just plain refuse. If I thought Skip was a ten I would've said so, but that way if I told Dean he was a ten someday, or that I loved him, he'd know I was telling the truth.

So it's my turn and I go to Dean, truth or dare, and he takes truth so I go, did that bother you just now, about Skip Pendleton?

He thinks about it for a little while, so of course I already know what his answer is and finally he goes, yeah, a little.

So I go over and give him a big hug and say, poor baby.

And he says, not really.

And Didi screams, stop it, no mushy stuff, not playing the game.

So then it's Dean's turn and I see him looking around and suddenly it's like clear as fucking Evian water that he's checking out Didi's body and wondering if she really would strip down. And I'm like, well, I suppose I can't really blame him, and I figure I've hurt his feelings so what the hell, you know, and so I say, go ahead, Dean, ask Didi.

And Dean goes, Didi, truth or dare and Didi looks around with this real world-weary look, like a movie star being asked to sign one more autograph, because usually we play this game with a whole bunch of guys and they're constantly daring Didi to take off her clothes. And she's like, okay, dare.

Dean looks over at me and I shrug and tell him to go ahead. And he scrunches up his forehead and squints at me, like—really? And I think, the thing that's really going to piss me off is if he wants to see Didi naked but he's too much of a wimp to ask. If there's one thing I hate it's dishonesty. Drives me crazy. I hate liars and hypocrites. And I'm not too big on wimps, either.

Take off your clothes, Dean says.

Not this again, Francesca says. I think I'm going to puke.

Is that all? Didi says. You could at least be a little more imaginative.

And Dean says, that's all, which makes the whole thing all right for me, the fact that he doesn't let her push him around. I mean, I'm a little bugged, sure, but I'm glad he's not a wimp.

So Didi does one more line and then stands up and says where? and Dean shrugs and goes, right there is fine. So Didi pulls off her shirt and of course she's not wearing a bra, and I hate to say it but she has these perfectly shaped breasts and then she takes off her jeans which don't have any panties underneath and I'm looking at Dean who is definitely impressed, which isn't surprising. He looks a little embarrassed, but he's not looking away either.

Didi goes, ta-da, like she's real bored, but she wouldn't do it if she weren't getting off.

Give me a break, for Christ's sake, says Francesca.

Didi shakes her hips, pirouettes like a runway model and then goes, okay?

Dean nods, very serious, like someone's asked him if he's ready to leave the art museum.

So Didi puts her clothes back on and at least that's over with for the night.

Francesca goes, it's been fun, boys and girls, but I've got to work in the morning.

Me too, says Jeannie. I'd almost forgotten she's still here.

And I look at my watch and it's two-thirty and I say, ditto, I've got class, I've got to get some sleep.

Nobody's leaving, Didi screams. No fair. I've been sharing all my blow with you and now you're just going to leave me all alone when I'm a shivering wreck. No fair. You all have to stay for a while and help me come down.

Actually, come to think of it, I couldn't sleep now anyway. I'm kind of a shivering wreck myself. I've been pacing the room for the last ten minutes and sucking down cigarettes and my heart's thumping like a fat girl on a trampoline.

Didi dumps out some more blow. Two more lines for everybody and then we'll take some Valium, she says.

I don't want the lines, I go. I just want the Valium.

No way, she says. Two lines for everybody. Including Francesca. House rules. And one more round of Truth or Dare. My turn. I earned my question.

Francesca goes, it's your party and you'll whine if you want to, and we all crack up.

Didi hoovers a monster line and then passes the mirror. She says, my turn to ask, shut up everybody. She turns back to Dean. He takes truth. She goes, two-part question. On a scale of one to ten, how would you rate my body and how would you rate Alison's body?

I'm like, you bitch, Didi. I'm going to kill you one of these days.

Dean looks like he's hoping for nuclear war to break out in the next thirty seconds.

Truth, says Didi.

Can I take the dare? Dean asks.

Nobody wants to see your body, Didi says.

I wouldn't mind, says Francesca, and Jeannie, who's trying to get her nostrils to work, says, me neither.

Rules are rules, says Didi. Truth.

Dean looks back and forth between us and finally he says, I'd give you both a nine and a half.

Give me a break, says Francesca.

Diplomacy is strictly against the rules, Didi goes.

So then the phone rings.

Dean jumps for it. Someone named Rebecca, he goes, wants to talk to either Alison or Didi.

I'm like, now what?

Rebecca says, Alison, is that you? Listen, you gotta help me. I need to get five hundred dollars quick or I'm going to get sliced up with a knife.

5

CARE OF THE SOCIAL FABRIC

So we're lying in Dean's bed, finally coming down on the Valium, but still grinding our teeth because they were only the five-milligram and Didi only gave us two. Semishivering. It's been one of those nights. I'm just beginning to really hate myself because I know I'm not going to be in any shape to go to class tomorrow and Dean's got to be at work in a couple of hours, poor guy, but then I think, well, we were saving Rebecca's life, right? It was a special occasion. It's not like I was just partying till dawn.

Suddenly Dean goes, are you mad at me?

And I go, about what?

And he goes, about daring Didi to take her clothes off.

I don't know, I say. Should I be? Do you want to sleep with her?

No, he says, I don't.

Truth, I say.

Really, he says. I don't. She's too weird. I can't imagine it. She's a harpy disguised as an angel.

That's exactly how he talks, I kid you not.

But you liked her body, I go.

Well, yeah, he says, I did. Can you understand that?

I'm not mad at you for that, I tell him. But I am mad at you for lying.

When did I lie? he says. He sits up in bed and looks at me with these big puppy eyes. He *is* cute. I wish I didn't have this stupid infection—I'm almost cooled out enough to have sex.

You lied, I say, when you rated my body the same as Didi's.

That wasn't a lie, he says, but he turns his eyes away from me when he says it.

Come on, I go, can you honestly sit there and tell me you think my body's as good as hers?

Sure, he whines. Jesus, you've got an incredible body.

I say, but not as incredible as hers.

Better, he goes.

I'm like, now I'm really getting pissed.

What did I do? he goes.

You're not being honest, I say. You're thinking one thing and saying another.

Not necessarily, he says.

Yes necessarily, I tell him.

In my experience this is one big problem with older

guys, they start to lose their spontaneity in their thirties, start saying what they think they're supposed to say instead of what they feel, sort of like hardening of the arteries. Like, we're all pretty much raving maniacs as kids, but then some of us get all conventional. Not me, that's why I know I'm going to be a great actress some day, I'm totally in touch with my child.

Alison, Dean goes, in this older-man kind of tone, let's just imagine that a guy had just met a girl he really likes. This is strictly hypothetical, right? But let's say that shortly after he meets her, and before he even knows her very well, somebody asks him, in her presence, who's prettier, her or, for instance, his former girlfriend. Right? Now, don't you think he'd be a real pig if he said, in front of this nice new girl, that his old girlfriend made her, his new female friend, look like Lassie?

I'm like, you think I look like Lassie, huh?

Dean's like, Alison! That's just an example. A deliberately extreme one.

So your old squeeze is prettier than me, is that it? I say.

He says, I'm just saying that even if I were lying, which I wasn't—truth isn't always an unalloyed virtue.

I go, a what?

Unalloyed, he says. That means pure.

And I'm like, no wonder I don't know it.

And he says, there are times when it's better to spare people's feelings, keep the social fabric intact.

And I'm like, the social fabric? What the hell is that? I go, is that like dacron polyester or something?

I mean really, he believes this shit?

Actually, it's more like silk, he says. It's a delicate thing.

It's like nonexistent is what I'm saying, I go. We're all just pieces of lint if you ask me.

That's very clever, Alison, he goes, hauling out the grown-up moan again. Look, he says, I'm just saying there's a reason for manners. The unvarnished truth isn't always what we need to hear. Diplomacy is what separates us from the animals.

I totally disagree, I say. I've grown up around liars and cheaters and I don't think there's any excuse for not telling the truth. I want to be able to trust you, but if I don't think you respect the truth, you know, then I'll just hit the road. You've got a nice vocabulary but I'm like, I insist on honesty. You should be able to tell me whatever you're feeling. If you think Didi has a better body than me you should say so. I can take it.

Dean says, and what if I do want to sleep with her?

Then you should, I go. Don't hold off on my account.

You don't mean that, he goes.

I do too, I say. I hope you don't want to. But if you do, you should.

There are some things you feel that you would never act on, Dean says, and there are some things you feel that you'd never want to say. Do you think I should sleep with everyone I'm attracted to? How far does this honesty go?

If I want to do something, I do it, I say. If I feel something I say it. Otherwise you're a hypocrite.

Have you ever wanted to kill someone, Alison? he says.

A lot of people, I go.

But you didn't, right? You can't act out all your impulses.

And I'm like, some of them I wish I had.

Dean lies back down and I can't even hear him breathing. After a few minutes I begin to feel bad about giving him such a hard time, especially since he was so great about helping Rebecca, so I roll over and curl up in his shoulder, then I kiss his ear and finally he leans over and kisses me on the mouth and one things leads to another and pretty soon we're in the same spot we were in the night before. I mean, I am one horny unit, but then the phone rings—for some reason Dean forgot to unplug it or turn on the machine, I don't know, maybe his friends don't call at all hours. I would've ignored it, but he picks it up and of course it's Rebecca. I look at the clock and it's 5:15.

What are you doing? Rebecca says.

I'm drinking tea with Princess Di, I go.

We're over at Didi's partying, she goes.

And I'm like, imagine my surprise.

She says, I wanted to ask you something but now I can't remember what it was.

I can hear Didi screaming something in the background.

So what's happening with you? says Rebecca.

Finally I get rid of Rebecca and apologize to Dean. He says it's okay and maybe we should get some sleep. What a wacky idea. I tell him he better unplug the phone. Becca will call back in five minutes once she remembers what she wanted to ask me. Probably she'll want to know the name of some kid who lived next door to us fifteen years ago or something like that. Or else she'll call up from the police station or the airport or from the apartment of some drug dealer who wants to kill her, like the first time she called tonight about three hours ago—it seems like weeks.

She's like, I need to get five hundred dollars quick or I'm going to get sliced up with a knife.

And I'm like, whoa, is this a joke, or what? Nothing would surprise me coming from Rebecca, but still, this sounds a little radical.

Alison, she goes, I'm not kidding.

So I get the address and then Dean and Didi and me hop in a cab. Francesca gives us seventy dollars and Jeannie has forty. Dean gets two hundred out of his cash machine and Didi gets a hundred, which is all she has left, and then we go and wake up our friend Whitney and hit her bank. Feels kind of like old times, scraping up cash to visit Emile—except I'm really scared for Rebecca and I'm thinking about some guy cutting her up while we're waiting for the damn computer at Chase Manhattan. *¡No más!*

So we fly up to Morningside Heights and Dean tells the cab driver the faster the trip the bigger the tip and finally we get up to this street of falling-down brownstones and find the right number. Dean says he's going to go up alone and I say, no way, I'm coming too, and Didi says she doesn't want to sit outside by herself. Dean's so cool, I mean, he doesn't even know Rebecca and he might get killed, I'm real grateful and I say later on I'll show him just how grateful I can be, but right now I tell him she's my sister and I'm coming up too. Then we hassle with the taxi driver, who naturally doesn't want to hang around. In this neighborhood, he says, you get bullets through the windows. Dean gives him some huge tip and asks him to circle the block four or five times and watch for us. Then we go up.

The front door is open already, busted on the hinges. The front hall is full of beer cans and crack vials. As we walk up the stairs I can hear the vials popping under our feet, snap crackle pop, breaking like little promises. We knock at the third-floor landing. After a while some voice goes yeah and I go, it's Rebecca's sister. The guy goes, you got the money? and I say yeah and then the door opens on a chain and these eyes look out, these dark, pinwheel eyes, and the guy goes, who are all these people? So we have this big debate at the door and he says he wants to see the money and I say I want to see Rebecca and finally she comes to the door and says, let them in for Christ's sake, Mannie.

So the guy opens the door and lets us in. He's holding this knife, just kind of pointing it at us in general, but it doesn't look like he'd really know what to do with it if it came down to that. He looks scared and sheepish. He's maybe my age, small and skinny, about the size of Prince, with that same ridiculous little mustache, not bad-looking actually.

Put the stupid knife away, for Christ's sake, Rebecca says. They've brought the money. She's drinking a beer, wearing a red Danskin top, these X-rated shorts and Reeboks. She looks like she's all set for aerobics, her hair up in a ponytail. I don't know, I expected her to be tied up or something. It's kind of an anticlimax.

Dean gives the money to Becca and she gives it to this guy Mannie and he shoves it in his pocket and then folds up the knife. I don't know why but I feel sorry for him. He looks so scared and lonely on the opposite side of the room from the rest of us.

We had an agreement, he says. She owed me that money fair and square. She was here last week. I trusted her for the bread.

You told me I didn't have to pay.

That was different, Mannie says.

Different than what? Rebecca says. You just thought you'd get to fuck me.

Mannie looks down at the floor. We had an agreement, he whines.

Becca says, let's get out of here, and then in the same breath she goes, if you guys have another hundred we can get an eighth for the road. I've got one fifty.

Rebecca is totally in character.

That's a good idea, says Didi.

So I don't know, it was hard to get the story out of Rebecca. She said she met this guy last week at the China Club and he gave her a quarter ounce and his phone number, so when she goes up there to get some more he demands five hundred dollars. I don't know what to believe, I really don't. Little Mannie is apologizing like crazy as we're leaving. Then he asks Becca to please call him, almost crying. I don't know what the attraction is—drug dealers, investment bankers, she turns them all into blubbering idiots.

Did anybody else think he looked kind of like Prince? I go when we're riding back downtown.

I thought he looked like Jesus, Rebecca said.

Of course I sleep through my classes. When I finally open my eyes long enough to focus on anything it's almost two, and I vaguely remember Dean getting up and leaving for his office. I grab the channel-changer by the bed and flip on "All

My Children." When I finally get my act together and go home it's three-thirty.

I'm about to take a shower because I smell like an all-nighter, then I think I'll take a bath so I can have a faucet orgasm. After all, I didn't get any last night. A faucet orgasm is pretty much the same principle as a bidet orgasm except upside-down. When we were growing up we had bidets in all the bathrooms and when I was about ten I accidentally discovered one of the things they were good for. After that I used to spend hours on the damn thing. This dump we rent doesn't have a bidet so I have to get in the tub and slide up toward the front, running my legs up the wall on either side of the faucet. Turn on the warm water and smile. Actually, you've got to get the water temperature just right first or you could really be in for a nasty shock. I've made that mistake a few times. This time I get it just right and I come three times before I get around to actually taking a bath.

After toweling off and dosing up with some baby powder, I flop down on the bed and next thing I know I'm asleep again.

I love to sleep. My dreams are so good, sometimes when I wake up in the middle of a really good one I go right back to sleep to see if I can get back into it. Once in a while it works. I don't think most people appreciate dreams enough. They don't remember or else they try to interpret them, you know, like they aren't any good unless they have some application in real life. I think you should just take them for what they are. I mean, I love sex dreams but if I believed this psych course I took in college, then all dreams are sex dreams, which is ridiculous. Believe me, I know sex when I dream it, and I'm about the last person in the world to underestimate it, but who represses their sexual desires anymore? Nobody I know. Well, maybe we sometimes resist the urge to jump on top of some guy in the elevator or on the sidewalk. But we probably give him our phone number for later that night.

Really, though, sex isn't the only thing in life or in dreams—I can hear some of my friends who are like, unbelievable, Alison admitting sex isn't everything. I used to be a bit of a slut. But anyway, about dreams, there are dreams about flying and swimming and eating and things that you can't even describe, which is what's so great about dreaming. I hate these people who try to make everything fit some scheme. Professors and shrinks. Francesca's parents really wanted her to go to a shrink just in case there was anything wrong with her, in case they screwed up somehow, so they can feel better about it in advance of even knowing about it and feeling guilty, so she goes twice a week and sometimes when she's real bored she'll dish out some really bogus crap about her childhood or her dreams and take the shrink for a horrible ride into fantasyland. Like, gee, I had this dream where my father was smoking a big cigar and stroking my inner thigh, gosh, what do you suppose it means?

When Jeannie comes home from work and wakes me up I've been dreaming this dream where the bunch of us from last night are all sitting around Dean's apartment playing Truth or Dare. My acting coach is there too. But it turns out that Dean's apartment is actually on the stage of the Public Theater and there's this huge audience out there watching us play Truth or Dare. TRUTH OR DARE is spelled out in flashing light bulbs over the stage and my acting coach has a microphone, he's moderating the whole thing, like a TV game-show host. . . .

Jeannie's in a real pissy mood and gets right on the phone to her fiancé, so I watch "Wheel of Fortune" in the bedroom. When she's finally finished discussing world literature and nuclear disarmament with Frank she hangs up and calls the deli to order some Diet Coke and a large bag of barbecue potato chips and a pack of Merit Ultra Lights. I stick my head out the door because I want to order a pack of cigarettes myself but she's already hung up. She picks up a copy of *Cosmo* and shuffles back and forth through the pages like they're playing cards that she's trying to seriously injure in the process. I think she's mad at me.

So I go back in the bedroom and call Dean and get his machine. I leave a message that's cheerier than I feel and then I call Carol, my little sister, but there's no answer. And then, like an optimist, I call Dad but of course there's no answer there. I'm such a sucker—every time I dial him I can't help getting this little tingle of hope. It's a miracle if I can even find him, but I sort of fantasize that he'll pick up the phone some day and say, is that you, Alison? I love you, honey, and I'm really sorry about the last fifteen years or so, I don't know what came over me but I'm better now and I'm so sorry. . . .

Jeannie picks up the phone in the other room while it's still ringing and says, oh, excuse me, really bitchy, and then slams it down.

There's no answer, anyway. After I hang up Jeannie calls up Alex, my old squeeze, it doesn't take long to figure this out because she keeps repeating his name and laughing real loud so I'll know who it is and what a great time she's having talking to my old boyfriend.

A few minutes after she hangs up Jeannie finally comes

in and sits down on the bed, viciously crunching away on her potato chips. I hate to see her expending so much energy on getting me to notice that she's not a happy unit, so I say to her, are you mad at me? I remember as I say it that Dean asked me that same question about twelve hours ago.

Who, me? she says, with a big fake look of horror. Mad at you? Why should I be mad at you? Just because you accused me in public of wanting to sleep with your boyfriend, is that any reason for me to be mad at you?

I bet Jeannie's been rehearsing those lines all day.

Well, don't you? I say.

No, I don't. For one thing I don't find him irresistible, no offense, and for another thing he's your boyfriend and some of us are loyal to our friends.

Well, I'm sorry, I say, I guess I was wrong. And I feel kind of guilty when she says loyal to our friends because I have been awfully hard on her lately, I don't know what's wrong with me, I love Jeannie.

And Jeannie goes what? The infallible Alison? Wrong? Impossible. God, I hate George Michael, she says, watching his video on MTV.

I could say, well, that's what channel-changers are for, babe, but instead I say, I don't trust men whose last names sound like first names.

Jeannie says, I don't trust men, period.

Well, at least it's not just me she's mad at. I ask her if there's trouble with Frank and she launches into this thing about how Frank suddenly told her he can't come up for the weekend which was the plan because supposedly the other tennis pro suddenly came down with a sick grandmother and he has to cover all weekend. I'm like, sick grandmother? give me a break. Or maybe the dog ate his homework, right? And not only can't he come up but he'll also be too busy to see her, she really wouldn't have a good time down there blah blah blah and Jeannie, not real surprisingly, isn't sure she believes him. She thinks something's rotten on the island of Hilton Head.

So I do my bit. Come on, I tell her, he's probably telling the truth, she should trust him, she's going to marry the guy and trust is the basis of marriage and she can always wake up really early Saturday morning and call him if she thinks he might be slipping around, see if he's actually home and if he sounds guilty. Or if she really wants to do a serious bedcheck she could fly down unannounced.

She says that's a great idea, it cheers her up, she decides to go for it and surprise dear old Frankie. She hugs me and I hug her back. She calls up the airline and reserves for an 8:00 A.M. flight.

You going to be able to wake up for that one? I say.

I may just stay awake, she says. God, this is great, I should be able to get to his apartment by ten, which is plenty of time.

She's dying to catch Frank in the act. It's nice to see her smiling again, but what a smile, all teeth and gums, like a piranha. She calls the limo service and books a car to pick her up Saturday morning.

Alison, she goes, you're a genius.

All this boyfriend stuff makes me think of Dean. I call him and get the machine again. This time I leave a really neutral message asking him to call me when he gets in, very demure and ladylike. That's me.

Jeannie and I talk for a while about what dickheads men are and then we watch some dumb TV movie, as if there's any other kind, I couldn't begin to tell you what it's all about because my concentration is shot, I'm thinking about Dean, wondering where he is. It's after nine so he's probably at dinner somewhere. I remember he said he likes Indochine so I call up there but they say he's not there. I try to remember the name of his old girlfriend. I could just call and hang up if he answered. . . .

Then I think, what am I doing? This isn't me. This is somebody else. I've been in lust for three days and I'm acting like a jealous wife. I can't believe this. I mean, I love men in general, I'm a huge fan, but I'm never going to make a fool out of myself over any one in particular. Not after Alex. So what's my problem? Maybe I'm just going to have to give up on old Dean right now. I don't need this emotional stuff in my life. I've got my acting, I've got my sanity.

Then I remember he said he'd call. So I'll probably hear from him, right? It reminds me of that song, if the phone doesn't ring you'll know that it's me. I try to concentrate on the so-called movie, Richard fucking Chamberlain looking soulful in his beard as per usual, exotic locations, I can't even begin to figure out what's going on, goddamn him it's almost eleven o'clock. I can imagine Dean looking like Richard Chamberlain in about twenty years. . . .

Settle down, says Jeannie after I accidentally spill the ashtray all over the covers. So I tell her about why I'm so bugged and she tells me don't worry, he's probably got some business dinner or something.

* * *

At two-thirty Jeannie's sound asleep and I'm still staring at the TV set, wide awake with no help from artificial stimulants and no hope of artificial depressants. I absolutely cannot miss class again tomorrow. I get up and look in the medicine cabinet. Midol, Tylenol, a lot of other useless shit. I find a couple of Unisoms inside an old Halcyon prescription and take one. Back in bed, I think about calling. Should I act mad? Just a little hurt, maybe? Should I be cool and not even call? That's what I should do. It would be uncool to call. But right now I can't even sleep.

The phone rings and I practically break Jeannie's nose grabbing for it. Jeannie goes, mumble mumble growl snore.

Rebecca says, hi, sis.

What? I go.

I just remembered what I wanted to ask you, she says.

Where are you, I ask.

She says, me and Didi are at some guy's apartment.

So what did you want to ask? I say.

She goes, you remember that nursery rhyme we used to say in school, I'm trying to remember the words.

Rebecca, I go, there were only about five hundred nursery rhymes we used to say.

This is the one about Miss Mary Mack, she says.

Oh, right, I go. Miss Mary Mack Mack Mack all dressed in black black black with silver buttons buttons buttons all down her back back back . . .

Yeah, she says, that's it. How does the rest of it go?

I'm like, that's all I can remember right now.

Are you sure? she says.

I don't know, I say, not right now.

I hate to admit it, but it's actually bugging me that I can't remember the rest.

Try and remember, she says, I'll call back later.

And I'm like, no way, don't call back, I've got class tomorrow. How's Didi? I ask.

She's out of her mind, Rebecca says. Completely insane.

I go, so what else is new?

She's got a drug problem, says Rebecca.

Which is pretty funny coming from her. Didi says the same thing about Rebecca. People who are really fucked up love having somebody who they can think is a little farther out on the limb.

After I hang up I call Dean and get the machine with his boring message.

Goddamnit, now I'm really mad. Still, if I show I'm mad he might just get really turned off and think, what right does she have, I've only known her three days. What I really am is mad at myself. He doesn't owe me shit, it's not like we have a relationship. God, I hate that word, it's the death sentence for fun. Like, now we're having a relationship, how should we act? It's almost as bad as marriage. Once you say those words you get rules and definitions and you start losing track of your feelings and then they die. It's like, as soon as *Time* magazine comes up with a name for something you know it's already not happening anymore, it's already over.

Why the hell should sex get all mixed up with emotions? Forget it. It's just skin rubbing against skin in the night. It's just contact. There's no need to get all soppy about it afterwards. Fuck Dean. Who needs it?

I mean, why does stimulation always lead to aggravation? Explain that to me, will you please?

I must've fallen asleep at some point because eventually I wake up. Jeannie's at work. I'm on my way out the door to class when I get a call from this guy Brad I met in L.A. He's in New York and wonders what I'm doing tonight. He's pretty cute, I remember. I think.

I don't know, I go, make me an offer.

He says how about theater and dinner, and I figure why not, it's Friday noon and I'm not the kind of girl who spends Friday night waiting by the phone, I'm sorry but there's no way, not for all the Deans in the world. So I say sure and he says he'll pick me up at seven-thirty.

So it's seven-fifteen and I'm trying to figure out what to wear, I have absolutely no clothes, when dickhead, my true love, calls. Just perfect.

Hey, he goes, it's Dean.

Could you spell that for me? I say.

Sorry I didn't get back to you last night, he says. I had a business dinner that ran late.

Yeah, I go. I put a lot of spin on it.

What are you doing tonight? he goes.

I'm like, I've got a date.

He sounds pretty surprised. I tell him I'm a popular girl, he should book in advance. He asks about tomorrow and I say it's possible, and then he says he'll let me go. He sounds so sad I'm practically crying by the time I hang up. I think about calling and canceling Brad, but it's too late, in fact the buzzer rings and I'm still half naked and I haven't even started my makeup.

We go to this play, *Liaisons Dangereuses,* it's all about French people cooking up these sexual conspiracies, it's not the sex they like so much as the planning and scheming to corrupt virgins and housewives, it's all mental, but the worst guy of them all, the hero of the play, falls in love in spite of himself with this woman he's trying to seduce on a bet and it really fucks him up.

Hey, tell me about it.

The play's fine, I enjoy it, but it turns out Brad is a totally different guy than the guy I was thinking of, he's not so cute and afterwards he has to drag us backstage to say hello to one of the actresses who's this great friend of his, and after we finally get back there and wait for all the other great friends of hers to have their little chat Brad goes, hi, Bradley Stone, and when that doesn't bring the house down—I mean, she looks at him like he's Chinese or something—he goes, we met at Morton's with Carol and Rick, and it's obvious she doesn't have a clue who he is. And then he has to drag me into this mess just to spread the embarrassment around and he goes, this is Alison Poole, she's an actress herself. . . .

I don't even want to talk about it. I wanted to just disappear, I would have gladly melted into a puddle right there at her feet like the wicked witch in *The Wizard of Oz,* leaving nothing behind but some goo and this sapphire brooch I borrowed from Jeannie that I have to hold on to because it keeps coming undone. I don't know, he meant well, but there comes a point sometimes when you know you're in dating hell, when you've just got to grit your teeth and get through it, and I knew this was going to be one of those nights. I wasn't into it anyway, I kept thinking about Dean, but I thought I owed it to Brad to make the effort to act pleasant.

Then we go to the Four Seasons where Brad makes a big stink about getting a fountainside table, and he keeps repeating his name like it's a household word. Dinner lasts for three or four decades, I don't know, Brad's basically telling me all about how the entertainment industry would grind to a halt if anything happened to him, God forbid. That's sort of the moral of every story. This guy's a legend in his own mind.

Plus I freak out when I feel on my lapel for the sapphire brooch and it's not there, but amazingly it turns up under the table, the fastener thing that holds the pin part of it is really loose, I'm like—gasp, the thing is only worth ten years' rent, so I just hold it in my hand and squeeze hard when I think I'm going to fall asleep from boredom.

Finally he pays the check and wants to go to Nell's and I tell him I've got to be up early which is not necessarily a lie since I'll probably have to shake Jeannie awake at dawn to get her flight, she sleeps like a corpse.

Anyway, Brad gets all pissed off. Just one drink, he goes.

And I'm like, Jesus, I've heard that line before but I don't say it, I just smile demurely and say it's way past my bedtime.

He just happens to pick this moment to tell me he has tickets to the U2 concert at the Meadowlands tomorrow night. And I go, I still have to head home.

At the door of my apartment it's thanks for everything,

Brad. When he realizes I'm not going to invite him up, he goes, I think it's pretty rude after I've taken you to the theater and a pretty spectacular dinner to just . . .

To just what? I say after this long pause. He stopped when he realized what he was about to say. I go, do you mean it's pretty rude to just run off without putting out? You expect a return on your investment, is that it?

That's a very crude way of putting it, he says.

Am I wrong? I go.

I don't really mind that he's not the guy I thought he was or that he has more hair on the back of his hands than on his head or even that he's wearing this big tacky Rolex President, but there isn't a bed in the world that's big enough for me and his ego both.

You liked me in L.A., he says.

But I'm sober now, I go.

He pins me back against the door. I know you want me, he says.

I'm like, I don't believe this shit.

You want me, I can tell.

This is great, it's like, so typical, girls always think they're less attractive than they actually are and guys always think they're more attractive. I didn't want to say anything before, but really, this Bradley is a toad. He'd have to be really rich or really powerful or really famous to look even halfway decent. And even then . . .

Come on, I know you want to, he's going.

How can you tell? I go. I'm dying to know.

I know women, he says. I go, right, like I know Swahili. He's got me pinned against the door and then he latches on to me with his horrible bony little mouth, I mean you could get paper cuts from this guy's lips and I don't even want to mention his tongue, we're talking reptile, it reminds me of this diagram I saw once in a magazine about these lamprey eels that glom on to salmon and suck their insides out. Meanwhile he's trying to force my legs apart with his knee, I can't believe the nerve of this guy, it would almost be funny if it wasn't so disgusting, but luckily I've still got Jeannie's brooch in my hand. I open it up and sink the pin into Bradley's butt. He screams and jumps back like I'm on fire and while he's trying to figure out what happened I slip in the door and run upstairs.

I call Dean and get his machine.

I know how I'm going to get rich, I'm going to invent a device that will destroy answering machines over the phone—you just push a button and boom, the thing blows up.

I vaguely remember hearing Jeannie come and go early in the morning. A little after noon she calls me up from Hilton Head.

Sure enough, she walked in on Frank and some bimbo in bed. Everything that wasn't nailed down she threw at them. Then she went after them with a tennis racket. When Frank's new honey ran out into the hall naked Jeannie put her clothes in the trash compactor and compacted them into all the beer cans and watermelon rinds. This nice little Ralph Lauren ensemble, right? There was a champagne bottle next to the bed left over from Frank's big romantic evening and Jeannie clubbed him over the head with it. He was bleeding pretty nicely when she left and now she's at the airport coming back home. I get her flight information and tell her I'll meet her at the airport.

Before I leave I call up Dean and he answers. I explain about Jeannie and tell him I'll have to cancel. She's going to need me tonight, I go.

Hey, I understand, he says.

She's really hurt, I go, she's been screwed over. I know it's not rational but it's like I'm blaming Dean, maybe because he's a man, maybe because he was out when I called last night.

Give her a hug for me, he says.

And I'm like, what's that supposed to mean, honey pie?

And he goes, just a friendly sympathetic kind of hug. On second thought, he says, why don't you make that a nasty, frigid kind of hug.

So how was your night last night? I go.

Group sex and intravenous drugs, he says. Nothing special.

Special enough to keep you out past two-thirty, I think, because that was the last time I called before I finally fell asleep, but for a change I decide to keep my mouth shut. Right now my main concern is Jeannie. I want to be there for her because she'll be there for me when Dean and his replacement and the guy after that are all history. Ancient history.

6

TWO LIES

'm supposed to be on a beach again, imagining intense heat and sunlight. St. Bart's or maybe Southampton. The smell of salt and cocoa butter, the gritty feeling of a sandy towel. A really great method actress, I suppose, could get a tan this way, projecting herself into a memory of a beach. Then you'd know you were pretty good, I guess. But I can't even work up a sweat right now, at this particular moment. It's a Friday afternoon and I'm in class, trying to do sense-memory. My concentration's shot. I'm thinking about Dean. I'm heavy in lust.

Last night we finally got to do it. We went to a movie, then dinner. Couldn't keep my hands off him.

For some reason I was afraid it wouldn't be very good. I mean, I hate these big dramatic buildups, they usually let you down. Patience has never been my middle name, I mean I got my first credit card when I was about twelve, and if I can't have something right away I generally forget about it. But this, I don't know . . .

I wanted to crawl inside of him and stay there. I wanted to disappear down his throat. I wanted to take all of him all the way up inside me.

Trouble is, this isn't doing my acting any good. My instrument is all out of tune here. I keep thinking about Dean running his tongue up and down me, vibrations going right off the Richter scale, instead of about the hot sun on this stupid imaginary beach. If only the assignment called for a sense-memory of outrageously good all-night sex I'd be made in the shade.

I'm not sure why it was so good—we didn't do anything really special. No video cameras, costumes, equipment or special effects. Just good old-fashioned sex, like the kind Mom used to make.

Rob walks by my chair and says, you're not giving me anything, Alison. He gave me this assignment because last time I flipped out before I could get into it.

How about if I do something with sex? I say.

He lets out this big sigh and goes, you're going to make a great porn star someday.

What do mean, someday? I say.

Alex and I used to make videos of ourselves. It was pretty outrageous, but definitely a turn-on. I don't know, I suppose some people would think that's weird. I guess it is. With my luck the tapes will turn up just when I'm about to win the Academy Award or something.

The teacher goes, get back to the beach, Alison. See if you can keep your mind out of the bedroom for just a few hours.

So I make like Annette Funicello. I start with the memory of the smell of Bain de Soleil Number 4, remember the feel of the hot sun, skin getting really hot, hands rubbing Bain de Soleil all over my body. . . .

After class I call Dean.

Hey, big boy, I say.

Hello, beautiful, he goes. I made a terrific trade today.

It must be all that good loving, I say.

I guess you inspired me, he goes. I made two hundred thousand before lunch.

I'm like, do I get half?

Actually I made it for a client, he says.

I go, tell him I deserve a commission at least.

I'll give you a big commission, he goes.

I'm like, how big?

We're both driveling idiots. We sort of drool and baby-talk for a while, then I tell him I'm going to tan, then shower and dress and he says he'll pick me up around nine.

When I get home Jeannie says, Alison, I've got to tell you something.

I'm like, if it's bad news I don't want to hear it. I'm too happy.

You want a line? she says. She's definitely wired.

No thanks, I say.

Poor Jeannie, she's really wiped out over this Frank

thing. He's tried to call but she won't pick up the phone and she won't let me tell him when she's here.

So what's up? I go.

We got an eviction notice, she goes.

I'm like, I thought you said you'd cover me this month.

Yeah, she goes, but we owe three months.

Are you crazy? I go. I gave you my half for the other months.

What are we going to do? Jeannie says.

What do you mean, what are we going to do? What happened to the money?

Jeannie starts to sob. Oh, Alison, she goes. I'm sorry. Please don't hate me.

Get this, it turns out that Jeannie's been taking the money I've been giving her and her father's been giving her and spending it before she manages to pass it on to the landlord. There was this Chanel skirt she had to have, it's only like eighteen hundred bucks, and she's been flying first class down to South Carolina, and then she reminds me I participated in consuming that quarter ounce she bought a few weeks ago and there have been some eighths here and some grams there since then, just to keep her going. A new set of golf clubs for Frank's birthday—that was a real good investment. One thing and another.

So get the money from your father, I say.

I can't, she goes. He'll kill me. What about Dean? she says.

Right, I say. I'm going to hit up this guy I just met two weeks ago for five thousand dollars? Think again, babe.

What are we going to do? Jeannie says as she bends over the mirror and snorts a big line.

I'm going out to do the town with Dean, I say. Then Dean's going to do me. The question is, what are *you* going to do?

That sounds harsh, but I mean, *really.*

Dean has tickets for this hot play but first he takes me to Petaluma for a drink. The waiter's Mike from my acting class, he tells me that Didi showed up at closing time last night, really fucked up.

She was probably just waking up, I say. She's not really good till after midnight.

Girl has a problem, Dean says.

The play is *Fences,* I've been wanting to see it all spring and I'm definitely not disappointed. It's basically about how a father can screw up the life of his kid and I'm like, absolutely.

There's this one incredible scene where James Earl Jones's son spits in his face. My acting teacher told us that at rehearsals for the play the guy who was playing the son couldn't bring himself to spit in James Earl Jones's face so the director started to insult him and spit in *his* face and tell him that James Earl Jones was nothing special. Right. That guy's so powerful he's like the ultimate father where you can't tell if he's God or Satan or what, and when the boy spits in his face you think lightning's going to come down and zap the kid into ashes. Afterwards Dean keeps talking about the structure and character development and I wish he'd shut up, I'm just thinking about that moment.

* * *

After the play we go to Nell's. I'm looking forward to show-ing up with Dean, making it sort of official, you know, like—here we are, everybody. Okay, so I'm an exhibitionist. Of course, it could be dangerous. On any given night there could be eight or ten of my old flames slipping around in there.

My friend Whitney is working the door. Whitney was like Phi Beta Kappa at some Ivy League school, she was really straight, studied all the time and then she went to Columbia Law School but one night Francesca introduced her to this guy in Elvis Costello's band and she disappeared for about two weeks and now she works the door and does some modeling on the side. She has two big guys with her. She points to people and the boys pull back the rope to let them pass. There are about fifty people waiting. I feel bad walking right in, but what can you do? Okay, that's not true, I feel good. It's a mean old world, right?

Whitney checks Dean out, winks at me and goes, not bad.

It's pretty crowded inside, considering it's only mid-night, but we get a table. A guy comes over and gives Dean a big hug and Dean goes, Alison, this is Phil, Didi's cousin. Phil's a big, athletic-looking guy. He's wearing a black T-shirt so you can see he's got this great young body but his face looks ten years older than the rest of him, like forty or something. He's got crow's-feet, wrinkles, skin that looks like it's seen a lot of wind from high-speed living.

And Phil goes, so you're a friend of Didi's. How is she? I haven't seen her in ages.

I look at Dean and he looks at me and we're both like, what do you want, the truth?

So I go, to tell you the truth I'm kind of worried about her.

What's the matter, Phil says, she looking for AIDS in all the right places?

You know how you don't like some people right away? Well, I don't know why but immediately I can't stand this Phillip.

She's been doing huge amounts of blow, I say. Every night, all night. She's got a real problem, I tell him.

Didi? he says, as if he doesn't believe me. Little Didi? I've seen her do a few lines but I can't imagine she'd really go crazy with it. What exactly are we talking about here? Because you're talking to somebody who ended up in detox for three months.

I'm like, good for you. I'm really impressed that you were such a major-league fuck-up.

Dean jumps in, he's such a diplomat, can't seem to stand unpleasantness between people, that's one of his big problems, he'd rather be pleasant than honest, I guess he didn't grow up like me where people were screaming and throwing cutlery at each other. Anyway, he goes, I've got to say I agree with Alison. Didi is pretty strung out.

Well, he goes, I'll check into it.

Hey, don't do us any favors. I'm really mad at myself for saying anything to this guy, and if he hadn't really pissed me off I would've made a joke out of it, but now I feel like I've betrayed Didi or something.

Phil makes like a tree, which is good because I could feel a major battle coming on. What an asshole, I say. What does he do besides aggravate people?

He's a stockbroker, Dean says. Relax, he says, and orders a bottle of champagne from the waitress with the soup-bowl haircut. I don't know, these downtown artsy coifs may get attention, but not necessarily the right kind. I don't think most guys are too keen on running their fingers through a fashion statement.

Anyway, suddenly I get a little tingle of tornado warning, like the air pressure drops radically around our table and sure enough a familiar voice screams *Alison* from a few yards away, then Francesca drops into the seat next to me, a natural freaking phenomenon—is that the word?—in green sequins and red beads. She's wearing this button over her tit that says THE DESSERT CART STOPS HERE.

I love Francesca, she's about the only person I know who has a sense of humor about herself.

My God, I'm so glad to see you guys, she goes, there's absolutely no one important or interesting here tonight, I was just getting ready to leave. Somebody told me Bono was here but I didn't see him. Hello, Dean darling, you're looking completely edible tonight. I'm absolutely starved. We went to some horrible Thai restaurant that just got a great review in the *Times*, me and Trey Burton and a bunch of other people and the restaurant had no bread. I told the waiter it's the fucking staff of life for Christ's sake. Can you believe it?

Rather ethnocentric of you, Dean goes.

You filthy boy, Francesca says, wash your mouth out with soap. She pauses to take a breath and do a quick surveillance of the room. Francesca is like one of those cartoon characters, I swear she can swivel her head three hundred and sixty degrees when she wants to see who's around.

Dean goes, so what are Mick and Jerry doing tonight, Francesca? I heard they were having a big party.

I take back all the nice things I said about you earlier tonight, she tells him. You're a jerk. When I have a party I'm leaving your name off the list.

Then just for good measure she turns on me and says, Alison, you're actually wearing a skirt and heels for a change. Did someone steal all your sneakers and sweatshirts?

It's true, I've got a little black leather skirt on, black silk top and decent heels.

And Cesca's like, you almost look like a grown woman. The way you usually dress, I mean, Dean may be a jerk, but unless he's really rotten in bed he deserves better than that.

He's fanfuckingtastic in bed, I say.

Go ahead, Cesca goes, depress me.

Have some champagne, says Dean.

And Francesca says, I don't drink, alcohol's got zillions of calories. Literally zillions. Later for you guys. I'm going home to try and scrape my makeup off. That's one way to lose five pounds quick and if I'm lucky it'll only take a couple of hours.

She kisses Dean, then me, then like a big green cruise ship she casts off her lines and steams away, blowing a kiss.

Speaking of weight, Dean says, there's no way you're a 34-B. He's wearing his extraspecial shit-eating grin, the one that he gets after a blow job.

What? I say.

And he goes, bra size.

How do you know what size I wear? I go.

He goes, I looked this morning before you woke up. You've got to be about three sizes bigger than that, he says.

I tell him, you don't know what it's like walking down the streets of New York alone with your tits. So I wear really small bras. It hides 'em. I can't believe you looked at my bra while I was asleep. You're weird, I say.

Dean and I are just getting kissy when suddenly out of the corner of my eye I see somebody ooze up out of the crowd and this familiar oily voice goes, Dean, how the hell are you?

Dean looks a little queasy, but I love it. I'm really glad to see Skip at this particular moment. I'm like, Skip, what a wonderful surprise. What an honor. I mean, gee, the great Skip Pendleton. Would you care to join our humble table?

Skip isn't exactly thrilled to see me, I don't think he realized who it was with her tongue down Dean's throat. But Mr. Polite takes a seat and tries to make the best of it. Dean's squirmy, but he offers Skip a glass of champagne and Skip says great! with this big fake heartiness. Men are so stuck inside these codes of behavior, they're like musicians who only know three chords. Emotionally they're punks. Dean and Skip are both playing at being good sports right now while mentally they're circling around each other like attack dogs. Skip's mind is going, I pissed here, this is my territory, how dare you piss here? And Dean's really upset because Skip got here first. So what does that make me, guys, the fire hydrant?

How are you, Alison? Skip says.

Never better, I say, looking at Dean.

Will you guys excuse me for a minute? Dean says. He heads downstairs. I don't know, maybe he's being nice and giving us a chance to make our separate peace or something, or else he's uncomfortable with the situation and can't deal with it. Or maybe he just has to take a leak.

You going out with Dean? Skip asks.

Yeah, I am, I say. He's great.

That's good, Skip says. I'm glad.

I'm thinking, sure you are, Skip, and then he waves to somebody on the other end of the room. He's always got his eye on the next thing, always checking to see if something better isn't just around the corner. He's ten times worse than Cesca. The only way to keep Skip's attention is to talk about him.

So Dean must've told you about the great time we had the other night, he says.

And like an idiot I go, when was this? I could've kicked myself as soon as I said it. Now Skip's got me. Whatever he tells me, he's going to know I didn't know it before. I hate to have him get the satisfaction of telling me anything about Dean.

It was wild, Skip goes. I think it was Thursday. I ran into Dean here about one. Neither of us was feeling any pain by that time, but we had a couple of bottles of champagne and then we went with our dates down to Automatic Slims. Had a great time.

I hear *our dates* and I know that was the whole point of the story but I'm not going to bite, I won't give Skip the satisfaction. He's going to tell me anyway. Thursday was the night I kept calling Dean and getting his machine. I woke up at ten and called and the machine was still on. He told me he'd been at a business dinner.

Skip's going, you know Cassie Hane, don't you? Nice

girl. Model. Not exactly a rocket scientist, but she's a lot of fun. I know Dean isn't really serious about her, though. Obviously he's a lot more interested in you.

I'm thinking, excuse me, Skip, but would you mind, like, stepping into an open elevator shaft on a high floor for just a second? I'm wondering if he suspects he got burned on the abortion deal. Or does he just think like three-quarters of the men in the world that any girl who sleeps with him should go to a nunnery afterwards and cherish the memory, or throw herself on a fire, or declare her vagina a national historic landmark and seal up the secret passageway forever after.

Anyway, he's out for revenge and he scored. He knows it, too. I'm so pissed at Dean I could cut his dick off. Not because he went out with this bimbo and probably screwed her. I'm mad because he lied and put me in a position where Skip could humiliate me.

My party's over at the front booth, Skip says. I really should rejoin them. Great to see you, Alison. Give a call sometime.

He winks in a way that makes me think he's serious. Probably he sees me as desirable again, now that Dean wants me.

This was definitely Thursday night? I ask.

I've already lost this round so I might as well get the information I need.

Let me think, Skip goes. Yeah, definitely Thursday, I had my tennis game the next day and I remember being hung over.

As soon as Skip clears out this guy Chuck Harnist sits

down and starts hitting on me. Like an idiot I slept with him one night so now he thinks I can stand the sight of him. Not that he's bad-looking, he could practically stand in for Tom Cruise, but when he opens his mouth he makes you wish you carried a roll of electrical tape in your purse. He's telling me about some stupid project supposedly in development with Paramount, like I could care less. Chuck's supposedly a screenwriter. He's one of these people who's always talking about deals, he's made a deal here and he's negotiating a deal there, but after you've known him a while you realize these deals are like a daisy chain where nobody ever actually has an orgasm, it's just a lot of lubricated friction. You sell an idea to a producer and he sells it to a studio and then the idea changes and then the studio changes and nothing ever happens except a lot of checks get written. Yada yada yada. Chuck has bored me to tears with this stuff a bunch of nights. Unfortunately, the last time it happened I was at his apartment when the drugs ran out and I was too lazy to go home, but if Chuck thinks I want to repeat the mistake he's out of his mind. I mean, it wasn't that good, honey. Frankly, I've seen bigger matchsticks.

So Chuck's yammering away and I'm thinking about how pissed off I am at Dean when suddenly I think, shit, where is he? Maybe he got really pissed off when Skip came over and actually left the premises. Or else he saw me talking with Chuck. He's kind of the jealous type, which is something I don't have much time for. I mean, what's the point? It's a lot of wasted energy, and my feeling when I'm out with a guy and I see some other girl hitting on him is like, great, if you can get him out the door, you can have him, I don't care. But first you've got to get him out the door, honey.

So I'm like looking around and thinking I better get rid of Chuck so Dean won't get all jealous on me and then I'm like, what's wrong with you, Alison? What do you care what that liar thinks? Dean's an asshole. Let him slink away on his belly like a snake. Good riddance.

Basically it's just that I don't want to be robbed of seeing the look on his face when I catch him up with his own lies. He can take a cab straight to hell as far as I'm concerned—I don't have to be lonely tonight, there's about eighteen guys here who would take me home in a minute. But I do want him to know that I know what a shithead he is.

Fucking Cassie Hane! That bimbo. That really pisses me off, I consider it a personal insult that I'd be placed in the same category as Cassie. A real smart girl, she's only a little less articulate than Sylvester Stallone. I mean, if he's going to fuck other women, fine, I don't mind, really I don't, but they better be at least in the as-wonderful-as-I-am category or how could he even consider it? Obviously the guy has no taste. That's what really gets me. If he thinks she's worth the price of dinner, how can he truly appreciate me?

Then I see him coming back across the room. I introduce him to Chuck and ask if he's ready to go and he says, sure, if you are. So I give Chuck this huge kiss for Dean's benefit, I can see him wince a little, he doesn't like that at all. You just wait, honey. Dean doesn't mind leaving early, though, because he thinks he's getting nooky. Dream on, babe. You wish. In the cab he kisses me and I let him. He tells me about some people he ran into on his way to the bathroom.

Back at his place he asks if I want a drink and I say no and he winks and goes, bed? and I'm like, sure, that sounds cool. Of course, there's bed and then there's bed, right? Like—you've made your bed, now lie in it.

When I come out of the bathroom he's lying between the sheets with his clothes piled on the floor. I turn on the TV and climb in with all my clothes on. He watches the last few minutes of Letterman with me but I can feel him getting restless over on his side. He clamps a hand on my thigh. Very subtle. When I start switching the channels he rolls toward me and starts kissing my neck and chewing on my earlobe, rubbing his crotch up against my hip. There's nothing sillier than a hard-on with no place to go.

I find an evangelical show. Brothers and sisters, Jesus loves you, blah blah blah. One of my mom's redneck boyfriends took us to one these things when I was eleven. He was a landscaper during the day and a stud at night and on Sundays he went to these religious revival meetings and blubbered about Jesus while this geek preacher healed everybody, casting out devils and throwing away crutches, shit flying all over the place. Eleven years old and even then I knew it was all a crock. This preacher was an amateur, I mean, give me a break, starting with my father I'd grown up around a better class of liar and cheater and con artist than this cracker. I've been lied to by the best.

Which reminds me. I suddenly go to Dean, he's kind of whimpering on his side of the bed, hey, I go, what are the three greatest lies in the world?

Is this a joke? he goes. He's definitely not into it. He's into getting into me.

But I'm like, no, not really. It's just kind of an old

proverb or something. You know. You're an expert on this subject. (This goes right past him.) One, the check's in the mail. Two, I promise I won't come in your mouth, and what's the third?

I forget, Dean says. I don't think he's trying very hard to remember. His eyes are glazing over. If you look closely you can see his IQ falling by the second. All the blood's draining out of his brain, headed south. Pretty soon he won't remember his own name. He's working his hand up the inside of my sweatshirt.

It's really bugging me what the third greatest lie is, but in the meantime I switch the channel to "Star Trek." Dean works his hand up under my bra strap and slides his hand in.

So tell me about Thursday night, I go.

The hand stops moving. Thursday night? he goes.

Thursday night, I say.

Was that the night I had a business dinner? he goes.

And I go, I don't know. Was it? You tell me.

I'm not sure, he goes.

And I'm like, maybe we should call Cassie Hane and ask her.

He lets out a big sigh.

Coming back to you now? I go.

He nods real slow and dramatic, as if he's a man who's been carrying this huge secret around with him for many long years through the rain and the snow and had bamboo shoots stuck up his fingernails by people trying to get this information from him but he didn't crack—and now that it's finally out there's nothing he can do about it so he's kind of glad to be relieved of the burden. I'm beginning to think it's Dean who should be the actor.

I say, why did you lie to me?

He's like, I don't know. I didn't want to hurt your feelings.

They're hurt now, I go.

I just . . . I made this date before I met you, he goes. I didn't want to blow her off.

You're a real sweet guy, I say, not wanting to hurt anybody's feelings. You're a real saint, aren't you?

I'm sorry, he goes. I guess I should've told you.

You shouldn't have lied about it, I go. I told you that's the one thing I can't stand. I'll be out the door so fast your head will spin. If you want to go out with other girls, fine. If you want to screw them, fine. But don't ever lie to me. Okay?

Okay, he says.

And wear a goddamn rubber, I say. I don't want to die from anything that comes via Cassie Hane.

We lie quietly on the bed, both on our backs looking up at the ceiling. It's the loneliest sight in the world.

Did you fuck her? I say. This time I turn and look into his eyes.

No, he says. He doesn't blink.

I don't believe you, I say.

It's true, he says.

I go, I'm not going to get mad at you. Believe me. I just want you to tell me the truth.

I just told you, he says.

You're lying again, I go.

No I'm not, he says.

Why didn't you fuck her? I say. Didn't she want to?

I didn't want to, he goes. I was thinking of you.

Well, you can forget about me for tonight, I say. Getting lied to turns me off.

I'm sorry, he mumbles.

I go, sorry for doing it or sorry for lying?

Both, he says.

So we do this manic depressive routine side by side in bed, both of us lying there like dummies for a while until we both start tossing and turning and yanking the sheets away from each other. Part of my problem is that I'm actually kind of horny. He got to my nipples before I let loose with the stuff about Cassie Hane. Finally I reach over and rub his hip, then feel for his cock, which gets hard in about three seconds, so I climb on top of him, slip it inside me. I hate to admit this but it feels good.

This isn't for you, I go, this is just for me. I'm still mad. I'm just horny.

He's not complaining. Dean may be a liar but he's not stupid.

7

JUST CONTACT

Amazing, I wake up before Dean, drag ass into the kitchen and find some oranges in the fridge, an electric squeezer on the counter. Back in the bedroom I climb up and sit on Dean's chest. I take a big drink of OJ, then lean over and dribble a little on his face. His eyes flutter open. This boy looks scared. Guilty conscience, I'd say.

Did you fuck Cassie Hane? I go.

He's freaked. He turns his head both ways, then tries to sit up, but I've got him pinned.

I want the truth, I say. Did you fuck Cassie Hane?

Alison, he pleads. I guess he finally recognizes me. Was it the face or the tits, I wonder.

Did you? I go.

Yes, he says, I did. He looks away.

Thank you, I say, climbing down off him. Thank you for finally telling the truth.

I go in the bathroom and take a shower. The shithead has all the latest shampoos and conditioners, I'm beginning to think dickface is a little teensy bit vain. I went out with this male model once, the guy had more Chanel makeup than I do, that was creepy. Most guys' bathrooms *are* strange, though, even when they're disgusting they have a sort of impersonal, unlived-in feeling.

Some kind of weird black soap that stings my vagina, which is a little bit sore to begin with, granted. That will have to go. I'm an Ivory girl. If I ever decide to come back he better have my soap, plus a refrigerator stocked with my favorite beverages—Diet Coke, Amstel, Cristal. Flowers. I think Dean the liar is going to have to pay for this little adventure. Hey, don't ask me how I know, I just have this feeling.

When there's finally no hot water left I turn off the shower and use all the towels. Out in the kitchen, Dean's dressed and making coffee. He looks like the boy whose dad just got home from work to hand out the spankings.

He's got his table set with place mats and everything, a plate of bagels and Danish in the middle, little jars of English jam that he stole from some hotel, probably, the *Times* and the *Post*.

I went out while you were in the shower, he goes.

Well, isn't that special, I say, checking out Page Six real quick. I give it a lot of spin, a big shot of sarcasm.

But at least he knows who's on top around here.

I gotta go to class, I say. I'll see you around.

Will you call me? he goes.

I don't say anything, I just shrug like, if it occurs to me in the course of my incredibly busy social whirl and my active and fulfilling sex life, maybe, possibly, if I'm near a phone at the time and there's nothing good on TV.

The thing about acting is, if you're good you should be able to get all of that into a shrug. I think I did.

He's like, I'll call you.

If you want, I say.

So I go to class and knock everybody dead, I feel really great about my work, I do this scene from *Crimes of the Heart* with this girl in my class. I'm the Jessica Lange character, Meg. Rob tells me to work on my breathing and wants us to do it again next week, but he says it felt like I was inside the role. That's high praise from Rob. Then Carol—she's like a housewife from the suburbs or something—gets up and does a monologue from *Broadway Bound,* the one where the mom is talking about the history of her dining-room table. She's droning on and Rob's watching from the back of the room.

After a while Rob shouts, she's in the attic.

Carol stops midsentence, she looks like she's been slapped. She says, do you want me to go on?

Rob is like, you're not inhabiting your role.

So I'm not shy, I go, who's in the attic?

Haven't I told you that story? Rob says, even though he knows he's never told us, it's like this big mystery. So while Carol is standing up there in front of the class with tears forming in her eyes, Rob finally tells this story about how this actress—really talented, right?—married a rich guy who wanted to make her a big star so he was basically buying her the starring roles in these plays, like he would put up the money for the plays if the director would let her play the lead. So one of the roles he buys for her is Anne in *The Diary of Anne Frank.* Well, this bimbo was so bad that by the time the Gestapo came knocking on the door to take her away the one guy who was left in the theater shouts—she's in the attic!

After class I stop off to tan. Work on that golden brown look that makes the boys so hungry. Get home feeling great, pick up the mail, June *Vogue* plus postcard from an old flame who's in California now, wants me to move out there. "Remember that bench in Riverside Park? Love, Trip." Trip's all right. I don't know, some girls get love letters, me, I get lust postcards.

In the bedroom I flip on "Live at Five" to check out the news. There's an update on the garbage cruise story—this barge full of putrid gunk from Long Island that's been sailing all around the western hemisphere looking for a place to dump and big surprise, nobody wants the shit. Now it's just been turned away from New Orleans or something.

I check the messages—a worried one from Dean saying he's really sorry, he wants to see me tonight and he'll call later. I try dialing Francesca but I'm getting this weird signal, then a computer-girl voice comes on and says, we're sorry, your service has been temporarily interrupted for nonpayment and I'm like, shit, not this again, fucking Jeannie. I don't know, this happens every other month, just about, and suddenly I'm cut off from all my friends and delivery service from the deli. Trauma city. Last time it happened we moved into a room at the Plaza for a couple of days and charged it to Jeannie's dad while we waited for the check to clear, but after he got that bill he called the hotel and told them basically to shoot us on sight, or at least not let us charge to his corporate account. Between phone calls and room service I guess we did do some serious damage. Rebecca was in Paris for some reason, some guy, and we had the line open to France for most of the afternoon one time, taking turns with Becca while the other one went down to Trader Vic's for refills and all these fat out-of-town businessmen thinking we were hookers. . . .

That's part of the problem now since Jeannie's dad is really fed up and he's closed the vault. But it's like, these goddamned fathers, they give us everything for a while and then suddenly they change the rules. Like, we grow up thinking we're princesses and suddenly they're amazed that we aren't happy to live like peasants? With me it happened a while ago, Dad suddenly cut me off when I dropped out of college to come to New York, he'd been cutting down for a long time anyway, bouncing checks on me and shit like that, but Jeannie's dad just suddenly started cracking the whip a couple months ago and it's really cramping our style. Our first year in New York it was great, there were always guys around to pick up the tabs, and I'd just sold my Alfa for cash when I moved from Virginia, plus Jeannie had all the major credit cards. I admit we abused them a little. Jeannie's AmEx card was practically transparent it had been run through the little machine so many times. That was our idea of exercise, the gold-card press. Back and forth. So then her old man canceled all the plastic and cut her down to fifteen hundred a month, which is, like, what does he want her to do, start selling her body?

On top of everything else I've been thinking of tormenting Dean a little more, but suddenly the thought that I can't reach him makes me a little panicked. I mean, he can still get me, we're still getting incoming, right? But after fifteen minutes without a single call I'm thinking, shit, maybe they shut off all our service, the pricks. Dean might be trying to call now. What if it's an emergency? I could be dying of a heart attack up here or something with no way to get help.

The phone rings and I practically swallow it whole. It's Rebecca. She sounds halfway sane at the moment, she's over at the Stanhope with this guy Everett. And she's like, can you believe it, he's saying we've got to move to a cheaper hotel or something, turns out he's not so rich after all and he's spent his life's savings on me in the last three weeks. I guess it's sort of touching, but anyway, he's proposing marriage and he wants to have my children blah blah blah.

Story of Rebecca's life. What is it about men, you take a guy who's scared to death of commitment, who never makes a date more than two days in advance, you throw him in a room with Rebecca, who's probably the most unfit candidate for matrimony and motherhood on the whole eastern seaboard, I guarantee you in five minutes he'll be begging her to have his children. She's babbling on, saying, and then there's Manuel. . . .

I go, that little drug dealer that looks like Prince?

She goes, yeah, he's practically camped out in the lobby, it's really embarrassing, the doorman has to keep throwing him out and he waits for me on the sidewalk and begs me to marry him, he's quit drugs for me—can you imagine anybody quitting drugs for me, of all people? And he's quit dealing supposedly which was the only thing he had going for him in my book and now he's enrolled in some job-training program. All this so he can make a respectable woman out of me, buy a little house in Queens or something with a white picket fence. I mean, please. I told him that like ridding the planet of nuclear weapons would be a more realistic kind of goal, you know? Maybe start with that and work up. What is it with marriage this week, guys are proposing left and right, have you got the *Post* there, I should check my horoscope. Hold on, it's room service. . . .

When she finally comes back I go, Rebecca, what do you do to them?

Who? she says, her mouth full of something.

Men, I say.

Treat them like shit, she says. Everett's sitting here pouting at this very moment. . . .

Listen, I go, I really need money, have you got any?

Not really, she says, and she whistles when she hears how much.

I know she's lying, I went through her purse one night looking for cigarettes and came up with three Swiss bank-books and two more from the Cayman Islands each with like five or six thousand in her name. I don't know where she gets it—guys, I guess—but she squirrels it all away in these banks all over the place and she's always crying poor.

What about Gran's pearls, she goes. You could sell them.

I don't want to do that, I go.

I'll buy them, she says.

I thought you were broke.

I mean I'll get somebody else to buy them, she goes. I have a friend who's in the jewelry business.

I go, which end of the business, stealing or stealing?

Gran's pearls are like this issue, I got them because I was her favorite and Becca has never forgiven me. She was furious. Since Gran died she's been sucking up to Pops so she can be in his will, but it's like she has this thing about the pearls, she wants them just because I've got them and Gran died before Rebecca could win her over.

Jeannie comes home and I tell Rebecca I gotta go and she tells me to think about the pearls, it's a triple strand of flawless twelve-millimeter pearls with a handworked platinum clasp. I'm like, yeah, I'll think about it. Thanks so much for the help.

When I hang up I tell Jeannie the phone's about to be cut off again and she goes, I know, we owe thirteen hundred bucks, and I'm like, shit, that's high even for us, were you and Frank having phone sex all month? and she's like, no, we were having phone fights all month. Then her eyes get all teary and I remember this is a touchy subject. I'm supposed to be sympathetic now that Jeannie's heart is broken.

Why me? that's what I want to know.

Alison, what are we going to do? Jeannie says.

You've got to call your father, I go.

What about your grandfather? Jeannie goes. He's loaded.

She already knows I'd never ask Pops for money. One of my principles is not to suck up to him, I don't know, he's like one of the few totally decent people in my life. The whole family is all screwed up but Pops has always been good to me and I feel like I'd spoil that if I started using him as a cash machine. Sometimes he sends me a check but I never ask and I probably don't write or visit as much as I should. Unlike Rebecca, who didn't have much time for Pops back when she was a kid, before she entered the economy in a big way as a major consumer. It's weird the way our childhood affected me and Rebecca—I find it really hard to tell a lie, it makes me nauseous, and she finds it almost impossible to tell the truth. Like everybody else in my family. But my baby sister Carol's practically normal, don't ask me how. So far. Sometimes I used to have this fantasy where I'd have Carol kidnapped by Australian bushmen or something and raised by them before she turned out like the rest of us.

Anyway, Jeannie knows I won't hit Pops up no matter what and I remind her.

You could always get another abortion, says Jeannie. Call Skip.

I don't know why, this really cracks us up, we both go into hysterics. I'm laughing so hard I'm practically crying.

Tell him the rates have gone up, Jeannie goes. Tell him it costs six thousand now.

We're like rolling on the floor.

I love Jeannie.

Why don't *you* get an abortion? I go.

But Jeannie says she hasn't slept with anybody but Frank and she never wants to speak to him again and anyway he wants to have kids, he'd just try again to convince her to marry him.

I'm like, Dean's feeling really guilty right now. He'd probably finance an abortion and throw in a free trip to Bermuda.

I fill Jeannie in on the whole Cassie Hane episode and she's like, fucking *men,* and I go, really. But after a minute I feel kind of guilty talking that way even though Dean's a liar and a wimp and a totally worthless shit, I really like him anyway. Jesus, I must be getting soppy in my old age or something. Next thing you know I'll be making goo-goo sounds and saying, *it's so precious* whenever a baby comes on TV. But don't hold your breath.

What are you doing tonight? Jeannie says.

And I'm like, I was thinking about letting Dean be my sex slave.

And she says, has he gone down on you yet?

And I go, that'll be my one of my first commands.

Let's make a list, Jeannie says.

And I'm like, whatever happened to my vibrator kit, anyway?

Suddenly the phone rings and we both dive for it and Jeannie gets it first but I pull it away from her and she's screaming in my ear.

So how's my little postmodern girl? Dean goes. That's what he calls me sometimes. I love it. Hearing his voice makes me real happy for about two seconds but then I feel a little pissed, right? because, you know, it's the same voice that lied to me. I'm being a little frosty during the chit-chat, so he gets down to important business, which is basically that Didi's cousin Phil has been looking into the whole Didi situation, I don't know how, and finally figured out that I wasn't bullshitting when I said she had a problem. Anyway, Phil already made an appointment for her with this specialist who's like the best in the world or something, but he needs our help. One thing he can't understand is where she's getting the money, he's talked to Didi's mother and father and they have no idea how she could be financing this big a habit—it's not like she has a job—and Phil wants to know if she's getting heavily in debt or fucking some dealer or what?

That's easy, I go. She was in that Pepsi ad about a year ago and she gets residuals. I've seen the checks in her purse, two hundred, four hundred, they come in a couple of times a week and she cashes them in about a nanosecond.

That's one mystery solved, Dean goes. The other thing Phil wants to know is who's dealing it to her. Does she have a lot of dealers or mainly one?

I can't tell him that, I go.

Dean goes, look, you want to help Didi, right? Phil isn't going to turn the guy in or anything. He just wants to call him and tell him not to sell to Didi anymore.

I go, Emile isn't like a social worker or something, you know. You expect him to just go, oh, dear, cocaine is bad for her, she's actually abusing it, well, that's very disturbing and I won't sell her any more?

Believe me, Dean says, Phil knows how to convince him.

I'm still a little dubious, I mean this seems to go against all the rules of friendship and drug abuse, but then I realize it doesn't really and if Didi winds up dead I'll be partly responsible, and Emile's a total creep and major reptile anyway. So yeah, okay, I tell Dean what he wants to know. But I also tell him that I don't see how in hell Phil's going to get her into rehab and I also say I'm really going to be furious if my name ever comes up. I know it's for Didi's own good, but I still feel kind of like I'm betraying her and I know that's how she'd feel if she ever found out.

So what are you doing tonight? Dean goes after we've taken care of the Didi problem.

And I explain to him that he's taking me out for an incredibly expensive meal and that he'll receive further instructions after he picks me up and brings me about two dozen long-stemmed red roses from my favorite florist.

We're still getting incoming calls a couple days later but I figure it's only a day or two before they cut us off completely. The landlord's lawyer has sent a letter telling us to be out by the end of the week. I'm like totally depressed. I don't even have subway fare. I'm so depressed I don't even go to class this morning—no way I'm walking sixty blocks, plus I just wouldn't be any good so I stay home and watch the soaps. When Jeannie gets in she's acting really weird, zipping around the apartment like a trapped bird or something, bouncing off the walls, tidying things, giving me shit for having my clothes thrown all over the place. Like, now what's her problem?

Finally she goes, Alison, I got my half of the money.

That's cool, I go. Did your father come through?

She nods.

Only half? I go.

My half, she goes.

Suddenly I don't like the way she's talking one little bit. Jeannie, I say, let me just point out for your benefit that I gave you the rent for March and April and you spent it. So let's not have any of this *my half* shit. If you're going to start using fractions on me then you better say my three-quarters or my seven-eighths.

122

Jeannie and the higher math. She never even heard of fractions until she started buying eighths and quarters from Emile.

Well, I could only get half out of my father, she goes. And that was on the condition that you pay the rest or else I have to find a new roommate. He thinks you're irresponsible.

I'm like, I must be dreaming. Has Jeannie lost her mind or is it me? I go, he thinks *I'm* irresponsible? Me? I didn't spend the goddamned rent money. Why does he think I'm irresponsible?

It was the only way I could get the money, she goes.

What was the only way? I go. Let me guess, you told him that I spent the rent money.

She doesn't say anything.

That's it, isn't it? You bitch, I go, I can't believe you'd do that to me. That's really the lowest.

It was the only way I could get any money out of him, she whines. He wouldn't have given me anything otherwise.

I'm like, you're such a liar, Jeannie. I'm completely surrounded by liars.

I mean, I know you can't trust men, and families are a lie from the start, based on the totally ridiculous notion that two people can be faithful to each other, but what else have you got in the world to count on besides friends? That's about it, in my book, and when your friends start lying and cheating on you, Jesus, it's hard not to be a total cynic.

It's like, you can't trust anybody, and if somebody you know doesn't fuck you over it's just because the price of selling you down the river was never high enough.

I'm sorry, Jeannie goes.

Just fuck off, okay? I go. I don't want to hear it.

Jeannie starts to cry. Oh, Alison, she blubbers.

She tries to take my hand but I push hers away.

I'll tell you something else, I go. If I ever fucked you over I wouldn't be a wimp about it and start bawling. If I ever decide to treat you like you treated me I'll know exactly why I'm doing it and I won't think twice and I'll laugh in your stupid face. That's the difference between you and me. You're a bitch but you're not even good at it. And you better be good if you fuck with me. Because when it comes to being bad, I go, I'm good.

Let her chew on that for a while. I'm out of here. I'm so mad I can't believe it.

I walk over to Dean's place which is like ten blocks but I don't have cabfare. I don't have shit. Thirty-five cents, four cigarettes and a barrette. Reminds me of that REM song, "It's the End of the World As We Know It."

I stop in front of a phone module, you could hardly call them booths, these weird little open-air units they have in New York now. Anyway, I call Francesca and get her machine—story of my life, talking to machines—which blows a quarter so now I've got like ten cents left. So I call Alex, my old squeeze, collect in Virginia. He answers and accepts charges and I'm like, I must be dreaming—something in my life today that didn't fuck up. Unbelievable.

Alex is like, Alison, what's happening?

And I go, what isn't happening? If it sucks, it's happened to me lately. I'm thinking of declaring myself a disaster area, you know, so I can get federal funds.

So I tell him about Dean and Jeannie and he's real sympathetic, I don't know, it's just nice to have someone on my side. We're best of friends now, I don't know what I'd do without Alex, jump out a window probably. When you've known somebody half your life and slept with them for a quarter, I mean—you get close. He knows me better than anybody. Same with him for me. He's family. Just ask Mom or Rebecca. They both were like, share and share alike. Popping up naked all over the place, like—oh dear, excuse me, I didn't know Alex was here, how very embarrassing, let me just very slowly cover myself with this teeny little towel after he's had a nice long look. I start thinking about this stuff while we're talking when he suddenly says, listen, Alison, would you be real upset if I came up to visit you guys?

And I'm like, that would be wonderful. And then suddenly I figure something out and I go, what do you mean, you guys?

And he says, you and Jeannie.

You don't even know Jeannie, I say. I mean, you've never met her.

I've talked to her on the phone, he goes.

You want to come up here and fuck Jeannie, I say. That's it, right? If that's the story, just say so.

I wouldn't even think of it if it wasn't cool with you, he says. Look, you sound upset, forget it, I'd never do anything to hurt you.

I don't know, at first it's like my stomach just drops out of my body and bounces on a little string just above the pavement. Alex was my first love. Hell, he was my only love and he helped me get over some things from my childhood, I mean when I met him my attitude about sex was what the early settlers must have thought about scalping—basically you'd rather be dead. Alex helped me over that, which is another reason this thing feels weird, him having the hots for Jeannie. If it were any other guy, no problem, hop right on. But then I think, well, why not, what do I care? If Alex wants to do it, he should, I don't believe in unrequited lust and it's not like we're going out anymore or like we have been for a long time. I can handle it, plus it would be good for Jeannie, even though I'm furious at her she's still my oldest friend on the planet and she hasn't been laid by anybody but Frank in years and just in case she's thinking of getting back together with him this should show her that a secure future with Frank is like two weeks in Philadelphia except longer.

Come on up, I say. It'll be good to see you.

I'll call my travel agent and talk to you guys tomorrow. Meantime, don't do anything I wouldn't do.

Which maybe rules out murder, obviously not much else.

I think Dean's doorman kind of likes me, he winks at me and lets me go right up. Guy's from one of those Communist countries that sounds like a disease, what's it called, where they used to have vampires and Dean's always loaning him money because he's completely in debt to these Korean gamblers who are going to kill him. Welcome to the free world, Igor.

Alison, Dean goes, when he opens the door. He's like, what a nice surprise. He looks a little worried, like he's got somebody in his bed already or something, but I guess maybe he's just nervous about where we stand or maybe it's my expression which probably looks like a psycho killer about now, anyway he lets me in, kisses me on the cheek.

What's the matter? I go.

I don't know, he goes. The bond market is really bad.

You losing money?

He nods. So here we are, two seriously depressed units. The phone starts ringing.

How about you? he goes. Are you okay?

Oh, yeah, I'm just super, I go, really sarcastic.

What's the problem? he says.

What isn't a problem? I go. That bitch Jeannie . . .

The answering machine picks up and after the beep I'm treated to this silky lingerie voice going, Dean, it's Cassie, returning your call. I had the greatest dream about you, I can't wait to tell you. I'll be in tonight. Call me, angel. Don't leave a kinky message, though, cause Peter knows my access code.

Dean shrugs, looking helpless, like—can I help it if they throw themselves at me?

Can I get you something? he goes. He looks kind of scared.

I'm just standing there in the hallway trying to decide what to do, whether to just turn around and leave. And I'm remembering that Cassie Hane goes out with Peter Finnegan, which suddenly is giving me some big ideas.

Alison? he goes. Are you all right? What's the matter?

Fuck me, I go.

What? he says.

Let's fuck, I go. Let's just go into your bedroom and fuck, okay?

So we do. So I go in and lie down on the bed and he comes in and undresses me and plays with me. I don't play with him but he doesn't seem to mind—he better not—he gets inside me and I clench my teeth and grind against him and practically carve my initials in his back. I have my eyes closed, I don't even look at him, and when I come it's good but it's not enough, not nearly, he comes with a sort of a shout and rolls off. I give him about three minutes, then I grab his cock and start yanking—he better have eaten his eggs today, he's going to need them, I pull on his cock like it's attached to a busted cigarette machine and I'm having a nicotine fit, he winces and gasps through his teeth, then I climb on top of him and hump and ride, he doesn't know how lucky he is, the jerk, horsewomen have muscles he never dreamed of, doesn't deserve, and after about ten minutes I come but I keep my mouth shut about it, this isn't one of those beautiful sharing experiences, this is something else entirely.

Then he comes. Alison, he goes. Alison Alison Alison.

That's my name. My parents gave it to me, the creeps. Alison Poole. I'm going to make goddamn sure he never forgets it.

I try. I want this to be enough, just this. Just contact, just friction. But it's not. It doesn't fix me the way it used to, the way you always dream it will.

8

SCENES FOR ONE MAN AND
TWO WOMEN

Get in touch with your child, Rob says at the beginning of class.

After our warm-up this guy does a scene from *Hamlet,* where Hamlet's trying to deal with the fact that his mother married this guy who killed his father. It sounds pretty good to me and the boy's really rolling, really emotional, and he has this great English accent, but Rob starts shouting at him about halfway through. He shouts, breathe! breathe! Your voice is up in your throat. Breathe evenly.

Finally Rob stops the guy, his name is Jim, and Jim's all sweaty and in tears and he starts wobbling around like he's going to faint and Rob says, what's with all the theatrics, all this huffing and puffing, squeaks and honks, it's all camouflage for something, what are you trying to hide?

So Jim looks real pained, he's trying to catch his breath and he says, I think I'm going to faint.

Rob says, you're not going to faint, that's more camouflage, stand up straight and breathe evenly. Okay, now, what's really going on here?

Jim shakes his head and shrugs and Rob goes, defense mechanisms.

Finally Jim gasps, defense against what?

You tell me, Rob goes.

Jim keeps saying he doesn't know and Rob keeps after him and finally he goes, this isn't about Hamlet and his father, this is about you and your father. It's all camouflage for feeling that your father wasn't strong enough, isn't it? Isn't that what's going on here?

Jim starts crying and finally he says maybe that has something to do with it. Rob thinks that the scenes we pick tell a lot about us. And I'm thinking maybe so, Jim seems to be really affected by this, or else maybe he's just playing along because it's a good scene, I don't know.

Acting's about honesty, Rob goes, after Jim has his cry. Don't be afraid of your feelings, he says.

So this girl who's new to the class raises her hand and she goes, I worry sometimes when I get into an emotion that I'll get totally carried away and I won't be able to stop.

Every natural emotion has a beginning and an end, Rob says. If we surrender to a predominant emotion in class it will run its course in a healthy way. Of course, he goes, if you're deeply troubled then you may not be able to stop and that *is* a problem.

Maybe it's my imagination, maybe I'm just paranoid, but it seems like he looks at me when he says this, I guess he's thinking about my little freak-out a few weeks ago, when I made like a spastic and had to go see the nurse. So okay, I never said I was normal.

Let me give you an example, Rob says, sitting up on his desk and folding his legs underneath each other—he used to study yoga in India before he decided to be an actor. Example, he goes, I sometimes have a fantasy of mowing down people on the street with a machete. I do. That doesn't mean I'm going to act on it. But it's something I occasionally feel. Not that I'm ever going to do it. A healthy adult can tell the difference between fantasy and reality. As a normal human being you recognize that you don't need to act on every impulse you feel. But as an actor you tap into the fantasy and use it. Of course, first you have to know the difference between fantasy and reality.

I raise my hand and I ask, how do you tell the difference?

He looks at me and says, Alison, have you ever considered therapy? I really think you should.

I'm serious, I go.

He goes, so am I.

So after this really wonderful day at acting class I get home to deal with the fact that my ex-boyfriend, the only love of my life, is arriving any minute to sleep with my roommate. This seems to me like a case where fantasy is leaking into reality in a serious way.

Jeannie comes home from work all flustered and excited

131

and I find out she's sent a car to meet Alex. I don't believe it, I don't mind her sleeping with my ex-boyfriend, really I don't, but we've got this incredibly serious deficit in this house, we're like Bangladesh or something, and she's ordering limos. I was down to my last dime until I made a little withdrawal from Dean's wallet. Foreign aid, right?

Jeannie spends the next two hours working on her eyes. Don't ask me why, but for some reason I think of this story I heard once about these two college roommates who hated each other—one of them was a friend of mine, actually—and one night she put some Nair hair remover in her roommate's mascara tube, you can imagine what fun that was.

Anyway, Jeannie's fixing her eyes, so I go down to the corner—my phone away from home. First I try Dean, no luck, then I try to track down my dad. I've got to get hold of some serious cash. I call his office in Washington and the secretary accepts the charges and tells me to try the farm in Virginia, he's down taking care of some horse business. Can I give him a message if he calls? she says.

Yeah, I say, tell him to get in touch with his child.

I'm kind of amazed that Dad's in Virginia because he hardly ever goes down there anymore, Mom lives there and they can hardly stand the sight of each other. You can't blame them, really, either of them.

Dad moved us out to the farm from Long Island after they separated, I was ten then. Before that it was a tax write-off. It's complicated, they're divorced and Mom still lives there but he owns part of it or something. It's a big white house with pillars, on a rise, seven or eight barns and stables spread out behind. It was a good place to be kids, all the land and horses. School was fifteen miles away and we'd always miss the bus and Mom could never get it together to drive us in, she was asleep most of the morning, totally zonked in her big pink canopy bed. When we were little we'd climb in and pretend it was a ship sailing off to England, where Gran was from, the chintz curtains were our sails.

I call the main house collect and Cliff answers. I ask if Dad's there and he says no. Cliff doesn't know where he is or when he'll be back. Mom and Carol are out shopping. I tell him to have my dad call me, then I hang up.

Cliff is probably my least favorite person in the whole world. He's Dad's right-hand man, he drives the car and beats people up or something. He tried to rape me when I was a kid. I was out in the stables and he cornered me, the only thing that saved me was I had the curry comb, I'd been brushing Eric the Red, and I finally whacked his face with it. I wish I'd hit him where it really hurt but I was so freaked out, his hands pinning me to the walls, and I ran like hell after I hit him. When I told Dad, he acted like he didn't believe me. And finally he said Cliff didn't mean any harm and told me to shut up about it. That's when I realized Cliff had something on him, that Dad couldn't afford to fire him. That's also when I realized that my father was a complete asshole.

I call Dean again and get his machine. Story of my life.

I don't want to be around to spoil the tender moment, Alex meeting Jeannie for the first time, so I fish out another quarter and call up Whitney to have a drink with her. Then I go back to the apartment and tell Jeannie I'll meet them later for dinner, but Whitney and I get really blasted and I keep trying Dean and getting his machine and so finally I go, okay, two can play that game.

The next morning I call up the apartment, I'm hung over as hell, and I check to make sure they're awake, I don't really feel like walking in on them when they're rolling around in bed, and Jeannie answers the phone all giggly like a newly minted ex-virgin or something and she says, Alison, come on up for breakfast, which is a zany idea, I don't think anybody's ever eaten breakfast in our apartment before. But then I remember, Alex loves the big breakfast production number, eggs and bacon and toast, the works, he'd cook up a storm most mornings, scramble five or six eggs just for himself, I'd be sitting there moaning over coffee and I'd say you're such a pig, Alex, and he'd say, I need my eggs if I'm gonna keep my baby satisfied.

I wonder if he said that to Jeannie.

I've got to say this is bugging me a little. Okay, I admit it. The funny thing is, I couldn't even stand the idea of sex, of having men touch me, until Alex.

He greets me at the door and gives me a big hug and even after everything it's good to feel his body and I know that I can forgive him, whatever happened it's no big deal, he's still there for me somehow, a way that Jeannie can't touch. He looks great, tan and dark and beefy. Jeannie kind of peeks out from the bedroom.

So, I go, when Alex finally lets go of me.

So what? says Alex.

You know, I say.

Jeannie says, I'm not the kind of girl who kisses and tells.

134

Right, I say, can I remind you who you're talking to here, I'm like your best friend and roommate, the one you always tell about your so-called kissing.

Let's eat breakfast, Jeannie says.

We decide to go out for a walk, Alex has never really seen New York, so we take him to Bergdorf's and make him buy us both some perfume. Then we go to Trader Vic's and have a couple of scorpions, we tell Alex about our wild weekend at the Plaza and then me and Alex tell Jeannie about the time we went to the Fontainebleau in Miami and flooded our room. Thinking about the weekend in Miami gives me a great idea, flooding the room wasn't half of what we did. Let's go to Forty-second Street, I say, and Alex is totally up for it, Jeannie's not so sure but she's really careful about showing it because she doesn't want it to suddenly become me and Alex again, she wants to stake her own claim.

So we walk down to Times Square. We're walking down Fifth and after a while Alex goes, what are all these people doing collapsed in heaps on the street? I guess we've been passing a lot of bag ladies and bums, and I'm like, I don't know, they're everywhere, and Jeannie goes, we've got a guy who sort of lives under the awning of our apartment building, which is true. When Alex sees the big black guy with the ski parka and the seeing-eye dog selling pencils out in front of Saks he stops and starts in on this big conversation, asking the guy where he's from and stuff. Jeannie's sort of embarrassed but I think it's cool, this is what I love about Alex, he's such a nut. Finally he buys a pencil and gives the man two bucks.

Alex is the total tourist, he sees the Empire State Building way down Fifth and he's like, wow, let's go up, and he's amazed when Jeannie and I say we've never been up it. So we promise we'll take him but first we go into this sex shop on Forty-second over by Port Authority after dodging all the drug dealers and pimps and Japanese tourists. There's five or six guys drooling over the magazine racks and they all sort of freak out when Jeannie and I walk in. Jeannie freaks out a little herself, she can't help looking like a nice girl from Princeton, New Jersey. Alex and I go over and start checking out the magazines, showing each other pictures and reading the titles. I pick up *Young Girls* and say, I'm going to buy this for my father.

And Alex says, yeah, really.

I can tell he's getting into being with me, we go back too far and too deep for Jeannie to understand and she's beginning to get a little upset about it.

I drag Alex over to the counter and make him check out the sex toys with me. The counterman is looking at us like he's afraid we're from Neptune or something. We start asking him to show us the stuff and how they work and what the features are. Meanwhile the perverts are slinking out of the store, they can't take it.

Finally we decide to get the four-pack vibrator sets, one for Jeannie and one for me, it comes with a battery pack and four attachments, the Super Stud, the French Tickler, the Rear-Ender and the Old Faithful. Alex pays. Anything to make my girls happy, he says.

We take Alex to Sardi's for a drink, we're trying to make sure we don't miss any of the touristy things to do. Alex wants to see some stars but the bartender tells us it's too early. The stars come out at night, he says and laughs like this is a great piece of wit. He's not bad-looking, though, maybe thirty, looks a little bit like Christopher Reeve. I don't even have to ask if he's an actor, you can tell from the way he talks he's been taking voice. He's overdoing the whole chest thing. We show the bartender our new toys and he gives us a free drink. When we're leaving he asks for my phone number, so I give him the Midnite Escort Service number, I memorized it for these kind of occasions.

Then we take a cab over to the Empire State Building and pay our two bucks and wait around in the lobby for the elevator with all these like families, moms and kids. Once we get on the elevator it smells like milk, I kid you not, and some little red-headed boy grabs my knee and gets gum all over my jeans. Freckle-faced, he looks like something out of a peanut butter ad. Another little kid starts bawling. I don't know, they talk about this maternal instinct, I can't say it's ever really hit me, but then I don't think it ever hit my mother either. I think she was just too lazy to put in her diaphragm some nights.

The ride up makes me really nauseous, my stomach gets left behind on the lower floors. We have to change elevators to get to the very top. Alex has his arm around Jeannie. She's telling him about her job and he's looking fascinated. It's really amazing the things we pretend to be interested in when we want to sleep with somebody. Sometimes I think conversation between girls and guys is all just foreplay.

To take my mind off how nauseous I'm feeling I say, hey Alex, what are the three great lies?

It's weird, he comes up with the same two I already know, except his second lie is a little different than my ver-

137

sion, it goes, I promise I'll pull out before I come, you can bet the moms in the elevator are really freaked out by this conversation. But he can't think of the third one either.

Finally we get up to the observation deck and pile out of the kiddie capsule. I'm really dizzy. Jeannie and Alex rush over to the fence to look out, there's like this chicken wire all around the platform and blue sky beyond. The chicken wire's so nobody will jump, I guess, and it reminds me of this thing I saw in a book of photos from *Life* magazine, this picture of a car parked on the street, the roof of the car molded around the body of a girl who'd jumped from the Empire State Building. She was wearing a long billowing skirt that fanned out like a huge lily across the top of the car, the kind of dress you'd wear to a ball or a fancy dinner, she was lying face down so you didn't necessarily figure out what was wrong at first, it was as if she was resting or floating in a pool, a girl without a trouble in the world. . . .

I don't look, I stand right in the middle of the observation deck and throw up.

9

DERBY DAY

Thank God I never slept with Tom Walker. That makes at least one guy in the room.

We're over at Tom's place for his Kentucky Derby party and the past is coming back to haunt me. The gang's all here. I mean, I can handle it, no problem, but the guys are all acting weird. I never said I was a virgin, did I? Somebody tell me if I'm wrong.

I come with Dean and Chuck Harnist is here, and he's jealous of Dean anyway, Chuck starts making these cracks like saying he's redecorated his apartment and then going, Alison, you remember how ugly it used to be, don't you? The ceiling, for instance? And Dean says something about redecorating Chuck's face—for a smart guy Dean can act just like a dumb guy sometimes. But Dean's got troubles, the bond market's going to hell or something and he's really worried.

So Chucky's with some girl he must have met in Las Vegas, although actually she's from Texas, even her lips look like they've got silicone implants. Her name's Tina, but she tells me her friends call her Teeny, and she kind of looks at her chest when she says this and she laughs and jiggles her tits and that pretty much tells you more than you'd ever want to know about her.

And I go, yeah? Chuck's friends call him Teeny, too, but they're not kidding.

And she goes, wow, really? What a coincidence! And Chuck turns a nice salmon color and gives me this lethal look.

And then who shows up but Skip Pendleton, just the guy I wanted to see, and amazingly he's not with anybody. I mean, for Skip this is news, this is practically gossip, you know how some men wouldn't think of going out of the house without a tie, well Skip wouldn't think of showing up at a party without at least one vacuous bimbo on his arm. And he wears the girl for the same reason as the tie, for decoration. Maybe there's somebody here he wants to nail. I don't know, the only unattached women are Didi, Jeannie and Whitney and they're all my friends and wouldn't let him touch them with a ten-foot pole. Well, maybe with a *ten-foot* pole . . . I remember I read somewhere that outlaw guy John Dillinger had one that was about a foot and a half long and it's preserved in the Smithsonian or someplace. Now that's what I call the Washington Monument.

Skip is giving me these looks which I do not appreciate at all, these fuck-me eyes. And he's acting really strange with Dean, talking down to him like he's a kid or something, lecturing him about horses and race track society, which is really bugging me. Jesus. My old boyfriend, Alex, he told me this thing that guys say about girls—find 'em, fuck 'em, fight 'em, forget 'em. So if that's what guys say, how come these guys—these so-called men—can't fuck me and forget me? I mean why do they all have to act like crazy Latins afterwards, hot tempers and long memories.

Anyway, Jeannie and I are sort of friends again, but I'm still pissed off at her and unless I can come up with some money soon I'm screwed. The big news on Jeannie, though, is that she's madly in love with Alex. I knew this would happen. Apparently they screwed twenty ways till Sunday— Alex and Jeannie—and Jeannie figured out what she'd been missing. So now she's in lust with Alex, she thinks it's this great romance but I hate to tell her, Alex has this problem with his attention span and I don't think Jeannie's going to be able to keep him interested past yesterday. Meanwhile we've still got this money problem. Francesca's going to loan me a thousand, she's the best, but I still need at least a thousand more. She's at some celebrity derby party but she's supposed to meet up with us later.

Didi's boring the shit out of everybody talking about rehab. Cousin Phil actually managed to drag her in the other night. The way he did it was by keeping her up for two days, feeding her so much coke that she felt even worse than she normally does. Then he let her sleep for a few hours, then woke her up and wouldn't let her go back to sleep till she promised to go in the next day and talk to the shrink. Phil says the pre-op cost him about a thousand bucks in blow and three days' work, but Didi's parents are going to pay him back. So now she's seeing this shrink in the afternoon and going to group therapy at night. It's really great, I mean, here she is, more or less awake in the middle of the afternoon, and she's talking about her drug problem and how she's got to stop. She talks about it all night long, in between lines. It's a start, I guess.

From my point of view the only thing good that's come out of Didi's rehab is that she doesn't look quite so good as she used to, she doesn't necessarily look like a sex goddess the last few days, even though she's still doing drugs it's like something crazy has gone out of her eyes, the tension's gone from her body and it's sort of defused her looks or something. I don't know, maybe it's my imagination, but the guys aren't really flipping out over her today like they used to.

So Becca shows up at the last minute, right before post time. She's already called about eighteen times just to let us know that she's coming, finally she dances through the door in this micro lycra red dress—just a sheath really, perfect for that 3:00 A.M. nightclub appearance, but like even I wouldn't be caught dead walking around in this thing in the middle of the day. But the boys love it and it gets so quiet for a minute you can hear the sound of tongues dropping and saliva splashing on the floor.

Becca's dragging some preppy guy in her wake, all neat and tidy in his blue blazer and bright green pants, but he seems a little dazed. This must be Everett, pigeon of the month, the poor son of a bitch. He looks like a harmless version of Skip. I hope to God for his sake he's hanging on to his gold card for dear life, has his stock certificates locked in the safety deposit box.

Hey y'all, Becca goes, doing her southern girl thing for

the occasion. Who's winning? she says. What quarter is it? I just love these sporting events. They're so sweaty.

All the guys laugh. Am I like missing something, or is this funny?

The prep goes, hi, I'm Everett, but nobody gives a shit. Everybody's colliding and tripping, trying to give Rebecca a seat and get her a drink. Becca's obviously wired and it's only like three in the afternoon or something. Really sick. I wonder how much she's got.

We're all sitting around Tombo's loft drinking mint juleps in front of this big projection TV. Tom owns a gallery or something, I don't know, he's from Kentucky. Big ugly canvases on the wall, wacked-out Italian furniture, great bathrooms though, both with phones, I could easily live in the big one. Maybe he needs a roommate. Somebody young, blond and beautiful to answer his phone. Two out of three, anyway—I used to be pretty good-looking, way back in the olden days before Becca walked in the room.

I don't know, lately I've had this fantasy about moving in with Dean, you know, but I just couldn't see giving up my independence like that, it would practically be like marriage and anyway he's never asked.

Becca takes me aside and says, I can get you three thousand for the pearls.

And I'm like, not for sale.

Why not? she goes. You never wear them.

And I go, Gran was the only one in our whole family I ever liked. Gran and Pops.

Don't be a bitch, Alison, she goes, I'm trying to help you here.

Who's buying them? I say.

And she goes, just a friend.

I ask her if she has any blow and she says she just ran out but she'll try to get some more.

Right.

Becca's lie reminds me of this story I heard from a friend of mine who's a musician. He's working on an album with, let's just say this Famous Blind Musician, right? My friend's a session man, plays great guitar. So he's been up half the night laying down tracks with the FBM and meanwhile every half hour or so the FBM walks over into the corner and snorts from a vial—doesn't even bother to leave the room. Like, I don't know, because he can't see nobody else can? And after a couple times of this my friend goes up and says, hey man, can I have a blast? Because, you know, he's tired and all and they're working together all night. So the FBM says, blast of what? And my friend is like, a blast of that blow. And the FBM goes, I don't do drugs. Even though he's holding it right there in his hand. But I don't know, he's blind, so it's not like my friend can point to it and say, there! Well, this happens two or three more times, and the FBM keeps saying he doesn't have any. So the next time this happens, my friend finally goes up and taps the spoon as the FBM's putting it in his nose and says, if you don't have any drugs what's this? And the FBM goes—hey, you're right, what can I say? So he offers my friend some and eventually my friend says, why did you say you didn't have any? And the FBM goes, what can I say? This shit makes you lie.

Meanwhile, Skip's asking Tom if he has Trivial Pursuit and Tom says he doesn't and Skip goes, that's too bad, and then Whitney jumps in and says, yeah, I love that game, and just because I know that Skip takes like this great pride in his

Trivial Pursuit skills I go, Whitney is a really good player, and Skip says he's the best—the macho asshole—and Whitney, she went to Yale or someplace like that, she says, someday we'll see and Skip goes, I'd kill you. What a total jerk. I mean, as if we care, for one thing.

Shh, quiet everybody, Tom goes. We're coming up on post time. This old boy takes his derby seriously. Or at least he pretends to. I don't know, I think it's just a way of having a little bit of identity, you know? Like wearing suspenders all the time or collecting art or something. I mean, it seems like everybody's always doing something to impress everybody else. Anyway, he's got all these complicated bets going with the other guys and they're all acting very serious and involved, even Dean. The weird thing is, I don't think he even knew the Kentucky Derby was happening until yesterday when I invited him to this party.

I'm not betting, but I know the horse I want. I want Demons Begone to win.

So we've got these seventeen three-year-olds at Churchill Downs and there's some really good-looking horseflesh out there, all carrying a hundred and twenty-six pounds, I'd just barely make the weight myself now, but back in my riding days I was like, a hundred and two pounds, skinny as a whippet. And our horses were older and tougher, these three-year-olds have delicate legs, I hope to God they all make it okay, I can't stand to see a horse get hurt.

The other thing I hate is the drugs. Our horses were so pumped up and tranked down and wacked out they make me and my friends look straight. It was really depressing, but we were just kids, we didn't really understand. But we knew something was funny. We saw what they were doing and just learned to live with it. Drugs for pain and drugs for speed and drugs for when they'd passed their prime and they were heavily insured.

It's taking them forever to get this thing going, I mean the race only lasts about three minutes and they've got to wring all the advertising bucks they can out of this thing, plus give everybody time to get to the betting window.

Demons Begone looks ready, he's real feisty, dancing high on his feet. Skip's like insisting he knows for a fact that they've been holding back this horse Alysheba who's going to blow them all away. Trust Skip to have the inside dope. I hope his horse finishes last. Dean's so cute, he's picked this horse named Capote, just because it's named after a writer and he likes writers and wants to be one someday. What a dope. There's also a horse named Leo Castelli, but Tom the hotshot gallery owner isn't betting on him. Tom's going on statistics. Dean's a romantic, which is just another word for a flake, but I love it. I guess you could say we've made up, and then some. I just want to be with him all the time and I talk about him and think about him constantly.

I'm totally in lust again.

Finally they're off already after about nine hundred commercials. Demons Begone takes an early lead and I'm like, all right. Capote's on the inside and then Leo Castelli. Suddenly I've got to pee, must be all those beer commercials. I slide out of the huddle and Tom's like, Alison! as if it's sacrilege or something to go to the bathroom and I'm like, I'll be right back. I slip inside this big marble bathroom which is like the tomb of some ancient emperor or something and suddenly I feel real dizzy and nauseous, I put my head down on my bare knees and I listen to the shouting and talk from out there, it's strange how you can be involved in something and then just step back out of it and it seems really distant and silly. I suddenly wonder how long it would take them to notice I was gone if I went out the fire escape or something. What if I just kept going, left New York entirely? I'm getting this really weird feeling like, I'm so involved in all this hysterical noise which is supposedly my life but it doesn't add up to anything, if you step back far enough it's just a dumb buzz like a swarm of mosquitoes. But everybody's life is like that, right? It's like, down there in Lexington, Kentucky, the derby's the most important thing in the world to all these people, but what does it mean, really? It's just a stupid horse race, right? From the planet Jupiter, none of it counts for shit.

I don't know, I think I'm getting my period or something. Half the time I'm walking around feeling totally nauseous, and the other half I'm wasted, which probably has something to do with it.

When I go back everybody's jumping up and down and the horses are coming to the wire. What's with Demons Begone? I go to Dean and Dean goes, pulled from the race, talking like a telegram so he won't miss the finish.

Pulled from the race? I go.

So Alysheba wins, followed by Bet Twice. I don't know which bugs me more, the fact that my horse dropped out or the fact that Skip's horse won. It just figures. Skip always has the inside dope. I'm like majorly depressed. In between shots of the winner's circle they're showing Demons Begone being led to an ambulance trailer, hobbling, fucked-up, dead tired.

Bleeding from the nose, his trainer says. Sounds familiar, right? Jesus. Pour me another julep.

I told you, Skip goes, coming up and putting his arm around me in this creepy possessive way. You should stick with me.

I go, fuck off, Skip.

Hey, just trying to be helpful, he says.

I'm like, yeah, right. You could really help me a lot by diving out the fucking window head first.

Dean comes over and goes, I guess it was pretty stupid to think a horse named Capote could go the distance. He says, it's a case of sport imitating life—brilliant start, pathetic finish.

Skip goes, that *was* pretty stupid, Dean.

And I go, don't you call Dean stupid.

And Dean's like, whoa! Alison, cool out, it's called kidding. He puts his arm on my shoulder and says, a kind of verbal sparring characterized by irony and hyperbole that often passes between friends.

I'm thinking, friends! You don't know who your friends are, Dean. Sometimes I don't know what I see in him, really I don't.

Who else is holding drugs? Didi screams. Doesn't anybody but me buy drugs anymore? I know you all still do drugs, you cheap, sleazy bastards. I'm going to be so happy when I quit and you're all still addicted but you won't have me to supply you with free toot. The magazines say cocaine isn't fashionable but they really mean you fashionable fucks don't buy it anymore, you wait for me to come over . . . you invite me over to your house so you can do my drugs and look down my shirt.

I go, you're half right, anyway.

Dean says, hey Didi, honey.

And she goes, what do you want, Shakespeare?

And Dean says, I wonder if you could give me the name of your drug therapist. The man is clearly a miracle worker.

And she goes, Rome wasn't built in a day, asshole.

And Dean says to me, in this low voice so Didi can't hear, no, but it *was* sacked in a day.

I'm like, what's that supposed to mean?

He shrugs. I was just thinking about that basketball player, Len Bias, he goes.

I remember, a couple years ago maybe, that was the kid who ODed on coke and died. That was one of those times where everybody got all aroused for about five minutes and all these politicians shook their fat little fists and pretended they actually wanted to stop the drug trade and then Sylvester Stallone got a new girlfriend or Reagan got a malignant pimple on his nose or something so everybody could forget about the dead basketball player.

Didi says to Becca, are you holding? Becca shakes her head and Didi says, liar, I know you are. Fine, she says, don't give me any. I don't want any, I'm absolutely quitting tomorrow and then I'll be laughing at you when you're still a shivering wreck. Then she says, hey, I've got a present for you and she gives Becca the card I gave her a few weeks ago, the one with the cocaine help-line number.

This cracks everybody up. Except Becca.

Tom tells me there's a call for me so I go find the phone which is this weird piece of sculpture made out cement and plastic.

Alison, Francesca gasps, you won't believe it, guess who's here?

I go, Len Bias.

Who? she goes.

Okay, I say. Elvis Presley.

She's like, no, really. I'm dying.

All right, I go, who's there?

Jerry, she says.

Unbelievable, I go, but of course I'm thinking—big yawn. Score one for the bimbo patrol.

I've been talking to her, Francesca says.

Does she speak English? I go.

Francesca goes, she's in the bathroom now but I'm going to talk to her when she comes out.

I'm like, why didn't you follow her in there, see if she pees like the rest of us?

So Francesca gets mad and I tell her I'm sorry, it's just a really stressful scene here, my horse lost, Didi's nuts, Rebecca's a time bomb and I've fucked everybody in the room.

Jerry's back, she whispers. I'll call you later.

Meanwhile Rebecca's climbed up on the coffee table, she's holding this bottle of Jack Daniel's over her head and saying, let's party. She looks like some really kinky version of the Statue of Liberty and nobody's asking her to come down, all the guys are trying to look up her skirt . . . that's the way things are starting to go, and it's only about five in the afternoon. I have a feeling it's going to be a real long night.

10

TRUTH OR DARE II

Reality is out the window by the time we end up back at Dean's place. It's like nothing can touch us as long as we stay high. Sitting down around the coffee table I'm having this déjà vu about a dream I had where Dean's living room is a stage and we're playing Truth or Dare for an audience.

Right after we walk in Rebecca's preppie asks what time it is—he's been holding on all night and he's probably wondering at this point if he's ever going to get laid tonight. Not that Rebecca hasn't already broken him in a little, I'm sure. Anyway, he asks the time and we all start booing and throwing pillows and cigarettes at him.

The usual suspects: Didi, Francesca, Rebecca, Skip, Ev the Prep and Dean. Jeannie crashed, I think Alex wore her out last weekend and I guess we lost Tom and Whitney at Nell's. Chuck and Teeny we ditched, said we'd meet them at some dumb restaurant where they were actually going to eat. Seems like days ago.

I'm like a shivering wreck. Totally nauseous.

The coffee table is full of beer and champagne bottles and there's three or four mirrors going around. And suddenly Didi goes Truth or Dare and that snaps me back into the real world in about a nanosecond. I'm like, uh-oh. Not a good idea.

Dean says, yeah, great idea, the horny bastard must want to see Didi's tits again. And Rebecca's all for it too, she's an exhibitionist from way back.

I take a quick look at Skip and he's looking back at me and I don't like his eyes one little bit. And I'm thinking, whatever those two things are you weren't supposed to ever mix together in chemistry class, they're about to get poured into the same beaker.

So the next thing I know we're in the middle of it and I am not a happy unit, I'm sweating bullets.

Of course Didi has to start, and of course she has to make trouble, so she picks Skip, who takes truth and Didi goes, two parts, how would you rate Alison in bed and, part two, did she go down on you?

Skip's loving this. But Dean isn't and neither am I. Finally Skip goes, I'd give her a nine.

What about part two? Didi goes, and I can see Skip isn't so keen all of a sudden because the fact is I didn't and if I weren't here the liar would go ahead and lie about it, but now he can't and he kind of shrugs his shoulders and says no.

Rebecca says, I can't believe Alison's a nine.

And Francesca goes, especially without going down on him.

Skip's turn, Didi shouts.

Me, me, Rebecca says. Pick me.

Okay, Skip goes, and of course Rebecca takes the dare and of course Skip goes, take off your clothes. So Rebecca jumps up and strips down, the guys are stunned and silent like they're in church or something while Becca shakes her booty, I've got to admit it's a nice package, you'd think she worked out about nine hours a day, if I were a guy I'd fuck her in a minute, it's a toss-up whether she or Didi has a better body, and finally the guys start giggling nervously and Becca puts her clothes back on real slow.

So then it's Becca's turn and when she goes Dean, he picks truth of course, the guys almost always pick truth. And Becca says, do you have a hard-on right now? and Dean says yes. Big surprise, with Dean all you have to do is like say the word nipple or something and he's ready to bust out the front of his chinos. Story of his life. Maybe he didn't get enough when he was younger. He told me he had a practically permanent hard-on from the age of thirteen to sixteen and how he used to get really nervous when class was ending because he wouldn't want to stand up and walk down the hall with an erection so he'd try to think about violence and garbage and stuff like that or else he'd sit in his chair like a moron and pretend he was rearranging his notebook or something.

So Dean picks Skip and I'm like, uh-oh. He says, do you still have the hots for Alison?

More specific, Didi says. Vague question.

Okay, Dean goes. Would you sleep with her again?

Skip goes, would I? Really smug, he smiles and finally says, you bet. And he and Dean lock eyes for a minute and I'm dying, I don't like what's happening here at all.

So Skip turns to me—I pick truth, I'm only a private exhibitionist—and goes, does Dean really satisfy you sexually?

And I go, yes, he does.

Skip leaves it at that, but he has this look like he just scored a point.

Boring, says Didi. She's vibrating at this really high frequency. Suddenly I notice this incredible thing—Dean has this weird expression, he's sitting on the floor with his legs under the coffee table and Rebecca is slumped in this really low chair right next to him and I see her reach down under the table and from Dean's expression it's like obvious that she's grabbed hold of his crotch. Dean has this slightly queasy expression when he looks up and sees me and I'm thinking, this can't be happening, but with Becca it definitely could be happening. She looks right at me, then lifts up her arm and sits back up in her chair with this ridiculous innocent look.

So I go to Rebecca, truth or dare, do you like the idea of seducing my boyfriends or is it just something that happens sometimes?

She goes, only if I find them attractive.

Good, says Didi. High reality quotient in that question and answer.

And I'm thinking about the time we were all sitting around in the hot tub in East Hampton, somebody's father's house, whatever poor bastard Rebecca was sleeping with that week, me and Alex, Rebecca and her squeeze, this was like two years ago when Alex and I were still going out, we were practically married for Christ's sake, it had been almost four years or something. Anyway, we're all in that condition where you can't tell where the water stops and you begin,.it's all like the same warm ooze, the four of us in the hot tub drinking Cristal wrecked on Quaaludes and we're like joking around about having an orgy and the next thing I know I feel a hand fishing around between my legs, I mean it could be anybody but I figure out it's what's-his-name, Trent, that was his name, and suddenly Alex is grinning and squirming around and we were all doing this underwater foreplay and it was cool, we were all friends and that was the point, and Alex is touching me too but it's just sort of giggly and casual. So like a jerk I decide to get up and take a pee, don't ask me why I didn't just pee in the water, so we're out in this kind of cabana deal and I have to get out and go to the bathroom next door. And I guess it takes me a while to find it or maybe it takes me a while to get the door open—I don't know, we were pretty fucked up at this point. I was, anyway, my whole body felt like a waterbed, so finally I get in and I'm just like washing my hands or something when the door opens and it's Trent, who's got this monster hard-on sticking out in front of him, I remember it cracked me up, like how can you walk around with that and not feel totally ridiculous? I remember thinking some things are meant to stay underwater, you know, and then Trent grabs me and sticks his tongue down my throat and I'm like, hey, we're outside the theater now, this script doesn't apply out here in the lobby and meanwhile Trent's trying to get my legs apart with his knee, I'm standing backed up against the sink and I pulled my face away and spotted the light switch just at that minute, it was this naked man made out of plastic and like the up-and-down switch was his crotch, very tasteful, right?—and it just sort of fit in with everything else. I kneed Trent in the balls and said, fuck off, I'm going to tell Rebecca if you don't chill out and he goes—holding his nuts and moaning—she doesn't give a shit, what do you think she's doing right now? and suddenly I'm running out to the hot tub and it's empty, there's no one there and I run up to the house, I rush up the staircase following these wet footsteps that get fainter and fainter and then disappear, I'm out of my mind, I start ripping open the bedroom doors, of course there are about twenty bedrooms in this goddamn house. I find them in Rebecca's room, they haven't even pulled the sheets up over them, I see Rebecca's face underneath him looking out at me like she was expecting me, her mouth open and glistening like something horrible coming up from the bottom of the ocean. . . .

Some impulses you should stifle, right? I never used to think so, I've always done whatever I felt like, I figured anything else and you're a hypocrite like I told Dean, but I don't know, here in the middle of this really ugly Truth or Dare session watching my sister grab my boyfriend's dick, thinking about her and Alex back then, thinking about some of the shit I've done recently, I'm beginning to wonder if a little stifling is such a bad thing. Right now I'd give my grandmother's pearls for a little white lie. The way this game is going, I'd give all my possessions for a dose of amnesia.

So I get up and go to the bathroom while Truth or Dare is raging around me. This is even worse than the fucking derby.

After a minute Dean knocks on the door and asks me if I'm okay.

It's all right, I say.

But actually I'm feeling like shit. I'm a shivering wreck, drunk and high and totally nauseous. I sit on the toilet for about ten minutes with my head on my knees, then I go back out.

Alison's looking wasted, Becca says.

A shivering wreck, Didi says.

She needs help, Becca goes. She hands me this ratty little card, I have to look real hard to focus on it. Big letters, H-E-L-P. Becca starts singing a chorus of "Help me, Rhonda" and Didi joins in for a second, then says, Ev-er-ett, tell the truth . . . how many girls?

Approximately twenty, says the prep.

Exact figures, Didi says. No rounding off.

Maybe twenty-two, he goes. By now the prep is looking really miserable and who can blame him?

So then he asks Dean, truth or dare.

And Dean says, I think I'll keep my clothes on, thanks. He picks truth.

No fair, Becca says. We want full frontal male nudity.

Everett says to Dean, am I crazy or did I see Rebecca grab your, uh, you know?

You ain't crazy, Dean says. He has this stupid smile.

God, Francesca says, I missed that.

Rebecca turns and looks at me. I was just checking his answer when he said he had a hard-on, she explains.

Rebecca the fact chekka, says Francesca.

It's Dean's turn, Everett says.

And when Dean says my name, I don't like the tone of

voice. He gives me this really unpleasant look. Truth or dare? he goes.

Truth, I say. I should've taken the dare.

And he says, have you slept with Skip recently?

I go, recently?

In the past week, he says.

I don't think I've ever wanted to lie so much in my life. But Skip's right here and he's not going to let me get by with it.

Didi, smelling blood, starts going, truth, truth, truth!

Everybody else gets real quiet.

Yeah, I say.

I look up at Dean, his eyes are this beautiful soft blue that sometimes looks like a tropical ocean. But now they look so cold.

I want to explain. I'd really like to tell him about it, I think I could make him understand. Not that I'm proud of myself.

Well, well, well, says Rebecca.

There's a knock on the door, which is great, anything to break this mood, a mass murder would make a nice change in the atmosphere here and Dean says, shit, probably my neighbor bitching about the noise. His voice is a little shaky but he's probably really glad to have the distraction of something normal to deal with because I can tell he's really upset and it's like breaking my heart. I don't think he expected me to say yes, he was just suspicious.

So Dean gets up to go to the door and Francesca is shaking her head like she hates to see her friend fuck up so bad, then she suddenly looks over toward the door and lets out this shriek and Skip goes, what the fuck! and Rebecca is like, oh Jesus, give me a break, Mannie.

Sure enough, it's the guy we supposedly rescued Rebecca from up in Morningside Heights last month or whenever it was. Except I think it was the other way around. He's got his knife out again. I don't know, it seems kind of harmless at this point, like sort of a gimmick, you know, his schtick. Some guys wear suspenders, Mannie the drug dealer always carries a knife.

He looks all hopped up, except Rebecca said he'd quit doing drugs so he could get a job and make an honest woman out of her, fat chance of that. And he's wearing a suit and a tie which seems weird, he doesn't look like he's used to it, he basically looks like he dressed up to visit his grandmother's house or maybe to try and impress the folks down at the immigration office.

He sort of zigzags into the room, crouched down low with the knife out in front of him, the way cops move on TV when they're expecting gunfire any minute.

Cut the theatrics, Mannie, Becca says.

And Mannie goes, you loved me.

I fucked you, she says. There's a difference.

Hey, what's this all about? Everett goes.

I got a job, Mannie says. You were going to live with me.

That was your idea, she says, not mine.

Come back, he sobs. There are actual tears running down his cheeks. He lowers the knife, which he's been pointing at Didi, lets his arms fall to his side. Please come back, he goes. It's really pathetic.

It was only one night for Christ's sake, Becca says.

Two nights, says Mannie. I never will forget.

Rebecca's like, whatever.

Obviously it didn't make quite as unforgettable an impression on her.

I guess he rates you a ten, says Didi, who keeps chopping lines like she sees this sort of thing every night.

Wait a minute, I want to know what's this about, Everett goes. He stands up and says, whoever you are, I think you better leave. Now. He looks at Rebecca for support.

He can do whatever he wants for all I care, she says, watching Didi lay out the lines.

Look buddy, why don't you give me the knife? Everett says. He's a pretty big boy, six two or so and built, I mean he probably played lacrosse at Dartmouth and this guy Mannie's about a foot shorter.

I don't know what happens next—the prep makes a move and Mannie freaks, suddenly the prep is holding his arm and there's blood dripping out from between his fingers.

Oh God, Francesca says.

Dean's been watching this, he's seen Mannie in action once before so he wasn't too worried at first, I guess, but now he comes up toward Mannie and says, look, give me the knife, Mannie. You know me, he says, I'm not going to hurt you, and just then Everett goes, I'm going to hurt you, you motherfucking spic, you cut me. And Mannie's looking like a trapped animal, I really feel sorry for the little guy, he's just confused.

He backs himself up against the window, pointing the knife at Dean and the prep, his arm whipping back and forth like a dog's tail. He kind of climbs up onto the windowsill and Dean's going, Mannie, calm down, okay? Let's talk about this thing.

And Mannie, he's breathing like a horse after a race, gasping for air, and he goes, please, Rebecca, I love you. Please.

God, the sound of his voice, this despair, it's like the saddest thing I've ever heard in my entire life, practically.

Rebecca leans over the mirror and snorts a line.

I'll hurt myself, Mannie screams.

Be my guest, says Rebecca.

Come on, Mannie, Dean says, real soothing, there's this big drama going on but of course I'm thinking about myself, I'm thinking about Dean, what a sweet guy he is, basically. I'm really proud of the way he handles things, unlike Skip, and I'm thinking, shit, maybe I've blown it forever, and all this is going through my head in about three seconds.

Then Everett makes another try for the knife.

Mannie screams Rebecca's name and then I don't know, suddenly he disappears, he's just gone, and Dean rushes over to the window and looks out. Oh God, he says, oh Jesus.

Everett is just standing there in a daze, bleeding and saying, he cut me, then Skip looks out, he doesn't say anything, he runs from the window to the coffee table and grabs Didi's bag and says, quick, we've got to flush this stuff before the police get here and I'm still having trouble catching up with the situation, I'm like—the police?

It takes me a minute to realize we're on the sixth floor and Mannie's jumped out the window.

11

HUNTERS AND JUMPERS

S o when Francesca calls I'm asleep as usual, I can't seem to wake up anymore. I could sleep forever. But I'm half dreaming and I hear Francesca's voice on the machine and she was already in the dream but the voice keeps saying pick up pick up and I'm thinking what did I drop, what did I lose, pick what up? Then I wake up enough to figure out it's the phone.

What? I go.

Alison, I don't believe it, I've been leaving messages on your machine for two days, where have you been? and I go, I've been sleeping.

With who? she says and I don't say anything.

Listen, she goes, you won't believe it, you will never in a billion years believe where I was Thursday night.

I'm like hanging on, holding my head and rubbing my eyes, and she goes *Alison,* really impatient, and I realize I'm supposed to act interested so I ask where.

Mick and Jerry's, she goes. Do you believe it?

I don't believe it, I say, like I could give a shit. I mean I'm glad she's happy but right now I have this headache and I'm feeling nauseous and I could give a shit about lifestyles of the rich and infamous. I'm a lot more worried about survival of the fittest, and like whether I'm going to make the cut or join the club for dinosaurs and dodo birds.

I feel. like shit.

Francesca says, it was so great, guess who I sat next to?

I pretend to listen for a while and then I tell her I gotta pee and swallow some aspirin, I'll call her later and I can tell she's kind of ticked that I'm not having multiple orgasms about her social coup, but I just don't care right now, so shoot me.

Maybe because she's mad at me she says, I saw Dean at Elio's last night.

I know there's more coming. Yeah? I go.

She goes, he was with his old girlfriend, Patty.

For some reason this doesn't surprise me. In fact, as soon as I hear it I feel like I already knew it.

When I don't say anything, Francesca says, he was a jerk.

Dean's not a jerk, but I don't feel like arguing.

Then suddenly I go, Francesca, what's the third great lie?

She's like, huh?

What's the third great lie? I go. The first one is the check's in the mail. Then, I promise I won't come in your mouth. What's the third?

But she doesn't know either. I tell her I'll call her back later.

I almost fall back to sleep but instead I get up and lurch to the bathroom, using the walls for support. I suck down three Extra-Strength Tylenols and then I look at my face in the mirror, it's all puffed out and blotchy, my tan's shot, my eyes look Chinese. I stand there for a while holding onto the sink feeling like I could puke, but it doesn't quite come.

The phone's ringing again, I forgot to turn the machine back on. For some reason I answer and it's Whitney. Alison, she goes, you'll never believe it (I'm like, why is everybody so sure I won't believe them, at this point I'll believe fucking just about anything), I was working the door last night and who shows up but Skip Pendleton with some thirteen-year-old bimbette on his arm. Well, you remember how he said he was such an expert at Trivial Pursuit and he'd kill me if we ever played? So he's like standing outside the rope expecting me to sweep him right in and I go, Skip, what's the year the Beatles first played Hamburg and what's the name of the club they played? and he's like, what? And I say, Trivial Pursuit, Skipper, and he says, I don't know and I say, sorry, then, you can't come in. He almost died, he's just standing there and I wouldn't let him in . . . I didn't . . .

She goes on and on and I'm thinking she sounds like an idiot. Yada yada yada. God, she sounds just like me. A few weeks ago this story would've had me rolling on the floor and slapping my ribs but now I'm hardly listening.

Isn't that great? she finally says.

I go, just great.

I knew you'd love it, she says.

That story is going to change my fucking life, I say.

Hey, I just thought you'd be interested, Skip and all, she says. No need to be such a bitch.

I tell her I'm sorry, I'm just sitting here desperately waiting for my period, I'll call her later when I'm feeling human again, though frankly if I never saw Whitney again it wouldn't bother me for more than a nanosecond.

I don't know, I don't seem to want to have anything to do with anybody who was there that night. But then, I don't seem to want to have anything to do with anybody, period.

It's been almost two weeks. I've only talked to Dean twice since then, once the morning after when he was at the hospital. He called to tell me that Mannie was stable but critical, whatever that means. About a week later I called him back. It was really awkward. We tried to make small talk. He said he'd talked to Phil and that Didi had been clean since the accident and she's started going to some church group down in Soho and she never wanted to see another line of cocaine in her life. I knew that already, I've been hearing about it day and night whenever I'm not crashed out sleeping. She calls me and preaches, which is probably why I'm so sleepy. It's all she can talk about, how bad she was then and how glad she is now that she's stopped and how Jesus is the man with the plan. Amazing Grace, how obnoxious the sound. I think I liked her better as a junkie. But I said to Dean, oh yeah? like I didn't know all this, because I wanted to talk to him and I didn't want him to hang up and we needed something besides ourselves to talk about. That's good, I said. Everett got a few stitches in his hand, Dean said. And he told me the police had closed their investigation.

They questioned all of us, and our stories were pretty much the same. At first they were sort of nasty about it, when they clumped in, it was obvious we were all fucked up, but by that time the premises were drug-free. What clinched it was when Mannie regained consciousness, he said it was his own fault. He said he'd meant to scare his girlfriend and that he'd slipped on the windowsill. Could've happened to anybody, right? In the meantime there'd been a few million new crimes in the naked city so the cops were happy to drop it. The whole thing was only a paragraph in the *Post* and the *News,* about how some nobody fell out of a window on the Upper East Side and lived to tell the tale. Jesus. Skip got twice the column space the last time he threw a party.

Rebecca split town the day after. She tried to leave the apartment before the cops got there but Dean wouldn't let her. The next day she was gone, I know because Everett called here looking for her. He told me he got five stitches where Mannie had cut him. A couple nights ago there was a crackly message on my machine from Rebecca in Lugano, Switzerland, where she's staying in this incredible hotel overlooking the lake, drinking champagne and eating radioactive chocolate. She said she's totally in lust, she'd met a great new guy. Story of her life.

Jeannie's in South Carolina visiting Frank. They reconciled after Alex called up and said he couldn't make it for the weekend and that he didn't think he'd be up the next weekend either. Jeannie's been working late and checking out china and silver patterns during lunch and I've been sleeping most of the time so we haven't really talked much lately, I'm not sure what's going on in her mind. It looks like I'm going to have to find a new place soon since her old man thinks I'm irresponsible and that the two of us are a dangerous combination. It's not really Jeannie's fault, I guess. She says I can stay as long as I need to find a new place, but Francesca told me I could move in with her and I guess a change is as good as a rest.

A few days ago some friend of Rebecca's called up, he said he was a jewelry dealer and that he wanted to buy the pearls, so I'm going to take them over tomorrow, I don't know what else to do.

My father says he's broke. Which is total bullshit but what can I do? Can you sue your father for nonsupport? He sent me a check for five hundred dollars—like wow, thanks Dad—but that was gone before I'd even cashed it. I owe everybody. The last thing Dean said to me was, do you need money? and like an idiot I said no.

I know, I've got to get a job, I guess I'll have to waitress—God how depressing, but right now I'm having trouble getting out of bed, I haven't even been to class in a week. Tomorrow after I go meet this so-called jewelry dealer I'm going to the doctor. I'd probably feel better about myself if I could go and work on my instrument, but I feel too shitty to bother, it's a vicious circle. Or is it cycle? Dean used to tell me these things. A few more months with him and I might even have started to feel educated.

Dean said he was buckling down to his work, really getting organized, going to bed early and waking up early, keeping a journal and working on some ideas for plays. I could tell that was kind of directed at me—blaming me for his wildness. There was this big slide in the bond market a few weeks ago and it really freaked him out, he's like a reformed sinner or something. It suddenly occurred to him they might show him the door before he'd socked away his first million. Not that I'm any expert on employment but maybe jobs are like lovers—one day they're boring and stupid but suddenly they're real desirable when you think you're getting dumped. I don't know, he'd just broken up with his long-time squeeze when I met him, he was all set to get down and be irresponsible. Now that he's scratched that little itch deep enough for a while and he wants to act like a grown-up again he needs somebody to blame for acting like a kid. When we'd stay up late he'd sometimes get in this panic, this big middle-class guilt thing about being a productive citizen even though the night before he'd wanted to be a bohemian, right? Then he'd take it out on me, get real weird in the mornings. I mean, I didn't tell him to stay up all night, he was right there chopping the lines and pouring the drinks.

Now, after a little run with the bad girls, it's back to the mature and responsible Patty. Enough of the postmodern girls, now he wants the good old-fashioned kind. Patty's like a banker or something. I can see her in her sensible shoes with her briefcase, or her Talbot's clothes on the weekends in the country, doing the crossword puzzle, sipping decaf, buying antiques. Pass *The New Yorker,* dear. Certainly, muffin.

Dean practically has all of Shakespeare memorized and he can handle millions of dollars a day of other people's money, he can be smart about other people but he's like a foreigner to himself. Sometimes I just wanted to stand him in front of the mirror and say, Dean, meet Dean. Sit him down with himself and translate what he says into plain American.

So that's Dean. Francesca's wrong, he's not a jerk. He is, but not really. I fucked up. I did something he couldn't get over, and you can't really blame him for that.

I don't know, he did the same thing to me, screwing Cassie Hane. I suppose that was why I did it. I called up one night a few days before our killer Truth or Dare session and asked him to take me out to dinner and he said he couldn't, he had to go out with some friends. What really pissed me off is he didn't give me any explanation. That was that. You know, he could have said who these friends were who were so important and so exclusive that they couldn't stand my company, but he didn't. I said fine, really bitchy so even Dean could tell I was pissed, and hung up. Then I waited for him to call me back and the son of a bitch never did. I was furious. I was so furious I called him back after half an hour to tell him. I got his machine. After that I called up Cassie Hane's boyfriend, Peter. I didn't say who I was, I just asked if Cassie was there and he said no, she had her own place and I said, you know how she got that Barneys' ad? Dean Chasen is real good friends with the guy who owns that agency. And he goes, who is this? and then I go, a friend, I hate to see her make an idiot out of you. Then I hung up. Next I call up Cassie and I do this southern accent I can do perfectly from all the girls we used to show horses with and I go, Cassie, honey, I hate to be the bearer of bad tidings to y'all but I saw you the other night with Dean Chasen and I just thought it might interest you to know that he gave me a nasty little infection. And she goes, who is this? but I'm already gone.

So when Jeannie came home and asked if I wanted to split a gram I said sure. When that was gone we went to the

Surf Club and Didi was there, and so was Skip. Skip was flirting outrageously, really hitting hard on me, all these steamy looks and sexual innuendos. I don't know, I had a bunch of drinks, at that time of night Magilla Gorilla can start to look good and Skip's no gorilla, he's pretty decent-looking, plus I was remembering that he was actually really good in bed. Plus I was so mad at Dean. That's what it was really all about in the end, when Skip and I were rocking the old sleigh bed back at his place, we weren't really screwing each other, we were both screwing Dean.

I wish I hadn't, but it's done now. I think about calling him, but I don't. I turn on the tube for a while and watch "All My Children." Then I go back to sleep.

When I go to the doctor's I tell her I just feel shitty and nauseous and I sleep all the time. She asks me about my period and I can't really remember. I've been on the pill since I started going out with Dean but sometimes I forget to take it and I can't really remember when I finished up the package. I don't know, for a while there—like a couple of months—I was using the old withdrawal method, which is about as safe as Russian roulette. After surviving that I figure I should do fine on the pill. My gynecologist keeps telling me I should make the guys wear rubbers but I hate them and so do they. Safe sex, right? That's like, truth in advertising, it's kind of a contradiction in terms.

So anyway, I think this doctor's barking up the wrong tree, but she takes some blood for a test along with everything else and sends me on my way without a single prescription for narcotics, which really depresses me, I'm going to have to find a new doctor. I mean, when I spend a hundred bucks I usually get off.

So I meet this guy at Jackson Hole who wants to buy the necklace. The short, balding type, maybe forty, he looks like my father. He has rotten skin, the pores in his nose are like the potholes on Second Avenue, you could lose a cab in one of those things. Real attractive, right? He's wearing this incredibly tacky diamond ring and a giant Rolex. If I had to list my least favorite things, jewelry on men would be right up there at the top.

After we sit down I take the necklace out of my purse—it's in this blue velvet case—and he puts it down on the table and starts looking at me instead of the pearls. He goes, your sister Rebecca is a lovely girl, I admire her very much.

I go, she's a big hit with all the boys.

And he goes, but I think you're even prettier.

You'd be the first if you really did, I say.

Just to give him a little hint about why we're here and all, I reach over and open the case for him. He picks up the necklace and holds it up to the light, sticks a little telescope thing in his eye and squints at it. I mean, this has got to be an act, I know damn well who he's buying these for, but she certainly went to a lot of trouble to make it look authentic, the bitch.

When the waitress comes around I order a burger deluxe because I haven't eaten in two days and frankly I'm starved and I figure I'll tell him I forgot my wallet. I'm feeling really dizzy, for a minute I almost black out, my vision gets all blurry.

172

After a while he says, nice, not bad at all. Then he looks up and says, did you know that pearls are a symbol of purity? and I shake my head, I'm scarfing my burger.

I bet you're pure, he goes.

And I'm like, right.

And he goes, I bet you don't go out with just anybody.

So finally I've cleared this big wad of beef out of my mouth and I say to him, actually I fuck practically anybody. But in your case I think I'd make an exception.

And he's like totally blown away that I'm talking like this.

So how much for the necklace? I go and eventually he offers me twenty-five hundred and I take it, he's got the cash right there—naturally a guy who wears gold jewelry would carry a huge roll of cash, right?—so I take it and make him pay for the burger and I walk out of the restaurant feeling dizzy and puke all over the sidewalk.

And this guy who's just bought my grandmother's symbols of purity comes out and watches me wipe off my face and goes, you wanna come back to my place and lie down for a while?

I hand over most of the money to Jeannie because even though her father came up with the back rent I still owe for the past month plus the phone bill and that pretty much takes care of my little inheritance. And of course she immediately decides we should buy a quarter ounce. But I'm the irresponsible one, right? Well, okay, I am a little irresponsible and I don't protest as much as I should about this idea. But I haven't really talked to Jeannie in ages and I really want to sort of clear the air, you know, I mean Jeannie and I go way back, plus I'm feeling so bad I don't think anything could make me feel worse and it's either stimulants or another twenty hours in bed.

We just sit around the apartment and talk all night. It's great. We start talking about Didi and how great it is that she's off drugs because she really had a problem, she was just way over the top.

Next we start talking about guys, naturally. Jeannie says she doesn't know, she's just not sure about Frank, does she really want to spend the rest of her life with this guy who was kind of dull to begin with and then betrayed her with a bimbo? Frank is pushing for a fall wedding and now Jeannie's got cold feet. I tell her she knows my feelings about marriage, I mean probably it works for people with really low expectations and about zero self-esteem, but show me a happy marriage and I'll show you one fool and one hypocrite. Like, I've got a late meeting tonight, honey, don't wait up for me. Okay, darling, don't work too hard.

I don't even mention that Frank has one of the smaller dicks I've ever experienced. Two inches of throbbing steel.

So after a while we talk about the old days on the horse circuit, that was where we got to know each other, sharing rooms in half the Hiltons of America, showing and jumping while everyone else was going to school and proms, riding all year long to qualify for the three big shows in Harrisburg, Washington and then Madison Square Garden, ordering room service and flirting with the busboys and the stable hands and the judges, and now it sort of feels like all of that's ending, I mean it ended a long time ago, a few years back anyway, but in a way we sort of grew up together on the road and in the saddle and moved to New York together and now I'm moving out to Francesca's and somehow I don't think I'll see Jeannie much after a while. She really sort of screwed me over but it still depresses the shit out of me, because whatever comes next it won't be the same.

And Jeannie is all excited about something she's saying, I've been half listening, something about horses, and then she's crying, saying, that wasn't fair, that was so unfair, I still think about it.

It turns out she's all upset about this one show out on Long Island when I won the ribbon for hunters. Showing hunters is very political anyway, it's all up to the judges. With jumpers if you jump clean it's strictly against the clock and more fun. The horses are thinner and they're fast and nobody can rob you if you win. Hunters are big fat beautiful animals and they're judged on form, supposedly. And I do mean supposedly.

So this one day Jeannie went before me, she was on this horse, Patrick Henry, he was beautiful and she had a great run, everything clean, I watched her from the stand and then I went out on my horse, Eric the Red. Eric was in this really rotten mood, I don't know why, then when I get out there and start jumping I realize he's lame. He banged two jumps early on and twisted once coming down. I was trying really hard to hold him up, he was pretty lame and I just thought, go for it, let's just get through this thing.

So me and Eric the Red won first prize in the class.

Something weird was going on in that judging booth, don't ask me what. Maybe my father paid somebody, maybe somebody liked the look of my ass in riding breeches, whatever.

175

It was so unfair, Jeannie goes. I never forgot that.

And I go, welcome to the world, Jeannie babe.

Because that's the thing about hunters and jumpers. The jumpers are fair, it's you against a clock. But showing hunters, it's political. Great preparation for life, right?

Let's face it, how often is anything fair?

Jeannie finally stops crying long enough to tell me she's always competed with me, even though she loves me she's always tried to outdo me in everything and never felt like she could, like this is news to me, and I go, it's okay really and for about three minutes we're best friends, everything's fine, and we talk about really silly and trivial things that seem important enough at the time and finally she says, I'm going to give you the best birthday ever and then she goes whoops, like there's been a big surprise planned and she blew it.

I sort of figured my friends would do something, I mean, I hoped they would. Ten days from now I'll be twenty-one. It seems like I've been on the planet a lot longer than that. Like who is that woman who goes around the country to Ramada Inns pretending to be some forty-thousand-year-old man, charging people hundreds of dollars to come listen to her speak in this fake baritone about the wisdom of the ages? Well, whoever she is she's an imposter, the real forty-thousand-year-old man is me. And I'm here to tell you, free of charge, that it sucks.

12

GOOD NIGHT LADIES

Of course with my luck it turns out I'm actually pregnant. The rabbit dies, so I have to visit the clinic for real this time. I can't believe it. And I don't have a nickel to my name, I owe everybody in the western hemisphere, I'm like a fucking Third World country—empty treasury, exploding birth rate. Jesus. And what's really depressing is I don't know whose it is, I mean, it could be Skip's and it could be Dean's. If this had happened a few months back there would've been like twenty suspects, but even two is too many. Francesca and Jeannie want me to call Dean, they say it's only fair. No way. I'd rather have the kid than call Dean, and I'm not about to have the kid.

I call Carol first, my sister, and she's really sympathetic,

I don't know what I'd do if I didn't have Carol to talk to sometimes and she says if I can't find the money anywhere else she'll get her boyfriend to cough it up, he's rich and she'll threaten him with a sex embargo if he gets difficult about it.

I go, where's Dad? and she says he's in Cancun with a new bimbo. Which is just great. Whenever I need my old man he's on some beach with a nineteen-year-old sex kitten. Story of his life.

Next I call my old man's office and his secretary claims he's in Europe on business and then she says, I just sent you the check for your school tuition.

And I'm like, incredible, I don't believe it. Something actually going right in my life for a change. I must be dreaming.

So I make an appointment for the next week and I use the tuition money which is kind of ironic because last month I used my supposed abortion money for tuition and now it's the other way around. And if that's not weird enough I see Skip Pendleton a few nights later, he's with some anorexic Click model and pretends not to see me. Meanwhile my breasts hurt like hell and I feel like I'm filling up like a water balloon. I try not to think about the thing inside me, I mean, even if it's a person instead of a fish I want to say, hey, believe me, I'm doing you a favor. You don't need this shit.

I'm so distracted that I totally forget the appointment is the day before my birthday. When I figure it out I'm like, what the fuck, I want this over with. They tell me I should be able to walk out of the clinic that afternoon and barring complications I'll be fine in a day or two. I tell them I've got twenty-four hours till the first day of the rest of my life.

* * *

Don't ask me why, I don't want anybody to think I'm getting mushy in my old age, but for some reason I decide to visit Mannie in the hospital. They've got him over at Lenox Hill, I walk over. Out in front these two old guys are having a wheelchair race down the sidewalk and people start cheering them on, these two guys must be in their eighties but they're really starting to cruise and people are jumping out of the way, then a nurse and an orderly come out and start screaming at them and chase them down.

Mannie's like a cartoon version of an accident victim, they've got him in this body cast, he's like a mummy in traction. His head is pretty well bandaged up but you can see his face and when I come in he opens his eyes, he starts smiling like a lunatic, I don't know if he remembers me or if he's just like a baby that smiles at anything.

So I go, it's Alison, Rebecca's sister. Then suddenly I feel bad, like I maybe shouldn't mention Rebecca, right?

He smiles, the guy's beaming like a headlight, either they've got him on some really great drugs or else he's glad to see me.

I'm really sorry, I go.

I know, don't tell me, I have a real gift for saying the intelligent thing.

I sit down in this chair beside the bed, just to give myself something to do. He's still smiling, it's beginning to drive me crazy, it's like he knows something I don't know, so finally I go, Rebecca asked me to send her best, she had to rush out of town for some important stuff but she wanted me to check up on you and say hello and all.

Which is totally a lie, I don't know why I say it, except maybe to make him feel better.

And after another few minutes of smiley-face I go, it was an accident, right? His face is really white, white and red where he's cut and stitched, he looks like some painting where the colors are all wrong and not true to life.

His mouth starts to move and I lean closer so I can hear what he's saying. Finally he says, in this gnarly whisper, tell her I love her.

And I'm like, what are you, nuts? You're crazy, you're really out of your mind. Listen, I go, I hate to be the one to tell you but she's actually a total bitch, she doesn't give a shit about you, she doesn't give a shit about anyone but herself, she hasn't even asked about you. That's what kind of person Rebecca is.

He's not really looking at me, he's looking through me, still smiling, and I say, what is it about her? I mean, tell me, I'm dying to know, this is really bugging me.

All he does is say it again—tell her I love her.

I say, I'm sorry, Mannie, I didn't mean that, it was just jealousy. Becca had to go out of town but she asked me to look in on you and everything. I'm sure you'll hear from her soon, I go.

I don't know if he hears me or not. I leave him grinning into outer space like some kind of Moonie, somebody way beyond your basic logic and facts. The thing is, he looks happy, which is more than you can say for the rest of us.

Francesca comes with me to the clinic. She's lost about twenty pounds in the last two weeks and she's looking great.

I make her promise not to call Dean no matter what. We sit around in this waiting room with *Mademoiselle*s and *Ladies' Home Journal*s on the coffee table in case we want to get some summer tanning tips or learn how to make a supermoist coffee cake that will drive hubby into fucking raptures and then they call me in and I undress, put on the little paper robe, climb up on the table, stick my feet in the nice cold stirrups.

I want drugs, I say, as soon as the doctor shows up.

I've heard they give you Demerol and I tell them I have this monster tolerance, forget about the correct dosage for my height and weight, but the doctor says for outpatients all they recommend is a local. I'm like, give me the express. She sticks a needle in my uterus and I try to do my sense-memory, I do a sense-memory of Dean just imagining him sitting in that chair of his where he reads and talking about Shakespeare or the stock market or something, I recreate the expressions on his face, his crooked smile, I put him right there next to me talking. Forget about sex—they're hoovering my insides out . . . the local isn't enough to kill the pain and it's hard to do my sense-memory, I can't concentrate, I keep losing the image, his face and his voice keep fading like something on a bad TV set in the middle of nowhere. . . .

So I try to remember that rhyme we used to say in school—Miss Mary Mack Mack Mack all dressed in black black black, but I draw a blank on the rest . . .

Afterwards it hurts like hell. They give me another incredibly painful shot to close up my uterus and after that it's cramp city.

Francesca takes me home in a cab and puts me in bed and Jeannie comes in with some ten-milligram Valiums and

I drift off into some kind of brain death for about sixteen hours.

Jeannie wakes me up a little after noon, she's bought me two dozen long-stemmed roses and my mail on a little breakfast tray, birthday cards from her and Carol and my mother and a bunch of other people. Nothing from my dad. Not even a fucking card.

Any messages? I go, and Jeannie says Francesca called to ask how was I doing, that's it.

So I just lie around in bed all day, I'm not exactly feeling too terrific, but why bitch?

My mom calls after five, she's very economical about little things like waiting for the rates to go down but then she'll spend a hundred and fifty dollars to have the poodle trimmed.

Happy birthday, baby, she says. You're all grown up now.

Thanks a lot, I go.

Did you get my card? she says.

I got it, thanks, I say.

Then she starts to tell me about her boyfriend, how thoughtless and inconsiderate he's been, how he's not sensitive to her needs, yada yada yada. She goes on and on, she's not blasted yet, but I can hear the ice cubes rattling at the other end of the phone. It's not like I'm not sympathetic, but it's a little depressing because maybe just this once on my birthday we could talk about me. I'm the kid here, after all, even if I'm supposed to be a big girl now. I'm the one who could maybe use some advice, and it makes me wonder, what's the point of being an adult, except that you can legally drink in all states of the union, my mom might as well be sixteen the way she talks. . . .

Finally I tell her I've got to get dressed for my party and ask if she knows where Dad is. She doesn't but she's sure he'll call.

Right.

At seven Jeannie says it's time to get dressed and helps me pick out my outfit, basic black, leather skirt from Fiorucci and a Kamali silk top, fishnet stockings, killer pumps from Bennis and Edwards that I borrowed from Didi a few months back.

You'll be raped on the street, Jeannie says after she checks me out.

I go, can't rape the willing.

That's my girl, says Jeannie.

I'm fine, I go.

Didi and Francesca have chipped in and got me a limo, so the four of us go over to Sam's and meet the gang there, a table for sixteen, the usual suspects. Rebecca's prep Everett is there, don't ask me why, he's like all mopey and it's like being at my birthday will at least remind him of Rebecca a little bit so he can keep being miserable. Plus Didi and Whitney and Mark from the tanning place and a bunch of other idiots who are all my friends sort of, and when I walk in everybody jumps up—happy birthday, Alison!—and I'm looking around thinking just maybe Dean will be there but he isn't and why would he be, really?

So we have this big dinner, I mean, some of us have this big dinner and some of us just keep going to the bathroom, Jeannie's got blow and so does Mark, Didi keeps screaming at us saying we're fucking drug addicts, she's really disgusted. It's amazing she doesn't even see that it's like pretty ironic, to say the least. When we all do a chorus of "Amazing Grace," she gets really mad.

Things kind of get out of control after a while. The prep tries to beat up the waiter, don't ask me why. He's one of those fighting drunks, plus his heart is broken. He offers to marry me at one point and I say, thanks, but I don't believe in marriage and he goes, I can respect that point of view, saying the words real carefully like he's afraid he'll drop them and they'll break. Then he offers to pay for the meal and everybody thinks this is a cool idea, suddenly he stands up and bangs on a wineglass with a spoon until he breaks it, so then he pounds on the table till he gets everybody's attention and then he looks around like he's not sure where he is until suddenly he remembers. He weaves his head like he's ducking a tiny plane that just skimmed the top of his hair. Then he goes, really serious, today is Alison's birthday.

Everybody goes wild and cheers, partly because it seems amazing that he can even talk or remember what the occasion is.

Today, he goes, Alison is an adult.

A lot of catcalls and hisses for this idea. The prep takes a direct hit—a piece of cheesecake on the cheek.

I'm serious, he goes. I mean this. I love this girl, no, wait, she's not a girl now she's a woman.

So of course Didi and Francesca start singing Bob Marley's "No Woman, No Cry."

Everett waves his arms for silence, his right hand is still bandaged from where Mannie cut him, he's like, I love her sister, but I love her too. I'd like to treat Alison and all of you to dinner because you're all friends of Rebecca's and I love Rebecca and I love all of you.

So everybody's cheering and throwing shit at the prep and I have this funny feeling about this offer. Sure enough, he remembers when the waiter brings him the check that he gave Rebecca all of his credit cards.

Later we go to Nell's and then the Zulu Lounge and then we end up at our place but it's too small and the prep says he's still got this suite over at the Stanhope, he can't afford to pay the bill so he keeps staying on. So we go over there, it's getting toward dawn by now and Jeannie takes up a collection and makes a run over to Emile's place. . . .

The party goes on for two days.

Some of the people disappear eventually, some come back the second night, two guys from this Australian rock band drop by for nine or ten hours and Emile shows up with fresh supplies, I guess we must've called him. Francesca keeps coming and going, trying to rescue me, at one point she offers to take me shopping at Bergdorf's with her Dad's credit card but me and Everett hold down the fort, sitting in the middle of the floor going, I can't believe somebody else feels that way—wow, I thought I was the only person in the world who felt like that—and him telling me about Rebecca and me talking about Dean while I burn holes in the upholstery of the Louis Cathouse chairs. We just can't talk fast enough to free up all these great thoughts we're having. Great minds sink alike, right? So at some point I ask Everett if he knows the three great lies. I tell him the first two while he sits there nodding like a guru or something with like the intense calm that only the truly crazed and manic can fake. Then I say to him, so what's the third?

That's easy, he says. The third lie is, I love you.

And I'm thinking, wow! of course. That's it!

And we have to phone in booze and cigarettes from this deli over on Lex because they've cut off our room service and I try to call my dad but I can never get him and I remember something about the management saying we would have to leave but we shined them on basically and after that I don't know, I think I got hysterical at some point, maybe I tried to jump out the window, suddenly it seemed like the thing to do.

Anyway, somewhere in the depths of my delirium tremendous I have this flash of sanity that says I am in bad trouble and I remember this thing in my wallet, so at some point when old Everett is draining his toxins I dig through my purse and then my wallet and finally come up with the card, which is tucked up behind the change purse with all these napkin fragments with the names and numbers of all the boys I never called and I crawl over to the phone and call out, call this number, the last four digits spell out H-E-L-P on the dial.

I think after that I talked to my father, I'm not sure, but anyway, eventually a doctor comes over to the suite, I don't really remember. . . .

And now I'm in a place in Minnesota under sedation dreaming the white dreams about snow falling endlessly in the North Country, making the landscape disappear, dreaming about long white rails that disappear over the horizon like railroad tracks to the stars. Like when I used to ride and was anorexic and I'd starve myself and all I would ever dream about was food. There are horses at the far end of the pasture outside my window. I watch them through the bars.

Toward the end of the endless party that landed me here I was telling the prep the story about Dangerous Dan. I had eight horses at one point, but Dangerous Dan was the best. I traveled all over the country jumping and showing and when I first saw Dan, I knew he was like no other horse. He was like a human being—so spirited and nasty he'd jump twenty feet in the air to avoid the trainer's whip, then stop dead or hang a leg up on an easy jump, just for spite. He had perfect confirmation, like a statue of a horse dreamed by Michelangelo. My father bought him for me and he cost a fortune. Back then my father bought anything for me. I was his sweet thing.

I loved that horse. No one else could get near him, he'd try to kill them, but I used to sleep in his stall, spend hours with him every day. When he was poisoned I went into shock. They kept me on tranquilizers for a week. There was an investigation—nothing came of it. The insurance company paid off in full, but I quit riding. A few months later, Dad came into my bedroom one night. I was like, uh-oh, not this again. He buried his face in my shoulder. His cheek was wet and he smelled of booze. I'm sorry about Dangerous Dan, he said. Tell me you forgive me. He muttered something about the business and then passed out on top of me and I had to go and get Mom.

After a week in the hatch they let me use the phone. I call my dad. How are you? he says.

I don't know why, it's probably bullshit, but I've been

trapped in this place with a bunch of shrink types for a week. So just for the hell of it I go, Dad, sometimes I think it would have been cheaper if you'd let me keep that horse.

He goes, I don't know what you're talking about.

I go, Dangerous Dan. You remember what you told me that night. After he died.

He goes, I didn't tell you anything.

So, okay, maybe I dreamed it. I was in bed after all, and he woke me up. Not for the first time. But just now, with these tranks they've got me on, I feel like I'm sleepwalking anyway and I can almost believe it never actually happened. Maybe I dreamed a lot of stuff. Stuff that I thought happened in my life. Stuff I thought I did. Stuff that was done to me. Wouldn't that be great? I'd love to think that ninety percent of it was just dreaming.

A NOTE ON THE AUTHOR

Jay McInerney is also the author of *Bright Lights, Big City*, *Ransom*, *The Last of the Savages*, *Model Behaviour* and *How It Ended*. He lives in New York and Nashville.

Ransom Jay McInerney
£6.99   0 7475 5366 1

Now brought back into paperback, *Ransom*, Jay McInerney's novel of exile ...

Living in Kyoto, the ancient capital of Japan, Christopher Ransom seeks a purity and simplicity he could not find at home, and tries to exorcise the terror he encountered earlier in his travels – a blur of violence and death at the Khyber Pass.

Supporting himself by teaching English to eager Japanese businessmen, Ransom feels safe amongst his fellow expatriates. But soon Ransom is threatened by everything he thought he had left behind, in a sequence of bizarre events whose consequences he cannot escape ...

'*Ransom* is cleverly written, intelligent, lively, concise and humorous. And it gives the reader that final buzz – it's serious' Guardian

'McInerney writes with superb economy of style, hoovering up the clutter of needless narrative. His world is effortlessly seductive' Irish Times

'McInerney is a superb and humane social critic' Newsweek

To order from Bookpost PO Box 29 Douglas Isle of Man IM99 1BQ www.bookpost.co.uk
email: bookshop@enterprise.net fax: 01624 837033 tel: 01624 836000

bloomsburypbks

bloomsburymagazine.com

Model Behaviour Jay McInerney
£6.99   0 7475 4233 3

'I'm sick of all this pointless glamour,' his glamorous girlfriend said. 'I want a simple life.'

If only Connor McKnight had listened. Now Philomena is off to California, allegedly on a fashion shoot, but he doesn't know where she is staying and a sinking feeling tells him that she might never come back.

'*Model Behaviour* does for the nineties what *Bright Lights, Big City* did for the eighties. It is just as stylish, just as sharp, not quite as sad, but, if anything, funnier. New York, New York: so good he nailed it twice' Independent on Sunday

'McInerney's novels, filled with the depiction of glamorous imbecilities and hilarious excesses, are acute about a certain kind of Manhattan amorality. They offer a swift, intelligent guide to the latest racket' Observer

'An intellectual *Ab Fab* – just as funny, but much deeper' Elle

'A comedy of dysfunction, a satire on a world in which Narcissus is God. Yet, beneath its running gags and scathing one-liners, there lies a more urgent critique of America's vain glory' Daily Express

To order from Bookpost PO Box 29 Douglas Isle of Man IM99 1BQ www.bookpost.co.uk
email: bookshop@enterprise.net fax: 01624 837033 tel: 01624 836000

bloomsburypbks

bloomsburymagazine.com

How It Ended Jay McInerney
£6.99   0 7475 5356 4

'Sharp, spare, exquisitely observed writing' Daily Mail

Discover a world of sex, excess and urban paranoia where worlds collide, relationships fragment and the dark underbelly of the American dream is exposed. A transsexual prostitute accidentally propositions his own father; a senator's serial infidelities leave him in hot water; two young lovers spend Christmas together high on different drugs. McInerney's characters struggle together in a shifting world where old certainties dissolve and nobody can be sure of where they stand.

'Metropolitan, middle-class young people grow up to learn that their triumphs will be hollow and their relationships false. McInerney flourishes amid the desolation: a kind of breezy, upbeat tone informs these dry, sardonic meditations on worldliness' Esquire

'Jay McInerney is the type of American novelist to whom English readers instinctively warm ... How It Ended **is the work of a fine writer on the top of his form'** Sunday Telegraph

To order from Bookpost PO Box 29 Douglas Isle of Man IM99 1BQ www.bookpost.co.uk
email: bookshop@enterprise.net fax: 01624 837033 tel: 01624 836000

bloomsburypbks

bloomsburymagazine.com